EXECUTIVE TREASON

Gary Grossman

ibooks

DISTRIBUTED BY PUBLISHERS GROUP WEST

A Publication of ibooks, inc.

Distributed by Publishers Group West
1700 Fourth Street, Berkeley, CA 94710
www.pgw.com

ibooks, inc.
24 West 25th Street
New York, NY 10010

ISBN: 1-59687-136-9
First ibooks, inc. printing October 2005
10 9 8 7 6 5 4 3 2 1

Cover design: M. Postawa

Printed in the U.S.A.

To Randy Kenton, Vin Dibona,
Jeffrey Davis, Michael Blowen,
Mike Brown, Jack Reilly, Robb Weller,
Betsy Goldman, Gene Roddenberry, Stan Deutsch,
Jeffrey Greenhawt, Glen Snowden,
Miss Gunning and Mrs. Seymour

– forever my mentors, my teachers,
my friends.

Acknowledgements

U.S. Navy Lt. Commander Greg Hicks, who pointed me in the direction of the South Pacific; John Gresham, whose authoritative knowledge of Specials Forces Ops and his ranking in the world of military history added to the detail and accuracy; Captain Barry Schiff, an extraordinary pilot whose experience with virtually every plane in the air, helped me on key scenes.

Additional thanks to Lt. Colonel Cynthia Scott-Johnson, Air Force Public Affairs; Jay Halfond, Dean of Boston University's Metropolitan School; and Linda Finnell at NBC. Also, Peter Loge, Senior Vice President of M&R Strategic Services. Peter had served as Campaign Manager to U.S. Representative Brad Sherman and Deputy to the Chief of Staff for Senator Edward Kennedy.

I also want to add my ongoing thanks to Sandi Goldfarb for her exceptional advice and assistance, as well as Debbie Supnik, Nancy Barney, Jacob Arbach, Fred Putman, Nat Segaloff, and my extraordinary agent at Broadthink, Nancy Cushing-Jones.

Of course, thanks to my wife, Helene Seifer, for her constant help and support; my wonderful children, Sasha, Zach, and Jake; and my mother, Evelyn Grossman, whose own political career helped shape my life. She will be with me forever.

Once again, I'm also grateful to have worked so closely with my remarkable and talented editor at ibooks, Dwight Zimmerman. In addition, I offer my personal thanks to ibooks Executive Vice President Roger Cooper who, has made this new career exciting every step of the way. I also must thank ibooks president Byron Preiss for having faith in me; not just once, but twice. His profound legacy in publishing and the arts will live on in my heart.

Finally, I want to express my sincere gratitude to the readers of my first novel, *Executive Actions*, for making me feel so welcome in the world of political thrillers. Your e-mails are wonderful. I truly hope I deliver on the good will you've given me, and that you'll enjoy *Executive Treason*.

RELATED GLOBAL NEWS

Reported in the American press
September 5, 2004

BRESLAN, RUSSIA—Attackers who seized more than 1,000 hostages in a provincial school may have smuggled in a large cache of weapons, possibly disguised as construction equipment, in the weeks before the takeover.

Reported in the American press
September 3, 2004

WASHINGTON—Despite its fervent denials, Israel secretly maintains a large and active intelligence-gathering operation in the United States, which for a long time, has been designed to recruit U.S. officials as spies and to procure classified documents, U.S. government officials said. FBI and other counterespionage agents have covertly followed, videotaped and bugged Israeli diplomats, intelligence officers and others in Washington, New York and elsewhere. "There is a huge, aggressive, ongoing set of Israeli activities directed against the United States," said a former intelligence official, familiar with the latest FBI probe, and who recently left government. "Anybody who worked in counterintelligence in a professional capacity will tell you the Israelis are among the most aggressive and active countries targeting the United States."

Australia Radio interview with Air Force Brigider General John W. Rosa, Jr., Deputy Director for Current Operations, the Joint Staff, about terrorists hiding in islands of Indonesia
March 20, 2002

"I don't want to be specific and tell you how or what we found but as you might expect, that is a vast, vast array of islands. Are there easy places to hide there? You bet ya."

Reported Maluku, Indonesia press report
July 2000

The Indonesian Navy Chief Admiral warned against those trying to smuggle weapons to warring groups in riot-torn Maluku. He told his staff to take stern action against intended arms smugglers. So far, the Navy had already detained 17 vessels in waters surrounding Maluku, confiscating weapons. Tensions in Maluku have been fueled by the arrival of 2,000 hard-line Muslim fighters from Java island, who have vowed a holy war against Christians. More than 3,000 people have been killed to date.

Reported in the American press
September 17, 2001

A high-tech Littleton, MA company, Viisage Technology, Inc. has offered the FBI free use of its face-recognition techonology to aid in the apprehension or identification of the persons responsible for terrorist actitivities in the U.S.

Reported in the American press
October 6, 2004

Representatives of Congress heard testimony today in special House Subcommittee Hearings on the Constitution that The Presidential Succession Act of 1947 remains the single most dangerous statute in the United States Code. Testimony termed the present rules of succession a "disastrous statute" and "an accident waiting to happen." Witnesses called for the repeal of the existing law, and the formation of a new operational model that would insure an orderly transition in the face of catastrophic events.

PRINCIPAL CHARACTERS

Washington

Henry Lamden, President of the United States
Morgan Taylor, Vice President of the United States
Lynn Meyerson, White House administrative assistant
Scott Roarke, Secret Service agent
Billy Gilmore, President's Chief of Staff
Bernie "Bernsie" Bernstein, President's Chief of Staff
Robert Mulligan, Director FBI
Jack Evans, Director National Intelligence
Louise Swingle, secretary to Vice President
Roy Bessolo, FBI supervisor
Beth Thomas, FBI agent
Presley Friedman, Head of Secret Service
Congressman Duke Patrick, Speaker of the House
General Robert Woodley Bridgeman, U.S. Marine Corps, ret.
Dan Shikar, FBI agent
Shannon Davis, FBI agent
Kelvin Lambert, journalist
Leopold Browning, Chief Justice, U.S. Supreme Court
Brad Rutberg, White House counsel
Mike Gimbrone, FBI agent
Malcolm Quenzel, Secret Service agent
Admiral Erwin "Skip" Gaston, U.S. Navy
General Reed Heath, U.S. Air Force
Captain Penny Walker, U.S. Army
General Jonus Jackson Johnson,

The CIA

Vinne D'Angelo, CIA agent
Faruk Jassim, CIA analyst
Backus, CIA analyst
Carr, CIA analyst
Dixon, CIA analyst
Bauman, CIA analyst

Boston

Katie Kessler, attorney
Donald Witherspoon, attorney
Paul Erskine, Starbucks employee

Australia

Mick O'Gara, electrician
Randolph Tyler, SAS Commander
David Foss, Prime Minister
Ricky Morris, SASR Tactical Commandeer
Chris Wordlow, Defence Chief
Ramelan Djali, President, Indonesia

Kansas

Elliott Strong, talk radio host
Darice Strong, radio producer

Los Angeles

Roger Ellsworth, LAPD Homocide Detective

Chicago

Luis Gonzales, Argentinean art dealer
Roger Alley, a driver

New York

Michael O'Connell, writer, *The New York Times*
Andrea Weaver, news editor, *The New York Times*

Tel Aviv

Ira Wurlin, aide to Mossad chief
Jacob Schecter, Director of the Mossad

Andrews Air Force Base

Lieutentant Eric Ross
Colonel Peter Lewis, *Air Force One* pilot
Captain Bernard Agins, *Air Force One* co-pilot

Shawnee Mission, Kansas

Charles Corbett

Indonesia

Commander Umar Komari
Musah Atef, soldier
Amrozi al-Faruq, soldier
Colonel Nyuan Huang

Russia

Aleksandr Dubroff, retired Politburo member, ex-KGB
Yuri Ranchenkov, FSB
Sergei Ryabov, FSB

South Pacific

Admiral Clemson Zimmer, Commander, 7th Fleet
Adm. Erwin "Skip" Gatson
Lt. James Nolt, Navy SEAL
Cpl. Derek Shaughnessy, Navy SEAL
Sgt. Mario Pintar, Navy SEAL
Julio Lopez, Navy SEAL
Harold Chaskes, Navy SEAL
Todd Roberts, Navy SEAL
Mark Polonsky, Navy SEAL
Brian Showalter, Navy SEAL

West Chester Township, Ohio

Bill and Gloria Cooper, retired couple

Damascus, Syria

Jamil Laham, a retiree
Rateb Samin, a visitor

Paris, France

Robby Pearlman, Canadian businessman

PART I

CHAPTER

1

Sydney, Australia
Monday, 18 June
4:20 A.M.

I t was the blinking LED that caught the electrician's attention.
"What's that?" Mick O'Gara muttered to himself.
If it hadn't been for the intermittent flicker, visible only because
it cut through the darkness, it would have gone undetected. The light
had flashed a moment after O'Gara killed the fluorescents in a storage
room on the basement level of the new 38-story Ville St. George
Hotel.

"Now where did you come from?" O'Gara turned the overhead lights
back on and looked around the crowded 14-by-20-foot room. He
waited about a minute. *Nothing*, he thought. The hotel electrician
shrugged his shoulders. He was about to leave when he decided to
give it one more moment, now with the lights off. Ten seconds went
by and he saw a red flash; dim and off to the right. He waited for it
to repeat, or cycle again. His patience was rewarded 30 seconds later,
though he couldn't quite pinpoint the location. A half-minute more—
"There you are! Up in the crawl space." The light appeared diffused,
indirect. "You're bouncing off something."

Mick O'Gara was one of the last hires in the electrical department
at Sydney's newest harbor-side luxury hotel. It overlooked both the
famed Harbor Bridge and the stunning Opera House. As a result, the
slim, 41-year-old man with a bushy moustache and long sideburns
pulled the dreaded graveyard shift. He had been poking around the
basement, tracing a conduit containing fiber optic wires. Guests on
the 33rd floor complained that their high-speed Internet connection

was out. It wasn't his specialty, but no one else was around, and he had the time to troubleshoot until his shift change.

Unfortunately, and for no good reason, the conduit continued above the ceiling in the small room, but the schematic dead-ended. *Another damned design flaw.* "Why can't they ever get it right?" Following it was going to be exhausting. After nearly an hour, O'Gara decided to leave the problem where he found it. That's when he noticed the red flash.

He trained his flashlight on the area in the far end of the room. The crawl space was a good three feet higher than his head. O'Gara, only 5'7", looked around the room and spotted a wooden cable spool, large enough to stand on. He dragged it over to the wall, stepped up, and peered into total darkness. O'Gara hit the void with the beam.

There, sandwiched deep into the opening, was a rectangular box, at first hard to see because it was either painted black or completely covered with black duct tape. He aimed the light at the top and then to the sides. It was wedged into an area no taller than 18 inches. He figured it to be about two-and-half-feet long.

O'Gara tapped it lightly with his finger. "Tape, not paint on metal," he said aloud. Curiosity was definitely getting the better of him now. The LED flashed again, illuminating the crawl space on each side for a fraction of a second.

The box wasn't connected to any outside wires. "Okay, you're not part of the phone system. And you're not connected to the electrical plant. But you've got something making you tick. So what in bloody hell are you?" He reached his right hand in about two feet, aiming his light at the back of the box. O'Gara searched for openings or identifying marks. There were none.

Just as his hand was tiring from stretching so far, the beam reflected back. He saw what looked like a small wire antenna, no more than three inches long, protruding from the back of the box. His arm ached, and he pulled it back. Once again, the LED flickered. "You're talking to someone, aren't you? A transmitter?"

O'Gara heard the sound of one of the elevator's pulleys engage directly above him. He looked up, then back to the box just as it emitted another red flash. "You're not talking. You're listening. Son of a bitch." His pulse quickened. The elevator moved again. He was amazed how loud it now sounded; right on top of him. Then he caught the sound of the gears working on another elevator to the left. A moment later, another to his right. He closed his eyes and remembered that in total there were eight banks, four on each side of a central artery inside the hotel.

He pointed his flashlight into the crawl space one more time. Now the details of it became more apparent. The box looked crudely homemade. The antennae was stuck out of the back, but bent toward the front. The light blinked every 30 seconds. Exactly. The regular frequency of the flashes told him it was either self-charging or scanning. He heard an elevator start above and across from him. It became more evident that he was under a critical focal point, a hollow shaft; the most vulnerable part of a large building. "Holy mother of God!" he exclaimed.

Mick O'Gara stepped down slowly. Very slowly. His green work clothes were dusty and drenched with sweat. He unholstered his Boost Mobile walkie-talkie cell phone from his belt. He was about to key the microphone when he suddenly stopped. "No, wait. The signal!" He didn't want to make a call, for the same reason passengers are instructed not to use cell phones on airplanes. The radio could interfere or interact with other electronics. In this case, it could set off the device.

The electrician slowly backed away and snapped the telephone onto his belt. He left the room, closing the door gently. It wasn't until he was upstairs that he punched in a number.

"Security," the voice answered.

"O'Gara. Listen carefully." He slowly explained what he had found.

The security officer swallowed hard and called the hotel manager, who didn't really know what to do. He phoned the CEO of the consortium that owned the Ville St. George, waking him from his sleep in the hotel penthouse. The CEO bolted upright in his bed as he followed the account.

"Are you sure?"

"Here, I'll conference in O'Gara." The security officer on duty connected him to O'Gara's cell. He heard the electrician's story firsthand.

Not knowing O'Gara, but not wanting to take any blame, the CEO phoned his regular Wednesday night poker partner, who happened to be the Sydney chief of police.

This is when it got more serious. The chief didn't hesitate waking the Australian Federal Police Commissioner. His must-attend seminars on terrorist threats had heightened his senses. The federal officer ordered the immediate evacuation of the hotel while he cradled the phone on his shoulder and pulled on his boxers.

All of this within 18 minutes of Mick O'Gara's find.

The Sydney police and national authorities had trained for such a contingency after concerns about terrorist attacks during the 2000 Summer Olympics. The country's defense command realized Australia could be an easy target for al Qaeda and even easy pickings for insurgent groups operating out of Indonesia and Malaysia. As a result, they developed an operational plan code-named *Exercise New Deal.*

In years past, terrorists struck symbolic targets, causing indiscriminate deaths. Al Qaeda changed the rules of engagement. 9/11 demonstrated their willingness to inflict heavy casualties on civilians and register greater fear and uncertainty as a strategic end.

Western nations now had a true understanding of the terrorists' objectives, even if they couldn't identify the enemy. Their ultimate goals were to devalue democratic institutions, weaken infrastructure, and supplant existing governments with moderate or fundamental Islamic rule. They attacked people and they targeted buildings. They couldn't win conventional wars, but took their holy fight to the new unconventional battlegrounds—civilian centers. Among the various landmarks identified as potential targets in Australia were the Sydney Opera House and the lavish hotels along the bay—including the towering cement, brick, and steel St. George.

An elite tactical unit was dispatched to the hotel.

Thirty-three minutes out.

They were backed up by the SASR—Australia's Special Air Service Regiment—which arrived by helicopter atop the St. George.

Fifty minutes.

By then, the night assignment editor at Sydney's Sky Television News had detected the surge of emergency chatter on the police frequencies.

Sixty-one minutes. The first of many microwave broadcast vans arrived at the hastily set-up police barricade a long block away.

Seventy-four minutes. Sky went live with a report carried cross-country.

"This is Sky Television News, approximately 200 meters from the recently completed Ville St. George Hotel, where a mandatory evacuation is now underway," the young reporter began. "Though we can't see it from our vantage point, our bureau, monitoring the police frequencies, reports an emergency of undetermined origin."

At seventy-nine minutes since O'Gara's find, the CNN night desk noted the coverage. With a special reciprocal arrangement with Sky, an editor patched the signal to his uplink and alerted Atlanta of the events that were unfolding half a world away.

Eighty-three minutes. A hot quick lead was typed into the teleprompter, and the Atlanta anchor read what was put before her.

"Breaking news from Sydney, Australia, where it is five forty-three A.M. Approximately eleven hundred guests and staff of the new five hundred thirty-five-room Ville St. George Hotel are being evacuated. There are unconfirmed reports of an electrical fire or the failure of an elevator. For details, we join Sky Television News with live coverage."

Far across the International Dateline, an overnight CIA officer at Langely, Virginia, monitored the news channels. Silvia Brownlee noted that CNN interrupted its domestic news for a story from Sydney. Using her remote, the fifteen-year veteran turned up the volume and jotted down the details.

Ville St. George. Sydney. Evacuation.

Brownlee added equal signs between the key words, and then wrote a large question mark. She swiveled her chair to her computer and typed in the hotel name. Then she clicked on a password-protected file. As she suspected, one floor of the St. George had been designed and built to White House specifications.

Brownlee called upstairs. Her boss needed to know there was an alert at a *Rip Van Winkle House*. Although she didn't know it, it was the most important phone call she ever made.

Los Angeles, California
Sunday 17 June
the same time

He wondered if anyone had stopped to think about the absurdity.

There it was, just on the other side of the chain-link fence: Rancho Golf Course. The home of the annual Los Angeles Police/Celebrity Golf Tournament.

Every spring the LAPD takes over the tees for a fundraiser that supports the Police Memorial Foundation. But Rancho Golf Course was also where O.J. Simpson used to play. That was the irony.

Simpson was on the greens as the jury deliberated his civil trial for the deaths of his ex-wife and her boyfriend. The case Simpson lost. He was also playing the day a single-engine plane crashed on the course just a few hundred yards away. One of the first things the two injured men heard as they were pulled out of their badly damaged plane was that O.J. was "over there."

Nat Olsen almost laughed at the thought. The police and one of L.A.'s most notorious citizens sharing the same $18-a-day public course. But he didn't laugh. That wasn't part of his character...not as the jogger today or the man he might become tomorrow. He was focused and waiting at the Cheviot Hills Recreation Park that bordered the Rancho Golf Course.

Olsen wore loose-fitting black sweats and gray running shoes that he'd picked up weeks ago from a secondhand clothing store on La Brea. The only thing that distinguished him from any other jogger was a pair of thin leather gloves. They weren't quite *de rigeur* for running, but they were definitely necessary for *his* particular line of work.

Affixed horizontally inside the zip-up top, at the small of the back, was a 4"-by-1" heavy duty, all-weather Velcro strip. It could self-adhere, but he'd sown it into the fabric for extra reinforcement. Another strip of the hook and loop tape was stuck to his Sog Specialty FSA-98 Flash II serrated knife. The $39 switchblade is lightning quick. It opens with a simple press of a thumb. The blade is under four inches and generally rated as a defensive slash-and-retreat weapon. But not in the hands of someone more experienced. Not in his hands.

Olsen certainly wouldn't have used such a simple over-the-counter purchase for something more difficult, perhaps on a worthier target. But this was going to a simple matter, reflected by a smaller fee than he'd recently been earning. Fifty thousand.

His quote was normally much higher, but so were the risks. Today's job required very little planning, though he always did more than required. Where others screwed up, he *never* did. The sloppy ones forgot that it wasn't just the kill, it was the exit that counted. He'd be as discreet in his departure as he was in his job.

To the normal passersby, he looked like a struggling and winded mid-to-late-40s jogger. He was neither struggling nor over thirty-five. If he chose, he could run for miles. But not today. With black hair extensions added to his closely cropped cut, dyed eyebrows and a foam rubber gut that put on an additional 45 pounds under his sweats, he easily passed as another middle-aged man trying to beat back the years.

He carried a Dallas license to prove he was Nat Olsen. He also created a convincing legend he'd share with anyone who stopped to talk. Nat Olsen was a nice guy, a Fidelity mutual fund trader relocating to Los Angeles. He was scouting a home for his family. There was nothing unusual about him; not a gesture or mannerism that would ever raise suspicion. He would pant, stop and start, double over, grab his sides, and shake his head and wish he was in better condition, just like so many others.

In reality, he barely taxed himself. Everything was completely planned out, rehearsed, carefully considered. Surprise would be on his side. However, he clearly understood that a daylight hit brought its own extra risks.

He had any number of ways to escape. Bicycles hidden both north and south of his intercept point. A car parked along a side lot off Motor Avenue. The Pico Boulevard bus. And his preferred method: simply joining a pack of other early evening joggers and going out inconspicuously.

He figured he had an hour more to kill. *Funny how that sounds*, he thought. Maybe he'd watch the golfers on the other side of the fence. He'd take his time and stay near his initial contact point. He'd politely nod to runners faster than him and stay behind anyone slower—like his target, who should be along well before dusk.

Lebanon, Kansas
the same time

"Let's go to the Midwest line. Hello, you're on *Strong Nation*."

"Hey, Elliott. This is Peter in Detroit. Long-time listener, first-time caller," lied the voice over the telephone. He was in a six-week rotation, either playing up to the audience with an anti-administration rant, or throwing in an incendiary left wing comment that would generate an hour's worth of bitter conservative reaction. He was there, like dozens of others, because Elliott Strong didn't count on his audience to provide enough controversy. The 52-year-old national syndicated talk show host, broadcasting from his home studio in the geographic center of the country—Lebanon, Kansas—had his ringers. They always helped.

Unseen to his millions of listeners, Strong took a sip of his hot Darjeeling tea and went through a quick set of mouth exercises that he watched in a mirror in front of him. This wasn't just a physical routine. Strong liked looking at himself during his live broadcast. It added to his performance and inflated his ego.

Strong also always dressed for his shows. Tie and jacket; sometimes a suit. He resisted the urge to install web cameras. He felt that the *magic* of radio presented more opportunity than television. He held the historic Nixon-Kennedy debates as case in point. Over the radio to an unseeing audience, Nixon was the clear winner—concise, authoritative, composed. To TV audiences, however, Nixon appeared drawn, tired, and evasive. Strong would resist TV, even though he knew the offers would be coming. His ratings were growing too fast to be ignored.

In the control room, Strong's engineer watched the meters, keeping them in the legal limits. Strong did less to modulate his opinion, openly criticizing public figures, while remaining vague about the details. He had only two other people on the payroll: his wife, who served as his screener, and his web master, who constantly updated the *StrongNationRadio.com* web site with right-leaning polls, editorials that supported his harangues, and links to like-minded Internet sites.

During broadcasts, the studio was off-bounds to everyone. No friends or visitors. No live guests. The shows belonged to Strong and his callers.

"State your case," the host said.

"What the hell's going on in Washington?"

Strong recognized the voice and smiled. Last time was on his late night show. Strong had become so popular over the course of the election and the controversial aftermath, that he now occupied two time slots: a three-hour afternoon shift, and another four hours overnight. Depending upon the time zone, he was carried live or replayed at a later hour. In 18 months, Elliott Strong had out-paced his rivals, and *Strong Nation* had become an extreme conservative mouth-piece for an audience who thought they were getting the news from talk radio.

"What's going on?" Strong said through a laugh.

"We've got a president we didn't elect and a vice president we voted out, that's what's going on. Both are part of the military establishment, which I don't remember electing. And now they're running everything. Two people, and as far as I can remember, Americans didn't give either of them their jobs."

The caller was pressing a nationwide hot button. Henry Lamden ran hard for the Democratic nomination and probably would have gotten his party's nod until Vermont congressman Theodore Lodge, clearly in second place, was thrust to front-runner status after his wife was shot on the campaign trail. A gunman fired just one bullet. It appeared to be a bungled assassination attempt. It wasn't.

Lodge quickly swept ahead of Lamden in a wave of sympathy. Lamden, a decorated Navy commander, became a reluctant number two on the ticket. The Lodge-Lamden team won the November election, defeating the incumbent president, Morgan Taylor. However, minutes before Lodge was to have been sworn in, he was killed on the floor of the Capitol Rotunda. The assassin, presumed to be the same man who killed Lodge's wife, had disguised himself as a Capitol Police officer. He escaped.

The rules of succession, enumerated in the 25th Amendment, required that the vice president-elect take the Oath of Office. To the surprise of everyone watching, Henry Lamden became President of the United States. He then proceeded to startle the country again with two revelations. The first: Lodge was not really an eligible candidate, but a sleeper spy, posing as an American. Second: former President Taylor, a Republican, would be his nominee as vice president.

The reporters covering the Inauguration were as shocked as the millions of people tuned to the ceremony.

Other countries have based their rule on a parliamentary system, where fragile coalition leaderships typically struggle through constant and predictable disarray, until they ultimately implode. This has not been the case with the U.S. Executive Branch. One party controls the presidency, with both the chief executive and the vice president representing the same party, though serving the entire nation. On the state level, there are instances where a governor from one party is elected along with a lieutenant governor from another. The scenario usually leads to infighting, a dubious lack of cooperation, and a recipe for political disaster. But in the case of the Lamden-Taylor administration, the new president made the controversial choice to solve problems, not to cause them.

Lamden sought to lay down the spirit of cooperation with his inaugural speech. The country narrowly averted a constitutional crisis, he told the people. America had elected a Russian-trained, Arab national sleeper spy as president. His ultimate intent: to end U.S. support of Israel and change the balance of power in the Middle East. Lamden explained how proof of the conspiracy was extracted by an American Special Forces team dropped into Libya just hours prior to the Inauguration. In a well-orchestrated assault, they took a building in Tripoli that housed the media empire of Fadi Kharrazi, son of the dying Libyan dictator, General Jabbar Kharrazi. Records proved that Fadi had not created the plan. He bought the three-decade-old operation from Udai Hussein prior to the fall of his father's regime. In Fadi's mind, the plan would have propelled him into a leadership position ahead of his brother Abahar.

President Morgan Taylor personally oversaw the mission and returned to Washington with hard evidence, minutes before the chief justice was to swear in Teddy Lodge. Taylor confronted Lodge and his chief aide, Geoff Newman, in the Capitol Rotunda. Newman grabbed a gun from a Secret Service agent. Before it was over, two law enforcement officers were dead. So were Newman and Lodge.

Back in Libya, Fadi Kharrazi made indignant denials. One week after the general's death in March, Fadi's brother, Abahar, assumed power. A week later, Fadi died in a car accident that no one witnessed.

Congress convened an unprecedented emergency session to begin its inquiry. Thousands of pages of testimony later, Morgan Taylor, on a strangely bipartisan vote, was enthusiastically confirmed as vice president. The United States had its first coalition government in more than a century.

Reporters dove into the history books for precedent. They were surprised it existed. John Adams, the nation's second president, served as a Federalist. His vice president, Thomas Jefferson, was a member of the unified Democrat Republic party. America's 16th president also ran on a coalition ticket. Abraham Lincoln, a Republican, had Democrat Andrew Johnson as his second VP.

"It's a *jackalope*," the caller continued. "I don't care if they did it way back when. We're talking about now. And I can't tell what kind of government we have. It's not Republican. Lamden is a liberal Democrat. And it's not Democrat. Taylor, who got defeated, is a moderate Republican, if you can call him a Republican at all."

"My friend, you hit the nail on the head," Strong said, nudging him on more.

"But it's even worse. They're moving us toward a military regime. Next thing you know, they'll be clamping down on our freedoms." The caller was beginning to sound the survivalist clarion call. "We're gonna have the army running the police, and the navy boarding everybody's boats. From the Great Lakes to Tahoe. I don't care where you live. And you know what they'll be after?"

"No, what?" asked the radio host in a smooth, soothing, encouraging voice.

"Our damned guns, that's what. From a governor we didn't elect president, and his vice president–master who's really running things...who we voted out."

"So you're not happy?" Strong said jokingly.

"How can any American be happy? The election was a total fraud. We should have a new one."

"But according to the Constitution, there can't be another election."

"Then what the hell can we do?"

This was just where Elliott Strong wanted the conversation to go. It would start simply enough. A question. Then a call to action. Then another listener would up the ante. An echo. More callers. A chorus. In the morning, a publicist for Strong's national syndicator would mention it to a few newspapers. It would make the wire services, certainly Fox News, and after that, the network news, CNN and CNBC. Then an e-mail campaign to the House and Senate, blogs, then...

"A good question. What *can* we do?" he asked, knowing the answer.

"Yeah. Well, why not another election? We elected a foreign spy, and now we got two losers. There's got to be something better."

Here was the moment. The seed needed watering. "The only thing I can think of...and I don't even know if it's possible...it would take an amazing effort...a really *Strong Nation*..." He loved utilizing the name of his show. "...to make it work. I don't know." The talk host drew it out. "Probably impossible. Unless..." he stopped in mid-sentence for impact. "Unless *we* band together." The operative word was *we*. It brought his listeners closer to the radio. "Then it could happen." He hadn't even hinted at the idea yet, but Strong knew that the truck drivers tuned in were mesmerized. The insomniacs lay in bed with their eyes now wide open. The conspiracy theorists were hanging on his words.

Elliott Strong had his faithful in the palm of his hand when he answered the caller's question.

Century Plaza Hotel
Los Angeles, California
the same time

"Goodbye, Mr. President," Lynn Meyerson said as she left the president's suite at Los Angeles's Century Plaza Hotel. It had been another tiring day; her fifteenth in a row. But she ate it up. In a very short period of time she had earned access to Henry Lamden, and now enjoyed what few others in the entire country could claim: The President of the United States appreciated her advice, and he shared his thoughts with her.

Meyerson was a staffer in the White House Office for Strategic Planning. She typically focused on project research that could culminate in pro-administration policies. This allowed her to be hands-on when it came to developing White House strategies, making her an obvious "inside source" for anyone on the outside. Not that she really touched much that was sensitive. Not yet. But other people didn't know that. Nonetheless, she had been fully briefed on how they'd try. Reporters would strike up conversations, build on seemingly chance encounters, and pull her into the young Washington social scene. It was all part of the game. And she would make great company. At 25, Lynn Meyerson had exceptional poise, genuine sincerity, great looks, and distinctive curly red hair that made cameras and men turn. She stood out of any crowd—a 5' 7", 118-pound beauty.

The FBI had cleared Meyerson into the White House and, even further, into the Oval Office. Each personal reference reinforced the view of the last. *She's dynamic. She has the political know-how to go far. She's a budding superstar, a natural-born politician.* President Lamden clearly liked the young woman's energy and enthusiasm and her willingness to express unpopular opinions.

Meyerson made it no secret that she wanted to work in government, especially the White House. She'd admitted that to her closest friends at Wellesley College. Her zeal earned her an interview her senior year. But what really counted was how she befriended then-President Morgan Taylor's secretary, Louise Swingle. It was the number-one rule to crack any company. The White House was no different than Microsoft. *Make friends with the boss's secretary.* Swingle took a liking to her and set up meetings with a variety of White House offices. Following the Inauguration, she got an offer with the Office of Strategic Initiatives.

Meyerson tried to send Swingle an exquisite assortment of exotic flowers. That's when she learned that things were as tough to get into the White House as they were to get out. The flowers ended up at Swingle's home.

President Lamden, nearly 40 years Meyerson's senior, talked with Lynn about her goals, but always kept everything on a business level. He agreed with the written assessments. *She would go far. Perhaps make Congress by her mid-thirties.* He heard that her friends were already egging her on about going after a Maryland seat in a couple of years. *And she'd probably win,* he thought. She had that much potential.

Meyerson paused for one more look around the suite at the hotel, named for Ronald Reagan. It was impressive. So was the president who now occupied it.

At first she laughed at the Stetsons he wore and the Montana stories he spun for her in their free time. Then she recognized that Lamden, like Lyndon Johnson, used his cowboy charm to make more important things happen. The lanky 67-year-old lawmaker could bring down a calf in a rodeo ring. She trusted that he had done the same with many a political opponent. Lamden was shrewd, tough. She was careful what she said to him. Still, she was impressed by the trappings and the access.

This is good. This is really good. She'd made it. She was traveling with the President of the United States, staying at the Century Plaza Hotel on Avenue of the Stars, and meeting some of the real stars who populated the avenue.

Most of all, she was thoroughly aware of the security measures surrounding the president with Secret Service agents always close by. Marksmen on the roof. The "football"—the attaché case with nuclear weapons codes and plans—always within reach. Bulletproof glass in the hotel suite and even the undisclosed evacuation routes through the Century Plaza's un-publicized secure corridors. When she really stopped to think about it, she truly was on the "inside."

Since she joined Lamden's administration, Meyerson spent nearly every day at the White House. This was her first trip away.

Henry Lamden was taking off shortly, but Meyerson wouldn't be on the plane. She'd requested a few days in L.A. "Well deserved," the president acknowledged.

"Good night, Lynn," the president said without casting eyes on the redhead. "See you back at the ranch Monday. We'll work on the first town hall meeting. When is it?"

"Fourth of July."

"I can just imagine the fireworks," he joked, not at all referring to the celebration. "Now enjoy yourself." He returned to his reading. "Go."

"Thank you, Mr. President. I will." She lingered for a moment. *He's looking tired. Hard week.* "You take care, sir."

He didn't hear her. Lamden was already deeply absorbed in a summation of upcoming legislation.

Meyerson smiled at the agents standing vigil at the door. "Night."

"You going for your run tonight?" one Secret Service agent asked.

"Yup. Then I'm cutting loose. Doing Melrose and catching a friend from Vassar at the Sunset Marquis Whiskey Bar." She didn't let on that it was really a blind date with a presumably drop-dead handsome aide to the governor of California. But a smile curled over her lips that might have given her away.

"That's all?" the agent asked like a friend.

She raised her shoulders and gave a coquettish shrug as if to say, *It's too early to tell.* Then she told herself, *I might not say no to anything.*

Cheviot Hills Recreation Park
the same time

Nat Olsen sat facing one of the three basketball courts. A pickup game was in progress on the court closest to him. *Probably lawyers and agents,* he thought. If they were star players in high school, they didn't look it here. Though it appeared he was following the game with great intent, Olsen didn't really care. He was focused well beyond the court, to the entrance of the park off Motor Avenue. He checked his watch. A young woman jogger would be along very soon.

Halmahera Island
Maluku, Indonesia

I ndonesia, in all its exotic beauty, is also viewed as an outlaw's
paradise. It is the world's largest archipelago, sitting astride the
equator between the Asian and Australian continents. The
sprawling nation covers some 3,200 miles of ocean.

The name Indonesia has its roots in Greek: "Indos" meaning Indian
and "Nesos" for islands. Two hundred twenty million inhabitants
make it the fourth most populated country, and the most populous
Muslim nation on the face of the earth. More than 17,500 islands rise
above the tide. Some are no bigger than a few yards. Others are the
size of Spain and California. Only 6,000 are inhabited. Most have
little or no infrastructure. Many have yet to be explored.

Indonesia is the proverbial haystack. Anyone trying to hide among
its islands becomes the needle.

The southernmost part of Indonesia, the province of Maluku, is
comprised of 1,027 volcanic islands and fewer than 1,700,000 people.
The vast majority are Muslim.

Not long ago, entire portions of Maluku were "cleansed" of Christians in a holy war staged by a terrorist group known as Laskar Jihad.
At its height in the late 1990s and first decade of the 21st century,
the movement had 10,000 followers actively engaged in arms smuggling, sniper attacks, forced conversions and circumcisions, and
massacres. An estimated 10,000 people were killed in the process.
Another 500,000 were displaced. Maluku is now strictly segregated
along religious lines.

Today, the most feared terrorist network is Indonesia's Jemaah Islamiyyah or JI. The group routinely preys on "soft targets": places where Westerners tend to congregate. It came to international attention after bombings at luxury tourist hotels in Bali in 2002 and Jakarta in 2003, and the Jakarta airport, also in 2003. Hundreds were killed in the name of Islam, mostly Australian and other foreign tourists.

Other terrorist groups also thrive in the region: the Philippines's Abu Sayyaf, with solid ties to al Qaeda; a Malaysian Islamist group, the Kumpulah Mujahedeen Malaysia; and homegrown insurgents who operate among the islands with little fear of ever being discovered.

None of the individual cells had the economic or military resources of a country, but for at least ten years, this was not a problem. Strategic strikes throughout the world had proven that open and tolerant societies were extremely vulnerable. Indonesia included.

Although the U.S. State Department designated JI as a Foreign Terrorist Organization, attacks in Indonesia are generally viewed as terrorism only if the victims are foreigners. Assaults against locals don't receive the same attention from the police, courts, or government, partially out of the belief that further reprisals from Islamic extremists will be worse.

However, the U.S. did send troops to Indonesia to help train the Indonesian Army (TNI) in counter-terrorism techniques. As a result, the TNI intensified offenses against JI strongholds. Laskar Jihad ultimately disbanded, but Jemaah Islamiyyah and other splinter groups continue to thrive, killing and scattering into the thick, mountainous jungles and dark, dangerous caves too numerous to catalogue.

The terrrorists live on ransom money, drug sales, and cash from the global terror network, including al Qaeda sources.

Widespread poverty contributes to further corruption. The police and military are regularly bought off. Lawlessness rules many of the islands. Kidnappings, bombings, extortion, and torture remain the terrorists' principal tools.

Americans interested in exploring the famed coral reefs of the Maluku Islands are urged by the State Department to seriously reconsider.

Umar Komari, commander of an emerging terrorist fragment October 12, is one of the reasons.

* * *

"Three million! And what do you come back with? One-third?" Komari shouted in Bahasa Indonesian.

Musah Atef offered only a muffled, "I'm sorry, sir," through the hood over his head. The haggard subordinate was prostrated before to his commander. Komari had his foot on his shoulder, his Luger at his temple.

Everything spoke to the Muslim tradition of dominance. Placing a captive on the ground, or putting a foot on him, implied the captor was God. The hood denoted shame for the captive. Fully aware of the cold barrel of the gun, Atef took special care to answer carefully. He had seen Commander Komari kill many hostages without remorse. Now four of his fellow officers watched him, fearing one day they would be in the same position.

"I'm sorry? That's all you can say?" Komari roared. Even those deeper in the cave would be certain to hear him.

"Yes, sir."

"The agreement was three million of the infidel's dollars!" the 47-year-old terrorist leader now whispered in his ear. The amount was not for general consumption, since he planned to skim a percentage as his own. "And you dared return with this?" Komari now shouted. He pressed his foot hard into Atef's shoulder blade, causing the young soldier to cry out and plead for his life.

Now Komari reached for Atef's backpack and spilled the contents on his back. He didn't have to count out the twenties—all in U.S. currency—to see how badly he'd been swindled by the corrupt Chinese colonel.

"Huang held a gun to my head just as you do, and he says the *Shabu* is no good. Low grade," Atef explained.

"Communist pig!"

"A pig whose paws can finger a gun."

"And you could not convince him otherwise?"

Atef raised his head as if to look at Commander Komari. "Convince him? No sir. There were only three of us. In the past we met only four of them. But he came out of nowhere in a fast amphibious craft with more men. Maybe twenty. His machine guns and cannons were already aimed at us. They could have blown our cigarette boat out of the water in seconds."

Komari spit in disgust. He'd been double-crossed, yet lucky to get his men back with at least some of the money. Still, he made Atef believe he would die for not trying harder.

"I should kill you now. That way I won't have to feed you. Your portions will go to someone deserving to live."

If he did pull the trigger, only his troops would hear, and that would serve its own purpose. No one else was nearby. Tonight, Komari's men were huddled in a mountain cave tucked into one of the four backswept peninsulas of Halmahera. Tomorrow they would be at another encampment—always moving, never providing a reliable pattern for the TNI.

Komari had greater knowledge of the North Indonesian island chains than any fisherman who worked the waters. He knew the tides, and which coves were safe and which were not. He also knew the interior trails, virtually frozen in time, where hunter-gatherer tribes lived as they had for thousands of years. And he had faith that he and his men could disappear for years, if need be, just like the Japanese soldier who went undetected on the island of Morotai for 28 years.

Komari cocked the trigger. At the sound, Atef bowed his head and pleaded. "Commander, it was different than each time before. The Chinese colonel broke his agreement with you. It is not my fault."

"Is it Allah's will then? You blame Allah?" Komari demanded, calling on the Arab belief that incidences are not a matter of cause and effect, but the will of God.

Atef shook his head.

"Then perhaps you are merely the messenger with the bad news? That our friends who manufacture the *Shabu* are providing inferior-grade product? That is why I should not end your life now?"

"Yes, sir," appealed Atef.

"Then go on. Beg for your life. But rest assured, your next words will determine your fate, for you have failed me and all who pray to Allah for the future of our independence."

"Sir, as Allah as my witness, this is the truth. Colonel Huang claims that not even the weakest can become addicted to our last *Shabu*. He says he must sell three times as much for the same money to be effective. So he pays us a third of your price. He threatens my head as you do, and he laughs. He tells me that I have a death sentence three ways: by his hand, by yours for not returning with the proper amount, or by the government if they catch me."

A smile rolled over Komari's face. He stroked his long, knotted beard. The length was a visible symbol of his faith; the longer the beard, the greater the faith. Commander Komari wore the beard of a truly devoted Muslim. He thought for a moment. Colonel Nyuan Huang was notorious for turning a moment to his advantage. He chuckled.

"Of course. If you had objected, he would have killed you on the spot. If you tried to escape with the drugs, then Huang would have notified TNI patrol boats. Given the right coordinates, they could have tracked you back to our camp. That would have been the other death sentence, right?"

"Yes, commander."

"And then we all would have been arrested, tried, and executed."

"Truly."

Komari was simply reciting Indonesia's laws regarding capital punishment, inherited from their former colonial ruler, the Dutch. It remains the mandated sentence for drug trafficking, whether opium, morphine, cocaine, or methamphetamines—the *Shabu*.

Komari was trumped this time. In turn, he would pay his factories less. Commander Umar Komari engaged the safety on his gun and holstered it. Atef took a long, relieved deep breath.

"You may stand."

Atef came to attention.

"And take off that hood, but remember how it feels."

The soldier complied, relieved to breathe in fresh air again. His mouth was filled with blood from a broken nose. His beard, shorter than Komari's, smelled of vomit from his beating.

"We shall check with our labs to see if this is true. Perhaps we shall make a quick, visible 'corrective step' to one worker for all to see. What do you think, Atef?"

The man was grateful to have his own life. He knew the best thing now was to agree with his commander.

"Whatever you choose, sir."

Komari slapped his man on the back. "Ever the diplomat. You shall praise Allah that you have lived to see another day. While you are the messenger with the bad news, you are not responsible for the message. At least not today. We must keep our Chinese friends happy.

It is their trade that funds the purchase of our weapons. And soon we will be powerful enough to deliver a message ourselves; a message that will make news, free us from our oppressors, and give Maluku our long-sought independence."

Atef bowed, patted his heart a few times in thanks, and backed out of Komari's cave, into the thick of the island jungle. The 22-year-old soldier felt the burning stare of his commander as he made for a waterfall to clean up the stench and wash away his fear. He would return. He believed in Komari and the cause of October 12, the date commemorating the glorious attack on Bali. If anyone would lead the charge to Maluku's independence, it would be Komari. He prayed he'd be alive to see it.

Century Plaza Hotel
Los Angeles, California
the same time

Lynn Meyerson laced up her sneakers and checked herself in the mirror. Her bright-green eyes sparkled. She widened them to see whether she wanted to touch up. *Nah*, she thought. *Fine for now*. She reached for her favorite barrette, one made out of an exotic blue-green oyster shell. She twisted her hair into a ponytail, shaped it into a bun, and clipped it up. Finally, Meyerson grabbed some crumpled bills from her purse along with a few other necessities. She stuffed them in her running shorts. The young woman looked in the mirror one last time, searching for the commitment she had made with herself. She saw her own strength and confidence reflected back.

Lynn Meyerson was ready.

So was a man in the park.

CHAPTER 3

The Ville St. George Hotel
Sydney, Australia

Immediately after the September 11th attacks in New York and Washington, the Australian government invoked the 50-year-old ANZUS mutual defense treaty. ANZUS, an anagram for the three signatory nations—Australia, New Zealand, and the United States—considers an attack on one nation an attack on all. However, the actual status of the treaty has been in question. New Zealand's refusal to permit U.S. nuclear-powered or armed ships in its ports resulted in the United States revoking its reciprocal ANZUS obligations to that country. Meanwhile regional terrorist attacks in Bali, Indonesia, and the Philippines, and activity in the Solomons, underscored the need for ANZUS protection.

Fear that the discovery of a bomb at Ville St. George might be merely a portion of a larger attack, the prime minister called an emergency cabinet meeting. Depending upon the success of the bomb squad, now at work at the hotel, ANZUS might be activated again.

The Sydney police bomb demolition team was in the storage room. The electrician had been dead-on. The container was suspiciously wedged in the crawl space. Black electrical tape covered what appeared to be a cardboard box. The LED fired a red burst every 30 seconds. There was no reason for it to be transmitting. The device *was* waiting for a signal.

The first question was, *how long?* They wouldn't know until they peered inside through a portable X-ray to determine the power of the storage batteries.

There was another, more critical question: *What did the batteries power?*

The next steps were textbook. Evacuate the building. Secure the site. Assess the immediate threat. Shield the radio from incoming signals. Disarm the bomb. Remove the explosives.

Space was limited. After the X-ray, it would become a two-person job.

The bomb squad used a Dynalog portable X-ray machine patched into a Sony laptop. It took a non-invasive video in wide angles and close-ups. The first scan, starting from left to right, revealed a package of 20 silver oxide, 1.55 V watch batteries with wires leading to a compact circuit board—instantly recognizable as a receiver. A lead went right to the antennae.

The officer at the monitor shook his head. "This thing could last for years." That was the unspoken good news. It probably wasn't intended for detonation tonight.

The next scan showed the really bad news: twenty soft, chalky bars, with the consistency of modeling clay, wrapped in cellophane. Each bar was twelve inches long, two inches across, and one inch thick. No one watching needed any explanation. The contents were comprised of cyclotrimethylene-trinitramine ($C_3H_6N_6O_6$). Properly manufactured, it went by a much easier name to remember: C-4. There was enough power in the plastic explosives to shoot a fireball through the elevator shafts, weaken the structural integrity of the new hotel, and bring it down.

"Okay, get the shield up, and absolutely no radios in here."

The SAS commander, Colonel Randolph Tyler, had quietly stepped into the room. He and his men came in unobserved in unmarked vans. The chief of the bomb squad nodded to him and gestured to the screen. They both knew how to read the information. No words were necessary. No one wanted to hear them, anyway. The local police and the Australian special forces had trained together.

Tyler signaled to the chief. He came to the opposite corner of the room.

"We've got to get a little smoke circulating out in the ether. There's a lot of press."

"Yeah," the Sydney officer noted.

"Let's cut the electricity to the hotel, starting at the top floors and working down. The emergency lights will go on for anyone still coming down. Then you get word out that a water main has broken under the building. We've turned off power simply as a precaution."

A cover story. Hopefully it would convince anyone with a finger close to the trigger to relax and stay with the plan—whatever it was.

"Good idea." the officer said.

He spoke to one of his men. Word quickly relayed through the chain of command. While the bomb squad worked to set up the radio shield, Tyler stepped out to make a call of his own. His message would be carried to headquarters, and on to Washington.

Langley, Virginia
George Bush Center for Central Intelligence
Monday, 18 June
the same time

Barely two hours after the box was discovered in the basement of the Ville St. George, and only 50 minutes following the first news report, Jack Evans was on the phone with the head of the Secret Service at the White House. He went right to the point.

"Presley, move Big Sky now."

"What?" Presley Friedman asked. "He's wheels up in another two hours."

"Move him now!" ordered the director of the National Intelligence Agency.

"Is this...?" The Secret Service chief didn't get to finish his question.

"Code: Rising Thunder."

"Copy that. Rising Thunder." The cryptogram was the president's own choice for a fast moving emergency.

"Yes," Evans barked.

"We'll get Big Sky on his way," Friedman responded. He was already typing the order into his computer.

The fact that President Lamden was staying in a specially outfitted suite in a Los Angeles hotel was exactly *why* he had to move. There was an evacuation at another hotel, with a similar suite, also dubbed Rip Van Winkle. That hotel was on the itinerary for President Lamden's visit in August, set by the Office for Strategic Initiatives.

"He'll be out in three minutes," the Secret Service director acknowledged.

"I'll alert the vice president and the speaker. Call me when he's cleared the building. Again, when he's on the road. At the airport and in the air."

Now Presley Friedman wondered about the exact nature of the emergency. He'd find out soon enough.

Los Angeles International Airport
the same time

Eric Ross had very few of the worries of the average American. His meals were covered. The same for his laundry bills. His clothes were provided. He had a per diem wherever he traveled, and he traveled all over the world without paying a dime to the airlines. It was a perfect deal for a private man with no family and few friends.

But Ross did have responsibility.

Eric Ross was a career U.S. Air Force officer. He served with the Air Mobility Command's 89th Airlift Wing, stationed at Andrews AFB, Suitland, Maryland. He had high security clearance and access throughout the base. He grunted more than talked, worked more than socialized. Cohorts who'd served with him could hardly say they actually knew *Rossy*, even after 12 years. But he wasn't there for his personality. It was for what he could do. Eric Ross supervised the maintenance of the two most important airplanes in the United States: a pair of specially configured Boeing 747-200Bs built at Boeing's Everett, Washington, plant.

The planes flew with the designation VC-25A and tail numbers SAM 28000 and 29000. In military parlance, *SAM* referred to *Special Air Mission*. These were definitely special jets.

When Ross's boss was onboard either craft, the radio call sign became *Air Force One*.

This afternoon, the planes were serviced and waiting at a satellite terminal on the ocean side of LAX. The president was in Los Angeles for two days of meetings with Western governors. Ross had to make sure they were ready to fly at a moment's notice.

Blindfolded, Lt. Eric Ross could successfully inspect the most hidden quarters of his SAMs. Performing specific diagnostic tests in the dark was part of his education. However, Rossy exceeded the minimum standards. He'd been trained behind closed doors by Boeing's top engineers. He had the reputation for being able to smell virtually *any* trouble. What he couldn't personally figure out, he could get help for, day or night, from anywhere on the planet. Ross had direct access to unlisted numbers of people with *very special knowledge.* Most importantly, he had the guarantee that there would always be an answer.

For years, the 44-year-old, five-foot-ten career officer passed on putting in for a transfer to far easier duty. He said *Air Force One* was his life. It called out to him. The last three presidents always felt better when they saw his name on the roster; better yet when he accompanied them in the air. And when the current commander in chief, still getting used to the trappings of his flying Oval Office, asked, "Is everything looking okay, Rossy?" the thumbs-up put him at ease.

The confidence came from the sense that these were Rossy's planes, and his hands-on approach to their care made the whole experience of flying on *Air Force One* more secure.

If Ross hadn't put in the 238 miles of wire in each plane himself, more than twice what is found in a typical civilian 747, he certainly acted like he had. They weren't just wires. They were *his* wires. And not just ordinary wire at that. These were lifesaving strands, with a shielding over the core to protect the planes' systems from any electromagnetic pulse—the kind generated by a thermonuclear blast.

Unless he was sicker than a dog, Ross traveled everywhere with the Airlift Wing. The planes couldn't be serviced by commercial aviation ground crews or even regular Air Force. Security reasons alone made that impossible. That's why Ross and members of the 89th were so vital.

According to the orders that had come down, the VC-25As were scheduled to depart for Andrews at 2215 hrs. Both planes. These days they *always* had to be flight worthy, 24/7. One ferried the president; the other was support. Ross couldn't pilot either 28000 or 29000, but he could ground them with a check mark in the wrong box.

In addition to their actual operation, Rossy had extensive knowledge of the history of *Air Force One*—actually a misnomer, because the call sign doesn't belong to any one plane. *Air Force One* is actually *any* airplane the president is aboard, whether it's a 747, an F/A-18 Super Hornet, a S-3B Viking, or even a Cessna. And once a president ceases being a president, through death or resignation, the designation of the aircraft immediately changes.

Such was the case on August 9, 1974, after Secretary of State Henry Kissinger read President Nixon's formal resignation letter and Gerald Ford was sworn in as the 38th president. Air traffic control in Kansas received the radio message from the plane carrying Nixon: "Kansas City, this is *former Air Force One*, please change our call sign to SAM 27000."

The lieutenant was not permitted to discuss classified information about the twin jets, or reveal details on anything already on the record. Occasionally, freshmen members of the White House press corps would try. *"Come on, Rossy. Where's the escape pod?"* There was none, but he would only smile and shrug his shoulders.

"How many parachutes does this thing carry?" Again, no comment, even though they were not equipped with parachutes. The dangerous slipstream created by the 747 in flight prevented their use.

"What about the range of this thing?"

"I dunno, pretty far," he offered, even though the reporters could find out on the Internet that the planes were capable of flying half-way around the world without refueling, and with midair fill-ups, they could probably fly indefinitely.

Ross was not known for volunteering much. But he did like telling reporters, "When you really come down to it, my job's pretty simple. I just have to think about the unthinkable and make sure it doesn't happen." For that reason and a hundred others on the official check-lists, *Air Force One* was gassed up and ready to go.

They were happy he was working for the good guys.

Century Plaza Hotel, Los Angeles, California the same time

"Mr. President, we have to go," said the lead agent, a 6-foot-tall bulldog of a man. The Secret Service agent closest to the president had gotten the message before Friedman was off the phone with Jack Evans. Word also had been radioed to the Air Force, which urgently launched a pair of F-15s out of Nellis AFB in Nevada. Already aloft were two Navy Super Hornets from San Diego, an E-3 Sentry AWACS Boeing 707/320, and a KC-10 tanker, all flying sweeping figure-eight patterns off the coast. Since 9/11, their contrails created a haunting white web above many of America's cities; a visible reminder of how the world had changed.

"What the...?" Lamden managed.

"This way, sir." The agent was absolutely insistent. "We have a *situation*. We need to leave the hotel immediately." He took Henry Lamden by the arm, making his intensions perfectly and immediately clear. Another agent fell in step on the other side of Big Sky. The Secret Service had come up with the designation name when they officially were assigned to guard him during the primary elections. It was an appropriate handle for the then-Governor of Montana.

Though they trained for this, Henry Lamden recognized that this was not another drill. This was the first time it really felt like an emergency. His heart quickened.

"Okay, okay. But I need to get...."

"We'll take care of everything, sir," the agent answered.

The president's guard force hurried him out of the secure suite at the Century Plaza Hotel. He noticed that the other agents looked equally as serious as the two men who flanked him.

The freight elevator door was open. Two more agents were posted there. Thanks to the use of an override key, they went down without stopping. Once in the basement, they proceeded along a planned exit route through a myriad of unmarked tunnels that led to a closely guarded garage exit and the waiting presidential limo. Lead and tail cars were already in place. The LAPD escort would have to catch up.

The agents pressed the president's head down, almost shoving him into his car. A second later they were screaming through the garage tunnels, faster than they'd ever practiced.

From the Reagan Presidential Suite to the backseat of the bullet-proof, iron-lined underbelly Lincoln: 2 minutes 45 seconds. Acceptable only because Big Sky was alive, and they were clear of a *Rip Van Winkle House.*

CHAPTER 4

Washington, D.C.
minutes later

"**M**ister..." the NDI hesitated over the telephone. This was still hard for him to get right. "...*vice president.*"

"Yes, Jack." Morgan Taylor responded to the Director of National Intelligence. "You don't sound happy."

"I'm not. We have a situation developing in Sydney."

"The evacuation at the St. George?" The vice president had seen the news. "Am I correct to assume there's no water main break?"

"Right. I hope the story sticks long enough to disarm about 20 bricks of C-4."

"Any idea who?" Taylor asked.

"No. Maybe there will be some signatures in the work. But my educated guess is al Qaeda. Maybe Abu Sayyaf. And if you want my two cents?"

"Of course."

"I don't think it was intended to go off today or tomorrow."

The vice president's mind raced. "The Ville St. George. Isn't that one of the hotels designated for presidential visits?" He hadn't stayed in it yet, but he was certain it was the venue for the upcoming nuclear proliferation conference. The session was already on Lamden's calendar, though not officially announced.

"Right again."

"August?" Taylor said after putting it all together.

"Yes, sir." Evans acknowledged. "It's a miracle some house electrician found the device now. SASR says it had enough battery power to keep the Energizer bunny going for years."

"Give me the wide shot, Jack. Short-term, long-term impact."

"In the immediate, all the Rip Van Winkle houses will be off limits for you and the president until they're turned upside-down. Long-term, millions around the world in security upgrades, from initial construction through identity checks on the lady who changes the toilet paper."

Morgan Taylor suddenly remembered the president was in one now. "Henry?"

"On the road as of seven minutes ago," the nation's chief intelligence officer answered. "We implemented Rolling Thunder as soon as we heard."

"Wise decision."

"Has Congressman Patrick been informed?" The vice president referred to the new speaker of the House, Duke Patrick.

"Next on the list."

"What's Homeland Security saying?"

"Nothing yet. But I don't think you and the president will be able to take a piss without your boys looking over your shoulders."

There was a knock at the door. "Mr. Vice President." Taylor recognized the voice of his principal Secret Service detail.

"Like clockwork, Jack," he said over the phone.

"Thank you. Secret Service wants you at the White House until the president is safely back. I'll have the speaker driven there as well."

Taylor didn't relish spending any more time than necessary with Congressman Patrick, but protocol dictated. Patrick, a self-made man and a fast decision maker, retired 12 years earlier from Dynlcom, a multi-billion-dollar Internet provider, with a billion of its profits. Taylor should have liked him, but politics drove them apart. Patrick went into Congress as a Republican, then five years ago recast himself as a "modern Democrat." That meant that as Democrats go, he was way right of center and suddenly someone to watch. *Duke*, as he liked to be called, wasn't even the kind of Democrat that Lamden could wholeheartedly embrace, but he was the man that the party looked to for the future. As speaker of the House, he was also number three in the order of Presidential Succession.

"Mr. Vice President!" the voice came more forcefully through the door.

"Yes, yes. I know. I'll be right with you."

"Get going, Mr. Vice President, I'll keep you posted," Evans stated.

"Before I go, give me your real sense, Jack."

Evans always appreciated Morgan Taylor inviting his personal appraisal. It often told more than some of the hard facts. "We got a lucky break, Morgan. No immediate danger to Henry," he used first names only with Morgan Taylor. "Next time we might not be so lucky. The enemy is getting smarter."

"But who's the enemy, Jack?"

The national intelligence chief answered before the blink of an eye. "Nothing's changed. Everyone."

Morgan Taylor wasn't good at being vice president. He knew it. What's more, most of the press within the Beltway also knew. *Hell, I should have just gone fishing!* he constantly told himself.

After running the country with the intensity with which he flew his Navy F/A-18s, this job was the worst. A typical day: Presiding over the Senate...enduring the hours of posturing from young turks he'd all but thrown out of the White House...shaking hands and not meaning it.

Morgan Taylor hated it, but it wasn't the kind of job you simply retired from. He accepted it for two reasons. First, he admired Henry Lamden. The second and real reason, decided in the instant that Lamden asked him, was that he had unfinished business. He claimed it was professional. Reporters speculated it was more personal. He was determined to find out who was responsible for stealing *his* presidency. Teddy Lodge was the end to the means, but not the means itself. Someone else had patiently manipulated the political process for more than 40 years. He had failed, which Taylor assumed would be hard for a man who counted on winning.

The same could be said for Morgan Taylor.

He won at Annapolis, graduating in the top ten percent of his class. He won in the air, as an aircraft carrier Super Hornet commander. He won on the ground, coming out alive after a crash landing in Iraq. That was thanks to a man who remained close to him today. He won in business as an executive for Boeing. He won in the Senate and he won the presidency.

Now 54, Taylor kept to a military regime and a military look. His weight remained a relatively fat-free 195 pounds, and his hair was no longer than when he was in the Navy. He exercised like he'd go hungry without it, and kept current in the cockpit of almost everything the Navy had in the air.

While he wore black pin-striped Brooks Brothers suits during work hours, he couldn't wait to get into loose-fitting turtlenecks, khakis, and a Navy flight jacket. Sometimes he wished he could chuck the suits in his closet altogether. He got close, but when Lamden asked him to remain in government, he unpacked his suits and sent them back for a pressing. For his Senate confirmation hearings, he wore his favorite, which was really hard to tell since they all looked the same.

Taylor testified that the country could not rest. When asked for proof, Taylor couldn't provide any. In fact, all the evidence in hand pointed to a one-time plot. But Morgan Taylor reminded the senators of the Islamic terrorist attack in February 1993. Their bomb below the World Trade Center towers damaged but did not destroy the buildings. Eight years later, with greater resolve and a deadlier plan, al Qaeda brought down both massive towers. "The same could happen with the United States presidency."

"No, this is not a time to breathe easier. Not a time to celebrate," he told the senators. "Not a time to think the country is safe. The American political process *is* the target now. The goal is to undermine America's foreign policy, destroy ties with our allies, and demolish our infrastructure. Our standing in the world can collapse like the World Trade Center towers." What he didn't say was, of course, the guiding political principal of the Moslem world: The day the Great Satan falls, the State of Israel disintegrates.

It was all so clear to Morgan Taylor. The press was right. It was personal.

So, Taylor accepted Henry Lamden's call. He testified before Congressional investigative committees, at his Senate confirmation hearings, then raised his right hand and once again swore on the Bible to uphold the Constitution of the United States, which he had done his entire military and political life. In doing so, he became the first ex-president ever to move into the number-two seat.

The new president gave Vice President Taylor wide-ranging, though not public, powers to do it. And he allowed Taylor to keep a unique asset on the payroll: a man by the name of Scott Roarke.

* * *

FBI Labs
Quantico, Virginia

"No, no, no. His jaw is bigger. Wider."

Secret Service Agent Scott Roarke slid his deep black coffee to the side of the standard issue metal desk, and leaned closer to the computer monitor. He pointed to the image on the screen—the work of FBI photo age-progression expert Duane "Touch" Parsons.

"Broaden it. And a bit more angular, Touch." Roarke said.

He'd spent a good deal of time with Parsons, whose nickname fit perfectly. Parsons had *the knack*. It was his *touch* that had convinced Roarke, and, in turn, President Morgan Taylor, that Congressman Teddy Lodge was not the man he claimed to be. Visual evidence, although not court-worthy, was in Parson's age-progression photographs.

Parsons lived at his computer day and night. Despite his weakness for Krispy Kreme donuts, ever-present at his desk, Parsons remained trim and fit. Roarke didn't know when or how he stayed in shape. *Maybe he's just one of those guys with a fast metabolism.* Whatever the case, Scott Roarke was happy he was at the computer.

Now the two men worked on another, perhaps more complex, though completely related, puzzle.

Ever since Roarke was a kid, plucked from a petty theft by an L.A. beat cop and given the choice to straighten out under the tutelage of a renowned Tae Kwon Do master or go to jail, Roarke listened to people in uniforms and experts. They took the form of drill sergeants in the army, officers in Special Forces, FBI investigators who really did know how to read evidence like the back of their hands, and most of all, his boss and mentor, Morgan Taylor.

These were the kind of men Roarke related to. And for good reason: He lived to see another day because of them. Yet, most of his experiences were not recorded in any official reports. Not his missions to China, Iran, Iraq, or Afghanistan. Not his work in uniform. Not his assignments in plainclothes.

Roarke stood six-feet even. He had a tight, muscular frame, but nothing that would draw attention to his strength. He always traveled with a Sig Sauer P229, but his smile disarmed almost everyone. His laugh did even more. And his flirtatious wit made him an extremely eligible bachelor.

Only a few women had actually gotten close to the small scar under his chin. These days, there was one woman in particular.

Roarke's dark brown hair showed no signs of gray. He hoped it would stay that way for awhile. He was 38 years old.

Roarke and Taylor shared a bond that superceded any visible delineation of duty—and for good reason. Roarke had saved U.S. Navy Commander Taylor's life in Iraq after a missile took out his fighter. Years later, then-President Taylor gave Roarke a strictly off-the-books job of coordinating counter-terrorism intel under a cloaked White House operation called "PD 16," for Presidential Directive 1600. Roarke was the charter member. Actually, he was the operation's *only* member. He moved about freely with Taylor's permission. Considering what he'd recently accomplished, the new chief executive wasn't about to change the natural order of things. Taylor's going-forward "arrangement" with Henry Lamden included the continued funding of Roarke's basement office.

Like always, Roarke was on his own. He clocked in at the Secret Service, but unlike the 900 other agents, he had special privileges and other duties. Most important to him, he didn't have to wear a tie. Next, he never had to stand vigil for endless hours while the president and other key members of the executive branch did everything from make speeches to screw their wives or girlfriends. He also didn't have to talk into his sleeve to other bullet-stoppers stationed around their perpetual targets. And he only reported to one man: Morgan Taylor.

Roarke had thought about giving it all up. A year ago, he was close to looking for a high-paying security job in the private sector. That was before he vowed—like Taylor—to clean up some unfinished business.

So Roarke continued to work in the shadows, poring over the reams of public testimony and classified documents that followed the death of President-elect Lodge more than four months earlier.

The assassin who killed Lodge had posed as a Capitol policeman. Ballistics had proven that an officer with fake ID pulled the trigger. Roarke was certain that he was the same man who shot Lodge's wife nearly a year ago—the very act that propelled a sympathy vote, and swept Lodge past Taylor in the election. He also placed the assassin at three other murders.

While the FBI had developed its profile, Roarke quietly considered his own. *Age 30-35, yet able to pass as almost anybody 20 to 60.*

Expert marksman. So good that people initially thought he blew the assassination of Teddy Lodge, when in reality he accurately hit his target, Mrs. Jennifer Lodge. An actor of sorts, with the ability to effectively disguise himself. Trained in dialects, allowing him to blend in with no notice. Definitely the muscle; probably not the brain.

The evidence pointed to a man with honed athletic abilities, a convincing manner, and an incredible understanding of forensics. With the exception of quite literally two missteps—a latent foot impression against a hotel wall in Hudson, New York, and another thousands of miles away along a riverbank in Utah—he left no clues. *A professional,* Roarke considered, *with very special training, including the precise eye of a marksman. But there was something extra-remarkable about him.* Roarke looked for a pattern in his work. *Bold strikes in the middle of the day—a main street, a river bed, inside a commuter train, and even under the Capitol Rotunda.* Every hit was different. There were no common denominators, except for the killer's keen ability to change appearances almost instantly.

As time wore on, Roarke developed an odd sense of admiration for the man's talents. *He knows it all. That means he was a great student with a great teacher. No,* he decided. *Different people, from different disciplines taught him...trained him.* While the FBI had their own profilers on the investigation, Scott Roarke was coming to his own conclusions. This was a man who was not only the perfect killer, he was a talented actor. He had two classical skills. Roarke realized he needed to look in two places to find him.

The man had murdered Lodge's wife, key in the plot to manipulate the congressman's rise to power, ultimately Lodge himself, and God only knows how many others. Taylor said it all after the Inauguration of Lodge's successor and running mate: "Find the assassin, and we'll find the man behind him."

First, Roarke needed to review whatever footage existed. The assassin had posed as a member of the Capitol Police, gotten access to the Rotunda, and at a key moment, made his shot. The still photographer at the Rotunda had nothing. Michael O'Connell, *The New York Times* reporter shooting a DV camera, only had the back of the killer's head from 20 feet away. Roarke found one quick shot on the pool videotape coverage from the Capitol shootout. But the camera never really focused on him. He was barely visible in a wide shot that panned the room—certainly not enough to make a true ID. He was turned to the side, his hat covered his forehead. He was out of the light. But there he was.

Roarke tried to glean something from the man's body language, his bulk, his posture. *Upright. Stiff. Alert. Watching everyone in one glance. Probably military-trained. Half of the puzzle.*

What do you look like? That was clearly Roarke's primary problem. There were descriptions. But each one was of a different man—all presumed to be the same killer.

A 20-year-old gang member. A 40-something businessman. An insurance agent in his thirties. A fisherman of undetermined age. One dark-haired, another balding, another gray. The Capitol policeman.

No fingerprints. No DNA. No photographs. The only evidence in common with some of the murders, but not all, was the size 11 boot print. Maybe even that was a red herring.

A different identity with every role he played.

Roarke needed to give him a name—a working identity. He thought for weeks, and then it came to him. *Depp,* for Johnny Depp. He decided on naming his quarry after an actor who always transformed himself *adeptly.* He even played a master of disguises in the film *Donnie Brasco.*

Depp fit him perfectly. It showed proper respect for a man Roarke realized he could never underestimate.

Roarke actually had provided a description himself. He'd had fleeting eye contact with Depp in the Rotunda when the killer was disguised as the policeman. But it was more likely that the assassin could pick Roarke out of a crowd quicker than he could spot Depp. That worried the Secret Service agent because it would give his prey a definite advantage the next time they'd meet, and he *was* certain— deadly certain—they'd meet again.

Touch worked with sketches of each "identity." They'd been drawn by FBI artists at the scene of Jennifer Lodge's death in upstate New York and the other killings he could be tied to. Now, he was reconfiguring the sketch based on Roarke's description. Once completed, it would integrate with the others in a computer program a Littleton, Massachusetts, firm, Viisage Technology Ltd., had provided after 9/11.

Clearly, all of the sketches portrayed vastly different men. But Roarke was personally certain he was looking for a lone accomplished killer. His goal was to come up with a reliable composite image; good enough to make Depp's mother proud.

"More like this?" Parsons asked after he'd made the changes on the jaw.

"Not sure." Roarke looked more closely. "No," he said on second thought. "Split the difference."

Parsons used his mouse to drag the jaw line out. Then he adjusted the shape of the chin to Roarke's specifications.

"Once I mess with one thing, I have to adjust everything else. You know, keep the face in perspective. Let me just play with it a bit."

"But his eyes still need..."

Parsons cut him off. "Do I tell you how to jump in front of the president or bust down a door?"

"No." Roarke saw where he was going.

"Then let me do what I know how to do."

"Your toys. Be my guest."

Parsons worked on a number of things. Thinning the eyes, making them colder. Raising the ears. Lengthening the nose. Everything connected with the last set of changes Roarke requested.

"So what exactly are we looking for in all of the pictures?" asked the Secret Service agent.

"*We*?"

"Excuse me. What are *you* looking for?" It was always like this with Roarke and Parsons.

"*I* am looking for common denominators to all the descriptions. I try them out. I grow them on a face, the computer whirs a little and tells me if I'm full of shit."

"And by the way, these are not *pictures*, so don't expect perfection," Parsons complained.

"Okay, drawings."

Parsons typed in a new line of code and sat back. "Sketches," he said, correcting Roarke again.

"Sketches. And?" Roarke asked encouragingly.

"And what?" Parsons replied.

"And now what's happening? You stopped."

"I stopped, but Ferret's working on it." Ferret was the Department of Defense's name for FRT or "face recognition technology," the program pioneered in the early 1990s, principally researched at MIT's Media labs. "The computer's thinking. It's scratching its hard drive."

Roarke looked confused for the moment.

"Its head, you dumbass. Ferret is scratching its head looking for commonality. And if this little project of yours crashes my computer, well, if you break it, you bought it."

"Uh-huh."

Parsons displayed a holier-than-thou attitude most of the time. Roarke learned to accept it. The 40-year-old FBI expert lived in a world of algorithms. He questioned everything and everybody. He never seemed satisfied that he'd be given enough time or information to properly solve a problem.

"You're all always in a rush. Every one of you spooks," he said.

"I'm not a spook."

Parsons ignored the answer. "Gotta have it now. Gimmie, gimmie, gimmie."

At least Parsons was right about that. Of course, time was never on Roarke's side, either. But the FBI graphic artist and programmer delivered, and that's what made him Roarke's go-to geek. Now the agent was back at Parson's door.

"You realize we'd both be better off if you'd give me something reasonable to work with."

"Sorry, but..."

"Photographs, Roarke. Photographs. Just once. Real pictures. Ever hear of film? Or maybe I can introduce you to a remarkable invention called a digital camera. Sony. Minolta, even Kodak's got it. Four, five, six megapixels. Amazing things."

Roarke knew this would go on for awhile. It was simply the cost of doing business with such a talent.

"What was I thinking?" Roarke sarcastically asked. "I'll go out, find, and capture Depp. Then I'll ask him to stand still for a second and say 'cheese.' Shouldn't be a problem. After that I'll pat him on the back and say 'thanks' and 'Oh, by the way, you can go back to killing important people now.' Then I'll post a real picture of him and see if I can track him down again. But wait. If I knew who he was and where he was, why would I be *here*?" It was time to re-ask his question. "What the fuck are you looking for?"

"All right," Parsons said shaking his head. "Using biometric technology designed to ID a person from distinguishing facial traits, the computer is trying to determine if there are any signatures common to each sketch."

"In other words?" Roarke asked, hoping to get a clearer description.

"Measuring characteristics, like the distance between the eyes, the dimensions of the nose, the angle of the jaw. Ferret's struggling to interpret data to create a template. Based solely on the multiple images, created by different people, the chances are slim that we'll get an accurate portrait. But since you ask, we're looking for face-to-face analogies. Are the eyes similar enough? The bridge of the nose? The lips? Teeth? The things that are hardest to cosmetically change. The program is processing distinct facial regions, encoding parameters from the rectified images, and attempting to establish a norm."

"And it works?"

"Sometimes."

"Oh, great."

"Well, that's the truth. I'd say Ferret works *pretty well* provided the materials at hand are good."

"Like a photograph?"

"Even then, it's no slam dunk," Touch allowed. "It's best when the subject's face occupies the whole image. Unless they're holding a number in front of their chest, you tell me how many bad guys will pose for the camera?"

"Back to my point. I got it."

"No, you don't. Not yet," the FBI expert complained. "Ferret recognizes the improbability of that. It's programmed to examine more complex images and sort out the extraneous, re-focusing on potential faces within any given field. Using a neural network-based face location system, it locates possible faces within an un-composed image."

"Then it works," Roarke said, hopefully.

"Depends on your definition of *works*," Parsons snorted through a laugh. "One of the first major applications was Super Bowl XXXV back in 2001. Everyone entering got their *punnum*'s scanned. Mind you, no one realized it was happening. But the FRT cameras clicked away as they went through the turnstiles. The digital pictures were fed to computers, which looked for possible matches with known criminals. Note that I said *criminals*. Boy, we live in a different world now," Parsons added as an aside. "Anyway, the software flagged 19 individuals. Some were just petty thieves. It picked out a ticket scalper or two. Most of the rest were just false positives."

"False positives?" Roarke needed some help with the explanation.

"Yeah. Falsely matching innocent people with database photos of perps. And then there's the problem of the reverse—false negatives."

"Not catching people even when the picture is in the system?"

"Bingo. That answer your question about it working?"

"Sort of. But it is an aid."

Parsons nodded agreement. "For me, yes. Some others out there wouldn't necessarily agree. There's a big debate on its use at airports. Concerns about the competency of Ferret delineating darker-skinned people in bright backgrounds. The effect of adverse lighting. Problems when there's high red content behind the subject. Whether glasses throw off the analysis. Scars. Tattoos. Head-on shots versus profiles. Everything matters."

"But now? Is it reliable now?" Roarke counted on an affirmative answer.

"Look, Roarke, with just sketches, you're not going to get what you came in for. There's no way to create a reliable extrapolation without at least one authentic picture. You realize the CIA and the Bureau don't have good pictures of most al Qaeda. Even when we access an archival passport photo from Interpol or other agencies, the programs still need further development to handle the aging process. You and I have been through that already."

Roarke nodded agreement.

"And the technology is still fooled by weight gains and beards. That's why it's taking so long. Too many geometric variations. Too much differentiation in age. Too much..."

Starting at the top of the screen, an image began to render.

"You were saying?"

"Well, the program reduces measurements of human faces to mathematical formulas or patterns in the data base. New software out of Stony Brook detects minute patterns of muscle movement in a smile. It's becoming one of the best indicators. Imagine that. A smile can be like a fingerprint. We call it a 'smile map.' And there are other facial landmarks that can come into play," Parsons continued more humbly. "Apparently..." he paused. A definite soft composite picture was resolving on screen.

Roarke smiled. "Yes?"

"Apparently, it detected enough landmarks to achieve a robust divination."

"In English."

"A crude prediction."

"Crude? Crude sounds real good to me right now," Roarke said.

"It's the best you'll get until..."

"I know. Until I hand over a real photograph. But this is going to help."

"Will you leave if I sharpen this up?"

"On my honor." Roarke held up three fingers: the sign of a scout promise.

"Why do I think you'll be back?"

Roarke stood and slapped Parsons back. "Because you know me."

Parsons waved him away and typed a prompt. The computer acted as if it had been given the equivalent of a stirrup to the hind quarter. Seconds later, a new image began to render. An almost photographic face gradually took shape, growing more real with definition. Colors and shading began to give it character. The chin was as Roarke remembered. The eyes deeper and thin. The rest was familiar, yet different.

The computer finished its work, and Parsons immediately saved it to the hard drive and printed a copy.

Speechless, Roarke studied the work. Depp looked to have an almost military quality. The composite depicted a man in his early 30s, Caucasian, computed with a muscular, chiseled face, a thin lower lip, an undistinguished nose, high cheekbones, thin eyebrows, close-set ears, short brown hair, and the cold eyes Roarke remembered. All in all, the likeness appeared very similar to Roarke in facial sculpture. Except for the scar under Roarke's chin and his short brown hair, they could be brothers.

"Well?" Parsons asked, fishing for a compliment.

"I don't know. I really don't know. It's different."

"Of course it is. As you said, your Mr. Depp *is* a master of disguises. But this may be as good a look behind the mask as you're going to get until you're face-to-face again."

Roarke peered into the screen. "Some of it seems right. Some of it...."

Parson's interrupted the thought. "Now let's see if he made the mistake of standing in front of a camera somewhere." Parsons saved the image to another program and typed in a new command. This time, Roarke let the photo expert continue without comment. Ninety-one seconds later, Ferret delivered the answer.

"I just accessed all of the known terrorists in the memory, along with state-by-state motor vehicle license photos, FBI records, newspaper archives, military IDs, and dozens of other sub directories. Here come the results."

The computer image reduced to one half the page, with the picture on the left and data on the right. Parsons read the analysis.

"Your man is a possible match to, let's see...." He highlighted a single line of text. "7,451,209 other subjects worldwide."

"Oh, fuck!" Roarke swore.

"And that's assuming he's even in the damned database. Wanna bet he isn't?"

CHAPTER 5

Cheviot Hills Recreation Park
Los Angeles, California

He was waiting for her.

Lynn Meyerson had already circled the Cheviot Hills Park and Rancho Golf Course once, a run of about three miles. Olsen planned to strike on mile six of her second lap.

He watched her still-powerful, long strides come into view again. She had circled the golf course, cut back into the park, and now darted across the grass near the parking lot. Her run took her between two baseball fields where Little League teams played. Olsen stood up from his park bench and stretched. Maybe she would have sprinting power left, he thought. He better be ready himself.

Meyerson took in all the sights and sounds while she ran. It relaxed her. With everything on her mind, it helped.

Closer again. He watched as she hugged the fence that separated the outfield from the greens, then followed a worn path toward the tennis courts, another 200 yards further. There she angled right, which took her by an asphalt basketball court. A few players stopped to catch a glimpse of the redhead. *She's not for you.* No one noticed when Olsen fell into step about 50 yards behind her.

Lynn rounded the recreation center. She heard a dance class. The door was open and young girls, probably no older than six or seven, were practicing ballet. She circled around again and ran in place just to take in the sight. About ten girls struggled to stay on their toes. It was sweet and almost comical. They were all dressed in pink tights and black leotards, their hair tied with pink ribbons. They did their best to please their instructor, a Russian immigrant, who had obviously worked with better students.

Lynn saw the pride in the faces of both the youngsters and the parents. She remembered the looks of her own mother and father, watching from bleachers just like the ones in the rec room. For an instant, it seemed like yesterday.

He suddenly slowed, rounding a turn along the path. The woman was jogging in place, distracted by something inside a building. Olsen rerouted to the sidewalk and leaned against a tree. He pretended to be out of breath. Thirty seconds later, she took up her run again, but he waited, not wanting to get too close too early. He noted how her breasts rose and fell with each step. He watched the firmness of her ass and the grace of her legs. He estimated how far away he was. *Sixty yards. Good.*

Meyerson continued running on a sidewalk that bordered the parking lot she'd crossed before. She gave her watch a quick glance. She figured she had another thirty minutes or so of good light. *Enough time to finish up and get back to the hotel.* She tried to be aware of the light and run when it was safe. All told, it would be a six-plus-mile course, covering the exact same path she'd carved out two days earlier and repeated the day before.

Now she cut left on the last arc of her run, down a road that rounded a dog park and to the empty park bench she'd spotted the previous day. She'd sit and rest there.

Fifty yards. Thirty. Twenty-five. The jogger behind Lynn counted down the distance as he closed in. The girl had paced herself the entire run, except when she stopped to watch the dancers. For a moment, he thought she might not continue beyond that point, but the ritual called out too loudly to her.

Twenty, he thought. *Fifteen.* He calculated his steps against hers. She took long, measured strides with her muscular legs that, no doubt, could still deliver a burst of energy in an emergency. But his approach wouldn't appear threatening. Exactly the opposite. In a few more steps she would hear his labored breathing; nothing unusual at the end of a day. It would announce his presence through a charade.

Now ten. Five. He caught up with her and matched her pace for 10 yards. After some heavy exhales, Nat Olsen managed a harmless "Hello." They were approaching an area about 40 feet long, with an incline that fell off sharply to the right.

"Hello," she said with little effort.

Ten steps later, "This used to be a lot easier."

She glanced over to him. *Oh man. Out of shape.* Another automatic look. This one to his ring finger. *Married.*

He caught the eye contact. *She'll be less on guard. Good.* "I want to meet the guy who said it's all about conditioning, not age."

Lynn gave him a reassuring nod. "You're doing fine. Only a little bit further."

Yes, only a little bit. He had managed to do the whole run without having had to talk with anyone else.

A few yards from the highest point of the incline, he grabbed his side and grimaced.

"You okay?" Lynn asked.

"I'll run through it." *Five more steps. Four. Three.*

They continued running in tandem for two more steps. Then he grunted, stumbled a step, locked his feet up, and tumbled down the hill.

"Hey!" she called out.

The jogger tumbled over four times and came to a stop precisely where he had planned, out of sight in the underbrush. Lynn automatically cut down the hill, calling out, "Are you all right? Need any help?"

He rose to his knees, his back to her. He nodded as if in pain, and waved for her to come down.

"Okay, maybe it's age, not conditioning," she joked, seeing that he was trying to regain his balance. "On my way."

Lynn was only a few feet from him now. She spoke softly. "Can you stand?"

For a moment, the caring in her voice broke his concentration; after all, she was coming to his aid. But he had agreed. The amount was set. Like always, half was already in his account. Instantly, any empathy for the woman evaporated.

He shook his head.

"Okay. Just take a few seconds, you'll be okay," she said, coming upon him.

Meyerson knelt down beside him, her arm on his shoulders. A thought flashed in her mind. *He's a lot more muscular than...*

Suddenly, the man reached his right arm in front of his chest, across his shoulder, grabbing her left wrist. Simultaneously, he brought his body down. With the combination of his forward motion and his hard yank, she flipped over his back and onto hers. In that one swift move, she lay flat on the ground, with shocked eyes staring into his. They were cold, peering at her from someplace darkly dangerous.

He's not sweating. He should be sweating.

He rolled on top of her, painfully pinning her arms down with his knees; his butt firmly on her pelvis. One hand went right for her mouth as she struggled to say, "Let me go!"

Lynn arched up her back, trying to toss him off. But she couldn't.

He's going to rape me! Her mind raced. *Oh my God!* She acted instinctively. *Kick him!* Lynn tried, but his weight and position locked her down.

It had already gone on three seconds longer than it should have. He had no desire to put the woman through any unnecessary agony. After all, it wasn't her fault. He knew where she worked, but little more. He didn't need to. All he had focused on were her habits, her rituals, and whether she carried Secret Service protection. The president's trip provided the perfect opportunity, although her regular jogging trail along the district's Rock Creek would have worked as well.

He had studied her as he did all his targets. He never considered them victims, just targets. This one was like most others, a creature of habit. In Washington, mornings were always the same. Out at 7:05. A Starbucks stop. A Metro ride to Union Station. An eleven-minute walk to the White House. Coming home depended upon the day. But he knew from his surveillance she always managed to run if the weather held and it wasn't too late. He followed her on weekends, noting that she dated rarely. No one special was in her life. It wouldn't have mattered anyway. He'd killed husbands and wives without so much as a second thought.

The method of dispatching the woman had been left up to him. She ran. So he'd find her while she was running. If it hadn't been this, it would have been something else. He'd been given only one additional instruction, which he would quickly carry out after. First things first.

He had decided that strangulation would be too slow. Slitting her jugular, too messy. A silenced shot to the head, too professional. He would do it like a gang member might in a rape.

In one effortless motion he reached under his sweat suit, pulled out the knife from its Velcro hiding place, and depressed the release. It instantly opened, and without further hesitation, he plunged it through her left breast, pressing through the softness, through her ribs, into her heart. He turned the blade slightly inwards to ensure he would cut across the ventricle, flooding her lungs with blood and killing her at least two ways.

She couldn't speak, but he knew by experience what her eyes were saying. *Why?* He leaned forward and whispered directly into her ear. "Are you wondering *why*?"

He was sure she tried to nod *yes*.

"Beats the hell out of me," he said coldly. And that was the truth.

CHAPTER
6

Tel Aviv, Israel
1058 hrs., local time

I ra Wurlin knocked on the solid metal door. Few people ever got this far. Fewer still passed through to the room beyond. For the last eleven years of his life, Wurlin felt two overriding emotions. He admitted to only one. He told his boss he was honored to serve him so directly. In his quiet time and private places, he felt cursed.

Now 51, Ira Wurlin wondered where his life had gone. He'd forgone marriage and raising a family to serve almost day and night as the principal analyst and aide to a man the West knew very little about. So, like the man he worked for, Wurlin led a secret existence. No children or grandchildren would ever be born to him and pass on stories about his exceptional service to their country.

He was an unimposing, ordinary man, the kind you'd never notice in a crowd. Thinning hair, glasses in bland, clear frames, a short-sleeved white shirt that would have looked better on him if he could lose 15 pounds. He was a blank man in a colorful world, and it was this virtual invisibility that made him so good at his job.

Wurlin took short deliberate steps, always with the same pace, which said all you needed to know about him. Work was his life. He slept more nights at his office than he did at home. He was an analyst. Only one man could fire him, and that wasn't going to happen. Yet, like every secretary, assistant, or even support staff in the complex, Wurlin wore an ID badge with a good-for-one-day-only computer chip. Try to traverse the halls without the proper chip, you were a dead man...or woman. There was blood on the walls to prove it.

A control officer watching a monitor three floors higher in the nondescript Tel Aviv headquarters always noted when a "blip" moved from one quadrant—it could be an office or a bathroom—to another. This blip was going where it was supposed to.

"Enter."

Wurlin didn't have to identify himself. Jacob Schecter knew he was coming, as he did so many other things. Schecter was head of Hamossad Lemodi'in Vetafkidim Meyuhadim. Israel's intelligence agency, Mossad.

"Ah, Ira," he started as if surprised, which he wasn't. "What do you have for me?"

Schecter had risen through the Israeli Air Force, the IAF, and flown on more unrecorded missions than those logged by paperwork. He was educated in intelligence specialty schools, though he never talked of his training or his experiences.

His wavy brown hair was longer than in his military years, but his wardrobe remained consistent with his military code: a tan, button-down, short-sleeve shirt and khaki pants. Nothing flashy, nothing that signified his supremacy in the Mossad or in the government. Tradition had it that even the identity of the Mossad head remained a secret as a matter of national security. Rumors flew. But rumors were usually wrong.

Jacob Schecter didn't have a birthdate or a birthplace. He looked to be in his late 50s, but even Ira wasn't certain. No Air Force friends ever visited, and he never spoke of a family; wife, children, or parents. Schecter might not even be his real name.

As Director of the Mossad, he had supreme authority over the security of Israel, guarding the nation from outside threats, gathering political, military, and civilian intelligence, and evaluating the information. He reported to only one person: the Prime Minister *de jour.*

The other focal point in his stark white room was the utilitarian industrial office desk, which contained visible locks and hidden sub-locks that Schecter alone could open. The only creature comfort was a very worn, coffee-stained leather chair. A picture of Israel's first prime minister, David Ben-Gurion, hung over his desk. Three clocks, representing current time in Washington, Tel Aviv, and—for historical sake—Moscow, were lined up at eye level on the opposite wall.

What wasn't visible was the metal lining within the walls. It effectively blocked eavesdropping devices and microwave signals. Even with that security protection, Schecter's office was swept by Mossad agents, not once a week or even once a day, but twice each day.

It was from here that Jacob Schecter sought ways to protect Israel's secrets and uncover those of his enemies...or his friends.

He was one of the most protected, most protective, and most secretive men in the world.

He was also one of the most aware. Except for today. He was trying to figure out the meaning of some unencrypted messages the Mossad had received via e-mail. Schecter laid them on his desk. There was no need to give them to Wurlin. He had already vetted the content over the last 72 hours.

"So, Ira, what is your opinion?" Schecter preferred first names. Trust mattered more than rank.

Wurlin didn't need prompting. They were scheduled to discuss the matter of the person they referred to as *Chantul*.

"Simple matters. Nothing more. We get a little bit of this and that."

"Grade?" asked Jacob.

"D. No better."

Schecter read the most recent seven-line correspondence again. "Interesting. And nothing."

"Like the last."

"Are we being wooed or baited, my friend?"

"I can't be sure. Not yet."

Wurlin took back the file. "The contact is traceable. That is what concerns me. Counter-intelligence could be back-channeled very easily."

"And traced here," the head of Mossad added. "I'm worried, not because it exists, but because it exists and says nothing."

Wurlin had come to the same conclusion. An uninvited operative was knocking at their door. *Why?*

"Verify every single word, Ira. And my orders stand. Do not respond. Nothing but silence from us."

"You are more suspect than before? This Chantul worries you."

"Everything worries me, Ira." He said it with a low, rumbling laugh, not a humorous one; the kind that signified his concern. "Now what else do you have today?"

Wurlin reported on a deep-cover Mossad agent who had infiltrated the Iran University of Science and Technology. An operation was in play to determine which Iranian professors were freelancing on the stepped-up nuclear arms program. Mossad wanted to know who they were, how dangerous their knowledge could be, and how they could be turned or neutralized. He would leave the final option open for Schecter. The briefing was another reminder that Israel lived day-to-day. They were surrounded by enemies and hated by most of the world. The country and its defenses were principally sustained through their high tax rates and their ever-tenuous relationships with the West.

As a people, Israelis stayed alive through an unparalleled determination and their government's reliance on intelligence. It was dangerous and time consuming to cast the net, but Jacob Schecter's spies succeeded where America's CIA failed.

Schecter continued to listen, but the news was always the same. *Bad.* Iran, Iraq, al Qaeda. Renewed anti-Semitism around the world. The French. Some days, even the Americans. That's what brought him back to *Chantul.*

He gave this freelancer a name; one with a specific biblical reference.

During the voyage of the Ark, Noah discovered that the lions had become far too dangerous. They liked dining on the other passengers. So he prayed to God, who answered him by sending the lions into a deep sleep. But soon, with lions asleep, rats quickly multiplied and made life on the Ark even worse. So Noah prayed again. God listened and woke the lion for one roar. Out of its mouth sprung a cat—in Hebrew, *chantul.* The creature, the first of its kind, was blessed with the timeless job of dispatching the rats.

This Chantul, his wily cat, came from another great lion. But as he sat and listened to Ira Wurlin recite the day's bad news, one thought continued to occupy his mind.

Who were the rats? He struggled over the same answer his American counterpart came up with. *Everyone.*

* * *

The White House Situation Room

"Hello, Duke," Morgan Taylor said, when the Speaker of the House entered the White House Situation Room.

"Mr. Vice President," Patrick replied in kind. "I see we've got a little excitement."

"Excitement we don't need." The comment served to deflate the speaker's enthusiasm.

"Perhaps a poor choice of words."

Taylor affirmed the admission with a nod. He then sat at the head of the long table and dialed the National Intelligence chief. "This is Taylor. Get me Evans. He's expecting my call."

Twenty seconds later, he was connected.

Duke Patrick looked on. He was 45, stocky, but not overweight. His one-inch heels lifted him to six feet. But it was his head of hair that made him appear even taller as well as distinguished. At the top and sides, thick fire-red locks; close to his ears, a band of gray. He was someone who caught the camera's attention in the way Teddy Lodge had the year before. Patrick was obviously annoyed to hear only half the conversation. He took the seat opposite the vice president and raised an eyebrow.

"What do we know, Jack?" Taylor swiveled the chair away from the speaker.

"The Australians have things locked down. They're working on getting the device out. It's not the kind of thing you hurry along."

"Understood. Are we getting one of ours there?" It was the kind of thing he used to order, not ask. The election had changed things.

"On the way," Evans stated. "The top explosive forensics guy from the FBI. But the SASR is a tight bunch. They know what they're doing."

Taylor was grateful that cooperation among the intelligence services had increased in recent years. "I'll give Foss a call." David Foss was the prime minister.

Evans agreed, then added, "I don't like this one bit. It's pure luck how the damned thing was found. And if it had gone off when expected..." He didn't finish the thought.

"Do you think we'll learn anything from the bomb itself?"

"We always do. Everyone who assembles one has a signature. Sometimes it's in the wiring, other times the marking on the C-4. It could be the casing, the type of electrical tape, or the solder. We'll be examining for anything and everything. And then there's the off chance we'll lift some clean fingerprints."

Taylor felt Patrick's eyes boring into the back of his head as Evans began to explain the chain of events. "Hold on a second." Taylor decided that Patrick should hear what made the situation *deadly*, not exciting. He turned back to the congressman. "Duke's with me. I'll put you on the box."

Patrick smiled, thinking he had won something. Taylor enabled the speaker phone. "Go ahead, we're both on."

"Hello, Congressman."

"Hello, Mr. Director. Nice to talk with you."

Nice? Taylor glared. Another faux pas. "Mr. Director," he said, reestablishing the seriousness, "this is a good chance for the speaker to get a crash course in international terrorism."

Vice President Morgan Taylor effectively cut the third most important man in the United States government down to size.

CHAPTER
7

Lebanon, Kansas
Tuesday, 19 June
12:05 A.M. CDT

The radio talk host potted up the cut of the Beatles' "Revolution."
He had adopted it as something of an anthem right after the
election, and unabashedly used it to keep his audience fired
up.

"Good morning, good evening, good night, America. It's been six
hours since I last talked with you. Six hours since the *Strong Nation*
gathered yesterday afternoon. Has your life gotten any better in six
hours? No," Elliott Strong said in the rambling soliloquy that opened
his late-night talk show. "It hasn't gotten any better because you
haven't done anything. Have you written your congressman? No.
Have you faxed the nightly news shows? No. Have you complained
about their liberal reporting? No. Have you gotten off your butts?
No, you haven't. So tonight you get to hear me. No open phones. At
least not now. If we go to the phones, I don't want to hear, 'Maybe,'
or 'I'll try,' or 'I'll get to it soon.' And definitely not, 'Oh, Elliot, I have
the carpool, my day is jammed, I wish I could.' I only want to talk to
people who are willing to tell me what they're going to do to take
back the country. If I don't get any calls, then you're just going to
have to endure me for four unending hours. Except for a few
important breaks for commercials," he added jokingly. "Like right
now."

The fact that Elliott Strong broadcast from the geographic center
of the contiguous 48 states was no accident. He wanted to visibly
channel American opinion from an appropriate location. What better

place than the epicenter? The site was marked by a limestone sign along Kansas Highway 191, a mile-long road that existed only for the purpose of leading visitors to latitude 39'50", longitude 98'35".

Actually, taking Alaska and Hawaii into account, the geographic center was in an even more remote area, near Rugby, North Dakota, but Lebanon, Kansas, was good enough for him. He had his satellite uplink, a web manager to run his dot-com, and a helicopter that could quickly get him to Hastings Municipal Airport in Nebraska, some 56 miles away.

Lebanon, Kansas, was not really representative of America as a whole. As of the last census, the population was 97.7 percent white, 1.3 percent Hispanic, 1.0 percent Native American. There were no African-Americans. Out of 312 inhabitants, Elliott Strong was the most famous. That's just the way he liked it.

"So what's it going to be? Me or you?" Strong looked at the phones. They were already lit up, but he wasn't going to give in that easily. The audience couldn't see. They deserved a good kick in the butt, and they were going to get it tonight.

"Okay, while you think about whether or not you're going to dial the phone, let's review what's happened in the world today. What you won't read in *The New* Yuck *Times—*" his joke "—and the rest of the liberal press."

Strong used the usual wire service copy, but his primary sources were the most right wing members of Congress and their aides, who briefed him on legitimate legislative issues and fed him outright political lies they wanted spread.

Strong would lay it all out—some as fact, some as rumor designed to undermine moderates and liberals, and some as plain malarkey. Each subject helped stir up the audience and make for a good show. Strong played the part of an increasingly fierce attack dog for the extreme right. They thought they had the better of him. He knew they didn't.

"*The New* Yuck *Times* reports that 98 nuclear devices from the *former* Soviet Union are still missing." He emphasized *former* in such a way as to suggest Russia was to be regarded as the enemy it was decades ago. Americans needed enemies to hate, and it was still far easier to wrap his message around the need to depose nations with un-American ideologies than attack faceless terrorists.

"Where do you think they could be?" he asked snidely. "Afghanistan? Chechnya? Iran? How about San Diego or St. Louis?" The thought hung in the air, silently, powerfully. The message was clear: Don't trust foreigners in your neighborhood.

"And speaking of Russia, what's going on there? Is anybody paying attention?" Strong asked with bombastic flair. "Hello? This should be front page news. But you won't find it in the leftist papers. No, sir. Not on CNN or the so-called progressive—that's double speak for liberal—talk shows. But, fortunately you've come to the *right* place." Strong went on to explain how the new Russian president continued to crack down on personal freedoms.

After a few minutes on that topic, he was onto another.

"Communist rebels struck again in Chile. Thirty-four dead freedom fighters, including a missionary." Again another veiled message, this time for the Christian right. "What year is it there? Nineteen seventy-one. President Lamden, why don't you put them away?

"And then there are those Pakistan, and Indian leaders. You pronounce their names, I can't. The liberals praise them for their courage to make peace. Give me a break. Like they're really out sipping green tea and playing chess. You know they're stockpiling more nuclear weapons. And if you think otherwise, then you've got to be smoking some really serious cannabis, which, by the way, is illegal. So when those mushroom clouds blow this way—you do understand the wind blows from West to East in the northern hemisphere—who do we thank? Taylor, for putting one over on us when he was president.

"And liberals keep trying to get us to believe that Israel's prime minister is happier than a clam at high tide. Well, my friends, that's just wrong."

If his audience checked the actual *New York Times* story, the opposite was true. Blanca Kaplov's troubles were widely reported. But that didn't matter. Elliott Strong put his claims out over the air, and his listeners took it as gospel.

"Believe me, that place is going to explode like a hot keg and *Mister* Lamden—" he hated calling Henry Lamden president "—is not going to be the Super Glue to keep things together.

"And Congress? They're forcing through one piece of anti-individual, big-government legislation after another. The country isn't going to look the same for your children. We're going to be living in a country formerly known as the United States of America. Mark my words, this administration is going to get to the 2nd Amendment this time around." There hadn't been a word of discussion about banning guns since either Taylor or Lamden took office. "It's not on the docket yet, but my sources tell me they have it in their sights.

"Which brings me back to what are *you* going to do about it." He became more agitated. "You know, I think you really don't want a strong nation," he said, a play on words. "Not really. You say you do, but you really don't. You're a bunch of sheep." He could just about hear his viewers chime in, *No, we're not!* "Sleepy sheep being herded around by a phantom administration; unelected, yet serving for four years. Four years!" he repeated. "The Lamden-Taylor White House holds you in its powerful grip...not because they have the power. Because you let them!"

Strong paused for maximum impact. "Oh sure, you're comforted by the illusion that you live in a democracy. You choose to believe that the Constitution—the law of the land—somehow sanctions this government. Every night someone wines, 'Oh, Elliott, aren't we a nation *by the people?*' Well, how can we be, when we didn't elect the two men at the very top! Every night someone e-mails me, 'But Elliott, we are a country *for the people.*' But how can we be, when both pretenders have no right to serve *us.*

"Interesting, isn't it, how the Lamden administration reads into the Constitution a definition of justice that suits them." Here he actually ignored Constitutional law. Lamden became president because of the Constitution. And Taylor was confirmed by the Senate, also under guidelines established by the founding fathers and ratified by the states. No matter. He didn't worry about the truth getting in the way of a good show.

"And they say we live in a republic of laws. Well, my friends, I ask you, again: Who elected them? Not me. Not you. Not one of us. Not a single person, either Republican or Democrat."

Elliott Strong's increasingly fiery delivery was drawing record ratings for the radio syndication company that sold his show across the country. As he liked to boast, "Now on three hundred forty-two right-minded stations."

He'd begun his attacks just ten days after the Inauguration. He provided the tantalizing words. His audience ate it up. And Strong's constituency grew every night. Not since the rhetoric of Father Charles E. Coughlin in the 1920s and '30s had anyone turned against a president with such vitriolic fervor. Not Rush, Savage, O'Reilly, or Hannity.

Like the egomaniacal Coughlin, Strong used the airwaves as a bully pulpit, blurring the lines between reality and fantasy, politics and opinion, winning converts and driving up ad revenue. It was all as calculated as his decision to broadcast from Lebanon, Kansas.

Elliott Strong's brand of talk radio existed, in part, because the Fairness Doctrine no longer did.

In 1949, the United States Federal Communication Commission mandated that station license holders were "public trustees." They had the obligation to provide reasonable opportunity for the open discussion of conflicting points of view on controversial topics.

The policy was born out of concern that broadcasters should not be permitted to use the airwaves to advocate singular political perspectives. The Fairness Doctrine required stations to present opposing points of view. Failing to do so could result in the revocation of an owner's broadcast license.

The doctrine worked in tandem to Section 315 of the Communications Act of 1937, a federal law, which required stations to offer "equal opportunity" to all legally qualified candidates running for any office if they allowed one candidate unpaid airtime.

The principle was further underscored by the 1969 U.S. Supreme Court case of *Red Lion Broadcasting, Inc. v. FCC*. The station, licensed to Red Lion Co., had broadcast a "Christian Crusade" program in which an author was attacked. When the author requested airtime under the Fairness Doctrine to respond to the claims, the station refused. The FCC ruled that the station had failed to comply with policy; a decision that was affirmed by the Supreme Court ruling. Red Lion lost the station.

The victory actually scared many stations away from covering *any* contentious topic. A so-called "chilling effect," opposite of the FCC's intention, resulted in less opinion on the airwaves—radio and television.

In the 1980s, deregulation fever swept the country, fueled by the philosophies and policies of the Reagan administration. The new Chairman of the FCC, appointed by President Reagan, vowed to kill the Fairness Doctrine. In 1985, he succeeded. The FCC argued in its "Fairness Report" that the doctrine might indeed have a "chilling effect" on public opinion, and could be in violation of the First

Amendment. Two years later, the courts declared in *Meredith Corp. v. FCC* that the doctrine was not mandated by Congress, and that the commission did not have to enforce all of its provisions. The FCC eliminated the Fairness Doctrine in August 1987, though its dominion over the area of talk was itself debatable.

Today, the broadcasting world is populated by hundreds of TV channels and the proliferation of radio stations. More than ever before. But due to further deregulation and consolidation of ownership, a short list of owners control the vast majority of stations.

Instead of the multitude of perspectives, the airwaves and cable channels are populated with only a few real voices, but hundreds of echoes. Legitimate political dialogue has been further eroded through budget restrictions dictated from the top of the vertically integrated companies. Now news is more widely debated than reported. Corporations have determined that it's far cheaper to have panelists shout at each other across a desk than to actually cover the complexities of a story in the field.

Which gets back to the death of the Fairness Doctrine. Once the FCC eliminated the guidelines, single-mindedness was allowed to rush to AM radio. Bullying flourished. In the process, talk show hosts, claiming to offer a forum for everyone's opinion, typically seek to reinforce their own. Hate found a home on AM radio.

"So what are you going to do?" Strong asked again. He caught the way he gesticulated in his mirror. Effective. Emotional. He loved it. It was as close to inciting a riot as he'd ever gotten and it made for great radio. Strong imagined how cross-country truck drivers, workers on the late shift, and insomniacs must be thrusting their fists in the air in support.

"You want to know what *you* can do?" It was usually *you*. "You," he knew sounded more effective, more personal, "are the government. Not the liberal Congress. Not a president *you* didn't elect. Not a vice president *you* booted out. Not the Supreme Court. *You* are the government. Do you have any real idea what that means?" He could almost hear his audience shout a collective *What?* "Ever hear of something called an Amendment?" He spelled it. "A-m-e-n-d-m-e-n-t. Do you remember what that is? Look it up. Google it." He sounded exasperated, as if he was complaining to a specific caller. But it was for all of his listeners. Twenty million letter writers. Twenty million complainers. Twenty million people who Washington hated to hear from.

"What is it?" he asked rhetorically. "It's the way you can change things."

The phone lines continued to blink.

"It's your right! More than that, it's your responsibility. Let me give you an example. Theodore Roosevelt. The twenty-sixth president of the United States. Courageous. A fighter. A Rough Rider. A leader of a truly *strong* nation. Here's what old Teddy Roosevelt said." He read from a paper.

"'Patriotism means to stand by the country. It does not mean to stand by the president or any other public official, save exactly to the degree in which he stands by the country.'" He read it a second time for impact. "Again, 'Patriotism does not mean to stand by the president or any other public official, save exactly to the degree in which he stands by the country.' Roosevelt told Americans, 'It is patriotic to support him insofar as he efficiently serves the country. It is—' and listen carefully, 'It is unpatriotic *not* to oppose him to the exact extent that by inefficiency or otherwise he *fails* in his duty to stand by the country.'" He repeated a phrase. "'It is unpatriotic not to oppose...' Very interesting, but TR wasn't finished. He proclaimed, 'In either event, it *is* unpatriotic not to tell the truth, whether about the president or anyone else.'

"That, my friends, is what you need to do. You. Each and every one of you who feels you've had enough. From the grassroots. From your telephone, your computer, your fax machines. Call and write your representatives. Tell them it's time for real change. If you don't, this injustice will continue. By the way, they think you won't do anything. The liberals are counting on it. Roosevelt said it, but he was just adding to what Thomas Jefferson had argued a hundred years earlier. He said, 'When the government fears the people, there is liberty. When the people fear the government, there is tyranny.'

"This government doesn't fear you. You fear the government. You fear a president you didn't elect and a vice president you defeated. When are you going to get that? They've taken over the country. It's executive treason!"

Elliott Strong could feel it. He knew his audience. By now they were leaning closer to their radios at home, or pulling out their pillow speakers and turning up the sound. For those driving, he had a fleeting thought about their safety. He didn't want to lose a trucker. They were a great audience, even if they didn't count in the ratings.

He'd absolutely make certain that his calls would remain on topic for the rest of the night. As momentum grew, the idea would spill over to other talk radio shows. More would listen in the West Coast repeats later in the morning. By 9 A.M., at least 100 congressmen, mostly from the heartland, should be inundated with a first wave of e-mails and faxes. Of course, all of their addresses and phone numbers were conveniently posted on the *StrongNationRadio* website.

He took a breath and smiled at his image in the mirror before him. "Now are you ready to talk?" He laughed. "I bet you are." He cued his engineer. "Let's go to the phones." The first caller came up. There were fifteen more holding and thousands redialing, trying to get through the busy signal.

"Hello, you're on *Strong Nation.*"

Washington, D.C.
12:25 A.M. EDT

The radio was on in the background: a cool jazz FM station playing saxophonist Dave Koz. Roarke was only aware of the soft voice of the woman on the phone. He was in the middle of his goodnight call to Katie Kessler in Boston. A glass of his favorite scotch, a 12-year-old Macallan, was in his hand.

Roarke phoned from his two-bedroom brick apartment in Georgetown, on the 2500 block of Q Street, NW. Katie lived on Grove Street on the north side of Beacon Hill, also in a brick apartment building.

"Come on down," he begged.

Almost immediately after meeting, Roarke and the sassy brunette had begun a coy dance, which ultimately led to her bedroom. The fact that their relationship was more about romance than sex amazed them both. No matter where Roarke went—whether it was cross-country or aboard an aircraft carrier in the Mediterranean, or moments before a late-night assault on a building owned by the dictator of Libya—Roarke thought about Katie.

"No, you move up here," the five-six, 28-year-old answered. Her voice was as playful and as sexy as her look, but the lawyer gave no hint of negotiating.

"I can't."

"And what makes you think I can?"

"You can. Besides," Roarke heard himself saying things he had never admitted to a woman before, "I want you here."

"Only in Washington?"

"That's not fair. I want you. But it needs to be here."

"And my job isn't important?"

"Of course it is. But you could practice on the Hill. How many job offers did you get after the Inauguration?"

"Look, Mr. Roarke, I got a very nice promotion, which I deserved. You've got flex hours, and you generally get to fly for free. So from my vantage point, it's win-win for me. All things considered, why don't you pop up here and make a girl happy?" Katie said seductively. She examined the rich color of her Kendall Jackson Merlot in the light of her bedroom lamp, and took a slow, sensual sip.

The combination of the words, the sound of his voice, and the intent had an immediate effect. She wore only a purple cotton camisole and plaid, drawstring pajama bottoms. Suddenly, the fabric was tickling her nipples, which had become erect. She caught herself squeezing her thighs together to contain her increasing arousal. She bet he was having an equally hard time.

This is how it went almost every night—the conversation and the excitement. She knew he wasn't going to leave D.C. Eventually, she might move to Washington and pick up one of the jobs that had been offered. But not yet.

"Counselor, you're taking advantage of me and America's taxpayers. Hell, I could be the subject of a congressional investigation."

"Don't worry. I have friends in high places," Katie giggled. She was referring to the Chief Justice of the Supreme Court. But of course, Roarke worked for the new vice president, with *special* consent that was well beyond the reach of Congress.

Katie and Roarke had met during his investigation into what appeared to be an assassination attempt on Teddy Lodge. Lodge's wife was killed, and Roarke's inquiry led him to the law firm where Katie worked. Ultimately, the Secret Service agent determined that one of the senior partners in the prestigious Boston firm might be involved. However, like many of the people connected to Lodge's early life, he was killed.

Roarke was instantly taken by Katie in every way: Her quick wit, her mischievous attitude, her beauty, and ultimately, the other charms she revealed to him. She had the means to tame the former Special Forces soldier and bring out a sensitivity in Roarke he hadn't known since childhood.

When he said he wanted Katie to move to D.C., he meant it. But his first impression of her never diminished. Katie Kessler came to her own decisions in her own time.

"Case closed," she added. "Now, did you have a nice day, dear?" she cooed over the phone.

"Interesting," he added in the way that *interesting* said much more than one word.

"Interesting good or interesting bad?"

"I worked with my buddy, Touch. Trying to come up with an FRT match for an *acquaintance* of mine."

Roarke was always careful what he said on an open line. Katie was still learning.

"FRT? As in Facial Recognition Technology? If so, big problem with privacy issues."

He was somewhat surprised she was conversant on the subject. Maybe he had said too much already. "Hey, I'm just trying to connect the dots," he added, probably too late.

"Don't you have any boy toys that are more reliable?"

"It's getting there." *Why's she doing this?* He noticed the sexual tension was turning cold.

"Yeah, then why is the ACLU all over it?"

"Katie," he chided.

"The guys using the technology surreptitiously take pictures of innocent people. They file them or they mistakenly ID perfectly honest citizens as illegals or criminals."

"Katie!"

She ran right through his objection. "We litigated a case right here; a detention at Logan. We won a nice settlement. And you know the Tampa tests failed to ID a single suspect. Michigan? There were reports that police used FRT to ID women for sexual reasons and even intimidate political opponents."

"You're lecturing me."

"I'm educating you about the abuses." She was quite familiar and disturbed with the use of the technology at airports, including the system installed at Boston's Logan after 9/11. "It submits innocent people to real-time lineups without probable cause, and often without a compelling security threat. Sounds Orwellian to me, and a violation of privacy."

"Like a fingerprint is a violation?"

"Fingerprints aren't secretly and automatically taken and instantly compared with others while you're walking through a line to get a hot dog. Did you know that every time you go to an ATM you're getting your picture taken? How far away are we from having those images instantly compared with criminals? Do you have any idea of the false arrests that would be made?"

"Sounds like a boon for attorneys, counselor."

Silence. Roarke wished he could have recalled the comment as soon as he said it.

"Look, maybe I just shouldn't get into my day," he said, trying to drop the subject. "I'm sorry."

"Hey, I'm only raising some of the legal questions. You might as well use a coin toss, it's about as accurate."

Roarke thought about the percentages Touch had told him. He was faced with far less than a 50-50 coin toss when it came to Depp.

He closed his eyes and softly said, "We're living in a different world, Katie. The bad guys look just like us."

The reference to Congressman Lodge wasn't lost on her. She knew that Roarke wanted to get the man who had helped conspire to subvert the American political process. FRT was a tool, and despite the debate, if it looked like it would help, she had no doubt he'd use it.

Maybe she could do something herself.

Cheviot Hills Recreation Park
Los Angeles, California
the same time

LAPD homicide investigator Roger Ellsworth walked around the body of the attractive, now-dead Jane Doe. Under high-beam police lights, he had made his first pass over the crime scene. Now he was prepared to note his observations into a mini-recorder.

"Age—approximately mid-twenties. Height—approximately five-seven. Caucasian. Light-blue tank top, khaki running shorts." He stooped over the wound. "Cause of death, apparent knife-thrust, horizontal, left-side, heart puncture wound." The details would come from the autopsy. "Subject possible victim of attempted rape." The young girl's jogging pants were pulled down to her knees, but not all the way off. Ellsworth looked at the path that cut above, about 20 yards away. Another jogger spotted the woman when he took a cigarette break, which always made him laugh. *Jogging for your health, and then you smoke.*

Ellsworth looked back to the victim. Her eyes stared up at him as if asking a question.

The veteran officer had seen the look dozens of times before. Too many times.

His forensics team would analyze her clothing for any residual evidence—hair, saliva, fabric particles, semen. On the surface, nothing was visible, except for some footprints a few feet away in the dirt near the closest tree.

The detective had long ago hardened himself against emotion. He was a 33-year veteran; only 18 months from retirement. Still, he found himself slightly perplexed. Although he didn't record his next thoughts, he did question why the woman's pants were not all the way down. *He'd have a hell of a time fucking her. Scared off?* Although he didn't think there was any penetration, he stated the obvious, "Internal examination required. Check for possible DNA match on record."

Ellsworth walked around the body. He surmised she was on a regular run. *Probably no ID.* He checked her back hip pocket, using a pen to open the fold. *Something here.* It rolled out. "Right rear pocket contains a lipstick container, and..." He fished out more. "A small sheet of wafer-thin blank paper with some words typed on it, a pen, and more crumpled paper." The first sheet had an odd quality to it. He'd seen it before, but he couldn't quite place it.

The detective removed an envelope from his jacket and carefully guided the items in with his own pen. He wrote on the outside, recording his words at the same time. "Marking contents of plastic bag taken from Jane Doe. Items A, B, C.: lipstick container—Estee Lauder *Sumptuous*—small folder paper inside, crumpled dollar bills." He added the date, time, and location, and made certain that another officer confirmed the procedure with his signature and a verbal description for his recording.

Ellsworth continued to survey the scene. *Someone would know her,* he said to himself. He figured it would just take a few hours or less to make the identification.

"Photograph and cast the footprints," he told a young lieutenant. They'd take a mold, though he'd never known it to lead to a conviction.

Ellsworth studied the crime scene again. It seemed odd that there was no sign of a struggle. *She was big enough to put up a fight,* he thought. *At least until he warned her.* But the dirt wasn't even dug up by her heels. *Wouldn't she have resisted?* The thought really nagged at him. *Her pants are down, yet there's no sign of resisting?* He knelt down to look for some evidence that she had. He shined his flashlight near her feet and where her hands would have grabbed for grass. *She would have resisted,* he said to himself again. *Somehow. There's always a moment....* But Ellsworth couldn't find any sign. *Unless...unless she was killed very quickly.*

CHAPTER

8

The White House
Tuesday, 19 June
7:15 A.M. EDT

President Lamden had taken extraordinary heat for selecting Morgan Taylor as his vice president. Not at first, but soon after. His own party leadership, though caught off-guard, publicly called him "bold and decisive." Privately, however, Democrats were astonished at the choice. The opposition quietly embraced the spirit of bipartisanship, yet word on the street said it would not last.

Still, the Senate confirmed the president's man—the former president. But *what and whom* did he represent? The American people who voted him out? Certainly not the Democratic majority. Even Vice President Morgan Taylor couldn't say.

"You know, Billy, some days I wish I never left Billings," he confessed to his chief of staff, Billy Gilmore. The president's appointee was definitely a *Billy*, a don't-call-me-Bill kind of Tennessean lawyer. He tried to keep the new president aware, alert, and proactive. But it was usually the other way around.

"Mr. President—what's the expression—if it were easy, everyone would be doing it?" Gilmore got the desired response from his boss. He slid into a seat opposite the president's austere desk and shuffled his papers—a handpicked collection of overnight press reports and MDBs (Morning Daily Briefings). Knowing what the public thought and what the press was telling them was just as important to the president as the facts.

"Australia SASR disarmed the bomb. They're going over it now. Could be Abu Sayyaf, al Qaeda. Don't know yet. Both scary possibilities. The thing was just waiting for a signal to detonate."

"Like having a sleeper spy running for president," Lamden added. "Tell Evans and Mulligan that from now on all announced travel plans are on hold."

"Got that."

"What else?"

"Alerts in Indonesia. Terrorist activity. Police disarmed a bomb in a nightclub. No real interest from the news nets here. About a graph or two in the papers." The chief of staff spoke in short bites. If the president wanted more, he'd ask for it. "Three dead in a suicide bombing in Baghdad. No Americans. Over in Israel, looks like Blanca is digging in. But she's all but lost the Knesset. I say Israel gets a new leader by next winter." *Was the president listening?* "And my Titans are going to kick butt this year."

This brought the first response from the president. "No way. The Seahawks all the way."

"Willing to put money on that, Mr. President?"

"So you add it to your memoirs that Henry Lamden bet in the White House?" he joked.

"I have to have something to sell my book."

"Hey, it's not my fault you decided to work for a boring old president."

Billy Gilmore shook off the comment. Lamden's presidency was anything but boring. But the president was looking more exhausted by the week. His doctors had adjusted his blood pressure medication just days before the last trip. Though not widely known, the stress associated with the office necessitated constant medical monitoring. Leveling it out through treatments and medications was on the minds of presidents' doctors since the formation of the Union.

George Washington's physicians determined he was inclined to have "gloomy apprehensions." John Adams and Andrew Jackson suffered recurring attacks of depression. President William Harrison was said to use stimulants to deal with the illnesses that ultimately killed him during his term.

Two months before Franklin Pierce's Inauguration in 1855, Pierce and his wife were in a terrible train accident. Although they only suffered minor injuries, their son was killed; practically decapitated in front of them. The president's wife believed that God had taken their boy so that her husband would serve without distraction. Pierce maintained it was punishment for his sins. He buried his sorrows in alcohol.

Abraham Lincoln's "melancholia" has been copiously documented, specifically his bouts of depression following the Union loss at Chancellorsville. Some historians noted that Lincoln even considered suicide.

Calvin Coolidge's despondency went unchecked largely because he wouldn't let anyone treat him. And Senator Joseph McCarthy's vitriolic attacks on Harry Truman sent Truman and his wife to a retreat in Florida. Truman noted that the stress was so intense that he yearned for a simple life running a gas station and waiting for his "quiet grave." And following a March 1992 physical examination, George Bush's White House physicians prescribed a more relaxing schedule to combat the stress the president had been under.

For Lamden, pressure came with the political mayhem he brought on himself. After all, he chose to lead a coalition government. Some pundits mused that the nation had its strongest leadership ever. The one-two punch from a pair of decorated Navy warriors made the United States a more formidable force in the world. The administration was experienced, bold, and obviously decisive. Others, like much of the broadcast media, disagreed.

"Now what's the great *vox populi* report today?" Lamden asked wanting to get beyond the MDB and into more fundamental "conventional wisdom."

"Well," Gilmore continued, almost as an afterthought, "no change from CNN, and about the same everywhere else."

"It's not CNN I'm concerned about, Billy. Not the big guys. What about the ducks?"

"The ducks?"

"Yeah, the ducks that are nibbling me to death."

Gilmore knew exactly what the president meant, but dismissed it.

"They're not important."

"Then why do we pay attention to them?"

Gilmore couldn't answer the question. Presidents did pay attention to polls, e-mails, write-in campaigns, editorials, and what was being said on the street.

"Billy, tell me who's creating policy in America today?"

"We are," he quickly offered.

"No. Try again."

"Okay, officially, the House and Senate—"

"Wrong again," Lamden interrupted.

"I don't know. You are."

Lamden laughed. "If only that were the case."

Gilmore, Lamden's strategist through the primaries, didn't know where this was going, but it was obvious the president was intent on making his point.

"Look, my life's an open book. CNN, Fox—they've all run specials. I've been on the cover of *Newsweek* or *Time*—what, six times since the Inauguration?"

"Seven."

"Sixty days after the election there was a pretty fair instant book out on me. O'Connell included a chapter in his book. Hell, A&E even did a *Biography*."

"That's all normal."

"Yes it is, Billy. Taylor had the same."

"Yeah, so have some key members of Congress, particularly those with over-the-top personalities like Newt and Tip."

"Exactly."

"Exactly what?"

"Our lives are open books." The president paused to consider another thought. "Not a book. A fucking tabloid rag. We can't take a piss without it showing up at the checkout stand or some cable news show that has thirty minutes to fill. Hell, they'll spend one segment just trying to figure out if I've got a good stream or I'm down to a trickle. Then the next segment is devoted to what that will mean to the market or a defense appropriations bill. The third segment is an instant Internet poll. And they wrap it up with an analysis of my declining numbers. And you think we make policy? Not on your life, Billy. We react to what's being said. To polls in the news magazines, *USA Today*, the networks, and to people tuned in to the Elliott Strongs of the world.

"You're overreacting, sir."

"The opposite, Billy," the president declared, working himself up more. "My acid reflux makes news. But what do we know about the people who write or broadcast the crap? Where's the *Biography* of these hate mongers? What about a *20/20* or *60 Minutes* exposé? Give me just one investigative book about Strong and the others who fall in lockstep behind him. Where are they?" He answered his own question. "Nowhere. And why? The mainstream press is afraid of becoming a target themselves. So these clowns set the national debate every single day and night. They do it pretty much unchecked. You know what's even scarier?" Gilmore didn't interrupt the president's train of thought. "They're becoming the real voice!"

"Nobody cares, Mr. President." The chief of staff was trying to calm down the president.

"You are so wrong, Billy. So deadly wrong." Lamden's nostrils flared. "*Everybody* cares! You tell me Limbaugh had no influence on Clinton's ability to govern? And when some conservative comment-ators turned on Bush after Iraq, that didn't affect his presidency?"

Lamden picked up a picture of his grandchildren. He sensed he'd gotten far too aggitated. He rubbed his arm for a moment, took a deep breath, and walked the length of the Oval Office before talking again.

"It's getting so we have elections three hundred sixty-five days a year. Hell, I got voted out of office again last night on Strong's show."

"He's a wacko," Gilmore quietly said.

"With a huge audience."

"All sharing one brain."

"Yes, his," the president emphasized. "That's the problem."

"So you were up last night."

"I was. On the flight back. And I recommend that we start tracking his broadcasts for our morning news briefings."

"Come on, it only legitimizes him."

"Legitimize him? Billy, he's already legitimate, with a legion out there. I don't know what his endgame is. Ego? Ratings? Bigger salary? I can't tell you that any more than I can tell you anything else about him. But somebody should. That man and his cronies are setting a *new* national agenda."

"Which is?" Gilmore asked skeptically.

"A constitutional amendment."

"Come on. No way."

"You don't think so?"

"Mr. President, you know the funny thing about nighttime?" Gilmore said trying to take the edge off the conversation.

"No, you tell me."

"That's when you're supposed to sleep. It helps. Rejuvenates you. I recommend you pick up the habit."

"You better hope I don't, Billy. Because there's a lot going on then that we have to pay attention to."

CHAPTER 9

Andrews Air Force Base
Suitland, Maryland

R oss walked around the plane that had taken him cross-country. His 243rd flight.

It was impossible not to be awestruck by *Air Force One*. No other jet approximated it. In some regard, it was like being aboard an aircraft carrier, the focal point of a flotilla.

On international trips, the twin 747-200Bs travel with at least 14 other support aircraft. A pair of two C-5 Galaxy heavy transports carry upward of 50 soldiers and staff, and ferry not one, but sometimes two or three bulletproof limousines. The extra vehicles can be utilized as decoys when necessary. In addition, the transports carry a fully outfitted ambulance and as many as three VH-60 helicopters with folding roto blades. Everything is packed inside the massive 35,000 cubic feet of available cargo space. The C-5's interior is so large that its 121-foot-long cargo floor is one foot longer than the distance flown by the Wright Brothers on their first flight at Kitty Hawk, North Carolina.

Depending upon the duration and purpose of a presidential excursion, two or three C-17 cargo planes can also be assigned, bearing dozens of troops and additional equipment. Three KC-10 Air Force tankers, modified DC-10s, along with an equal number of smaller KC-135 tankers, keep the entire entourage fueled.

Rounding out the air show is an additional 747 dedicated to the press and an E-4 operational flying command post, ready to be activated as a working hub for the United States government in the event of a national emergency or a nuclear attack.

Ross knew the name of each and every man and woman assigned to the president's Secret Service detail, both the uniformed officers and those in plainclothes. Their vehicles, equipped with non-standard extras, flew inside the bellies of the C-5s.

The presidential retinue also included about 12 rotating reporters, each of them with their own means to phone home. *Air Force One*'s crew numbered 26. Including the cooks and the press pool, upward of 102 souls flew with the president.

As many as 1,000 people traveled with President Clinton when he visited Vietnam in November 2000. And as few as one other when President Morgan Taylor's two-seat F/A-18 became *Air Force One* when he flew to the Mediterranean prior to the Special Forces assault on Tripoli.

The $650 million that went into getting the two 747s into service was just the beginning. It takes millions more every year for maintenance and upgrades. The exact cost of operating SAM 28000 and 29000 and the associated fleet of aircraft and personnel remains classified.

The 89th Airlift Wing proudly considered it "the safest aircraft in the world." Air Force Lt. Eric Ross swore by the boast. He was completely certain that if anything was ever wrong, he'd personally know about it. However, it was getting harder and harder to keep track of every detail. That meant that Rossy had to trust others for their correct judgment and professional care. He couldn't supervise all of the electronics and avionics. And though he didn't tell anyone, that very fact scared the living hell out of him.

Chicago, Illinois
12:00 Noon CST

Luis Gonzales stepped off the jet way at Chicago's O'Hare, clutching a brown leather attaché case. The 3-hour and 55-minute flight from Mexico City went quickly, but he still felt exhausted. It wasn't because of his nonstop United Airlines flight. The previous year had begun to take its toll.

The Spanish-looking Gonzales managed a little sleep in his first-class seat. It was something he wasn't supposed to do for deeply religious reasons, but of course, no one knew. To the world, or the few people who actually did business with him, Gonzales was an art dealer with a handsome bank account, worldwide clients, and large portfolio. His transactions were mostly anonymous. He rarely appeared at a showing, instead choosing to bid and make his purchases over the Internet or through intermediaries. Gonzales had saved for years, tucking millions into accounts that he rarely touched. He lived a private life, in a Lake Shore Drive condominium that only recently had become his principal residence.

He spotted his driver. He was a big man; 6'5"—impossible to miss.

"Mr. Gonzales, may I take your bag." He reached for the burgundy tweed Hartmann.

"Thank you, Mr. Alley."

That was the extent of the conversation. The driver worked for Gonzales for a number of years, and he knew not to talk with him in public.

At midday, they made the 32-mile ride in under 50 minutes. The driver parked in front of the 26-story, lakefront building. Gonzales waited for him to open the door. Minutes later, they were both inside the luxurious condo. 19G. Gonzales didn't speak yet. He needed assurance from his man, who was more bodyguard than driver, that all was well. Like Gonzales's other assistants, Roger Alley knew how to sweep the surroundings for bugging devices.

"Are we okay, Mr. Alley?" Gonzales asked.

"Yes, sir," he said after checking with two other guards. "We're fine, Mr. Gonzales." The hardest part for the bodyguard and the rest of the staff was remembering their boss's new name, and their own.

"Good."

Gonzales was almost 64. But in many ways he was no different now than when he was 10, 20, 30, or 40 years ago.

His deep, commanding voice always got what he wanted. Though the length and color of his hair changed, moustaches and beards appeared and disappeared, and glasses came and went, nothing could ever hide the utter coldness in his eyes.

Gonzales spoke six languages fluently. Spanish, of course. English, French, German, and Russian, plus one that he hid from almost everyone—Arabic.

He didn't smoke or drink. Personal chefs, who were especially good with knives in and out of the kitchen, catered to his narrow culinary whims. When he did eat out, he never ordered off a standard menu. He shunned small talk. Every word always counted. He only saw women for personal pleasure. They never saw him a second time, which was probably a mutual decision.

Few people knew Gonzales. Those who worked for him never got close. They were loyal to their ruthless boss and recognized they served him at his pleasure—*for life.*

"What's happening in the news?" he asked.

"Haven't heard much today, but I do have the recording you wanted."

Gonzales walked to his study and closed the door. Once he was alone, Gonzales sat on a Massagenius 702 Electronic Massage Chair, reupholstered in a soft Spanish leather. He adjusted the chair's incline and stretched out. With one remote, he set the chair back to a slow, relaxing rolling pattern; with another, he turned on the CD that Alley had burned.

Luis Gonzales, formerly Ibrahim Haddad, eagerly listened to the 12-hour-old recording of *Strong Nation.*

Los Angeles, California
the same time

"No ID. No missing persons yet?" Ellsworth phoned in, hoping for a quick identification. He figured that finding the murderer was going to be next to impossible without serious lab work, but getting a positive ID on his Jane Doe would at least provide a starting point.

"Nothing," the overnight supervisor reported without emotion.

"You mean to tell me that after twelve fucking hours we have nothing on a missing woman in Cheviot Hills! A redheaded jogger in the middle of the whitest park in all L.A.?" The L.A. detective was furious.

"Well, we had a little problem."

Sweet Jesus, we better not blow this, Ellsworth thought.

"We were short because of the Lamden visit. A whole bunch of the force was on OT. After the president hightailed it for the airport last night, command cut them loose." He kept the real bad news for last. "So the fingerprints haven't been delivered yet."

CHAPTER

10

Boston, Massachusetts
Offices of Freelander, Collins, Wrather
Tuesday, 19 June

One name had been dropped from the law firm's marquee: *Marcus*. The decision was costly for many reasons. Reputation aside, the change amounted to $212,453.25 in the redesign of the logo, new stationary, business cards, editorial corrections to all of the Web site biographies and listings, and the five-foot, gold-plated lettering that hung over the entrance to the building.

Heywood Marcus had represented the Lodge estate. He was also a conspirator in the plot to take the White House. Now he was dead—the work of the man Roarke sought to identify.

Last night, Katie Kessler argued with her lover about the very means he wanted to use to find the killer. As she walked under the new marquee, she considered what she could do to help. *Our first argument.* Then she laughed to herself. *Son of a bitch. He did it again. He's so damned good at it, too.* Roarke made her question things that less than a year ago were so easy to decide.

Katie took her lunchtime in the research library where they'd made their initial discoveries together. She stayed there through the afternoon, pouring over Nexus/Lexus research on the use and abuse of FRT technology. She searched for cases where it resulted in bonafide arrests. She read arguments in support from police chiefs, and narratives spelling doom from civil libertarians.

Facial Recognition Technology wasn't going away. But Katie Kessler struggled over whether it was *getting in the way.*

She read editorials with dire predictions of Big Brother scenarios: how one day, surveillance cameras will be mounted on every street corner; how pedestrians will be photographed and analyzed in their own neighborhoods.

She also found cases where FRT had identified real criminals, one who had procured 17 fraudulent driver's licenses. Katie read about its widespread and successful use in more than 80 casinos, on school property to track potential child molesters, and at airports where suspected terrorists had been detained.

On balance, she wished she had better researched her topic before she spoke. She came to the personal conclusion that FRT shouldn't be the sole basis for arrest. But it could be an effective instrument in helping to identify and track suspected criminals and their movements.

At 4:15, she set the privacy issues aside for good. *Christ, he's turning me into a Republican!* If Roarke found his man through FRT matches, she'd live with her personal quandary.

What Katie didn't know is that while she was working, she was also being observed by three cameras. The law firm's security department eyes were always on, a result of technological upgrades installed in the last few months. The partners and staff were politely notified that some additional cameras were installed to prevent break-ins and theft. She never considered that the network was far greater than advertised, and that they'd ever be used for internal spying.

"Sir," the security officer reported over the phone, "you asked me to keep you informed on any of Ms. Kessler's prolonged studies."

"Yes," said Donald Witherspoon, an officious, but rising young attorney who organized the effort to equip the building with state-of-the art surveillance measures. Roarke had met him and concluded he had *asshole* written all over him. Kessler resoundingly agreed.

"Where is she? What is she doing?"

"She's in the library." He zoomed in the hidden camera behind her, reconfirming what he'd already discovered. He switched to a second and third angle. "Ms. Kessler is reading up on something called FRT. The print is a little too small to tell for sure. But she's scrolling through some cases or opinions. We have to get some better lenses in there, sir."

The security guard's explanation made Witherspoon sit up. He called up an office log on his computer. *Kessler. Kessler.* He found her name and scrolled down her current assignments. Nothing associated with FRT. *What's that cunt up to?*

"How long has she been at it?"

"About four hours. Nexus/Lexus. Google. Harvard Law Library online. She's got a pad full of notes."

Notes for a case she's not working on? This worried Witherspoon. She'd been seen with the Secret Service agent. There were even rumors that she had made a quick trip to D.C. the morning of the Inauguration, the morning that Teddy Lodge was killed. *Why?* Kessler never spoke about it, but she didn't deny she was seeing a man in Washington.

"Thank you, Freddie. I'll just go down and say hello. But it's all fine, and I appreciate you keeping me posted."

"Yes, sir." The security officer hung up and turned to his other cameras.

"Good afternoon, Katie," Witherspoon said, feigning real interest. He looked like he had reason to be in the archives, with two thick volumes in hand.

Katie looked up. "Donald."

Witherspoon busied himself for a moment, returning the books to a shelf. When he finished, he was standing directly behind her.

"Some pressing case? You seem really engrossed."

"Naw. Just researching." *Butthead.* "Stuff for the future."

The computer screen displayed a Florida newspaper extract. It confirmed what the security officer had described.

"Staying ahead of the curve, huh?" he offered.

"Yup."

"Interesting stuff?" he asked.

"Some."

He looked at her yellow pad.

She sensed his eyes bearing down, and Katie quickly turned to the next, blank page. "If you don't mind, Donald," she said, swiveling in her chair.

"Citing some *future* client privilege, are we?"

"I just don't like it when someone starts breathing over me."

"Sorry. Anything I can help you with?" He paused, then decided to add, "For the sake of the firm."

"No, thank you, Donald."

"Who did you say it was for?" he asked, trying to draw her out.

"I didn't." *Too many questions,* Katie thought. "Like I said, it's just research," she added sharply.

Katie turned away and typed in an innocuous, unrelated research parameter. The screen immediately came up with a list of new links.

"Well, let me know if I can help. We newbies have to stick together. After all, someday we might make partners together."

In your wet dreams. "Never know," she offered aloud.

Witherspoon leered more than smiled, and left. Although he wouldn't do it immediately, there was one call he'd make from a random public phone. Slowly, carefully, unobserved. He'd report just the kind of behavior he was told to look for, from the only person he was instructed to watch: Katie Kessler.

CHAPTER

11

Chicago, Illinois

"**Y**ou want to know what *you* can do?" Elliott Strong asked the caller on the tape. It was Gonzales's second time listening.

"Yes."

"*You* are the government," Strong explained. "Not a liberal congress. Not a president *you* didn't elect. Not a vice president *you* booted out. Not the Supreme Court." The usual rambling. "*You* are the government. Do you have any idea what that means? Ever hear of something called an Amendment?"

Gonzales laughed. Strong spelled out the word. Then the host added, "It's one of the ways you change things. A bit slow for my taste, but it works."

Elliott Strong had been putting ideas in people's heads for sixteen years, the last six of them as a nationally syndicated host. It was hard for even the most faithful listeners to say they knew much about him. They just liked what he had to say.

Occasionally he dropped a thought or two about how he lifted himself out of the horrible life his parents led. He admitted that they were unskilled migrant workers. Real card-carrying white trash, forced to follow the sun and the seasons to scrape out a pitiful living.

Strong often recalled how he couldn't wait to escape his parents' reach. His father beat him until the day he finally fought back. His mother died of emphysema but it was hard for him to care. She never showed any love for him whenever his father was around.

So, according to Strong, he retreated into books. He read everything in sight, from American and world history to travel and political nonfiction. He worked on his speaking voice, realizing he wouldn't become anything if he couldn't communicate. He recounted the story every year on the anniversary of his first day in radio.

"It was on my seventeenth birthday. I hitched a ride to Fresno in a navy blue Ford pickup truck that stunk from lousy cigars and nickel beer. I would have gone farther, but when I couldn't stand it any longer, I said, 'Pull over there!' I don't think he ever came to a complete stop. I jumped out, and he took off. I walked for about a mile or so and came to a radio station. It was a little single-story Navajo white building with bright blue call letters over the door. That, my friends, was Mecca. I marched straight into the offices of that 1,000-watt station and said to the first person I saw, 'Hi, I'm Elliott Strong. And I'm here for a job.'"

Strong never embellished his story. He always told it the same. "There was a girl. She was twenty-one and beautiful, with a full head of blonde hair done up like Farrah Fawcett's and lipstick the color of the reddest rose, with lips just as soft. She was unbelievable, but then again, I was seventeen. I'd never seen anyone like her.

"'And you are?' She asked"

"'Elliott Strong, miss. And I'm ready to start my career in broadcasting.'" This is the point where he always broke up telling the story. "I had dusty overalls on, a plaid shirt and worn boots. She must have wondered which tractor I'd fallen off."

"'Doing what? Mowing the lawns?'"

"'If that's what it takes. Yes.'"

"The secretary took some pity on me. She gave me a soda, and went into the general manager's office and closed the door. I heard some laughter. After a few minutes she came back out, followed by this older man. Maybe he was forty, maybe fifty. What's a kid know? But he was wiping his mouth, and believe you me, he didn't get rid of all the lipstick. That's when I realized she was more than just his secretary."

"'Gina tells me you're ready to get into radio, son.'"

"'That's right. I can read real good. You'll see.'"

"'We don't need anyone new. I've got a fine staff here. Some of them have been with me for almost a year. Anyway, it's "I can read *really well*."'"

"'Thank you. *Really well.* You'll never have to tell me that again, sir. Honestly.'"

"'No, I don't imagine I will,'" the manager said.

"'And I don't need to go anywhere. I can wait for one of your announcers to leave. You won't have to look around. In the meantime, I gather the grass needs some attention.'"

"'See,'" the secretary whispered. "'He's cute. Why not?'"

"The man nodded. 'Okay. Overstreet's the name.' He offered me his hand.

"'Elliott Strong, Mr. Overstreet. Pleased to meet you.'"

"'Where are you from?'"

"'Here and there.'"

"'Well, now you're here. By your appearance, I'd say you're pretty comfortable in the great outdoors. That's where I do need some help. Buck-fifty an hour. Cash, which I think you'll appreciate.'"

"'How much do your announcers make?'"

"He laughed. 'Buck fifty, but we take taxes out.'

"'Sounds fine to me. Keep my seat warm.'"

As Strong told the story, he was doing the graveyard shift in under four months. By the end of the year, he was also getting a little extra from Gina on the side.

Over the next six years, he earned his high school equivalency and lived the life of a gypsy disc jockey. Fresno to Prescott, Arizona to Bakersfield, California, and on to Sacramento and Phoenix. Along the way, he audited as many college political science courses as possible. When he got bored with straight announcing and spinning records, he moved into talk radio with a bright, witty, fast tongue and a conservative point of view. He found himself in the right place at the right time, when radio made a sharp turn to the right in the mid-1990s.

"That's right," the broadcaster continued on the tape. "Amend the Constitution. Just like you did a few years ago. Or don't you remember that battle? Now there are twenty-eight Amendments. How do you think they got there? Out of thin air? Materializing on parchment in the National Archives?" He was on one of his rants. "As Americans, *you* decide how to live your lives. We decide. Not somebody waiting for "Hail to the Chief" as a cue to walk down some red carpet...

someone whose only connection with the people is through the windows of his stretch limo.

"You decide, my friends, just as all the colonists decided they didn't want the British to be running things here. They didn't want to support some clown in a crown thousands of miles away who said, 'Pay the taxes or go to the stockades.' And Americans before you said that presidents aren't kings, so they can't serve for life. Your parents and grandparents decided that in nineteen fifty-one when they voted state-by-state to limit a president to two terms. No more dynasties like Franklin Roosevelt's. No imperial presidents. And how did they do it? By amending the Constitution. For the record, it's number twenty-two. Go look it up."

Gonzales heard him take a sip of water.

"Two terms. Not three. Not four. Eight years. That's all. But look, we're on the verge of a dynasty again. This Lamden-Taylor thing could take us another twelve years. Count along with me. Twelve more years between them. Sixteen in all. We had Taylor's first four. Now Lamden-Taylor for four. Who says it won't be a Taylor-Lamden or Lamden-Taylor switching off for the next eight after that?"

Strong didn't bother to consider Lamden's age, which made his argument highly unlikely. Nor did he suggest that perhaps they wouldn't want to run. He had his agenda and he went for it.

"Did you vote for the repeal of the twenty-second Amendment? I sure didn't. Nobody has." He failed to mention that Ronald Reagan actually floated the idea during his term stating, "I have come to the conclusion that the twenty-second Amendment was a mistake. Shouldn't the people have the right to vote for someone as many times as they want to vote for him?"

There was no response from the caller on the tape. Strong had dropped him well into his speech. But the host still acted as if he was there; appearing to talk one-to-one, but actually reaching millions of individuals.

"So you amend the Constitution. You rewrite the law of the land. You change it. You, replace them with leaders we want, not ones who are the poster children of the military-industrial establishment." A familiar rallying cry for Strong. "Go to our *www.StrongNationRadio.com or www.ElliottStrong.com* Web sites. All the e-mail addresses, phone numbers, and fax numbers are there. The White House. The Supreme Court, and each senator and congressman. All of them.

You're going to write them and call them, and tell them how you feel. By Monday morning they'll get a real sense of what Americans are thinking. What *we're* thinking. What *we* want." Each phrase came quicker, with more passion, with greater authority. Strong wasn't asking. He was commanding.

"You can do it!" He slammed his fist down hard. Punctuation. An exclamation point to his lecture.

"You can do it! You live in the greatest nation in the world. You live in America where your voice counts." He pounded his fist again. "Let's start acting like God-fearing Americans instead of some third-world peasants. We don't have to take it anymore. We'll be right back."

A commercial for a foreign automaker came up.

CHAPTER

12

Staritsa, Russia

A leksandr Dubroff looked like any of the other old men digging for mushrooms in the ankle-deep mud. A hint of his denim shirt was visible under his nearly worn out khaki vest. *It's not worth the money to buy another,* he thought. *After all, how many more years will I be at this? One, maybe two?*

His vest, shirt, and worn corduroys were covered by a leather, fleece-lined coat; underneath it all, long johns. He wore his favorite beret, a ragged brown checkered gift from his wife, Mishka, the last year of her life. The hat, like her memory, fortified him against the early morning chill.

None of his clothes gave away his status. Not that status mattered anymore.

Aleksandr Dubroff had long ago retired from the Politburo, the Central Committee of the now-defunct Soviet Union. At that time he was a good three inches taller than his 5'7" frame today. He had been one of the elite, a man who set Soviet policy and ran the country. He left, not because he saw the end of Soviet life coming, but because his beloved Mishka needed him. They'd been married for just over 46 years when doctors told him she would not see their next anniversary.

So Dubroff decided to spend every remaining minute with Mishka. They moved to their state-provided dacha, in the wooded Tver region, about a four-hour car ride outside of Moscow.

Despite Dubroff's diminished stature, he was still strong, a barrel-chested man with bushy, black-as-night eyebrows that jutted out a full half-inch, and a thick salt-and-pepper moustache to match. His face was lined with age, but red cheeks always projected a cheery manner. Over the years, too many people took that for a jovial, soft demeanor. They were wrong—some of them, in fact, *dead* wrong. As a retirement present to a trusted friend of the Party, Soviet Premier Nicoli Andropov renovated Dubroff's dacha. That meant he and Mishka would enjoy electricity and a generator, hot running water, and an indoor bathroom. By neighbors' standards, they'd live in the lap of luxury.

"All the comforts of home," the Premier told him at his goodbye party. "You and your Mishka should be comfortable."

Dubroff thought the rest. *For as long as she has.* But he said, "Thank you, Mr. Premier. I can't begin to express our sincerest gratitude."

"No, Sasha. We, the people of this great country, are grateful for your dedicated service. From your defense of Russia to your tireless work for the Party."

Tireless work for the party said it all and said nothing. Some of the other Politburo members had known of Dubroff's earlier work. Others only heard the rumors. And others still, like Mishka and the other wives, were told to ignore the lies of the West. It was easy to do. Aleksandr "Sasha" Dubroff always looked so cheery.

Now most of his colleagues from the old days were gone. He even outlived the Soviet Union and its measly pension by decades. Had he not created his own savings in Dubai banks, he would have gone hungry years ago.

But now Sasha Dubroff foraged for mushrooms, anonymous to everyone around him. He picked his way through the wetlands, slicing away the dry branches above with his razor-sharp knife.

Every spring and fall, Dubroff returned to the marshes, but not because he really liked mushrooms. It was the hunt—like in the old days when he looked under different kinds of rocks. Here he found Beilee, Podberiozouik, Gorkoshkee, and Maslikyonok.

When he started, an old mushroomer—even older than him—said, "Only the *Seeroyejhka*—the fresh, edible ones. The pink, lilac, green, red, and maroon-cap mushrooms."

"How will I know the poisonous ones?" Sasha asked. He knew a great deal about dispensing poisons, but he didn't care to die consuming any himself.

The old man pointed to some intriguing looking mushrooms with his walking stick. "The ones that are most likely to catch your eye. The ones that you laugh at because they remind you of dicks and balls, or the ones that appear to be umbrellas for dolls. Look, but don't touch."

Dubroff explained he had just seen a woman carry those types away. The old man laughed. "Of course, of course. In the hands of someone with *the knowledge*, the poisons, once dried, can dull arthritis or migraines. But beware if you just add them to your greens. Your salad days will be over," he joked.

In recent years, Dubroff, like the old man before him, instructed newcomers and tourists in the ways of the dig. Now, *he* was the old man with the walking stick, the lumbering pensioner who had a simple answer when strangers asked about his work. "Oh, a little of this. A little of that." No one needed to know more.

Los Angeles, California
late afternoon

"I have something." The call was from the LAPD lab technician.

"Say again," Ellsworth radioed.

"Something on the Jane Doe." He sounded nervous.

"Okay, go ahead." Ellsworth was a good way crosstown in his squad car.

"I don't think you want me to do that, sir."

Ellsworth only needed to be told once. They were on an open transmission—open to other police officers, and open to amateur eavesdroppers.

"Where are you?"

"Heading west on Wilshire. Before Hauser."

"Copy that."

The LAPD detective looked in his rearview mirror and waited for a car to pass. He moved into the left lane, continued another short block, then made a sharp U-turn in front of the County Museum. He now headed downtown, due east, toward the LAPD lab.

"I'm about twelve out."

He flipped on his siren and picked up his pace. A string of lights ahead just turned green.

"Make that ten. See you when I get there. Out." The call ended.

Cars and trucks pulled to the side as Ellsworth sped downtown. He focused on the one thought foremost in his mind. *What the hell is the "something?"*

Chicago, Illinois

After a late breakfast, Gonzales returned to his study. He told his men not to disturb him. The art dealer locked the door and logged onto his computer.

With a few fast keystrokes, he was through Google and deep into eBay, searching the rare art auctions for a specific bid on a recently discovered, previously unknown oil painting depicting *Konstantin's Battle at the Bridge of Milva*. The unknown artist had captured the grotesque detail of a Russian battle. Gonzales had acquired the oil on canvas some years earlier and now offered it for ten days, with a starting bid of $25,000. Forty-eight hours remained in the auction. It might be priced too high. He wanted to sell it, and perhaps would. But he was most interested whether an Internet bidder got in an offer of exactly $27,777.

He scrolled to the bidding history. One offer at $25K. *Not bad.* Another at $25,400. *Even better.* He continued scrolling and saw what he was looking for.

$27,777—a confirmation of a different transaction.

Beside it, an e-mail address that would be dead—like a woman in Los Angeles. He was completely certain of that.

Gonzales smiled at the results. He'd sell the painting for $25.4K, and the job he commissioned was successfully completed. He'd even use the eBay sale to help cover the final payment.

If anything, Gonzales was a man of his word. He typed a new Web address and logged onto the first of four shelter bank accounts; the last one ending up in a secure Lichtenstein bank. It wasn't in the millions as he had paid before, but then the job wasn't as big as some of the others. However, if the news broke on the front page of *The New York Times*, he'd pay an additional, agreed-upon bonus.

Gonzales quickly calculated. Over the past year he'd released $2.6 million to the man, each payment going to a different numbered account. And his spending spree wasn't over yet.

* * *

LAPD Lab
Los Angeles, California

"So what is it? Do we know who Jane Doe is?"

"Yeah, and she's not local. That's why no missing persons," the 46-year-old former Northrup engineer reported.

"I ran the fingerprints figuring we'd find her through motor vehicles. Not California. Guess where?"

"Dunno."

"District of Columbia. Your Jane Doe has a name, too. Meyerson, Lynn. Twenty-five." He read off the birthdate and address.

"Just moved or visiting friends," Ellsworth concluded.

"I don't think so," Cullin replied. He looked up from his computer and handed a sheet of paper to Ellsworth. A phone number was written on it in longhand. "A few minutes after I made the computer hit, the desk told me I had a phone call. I took it, and this guy asked me who I was and—"

Ellsworth interrupted. "Who you were?"

"Yup. And why I was looking into this particular woman."

"Jesus, who was it?"

"You're going to find out yourself. And if you ask me, I think you stepped into some messy shit. That's the number. After I explained why I made the inquiry, I was *ordered* to have the investigating officer dial this specific number."

"You were ordered, who in hell..."

"Now you need to do it," Cullin said, not answering the question.

"A two-oh-two area code." *Washington?* "Come on, Cullin. Help me out here. Who the fuck is it?"

Cullin stood up and motioned for Ellsworth to take the seat. "The Director of the FBI."

The technician left without another word. He wished he hadn't been the one assigned to the computer this morning.

"Hello." Ellsworth began tentatively. He thought about telling his own chief about the call. *He's the one who should be doing this. Whatever "this" is.* Ellsworth felt he was way too low on the food chain to know how to talk to the director of the FBI. But the instruction was clear. Call. Right away.

"Mulligan," the voice answered.

"Sir, I'm Detective Frank Ellsworth, LA...ah, Los Angeles Police Department. I was told—"

"Yes, Detective. Have you talked with anyone?"

"Well, sir, Mehegan. My lab man."

"We spoke. Anyone else?"

"No sir, but—"

"You will notify your chief and no one else. Is that clear?"

Ellsworth didn't answer the question. Instead, he challenged the command. "Pardon me, sir, but with all due respect, I believe that will be my department's call."

"Detective Ellsworth, it is *not* your department's call. It is not *your* call. You will do as instructed. I'm certain that your supervisors will agree."

"With all due respect—" Ellsworth began again.

"With all due respect to you, Detective, the woman you found is quite important."

This silenced Ellsworth.

"My team will be coming in to observe the autopsy and participate in the investigation. The information may be sensitive. Do you understand?"

Ellsworth looked around the room. He was alone on the phone with the head of the FBI, and something was extremely out of the ordinary. He wasn't sure what to say. He decided to go by the book. "My department will cooperate with the Bureau. We will expect the same in return."

"Appropriate response, Detective. Now, in the spirit of cooperation, was there anything unusual about the crime scene?"

Chicago, Illinois
the same time

Witherspoon's phone call triggered a number of reactions from the man who retrieved the message.

Gonzales already knew that the Kessler woman had developed a relationship with the Secret Service agent named Roarke. But the information led him to believe that Roarke was now *personally* pursuing *his* man. In his experience, personal vendettas were dangerous; far more dangerous than an investigation in the hands of a nine-to-five civil servant. The latter usually didn't take his work home. Roarke would look far further, consider possibilities that others would ignore or dismiss. And now Kessler was helping.

Luis Gonzales would have to give this thought.

CHAPTER

13

Maluku, Indonesia
Wednesday, 20 June

U mar Komari did as promised. He took one scrawny, diseased man out of the makeshift Shabu manufacturing plant—actually little more than a hut with a tin roof and the requisite burners—and beat him in front of his co-workers. He chose the man partly because he was the first to have eye contact with him, and partly because he had three worthless daughters who would not serve the cause for which Allah had chosen him. So, the sins of the daughters now fell on the father, and Amjad Mohammed suffered a twenty-minute caning which left him weak, yet alive. With the last lash, he collapsed on the floor and broke his nose.

"If you want to feed your pitiful family, you'll get on your feet and return to work!" Komari ordered. He signaled for a fellow worker, little more than a slave, to help him up.

"Do you see what happens when you fail?" Komari shouted to the other twelve half-starved men. "You are punished. This time, one of you. This time, he lives. The next time, you will all feel the bite of my stick. And two of you will die."

Amjad spit out the blood that had filled his throat, and forced himself to a wobbly stance. He diverted his eyes for fear of further reprisal.

"From now on, you will triple your output because you have shorted me. And it will be the finest Shabu you have ever produced."

No one dared object.

"I don't care which one of you is guilty. You all share the burden. Everyone works harder, or you die a traitor's death."

Komari had another stop to make—an arms supplier 25 kilometers away, across a stretch of calm seas. He would be lucky if he got half his order of AK-47s, 40-mm GP-25 under-barrel grenade launchers, Russian-made VSK-94 sniper rifles, semi-automatic high-velocity 9x21mm Gyurza pistols, and the most prized possessions: Stinger missiles.

He would not be getting the tube-fired missiles he sought or all of the Kevlar-piercing ammunition. The new cache provided him with less than enough weapons to turn his growing army into a formidable force. Komari also had to buy food and medical supplies for his men. Because of failures on the manufacturing side, his dream of raising a mighty sword for Islam and striking a deadly blow in Allah's name was delayed. The Christians in the Malukus would live awhile longer, perhaps through late August. Then he would cleanse his beloved islands of the pagans. Portuguese, Spanish, and Dutch blood would flow from the fishing villages into Jakarta's gutters. A reborn Indonesia, a fully Muslim Indonesia, would rise, and the world would acknowledge the name Komari.

As Komari brushed by Amjad Mohammad, the beaten man struggled to stand. He kept his eyes lowered, but a small curl formed at the corners of his mouth. It made his swollen face hurt. It wasn't the kind of expression that suggested happiness. It was more relief. However, Komari read only insubordination.

A smile? He dares to ridicule me? In one swift move, Komari unholstered his pistol, and with absolutely no remorse, put a bullet in the forehead of the slave laborer.

"Let that be a lesson for all of you. I am Commander here. I will not abide insolence." To his own shocked men, he demanded, "Take him out."

Washington, D.C.

"Alma, get me in."

In the first months of Lamden's presidency, Alma Coolidge had already put through calls from the country's biggest political egos and the world's greatest leaders. In order to reach the President of the United States, they went through her first. Everyone. Congressmen, kings, dictators, prime ministers, department heads, and Boy Scout leaders. Most people knew her by her first name. The FBI chief did. She could distinguish between a calm greeting, noting no real sense of urgency, to a rapid-fire, curt hello, which didn't invite any small talk in return. She measured the importance of each call by the tone of the first words. She'd been tutored by the best, Louise Swingle.

The FBI director's intent was unmistakable. He didn't invite anything other than a proper business response.

The president's secretary clicked to a screen showing the day's calendar. "Five forty-five, sir?"

"Earlier."

It wasn't a question. Robert Mulligan needed to see the president immediately. Alma didn't ask for a reason. She quickly scratched a note to herself on her phone log. She'd move a meeting with an FCC commissioner.

"Thirty-five minutes, Mr. Director? Twelve fifty?"

"Good."

"Can I have any lunch waiting for you?"

"No."

His answers were all short and deliberate. The hair on the back of her neck prickled her skin.

"And would you like Mr. Gilmore there?"

"No."

The president felt better when his chief of staff, his confidant, was present. She thought he might want to reconsider.

"Are you certain?" she said matching his delivery. Telling more than asking she continued, "You know that the president values his opinion."

"Thank you, Louise. Tell him I want fifteen minutes alone. After that, he might want to have Billy around, Evans, and, hell, maybe the CIA chief and the whole National Security Council. I'm on my way."

Robert Mulligan scanned the notes he took over the telephone from the LAPD officer. His folder also included an e-mail jpeg of the victim. It would be difficult for the president to view, but part of the process of identification was confirmation. Henry Lamden would have to look at the startled and pained expression on a young and beautiful face; an expression frozen forever. Fingerprints and dental records would also provide indisputable proof.

Mulligan framed his thoughts in the backseat of the six-minute chauffeured drive from the Hoover Building to 1600 Pennsylvania Avenue. On some level, Meyerson's death was like hundreds if not thousands of others every year: a woman attacked and killed in the act of robbery, rape, or attempted rape. He could have someone research the exact statistics, but it didn't matter. What made her death different, notable, and newsworthy, was the fact that this victim worked in the White House, directly under the eyes of the president. And then there was his *other* concern.

Right after talking to Ellsworth, Mulligan ordered his Los Angeles team to work with the LAPD. With his next call, he sent his most experienced D.C.-based investigator to Meyerson's apartment.

Alma Coolidge tried to read the FBI director's expression as he entered. There were no signals, but there were no pleasantries either. The FBI head usually chatted with the 58-year-old mother of five. He'd normally ask about her children and grandson, her mother, and her husband who worked as a cab dispatcher. Not today.

"Alma."

"Mr. Director."

She didn't get anything more. He hurried past her desk, only calling out a thank you with his back to her.

He knocked on the door.

"No need, you can just go in, sir," she said. "The president is waiting for you."

Coolidge had alerted Henry Lamden that the FBI director had been absolutely insistent on seeing him right away. Not ever liking to be blindsided, a carryover from his days as a battleship captain, the president asked if Mulligan gave her any reason for the unexpected visit.

"No, sir. I tried."

The "no" meant trouble. He could feel his heartbeat quickening.

As Mulligan entered, the president's secretary could see Henry Lamden gazing out the window. She understood that somehow the very act of looking into the Rose Garden instinctively became a way to deal with the unknown. The openness of the grounds provided every president the way to surround impending troubles with natural beauty, if only for a moment.

Mulligan closed the door.

"Mr. President, thank you for seeing me on such short notice."

The president didn't turn around. As if reading the FBI director's thoughts, he began, "Imagine what Lincoln thought as he looked out these windows. Do you think he found any solace in the Garden while America was at war with itself? What about Woodrow Wilson, when he desperately tried to convince the country that the League of Nations was a good and necessary idea? Or President Kennedy, at the brink of a third World War? Where were his thoughts? Out there? Wishing he could be playing in the fall leaves with his daughter, Caroline?

Lamden slowly walked away from the window, and greeted the man he had asked to stay as head of the Federal Bureau of Investigation. "I understand you have something urgent."

"Yes, Mr. President."

"Then put your things down, Bob. A pleasantry first. How are Molly and the girls?"

"All fine, Mr. President. And Joanne?"

"Missing the ranch. Like me. Now sit. Please. Some water?"

"No, thank you." Mulligan gingerly crossed the magnificent rug that lay in front of the president's desk in the center of the Oval Office. The chief executive's seal was woven into it. Guests automatically walked over it lightly, out of a sense of guilt. He took a seat in one of the two modest cherrywood courthouse chairs. He removed a sealed document and placed it on his lap.

Lamden took his favorite seat, a handcrafted, button-tufted, brown leather Teddy Roosevelt Room chair from the Kittinger Furniture Company. His choice. The president noted the file, but didn't ask about it yet.

"And you, Bob. You're doing okay?" he asked.

"I'm fine, sir." He was still getting used to his newest employer—different, more measured than his predecessor. "But I'm afraid I have some bad news."

Lamden had heard these words many times before. They were never a good start to a conversation. From his navy days, it usually meant a pilot was down, a helicopter was lost; incoming fire. Now the president realized this was his first time, as commander in chief, anyone started a conversation that way.

"Come sit down and tell me about it." The president reached for the same warm words he had used years earlier.

Mulligan obliged. He realized he hadn't forged a real relationship with President Lamden. *Go slowly*, he warned himself. He wondered whether Lamden truly had what it takes to be president. Could he exert the ultimate authority? Would he be willing to use extreme measures? A voice told him *no*.

Upon becoming president, Henry Lamden agreed to Morgan Taylor's first recommendations: that the FBI director remain at his post; the same for three other key cabinet members—Secretary of State Norman Poole, Attorney General Eve Goldman, and Homeland Security Secretary Norman Grigoryan. However, Lamden made two notable changes. He elevated CIA Chief Jack Evans to the higher post of national director of intelligence, and appointed David Jaburi, a second-generation American and devout Muslim, as secretary of the Treasury. It was a calculated move designed to demonstrate how America embraced people of all faiths. That fact that Jaburi worked with Eve Goldman, a Jew, was a positive lesson to the Muslim world.

"Go ahead, Bob."

"Sir, a junior member of your Office for Strategic Initiatives was killed last night."

Lamden tensed.

"Who?" the president quickly demanded.

"A young woman. I only met her once myself. Lynn Meyerson."

Lamden closed his eyes, lowered his head, and whispered, "Oh, my God." Without looking up he asked, "How did it happen?"

"She was jogging in L.A. Apparently stalked and attacked. We're still looking at the initial evidence."

"She left my suite to go running. I gave her time off," the president said in a self-confession.

"Yes, Mr. President. I know."

The president's shoulders collapsed under the impact of the news. He thought about Lynn's promising future, now gone. Her energy. Her desire to succeed. He buried his face in his hands. "Tell me what happened."

"As you noted, she left the Century Plaza Hotel shortly before your departure. She was seen running down Avenue of the Stars to Pico Boulevard, and into a local park. At some point, she cut into an adjoining golf course. That's where she was assaulted."

"My God! I drove right by there on the way to the airport." Henry Lamden looked up. His voice cracked as he continued. "How did she die?"

"She was stabbed, sir." He paused, as if reading the president's mind. "And no, we do not believe she was raped." He paused. "Though it appeared that was intended."

"So there was a witness who interceded?"

"Possibly."

"But he still took the time to kill Lynn?"

"Yes. And we don't know why."

Mulligan turned to a page of his own notes, scanned them, exhaled, and mustered the courage to proceed with what he had to say.

"Mr. President, I have to ask you something. If, after you hear my questions, you believe you should consult White House counsel, then I advise you to do so."

The president's mood suddenly changed. Armor went up. "Say what you mean, Bob."

"I need to ask what every reporter will also be asking you. Three important questions." Mulligan was a former prosecutor, a devilishly manipulative courtroom attorney. He had his cross-examination down. He fixed an unblinking stare on the president, trying to read his very thoughts.

"There have been hundreds of similar deaths this year that the media will show no interest in. This one is different. The victim worked for the government. She worked in the White House. And she worked for the President of the United States. You."

"Get to your questions, Mr. Director." Lamden now showed dismay over where Mulligan was heading.

"Mr. President, did you have any relationship with this wom—?"

"No!" the president shot back before the final word was off the FBI chief's lips. "That's one. Next."

"Sir, can you shed any light on why anyone would want to harm Ms. Meyerson?"

"No, I cannot. For Christ sake, she was the most liked person here. Two."

"Did she have access to any classified information?"

This caught him off guard. "Classified information? Well, I suppose a lot of what she touched could be considered classified. Hell, she was in Strategic Planning. Where are you going with this, Bob?"

Protocol usually demanded you never answered a president's question with another question, but Mulligan did.

"What kinds of things, Mr. President?" He voice was more urgent.

"Schedules. Strategies. Secrets."

The president locked onto the eyes that were scrutinizing him. It was a look that Robert Mulligan would long remember. It was still, serious, and final.

"Mr. Director, Lynn Meyerson was a fine young woman with a bright future. She was a trusted aide with access to the President of the United States. And, as you damn well know, almost everything we talk about in the Oval Office could be considered classified until it's in the press. Now before you hear another word from me, it's your turn. What the hell is going on?"

CHAPTER

14

Washington, D.C.

FBI Agent Roy Bessolo parked his customized black Suburban on Columbia Road NW, directly across the street from Meyerson's apartment. It was his second time up the hill today. His first was a drive-by surveillance run on his own. Now he had his entire team.

Meyerson lived alone a few blocks from Dupont Circle, in a one-bedroom walk-up. Her apartment was on the fourth floor of a century-old five-story brick building on 18th Street in the Adams Morgan neighborhood. Higher priced condos lined the street. Meyerson's building hadn't been converted yet.

"There it is," Bessolo told his passengers. "Right over the video store."

His team assessed the exterior. Chunks of brick and mortar had fallen away. Workers had tried to patch the façade with plaster, but the structure desperately needed work. Individual air-conditioning units hung from windows, indicating that there was no central HVAC.

"I've got the specs." Earlier, Bessolo pulled the name of the owner, the money he owed on the building, and information on all the occupants. They were 20-something students: some from Georgetown and GW, a few of the "bridge and tunnel crowd" from the University of Maryland, a collection of junior hill staff, and some young attorneys. Bessolo ordered up more detailed information on each of the tenants, including what they paid in rent, their personal debt, and whether they had any record. Meyerson's monthly nut was $1,980. She had no roommate. *She's getting hosed,* he thought. Bessolo was the father of a 23-year-old daughter and he worried about such things. It was the only sympathy he'd show for Lynn Meyerson that day.

"We wait here until we have the warrant. Then we move." Bessolo was pissed. He was ready to go and the fax was still to come. He took the time to review procedure.

Roy Bessolo issued his instructions the way he did everything: military, direct, monotone. And what his voice didn't say, his appearance did. Marine crewcut. Marine physique. Marine barrel chest. The only "ex" was his active duty status. He was as strong today as he was at the peak of his training.

"Let's go through this once more."

The team had already reviewed their assignments, but Bessolo was a stickler for proper procedure.

"Thomas. You start with the head. Tag prescription medications, illegal substances, birth control pills. Everything. Then you've got the subject's bedroom. All the drawers. What's visible and what's not. Hidden compartments. Everywhere."

"Everything, everywhere," said Beth Thomas, one of the FBI's brightest criminologists, and the only woman in the bureau to hold a Ph.D. in the subject.

"Shik, you're in the kitchen and living room. Drawers, cabinets, bookcases, desk. Over, under, around, and through."

"Behind?" asked the agent.

"Behind," Bessolo answered. "Anything outside the bedroom is yours." Bessolo knew his man would not miss a square inch. Agent Dan Shikiar was the team's most detail-oriented agent.

"And Gimbrone, get into her computer fast, but carefully. Watch out for any embedded viruses that could be set as traps. I need to see what's in there. Pull up everything on the subject's computer. Read, copy, report. In-boxes and outgoing."

"Yes, sir," the third member of the team acknowledged. Like the others, Mark Gimbrone was an expert. His discipline—hacking and cracking.

"Thirty minutes, people. I want a continuous narrative. I'll be monitoring each of you." The team's microphones were all fed to distinct digital tracks in the black, windowless van. "I want to know that this woman is cleaner than a baby's butt." He left out the important fact that she was no longer alive; a calculated deceit in order not to color their thinking. "Am I clear?"

He got the obligatory affirmation he sought. "One bit of intel for you, the rest you fill in for me: Our subject works for Uncle Sam. Find me anything that compromises her. Or give me your assurance she's on the home team."

The fax machine started to print out the court authorization. Bessolo grabbed the sheet when it finished printing. "The United States District Court for the District of Columbia says one, two three—greenlight!"

One by one, the team exited the tricked-out van parked in front of a bank. Beth Thomas was the last to leave. She ducked back in when the others were out of earshot.

Bessolo shot her a confused look. "Agent Thomas?"

"Just a question, sir. Off the record?"

At first, Bessolo showed annoyance. But since he openly encouraged his team to speak their mind, he acquiesced. He reached over and paused her discreet audio channel on the computer recording. "Two minutes."

"Less," she began. "You always told me to keep my radar up. Well, my radar's up. Warrant aside, are we examining a crime scene or spying on a citizen?"

"We have an assignment. That's all you need to know."

"Nothing else?"

"Nothing else."

She knew he lied very, very well.

"Same answer on the record, Roy?" she asked using her boss's first name.

"Agent, do your job. And don't ignore anything. You go in with an empty canvas and paint me a fucking Rembrandt."

He pointed the computer mouse at the record icon and left-clicked. The conversation was over.

"Scott..."

The phone call caught him while he was walking into the Pentagon. Recognizing the voice, he stopped just shy of security and returned outside. It was Louise Swingle, the vice president's secretary. She kept him plugged into relevant administration issues. Morgan Taylor insisted on it, and the new president had agreed. Roarke's access to breaking information was critical.

The conversations were always lighthearted and cryptic.

"What's up?"

"Where are you?"

"About to see Penny." Swingle knew all about Captain Penny Walker. She was one of Roarke's deep contacts inside the Pentagon, and an old girlfriend.

"Are we conducting business today?" she asked mockingly.

"Nothing but."

Roarke wanted to see if Penny could run a search on military veterans who might overlap one or more aspects of Depp's profile. She was a master detective assigned to the Defense Intelligence Agency, who did all of her work on one of the Pentagon's most interconnected computers.

"But if you need me now..." he began.

"No, just wanted to know if you heard the rumors?"

"Rumors? Nothing beyond the hustle out of L.A. a few days ago."

Her sudden switch to business clearly suggested this wasn't a conversation to continue on an open line.

"Why don't you hit *home* later." *Home* was the vice president's office. "There's something else."

Louise Swingle never said anything that didn't have meaning.

"You sure this can wait?" he asked.

"Yes, but don't take all day. Bye-bye."

With that he hung up and proceeded to security. Even his Secret Service ID didn't earn him a quick pass. Not these days.

"Okay, Penny, do your stuff," Roarke said after the preliminary explanation.

Penny was a slender, 5'6" blonde beauty. Her looks always made men take notice; Roarke had. But her uniform usually made them stop and think twice. Roarke hadn't. She was a U.S. Army captain assigned to intelligence. Two years earlier they had had a whirlwind relationship, all sex and no romance. At the time, it was what both were aching for. However, Penny understood that Roarke needed more than she would ever give him. That's why she was happy he'd found Katie Kessler.

Walker finished typing. "Anything else you can think of?"

Roarke looked over her shoulder at the parameters he provided for her search: *Caucasian. Ex-military. Marksman. Age range 28-40.* Nothing more than possibilities. She also included approximate height and weight variables, and a composite picture created by Touch Parsons.

"Will the computer ignore the picture if it comes up with positives on these aassumptions alone?"

"If that's what you'd like." She altered her typed prompts. "You know how I like to make you happy." She looked back and blew Roarke a kiss.

"Then add in theatrical makeup as another parameter."

"Geez, you're easy these days," she cooed. "She must be very, very good."

"She is," Roarke said smiling. "And thank you."

Walker sighed. "Oh, what could have been." She turned back to the keyboard. "Well, sweetheart, since I struck out with you, at least let's see if I can come up with Mister *Wrong*."

Antiguilla

The sun beat down on the pristine white sand at Antiguilla's Cap Juluca resort. The British West Indies facility is tucked away on a private self-contained enclave, spread along two miles of the Caribbean coast. Singles and couples alike flock to the Moorish villas, feasting in the five-star restaurants, working halfheartedly in the fitness center, diving, surfing, water skiing, sailing, or finding other more personally gratifying indoor sports.

Some of the vacationers were sprawled out, engrossed in paperback editions of Tom Clancy, Michael Palmer, Vince Flynn, and Dan or Dale Brown books. It might be another month until the next great beach reads were due, but here in paradise it was perpetually July.

One strikingly beautiful woman sitting on a straw mat spotted a snorkler emerging from the 85-degree water. She was awestruck by his 6-foot-plus frame, a magnificent physique, his blonde locks, hairless body, and his drop-dead good looks.

She wondered what he did. He was obviously successful. *Lawyer. No. Maybe a professional athlete. A quarterback.* She wished she knew sports better. *He could be anything,* she thought.

Part of her evaluation was right. He was successful and very athletic. In fact, a few nights before, he'd been a jogger. But after catching a 10 P.M. plane from LAX to Miami, and then a connecting flight to Antiguilla, he became someone else entirely.

If the woman, wearing only a bikini bottom, were lucky, she'd *never* discover what he actually did for a living.

Now, with his eyes fully adjusted to the glare, he saw her. He read her unmistakable interest from 20 yards away. He laughed to himself. *A redhead. Imagine that.*

"Hello," he said.

"Hello," she replied with a flirtatious smile. She lowered her eyes; a coy signal that he could do the same.

When she looked up again, the woman noted that he had taken her cue and found what she had invited him to see. Soon the stunning redhead would hear that this great catch out of the sea was a shark. He'd even have a convincing conversation with her about his career as a lawyer, or rather the identity that he'd stolen. Most importantly, over the next week, he'd show her a very good time. All on his dime. After all, money wasn't a problem.

CHAPTER 15

Washington, D.C.

S hik used his small lock pick to open Meyerson's 800-square-foot apartment.

"We're in," he said for the recording. "Let's get to it."

The team split up according to assignments, each making instant value judgments about the woman and her life.

Shik began in the kitchen. "Small. Old appliances. Grease caked in layers on the oven." His overall assessment: "Not a cook." He found her checkbook in a shoebox, along with a stack of bills. She had a balance of $2,438.32 that would have to be checked with the bank. But on first blush it appeared she lived hand-to-mouth, month-to-month. He radioed in his observation.

Beth Thomas went straight for the bathroom. To a woman, the bathroom said a lot. This is where the FBI agent would formulate the personal side of the subject. The bathtub caught her eye. "We have a guilty pleasure here or a bad back. Whirlpool Spa connected to her tub." Her search of the medicine cabinet produced a bottle of a muscle relaxer. "Five mg Flexeril. Vicodin, too. Ten mg. It's a back issue." There were also decongestants. "Allergies," Thomas continued reporting. She noted condoms and essentials from a Bobbi Brown makeup kit. Most of the things were missing. "The medicine cabinet doesn't have everything I'd expect. Subject is likely away."

Bessolo radioed up. "Any Estee Lauder?"

She looked again. "No. Why?" Bessolo didn't volunteer an answer.

Shik had his screwdriver out, and removed the plates on each of the wall sockets. Wearing a light on his cap, he peered inside each one. Next he checked the light fixtures. From there he went to the living room, examining the telephone and fax machine. He set up a small black box next to them. The onboard LEDs remained green. No bugs or wireless cameras. "Living room is clean." He followed the same routine in each of the other rooms.

Beth Thomas ignored him when he came into the bedroom. She was busy with her own analysis. "Walls patched up. Hardwood floors worn, but recently polished. I'd say she cares about her bedroom, but doesn't have money to work with. Assumption: She needs more money, or is afraid to spend what she has." Her walls were painted in a light blue, the ceiling in white. She'd hung a poster depicting wellesley college in its fall splendor, and tacked on a cork board, a collection of pictures that she'd taken with government officials and international leaders. So far, these were the most interesting finds.

"Photographs suggest that subject may work for the U.S. of A. With access." Beth studied the photographs. Senators, congressman, the Ambassador to Israel. Even President Lamden. "High up." No casual pictures. No single pictures of boyfriends.

Bessolo listened to the commentary in the van. He tapped his fingers to a tune he quietly hummed. His team members, blind from the beginning, were making solid observations. But what would they find that he didn't already know?

Shik returned to the living room after completing his electronics sweep. Now he could concentrate on the physical information. "Personal touches everywhere." He examined some tabletop sculptures. "Woman is an artist. Signed and dated work. Recent." He remembered seeing a poster in the bedroom. "Likely college art classes. Living room decorated artfully. Flea market finds on the tables. Lamps, vases, mobiles, all reworked, distressed, and displayed. She probably watches the junk-to-funk shows on HGTV and DIY. Her cable company can confirm viewing habits. Functional, inexpensive, out-of-the box Ikea furniture. A few throw rugs to pull the space together. Artistic hand. Creative," he said on mic. "Boxes in the living room." He looked around. "I'd say about a dozen." He opened one. "College books. She's still moving in. Betcha she's too busy at work to get this done." The mainly empty shelves reinforced the point. The only volumes in use were history books, non-fiction and fiction, DeTouqeville to Vidal. "History buff. American history." He examined the pages. "Individual words highlighted in yellow marker."

Bessolo heard the comment. *What words?* He made a mental note to examine the book himself. Codes are often developed through words in a book. Both sender and receiver work from the same source to communicate. *A message?*

Beth still worked the bedroom. "Subject's bed faces the windows. Morning sun. Sheer drapes. Very little privacy, but not much of a view from the condo across the street. Going to check out the closet now."

Meyerson's closet was another thing entirely. There simply wasn't enough room for a woman's clothes. Beth looked at everything, moving each item carefully. Like the other members of Bessolo's team, she wore latex gloves.

The closet overflowed with any number of requisite black and gray pantsuits, two conservative knee-length black business skirts, two black cocktail dresses, one mid-knee skirt, a collection of blouses and sweaters and basic athletic clothing. She was about Beth's size, in good shape, except for her back problem. But the jogging shoes suggested she ran to keep fit. "Nice taste. Very presentable. Professional, moderately conservative. Jogs or walks for exercise. Damn, it's cramped in here." She felt a twinge of sympathy, then looked for the natural space to store more clothes. Thomas found it. "There's more under her bed."

Meanwhile, Gimbrone followed the wiring in the living room, a few feet from Shik. "Flat-screen TV, hooked up to cable. Multiple phone lines." He crossed over to the bay window, where Lynn had her desktop. He checked the hookup. "Cable modem to a three-year-old Dell 4600C. MP3 player patched into the system's speakers." He powered up and immediately discovered a wall. "Shit. Password protected." He grimaced. "Sorry about that, boss."

Bessolo didn't worry. In his opinion, *just a temporary obstacle.*

"Now the bed," Thomas explained. "Queen." She felt the springs. "Sleeps on the right side. Alone." The information in the pictures, the clothing in her closet, and the college poster gave her enough intel to make an educated guess. "I'd say we've got a young Congressional aide or government staffer—maybe working for someone up the food chain. Works all the time," she felt the bed again, "and doesn't have a steady boyfriend." Beth knew the feeling.

Right again, Bessolo thought from across the street.

Slowly and surely, Bessolo's squad compiled an accurate snapshot of Lynn Meyerson. Now it was time to see if they'd find any blemishes in the picture. He counted on it.

Mossad Headquarters
Tel Aviv, Israel

"Then tell me, Ira. You've read the communiqués. Travel plans? Fleet locations? Pending legislation? Why aren't I celebrating?"

Wurlin smiled. He was quite prepared to volunteer his opinion. Walk-ins were his specialty. They always had a personal reason for offering themselves up. Sometimes it was their urge as a Jew to connect with Israel; other times, an individual epiphany brought on by a news story, a teacher, or a book. Something as simple as that. Loyalties also swung because of deaths of loved ones. There were often two other reasons: money, or the sheer, addictive lure of living on the edge.

"I have been thinking about it. Chuntul shows no level of sophisticated technical expertise here. Detail is lacking. And as we both suspected, the information is publicly available if you know where to look. These are simply teasers. Dainty bites to entice us, to suggest how close she is to greater information."

"In such an open manner?"

Wurlin laughed. "Our own Web site invites people to e-mail us to become agents." The Mossad discovered that even they needed to find new ways to recruit.

"So, where does Chantul work?"

"State Department. A key senator. Maybe somewhere in the White House."

This piqued Schecter's interest. He hadn't considered that. It had been a few years since they had someone close to an American president.

"But you say there's no real level of intelligence."

"No. Not yet."

"No names?"

"Just what you've seen, Jacob," Wurlin replied. "References to Papa Bear, Baby Bear. Things like that. And what we've already discussed. Legislation that could have an impact on us."

Schecter pursed his lips. "Money or conscience, Ira?" He then phrased it differently. "Will we get a bill?"

"Can't say yet."

"Create a short list of likely candidates," the Mossad Chief ordered.

"Already on it."

"Good. I want to know who this Chantul is. I still have a bad feeling about this. Nothing you've presented is making it go away."

Washington, D.C.

Gimbrone peered at the 17-inch computer screen. He'd already tried the passwords most used by people—the ones that required little or no thinking. *1-2-3-4-5, A-B-C-D*-E. The third one worked. *1-1-1-1-1*. Once in, he called up the most recent word docs—all innocuous files. Then he scanned through hundreds of cookies recorded in Windows Explorer. "She shops online," he reported to his recording in the van. "Some travel destinations checked out: France, Italy, Israel. No porn sites."

Now to her Internet account. She subscribed to Comcast. He tried the winning password again. It didn't work. Nor did any of the other likely choices. He tried combinations of birthdays, family names, and other obvious combinations.

"Anyone have any ideas? I'm stuck," Mark Gimbrone admitted. He turned to the team because that's what Bessolo had taught them. Individually, they were all highly trained agents, but they were part of a bigger team. They knew when to ask for help.

Certainly another court order could get them into her account through the provider. But Bessolo wanted information now.

Bessolo, monitoring the conversation over the wireless, radioed back. "Come on people. We might have company soon."

Pictures, Beth Thomas thought as she walked into the living room. Having examined her most intimate apparel, she was probably developing the strongest sense of their subject. "Hey, anyone seen any photo albums? Might be something in one."

"Don't know. Try the boxes," Shik offered.

It took Thomas a few minutes to find two albums filled with laminated pages. "Let's see what these tell us, missy," Beth softly said to herself.

The FBI agent leafed through the pages, going back in time through internships, college, high school, and earlier. That's when she spotted it: A photograph of a then-12-year-old girl holding an apricot toy poodle. *Her allergies! Of course she'd have a poodle or another non-allergic dog as a pet. Not a cat or a long-haired dog.*

Now for a name. She went to another photo album. On the third page she found the teenager eating a piece of cake. She looked closer. There was the dog; a puppy. Frosting was smeared over its muzzle. She studied the photo more. A number was visible on the cake. *They were celebrating the dog's first birthday!* One more look.

Beth swung her backpack around and off her shoulder and removed a plastic kit containing a magnifying glass.

The name on the cake, a blur to her unaided eyes, became clearly visible.

"Try Buckets," she called out.

"What?"

"Buckets. B-U-C-K-E-T-S."

"What the hell is that?" asked Gimbrone.

"A password, you idiot!"

"Buckets?"

"Buckets," Thomas repeated.

Seven letters later, Gimbrone was into his subject's e-mail account. "Well what do you know," he said under his breath. "Nice going, Thomas. How'd you pull this one out of the hat?"

Thomas smiled. "Woman's intuition," she slyly said. But it was nothing of the kind. One of the leading passwords, and easiest to remember, is the name of a first pet. That's what credit cards, bank accounts, and online services even recommend. Thomas also knew the old joke about porn stars taking the name of their first pet and the street where they grew up to come up with an exotic stage name.

"Son of a gun," was all that the computer wiz offered in return.

The criminologist flashed a satisfied smile and joined Gimbrone at the computer. A minute later, after scanning a list of deleted e-mail, Beth tapped the screen. "There. What's that?"

Gimbrone opened a recent outgoing mail and read through it. "Uh-oh."

Bessolo keyed his mike. "I heard that. Speak to me."

Gimbrone reached in his backpack for a backup Zip drive.

Bessolo called again. "What's going on, people?"

"Going to back up the hard drive before I look any further," Gimbrone explained. He plugged in his accessory, but before he left the Internet, he decided to read the contents of the e-mail again.

Bessolo was getting annoyed. "Gimbrone!" he said in a raised voice. "What did you find?"

"Sir, why don't you lock up and come on upstairs. You're going to want to see this."

CHAPTER 16

Washington, D.C.

"**W**hat's up, Louise?" Roarke asked.

"The vice president wants you to see this." She handed him a CIA briefing on the Ville St. George discovery and the subsequent evacuation.

Louise Swingle greatly respected Scott Roarke, a man who received no public recognition for his work, but who deserved the gratitude of his nation. Roarke was the Special Ops soldier who rescued Morgan Taylor after his Super Hornet took a hit and crashed in Iraq. More recently, he helped prevent a White House coup. Even she didn't know the depth of this involvement, but Morgan Taylor's secretary did recognize his importance.

Roarke read the report. It went way beyond the news reports of the Sydney Hotel evacuation. On the second page, he came to a section that detailed the discovery of C-4. The summary explained that the bomb squad took more than four hours to meticulously disassemble the explosive device, expose the critical wiring, and disarm the mechanism. It also noted the cover story. It concluded with the revelation that the President of the United States was scheduled to stay there in August.

"Okay, consider me informed."

"He awaits," the 55-year-old secretary said.

"Then buzz me in, Louise."

Swingle typed a note into her computer. The words simultaneously appeared on a screen on Taylor's desk. After a moment, the letter "y" showed up on her desktop.

"He's all yours."

Roarke tipped two fingers to his forehead in thanks and charged through the door. The CIA report was in his hands.

"Boss."

"Hello, Scott." The vice president put down the papers he was reviewing. "You know, part of my job as President of the Senate is to read these damned things. Let me tell you, they don't pay me enough."

Roarke let out an agreeable laugh. Taylor got right down to business.

"Let me take those and give you something else to look through," the vice president said. "Grab yourself a cup of java. Then you have a go at it."

"Okay." Roarke gave Taylor the CIA report and went to the pot of freshly brewed coffee.

"You might want something stronger by the time you're through."

Roarke raised his eyebrow out of curiosity. If news troubled Morgan Taylor, it was bound to trouble him.

"Is this related to the hotel bomb?" Roarke asked through his first careful sip.

"No. It's simply turning into a very busy day."

The vice president invited Roarke to sit in one of the hardwood chairs from Thomas Jefferson's term that he brought over from the White House. He handed the Secret Service agent a brown folder held together with a metal strip on the left side.

Roarke took the file and rubbed his thumb over the FBI insignia on the cover. Below it, in bold caps, was the warning:

TOP SECRET

Before reading he flipped through the time-stamped pages. There were eight in all, and the file was only hours old.

"This feels hot," he said, trying a joke.

"Don't burn yourself," Taylor replied.

Roarke carefully read a summary paragraph. A staff member of the Office for Strategic Initiatives had been murdered in Los Angeles. He didn't recognize the name. But it already wasn't good. "A bungled rape."

The word "bungled" sent the first shiver through him. He looked up at the vice president. Taylor, busy again with his own reading, wasn't paying attention to Roarke.

Bungled. Roarke thought for a moment. *Bungled? There's something about that word.* His right hand automatically moved inside his blue wool sports jacket. With the simple reflexive motion, he felt his holstered Sig. The pressure of the gun heightened his sixth sense. *Bungled. That's how they described the death of Teddy Lodge's wife. A bungled assassination attempt of the Congressman.*

Roarke returned to the report. It contained a combination of the LAPD account of the murder of a Jane Doe, later ID'd as Lynn Meyerson, Washington, D.C. resident. He didn't know her name, but a biography cleared up exactly who she was and what Meyerson did for a living. Roarke now understood why he was called in.

Next was a report from a name he did recognize: Roy Bessolo. In Roarke's estimation, Bessolo was *the Neanderthal*—a boorish, argumentative brute. But he was also a solid FBI field agent. Bessolo wrote a summation of his team's search of Meyerson's Washington apartment. They found e-mails on the victim's computer. The exact transcripts of the correspondences were not specified, but the report indicated that "due to the contents, the agency has sealed the subject's apartment and an investigation into suspected espionage activities is proceeding." The use of the word "subject" was also a tip. *But to what?*

There were no further conclusions.

Roarke closed the folder. Now for some questions.

"Did you know this woman?"

Taylor carefully put the cap on his pen, turned over the papers he was reading, and slowly responded. "I spoke with her on the phone a few times."

"And your impression?"

"Very smart. Well liked. Well connected. I've seen a lot like her over the years. Seemed like she could be on a fast track. Congressional material."

"And these e-mails? What were they? Mulligan's brief doesn't say."

"And it won't."

"Dirty laundry to the folks back home?"

"Worse. I'd term them more like *contacts*. Evans and Mulligan are knee-deep into it now."

"So what do you need from me?"

"You're going to tell me how worried Henry and I need to be."

Chicago, Illinois

Luis Gonzales perused *The Washington Post* and *The New York Times* Web sites. Nothing broke yet. It was only a matter of time. *Maybe on the nightly news,* he thought. If not there, cable, and eventually Internet bloggers. He could even arrange for a sketchy leak to cause some chatter. He laughed to himself. *These days, so many people could own a big story in so many ways.*

CHAPTER 17

Andrews Air Force Base
Suitland, Maryland
Thursday, 21 June

A*ir Force One* was more than an airplane. It was an airborne extension of the government. A flying White House. An office unlike any other in the world.

President George H. W. Bush flew the maiden flight of 28000 out of Andrews on September 6, 2000. The plane bore the distinctive blue, silver, and white look created for President John F. Kennedy's *Air Force One* in 1962 by designer Edward Lowey.

The sheer size of the 747s have inspired articles in every major newspaper in America, to books, television documentaries, and a variety of Web sites. Lt. Eric Ross knew every detail. Yet, not a day went by when he wasn't impressed by the commanding presence of the planes. Six stories high. The fuselage nearly the length of a city block at 231 feet. A bulge in the nose to handle midair refueling. SAM 28000 and SAM 29000 could slice through the air at more than 600 miles per hour, powered with 56,700 pounds of thrust by each of the four General Electric CF6-80C2B1 engines. The wings carried 53,611 gallons of fuel, accounting for a takeoff weight of 833,000 pounds. They were magnificent machines.

The planes were reconstructed by Boeing with a three-level floor plan.

From aft to stern, Level 1, the uppermost space, contained the cockpit. Behind it was a small galley, a lounge, and then the communications center with a stairway leading to Level 2.

At the front of this level, in what would be the First Class compartment of a commercial 747, was the president's office, appointed with light weight, but comfortable furniture. Off to the left, or port side, was a medical station. Farther back, a smaller lounge, and stairs which led below to Level 3. There was another set which returned to Level 1, and an even larger galley.

Directly in the front of Level 3—the lowest floor—was the Presidential Suite, including compact sleeping quarters. Moving toward the stern, the cargo area was actually split into two levels where equipment, supplies, and any number of specialty items were stored.

Though it occurred shortly before Rossy's watchful tenure, everyone who served aboard *Air Force One* knew about *the day:* January 28, 1998. President Clinton was on a whirlwind Midwest trip. He'd just completed a speech at the University of Illinois in Champaign, and was preparing to take off from Willard Airport for the next leg. As his Boeing 707, tail number 27000, taxied into position, the landing gear slipped off the runway into soft ground. The plane's engines revved and the crowd watched. But *Air Force One*'s wheels sank into the muck. President Clinton found alternative transportation on a backup 707 which was flown in. Ever since then, the Air Force established new safety procedures and everyone's job became much harder, Rossy's included. The lieutenant was acutely aware of the importance of each detail, whether *Air Force One* was on the ground or in the air.

Today, he didn't think he'd be flying, although after 9/11 it was anybody's guess.

There are generally five ways that an important story makes the news. A reporter is at the scene and files an account. An eyewitness tells a story to a reporter who then reports. A story pops up through a police reporter. A reporter is given an on-the-record tip by a quotable source. The final option is particularly popular in Washington: A story is leaked by an unnamed source.

And that's the way the first news about Lynn Meyerson hit *The Washington Post*.

> The FBI is investigating the death of a government staffer who may have been employed in a key administration post. The victim, identified only as a woman in her mid-20s,

allegedly suffered a fatal knife attack while jogging in a Los Angeles park. A source says the FBI is investigating whether she may also have had information on a security breach at the White House level. Neither the FBI nor Justice Department would comment.

The eight-line *Post* news brief was enough to catch Michael O'Connell's eye 212 miles away.

The New York Times
New York, New York

O'Connell was a reporter for *The New York Times*. By every account he was on his way to a Pulitzer for his reporting of the Lodge investigation. He'd earned an invitation from then-President Taylor to tag along as the chief executive flew to the Mediterranean to secure evidence that would bring Lodge down. Instead of seeing Lodge's arrest, O'Connell was a witness to his death.

Unwittingly, the reporter's glowing coverage of both Lodge and his campaign manager helped further the campaign. Taylor also figured he was the best person to chronicle the real story. His inside account became a series of seventeen front-page stories and the basis for a book that came out on the anniversary of Jennifer Lodge's death. Not since Woodward and Bernstein had a newspaper reporter been so quickly catapulted to such national, if not international, attention. A residual benefit was that O'Connell now had access to Vice President Morgan Taylor and the man who looked after him the most, Secret Service agent Scott Roarke.

He dialed an unpublished cell phone number. It rang twice.

"Yes?"

"Roarke," he blasted into the phone. "O'Connell."

There was no immediate response. O'Connell figured it was either a bad line or the agent was assessing whether he wanted to talk. If he didn't, it was probably because he'd already made the right call.

"Roarke?"

"Yup," he finally heard through the sound of traffic.

"Are you out on your morning run?"

"Yes." Roarke was jogging along the Mall. "So, what's up?"

"Got a question for you."

"How am I?" Roarke said without breaking stride.

"Naw. You know I don't care."

Silence.

"Just read a blurb in the *Post*. Making the wires now, but without any more details—about a government employee stabbed in Los Angeles. A woman. I thought maybe you might know something about it."

He waited for a reaction that didn't come.

"Killed."

Still no response.

"A woman."

"And?" Clearly, Roarke wasn't about to volunteer any information to O'Connell.

"...*Information on a security breach at the White House*... You don't see a phrase like that everyday."

"What?" Roarke said. "What did it say?"

O'Connell knew that *What did it say?* was a vastly different question than *What investigation?* He took it as a cue to push more. "Come on, Roarke. What do you know?"

"Haven't seen the paper yet."

"So you haven't heard about a woman in the administration being killed? And nothing about an FBI investigation?"

"What did it say?" Roarke asked sharply.

"See for yourself. Page three."

A few seconds later O'Connell heard the sound of papers rustling. Must have been a news kiosk nearby. He was certain Roarke uttered a quiet, "Oh, shit."

"So?" O'Connell asked.

"No."

"Nothing?"

"Not my job."

"Not your job to help me or not your job to look into it?" the reporter asked.

No reply.

"You know I've got to run this down. And I won't be the only one. A death and a security breach at the Oval Office."

"It didn't say that!"

"Pardon me," O'Connell replied. "The White House. There's more there."

"Be my guest," Roarke said.

"How about an arm's length relationship. You see what you can find out, we share information. Quietly."

"I can't do that."

"You did it before."

O'Connell was correct, but it was on Roarke's terms.

"Come on, off the record, Roarke."

"On the record. I've gotta go. Another time, O'Connell." Roarke ended the call.

O'Connell stared out into the city room of *The New York Times,* unable to fathom the full significance of the story or that a killer was going to make a bonus because he would soon put it on the front page.

Washington, D.C.
a short time later

Scott Roarke flashed his Secret Service ID to the FBI agent posted at the police tape. He was cleared to move into the building. That's when he spotted Bessolo climbing out of the van. He sucked in a breath and called out. "Hey, Bessolo!"

Ever since their run-in over whether Congressman Lodge was responsible for his wife's death, the two had been at each other's throats. The fact that Roarke had been right didn't ease the situation. Roarke took it on faith that Bessolo was a smart investigator, maybe one of the FBI's best, but for some reason he had a bug up his ass over Roarke.

Now Bessolo saw Roarke. If he hesitated to think about what he was going to say, it didn't help. "Hey, Captain America, what are you doing here?"

"Just what I'm told." That was enough to give him a free pass. Roarke met the FBI investigator, and together they walked inside. "What do you have?"

"Not quite ready to discuss anything," Bessolo said picking up the pace. He had no intention of briefing Roarke. First, he'd make a report to his boss. Robert Mulligan would then have to notify the president and then Attorney General Goldman. "So, Special Agent, how about you just run along and take your conspiracy theories with you."

"Hey, come on. You know why I'm here."

The arrival of Roarke immediately changed the game plan. "Look Roarke. You work for somebody. So do I. How about I tell my boss what I come up with. Then my boss bucks it up. Just like it's supposed to be."

"Tell your boss what?"

Bessolo realized he'd already said too much. "I gotta go." The FBI man turned away and continued his walk to the entrance of the apartment building.

"Tell him what?" Roarke shouted on the run. Bessolo stopped again and got right in Roarke's face.

"That she wore pink panties and played with a vibrator," he said, hoping that would end it.

Roarke ignored the comment. Instead, he reached for the door handle. "After you."

The two men walked up the stairs to the fourth floor without another word. When they entered Meyerson's apartment, Roarke saw that three of Bessolo's squad were busy working; their second day. Two were cataloguing personal items and a third was at the computer. Roarke assumed they'd already downloaded the computer's entire memory. Now they were drilling deeper into the details.

"What have you found?" he asked the man on the computer.

The FBI agent looked at Roarke, and then to his supervisor.

"You probably want to see this." Roarke dug into his pocket and produced his Secret Service ID.

Mark Gimbrone examined the card. It wasn't enough. He turned to Bessolo for approval. He got the condescending *no* he expected.

"Okay then, what if I just quietly watch. I don't get in the way. You don't get a phone call. Mind if I just look over your puppy's shoulder then?" Roarke asked Bessolo. "Promise, I won't disturb him."

This time, Bessolo shrugged and said, "Look, don't talk."

"Thank you," Roarke answered as impolitely as possible.

Gimbrone went from one program to the next, scanning the in- and out-boxes, the recently deleted messages, and Web searches. After ten minutes, Roarke pulled up a chair to get more comfortable. His host seemed to skip a number of things that Roarke showed interest in. The third time it happened, he tapped the screen.

"Mind if we spend a little bit of time on that?"

The FBI man snorted and clicked off the screen.

Roarke leaned forward and whispered in his ear. "You don't know me, do you?"

Without looking, Gimbrone nodded *no.*

"I didn't think so. A lot of what I do doesn't get public notice."

Gimbrone's ears perked up. He swiveled his chair around.

"I'm Taylor's boy. The one who gets to go anywhere and do anything. You might have heard about some of my assignments. None of which, of course, ever happened."

Recognition spread over Gimbrone's face. *Libya. The Capitol. The man who saved Taylor. The man who stopped Lodge.* They all came to mind.

"So, may I please take a look," Roarke continued in a whisper. "Quiet as a mouse, just like I promised."

There was no longer any question. He returned to the computer and typed in the command that brought the e-mails back to life. The FBI agent extended his palm, inviting Roarke to examine it closer.

Roarke patted his back in thanks as he read the first e-mail address, the time and date, and a completely incriminating message.

"Holy shit," Roarke said, suddenly making a friend.

Gimbrone agreed. "And there's more. Info on pending bills, military intel, travel schedules for the president and the veep. All a bit obtuse, but recognizable."

"How many are there?"

"Six," the FBI agent volunteered.

"All to the same recipient?"

"Every single one. From the first 'how do you do' to the last, just a day before she left for California."

Roarke looked around the room. Bessolo's team was tagging and bagging items. He recognized Beth Thomas. She'd be another good one to befriend. No doubt she was analyzing pictures, dinner receipts, and phone logs; the process could go on for weeks. Meanwhile, the story would take on a momentum all its own, and even though Vice President Taylor had no hand in Meyerson's hiring, he'd undoubtedly feel the heat.

Roarke wanted to help, but he wasn't sure how. As he craned around Gimbrone, the word *bungled* nagged at him again. *Why?* he wondered.

His thought was interrupted by the vibration of the cell phone in his sports coat pocket. *A 617 number. Not Katie's.*

"Hi, Scott. Catch you at a bad time?" It was Katie.

"In the middle of some stuff." He backed up two steps and turned to the side for a degree of privacy. "Where are you?

"Out." There was some nervousness in her voice. "But if you're busy we can talk later."

Roarke noted the undercurrent. "Is everything all right?"

She hesitated, then answered. "I guess so."

Roarke hadn't heard concern in Katie's voice, even veiled concern, in months. "Need to talk?"

"It can wait."

There is something. "You can do better than that. What's up?" He was sure he heard traffic noise. "Where are you calling from?"

"Outside. From a phone at Faneuil Hall. Can you believe it?"

"What about your cell?"

She didn't answer the question. "Look," she said instead. "You're busy. It's just a question. It can wait."

Roarke rubbed his chin with his free hand. They hadn't been together for awhile. Maybe he could hop a flight later in the day.

"Hey, you, I can be through in a bit. Wanna play this weekend?"

"Do I!" she exclaimed. "Really?"

"If you want me."

"In *every* possible way." She rushed to the next question. "How soon?"

Roarke continued to chat with his cell in his left hand. Since he didn't want to take his ear off the phone to check his watch, he simply stepped forward to the computer screen. Windows displayed the time on the extreme lower-right corner.

"...Two fifteen. I could be on the four-thirty. Meet you at our usual for drinks, say at..."

He stopped in mid-sentence, peering closer to the screen. *The time.* He looked at his watch, then the screen again. *Two fifteen.* He reached forward to tap the screen, wanting Gimbrone to see what he just noticed. But the agent pushed Roarke's hand aside, not allowing his finger to touch the liquid crystal monitor. The minute flipped to 2:16.

"At?" Katie asked. "Oh, hello? At?"

After the long pause, Roarke continued, but his focus completely shifted. "Sorry. Gotta get back to you," he said abruptly forgetting her concern. "There's something I have to look into."

The White House
the same time

The president's secretary cleared Robert Mulligan right in again. Not wanting to waste any time, Mulligan removed a folder from his briefcase the moment he stepped into the Oval Office.

"Mr. President."

"Bob."

The pleasantries were over.

"I take it you have more?"

"Yes. We found a request for a meeting in one e-mail. A time. A date. A place."

"Spare me the guessing. Where?" Henry Lamden demanded.

"Los Angeles, Mr. President. Around the time Meyerson was killed. That could be why she carried lipstick on her run."

"What?"

"To put a message in for a dead-drop."

"Have you found any reply from a handler."

"Online, no. But considering she was sending messages out on her PC, I'm not surprised. However, we did find some tape stuck under a park bench near where she was killed. It was right where another jogger reported seeing her sit down the day before."

Neither man had taken a seat. Mulligan passed the folder to the president, but Lamden didn't open it. Instead, he went to his desk and held up the morning *Post*.

"You want to tell me how the story got out, Bob?"

Mulligan knew this was coming.

"I don't know, sir."

"You don't know."

"No, sir."

"You better find out."

The director already had a team scrutinizing phone logs in and out of the bureau, but he decided that it would be better to agree now. Lamden had every right to be upset. Only the FBI knew about Meyerson's correspondence.

"While I have your undivided attention, Bob..."

"Yes, sir?"

"How the hell did you clear this woman for office?" the president demanded. "No background checks? No hint of a personal political vendetta? Resentment? Nothing showed up?"

"We investigated Meyerson before she came to the White House. Everything was clean—her family, her school, all of her contacts. No Zionist leanings. But apparently we missed one thing. One very important thing."

"You're damned right you did."

Roarke spun around and searched for Bessolo. He caught the field investigator in the bedroom, examining lipstick containers he found deep in Meyerson's dresser. "Hey, Roy, I need you to look at something."

Roy? Roarke never called him *Roy* before. "What?"

"Just come here."

Bessolo hated the idea of cooperating with Roarke, but he was smart enough to know that Roarke would ultimately get anything he requested.

"What now?"

"The e-mails. You should see a couple of them. The most recent."

"Already have."

"Then check them out again. Particularly the last two or three."

"I'm busy."

"Okay, then, but I need Gimbrone to print them out for me," Roarke said.

"They don't go anywhere!"

Bessolo's inclination was to throw the Bobbi Brown lipstick container on the floor to show his anger. But everything was considered evidence.

"Nothing leaves here."

"Sometimes I think you stepped out of the wrong building."

"What the hell's that supposed to mean?"

"Natural History instead of the FBI."

Bessolo didn't get it.

"Never mind. Can you just do this the easy way for a change? Allow Gimbrone to print out the damned e-mails for me."

"Why?" Bessolo asked, deciding to be more difficult.

"You'll see why," Roarke said, forcing a smile. "Pretty please."

Bessolo stormed past Roarke while Roarke remained in the doorway between the two rooms. The two FBI men talked to each other. Two minutes later, Bessolo was back with printouts.

"Here you go, Sherlock."

"Thank you," Roarke said, not giving into the comment.

Roarke read the header of the first e-mail. "Okay," he simply said. He put it behind the next sheet and continued to scan the remaining pages, one after another. It took all of 15 seconds.

He handed them back to Bessolo with an interesting upturned grin.

"So you're a fucking speed reader. I'm impressed."

"No. I saw what I was looking for."

"Pray tell, what was that?"

"Look at the header."

"Which one?"

"Take your pick."

Bessolo held up the first page. It didn't look any different than the last time he'd read it.

"And the next one." Bessolo complied.

"And the rest."

The FBI agent read them all. If there was anything specific he was supposed to catch he failed to recognize it.

"Okay. I give up. What magical thing have I missed?"

"Nothing on the pages. It all looks like she sent them out in the middle of the night."

Bessolo checked the time stamps on the header. 3:11 A.M. 2:24 A.M.. 4:56 A.M..

"Yeah, so?"

"So, what time is it now?"

Bessolo was becoming more irritated, but he looked at his watch. "It's two-fucking-twenty in the middle of the fucking afternoon."

"P.M.?" Roarke asked.

"P-fucking-M," Bessolo shot back.

Roarke leaned around Bessolo and pointed to the computer in the living room. "Really? Are you sure?"

Staritsa, Russia

Aleksandr Dubroff nursed his bottle of vodka for over an hour. At this time of night, alone, as he had been for 24 years, he worked on another hobby. When he was 83, he bought himself a computer. Two years later, he was proficient at surfing—as the Americans called it—the Net. *If only the phone lines were more reliable in his dacha. Better yet,* he wondered, *when will Russia step into the 21st century and be wired with high-speed lines like the West, Japan, South Korea, and even the smallest European villages?*

"This will come," government spokesmen often said. *Propaganda,* he said to himself. Time had really not changed Russia.

So, almost every night, his service was interrupted. Dubroff learned to quickly save files and pour through them, waiting for the intermittent service to return. He was amazed at what he found. Decades-old Soviet secrets now there for everyone to see in Times New Roman English text. There were complete accounts of Russian space disasters, exact figures on the industrial and agricultural failures of the Soviet Union, hundreds of Web sites devoted to the most degrading pornography, and more sites that outed *him* as a KGB agent.

He checked accounts that detailed means that *he* used to extract information from informants, enemies of the State, and traitors to the Party. He was amazed what people uncovered. As Dubroff read on, he remembered each interrogation, each face, each admission. Throughout his service he had been proud of his accomplishments, but now, reading the stories, he appeared to be a psychotic torturer; a war criminal. *How could this be?* These were not the appalling, inhumane acts chronicled in these pages. *It was my duty to get information. That was all.* But that was not *all.* Dubroff knew it.

Every night he searched for new references. Fortunately, no reporters had searched hard enough to actually find him. That would be difficult. His telephone was unlisted. He never received a phone or electrical bill. They were paid for life through his pension. The little mail that he got came to a postal box, and his pension checks were issued by first initial only, then last name. Dubroff hadn't talked to anyone in government for years. *I'm one of the walking dead. A remnant of the old guard. Probably lost to them all.*

Dubroff was quite right to assume he was lost to humans. But he was not lost to the system. He was not lost to SORM.

Washington, D.C.

"Let's take a walk," Roarke said, after Bessolo returned from his second visit to Meyerson's computer.

The FBI field supervisor didn't object, but he was confused; confused enough to want to learn what Roarke was thinking. The two men went downstairs and out the front door without talking.

"Where to?" Bessolo asked.

Roarke motioned to the left. Once clear of the building, the police tape, and anyone who might have closely observed them, Bessolo spoke up. "Okay. You better take me through this. So the clock's wrong on the computer. I got that much. What's the big deal? I can't get my damned TIVO to work."

"It's not just wrong. It's exactly wrong. By twelve hours. A.M. for P.M."

"So?"

"So the last e-mail was what? Four fifty-six A.M.?"

"Yeah," the FBI agent in charge replied.

"A.M., like in the morning."

"Right."

"The next day she left for L.A. on *Air Force One.*"

"Yes," Bessolo said, sliding his answer across three syllables.

"And presuming the clock was right, she sent it out at four fifty-six A.M., why was it two fifteen A.M. when we just looked at the time?" Roarke stopped walking. Bessolo automatically did the same.

"I don't know."

"I do." Roarke took a half a step forward and lowered his voice. "She never sent out an e-mail at four fifty-six A.M."

"Of course she did."

"She didn't send one out then, and I'll bet you she didn't send out any of the others, either. Someone else did. Someone else came in to her apartment during the day, reset the clock on the computer to make it look like it was in the middle of the night, and then hit *send*."

"You're full of shit, Roarke."

Roarke moved closer. "Who knows, maybe the clock got adjusted back correctly every time except for the last. Something happened. The person got spooked. Maybe he got tipped off she was coming home early. I'd want to check that if I were you. Maybe he just fucked up."

"And maybe you should realize we've uncovered a stinking spy cell."

"Like someone wants you to think!" Roarke shot back. "Look, Roy," he said without an ounce of gentility. "It's a simple thing, but it makes sense. The girl was killed, not because someone was trying to rape her. There was never a rape. It wasn't dark yet. She was killed. The path led you right to her apartment, and you found what you were supposed to find."

For once, Bessolo didn't lob back a quick and asinine retort.

Roarke continued. "And the story broke. I take it nobody on your team leaked it."

Bessolo delivered his conclusive answer through an ice-cold stare.

"Another part of the plan. It's all choreographed."

"But she did send classified information," Bessolo maintained.

"Did she? You tell me if anything really worthwhile got out, or whether it's old news, or a rewrite of a *Popular Science* article, or a grab from a Clancy novel. Like they say, it's not my job. Why don't you check it."

Bessolo couldn't argue the point any longer. Roarke was right. Something wasn't adding up. "Across the street," Bessolo stated. "Let's get some coffee."

They waited a moment for the traffic to open up, then jaywalked to a coffee shop. As they reached the curb, Bessolo stopped again. He had a knot in the pit of his stomach. "Assuming for half a second that your cockamamie theory is partially right, why go through all of this?"

"I don't know. I'm not the political science major, but just off the top of my head?"

"That'll do."

"Embarrass the hell out of the president?" Then it came to him. "No, bigger than that."

"What?" Bessolo asked.

"Complete an unfinished job. Undermine our relations with Israel and bring the administration down."

They walked by a bank before coming to the coffee shop. It was a small mom-and-pop establishment that somehow carved out a loyal customer base in an otherwise-Starbucks world. Bessolo and Roarke both ordered black coffees. While they waited for their drinks, Bessolo scored a metal table outside the shop, diagonally across the street from Meyerson's apartment building. Roarke brought over the cups and took the seat facing the storefront. They spoke softly.

"So, do I take it you're willing to consider the possibility?" Roarke asked.

"You can assume anything you want. I just work with the evidence."

"Never beyond the evidence, Bessolo? You never wonder about things? Come on, this is Washington. There are at least two reasons for every action."

"Hard evidence, Roarke. Rock solid," Bessolo replied.

Roarke looked away, surprised he was even trying to have a conversation. That's when he noticed the bank a few feet away. He leaned to the left to get an unobstructed view, then shifted his glance to Meyerson's building. Then he studied the front of the bank again.

"Excuse me for a second."

Roarke stood up and walked to the front, stopping at the outdoor ATM. From there, he looked over his shoulder one more time. *Right across the street.*

"Bessolo!" he called. "I need you for a second."

"Forget it. I'll cover the coffee." The FBI man figured Roarke had forgotten his ATM card. Then he grasped what the Secret Service agent had already realized. *Shit. The ATM camera!*

New York Times City Room
New York, New York

Michael O'Connell retrieved a message on his voicemail from an anonymous caller. The man described himself as someone who had special information regarding a story in *The Washington Post.* "It is twelve twenty P.M. now. I will call back every ten minutes. Pick up on the first ring. I'll hang up by the second. If by six calls you have not answered, I will take what I have to *The Washington Post.*"

"Oh, shit!" he cursed aloud, catching the time. One-twelve. Sources were manipulative bastards, and this one seemed to have a special agenda. *One more chance,* he said to himself.

At 5:20 exactly, the reporter's phone rang. O'Connell grabbed the headset, nearly knocking his phone over.

"O'Connell. Who is this?"

"Never mind. I have some new information."

"What kind of information?"

"The kind that you like, Mr. O'Connell. Deeply troubling. About Israel."

Washington, D.C.

Morgan Taylor wished he had done what he originally intended after the Inauguration: retire to some secluded fishing hole. But in the moments following Lodge's death, the man next in line to be president—Henry Lamden—asked him to stay. He appealed to Taylor's sense of duty, arguing the country needed him. With the smell of gunfire still in the Capitol, Taylor agreed. Now he questioned the whole bloody decision.

Taylor hated babysitting the Senate. He hated being number two. He hated being viewed as a functionary. And he hated being a desk jockey. Ever since flying sorties off the deck of a nuclear carrier, he was used to being in control. *Always.* Until now.

So when Scott Roarke said he needed to see him immediately, he welcomed the excuse to skip out on the Senate.

Roarke had already phoned Katie to say he'd be at least two hours late. He still expected he'd make it for a late dinner. When she asked why, he cryptically offered, "Allergies. My nose is itching again."

They had worked out a variety of codes between them. This was one of the important flags. *I'm onto something.*

"Boss," Roarke said, barging into the vice president's office as if it were his own, "I need to run something important by you."

"The floor's yours," Taylor said. There was no offer of coffee.

"A little Q and A, boss."

"Go," Taylor said. He settled into another of his favorite chairs. This one, a 19th-century captain's chair, which had belonged to Admiral Halsey when he served aboard the USS *Enterprise*. Roarke did the pacing for everybody this time.

"The killing of Mrs. Lodge, the act that launched Teddy Lodge's bid for the White House. What was that called?"

"I don't know what you mean."

"How did reporters describe it?"

The vice president was not pleased with Roarke's dialectic approach. "Just get to it, Scott."

Roarke noted his objection. "The press called it a *bungled* assassination. Everyone thought the killer was out to get Lodge. They said it was *bungled*."

"And?"

"Lynn Meyerson."

"Yes?"

"Sexually assaulted. In broad daylight. In a public park. Below a jogging path. Maybe somebody broke it up, made a noise, shouted. But guess what?" He didn't wait for an answer. "I don't believe it. No one's come forward to confirm it. And you've heard what they're calling it?"

Roarke had his mentor's undivided attention. Taylor thought the word as Roarke stated it.

"Bungled!"

"Where are you going with this?"

Roarke told him.

that night

"So it was a busy day," Katie began on their nightly phone call.

"Very." He couldn't explain how busy.

"Is the weekend out?" she asked.

"No, still planning on coming up. Seemed like you need a little TLC." He was obliquely asking about her manner earlier on the telephone.

"Listen, I've got to feed the cat. Can we talk later?" Katie asked hurriedly.

"Sure," Roarke said, aware of an undercurrent of tension. "Love you."

"Love you more."

Katie had no cat.

Seven minutes later, Roarke's phone rang again.

"Hon," Katie said over the noise of traffic.

Roarke heard the cars. "What's wrong?"

"Well, probably nothing, but...."

"Where are you?"

"A phone booth at Cambridge and Charles."

Roarke closed his eyes and pictured the spot. It was just outside of a drugstore, near the Longfellow Bridge.

"You called from a phone booth before, too. What's the matter?"

"Scott, would I know if my phone was being tapped?"

"Tapped!" He suddenly bolted upright from his chair.

"Does it have a different sound?" she wondered.

"When did you notice?"

"Two days ago."

Roarke mentally reran their conversations together. *Two days ago? What the fuck did we talk about? Two days ago?*

"Maybe I'm imagining things..."

He raised his hand to stop her, even though she couldn't see him. "Hold it!" He quickly organized his thoughts. "Tomorrow, you're going to get a flower delivery. The people will fuss all over you, and it'll take a little time. You'll invite them into your office. Casually close the door. They're going to check the phones. They can do it very quickly. They'll do the same at your home, so don't alarm your apartment."

Katie became more nervous. This was real. "I don't know," she said nervously.

"Everything will be fine. I promise. And you can keep the flowers. They'll be from me."

Roarke's father used to joke that his boy was like a salmon—always forcing himself through the surging current. That current took on many forms.

As a kid, Roarke stood up to the gangs in his neighborhood. Having a black belt in Tae Kwon Do from Master Jun Chong worked in his favor.

Years later, his Special Forces training made him lethal. Anyone who didn't get out of his way never got a second chance.

Now, Roarke's instincts were taking him upstream again, into more troubled waters.

Roarke called his friend Shannon Davis, who quickly and easily arranged for an FBI team, disguised as florists, to go in and sweep Katie's office. When they finished there, they'd do the same thing at her apartment.

Assuming that she was right and her phone was tapped, Roarke had three immediate concerns: *Who? Why? And what did they expect to find?*

CHAPTER
19

Maluku, Indonesia
Friday, 22 June

Nutmeg and cloves. The exotic spices could have been the Holy Grail, considering what nations went through to locate their source.

Indian, Javan, and Arab traders introduced the spices to Medieval Europe. They were valued for more than merely the flavors they added to food. The cloves, called *cegkeh* in Indonesian, are the pungent-scented, pale-green flower buds of the *syzigium aromaticum* tree. Picked and left to dry to a dark brown, their chemical properties preserve meat. Therein lay its real value. As a result, in an age long before refrigeration, every major seafaring nation of Europe sought to locate the natural growing grounds and control the market.

The quest sent Columbus in search of the fabled Spice Islands. But, of course, he ended up in the New World. The Portuguese, credited as the first actual Europeans to set foot on the South Pacific islands, couldn't hold onto their spoils. Other sailors, under the flag of Spain, moved in. They introduced Christianity and terror. In 1861, Holland took control, establishing the United East Indies Company. The Dutch mercilessly ruled the islands, killing the indigenous people, leveling plantations where natives rebelled, and enslaving those they kept alive. The Dutch subsequently drove out foreign rivals, thus delivering huge profits home in their monopolistic, dictatorial exploitation of the Spice Islands.

The Dutch strongly believed they had made a lasting conquest. However, years of warfare, starvation, and depopulation accompanied the autocratic Dutch rule. Their dominion continued until they presided over most of what eventually became the Republic of Indonesia. But it was the marketplace that unseated Holland's ruthless monopoly of the Spice Islands, not a coup. Gradually, smugglers managed to ship the islands' seeds overseas. In time, the world no longer needed to rely on Banda, Ternate, Ambon, and Maluku for the answer to food preservation. They could grow the spices closer to home.

What little trade remained into the 20th century virtually disappeared with the Japanese occupation in World War II.

The Japanese ousted the Dutch in just under 10 days. Initially the conquerors were welcomed. But Japan immediately established an even more brutal rule, marked by further famine, slavery, and executions.

Two days after Japan surrendered to the Allies, Indonesia proclaimed its independence. The government was loosely held together by an unstable coalition dominated by the Socialists and the conservative Muslim Masyumi party.

Sukarno emerged as the first president. He established a "guided" democracy, which fell apart through regional and factional problems. In 1959, he assumed full dictatorial powers, and four years later anointed himself President for Life. He cozied up to Communist China and withdrew Indonesia from the United Nations.

Despite his self-proclamation, Sukarno did not remain president. A 1965 coup d'état led to the military takeover by General Suharto at the cost of between 500,000 and a million dead. Suharto had opposed the pro-Communist policies, and became first acting president and then president in 1968, supported by students, the Army, and Muslim factions.

He remained in office, re-elected every five years, until he resigned in 1998 amidst allegations of corruption, which were later dismissed.

In recent years, Indonesian governance has changed numerous times. As a result, good PR alternates with reports of terrorism; adventure travel features compete for print space with stories chronicling human rights violations. As for Maluku's two million inhabitants—they largely live in poverty.

To this day, cloves and nutmegs remain a limited export of Maluku. Commander Umar Komari sowed other seeds—seeds of terrorism. He was driven by personal devils: the desire to punish the world for exploiting the Malukus and slaughtering its people. He was also determined to establish complete Muslim control over the Christian non-believers.

He examined the weapons from the last transaction.

"Pitiful. Barely bows and arrows," he told his subordinate, Musah Atef.

"*Shabu* production will pick up. Soon, the Chinese will deliver our missiles. Jakarta will tremble and tumble. We shall have our way."

"Allah be praised," the terrorist proclaimed.

His men echoed their reverence with the same words.

Komari had made promises to hungry men; men who followed him for food and believed in his cause. Word spread through the islands. More recruits came daily. His ranks had swelled. Komari scattered his camps and supplies over dozens of islands on the east side of Halmahera and throughout the coves of Maluku's peninsulas. His enclaves were invisible to many probing satellites, but not all. Arms and food remained the only obstacles between Komari and the coup he planned. Komari would secure both.

The White House
Washington, D.C.

When Henry Lamden ran for office, he had no real conception of how much bad news presidents had to hear. Now, five months into the job, the next phone call was not entirely unexpected.

"Mr. President."

"Mr. Prime Minister," Lamden replied. "It's good to hear your voice. I look forward to meeting you in August."

"Quite right. I understand we're to have dinner."

Lamden had the schedule in front of him. The schedule prepared by Lynn Meyerson. "Yes. It's in ink on my calendar."

David Foss was a career politician and Lamden's senior by a decade. Like the American president, he had military service, retiring with the rank of general from the Royal Australian Army, Royal Queensland Regiment. During his tour of duty he served in East Timor, Malaysia. As a civilian he became a military analyst for Australian television, a political commentator, and eventually the host of a weekly news-magazine before he launched his own grassroots campaign for political office. Now, nine years later, he was head of the Liberal Party, and Prime Minister of Australia.

There was a "but" coming. The president could sense it.

"Very good. We'll have much to talk about then. But..."

There it is.

"...there's something we need to discuss in advance of our session."

"Certainly, Mr. Prime Minister."

"As I'm sure you know, a number of years ago Australia entered into the MOU."

Lamden was familiar with the term, but only because Billy Gilmore made sure he had all the PM's possible agendas in front of him. MOU referred to the Memoranda of Understanding on Combating International Terrorism. Australia, Malaysia, Indonesia, and Thailand signed the agreement in 2002. The teeth of the bilateral pact came from the commitment to combat terrorist financing and money laundering in the South Pacific, another outgrowth of the 9/11 and Bali attacks.

"Yes," was all the president said.

"Well, the Ville St. George discovery has us rather concerned. We don't know who is responsible. However, our neighbors, some of them heavily populated by our Muslim friends, have confidentially shared with us an increase in telephone and Internet chatter that we all deem disturbing. My own intelligence contacts from my Royal Army days claim that all is not well. Al Qaeda, Abu Sayyaf, Moro Islamic Liberation Front, and many others are growing richer through drug trade. They all seek glory and much more than—what do you typically call it? Fifteen minutes of fame?"

"That's it."

"We may strike down one evil serpent, but this Medusa springs forth another...and with it, long tentacles that reach well within our infrastructure. This week, the Ville St. George. Next week, who can say?"

"Truly worrisome, Prime Minister Foss. You have identified a threat that we must join hands to destroy." Lamden felt the discussion was about to take a more serious turn.

"What a perfect segue, Mr. President. And quite to the point of my call," Foss replied. "As a signatory to MOU, I am prepared to invoke the terms of the ANZUS Treaty. We view the St. George bomb as an attack, foiled perhaps, but an attack nonetheless. An attack on Australian soil. An attack on the Australian people. Conceivably, Mr. President, even an attack intended for you."

Henry Lamden couldn't disagree. "What level of assistance are you requesting, Mr. Prime Minister?" he directly asked.

"Mr. President, nothing short of a greater presence by the Seventh Fleet. We need help covering the terrority."

Lebanon, Kansas

"Try thinking like a liberal. Don't hurt yourself. But try. Oh, you'll have to throw all reasoning out the window. But for the next hour, let's see if you can. It's open phones, and I want you to call in and try out any bit of liberal logic you have for keeping Lamden and Taylor in office."

It was another one of Elliott Strong's games; a reliable trick that would serve to ridicule his targets and rile his audience. For the host, it was a sucker pitch to the plate. His listeners would hit it out of the park.

"No one?" he said, baiting them. "Come now, millions of you out there and no one wants to be a liberal? How did these guys get in office if there's no one to support them?"

Of course, callers were lined up. He just wasn't ready to release them.

"Maybe you need a little nudge." He cleared his throat and added a phone filter to his own voice with the flip of a switch on his audio board.

"Hello, Elliott?"

He cut back to his normal voice. "Yes, you're on *Liberal Notion*." He laughed at his own creativity.

"Yes, I represent the Urban Spotted Owls League," he mockingly offered.

Then another dialect: "Hello, Elliott, I think we've got too many prisons."

"And I'm a truck driver," he added as a woman long-hauler on a cell. "I personally feel we should cap interstate highway speeds at 45 mph. That or give California back to Mexico, which would shorten the mileage cross-country."

Strong gave it a good five minutes. Then he went to his calls. Calls like, "As far as I'm concerned, it's good that the president hired foreign spies. That way the enemy doesn't have to subscribe to *The New York Times*." And, "You want to know why Lamden always looks so good on TV? Just ask his *Taylor*."

After an hour, Strong called an end to the fun.

"Stop! I can't take it anymore! It's too hard to think so idiotically. I know you're asking yourself, how do people do it? We're all the same, but how can we be so different? So different in the same country? How can we see things so clearly, but your liberal neighbor, or your kid's teacher, or that anchorman, or the bank teller who takes your money, see things so wrong? How do Lamden and Taylor still have their jobs?"

Thanks to the current law, everything Elliott Strong said was protected speech. It didn't require rebuttal.

"It's beyond me." He shuffled some papers. "Gotta go to a commercial. When we come back, I'll tell you about a call from the White House press office today. You're gonna love this."

"So listen to this. A junior level White House press flak calls and says, 'Mr. Strong, you've clogged up our fax lines, and there are too many e-mails for us to conduct the nation's business.'" The host put extra sarcasm on "the nation's business."

"I replied in my most courteous voice, 'Why, isn't it the nation's business to consider what Americans have to say?'

"'Yes, but....' the press aide tried to blabber. I'll spare you the rest of his whining. But let me tell you, I got the same thing from twenty-seven members of Congress today. 'Can't do our work. Overloaded the fax machines. Can't get through the necessary e-mails.'

"Ladies and Gentlemen, citizens of *Strong Nation*, this is unbelievable. We are the nation's business. We are their work. We are necessary. We are the boss. Not them. They serve at our pleasure. By our vote. They represent us. We are the constituency. They are the representative arm of the people. Where do they get off? Where in hell do they get off telling you that your letter isn't necessary. It's not America's business?"

Listeners heard Elliott Strong take a long, quenching sip of water.

"I'm sorry. I'm just so wound up. These people. They're not in charge. They're not the boss!" he repeated with more conviction. "They are *not* my boss.

"And this idiot at the White House told me to stop handing out the phone numbers and e-mail addresses. Can you believe that? Their own published numbers." He cleared his throat to make the next point. "Excuse me, *our* own published numbers. The White House. Each and every member of Congress. Those are numbers we use to communicate with the government—the government we put there! But guess what? You haven't done it enough! Let them complain. Let them realize this is just the beginning. Because maybe one in ten thousand of you wrote or called to state why you want a Constitutional Amendment to end this mess. But that's not enough. They haven't even seen the iceberg yet, let alone what's under it.

"Well, I'm keeping the numbers on the Web site. You go there and get them. No, let me make it easier for you. We'll go to a commercial and when we come back, I'll read them to you. And I'll do it at the top and bottom of every hour. Because this administration is the *Titanic,* and you're going to send that iceberg right in its path.

"We'll be right back."

CHAPTER

20

Washington, D.C.
Friday, 22 June

There wasn't even the question of the president attending the Meyerson funeral in Lewiston, Maine. No one connected with the White House went to the small New England town. No apologies were expected or given. The story had already broken nationally.

First, FBI Director Robert Mulligan dropped the bombshell on the president. Then came the brief *Post* story. But it was O'Connell's article in *The New York Times,* obviously based on an informed source, that gave it a life of its own. He'd pieced enough denials together to fashion a compelling argument.

> **Neither the White House nor the FBI will comment on the investigation into the death of administration staff member Lynn Meyerson, killed last week in Los Angeles. A source close to the inquiry says that Meyerson may have passed classified information onto Israel's intelligence agency, the Mossad.**
>
> **Meyerson, 26, was assaulted while jogging in a public park. Police in Los Angeles are cooperating with the FBI. The victim worked in an administrative capacity in the White House Office of Strategic Initiatives. According to an inside source, she had access to sensitive documents, and was in Los Angeles with President Lamden.**

O'Connell didn't report everything he was told, strictly because he couldn't confirm what the source provided. However, the words he did use said enough to frame an explosive front-page story and one hell of a national tempest.

Mossad Headquarters
Tel Aviv, Israel

"We have a problem, Ira," the Mossad director began. "Sit down and read this."

Jacob Schecter slid the intelligence briefings across the desk to his number two. The salient points were highlighted with a yellow marker.

> **"...passed classified information...Israel...spy...White House Office of Strategic Initiatives...inside source...sensitive documents."**

The rest of the briefing, culled from wire-service stories, *Washington Post* and *New York Times* articles, and opinion from Mossad agents working inside the embassy in Washington, filled in the details. Everything led Wurlin to the same conclusion that Schecter already made.

"Chantul?"

"Yes, Chantul," the Mossad chief said without equivocation. "If she left any trail, which is likely, then Evans will discover it. I assure you we will hear from him in the strongest possible terms. And if this should become public, even Evans will not be able to contain the damage."

"Yes, Jacob."

"Two immediate things. One, seal all the Chantul files. No one has access. Two, get me information on this woman. Her life, her motives. Everything we didn't know about her when she was alive, I want to know now. I want to be prepared for the call when it comes. I want information and ammunition. And I want it right away!"

Washington, D.C.

The White House press secretary offered obligatory answers at the morning briefing. "Yes, Ms. Meyerson was employed by the White House Office of Strategic Initiatives...Yes, she handled various materials relating to presidential programs...No, those programs cannot be discussed...Yes, we are working with the LAPD in their investigation of Ms. Meyerson's death."

So far even O'Connell hadn't dug deep enough to uncover names, dates, and places. But President Lamden and his chief of staff, Billy Gilmore, had no doubt they were living on borrowed time.

Evoking the rhythm of Senator Howard Baker's famed interrogatory during the Watergate Hearings, Lamden demanded of his FBI chief, "What do you know, and when did you know it?"

"We're just piecing it together now, Mr. President. We don't wiretap the lines of people who have been cleared. We have to have cause. There was none."

"And the CIA?"

Mulligan shrugged his shoulders. "If they had, they didn't tell us."

National Director of Intelligence Jack Evans had already assured the president there was never a reason to suspect Meyerson.

"Then how the hell did any of you miss this? What kind of lame-ass background check did you do?" Now Lamden yelled louder than any president Mulligan had ever heard. "And what was this woman doing in *my* White House?"

Lebanon, Kansas
later

"And now this! Oh, there's trouble in paradise, my friends. Trouble indeed," Elliott Strong said, raising the controversy to a personal attack on Lamden. "Unless you were lying under a rock in the last twelve hours, you probably heard this one. It's a doozie. And I wouldn't want to be Henry Lamden tonight."

Strong had his *New* Yuck *Times* in front of him, but this time he didn't malign the paper. Instead, he quoted from it. "Front page, no less. And from the renowned Mr. Michael O'Connell. This is big, my friends. Big." He read the story verbatim, emphasizing key words to make his point.

"Are you getting this? A member of the Lamden-Taylor dynasty now accused of leaking secrets to an ally. To Israel, no less!"

Listeners heard Strong rustle the pages as he turned to an AP account, then to CNN's latest online report, and another from Fox

News. "We have an unrestrained imperial presidency, and low and behold, another country has its hand in our cookie jar. You're going to hear shock and denial from the administration. But you tell me. A woman is killed while jogging. She happens to have been—dare I say— a spy?" He added only for legal purposes, but well set off from the rest of the sentence, "...allegedly."

"So who killed her?" He was fully revved up again. "I bet this is going to prove interesting. A modern-day Mata Hari tries to sell us down the river and she's killed. Now who would possibly have cause? A rapist in broad daylight? Come now. You think we're going to buy that story, Mr. President?"

He could just about hear everyone say, *No way!*

"So tonight, *Strong Nation* asks: Henry Lamden, who was Meyerson working for? How was she killed? And when are you going to accept the blame that you are responsible? You, Mr. President. You and your cronies. You are the reason that we're failing as a country. You are what's wrong with America. You. And you have to go!"

CHAPTER 21

The White House

"**A** goddamned Mossad agent in the White House! How?"

"Mr. President, you know it's not confirmed," Jack Evans told the president.

"Bullshit. *The New York Times* reported it. The *Post*. The networks. And someone inside the FBI told them. What the hell will denials accomplish now? Jesus H. Christ, aren't these people supposed to be our friends?"

The Director of National Intelligence decided to bite his tongue. Besides, he didn't have the freedom to interrupt this president the way he did the last, who was sitting beside him. He let Henry Lamden do what he needed to do: fume. That was Billy Gilmore's advice to him in the hall.

"I'm this close." Lamden held his forefinger and thumb almost together. "This close to throwing their ambassador right out on his ass and canceling—what do we give them? Four billion a year in aid?"

"More," Gilmore addeed. "Six-point-three billion. About seventeen million a day."

The number made Lamden, a die-hard supporter of Israel, even more furious. "In my fucking White House! How the hell did this happen? Will someone tell me?"

Evans didn't volunteer an answer. Neither did National Security Advisor Bird and FBI Chief Mulligan. Only one other man could possibly speak: Morgan Taylor.

The vice president rose out of his chair. The very act made Henry Lamden sit down on the couch.

Morgan Taylor spoke calmly. "As NDI said, we're still trying to get a handle on this."

Evans seconded the comment. Mulligan, on the other hand, shifted in his seat. His man was still unconvinced about Roarke's theory. For now, Bessolo argued that the time shift might be nothing more than a computer glitch and Meyerson was guilty as sin.

Taylor addressed Jack Evans. "Jack, have you fully briefed the president on our own operations?"

Evans shot him a quizzical look.

"In Israel," Taylor added.

"What operations?" Lamden demanded.

Evans cleared his throat. "Not yet."

Lamden became more furious. "Not yet *what*?"

"Mr. President, it's fairly standard," Evans started. "We just don't talk about it. But we have our own people in the Israeli government. Working within the Knesset."

"Oh, for God's sake."

"For years. We do it. They do it. So I wouldn't be too hasty with—"

"Excuse me," Lamden continued. "Hasty? *You* are not to tell *me* what to do!" he shouted. "Do you understand, Mr. Director?"

Evans noted his mistake. "I'm sorry. I didn't intend it that way. You have every right—"

He didn't get to finish the thought. The president interrupted again.

"You're damned straight I have. And for that matter, I want to know exactly where you have placed your agents!"

"Are you certain, sir?" the National Director of Intelligence asked, shifting his eyes uncomfortably toward Morgan Taylor.

The ex-president got the signal. "Henry," he said quietly, "sometimes it's better we don't know everything."

Lamden was not to be dissuaded. "Don't give me that goddamned Republican deniability bullshit. I'm in charge!"

Morgan Taylor had never seen this side of Lamden. But then again, Henry Lamden had never faced such pressure before. *I have to calm him down,* he thought.

"Henry, Jack can pull all the information you want. But reading it exposes you and the entire government. Let's you and I sidebar this for later. Okay?"

He got a reluctant wave of the hand to move on. That's when Taylor noticed that Lamden was beginning to perspire profusely.

"Henry, are you okay?"

"No, I'm not okay. I had an Israeli spy right here in my office." The president realized beads of sweat were forming on his forehead. Lamden reached for a cloth napkin. After patting down, he poured himself a glass of water from the pitcher on the table beside him.

The president's chief of staff took the opening to speak up. "So what you're recommending is that we should simply forget about this and ignore the fact that we have a spook inside the Mossad?"

"Spooks. And not inside the Mossad. In the government. And I'm not saying we ignore it," Taylor offered. "I think we should be indignant. Call Jacob Schecter. But the call should come from Jack. Not you or me, or the president."

"He's right," Evans added. "I can get more done. Maybe a trade-off. Information. An apology."

"You better get an apology. A big fat public one."

"We will demand it, just like before."

Lamden shook his head. "You mean this isn't the first time?"

"Far from it," Taylor said, jumping back in. He was actually surprised the president didn't know about the cases. "And it surely won't be the last. But Henry, if we make too much of it, it could be the thing that brings down Blanca."

"I don't..." He started to say "care" when Taylor held his fingers to his lips.

"Yes, you do, Henry. You have to. And you will."

"Now you're telling me what to say and think. I don't work that way, Morgan."

"Politics and poker, Henry," the vice president said with a slight laugh.

Lamden didn't get the meaning.

"A song out of an old Broadway musical, *Fiorello,* about New York Mayor LaGuardia in the thirties. There was a lyric that said if politics and poker ran neck and neck, politics might be the better bet because you can usually stack the deck...or something like that," Taylor explained. "It's the way things are. Sometimes we stack the deck. Sometimes it's stacked against us. Over the years we've held the most high cards."

"Go back to your earlier point. This isn't the first time?"

Taylor deferred to the FBI chief.

"Not by a long shot," Mulligan said off the top of his head. "I can give you bullet points."

"Why don't you do that, Bob," the new president said angrily.

"Okay. Not going all the way back..."

"Start wherever you want."

"Nineteen seventy-four. And for the sake of argument, I'll preface this with *alleged*. It's best we leave it at that," Mulligan advised. "The Ford White House. We were looking into selling AWACS to the Saudis. The proposal was consummated by Reagan, but in the process we traced possible leaks to the Mossad. You want to know their possible motive?"

"It would be nice to know," Lamden growled.

"The Israeli Air Force didn't particularly like the idea that their flights could be tracked by the Saudis, which they could have been."

"You started in seventy-four. Why do I feel there's more coming?"

"Because there is," Mulligan continued. "During Carter's administration an *alleged* operation by a Mossad burglary unit—the *Keshet*, or 'Arrow'—against National Security Advisor Zbigniew Brzezinski. There were rumors that he was anti-Israel, and the Mossad wanted to know what was our possible intent."

"More?"

"More, sir. Reagan. Second term, through George the First. This time it was believed that James Baker was the surveillance target. Same reason as with Brzezinski: fear that he was anti-Israel. And then the Jonathan Jay Pollard case. Pollard, a former U.S. Navy analyst, was convicted in 1986 of selling sensitive U.S. military intelligence to Israel. He was given a life sentence. It was rumored that Pollard reported to someone higher in America's intelligence community, but no 'Mr. X' has ever been unmasked, if one even existed. Still, Pollard's conviction cooled contact between the CIA and the Mossad.

"Now, let's go to nineteen ninety-seven. The CIA, the National Security Agency, and the FBI searched for an Israeli spy, thought to be operating within the Clinton administration. The story broke in *The Washington Post*, but the hunt for the mole abruptly ended with no clear conclusion. There's more, but believe me, I'd rather not get into it."

Lamden looked more and more upset, but he urged Mulligan to continue.

"Okay, flash forward to the Clinton impeachment hearings. There were reports that the Israeli's might have eavesdropped on conversations between Clinton and Monica."

"Oh, great," Lamden said.

Jack Evans went on. He recited the history from memory. "The next major flurry occurred in June two thousand one. This time, the buzz was over some one hundred Israeli students and employees of high-tech companies. According to reports, all of the subjects were questioned; some were said to have been imprisoned. The Justice Department acted on information that the Israelis may have been tasked to track al Qaeda terrorists on American territory. Although unconfirmed, this wouldn't be inconsistent with the Mossad's activities in other parts of the world."

"Meaning?" President Lamden demanded.

"That Mossad agents ran successful operations in Belgium, Norway, Jordan, and Egypt. And sometimes more publicly than privately. Over the years, Israel's prime ministers consistently declared their willingness to hunt down terrorists and the enemies of Israel anywhere.

"And since nine-eleven, we've arrested or detained about sixty Israelis under the Patriot Act, or for immigration violations. Some of them failed polygraph questions when asked about alleged surveillance activities against and in the United States."

"Mossad?"

"Maybe, Mr. President," Evans replied.

The president had spent the last half-minute shaking his head. When Evans finished, the room fell silent. Finally, Taylor spoke.

"As I said, Henry, it's the way things are. Just the best of friends spying on each other."

"So what do we do?" the new president asked.

"We quietly negotiate a way out of this so that neither you nor Blanca are harmed," Evans volunteered. "Maybe it's a cover story. Maybe we explain how we've been testing each other's security against possible terrorist infiltration. The girl comes out as a hero."

The president still wasn't onboard.

"We develop a plausible legend," Evans added. "And we leave it at that. It goes away."

Billy Gilmore disagreed. "This isn't going to go away. She's becoming the new Vince Foster; a lightning rod for anti-administration hate."

The president had a pained look on his face. "She seemed so good. So nice."

At first, no one offered a rebuttal, but Taylor shot Evans a look. *It was time.*

Morgan Taylor casually worked his way to the center of the room, a place where he was extremely comfortable. The very act drew everyone's attention.

"We don't know she wasn't," Morgan Taylor said, hardly above a whisper.

"What?" Lamden asked.

"We don't know she wasn't loyal," he said, clarifying the point. "You all know Scott Roarke?" The comment was really intended for Billy Gilmore, who had only a cursory understanding of what the man did. "He believes the woman was intentionally killed." The proposition had the effect of sucking all the air out of the room. The president's men gasped audibly.

"Why? For what goddamned reason?" Gilmore asked.

"To discredit the president. To discredit us. Maybe even America."

Evans piped up. "And Israel?"

"Perhaps Israel, too," the vice president added.

"I don't follow," Gilmore said.

"She *had* to be killed in order for the story to break and for everything else to unravel." Taylor explained his logic and concluded that Evans needed to have a no-bullshit conversation with the Mossad chief. "Jack, you have to hit this straight on."

"Yes, sir," he said, as if he was still addressing Taylor as the president. Lamden caught the tone.

"Tell them that if they had nothing to do with her death, they still better take heed. As Mr. Roarke reminded me, we have enemies with *unfinished business.* Israel may be the ultimate target."

Tel Aviv
Mossad Headquarters

Jacob Schecter expected the call. In fact, he was surprised it hadn't come sooner.

His aide, Ira Wurlin, listened on a separate headphone. He correctly concluded that Evans would not be alone, either.

"Hello, my friend." They had only met once, briefly, unofficially and secretly in the Netherlands. Schecter had not yet assumed control of Mossad. But even so, it had not been a pleasant meeting, and they were *not* friends.

"Hello Jacob," Evans said. "You must know why I am calling?"

"Yes, I do. The investigation of the Meyerson woman."

"Well, thank you for sparing me your legendary wile."

"We are both busy men, Jack."

"That we are, Jacob. Then to the point: What can you tell me about her?"

"Only what I read in your newspapers."

"As you said, Jacob, we're both busy men. So cut the bullshit."

They were on a secure, scrambled line, but Schecter never liked discussing such business over the phone.

"I would prefer that this conversation continue in person."

It was a punt. Evans and Schecter wouldn't meet. Since becoming head of Mossad, Schecter hardly ever stepped out of his headquarters, let alone traveled. It would be far too dangerous.

"What do you propose?"

"Twenty-four hours. Italy." He knew the principal locations around the world where the Mossad could surreptitiously guarantee the safety of a meeting. "Positano."

"Not possible," was Evan's reply. "Far too quick."

"Now it's your turn to cut the bullshit, Jack. Your planes fly as quickly as ours. Twenty-four hours is ample. Even generous."

"The Sabbath, Jacob." Evans reminded Schecter that they were coming up on Saturday, the Jewish day of prayer.

"We'll all have more to pray for after our men talk."

"Twenty-four hours it is," Evans conceded.

"Send someone we will know," the Mossad chief continued without any pretense of fellowship. "If it's an unfamiliar face, there will be no meeting."

"Your people will recognize my man."

"And you?"

"The same."

"So our people will meet and clear this matter up."

"We will discuss what we can discuss. I will notify you as to the exact time and place in two hours. You have my word that we will work together to make it a safe meeting."

"And productive," Evans sharply stated.

"It is in our best interest, as you will soon see."

"Yes, it is."

Next, Jacob Schecter adroitly sent a shot across the bow. "And it is in your best interest to find out who leaked this story. There will be further embarrassment until you are able to do so."

Evans let out a breath. "We are working on that."

"Good. We shall make this the basis for renewed dialogue."

"I look forward to that, Jacob. But first things first."

CHAPTER

22

Staritsa, Russia

Aleksandr Dubroff was becoming more proficient. One Web site would lead him to another. Now he was onto what the Americans called *blogs*. He discovered a number of them dedicated to Soviet spies. Somehow, more information was showing up about him. Just as the mushrooms grew each night, so did his angst.

Unspeakable acts? I was loyal to the Party. I was doing my job.

But now he wondered what it all meant. The Soviet Union was gone. The government that had deceived its people for 70 years was relegated to history books...and the Internet. He had served a financially and morally bankrupt government...a government that had murdered its own citizens on a scale that rivaled Adolf Hitler. And Dubroff had been part of it.

For most of his life he felt it was an important part. Yet now, with only mushrooms and computer extracts to measure his remaining time, and his beloved Mishka becoming a distant memory, Dubroff questioned the value of his life.

Dubroff remembered how Mishka would comfort him. She would place his head on her lap, rub his forehead, and stroke his hair when he came home, pained by the work he could never explain. "You are upset, my love. Ask them to transfer you," she urged him. Finally, he followed her advice. He requested a job in administration. The KGB complied and for sixteen years, from the mid-1960s until the late '70s, Aleksandr Dubroff taught at the agency's spy school. Within five years he was named supervisor of a special curriculum, one that gained prominence in the twilight years of the Soviet Union.

Aleksandr Dubroff was the Chief Intelligence Officer of The Andropov Institute's Red Banner Curriculum, the man who oversaw the secret Soviet cities known as *Zakrytye administrativno-territorial'nye obrazovaniia.*

Washington, D.C.
later

"Can you run through those again a little slower?" Bessolo asked. As a courtesy, the bank allowed him to review the ATM still frames. It saved him getting a warrant. Bessolo managed a hard-pressed "Please." He was not used to being so polite, but the FBI investigator needed to put on a good face for the video editor. Besides, the twerp on the computer seemed clueless. He might as well be nice.

The disk contained a series of pictures, not continuous moving images. However, played in sequence, there was a degree of movement. The date/time stamp burned into the images helped narrow the search. He looked for daytime activity at Meyerson's building. Sometimes the view was blocked by a customer who stood at the ATM machine. Other pictures showed a little more. Bessolo scanned for activity across the street that outwardly might seem normal: a delivery truck, a courier, a plumber. The chances of seeing anyone were slim. The ATM camera only snapped an image when a customer inserted a card.

On Roarke's insistence, Bessolo looked for frames starting from three days before the last e-mail went out. It was tedious work. But an hour into the job he shouted, "There! Behind that woman. Can you make out the van?"

The technician stared at the screen. "Not on this still. Let's see if it's in another frame." He stepped through the next few frames, noting the time code burned into the upper left corner. "It's lunchtime, so maybe we'll get lucky." Bessolo grunted. "Here we go." He stopped at a frame with a customer turned to the side. For one shot, the camera had an unobstructed view of a white van. "Bingo." A Time Warner logo was clearly visible.

Bessolo typed an e-mail into his Blackberry and simultaneously asked the young tech for a printout of the frame. When he was finished, he said, "More. Let's see how long that van stayed there, and who gets in it."

They got the easy part. The cable TV truck was partially visible through another 23 minutes of bank transactions. Then it was gone. They missed a shot of the driver. *Quick for a cable visit*, Bessolo thought. He sent another e-mail out.

"Can you do me a favor," he asked as politely as he ever asked anything.

"I'll try."

"Now that I know what we're looking for, see if this truck shows up any other day. Also try to spot anyone wearing a cable company uniform. I don't want to assume that the only time he paid a visit was when he got a good parking space."

"Cool," the young operator said.

"Roy, you're gonna love this." Gimbrone caught Bessolo on the way to his office. They talked as they walked.

"Something already?" he asked.

"Yup," Bessolo's team member continued. He explained that it took four phone calls to Time Warner to get the information. Ultimately, it was an easy question to answer. "They don't handle the block."

Bessolo stopped in his tracks. "What do you mean?"

"There's no way a Time Warner tech would be at Meyerson's address. Their coverage ends a block away. Comcast has the lock on the block."

"How do you know?" Bessolo asked.

"Her e-mail account. It's through Comcast, remember?"

"Son of a bitch!" Bessolo exclaimed. He was mad at his own stupidity.

"Pardon?" Gimbrone asked.

"Roarke."

"Come again?"

"That son of a bitch Roarke was right again."

Bessolo sent Gimbrone back to the phones. "Make some calls for me. Is there any reason they'd dispatch a technician there? Ask whether a Time Warner employee has any reason to visit her building. A relative? A girlfriend? Hell, even a boyfriend? I don't care what their orientation is. Just tell me if there's any reason someone from Time Warner would be parked in front of her building. And get me the records of all their vans for the day. I want every vehicle accounted for between the hours of noon and two."

"On it, chief," Gimbrone said, scurrying down the hall.

Bessolo closed the door to his office and turned on CNN. He thought more clearly in a room filled with sound. It actually helped him focus.

Gimbrone's simple finding suddenly changed everything. This might not be an investigation into a spy ring, at least not one involving Meyerson directly. By all accounts, Meyerson was framed as Roarke suggested. He re-ran the conversation with the Secret Service agent. *Was it to draw attention to the president? Or to divert attention from something else?* Both could be plausible. He decided to go online and read what was being reported.

The New York Times City Room
New York, New York

Israel. O'Connell ran his hand over his chin and pondered the possibilities. Reports of Mossad infiltration into White House affairs had been around for years. He'd read a number of the stories, most notably a 1998 inquiry into alleged hacking of White House computers during intense negotiations on the Palestine peace process. Virtually undetectable chips were said to have been installed during the manufacture of the computer boards bound for the White House. The chips made it possible for outside eyes to tap into the data flow. At risk were communications between the president and senior staff in the National Security Council concerning the major issues. O'Connell learned the information may have been transferred to Tel Aviv as often as two or three times a week.

There was no doubt in O'Connell's mind. The young woman's penetration could be more explosive than imagined. His source sounded completely credible on the telephone and the subsequent noise out of the Capital bore out the facts. Washington was abuzz over Lynn Meyerson.

Forget Roarke. I'll go to Taylor.

"Hello, Louise, this is Michael O'Connell." He swallowed hard. "At The *Times* in New York."

"Of course, Mr. O'Connell."

"So nice to hear from you again."

"Michael. Please. Always Michael. Say, is the vice president available?"

The automatic armor went up. "No. He's out of the office."

"I'd like to talk to him."

"Certainly. I'm sure he'd enjoy saying 'hi' to you again, Michael."

"It's actually not a social call."

"Well then, can I tell him what it's regarding?"

"Yes." He had to say something. "I would like to confirm some information I received."

"Oh? From?"

Swingle's attempt to play detective didn't go anywhere.

"I really do need to speak to him." He turned his wrist to look at his watch. "I'm on a deadline."

"Like always, Michael."

He laughed, realizing that the excuse of a deadline palled in comparison to Taylor's demands. "Do you think it would be possible?"

"Look, Michael, why don't you just tell me what you need. Take the guesswork out of it."

"Certainly, Louise. The Meyerson death."

"Let me see what I can do, Michael."

The *Times* reporter believed, on reputation alone, that Louise Swingle could produce Morgan Taylor out of a hat. But he didn't know he'd have to wait longer than expected for his return call.

"I'll be right here."

"Okay, I know the flowers arrived," Roarke said in a cheerful voice. And...?"

Shannon Davis was on the other end of the phone. "Well, you have one smart lady."

"I know that."

"And she's way too smart for you."

"Thank you, Dr. Phil. But can you get to the punch line. I'm driving. And it's too dangerous giving you the finger."

Davis got to it. "Both phones are bugged. Office and home." The FBI man explained the type of devices and their range. "The transmitter at her apartment can reach two to five miles—maybe more, since she's high up on Beacon Hill. The one at work is even more troubling."

"It can transmit farther?" Roarke asked.

"Just the opposite, pal. Weaker. Internal. Designed to kick out a signal only across a few floors. Short range, within the damned law firm."

"Oh, shit."

"By the way, we left them in place. No need to tip anyone off."

The text message came through Katie's cell phone. She lit up when she saw it:

> Dinner and kisses. Usual place. 2nite eight-thirty.

CHAPTER
23

Boston, Massachusetts

Katie was three delicious sips into her Lemon Drop martini when she saw Roarke walk into their favorite haunt, an intimate restaurant at the base of Boston's Beacon Hill called 75 Chestnut. She'd already licked off some of the sugar on the rim of her glass. He was guaranteed a sweet kiss.

A new host at the front desk asked, "Table sir?"

"It's okay. I'm joining someone." Roarke scanned the room and found Katie sitting farther inside. She'd purposely left the seat against the wall for him. She'd learned on their first date that's where he needed to sit. "Right over there," he told the host.

Roarke caught Katie's eyes. He smiled broadly and maneuvered around the other patrons. When he reached the table, he leaned in for a simple peck. Instead she locked him in a deep, passionate, delicious kiss.

"Mmmm," Roarke sighed. "That's your hello?"

"Uh-huh," she said, smiling.

"Okay, my turn." Roarke began to move forward again, but she held a finger up, licked it, traced the martini glass, and placed the sugar on Roarke's lips.

"Now," Katie said closing her eyes.

They hadn't been together for nearly two weeks. "I think dinner's going to be very quick," he said, taking his first breath.

For an appetizer, they shared a warm goat cheese and spinach salad with roasted pecan and bacon dressing. The taste was just right, but the experience wasn't as sensual as when they came to the main course, lobster scampi over a bed of saffron rice and vegetables. The desert completely put them in the mood. They fed each other little, sexy spoonfuls of ginger-lavender crème brulee.

No lingering tonight. Roarke wanted to be within Katie's deepness. Katie needed Roarke's strength. They were at each other the moment they walked through her door. Neither worried about the tapped phone. Anyone listening would hear the Dave Koz CD over them. Roarke make sure the phone was right next to a speaker. Anyway, they didn't care...not as they made love on the floor to the smooth jazz...not as Katie wrapped herself around his waist when he carried her into the bedroom...and not as they gave into each other's pleasures in joyous moans.

They made love through the night, resting through need, then awakening again. The smell of the flowers left by the FBI was Roarke's only reminder that something was wrong.

CHAPTER
24

Washington, D.C.
Saturday, 23 June
2:15 P.M. EDT

T he Secret Service chief raced through the pages. The protocol
was all there. Notify the vice president. Move him. Locate and
brief the Speaker of the House, the president pro tempore of
the Senate, and each of the cabinet members. Call the chief justice.
The same for the National Security advisor, the NDI, DCI, and the FBI
chief. Finally, hand the PR problem over to the White House press
office.

The procedure was the same whether it was in the middle of the
night or during the World Series. The only difference was that Presley
Friedman decided to tell Morgan Taylor in person. That added an
extra 17 minutes.

The Secret Service agent guarding the vice president's residence at
the southeast corner of 34th Street and Massachusetts Avenue had
just been alerted that Friedman was on the way. Though he didn't
know why, the fact that he was coming at this early hour was an
indication it was serious.

"Good morning, sir."

"Sanchez," the chief said. The directness hinted there was nothing
good about it.

Another career agent on the inside, Malcolm Quenzel, also alerted
to the visit, greeted Friedman in the same manner, and received the
same clipped answer in return.

"Is the vice president still sleeping?"

"Yes, sir."

"I need to wake him."

"This way, sir," Quenzel responded.

It had been three years since Presley Friedman had been inside the VP's quarters. Although the home was built in 1893, it was still a relatively new vice presidential address.

For 81 years, Number One Observatory Circle was home to whoever served as the Superintendent of the United States Naval Observatory. In 1974, Congress called in the moving vans. The vice president, who until then could live wherever he wanted, would finally have a government pad.

Not that anyone wanted to rush into it. The roof leaked, there was no central air conditioning, the wiring was not up to code, and the fireplaces were a hazard. While Gerald and Betty Ford were going to be the first to be eligible to move in, they were spared the pain when Richard Nixon resigned.

President Ford's VP, Nelson Rockefeller, wisely decided to remain in his own lavish Washington home. So contractors tore into the walls. Three years later, the renovated residence had its first occupants, Vice President Walter Mondale and his wife.

Now, three decades later, it was Morgan Taylor's. However, he hadn't changed a thing since the day he and his wife moved in. That was a sure sign that Taylor really didn't consider the Queen Anne–style house a home.

Presley Friedman and the nighttime agent-in-charge walked up the stairs to the second-floor master bedroom. Along the way, they passed paintings of America's vice presidents, some who had become presidents, including Truman, Johnson, Nixon, and Bush, and others who hadn't succeeded to the presidency. There was no portrait of Morgan Taylor. Word in the White House was that he banned "the so-called housepainters" from sitting him down.

At the top of the stairs, Friedman and Quenzel followed a hallway to Taylor's bedroom. Another agent was posted by the door.

"The vice president and Mrs. Taylor are still asleep, sir."

"Time for a rude awakening," the Secret Service chief answered. He knocked hard on the bulletproof door. "Mr. Vice President, this is Presley Friedman. I must speak with you."

Morgan Taylor was a light sleeper who always bolted awake, a habit left over from his years as a Navy pilot. He recognized the voice. "I'm up, Press. Be right with you."

True to his promise, he unlocked the door in under two minutes. He wore an Adidas sweatsuit and sneakers. His breath was fresh and he appeared robust; hardly the look of someone rousted out of sleep.

"What is it?"

"Can we talk, sir?"

Taylor recognized the urgency. "Yes, come with me. Coffee?"

"Actually, that would be great."

Taylor held up two fingers, and Quenzel radioed the request to the kitchen. A pot would be sent upstairs immediately.

Taylor invited the chief into the study, an austere oak room filled with bookcases that contained a complete library of vice presidential memoirs and biographies. It was a constant reminder to Taylor that he hadn't started his. He'd already turned down a multi-million-dollar advance, believing he had a great many chapters yet to live.

Friedman began looking at the titles while they waited for the coffee.

"You know, Press, the Mondales started the collection of books here," Taylor said, noting the agent's interest.

"No, I didn't, sir," Friedman politely responded.

"The books were in the living room for years. Now there are too many to keep in one place. Hard to believe so much has been written about the worst job in the country."

Friedman laughed politely. No doubt the news he was about to share would show up in Taylor's biography one day.

The coffee arrived and Taylor closed the door.

"Well, what's so important you need to come by in the middle of the night?" He motioned for Friedman to sit down. He didn't.

"Mr. Vice President, the president has suffered a heart attack. Less than an hour ago."

"Oh, my God!"

Taylor expected to hear important news, but he never anticipated this.

"What's his status?"

"A coma, sir. You'll have to speak to the White House doctors. And you'll need to come with me." Friedman had faithfully served Morgan

Taylor through his term as president, and he didn't hesitate adding his next comment: "You're going home."

Walter Reed Army Medical Center
Bethesda, Maryland
The same time

Henry Lamden lay in the ICU at Walter Reed Army Medical Center. He was incapable of making any decisions, let alone presidential ones. The country needed a president. The Constitution required it. By the time most of America woke up, they would have a new one.

The issue of presidential disability was first considered by John Dickinson of Delaware, during the creation of the Constitution. As the Founding Fathers debated the structure and organization of the document that was to shape the new nation, they conceded that the leader, a president, might not be able to fully or adequately administer the duties because of a "disability." Once raised, Dickinson simply put forth the question, "What is the extent of the term 'disability' and who is to be the judge of it?"

This was before the authors of the Constitution even came up with the idea of a vice president.

The issue was further addressed in Article II, Section 1 of the Constitution. The language provided that only the vice president succeeds the president. Beyond the vice president, the precise order of presidential succession has changed over the years. The current law of the land was codified in 1967 with the passage of the 25th Amendment. Once ratified, the amendment directly addressed *how* the president is succeeded, and the means for the vice president and the Cabinet to remove the president from office due to incapacitation.

* * *

Cabinet Room
The White House
three hours later

No one spoke. Some of the men had taken the time to put on ties; most had not. Eve Goldman, the attorney general and the only woman in the president's Cabinet, had her brown hair down and only a light blush. Everyone looked like they had been rousted out of bed, which is precisely what happened. Not one of the people at the table had been told the nature of the emergency meeting.

Morgan Taylor entered from the Oval Office. He carried a leather-bound book. The door closed behind him. *Odd,* thought Goldman. *The president should follow...*

Her observation was interrupted by Morgan Taylor clearing his throat as he took his old seat—the president's seat—at the middle of the oak table.

"If you'll pardon my abruptness," Taylor looked at every one of the Cabinet members, "We have a difficult task. A responsibility. A duty." There were audible gasps in the room. "President Lamden has suffered a heart attack. Very serious. Life-threatening. He currently cannot function as President of the United States."

Taylor stopped, respectful of the fact that the Cabinet members needed time to process the news. Showing equal respect, the cabinet secretaries did not interrupt him. This was not surprising, since most of them had served under Morgan Taylor.

"Doctors are attending to Henry now." Taylor's use of the president's first name felt completely appropriate in the moment. "I've talked to the senior cardiologist on duty. Henry has been unable to communicate since arriving at Walter Reed. As I'm sure you know, the White House has a specialized response team. The chief physician from Georgetown is already on site. Others are on the way from around the country.

"Henry is in ICU. We might want to send him our prayers now."

Morgan Taylor closed his eyes for a half-minute. When he opened them, the ten men and one woman were all looking at him.

"Eve," he said to the attorney general, "I have a copy of the Constitution for you." He slid the bound volume across the table. "I would appreciate it if you would read the 25th Amendment aloud, and outline the process we are to follow."

In all of Eve Goldman's 54 years, this was by far the hardest thing she ever had to do. The former senator from Delaware and mother of three raised her reading glasses, which were attached to a beaded chain that hung around her neck. "Begging your pardon, sir, I think I should begin with Article II, Section 1."

Morgan Taylor nodded. "Quite right, Madam Attorney General."

She thumbed through the pages, finding what she needed.

"In case of the removal of the President from office, or of his death, or inability to discharge the powers and duties of the said office, the same shall devolve on the Vice President and the Congress may by law provide for the case of removal, death, resignation, or inability, both of the President and Vice President, declaring what officer shall then act as President, and such officer shall act accordingly, until the disability be removed, or a President shall be elected."

Goldman removed her glasses and addressed the room. "The exact order of succession has changed over the years. Now, according to the terms of the 25th Amendment, the speaker of the house will be next in line after the vice president. Has the speaker been notified, Mr. Vice President?"

"Yes." Taylor looked at his watch. "He should be arriving within a few minutes. He'll be briefed then."

"Then I'll continue." She turned to the 25th Amendment, near the end of the volume. "I'll paraphrase first, then read verbatim. Section 3 stipulates that during a period when the president believes he will not be able to serve as president, however temporarily, he may declare himself *unable to discharge the powers and duties of the office,* at which point the vice president must assume the office as acting president."

She addressed Morgan Taylor. "Mr. Vice President, President Lamden is unable to make this decision for himself?"

"Affirmative. He cannot."

"On your word?" she asked sharply.

"On the diagnosis of his supervising physician." Taylor didn't mean his comment to sound curt. "I'm sorry. Before we do what we must do, you will hear from him on the phone. We will also get confirmation from FBI Chief Robert Mulligan at the hospital. You may discuss the prognosis with the lead physician."

"Thank you. You understand we must have that confirmation."

"Absolutely. I expect nothing less."

"Then I'll move on to Section 4 of the 25th Amendment. This permits the vice president, together with a majority of the members of the cabinet to..." She paused, choking on her own words. "Excuse me. This is quite difficult." She reached for the water in front of her. "This permits the vice president, together with a majority of the president's cabinet, to declare the president incapacitated and thus incapable of discharging the duties."

"Is that is our purpose here?" asked Secretary of State Norman Poole.

"Exactly," Morgan Taylor answered. "You'll need to take a vote."

The position is termed "acting president," so decreed by the 25th Amendment to the United States Constitution because it is a *temporary* office.

Morgan Taylor made it very clear that's how he saw it. They were not ousting Henry Lamden. Taylor was replacing him, with full presidential authority, until which time President Lamden could resume his duties. The actual amendment allowed the president to declare himself *unable to discharge the powers and duties of his office.* Under such circumstances he could and must voluntarily relinquish the office. Unfortunately, as Taylor explained, this was not the case.

Lamden was very ill. History was being made, and history would be the judge of the vote in the cabinet room.

After consulting with the president's physicians, Eve Goldman, also a former Harvard law professor, provided a primer on presidential transference of power.

"There's actually not much precedent. Before the passage of the 25th Amendment, Dwight Eisenhower suffered a heart attack in 1955. But he failed to relinquish control to his vice president, Richard Nixon. We could spend a fair amount of time talking about their relationship, but let's leave that for another day.

"There was, of course, LBJ's succession upon the death of President Kennedy. Then all was quiet until 1981, when Ronald Reagan was shot in an assassination attempt. Vice President George Bush decided not to invoke the 25th Amendment. However, in 1985, Ronald Reagan underwent colon surgery to remove cancerous polyps. He voluntarily declared his temporary incapacity to the Speaker of the House and president pro tempore of the Senate, the first time an element of the 25th was invoked. Vice President George H. W. Bush acted as president for nearly eight hours. Presidential authority was transferred back to Reagan upon receipt of a second letter transmitted by the president.

"In June 2002, President George Bush similarly declared himself unable to discharge the duties of the office prior to his colonoscopy. Vice President Dick Cheney assumed control for just under two-and-a-half hours while the president was sedated.

"I don't think anyone in this room would argue the fact that this is clearly different."

Morgan Taylor thought to himself that he really did miss the job. He missed the authority and the responsibility. But he didn't want to serve as president this way.

"Mr. Vice President, is there anything you want to say before we take the vote?" Secretary of State Norman Poole asked.

"The press will want to know how you voted and what you thought. Some will even question whether this is a coup of some sort by a defeated president. You can tell them that we are doing what the Constitution requires. You are not electing or appointing me president today. We—together—are deciding by majority whether or not President Lamden is incapacitated. Even though the powers and duties will be transmitted to me, it must be clear *that*—and *that alone*—is what we are doing. Am I correct, Eve?"

"Yes," the attorney general replied.

"What do we call you, sir?" the Secretary of Interior asked, not really knowing.

Once again, Taylor deferred to the attorney general.

"According to the Amendment, the acting president is to be accorded the protocol consistent with the office," she answered. Eve Goldman stood up. She straightened out her black silk suit and tugged at the starched cuffs. She gave Morgan Taylor a respectful nod. "He will be—Mr. President."

Morgan Taylor worried about two men as the Cabinet offered their support: the one he replaced, who was deathly sick, and the one who stood to replace him. Speaker of the House Duke Patrick.

PART II

CHAPTER

26

Washington, D.C.
The White House Press Room
Saturday, 23 June
8:00 A.M. EDT

"**L**adies and Gentlemen," press secretary Bagley began, "I have an announcement of utmost importance. When I'm finished with the statement I will take questions. There will be another press conference at ten A.M. Eastern Daylight Time."

Bagley was a former radio announcer and newsman himself. Many of the reporters had been colleagues. But no one could be considered a friend anymore. He realized that as he looked into their hungry eyes.

"At oh-Three-one-five hours, three fifteen A.M., President Henry Lamden fell ill. Mrs. Lamden notified the Secret Service that her husband had difficulty breathing. A medical team was at his side within four minutes. Doctors at Walter Reed Hospital have since determined that he has suffered a serious heart attack."

Camera flashes popped. The pool video camera fed the television routers that linked to each of the major broadcast and cable news operations. Radio news operations were similarly hooked up. The pounding sound of laptop keys were audible all the way up to the podium where Bagley nervously stood.

Two dozen reporters called out simultaneously, but the press secretary thrust his hand up.

"President Lamden is in guarded condition. You will hear from his doctors shortly."

Hands shot up in the air. More shouts. But Bagley continued.

"At four fifty-five A.M., the terms of the 25th Amendment were invoked and the Oath of Office was administered to Vice President Taylor by Chief Justice Leopold Browning. Mr. Taylor is now serving as President of the United States. He will address the nation later today."

By the time Bagley was onto the questions, NBC interrupted the *Today Show*, and ABC cut into Good Morning America. The same was true at CBS and the news channels, which went live from the White House. Morning shock jocks across the country were handed bulletins. They immediately changed their tone. Text messages fired across cell phones.

Within 12 minutes, the loudest voices on the air launched into their opinions. The echoes followed. People looking for real news on the transition would have to wait as the airwaves filled with uninformed wall-to-wall talk.

Boston, Massachusetts

Katie began to slip out of bed as quietly as she could. She thought Roarke deserved extra sleep after last night. She slid her legs to the left, then slowly rolled to her side, letting the sheet fall back to the bed. Katie propped herself up on her arm, rising to a sitting position. She turned back to look at her lover. *No,* she thought. She'd had lovers before, the first at 18. *Scott is so much more than a lover.*

She watched him breathe, quite proud that she had actually gotten this far without waking Roarke. He slept so peacefully. Roarke's head was turned to the side. He lay on his back. His left arm was still extended forward, where Katie had snuggled for so many hours. His legs were spread apart.

He's the first real man I've known. Scott's the only man I want to know.

She decided to stay in bed. Katie rolled back around, snuggled into his arm again, and reached under the sheets to find him. He stirred. Simultaneously, she nestled into his neck and kissed him. Leaving Roarke was not what she wanted to do. Not for a short time. Not forever.

Neither was sleeping.

* * *

The White House
The Oval Office
the same time

"Good morning." Morgan Taylor wore one of his Brooks Brothers black pinstripe suits. He opted for a subdued maroon tie over a white shirt. His voice was calm and reassuring as he sat at the desk in the Oval Office. Pictures of President Lamden and his family were visible behind him. He intentionally kept them in view. "This has been a difficult day; a day of transition. My good friend, and *our* president, Henry Lamden, suffered a serious heart attack late last night. He remains in intensive care, and with our prayers and God's help, he will be back where he belongs—in this seat, with years of good work ahead of him." *Soon* was noticeably absent from the sentence. "However, for now, our forefathers have provided us with the means to continue the normal process of governing our great nation.

"As you have probably heard on news broadcasts throughout the day, I have been sworn in as president, until such time that President Lamden is well enough to return. His doctors tell me they are hopeful, but it will take time.

"Commentators are wondering, as you must be, whether my service will precipitate a change in policy. Circumstances make that an obvious question. While it is true President Lamden and I are from different political parties, we represent the American people. He asked me to join his administration in the spirit of unity. I now sit in *his* seat, promising you that unity, not politics, will be the mark of my leadership."

Taylor had struggled over the words in his speech. He wanted to convey the feeling that there would not be a fundamental change in the direction of the executive branch, while also stating that he planned on governing.

"We have much to accomplish. And yes, I will consult with President Lamden and turn to him for advice and counsel when his doctors allow. When he has recovered, I will step aside and welcome *our* president back to the Oval Office."

Minutes before his speech, specialists at Walter Reed told Taylor that might never happen.

Boston, Massachusetts
an hour later

"I insist. You go. I'll make some calls. Check my e-mail. Slip into one of your dresses."

"Oh, stop that," Katie said.

"Okay, okay. I just want to know where all the zippers and buttons are," Roarke answered.

"I'll be happy to point out each and every one, but I think I can honestly say that's not a problem for you, Mr. Roarke. I've seen what you can do in the dark." They both laughed. "Come on," she continued. "You won't have to do a thing except duck under the jib. I'll be gentle."

"Thanks, but no thanks. I'm a landlubber."

"Please."

Roarke laughed. "You're pouting."

"No, I'm not."

She was.

"You are."

"I'm not."

"You are, and it's okay. I haven't seen that before. It's a good look for you."

Katie frowned. "It is?"

"Yes. And I know why." He reached across the breakfast table, pushing aside the coffee cups and maneuvering around the spinach omelet Katie prepared. "You came back to bed this morning because you don't want us to be apart."

"I didn't do any such..."

"Shhush."

She stopped. *No one has ever known me like you do,* she acknowledged by squeezing his hand.

"You did, and I'm very glad. But if you think I'm pushing you away now, I'm not." Roarke gently squeezed her hand, communicating the same love. "So, go sail. If I finish quickly, I'll come down to watch."

"Promise?" she said softly.

"I promise." Roarke rose. "Come here, you."

She stepped forward, and Roarke pulled Katie into her arms.

She loved the feeling of his arms around her body. He could hold her so tightly, yet his touch always seemed tender. He was certainly more fit than anyone she'd ever known, but he had a softness that made sleeping in his arms absolutely wonderful. And while she had no doubt he had killed, his eyes were warm and inviting. Scott Roarke was full of these kinds of contradictions. Katie believed no one else had ever gotten so close to him. As far as she was concerned, no one else ever would.

They locked in a long, engulfing kiss until Katie reluctantly pulled back.

"You win," she said, trying to catch her breath. "I'm outta here. Besides, I think I could use the fresh air."

"Good. Now go."

Katie pulled the few things she needed together, tucked a Red Sox T-shirt into her tan shorts, tied her sneakers, and straightened up.

Roarke thought she looked just great. It was getting harder to be without her.

"Later," Katie said. She went to the only door of her Beacon Hill apartment and unbolted the lock. The sound only served to remind Roarke that he wished there was a back door. He *always* wanted to know there was another way out of every place. The thought blocked her goodbye from sinking in, but as she closed the door, Roarke did hear Katie add, "And leave my dresses alone!"

The wind was perfect. It blew across the Charles River at 11 knots, filling the 55 square feet of Katie's Vanguard Laser sail. The Community Boating program had a fleet of some 70 boats, any of which where available to Katie for only $175 a season. Her rented 130-pound craft reached 20'1" into the midday sky. She preferred the speedy single-skipper Laser rather then one of the family-sized Rhodes 19s, Cape Cod Mercury sloops, or 14-footer 420s. Anyone, no matter the age, had access to the same craft throughout the season, providing they passed the appropriate tests.

She took to the Charles from the first of April through the end of October. Katie's friends knew that this was *her* time. That's why Roarke insisted that she go sailing. Colleagues at the office also recognized that even if she was swamped with work on Saturdays, only bitter cold or stormy weather would keep her from getting out on the water.

Katie was a good sailor, with no greater aspirations than just to have fun. She wished that Scott would share *this* passion with her. While the boat skipped over the Charles, banking before the Longfellow Bridge near Boston's Museum of Science, she imagined how incredible he'd look in his T-shirt, with the wind blowing through his hair. The very thought aroused her. But she'd have to live with the fantasy. Roarke was adamant. She could have the water.

The Charles was relatively clean these days, thanks to the successful efforts of the Charles River Watershed Association. No longer was it the river described in the old rock song, "Dirty Water." Beginning in 1965, the year before the Standells' song reached Number 11 on the charts, the organization began to monitor pollution and push for improvements. Swimming was still prohibited by the Metropolitan District Commission.

Accordingly, it would be unusual to see anyone take a plunge into the Charles River basin between Boston and Cambridge. However, a man in a wet suit and scuba tank *with* an MDC lanyard strung around his neck was another thing. The diver looked official. Nobody took any notice as he slipped below the surface.

Roarke left Katie's apartment. He wanted to use his own phone; definitely not hers. He placed the call to Army Captain Penny Walker's direct line. *Come on, Penny,* he said to himself. She'd left an encouraging, though cryptic message on his cell phone: "Scott, got some things to go over with you about your boy. Get back to me."

He'd missed her call when he was in the shower with Katie. Although they couldn't get into specifics now, Roarke was eager to hear the headlines.

"Walker," she said, picking up on the third ring.

"Captain, you rang my chimes?"

She recognized his voice. "That was years ago," she responded in a far sweeter voice.

"Ah, yes. Anything?" he said, getting right to the point of the call.

"Affirmative. Where are you?"

"Boston."

"Of course, what was I thinking?"

"Only of work, Captain Walker, which is why you called."

"Well, here's the latest. Assuming for the moment, perhaps incorrectly, that your very adept Mr. Depp is an American, and his very special training was done at taxpayers' expense, I've focused on former Rangers, Seals, and Green Berets and not the happily married, retired types—only the ones who would have more likely gone into mercenary work or fallen off the radar altogether."

"So, we're alive and well?" Roarke asked without showing any excitement. He knew how labor intensive the process was.

"That's a matter of semantics, Mr. Roarke."

Her answer didn't make sense. "What do you mean?"

"Let's just say with those parameters alone, and factoring in a close identity to the sketches, we're down from tens of thousands to about six hundred fifty potential characters. Now throw in your random factor—acting. I cross-referenced high school and college yearbooks, local newspaper archives, even made some phone calls on any of the ones who might have smelled the greasepaint or heard the roar of the crowd somewhere along the line. The list gets smaller, but not by much."

"So where's the semantics, Penny?"

"More in your question than my answer."

He forgot what he had asked. "Wanna help me?"

"You said *we're alive and well.*"

"I did."

"And?"

"I like some of the dead guys better. Our man is very much alive, Penny."

"I'm just sharing data, sweetheart."

"Pull it all up. I'll see you later today."

"Before or after you stop in at the White House?"

"The White House?" Roarke asked. He'd only been there twice since the Inauguration.

"Yeah, the White House."

"Why?"

"Where have you been?" She laughed. "Wait, I know the answer to that."

"Penny!" There was urgency in his voice now. "What's happened?"

CHAPTER
27

Lebanon, Kansas

"**N**ot once did Taylor say anything about the campaign to get him out!" Strong shouted into the microphone. "Not once did he acknowledge the fact that millions of Americans *do not* consider him *our* president any more than we considered Lamden *our* president."

He slammed his hand on the table. Actually, Strong couldn't have hoped for better news. It all played so well, like pieces of a complex puzzle fitting together. He reached for another piece that could be slid into place.

"And another thing. Am I the only one who's noticed that the whole Lynn Meyerson thing has disappeared from the news?" Strong asked. He raised the question, certain that his listeners would hear *conspiracy*. "I mean, one day there's front-page news that an innocent young member of the Lamden White House was killed in an apparent rape in Los Angeles. Then we hear—oh, by the way—maybe she wasn't so innocent. You see, she could be a spy, leaking classified intelligence to the Israeli's. The story starts on the front page. It gets airtime on the news networks. Then what happens? The reports get shorter, the coverage gets slimmer. Lynn Meyerson moves way inside the newspapers. No more pictures. Then she's off the network news shows entirely. Now? Poof! The story's completely vaporized. How about that for some instant Washington magic."

He used one of his mocking voices. "Oh, Elliott, the FBI says she wasn't a spy. It was just a rumor. Can't you let the poor girl rest in peace?"

Strong returned to his own voice. "No! No, no, no, I can't. Look at the facts, people. This woman was taken out! She was killed while she was jogging. I can't tell you by whom. But I've got a short list. Us or them. We wanted her dead, or she was going to turn on her handlers and the Mossad took her out. Read between the lines in *The New Yuck Times*. It's all there." It wasn't.

He cleared his throat. "As hard as it is for me to admit, this is one time that I'll have to go with *The Times*. But just when they start getting into it, what happens? A few calls get made by the White House, the FBI, or the CIA. Why? Because we have to maintain our good relationships in the world." He didn't have to say Israel.

"So who's left to report this cover-up? Looks like it's me. Apparently no one else is interested in finding out the truth." Strong knew otherwise. Very soon, other hosts would join the conspiracy bandwagon. Lynn Meyerson would become the lead debate on the beltway talk shows. Her face would return to the front page, and the Internet bloggers would have a field day.

"America, when are you going to wake up?"

Positano, Italy
later

Jacob Schecter chose Positano because of access. There wasn't much. Only one road led to the town. Boats could be checked easily. And Mossad snipers could hold the high ground above the old Mediterranean city.

The food was also good, particularly at Chez Black, right at the base of the steeply terraced town.

This is where Ira Wurlin and Vinnie D'Angelo would meet over pasta, the catch of the day, and the local wine.

Positano sat on a tight cove along the Amalfi Coast. The warm waters of the Mediterranean Sea lapped up onto the small, black volcanic rock beach. The city hugged the wall of a hill, as did many Italian towns. The lowest level, the site of the meeting, was only reachable by foot, small cart, or boat.

Wurlin flew to neighboring Naples and boarded the 1345 Metro Del Mare hydrofoil for the one-hour cruise to Positano.

D'Angelo converged on the meeting via an F/A-18D flight to the USS *Harry S. Truman*, which patrolled 92 nautical miles offshore. From there he hopped a Seahawk to a farm near Amalfi, a few kilometers up the coast. A black Fiat was there to meet him. His driver was a CIA man out of Rome. Though he didn't see others, he knew they'd be there.

Vinnie D'Angelo was a utility player for National Intelligence Chief Jack Evans. He'd been with him since Evans ran the CIA. No one, including his boss, kept a written record of D'Angelo's accomplishments. But his ability to write and speak letter-perfect Spanish, Arabic, and Mandarin made him one of America's most valued intelligence officers.

D'Angelo had served in Army Special Forces. That's where his professional dossier ended. He was a friend of Roarke's, though neither man ever talked about their service record. Their most recent collaboration: a little incursion D'Angelo helped throw together in Libya.

Wurlin was already seated at a table at the rear left corner of Chez Black by the time D'Angelo arrived. A bottle of a rustic red sat squarely at the center of the checkered table cloth. A gentle sea breeze kept the restaurant comfortable. Light early evening waves rolled over the volcanic rocks of Mermaid's Beach barely 25 yards from the restaurant. The calming sound set the tone for the greetings.

"Hello, Vincent," Wurlin said, rising to greet the CIA agent. Standing was a cue for the two Mossad bodyguards to close the sliding partition that separated their space from the general dining area.

"Shalom, Ira. You look well."

"Thank you, but not nearly as good as you. I don't get to travel to the places you do, or get the exercise."

It was a veiled hint that the Mossad knew D'Angelo took part in the Tripoli assault.

"I am truly sorry that President Lamden has taken ill. What can you tell me?"

"I only know what I'm told. He's in intensive care."

"Please convey my prayers and the prayers of my country."

"I will," D'Angelo said.

After another minute of awkward conversation, Wurlin looked at the menu.

"Shall we order some dinner?" the Israeli proposed. "The pasta with zucchini is fabulous, or perhaps the day's catch. Then we can get to business."

"With all due respect, Ira, my country considers our business more important than a leisurely dinner. If we still feel like eating later, then we'll order," D'Angelo said emphatically.

"At least the wine." It was not a question. He began to pour. "I chose the *Lacrima Chrisi* from the De Angelis Brothers vineyard nearby."

"*Lacrima Chrisi?* Tears of Christ?" D'Angelo asked, quickly translating the Italian.

"I forgot you were a linguist. Quite right. Would you say it's an unusual choice from a Jew?"

"Not one who is known as a wine connoisseur."

Wurlin laughed. "I see that the CIA has been extra diligent in its research, too."

"Always."

"Well, to the *fruits* of our labors."

D'Angelo did not raise his glass and join Wurlin in the toast.

Wurlin ignored the slight and examined the color—a rich, brilliant red. The Israeli then inhaled the bouquet. "Very nice," he offered. He took a sip and swirled it across his taste buds. "Umm. Real original flavors to this rosso." He swallowed and took another, deeper taste. "I like this. Did you know that the grapes are descended from vines brought to southern Italy by the Greeks twenty-five hundred years ago?" He enjoyed another sip. "Are you sure you won't try it, Vincent?"

"We have business, Ira."

"In time, my friend." He savored the next sip. "Ah, plum and cedar. Black fruits. It'll go well with anything on the menu. But more than just the wine, its origin fascinates me. Not to bore you, but the grapes are harvested at the base of Mount Vesuvius. As legend has it, the wines of Vesuvius were named because Lucifer was cast out of heaven here, causing Jesus to cry."

D'Angelo swirled his glass, though he didn't take a sip. However, the subtle spices called to him.

"A wine called De Angelis," the Israeli noted. "It's so similar to your name. Quite a coincidence that *you're* here?"

D'Angelo reached for the bottle and turned the label so he could read it. *De Angelis Bros. 2003.* "There are no coincidences in our work, Ira. I must congratulate you on your ability. You correctly deduced that Evans would send me." He spun the bottle around so the label again faced Wurlin. "Very astute. Or maybe it wasn't a deduction at all. Perhaps the Mossad has eyes and ears deep inside the United States."

"Oh, Vincent. You give us too much credit."

Boston, Massachusetts

T he black, streamlined SeaQuest Thruster flippers propelled him
under the Charles. Ten kicks, then a simple glide. He counted
and repeated. The flippers' center blade channels guaranteed
maximum propulsion when he needed it. Right now he was in no
particular rush. He was a good swimmer. He had time, and he had
the air. He carried a pair of 3000 psi tanks on his back, good for 50
minutes at shallow depth. They were strapped into his Mares Jubilee
backpack, which gave needed tank stability against the twisting moves
he was bound to make.

His principal concern was staying low enough not to get swiped
by the hull of the boats above. It became particularly tricky when he
had to pop up to get his bearings, look for the woman's Laser, only
to quickly drop back down. He'd already come close to her, about
twenty feet, but he wanted to wait until she was feeling tired. He also
plotted where she liked to make her turns. His best opportunity would
be about three-quarters of the way across the river, just as she came
around the Cambridge side. There, the woman slowed for the first
part of her turn, timed her cross under the jib, then shot back, pulling
the line hard and leaning over the side. That's where she would be
the most focused and the most off-balance.

He kicked again through the murky, but no longer toxic, Charles.

Katie brought her boat around, setting a course toward the Longfellow
Bridge, near the dam that held back the salt waters of the Atlantic.
The warm wind blew through her shoulder-length hair. It felt like

Scott's fingers. She wished he had joined her on the Charles. Maybe one day.

Roarke figured everyone at the White House was busy with the transition. That's why he hadn't been called. But he resolved never to be so disconnected from work again. He should have checked in or at least listened to the news. Louise wanted him to get a Treo or Blackberry, but he really hated e-mails and text messages. Too many distractions. Now he realized he needed a better way to stay in touch. There was one thing that nagged at him since Walker gave him the news. If the FBI wasn't already on it, they needed to be.

Roarke checked his watch. 1245 hrs. He could grab a seat on the two o'clock American flight with or without a reservation. *Better write a note*, he thought. He stopped at Katie's desk at the far end of the living room, a few feet from the apartment entrance. He used her stationery and pen and wrote, *Sorry, honey. Got some news. You'll hear about it. I'll call you tonight. I love you...more.*

He taped the note to a pillow and put it on the floor of her hallway. He felt guilty about rushing out without saying goodbye. *Another new feeling.* Was it complicating his life or making it better? *Better*, Roarke told himself.

The scuba diver was barely fifteen feet from Katie on the last pass— close enough to make it in seven or eight kicks. But not this time. Another boat forced him to plunge down and abort.

Katie had been out for almost forty minutes. She was more tired than usual. She felt it as she ducked under the mast and leaned back to balance her craft. Then it came to her. *Scott.* They'd been up for hours during the night, playing, loving, talking. She really wished he was here now. *No, I wished I'd stayed with him.* The thought evaporated with the sound of what she believed was a hard knock against her Laser. *What?* She let out the sail and turned to the left. Simultaneously, an unseen hand came up to her right side, but missed her due to her turn. As the boat picked up speed, the hand, and the diver attached to it, slipped back under the water to wait a few minutes more.

Katie was sure something smacked her hull, but nothing was there. *Probably a piece of wood.* She looked around to make sure. Only the wake of her boat with the telltale bubbles was behind her.

The diver shook off the vibration he still felt when the woman's boat hit his air tank. He was lucky. And he learned something. *Hands first, not back.* The next time he would be more careful. He would do his job and collect his money. He checked his regulator. Twenty-three more minutes of air. *More than ample.* He'd only need fifteen. He'd go down again, wait the eight minutes or so, and then kill the woman in the Red Sox T-shirt.

Positano, Italy

The interior of **Chez Black** was empty. The Mossad agent paid the proprietor to keep the interior clear. A "Private Party" sign went up at the entrance. For the next hour, patrons would have to be content sitting outside.

Wurlin's men also circled the perimeter of the restaurant, observing everyone. Other unseen agents looked through the telescopic sights on their rifles.

D'Angelo leaned forward. "You want to hear it the statesmanlike way or in my words, Ira?"

"I think we can suspend with the formalities," Wurlin replied.

"My sentiments exactly. Your presence in my country is not acceptable."

"I could say the same..."

"Stop," D'Angelo said emphatically.

Wurlin was completely prepared for a dressing down, but not the anger that D'Angelo brought to the table. After all, this is how the game was played.

D'Angelo inched closer. One of the Mossad agents keeping tabs from across the room got concerned. He took a step toward D'Angelo. Wurlin instinctively saw him and shot a sign not to worry.

"Jacob has gone too far this time," D'Angelo said. "He's risked everything, and he's lost. We will demand that he step down, that Israel make a formal, public apology, and that you immediately withdraw all of your other agents operating within our borders.

"Recruiting this Meyerson woman was an unconscionable act of espionage. Within the White House, no less! Never has there been such a blatant attempt to spy on an ally. Never!"

Wurlin opened his mouth again. He was met with a sharp, "No! I'm not finished. Your government has been warned in the past. During the presidencies of Carter, Reagan, both Bushes. Consider this the last warning, Ira. No more. This time there will be consequences!"

D'Angelo moved even closer. "Prior to his heart attack, President Lamden authorized the freezing of all pending legislation relative to Israel."

"He can't!" Wurlin exclaimed.

"He did. That was a preemptive move to forestall Congress from cutting off aid altogether. Imagine your world without the United States. And believe me, where Lamden might have controlled the House and Senate, Taylor will have a harder time.

"You went too far, Ira. Too deep. Too close."

D'Angelo more than made his point. He reached for his wine, took a long, slow sip, and prepared for Wurlin's denials.

"Vincent," the Mossad agent began with measured calmness, "you may not accept this, but as a friend I have only the truth for you." He produced an envelope from his sports coat. "I have a letter signed by Prime Minister Kaplov that swears this Meyerson woman was not a Mossad recruit."

D'Angelo took the envelope, but did not open it.

"Yes, we received unsolicited e-mails from her. They were sent in a dangerous, open way. Plainly stupid. We never responded. We never proposed a meeting. We never requested information. I suspect you know from traceable and recordable communications that the contact with us provided worthless intelligence. From our point of view, we could have secured the same thing by reading the Drudge Report."

He now stared at his opposite number from the CIA. "And if you haven't been informed of that fact, I recommend you ask."

D'Angelo looked away. He didn't know, and he would check.

"She is not ours Vincent. And if you want my personal opinion, which you probably don't, I think we were both set up. This entire affair was orchestrated for public consumption. For your six P.M. news shows and your talk-radio pundits. Just look at the commotion in your press. People everywhere are calling for Lamden's resignation.

We've heard these broadcasts, too. Hate is spreading in your country. Of course, we're the target." Wurlin raised his voice. "The target, Vincent, not the reason!"

D'Angelo remained silent. This was not going the way he assumed. Suddenly he had more questions than answers.

"Come now, Vincent. Uncoded e-mail over the Internet? We've done our homework on Meyerson since her death. Phi Beta Kappa. Wellesley. Four-star recommendations. Congressional material. Why would such a smart woman do something so stupid?"

"Late-blooming religious fanaticism?" the CIA agent responded. "Lack of sophisticated knowledge for the rules of the game. We found her with flash paper and a container near a dead-drop. And, as you acknowledged, it's all on her computer. I can also tell you about the things you didn't get to see: Internet downloads on Israel defense spending, wire service stories on Palestinian terrorist activities in the past six months, editorials on the reduction of American grassroots support for Israel. Naïve, yes. But she was passionate about Israel's survival, and she worked in a place where she had access to secret, politically damaging intelligence. So, to answer your question: stupid? Perhaps. But Lynn Meyerson was driven by blind allegiance, Ira. That's what makes a smart person do stupid things."

D'Angelo finished his rebuttal. Wurlin did not respond immediately. Instead, he poured another glass for himself.

"Perhaps it is time to win back your faith, Vincent."

D'Angelo cocked his head with interest. This was another unexpected comment.

"What do you have in mind, Ira?" He poured the wine that he had refused to take from Wurlin.

"Well, I believe it's something your government will be interested in. Considerably valuable information."

D'Angelo tipped his glass forward, not so much as a toast, but a rapprochement.

"I see I have your interest." He spoke softer. "Well then, we have information on a man your government seeks. A one-time Romanian national, though he holds no allegiance to that country. Most recently he resided in Florida, at a place called Fisher Island."

D'Angelo straightened up and fought off a shiver.

"A man," Wurlin continued, "who went by the name of Haddad. By our accounts he was rather influential in your last national election."

"What?" D'Angelo asked. "Where's this information from?"

Ira Wurlin laughed. "Maybe you don't give us too much credit after all." He laughed at his own callback. "It's from *authentic* Mossad agents inside your country, Vincent. Not make-believe."

CHAPTER
29

Boston, Massachusetts

K atie flew across the Charles with the afternoon breeze. She was in her westbound lap, skipping across the water some 200 feet from Memorial Drive on the Cambridge side. She made a wide sweep in front of the Mass. Ave. Bridge, adjusting her sails into the wind. Now to dart up the Boston side. She glided along the Lagoon, carved out in a 1930s renovation of the riverbank. Rows of three- and four-story brownstone condominiums stood along Beacon Street to her right. She quickly made her way back to the Hatch Shell on the esplanade where the Boston Pops often played.

That's where Roarke spotted her.

"Hey!" he yelled. "Katie!" He decided he wanted to say goodbye in person, not through a note.

"Katie!" he screamed again. She didn't see him, and she certainly couldn't hear him. Although Katie was no more than 120 feet away, the onshore wind obscured his calls.

Roarke ran along the grass toward the Community Boathouse where Katie had launched. *Maybe she's on her way in now.* But Katie sailed beyond the dock, toward the Longfellow Bridge.

Roarke walked to the edge of the dock. Two young boys, no more than twelve, were just coming in. They handled their sloop like pros. Roarke stepped to the side, away from their sail. In that one moment, he lost her.

Come on, where'd you go? He scanned the river for the woman in the red top. He didn't spot her, but he did see what appeared to be a log. It suddenly popped up above the surface. He panned his field of view to the right. *There she is.* He relaxed. Then he calculated Katie was on a trajectory that would intercept the piece of wood. He wondered how safe that was for boaters. He was about to ask the boys, when a light flare caught his eye. It came from the same place, just ahead of Katie. He strained to look, squinting to sharpen his view.

It's not a log. It's a diver. As quickly as he realized that, the diver was gone. It was no less dangerous than a log, but the swimmer must have seen her coming.

Roarke continued to track Katie's boat. Once more, he had to step away from the boys who, by now, were tying up at the dock. The diver's head emerged from underwater again. It seemed as if he swam underwater to get even closer to her. *Why? He had to see Katie. Impossible not to. He should have changed direction. But...*

All of Roarke's senses fired at once. A dangerous situation was developing. Possibly for the diver. Definitely for Katie. He screamed out as loudly as possible. "Hey! Move!"

The boys froze in place.

"Katie!"

The man who ran the MDC boathouse peered out from his window.

"Watch out!" Roarke yelled.

Katie continued on her course. She still couldn't hear him.

Roarke reached for his Sig Sauer. *A warning shot? A bullet in the air...too dangerous.* He shifted his attention. "Boys! Get me out there!" He pointed where Katie's boat would intersect with the diver.

"What?" they asked together. They were genuinely scared.

"Get me out there fast!" Roarke ran onto the end of the dock.

"But why?" the youngest asked.

By now the Community Boathouse manager had come out. He was an old sailor who had weathered a lot of storms off the North Shore seas, and handled his share of drunks in Glouchester bars. He carried a beaten-up Louisville Slugger baseball bat.

"Just hold up a minute there, mister. Leave those kids alone."

"Guys! I can't sail," Roarke said, ignoring the man. "I need you to get me out there!" There was real urgency in his voice."

"I don't know," the older, more responsible boy said sheepishly.

"My girlfriend's in trouble," Roarke added. He turned his attention back to the water. "Katie!"

"I don't know," the boy said again.

The situation looked worse. The swimmer kept adjusting to Katie's run.

"Look, I need your help!" Roarke bent down and grabbed their boat.

"You hold it there, mister." It was the old skipper. He was on the dock, about 10 feet from Roarke. His bat was up high, ready to take a swing at Roarke. "You're not going anywhere with those boys."

Roarke rose up quickly, his hands simultaneously slipping into opposite sides of his tweed jacket. He thought about removing his automatic with his right hand. Instead, he reached for his Secret Service ID with his left.

"Secret Service. Stop!"

The man froze in place, but mostly out of disbelief. "What?"

"I need this boat. These men will take me out right now."

"Oh, boy," Roarke heard the youngest say.

The manager didn't really know what to do, so he did nothing.

"You're really a Secret Service agent?" the boy questioned.

Roarke turned around. "Yes, now please!"

"Climb aboard."

Roarke gingerly stepped into the 17-foot craft. The sailor now made a gesture toward them, but Roarke waved him off. At fifteen feet from the dock, Roarke tried to get his bearings.

"You should sit down, sir," the older boy said.

Roarke didn't need the encouragement.

"And you better take your shoes off."

CHAPTER

30

Boston University Metropolitan School

T*his guy's crazy,* Bernie Bernstein said to himself. He put down a paper one of his students had written about the host of the radio show *Strong Nation.*

This was Bernstein's first teaching assignment at BU. His office on Bay State Road overlooked the Charles River just west of the Mass Ave. Bridge. He joined the faculty as a part-time professor after leaving the White House. After four years as Morgan Taylor's chief of staff, he accepted a teaching job. He encouraged his Government and Ethics students to reach beyond law books to find foundation for their legal arguments. One of his students decided to tackle a challenging topic: *Was the Fairness Doctrine Fair?* He drew a through-line between the debate over The Red Lion Case to the state of talk radio today. In doing so, he analyzed the phenomenal rise of Elliott Strong, or as the host considered himself—America's leading "Voice of Reason."

Bernstein was aware of Strong, but he hadn't listened to his show in a long time. His student's paper made the man Morgan Taylor affectionately called *Bernsie* more interested than ever.

According to the report, Strong's radio show was having a domino effect: other broadcasters were listening to him and following his lead. Strong's political bias made for good radio. And good radio, largely unregulated, made for great ratings. Since every radio host in the country lived for ratings, the Strong rhetoric appeared to be a formula worthy of imitation.

The student provided the statistics. Four hundred fifteen percent growth in audience in the six months dating back to January of the current year, according to the Arbitron rating's service. Strong reached an estimated 21,450,000 listeners in late night, far more than King, Bell, or Nouri ever pulled. His daytime ratings trounced the competition. His audience remained with Strong for an average of 47 minutes, longer than any other talk host in the history of the business. The number of stations that carried *Strong Nation* continued to grow by the week.

Crazy like a fox. The ex-president's chief of staff was learning from a graduate student the first rule of talk radio: Stay on the good side of the hosts. Somewhere along the line, the administration wasn't. Now he wondered whether Strong could be stopped.

The student raised the same rhetorical question in his paper. The immediate answer was *no.* "Contemporary talk radio is the Frankenstein born out of deregulation," the student maintained in his paper. "It took its first, unsure exploratory steps with the relaxation of laws that had previously guaranteed a multiple of opinions on the airwaves. It came of age with the demise of true local community ownership, and it matured with the encouragement and support of the political right."

Even Bernstein had to admit he'd used people like Strong to help Morgan Taylor. Did he control them? *No,* he had to admit. It had worked for Bernstein as long as the president wasn't the target. He believed, perhaps naively, that they'd never turn on the man who most closely represented their politics. But he was wrong. There was no loyalty among the thieves of the airwaves. They'd stolen the meaning of true political debate. It was all in the student's report. It had happened years ago. Now it seemed that Morgan Taylor would be the catalyst for Strong's highest ratings ever.

After reading the paper, Bernstein went on the Internet. It was all there. His student had done his research well. Bernstein considered calling Elliott Strong himself. Maybe he could get the talk host to ease up. But who was he now? *A teacher with no political clout. Another former White House staffer.*

Instead, he decided to phone an old Georgetown classmate: the CEO of the company which syndicated *Strong Nation.*

"You have to understand, the entire world of radio is different today. And it's probably all due to one man," Charlie Huddle explained.

"Limbaugh?"

"On the nose. And it's not because he's a blowhard. He was the first one to listen to an audience that felt unrepresented by the mainstream media."

"Come on, Charlie, he doesn't listen to anybody. Nor do—"

"You asked my opinion, Bernie, let me give it to you," Huddle said, cutting him off. "Generally speaking, conservatives were always labeled. Liberals were not."

"What do you mean?" Bernstein asked over the phone.

"Well, news anchors would read lines like, 'Conservative *firebrand* Newt Gingrich clashed with Senator Kennedy.' Gingrich had a negative branded to his name, while there was nothing for Kennedy. Why not?"

"Charlie, it's just an adjective."

"It's more than just an adjective. It was a way of thinking. And guess what? This isn't from me. Google 'Brian Williams,' you know, the anchorman. In a C-SPAN interview a few years back, Williams acknowledged that for decades many people felt like they were unrepresented. No one talked *to* them or *about* them; no one until Rush. Suddenly, the right had a savior for three hours a day; a voice that said what they were thinking. Limbaugh found that listeners, sick and tired of getting their news filtered through a liberal bias, were thrilled to have a spokesman who was one of them."

"Come on, Charlie, it's not that simple," Bernstein argued.

"No? Then why did he catch on so successfully? Again, Williams said it. I'm surprised you missed it. There probably wouldn't be a Fox News if Limbaugh didn't give conservatives a voice."

"That doesn't give Strong the right to lie."

"Lie?" The syndicator challenged him brazenly. "Is it a lie because you don't agree with what he says?"

"It's a lie because what he's saying isn't true."

"Strong complains that nobody elected Taylor president. Is that a lie?"

"No, but—"

"He says that the way the Constitution looks at succession is outdated. You have to agree with that, Bernie."

"Out of date, but not something to step on and grind into the ground. That's what Strong is propagating."

"No, he's just coming at it from a different political perspective than you."

"Don't give me that!" Bernstein complained. "He's dangerously close to calling for the overthrow of the American government."

"Bernie, do you actually listen to Elliott?" He sounded patronizing now. "He's not trying to overthrow Taylor, he's asking people to exercise their right. He's giving listeners a platform to talk about change. It was okay when Kerry got airtime during the Vietnam War when he wanted Nixon out, but it's not okay for everyday listeners to get a few minutes on the air? Bernie, it's talk radio. It's just a show."

Bernstein was completely annoyed. He returned to the essence of his call without any hint of friendship. "So you won't do anything?"

"Do anything?" Huddle laughed. "We *are* doing something, Bernie. We're practicing the First Amendment, and making millions of dollars doing it."

CHAPTER

31

Boston, Massachusetts

The scuba diver surfaced again with a quick kick of his flippers. *There she is.* The woman's boat was coming around. *This time,* he solemnly said to himself. *This time. It'll be over in under a minute.* The instant he stopped kicking, his body slipped under. In another few moments he'd bob back up, grab her at the point she was most off-balance. Then...

Katie could have sworn she heard her name called. *Scott?* Her head was into the wind. She smiled and wrote it off. *This is what it's like when you're really in love.* Now there were only the natural sounds— her Laser skipping across the Charles and the sail billowing in the breeze like a puffy cloud. Katie angled out of the arc on what she decided would be her last turn. She ducked under the boom, swapped hands for control of the rudder, and leaned sharply over the edge of the starboard side to balance her craft. Her legs were stretched out across the width of the hull. The boat was stable, even if she was not.

Now! He kicked and shot straight up. He actually admired her skills as a sailor. She picked her spot to turn and hit it every time. It made his job easier.

Three feet. Two feet. One more hard kick. He needed more than his head above water this time. *There she is.* He saw the woman gliding across the river right in front of him. He reached out. The top half of her body was extended well out over her craft. *So easy.* With that thought, he grabbed the back of her shell with one hand and yanked her hair with the other.

It happened too quickly for Katie to process. First she felt herself falling backward. There was no time for corrective action, only an automatic cry. Luckily, as she went over, Katie had the good sense to suck in a breath of air. When she hit the water, she realized that she hadn't just fallen overboard. She was being weighted down. Katie kicked and grabbed at the water, trying to resurface. But she was unable to right herself. She continued to sink.

Katie squirmed and tried to twist her head around. She felt a sharp yank on her hair. It was so powerful that it did what she couldn't do herself. It turned her around. Below her, pulling her, was a man in a wetsuit, goggles, and scuba tank. She flailed her hands, but she was no match for the man.

Still, she fought against his power. But each time she struggled she used up more air. The man pulled again. Katie looked up. The light from above dimmed as he dragged her farther down. Her body ached. She desperately held onto her last breath and suddenly was overcome by a final realization: She was going to die. Here and now...without sharing her life with Scott.

Scott. She imagined Roarke swimming toward her, reaching out, taking her into his arms. The thought brought a sense of calmness to Katie. She reached out to the image of the man she loved, wishing he were really there.

Less than 20 seconds after Katie went under, the boys steered to where she'd been pulled over. Roarke had clearly seen it. He knew what he had to do.

He dove in and kicked hard. Bubbles from the diver's tank showed him the way. *Air!* It's what the diver had, and exactly what he and Katie needed. His mind raced. *How?* He couldn't fire his Sig.

Despite what's depicted in the movies, discharging a bullet underwater can be as dangerous for the shooter as it is the intended target. It doesn't do much good for the weapon, either.

The effects had been drilled into Roarke. Shock/pressure waves could severely damage the shooter's eardrums as the blast is amplified underwater by a factor of four. The chamber can explode sending shrapnel backward as well as outward. The pistol might blow up in the shooter's hand. The bullet may not follow the intended course. Or, in this case, it could strike Katie.

Roarke's gun was out of the question.

The killer's flippers could have taken him beyond Roarke's reach, but he swam slowly, not knowing he was being pursued. After all, time was on his side. He just continued to drag Katie lower. The more he did, the less she resisted.

The midday sun shot beams of light through the Charles. Roarke swam away from Katie's outstretched arms. It was the most difficult thing he'd ever done in his life. To save her, he had to ignore her. Roarke needed to come around the diver's blind side.

Roarke kicked harder. He was glad the kids told him to lose his shoes. *Faster!* he willed himself.

He swam under Katie. *Deeper.* With hardly any air left and all the power he could muster, Roarke rammed his head into the diver's kidneys. The regulator instantly popped out.

Roarke figured that he couldn't survive a fight more than a few seconds. That's when the odds tipped against him. The man pulled a five-inch blade from a sheath on his leg; somehow he still held onto Katie's hair. Roarke instinctively drifted away. The hesitation gave the diver the opportunity to reinsert the regulator and take in more air.

Enraged, the diver swam forward, his arm outstretched, the knife blade catching the light from above. But he moved slower than he wanted because he had Katie in tow.

As if in a slow-motion aqua *pas de deux*, Roarke faked to the left and leaned right, dodging the first thrust. But sensing Roarke's next move, he lunged forward. Roarke kicked away, but not quickly enough. The knife grazed Roarke's left calf.

Roarke jerked backward. He fought the temptation to look down at the wound. Instead, he let his body relax. He dropped his arms to his side, giving the diver an easier, stationary target.

Jun Chung had taught him what to do, albeit on dry land and on a gym mat. The lessons from his Tae Kwon Do master in Los Angeles seemed like a lifetime ago. It might be if he didn't execute the next moves correctly.

"Slow or fast makes no difference," the Tae Kwon Do master had explained. "It is the point of contact. Concentrate on force, not speed."

Roarke heard Master Chong through the water, through the years, and through his pain. *Concentrate on the force. Force, not speed.*

As the attacker pushed through the water, Roarke dodged right, twisted his body and reached forward with his left hand. He gripped the assailant's right wrist, held it, then with his own right hand coming into play, he forced the man's knuckles unnaturally backward. The killer struggled to free himself, but he couldn't. He let go of the knife and tried to kick away. Again, he couldn't.

Roarke increased the force, still remembering *force, not speed.* With his left hand still on the man's wrist, he released his right hand, extended his whole arm flat against the killer's arm, elbow touching elbow. He bent the arm against what nature intended, and it broke. Roarke heard the amplified crack through the water.

The man suddenly drifted upward. Roarke kicked to stay with him. Accelerating, he extended the fingers of his right hand straight out, held them tightly together, and drove them directly up and into the man's unprotected Adam's apple. Roarke pulled away and repeated the move, further drilling his fingers into the man's neck. This time he felt bone crush. But he was not finished. Now with his left palm flat, he slammed up into the man's right lung, instantly collapsing it.

The attacker's mouth opened; an automatic reflexive motion. This had a serious effect underwater. He gagged and gasped. But the Charles River filled the space that hungered for air.

Roarke and the man who wanted to kill Katie were inches apart. Roarke ripped off his face mask. There was nothing the scuba diver could do to stop him. Not anymore. Roarke stared into the lifeless eyes and recorded the face.

He took in a lungful of air from the regulator that hung over the dead man's shoulders. Now for Katie. But Roarke couldn't find her.

CHAPTER

32

Boston, Massachusetts

U *p or down?* Roarke needed to see better. The mask was still in his hand. He put it over his face, and using the scuba mouthpiece, he cleared out the water.

Up or down? He didn't know. Roarke held the dead man close in order to suck in another breath.

Up or down? Down was dark. He didn't even know the depth of the river, or how far Katie could have sunk. *If she went down?*

Roarke replayed the pursuit and the fight. *Katie reached out. Her arms were there. I swam around her. Did she see me and give up? I rammed him. He held onto her.* Then the final blow. *Where did she go?*

He remembered that the man had begun to rise in the water. *He let go! Katie must have gone down.* Down to where there was only darkness.

Roarke looked up to the light. He saw the outline of two boats: Katie's and the boys. And then a splash. One of the boys was coming toward him.

He turned away. He'd given too much thought to where she was. Roarke had to go deeper. He took one more blast of air, let the dead man go, and dove. As he kicked, he thought he felt a fish brush his foot. He hadn't seen any, but there definitely was a tickle; a touch of some sort. He kicked again and swam farther into the darkness. The feeling was there again.

Roarke glanced back. It was really too dark to see anything, but he felt the sensation once more. It was like a touch...a touch that moved up his body until it was on his hand...a hand holding his hand.

It was Katie.

Maluku, Indonesia

T he drug production increased by 60 percent over two weeks. *It's amazing what people can accomplish when they want to live,* Commander Umar Komari rationalized. Soon he would set up another transaction. This one would finally leave him with the cash to complete his purchases. Drugs to cash. Cash for weapons. *What a wonderful world.*

Komari expected to have firepower to take and hold a moderate-sized, poorly defended Indonesian city. But for bigger gains he needed more men. More men meant more supplies. His solution lay in the history of his own land. The terrorist commander took a page out of the Dutch conquest. Night after night, the colonel dispatched his forces into villages in neighboring islands to steal what they needed. The more fathers and husbands saw hungry mouths at home, the more they turned to people who had food. Of course, they were the very forces that stole from him in the first place: Colonel Komari and his men.

And so the militia grew.

"You see," he told his lieutenant, Musah Atef, "it is a simple matter of supply and demand. We can put the hunger in their bellies. Now comes the real challenge. Can we put the hunger in their hearts? What will it take to transform ditchdiggers into Muslim warriors? We must quickly teach them that our Jihad is their one true calling. By giving them a reason to die, they'll have a reason to live forever. We must do that, Atef. We must do that without delay."

Komari closed his eyes and visualized the success of his mission. "The edge of our sword will slice across our homeland, and the words of the Prophet shall be on everyone's lips. We will drive the non-believers from our midst, and the one true God will look over you, your children, your children's children, and for all who follow."

Colonel Komari ranted on endlessly, as despots do. His minions pledged they'd follow, as obedient sheep would. And night after night, the ranks of Komari's personal army swelled. His plans grew bolder by the week. He had seen other noble soldiers of Islam strike deadly blows against the infidels. Bin Laden. Hussein, in his day. Even his brother miles away shared his passion against the Great Satan, the Christians, and the Zionists.

The day will come. Soon he thought.

Komari ended every speech the same way. "Have no doubt: Have no fear, my people. From this, our one little island, we will form a new nation. A nation true to Allah. And no one will stop us."

The South Pacific

The 7th Fleet's area of operation is immense. It stretches across more than 52 million square miles of the Pacific and Indian Oceans. The borders frame much of the globe. The fleet patrols west of the International Date Line to the east coast of Africa, north from Kuril Islands off the coast of Russia, and far to the south, to the Antarctic. The Navy conducts at least 100 exercises a year in the Pacific theater, not only as a way to strengthen bonds with allies, but to keep the fleet at a high state of readiness.

President Lamden's order to deploy elements of the 7th Fleet to the waters between Australia and Indonesia put American Super Hornets within hours of both nations.

Taylor honored the commitment without hesitation. One of his first acts as chief executive was to call Prime Minister David Foss. He pledged his support and reassured the PM that the fleet, under the command of Admiral Clemson Zimmer, would answer any call. President Taylor also added a personal aside. As a Navy commander and an F/A-18 pilot, he participated in one training mission with the Australians—INDUSA RECONEX. This bilateral reconnaissance exercise took him into Indonesia and familiarized him with the region.

President Taylor reaffirmed the promise that America would maintain a highly visible presence in an area 14 times the size of the continental United States. That meant that Adm. Clemson constantly would have to move his pieces—some 40–50 ships, 200 aircraft, and about 20,000 Navy and Marine Corps personnel—on a floating chess-board. This included coordinating with the local military forces, transoceanic freight trade, and pleasure craft.

At the back of the PM's mind was whether or not the U.S. could help in time. Australia was now in the terrorists' crosshairs. They'd targeted the hotel scheduled to hold a multinational conference. God knew what else could happen.

Boston, Massachusetts

"That sonofabitch!" she cursed as soon as they got in an FBI car. Roarke had warned Katie not to say anything until they were away. "The fucking sonofabitch, Witherspoon. He did it."

"Take it easy. You don't know that." He wrapped a blanket around her, then checked the bandage on his leg.

"Yeah?" She was furious. "Who else? It's Witherspoon."

"Why?"

"He caught me looking up case law on FRT. He probably—no, not probably—he *definitely* figured out what I was doing and who I was doing it for!"

"Oh, God, I'm sorry, Katie," Roarke said."

The danger was beginning to settle in. "Scott, he tried to have me killed. You could have been..."

He held her in his arms, warming and consoling her.

She whispered through her shivers, "You know he bugged half the law firm? Installed cameras everywhere. He called it security."

"A chip off the old block?" Katie didn't get the reference. "Like his mentor—the recently departed Haywood Marcus." Roarke referred to the late partner of Freelander, Connors, Wrather & Marcus. Marcus had represented the Lodge family estate. He was killed in the North End by the man Roarke presumed to be Depp. "You are making a lot of accusations, counselor. Are you sure you want to go there?"

"Do I ever!" She unraveled the blanket and used it to dry her hair.

By now, the car was moving west on Storrow Drive, away from her apartment. "Hey, where are we going?" she asked.

"Someplace safer," the FBI agent said from the front.

Katie looked at Roarke, expecting more of an answer.

"For a while," he explained. "Until we sort things out."

"You mean until you get Witherspoon!" She surprised herself with what she said. "I mean, until you arrest him."

Roarke looked directly ahead, not answering. He let out a tension-filled breath. It hardly cleansed him. Katie turned to her own thoughts. She retraced all of the steps in her mind; steps that tied Witherspoon and Marcus together.

"I can't believe I never realized it before. I'm such an idiot," she said.

Roarke took her hand. He worried what would happen when the experience fully caught up with Katie. Her anger would mask the shock for only so long. *She can't be alone.* He decided to stay with her. He'd think about what to do. *Some way to flush Witherspoon out.* But for now, his mind went back to his first encounter with Witherspoon. He remembered how much he instantly disliked the man. He didn't seem dangerous when they met a year earlier. He simply represented the worst in lawyers. Katie showed him the best.

Roarke took Katie back in his arms for the rest of the ride to the safe house, a 200-year-old farm in Lexington. They talked about Witherspoon for the rest of the afternoon and into dinner. They took the discussion to bed a few hours later. Katie propped her head up with her arm—still too angry to realize she'd been so close to death.

"Why?" she finally asked her boyfriend. "Why, Scott?" Tears finally filled her eyes.

Roarke sat up and leaned over her. "There's always been someone at the top of all this," he said softly. "We have an assassin doing his work and functionaries below him. On one level, Marcus. Then, if you're right, Donald Witherspoon. But who knows how far it goes after him?"

"They can't all be sleeper spies."

"No," he answered. "I don't even think Witherspoon was. But people trying to get rich? That's another story. They don't know why, they just get sucked in. Marcus either brought Witherspoon in, or worse, he was recruited by our number one. My guess is that Donald Witherspoon operated independently, maybe even unknown to old Haywood Marcus himself."

"A mole?" she asked.

"Yes, exactly." Roarke's eyes lit up at the thought. He suddenly felt he might have a shortcut to Depp. "A mole we can trap. We can..."

He stopped. Katie was crying now.

"If you didn't come to the Esplanade to say goodbye...."

"I know, sweetheart. I know."

Roarke rocked her in his arms. For the hours that followed, they shared each other's tears, and declared through the deepest kisses and the most passionate love their commitment to one another.

As they fell asleep, Roarke tried to push an image out of his mind. *Not tonight*, he said to himself. *Not now.* He didn't want to see Depp's face. But it kept forming and it wasn't the man being dragged by a grappling hook from the bottom of the Charles.

At 5 A.M., Roarke called a special number. He bet the man at the other end would be up already, too. He was right.

"Boss."

"Hello, Scott. I heard I'm not the only one who had an unexpected day." Morgan Taylor was in the Oval Office reading the updates he requested from each of the Cabinet members. "Is Ms. Kessler okay?"

"Yes, shaken, but she's remarkable."

"You're very lucky," the president said.

Roarke corrected him. "She's lucky."

"You are, to have her."

Roarke had to smile. "Yes, very lucky."

"So what's your theory? I read the FBI report and saw the pictures of the dead man. He's not your guy, is he?"

"Nope. But Katie is certain that one of her colleagues is responsible for the attack. Donald Witherspoon, a Marcus lackey."

"And you agree?"

"Well, it's plausible. I'd like to let him stew for a day or two. Make him feel uncomfortable."

"Why?"

"A nervous man makes foolish mistakes."

"Turn it over to the FBI, Scott. No stove piping. You don't need to—"

Roarke interrupted him, something he never did. "Yes, I do."

"I understand," the president acknowledged.

"Thank you, sir."

The president raised his eyebrow, unseen to Roarke on the phone. Roarke rarely said *sir.* "Go on."

"Well, now I have one for you."

"Yes."

"President Lamden?" Roarke declared. "Was it a heart attack?" He could ask the question over the scrambled phone line.

"The doctors are quite certain. Yes."

"A *natural* heart attack?"

President Taylor was caught short by the question. Roarke reacted to the silence.

"Yushchenko." The name was enough of an explanation. When Viktor Yushchenko ran for president of the Ukraine, he was poisoned with the dioxin TCDD, a key ingredient of Agent Orange. The plot failed to kill him, and he lost. The nation's Supreme Court determined that the election was fraudulent. A new election put Yushchenko back on the ballot. The electorate made him president.

"Are you thinking that terrorists...?"

"Not terrorists. Terrorist, singular. Or assassin," Roarke offered.

Taylor hadn't considered the possibility. He didn't know whether Lamden's doctors had, either.

Lebanon, Kansas
Monday, 25 June

Elliott Strong did more for talk radio than the legends who came before him. Out of respect, he often referred to them on the air. On the other hand, he didn't thank the people who quietly fed him information and talking points on an almost daily basis. He never mentioned that he knew which congressmen and senators were vulnerable to a barrage of constituent complaints. He failed to disclose how he had a seemingly sixth sense for what argument would provide the next flashpoint for Capitol Hill debate.

Strong wasn't the first to have inside briefings. For years, critics of conservative talk argued that Limbaugh and the other like-minded hosts must have had a cozier-than-cousin relationship with the Bush administration. But unlike many of his predecessors who once wore the crown of AM talk, Elliott Strong did not support the president. Any president. Not the Republican Taylor. Not the Democrat Lamden.

He served another master. He attacked *anyone* who purported to have an international view rather than a national view. He went after those who advocated free trade with China and full restoration of relations with Vietnam. He dismissed the very existence of the EU, the European Union. He questioned America's constant effort toward unseating contemptible dictators and installing "pro-American stooges," as he called them. And he questioned the unquestionable: Israel's politics.

Elliott Strong walked the line, never crossing over directly. He was always careful with the way he put things. He talked about the Jews, but he asked, "What are *those people* thinking?" It was always *those people*. Subtle, but effective. Most of all, he vigorously fanned political fires only to get out of the way of the flames.

"Well, well, well, what do we have? A sort of new president in the White House. You never know what you'll find when you wake up. So now it's a Republican again. Correct me if I'm wrong, didn't America vote this guy out last year? Is this some sort of *Twilight Zone* mockery of the Constitution?"

In reality, it was the Constitution that legally gave Morgan Taylor the reins of government. However, Strong ignored the law of the land when it was convenient—like today. He twisted the meaning of the laws and lied to turn millions of Americans toward his way of thinking.

"So Taylor's back. The old commander landed again at 1600 Pennsylvania Avenue. Quite frankly, I'm stumped." He wasn't really. Strong stretched his jaw, watching himself in his mirror. He was just getting loosened up.

"Ladies and gentlemen, I'm telling you, it's arrogance of power. What we have here is a supreme arrogance of *absolute* power, spying from *those people* and cover-ups. Taylor—" he dropped his voice as if to cast suspicion "—somehow back in office? Just watch, in the coming days, you'll start seeing changes. A little here, a little there. Taylor will put his cronies back in—the old Taylor team reunited; an imperial presidency that won't care about you. Trust me. That's what we'll be seeing, and only you can get them out!

"I suppose we can only blame ourselves." Strong let himself sound defeated, only to raise his voice after a dramatic pause. "But I'll tell you right now, it's not too late. No way! There's time for more calls, more e-mails, and more faxes to Congress and the White House. Now more than ever. My friends, this is a battle we must win. We need a Constitutional Amendment that will fix this once and for all!"

He cleared his throat on the air. "So you wrote before. You wrote your own congressman. Your own senator. Well, pick five more now. It's your job, ladies and gentlemen of America. Take one hour each day, every day, and do it."

He went to a caller, and took a forkful of mushroom pasta.

CHAPTER 34

Staritsa, Russia

How ironic, the old *mushroomer* thought. Pravda *—the principal Soviet newspaper.* Pravda meant *truth* in Russian. *There was hardly a word of truth in it. Maybe the weather forecasts and the soccer scores, but never the news.* Now, decades after the fall of the Soviet regime, the concept of truth was finally meaning something to a former Politburo member.

He came to this newfound opinion because of lies perpetrated on the Internet by people who described *his* role in the Soviet government.

Former KGB operatives had cashed in, selling their stories and speculating about things they knew little about. Some colleagues relocated to the United States, others ended up in England. Too many told things that should have remained secret. A few wrote about Dubroff's role in the intelligence agency and the programs he had supervised. They separated themselves from heinous crimes, but willingly attached Dubroff's name.

He slammed his fist down on his old oak desk, nearly tipping over his 14-inch computer screen. "Traitors!" he screamed. "Lies. They rewrite history and wash their own hands of blood at my expense!" He read on, thinking to himself, *We had to protect the country. Defend the Motherland from the Capitalists. What did the poet Nikolai Nekrassov plead? "You are poor and abundant, mighty and impotent, Mother Russia."*

It was my duty. My responsibility. My job. He read on. More hits. More revelations. More lies. The Internet was the new *Pravda.*

Aleksandr Dubroff's English was spotty. It took him time to comprehend the things he read on the Web. Learning as he went, he entered his name on the Google search engine. A few lines of text came up under the sub-heading *Author's Inquiry*:

Information sought on the life of Aleksandr Dubroff. Member of Soviet Politburo. 1979–1985. Master spy KGB 1964–1979. Chief Interrogator for First Directorate 1964–1973. Allegedly responsible for the deaths of more than 400 prisoners. Operations director, Andropov Institute, 1973–1979. Former Russian Army Colonel. Local magistrate. Widower. No children. Status unknown. Presumed deceased. First-person interviews with survivors' families, former Soviet officials sought.

The extract was posted by a British writer soliciting information for a new book. A biography. Dubroff was tempted to e-mail back an emphatic, "Fuck you!" But he did not. Instead, he stared at the screen for nearly thirty minutes, re-reading the inquiry, seeing how his life was reduced to a handful of words, cold words, including the one word—*Widower*. His whole time with Mishka reduced to one word.

At 0330, Dubroff pushed his chair away from the computer. He rubbed his eyes and went to his lonely bed. He still reached for his beloved, wanting her warmth beside him, but he had only her pillow. He spoke softly into it, as he did every night. But this time, he asked for forgiveness. She had never known what he had done in the name of the Motherland. Now his crimes would be published by someone who would never understand, never know what it was like to faithfully serve.

As soon as he fell asleep, Dubroff became absorbed in a vivid dream. He was at the head of a classroom. A blackboard was behind him. A TV patched into a three-quarters-inch videotape machine played an episode of an American police show. He listened to it through his sleep. Something called *Starsky & Hutch*. Students, some very young, some older, sat on chairs, spread out in two rows of a semicircle in front of him. He spoke to them in perfect English. They listened, but they wrote nothing down.

"You will learn to think as an American," he told them in his dream. *"You will become an American. You will take your place in American society. Marry. Have a family. But you will remain a citizen of the Soviet Union, one day being summoned to duty, forsaking all you have*

acquired. All who are near to you. You will feel your Russian blood course through your veins again. You will fulfill your mission."

He saw the faces of his students. Attractive young men and women. They were being trained to head businesses, to become lawyers, to rise in government as judges, mayors, and congressmen. He could see them all so clearly. While he wasn't aware of their exact assignments, he knew them all by name—their new American names. He went around the room, one by one, saying hello to the old students in his dream.

Simonson, Curtis, Maxwell, Greer, Luber, Hale, Blair, Chantler, Gerstad, Ford, Gillis, in the first row. Twelve others sat behind them.

One young man, no older than 15, peered over someone in front of him and smiled. It was a friendly, winning, engaging smile. He nodded. Dubroff remembered that he was a remarkable student, maybe even his prize pupil. *This boy was going to do great things,* he dreamed.

Dubroff smiled back. Suddenly, the lights in the classroom darkened. Everyone disappeared except for the young student and Dubroff. Without warning, the boy's face disengaged from his body and floated up in front of him. The smile morphed into a horrifying grin. *"You were such a good teacher, Sasha. You nearly brought the Capitalists to their knees. Did you even know it?"*

Dubroff was now outside of his body, watching himself in his own dream. *"No. What do you mean?"*

"We got so close."

"Close to what?"

"Our dream."

In the next instant the entire class was visible again. The boy slowly moved back into place.

"Close to what?" Dubroff asked again in his sleep. *"Close to what?"* he was now mumbling aloud.

Dubroff opened his eyes. The image of the face was still before him. A young, handsome boy. So familiar. So intense. But that was more than 40 years ago. *Close to what?* Then Aleksandr Dubroff remembered the visiting student.

For nearly two decades, everyday Russians enjoyed a sense of freedom. The government stayed out of people's lives, and anyone with the money could travel throughout the country. But recently, soldiers with .45 mm Stolbovoy St-8 automatic rifles were taking up posts along the major highways and the transportation hubs. At the same time, newspapers and television barely concealed a conspicuous slant toward Kremlin attitudes, shunning the more populace points of view they'd exhibited.

A sure sign that Russia was in the midst of change: an occasional click on the telephone line. It took a trained ear to catch it. Even in his eighties, Aleksandr Dubroff had the knack. The government was eavesdropping again. The signs all pointed to an unequivocal fact: the country's new president was clamping down.

Putin was the first. He'd taken advantage of America's preoccupation with Iraq and the war on terrorism to quietly dissolve Yeltsin's democratic gains. What Vladimir V. Putin didn't do, his successor did. He elevated many Federal Security Service officials into high-level government positions. He arrested hundreds of foreign spies. Some fell out of windows just before FSB thugs left. Most were sent to Moscow's notorious Matrosskaya Tishina Prison. Jews were targeted again. People spied on one another like the old days—in private industry, in political parties, and in government offices.

Of course, the rollback on freedoms was sold as reform. The Kremlin explained away the FSB intrusion in everyday life as a necessity to protect the nation from terrorists. Dissidents in the Ukraine gave Putin the justification to clamp down. In light of further turmoil in the East, ever-expanding terrorist attacks in Moscow, and the very basic realization in the Kremlin that Russian rule demanded strong tactics, the new Russian president turned a deaf ear toward democratic principles.

Dubroff retired before the Soviet Union fell. At the time he quietly applauded its demise. After thirty years as a party member, twenty as a KGB officer, and the last six as a respected member of the Politburo, Dubroff came to realize that Communism would not survive the millennium. He envisioned an age of reformists. But he had no doubt they would have great difficulty ruling. He foresaw elections and a fragile democracy. Borders would open up and foreign money would pour into Russia. So would organized crime. Post-Communist Russia would be ripe for drugs and prostitutes. It seemed so inevitable to him.

He also predicted that the Soviet states would eventually resist home rule. The suppressed Muslims would align with their Middle East cousins. He saw it all coming. He saw the chaos, and he predicted the day would come when Russia would have to restore authoritarian rule.

It was unfolding now.

Russia was returning to its more familiar, brutal, autocratic roots. It was the best way to control dissidents. That meant an increase in military spending, heightened authority for the secret police, and the eradication of basic freedoms. In this *new-new* Russia, the FSB, like the KGB of old, had to discover what potential enemies were doing.

This Russia wasn't built on bogus five-year plans and state-owned industry. It was taking the form of a free-market dictatorship.

Elections were not necessary unless and until the president declared the need. Representatives served at the pleasure of the nation's leader. The legislature was little more than a rubber stamp board of trustees. Information flowed to the top, not down through the press to the people. This was the Russian way.

To Dubroff's mind, the Soviet Union failed because it excluded the West. It had been in the throes of death for years; hanging on with left-over Cold War political currency and very little cash. When both ran out, the system collapsed.

Dubroff believed that international trade was the key to Russia's long-term survival, no matter what the Kremlin needed to do to maintain domestic order. But the newest regime was gradually closing the nation off again. *Fools,* he thought. *What will that get us? Nothing but a new age of economic instability.* To him, the only way to save Russia was to forge lasting partnerships with the West.

However, Americans were beginning to interpret Russia's actions as a sign that the Cold War was *not* over. This empowered right wing political causes, most notably fresh talk of Star Wars defense systems.

Dubroff studied Machiavelli. American leaders needed enemies and wars to maintain their influence over the masses. In that respect, they were no different than the Russian government. In Dubroff's view, recent administrations perfected that particular political art. The Taliban, al Qaeda, and Saddam Hussein all helped sustain conservative power in America. President Taylor, a former military man, took exception with Russia's soft stance on North Korea's nuclear stockpiles, Russia's lack of support for America's war on terror, and Russia's inability to account for its own missing weapons of mass destruction.

While the real fight was with Arab terrorists, many political factions in America didn't want Russia as a friend. For the time being, U.S.

businesses were knocking on Russian doors. But the Kremlin was seizing private businesses, and the climate was rapidly chilling. That's why the infantry had taken to the streets. That's why the phones were being tapped. That's why Aleksandr Dubroff was worried for his country more than ever before.

Then an awesome truth hit him.

Years after he retired, the pieces were coming together. *How could they?* But of course he knew the answer. He had sown the seeds himself.

The plan seemed so preposterous years ago. It had been a simple money play for Russia. Arab money. Millions. He remembered giving it zero chance of surviving. And yet, it had. Maybe not all of it, but certainly the most elegant part.

After 40 years his work—*his*—was about to come to fruition. *Not all of it, but some. How?* he asked himself.

By accident, he followed the progress on the Internet. He couldn't believe it. And yet, soon America's view of the Middle East would be immediately and inextricably altered. And who would the United States single out as the new evil in the world?

Russia.

Aleksandr Dubroff shuddered. The results would be disastrous. Moreover, Russia, which battled Muslim fundamentalists in the eastern states, could hardly stand alone in a fight against Arab extremists. It needed the U.S.

Dubroff could not turn to his own government for help. He'd be branded a traitor for having had a hand in a plan that was, unintentionally now, so detrimental to Mother Russia. He had to do something. Somehow he had to expose this awful thing. He had to communicate with a credible contact; someone who could surreptitiously reach the American leadership. *Who?*

CHAPTER
35

Los Angeles, California

Bernstein's call gave Charlie Huddle the idea. After mulling it over for a few days he decided it was time for the mainstream press to acknowledge Elliott Strong's impact. *Actually,* he mused, acknowledge *wasn't necessarily the correct term for a vanity ad buy.*

Strong had surpassed all late-night radio numbers established by Larry King, Art Bell, and George Nouri. He was the first radio nighttime host to also carve out a significant daytime audience. And he was the principal political pundit on the air, overshadowing every other voice. That was worth touting in full-page ads in *USA Today, The Philadelphia Inquirer, The Boston Globe, The Los Angeles Times,* and most of all, *The New York Times.*

Huddle's ad sales department asked for quotes. The normal combined rate card price for all the ads was well over a half-million. Yet, because this was the first time Strong's syndication company explored buying advertising space, the liberal papers were willing to discount the rates. "Glad to have you!" was basically the word. Huddle laughed when he saw the memos. *So much for politics!* he thought.

He personally oversaw the production of the ad, sending it back eight times for rewrites. In its final form it was simple and powerful—a full page with very few words; all of them *strong.*

YOUR FRIENDS AND NEIGHBORS
LISTEN TO
ELLIOTT STRONG.
DO YOU?
STRONG NATION.

He was told that it would take a little time to coordinate a buy that would simultaneously run in the first section of all the papers. Huddle gave them the target date. It would be worth the short wait.

CIA Headquarters
Langley, Virginia

Jack Evans also communicated in just a few words. His directive to Vinnie D'Angelo: "Find Haddad!" To others, he said D'Angelo was to be given access to CIA, NSA, and FBI files. The same message was sent to the corresponding branches in military intelligence.

All of that was fine, except for one thing: D'Angelo didn't know where to start. The Mossad had given him only sketchy information. Haddad was said to be a Jordanian by birth, a naturalized American citizen, and a very successful international businessman. He was the likely Arab connection to the Russian sleeper spy network.

Who the hell is he? Is he still alive? He felt certain he knew the answer to the second question. But what about the first? This is what he asked himself as he walked into the office area the CIA designated for his investigation. He was met by a young, enthusiastic, Middle Eastern-looking man and a roomful of other analysts.

"Good morning, Mr. D'Angelo," said Faruk Jassim.

"Ah, good morning." Five people were busy at work, six including Jassim, who was closest to the door. Their faces were buried in computer screens. It seemed like they had been at it for hours, and yet it was only 6 A.M.

Jassim smiled, noting D'Angelo's reaction. "A little surprised?"

"Yes."

"Well, Director Evans figured you could use some pencil pushers. We're here to help you."

"Whoa. I guess so." D'Angelo offered a grateful hand to his new best friend.

"We've just begun, so please give us some start up time."

"Hell, it looks like you've been at it for days."

Jassim laughed. "We gear up pretty quickly. But then you have a reputation of being able to do the same thing." The 28-year-old Arab-American smiled. His comment would not garner a response. "You'll get to know everyone really well. But here's the primer." He raised his voice, getting everyone's instant attention. "Heads up!" The team obliged. "If you haven't already noticed, this is *the man*."

D'Angelo heard a few muted hellos.

Jassim pointed out the team members. "Carr is all over banking. Say hi." The only woman of the group, a 32-year-old brunette, waved. She was deep into her computer screen. "If he had a bank account anywhere in the world, she'll find it, track every deposit and withdrawal for the last forty years, and get you some head shots to boot."

D'Angelo walked over and shook her hand, quickly memorizing her name and details about her appearance. He always made fast assessments of everyone he met, cataloguing impressions, from looks to skills. He did the same for the others Jassim introduced to him.

"Dixon will be your liaison with the FBI. He's already got some news for you that we'll go over when you get settled. Backus can read a satellite picture down to a foot." He had a game of Spider Solitaire up on his screen, with no signs of regrets. "Don't worry, he's waiting until we give him some times and dates to work with.

"Bauman is our historian. Evans feels that history somehow plays into this guy's story. He's the analyst who'll go through the files that came back from Libya."

Jassim read D'Angelo's face. He assumed the agent had been on ground for the assault. If he hoped to get a glimmer of an admission from the agent, he didn't.

"And Holt is our resident ciphers expert. If there are codes to be found, he'll find them. If anyone can crack them, he will. By the way, we're all about last names here. I think I'd have to read their IDs to tell you their first names."

"And your expertise?" D'Angelo asked Jassim.

"I did save the best for last. I'm your Middle East expert. I have the feeling we're going to be spending a lot of time together."

CIA Headquarters
hours later

Jassim made good on his first promise. Dixon tracked down 53 Ibrahim Haddads in the United States and eliminated 52. "Our man lived in Florida. Fisher Island, off Miami," Dixon explained.

"I made a call," Jassim interjected. "He hasn't been there since January."

"Let me guess. January nineteenth or twentieth," D'Angelo said.

"Correct," Dixon added. "Here's more. He owned a sixty-four-foot Aleutian AC-64, which he moored at his condo dock. Quite to your point, it was there on the nineteenth. It was gone on the twentieth. It hasn't been seen since."

"We need a warrant. I want to go through his home today."

"We're on it, Mr. D'Angelo."

"'Chief' will do."

"Chief," Dixon added. "Along with your ticket. You're on a thirteen fifteen flight to Miami out of Dulles. The FBI will meet you at the airport."

"So much for my first day in the office," D'Angelo said.

CHAPTER 36

Fisher Island, Florida
later that day

If the FBI thought that lifting fingerprints was going to be easy, they were wrong. A cleaning team had been hired to dust, wipe, and Lysol everywhere and everything. It was in the condo record book. January 21. And if that weren't enough, another crew from a different cleaning company was hired to do the same thing on the 23rd. Another two days later. There was another notation in the record book that allowed a fourth cleaning crew to throw out all the silverware and dishes. In D'Angelo's mind, it meant that Haddad had everything systematically removed that might produce latent fingerprints.

Nonetheless, the FBI team, headed by the near-legendary Roy Bessolo, was determined to find something.

Bessolo barked orders like he hated everyone in sight. But D'Angelo knew otherwise. This unit was completely dedicated to their boss.

As D'Angelo surveyed the 8500-foot, two-story condo, he was struck with the thought that it was in such pristine condition, it could serve as a model apartment. But condo fees had been prepaid for two years. No one other than the cleaning companies had set foot in Haddad's apartment for seven months.

"Any papers?" D'Angelo asked as they walked through the study.

"Nothing," Bessolo said. He noticed a few scratches on a desk. "He had a computer here. That's long gone. And not a damned sheet of paper." Bessolo spotted a liquor cabinet across the room. "Hey, Beth, dust inside that cabinet," he called out. Beth Thomas gave him a thumbs-up.

D'Angelo walked over to the cabinet. Bessolo needed one good fingerprint, but the CIA agent had his first clue. The shelves were full of bottles, four rows deep. *Water!* "What do you make of this, Bessolo?" he asked.

The FBI field supervisor looked inside. "Ah, fucking teetotaler?"

"No. A devoted Muslim."

Boston, Massachusetts

Donald Witherspoon made his first inquiry just before eleven.

"Has anyone seen Katie? Katie Kessler?"

"No," said one aide. "But maybe she's in the archives."

"Haven't been by her office yet," said a junior attorney.

He heard basically the same thing from everyone else, but Witherspoon tried not to appear overly interested. Just a question here and there.

By 2 P.M., he was satisfied she wasn't coming to work. No one heard from her, not even her closest associates on the floor. By four, he checked in with a source at the D.A.'s office who let slip that somebody drowned Saturday in the Charles. He wasn't sure if a body was recovered, but apparently the Boston Police stepped aside for the FBI, which he said was "unusual."

That would be about right, Witherspoon thought smugly. *Her boyfriend would have called the troops.*

The absence of any real news led Witherspoon to assume that "the accident" was getting some high-level attention, and Kessler's name was being withheld for a time. Certainly someone at Freelander, Connors & Wrather would get a call later today after her family was informed. Then he'd hear.

But that call did not come. Nor did it the next day, despite growing concerns at the law firm.

It was Roarke's idea to make Witherspoon uneasy. He calculated that the silence would be maddening. Silence about Katie. Silence about the assassin. He ignored that fact he also was causing her friends to worry.

But Roarke was right. Witherspoon made more phone calls to the D.A. Nervous ones. He then tried her parents. Thanks to Roarke and Katie's convincing, they took an unscheduled vacation to Maui—all on the government's dime. As a result, there was no answer at their house, either. Not even voicemail.

Witherspoon now called the police directly. "Nothing, sir." All of his calls were logged.

The arrogant young attorney went from smug and confidant to unsure and jittery.

Roarke used the time to confirm his own suspicions. The photo of the dead man was sent to Touch Parson.

"This is one ugly corpse," the FBI photo analyst complained over the telephone. "Is this your work, Roarke?"

"Touch, just tell me. Is he or isn't he?"

"Isn't." Katie's assailant was not Depp.

Washington, D.C.

While the doctors tested President Lamden's blood for any possible traces of toxic substances, the FBI backtracked each meal he'd had 72 hours prior to his heart attack.

The two dinners on the rubber chicken circuit—state affairs where he just pushed the food around the plate—were quickly ruled out. By habit, Lamden only drank the water. They were from bottles brought by the Secret Service.

His only other dinner, his last, was from the White House kitchen, prepared by the president's personal chef. Nonetheless, everything in the kitchen was hauled away for testing, which essentially wiped out the White House stock.

The FBI echoed what the doctors at Walter Reed explained. Analysis was best if immediate. It was now days later. Lab technicians, supervised by the Secret Service, complained about the delay. At first, they weren't even sure what they were trying to detect. "Try testing for Sodium Morphate," Roarke told them from Boston. "*He* used it before."

"President Lamden?"

"No," was all the Secret Service agent said. But the *he* Roarke inadvertently mentioned was only one man.

Boston, Massachusetts

A tanned vacationer with a 10-day stubble on his face stepped off a flight from Miami. He wore a short-sleeve Tommy Bahama blue-and-green print shirt, khakis from Banana Republic, and black boots.

He looked like any number of other vacationers. He was probably more relaxed than the rest, though. He and his redhead had extended their stay at Cap Juluca. He'd never fucked so much in his life. But when his consort received a call that her mother was sick, she returned to Philadelphia. He went onto Dallas, for no particular reason. There, he checked into the Marriott and logged onto an eBay sale. Through the cryptic wording, he learned that his principal employer had an urgent communiqué.

"Damn!" he said. He wasn't anxious to get back to work. Quite the opposite—he thought he'd travel more. French wine country, Scotland, Ireland. No big cities. Nothing in the U.S. for a while. But the message, encoded in an eBay Web site, was clear. The job would take just a few days of preparation and execution. *Execution, how appropriate,* he thought.

He shrugged and e-mailed his acceptance. He figured he could fly to Paris just as easily out of Boston.

CHAPTER

37

Staritsa, Russia
Tuesday, 26 June

After living in a closed society and perpetrating the notion that everyone is being watched, it was impossible for Aleksandr Dubroff to think otherwise. The KGB no longer existed. But from what he read on a number of foreign Internet Web sites, the FSB (Federal'naya Sluzhba Bezopasnosti, or Federal Security Service) had eyes everywhere. He sat back in his chair, looking at the screen. *Maybe they watch more than the KGB did,* he thought. *More than any of us could have ever imagined.*

It only made sense. Russia was Russia. Communist or not, this is what the Kremlin knew. This was how the people lived going back to a time before the Communists, before the Bolsheviks, even before the Tzars. There were always people watching; always people listening. That's why he never talked about his work with those he met in the forests of Tver or on the streets of Staritsa.

As a quiet, mushroom-picking government pensioner, Dubroff wanted to believe he had been forgotten by the system. Yet, in his day, if he had been monitoring someone else undertaking such deep research, bells would have gone off from Starista to Moscow. *Is there someone like me now? Someone with a raised eyebrow? Someone suspicious enough to call me in?*

Whatever he *wanted* to believe, the reality was that, according to the rules of the game, Aleksandr Dubroff just declared himself an enemy of the State. He had no idea how right he was.

Acting very much like the KGB, the FSB spied on its citizens via a little-noticed Orwellian Internet plug-in dubbed SORM.

The program was initiated by President Vladimir Putin, a former KGB agent himself, five days into office. With the stroke of a pen, he broadened the scope of the 1995 Law of Operations Investigations to give the tax police, the interior ministry police, parliamentary security, the border and customs patrol, and the Kremlin the rights to monitor the private correspondence of all Web users in Russia.

By 2000, the FSB had the technological wherewithal to discreetly observe the actions of Russia's then 1.5 million Internet users. Currently, there were millions more. The government responded by setting up a spy network to manage the surveillance.

Originally, the law gave only the FSB the authority to monitor private correspondence, whether through letters, cell phone traffic, or e-mail, providing the agency first obtained warrants from the court.

The actual oversight fell into the hands of a new department: the System for Operational-Investigative Activities or SORM. The cost of the operation was footed by Russia's own Internet Service Providers. The ISPs were immediately required to install so-called "black boxes" through which all of their electronic communication flowed. Once hot-wired, the traffic would, in turn, be routed to FSB headquarters.

The ISPs also had to pay for the technology and cover the cost of training FSB officers who analyzed the data. Service providers that didn't cooperate created their own problems which the FSB dealt with expediantly.

Not that Russia was alone in such Internet eavesdropping. The United States employed the secretive Eschelon system through the National Security Agency. The program is capable of monitoring, cataloguing, cross-referencing, and storing billions of electronic communications from around the world.

The principal difference, even recognized by Eschelon's critics, is that the American system is not inherently "coercive." It does not force private industry to cooperate. In other words, the U.S. telecommunications companies are not required to hook into Eschelon.

However, in Russia, the spy technology reaches into citizens' homes through the telecoms. And virtually every agency with a reason to spy has access to who's on the Internet, what they look at, and to whom they talk.

If this weren't enough, a new SORM application was established five years after the initial declaration. SORM-2 now affords security agencies the means to sidestep legal procedures. Prior to the change, warrants were necessary in order to tap private communications.

Once more, Russia was becoming a fully functional, though smaller, human rights-violating police state.

How did the others communicate their secrets to the West?

Dubroff was baffled. Having logged onto foreign Web sites on the subject, he knew a little about SORM, so took special care with his searches. He also avoided e-mail.

It wasn't paranoia, it was experience, born in his belief that *this is just how things are done.* The people can't be trusted, so the government must monitor what they do, where they travel, and whether they are a risk to the state.

Dubroff was more than a mere mushroom digger who couldn't see the forest for the trees. He could see the danger that lay ahead. He had information to share with the West. Getting it to them was the challenge.

How? he asked himself. *What's the best way?* Dubroff started thinking like a traitor. But the question really was: a traitor to what?

Lebanon, Kansas

"On the phone is a man you are going to want to listen to tonight, my friends. Why? Because he has a message for you. A message you may not want to hear, but you better, if you care about America."

Elliott Strong delivered the last words slowly and with unmistakable conviction. "Let me tell you about General Robert Woodley Bridgeman." Elliott Strong rarely had guests on the air. His show almost exclusively catered to the callers. But it had been decided. The former decorated general asked for airtime. And Strong would give it to him. Over the next few months, he was going to become a very familiar voice on the airwaves. First radio, then television.

"General Bridgeman is one of the most decorated American heroes of the war in Iraq. A Purple Heart, a Navy Cross, numerous commendations for bravery. His men faithfully followed him into war. Cities like Baghdad, Fallujah, and Mosul. Dangerous places. He did the kind of work that's not for the faint of heart. You want to know about his heroism, just go to the Internet. I stopped counting after finding four hundred twenty-six individual Web sites that chronicled the exploits of this great man. Log onto my Web site. We've linked up a few you'll want to check out," Strong added.

"Before Iraq, General Bridgeman served in the infantry in Desert Storm. My sources tell me he also participated in a number of classified missions into North Korea. I don't suppose he'll talk about it, but rest assured, it's because of brave hearts like General Robert Bridgeman that America remains secure today. He fought for you, my friends. He put his life on the line for your freedom, for the United States of America. Now he joins us tonight.

"Welcome to *Strong Nation*, General Bridgeman. It is an honor to have you with us."

"Good evening, Mr. Strong The honor is mine. You do a great service yourself for your country," the general said with a warm, trained, and modulated deep voice.

"Thank you. Let me get to your record," Strong said, wanting to establish firm ground for his guest to stand on. "You were directly in the line of fire."

"Yes, sir."

"Time after time you not only issued the orders, you led attacks on enemy strongholds risking your own life."

"I suppose I'm from the old school. Lead by example."

"I don't suppose your command was always happy with that."

"I brought more men home because of my decisions in the field, Mr. Strong. I was there. They weren't," he responded. Bridgeman sounded decisive; the hallmark of a leader. With just a few words so far, he exuded authority and warmth. His voice had a timber and quality that inspired. Listeners had no trouble making the leap of faith that troops under him would follow the general to the gates of hell. Thousands of Strong's listeners were already logging onto the *Strong Nation* homepage to read about Bridgeman. The first thing they saw was a photo of a handsome 6'2" warrior in full battle regalia, with a crooked, Harrison Ford smile. He had jet-black hair, cut to military length, and long, dark eyebrows that connected in the middle. The photo wasn't a posed studio shot. It worked better for that reason. The general's face was bathed in the afternoon sun. Behind him, a dynamic, bright-red glow of a burning building in the center of

Baghdad. It could be presumed that Bridgeman and his men were responsible for the explosion.

"As a career officer in the United States Marine Corps," Strong continued to recite, "you always chose the front lines over a Pentagon desk. I take it you had opportunity to return to Washington."

"I did. Through the years I faithfully served in the United States Marine Corps, I believed that the command was solid. The right decisions were being made by the right people. I could do no better there. But perhaps I could do better than others in the field."

"And so you stayed, declining offers to come in."

Listeners heard a laugh. "I suppose my beautiful wife Lily would have preferred me home, but she would have gotten tired of me in no time. That's why we still have the magic after 35 years." A second picture on the Web site showed the general and his wife together at a Marine function. He was in his dress uniform and she was in a conservative, navy blue suit and a bright red silk blouse, set off by a string of fine white pearls. Lily, the daughter of a Texas representative, had Southern grace and poise. She looked positively perfect on the arm of the general. She was nine years his junior, which made her 48.

A smart listener would have realized that the conversation was completely structured. Each comment led to another scripted layer. Each layer was reinforced with a graphic, a paragraph, or a link on StrongNationRadio.com. The only thing missing online was the payoff to the conversation. That would come midway through the second half-hour of the interview. And when it did, Strong's webmaster would click a key that would immediately load the news at the top of the homepage and simultaneously send it out to the major news organizations in America along with Reuters in London.

"Now you're a civilian. What, only three months?"

"Almost," Bridgeman said. "Just shy of three, though it feels like ten years already. Lily's got me redoing the house. Let me tell you, when it comes to giving orders, my wife is at the top of the chain of command."

Strong gave a hearty laugh. "I suppose that does take some time to get used to."

"Well, I'm doing my level best. And I'll tell you, it's not so bad. I've got my home, my loving bride, great neighbors, and a wonderful community."

"Where have you settled, General?"

"The same house Lily and I moved into when we first married. We're in Tyler, Texas. You can find us easily enough. Follow the smoke down Elm Tree Circle, like our friends have. We've got the barbeque going in the backyard almost every night."

The next picture on the Web: Bridgeman behind his barbeque, serving up ribs to very familiar Texans who have gone onto prominence. The effect of the photo immediately notched up Bridgeman's political cache.

"But I gather that you're not just going to settle into the life of a chef."

"No, sir, I'm not." The tone changed. "A few moments ago I spoke about the leadership I served under. How solid it was. How secure as a nation we were. Well, I can't say I feel the same way now. I think your listeners would agree. I love my life in Tyler, but even that is at risk. Maybe not today or tomorrow. But day by day, life gets more precarious. So I have set a course that Cervantes spoke of when he wrote, 'The brave man carves out his fortune, and every man is the son of his own works.'"

"So, as a civilian, you are taking a stand?"

"I must, Mr. Strong. For to do nothing now would be tantamount to opening the door to ultimate disaster. And you have kindly afforded me generous airtime to address my concerns on national radio. After tonight, I'll take it further."

"Further?" Strong asked.

"To where the problem resides."

"Which is?"

"Our nation's capitol. Tomorrow at four P.M., I will hold a press conference in Washington, D.C., at the base of the Marine Corps War Memorial to the Armed Forces at Iwo Jima."

"Why the Iwo Jima memorial?"

"Because I feel I can speak for the fighting men who have laid down their lives in the name of our great country. The memorial is a lasting symbol of a nation's gratitude for the honored dead. Certainly, it depicts World War II Marines in one of the most famous battles of the Pacific Theater. But it also represents the dedication of all service men and women who, since seventeen seventy-five, have given their lives in defense of the United States of America.

"You'll be giving us an indication of what you'll be talking about tomorrow, General?"

"Well, I can't think of a better place to reach true Americans than through your program, Mr. Strong."

"Please, it's Elliott."

"Elliott," the general replied.

"Before we get to specifics, a few questions if you will," Strong asked.

"Of course, my pleasure."

"You've suggested that America is not on a course that you can embrace. Is it the leadership in Washington, the politics, or the nature of things that worry you?"

"That's actually a very complex question, Elliott. I think the people are on the right course, with the moral values that matter—the values that define what it is to be an American: to be the center of the free world. To be free. To have the right to life and liberty.

"The majority with the moral compass have no trouble finding their way. But for many of our elected officials, it is a different matter. They are plugged into high-voltage power in Washington. They extend their hands out to us, but ask us to step into the rain. As you know, it's a deadly combination."

"Do you take issue with Lamden-Taylor?"

"On every count."

"And do you question the legitimacy of Morgan Taylor's ascension to the presidency?"

"I do."

"Can you elaborate, General?"

Bridgeman did not miss a beat. "Yes, I can."

The dialogue was proceeding exactly as rehearsed. Strong covered the points in order. He provided a friendly, non-confrontational environment for the general to express his views. The conversation was drawn out to maximize the impact, but it never detoured from the established outline. Bridgeman's job tonight was to create water-cooler conversation for tomorrow. The goal was to leave the listeners with a sense of confidence through short, clear answers. They would be measured by a serious delivery. General Robert Woodley Bridgeman was already accomplishing both.

"Morgan Taylor has to go."

FBI labs
Quantico, Virginia

"Your gal Friday from the Pentagon sent over some stuff. She's a lot nicer to deal with than you, Roarke."

"And a bit more dangerous," the Secret Service agent told Touch Parsons over the phone.

"But she sounds so nice."

"Army Intel. She'll suck the eyes right out of your head. She knows more things about you than your mommy. And what she doesn't know, she'll find out one way or another."

"Well, turnaround's fair play. You see, I've done a little checking up on the good Captain Walker, too. Thirty-five. Good-looking. Career field officer until she became a desk jockey and a computer junky. Maybe you could fix us up."

"Oh, Walker will love knowing that you've spied on her. News like that will get you real far. Broken collarbone, smashed kneecaps. You'll be lucky if your balls are still attached when she's through with you."

"Yah, then why did she check me out on the agency Web site?"

"You hacked into a DOD computer?"

"Due diligence, Agent Roarke."

"Why?"

"Because I can. So why don't you play matchmaker and let me take my chances? I haven't had a date in two years. It's the least you can do since you fucked up the rest of my life with your half-baked ideas."

Roarke was actually amused by Parson's schoolboy hots for Penny Walker. As far as he knew, she hadn't been serious with anyone for a long time. He thought about it for a moment. *They just might hit it off.*

"What will you give me?" Roarke asked.

"What do you mean?"

"What will you give me?"

"I don't understand."

Roarke's voice grew serious. "I want Depp."

Parsons, noting the change in tone, responded in kind. "I'm doing the best I can."

"Then plan on working late over some java as soon as I get back to D.C."

Boston, Massachusetts
Wednesday, 27 June

Paul Erskine could make a mean cup of coffee. He'd worked at Starbucks in Rapid City, Tulsa, and San Francisco. This particular Starbucks in Boston's financial district suddenly had an opening. One barista on the early shift didn't show up the very morning Erskine applied. "So, if you're good and you can handle the five-thirty A.M. shift, the job is yours," the manager told him.

"Put me on. See for yourself. I think you'll be happy," Erskine proposed. His Southern accent made him all the more friendly.

The manager took Paul up on the offer. Erskine delivered the speediest, friendliest, most organized effort the manager ever saw.

"If you need references..." Erskine said after the demonstration.

"No, you've got the job! You can start in the morning."

"Well, bless your heart. Thank you. I appreciate it."

The manager was quite happy to have someone he didn't have to train; someone with some maturity. Erskine was in his 30s and obviously something of a wanderer. He wore a nicely pressed white shirt, fairly new blue jeans, a bead necklace, and two of the yellow rubber bracelets that signified support for cancer patients. His long brown hair was pulled back into a ponytail and large aviator glasses framed his face. He had a five-day stubble that completed his bohemian look. The manager noticed that he didn't have a wedding ring, a signal that Erskine was probably one of the typical coffee hobos who explored America by taking jobs at coffee grinders.

The most important thing was that he'd worked in Starbucks before and he knew the drill. That counted immediately. Erskine had proficiency, that was certain. And he had speed. The added bonus was his personality. *Just right for the morning crowd.* The earliest commuters started crowding his doors at 5:45. The biggest crunch was between 7:45 in the morning and 8:30. Erskine was a godsend.

"What's your phone number?"

Erskine recited it. "But you won't ever need it. I'll be here on time."

The manager laughed. "Just in case we need you for a second shift."

"Anytime."

With that, they shook hands. "See you tomorrow," Erskine said with a broad smile. "And thank you very much."

The newest barista at the Starbucks across from some of Boston's most prestigious law offices walked out, very pleased that he'd scored the job he wanted the most.

CIA Headquarters
Langley, Virginia

D'Angelo mulled over the latest hourly report from the FBI. Bessolo had his prints—one from inside the liquor cabinet, another on the refrigerator door, a third on the bathroom toilet handle, and a fourth on the inside of the bedroom closet door. *So much for spotless cleaning*, he thought. Three were the same: the cabinet, the bathroom, and the closet. But none of them matched the fingerprint on file for Ibrahim Haddad's passport. He didn't have a driver's license.

This told D'Angelo that either the common print was not Haddad's or that Haddad had someone else apply for the passport. He wrote off the fingerprints. They'd need more.

D'Angelo assembled his team. They worked around a bulletin board in a bullpen section of their CIA office. "Okay, let's put everything on cards and get them up.

"Here's what we have," D'Angelo stated. He started writing. After one card, Jassim took over.

"Let me do that. You dictate."

"Are you trying to tell me my handwriting sucks?"

"Yes," Jassim said.

"No argument there. All right, here goes in no particular order," D'Angelo said. "First me, but feel free to chime in. One: Haddad stayed inside most of the time," Jassim wrote down the key words or phrases. "Two: no social contact. Three: he was always accompanied by bodyguards. Four: he ate at home. Five: he didn't use the condo facilities. Six: he never showed up for functions." He stopped to let Jassim catch up and then asked, "Comments? Additions?"

"None yet. Keep going."

"Seven: secretive to the point of reclusive." Next, he handed over a picture that needed to be added to the cards. "Eight: he's a big guy, too." He pointed to a man walking by a family posing for a picture. It was a still frame from a DV, shot by a condo owner the previous summer. Haddad was clearly visible. "We have the whole tape."

Jassim put it next to Haddad's enlarged passport photo.

"That's nine. He traveled."

"I can help you there," Bauman said. "I pulled a mess of files from Immigration. Haddad made an almost yearly trip to the Middle East. All listed as business."

Jassim wrote *Middle East travel* on a card and tacked it up.

Bauman continued. "We're checking back beyond ten years, but it's harder to document. With so many airlines gone, who knows what's even out there. But we're talking with the companies still around."

"Including the British and French carriers?" D'Angelo asked.

"On it. Lufthansa, too. The Moscow desk is also running Haddad's picture for us. Same for Tehran, Baghdad, Damascus, and Riyadh."

D'Angelo turned to Carr. "What about banking?"

"Working on it. Lots of large transfers through Switzerland and the Islands. Still tracking them. Looks like elaborate precautions. It's gonna be harder than I thought."

"Just keep at it."

Carr didn't need to say *yes*.

"Anything else?" D'Angelo asked the group.

Holt shook his head no. The FBI report covered his area. He polled the rest of the team. More *no's*.

"Okay, then. Let's start each day this way and powwow again before we split at night. Remember, consider everything important. Nothing should be viewed as insignificant."

There was no argument there.

After the team went back to their cubicles, D'Angelo looked at the cards. A picture, though incomplete, was coming together. He decided to make two calls: his boss, and his counterpart at the Mossad.

The Washington Mall

A light summer rain fell. About 15 network camera operators, representing the major broadcasters, kept their equipment dry with umbrellas and plastic bags. The general's handlers allowed everyone to put their own microphones on a six-by-eight platform. They could have used a pool feed, but Bridgeman wanted the look of multiple microphones. Elliott Strong would talk about it later.

Robert Bridgeman wore civilian clothes—a navy blue jacket, gray pants, and an open-collar white shirt. He passed up an umbrella, choosing to stand in the elements. The only concession he had to make was to not touch the metal microphones or their stands. It might make for good newstape, but Bridgeman wanted people to remember what he said, not how he looked if shocked.

There was no formal program or introduction.

"Good afternoon. I won't keep you out here too long, but maybe the weather is underscoring what I have to say today. We are not living under sunny skies."

Bridgeman had just begun and he already gave the newshounds a great lead-off sound bite.

"I have only a few words; however, they carry great weight. I believe the United States has lost its compass. I believe the will of the people is not being served. I believe Washington is isolated and our leaders do not want to hear what *we, the people,* have to say. I believe there is only one way to demonstrate, beyond the shadow of a doubt, how united we stand. I call on all Americans everywhere to join me for a march on Washington. Not just a march...the largest assemblage in the history of the United States. We will show this self-anointed government that it is time to have a national referendum on the presidency. We will show legislators that if they don't change the rules of succession, we will change who we send to Washington."

"Join me in our nation's capital on Saturday, August eighteenth for a march to bring America back home."

The whole notion was revolutionary. Every reporter on the spot secretly loved it.

Lebanon, Kansas
that night

Elliott Strong's phone lines were clogged. People called from every corner of the country. *The news,* as it was being called, spread across the country like a firestorm, igniting interest in Elliott's ever-growing *Strong Nation.*

"So, you heard it. What does it mean to you?" Strong asked at the top of the hour.

Listeners responded as one:

"It's great."

"Finally!"

"Somebody's going to do something about all this."

"Sign me up."

"Me, too."

"I'm in."

Elliott Strong took dozens of calls. Quick ones. Affirming ones. All supportive. All angry. General Robert Woodley Bridgeman struck an emotional chord, and Strong's viewers were singing his praises.

The news was also on ABC, NBC, CBS, Fox, and CNN. The daytime roundtable cable shows were making it the central topic. Bridgeman was booked for Larry King at seven. Everyone wanted him. They couldn't wait to score an interview with a retired Marine war hero who basically called for an immediate national referendum on the presidency. And they wanted to talk to him about whether he was going to run for president.

Now all the principal news organizations were also paying more attention to the radio host who broadcast from the geographic center of the country.

"You march. You go to the Capitol, the Mall, and the White House with General Robert Bridgeman," Elliott Strong preached. "Not a thousand. Not ten thousand or a hundred thousand. Not a million. Show them what Americans really demand. We do it the Strong way. We do it with five million Strong."

By the end of his broadcast, the slogan *Five Million Strong* was embedded in the minds of his listeners.

CHAPTER

38

Washington, D.C.
Thursday, 28 June

"**A**ccording to the doctors at Walter Reed and the lab reports, no toxic substances were evident in the president's blood," Mulligan told the president. "Nothing in the White House food or water. Nothing untoward in the White House stock. The short version, sir: President Lamden was not poisoned."

"Are you absolutely positive?"

"If you're asking if there is any margin of error, the answer is yes, due to lateness of the toxicology tests. That stated, the labs feel they would have found some evidence if it existed."

Taylor was relieved. He thanked the FBI chief and hung up. Nonetheless, the possibility that Roarke raised was enough for him to question the procedure and standards for how the President of the United States is safely fed, either in the White House or in White House–supervised kitchens.

Maybe it didn't happen this time, Taylor considered, *but we are vulnerable.*

Taylor decided to draft a directive that would result in a comprehensive study of the White House food chain. Where does the food come from? How is it protected? Who oversees the process?

Certainly some procedures existed, but he asked for recommendations to improve the safety standards.

His request went to the Office of Strategic Initiatives. Ironically, it might have gone to Lynn Meyerson's desk.

CIA Headquarters
Langley, Virginia

"Are we sharing?" D'Angelo asked. It was a necessary question.

"Sharing means we both benefit. What is the benefit to us?" Ira Wurlin responded over the secure telephone line.

"Perhaps the security of your country."

The silence on the line from seven hours away indicated how serious the declaration was taken.

"We're sharing," Wurlin finally said.

"Then I'll start. We've located Haddad's home. He fled the country. January nineteenth—possibly after being tipped off; probably after watching the news. His yacht disappeared. Probably scuttled. Haddad has vanished. He laundered money here to Kingdom Come, and we think he's hell-bent on bringing Israel down."

"What is the basis of your theory?" the Mossad officer asked.

"My team has been analyzing the papers recovered in Libya. Haddad is not mentioned by name, but there are clear references to a Syrian who worked for Hafez Al-Assad as a go-between with the Russians for the development of sleeper cells. Haddad has also shown up in phone records with the lawyers who represented the dearly departed Congressman Lodge. In our estimation, Haddad could be this Syrian, even though his papers show he became a U.S. citizen thirty-one years ago."

"So what are we sharing? You seem to have done very well on your own, my friend," Wurlin said.

"Quite to the point. You will be sharing what you can find from your very well-placed Mossad agents in Syria."

"You ask a great deal," Wurlin replied.

"I ask for your cooperation. Nothing less. There is still the issue of Mossad agents in the United States."

"I thought we put that to rest," Wurlin said.

"You may have, not the American public." D'Angelo wanted Wurlin to fully understand the next point. "I'm sure you agree, the press doesn't need any encouragement."

"I will see what we can do. We'll talk soon."

"When?" D'Angelo asked impatiently.

"Soon."

CHAPTER 39

The White House

"**B**ernsie, I want you back." Bernie Bernstein glanced around the Oval Office, noting how Lamden and his wife had redecorated the room. It was warmer than Taylor's days, full of flowers and grandchildrens' pictures. He wasn't surprised to see more photographs of democrats and JFK's famed desk, the one that John-John and Caroline played under.

"Mr. President, I'm flattered, but it's not going to look good. You can't dump Lamden's key staff so quickly."

"Jesus H. Christ, Bernsie." Morgan Taylor leaned across the desk he inherited and rubbed his hands together. "If I cared about what looks good, I wouldn't be inviting a tired, overweight, contrarian asshole like you back into public life. But the fact of the matter is that I plainly don't care. I need you here."

"What about Gilmore? He's pretty damned knowledgeable."

"He's not you. And that's *his* admission. He's willing to step aside. Besides, he likes the consultant money."

Bernstein laughed. "I don't know, maybe that's the job I want."

"Look, the chief of staff is either going to be my wife or you. Honestly, I think I argue *less* with you."

Bernstein laughed. Morgan Taylor had a wonderful relationship with his wife. "Come on," he said. "The real reason is I don't complain when you swear and smoke."

Bernie "Bernsie" Bernstein had been President Morgan Taylor's sounding board for the previous four years. He sided with the president only half the time, but he always helped Taylor reach the right political, moral, and diplomatic decisions. He left the White House when

Henry Lamden took office. Unlike some of the Cabinet members who stayed on, there was no place for Bernstein, so he accepted a long-standing offer to teach law part-time at BU.

"What about my commitments, Mr. President?"

"I already called your dean. You're excused."

"You did what?" Bernstein said, only partially surprised.

"Halfond was okay with the arrangements," the president said.

"What arrangements? Nobody told me."

"I said that you'd be available to lecture once in a while to students here. We'd set up a special governmental studies program. He was quite impressed and saw the promotional possibilities in it."

"He said, yes *before* you asked me?"

Taylor turned serious. "Bernsie, I really need you with me. I don't know how long it'll be. Maybe for the long haul."

That answered Bernstein's immediate question. "Doesn't look good?"

"Don't know for sure. Based on what the doctors tell me, coming back to work full time may be out of the question."

"A few things for you then, if you don't mind."

"Shoot."

"You have to come clean on everything you know about this Meyerson investigation."

"Agreed."

"We work out a plan to patch up your differences with Congress. They're on the other side of the aisle."

This request was harder. "I'm asking you to come back as chief of staff, not White House magician," Taylor responded.

"You agree to try."

"I'll try."

"And finally, you promise, you absolutely promise, that you'll listen to me."

Taylor laughed. "Listen to you? Are you fucking kidding?" Taylor finally sat down at the famous presidential desk. He pushed back into the leather seat, realizing it wasn't the right fit, but he could live with it. "No way!"

Bernsie smiled. He was feeling happy to be back in the thick of it. Things were just the way he liked them. "Mr. President, I'll take the job."

With that business behind them, Morgan Taylor moved onto his next meeting. He invited in the intelligence czar. Jack Evans was only half surprised to see Bernsie Bernstein.

"Bernsie," he said in greeting.

"Mr. Director," the newly reinstated chief of staff replied. "Like old times."

"Only worse." He had a folder with him that he put on the president's desk. The comment wasn't a joke.

Taylor opened the folder, but did not look at it.

"I'll save you the heavy reading, Mr. President. Let me fill you in about D'Angelo's meeting with Ira Wurlin, number-two in the Mossad under Jacob Schecter. They had a face-to-face talk about the Meyerson allegations and our own issues with their spy apparatus operating here."

The president looked at Bernsie, who took a seat.

"Starting with a general fact...the Israelis have their spies in the United States, just as we have ours in their country. We try to protect against their infiltration. They do the same. We succeed more often than not. They find some of ours. Usually, no one gets hurt."

"To the point, Jack. What about Meyerson?" the president asked.

"They're knee-deep in a lot of agencies. But not here. At least not with her. Meyerson is not theirs."

The president closed the folder without reading a word. "You're certain?"

"Let's just say I believe what Wurlin has reported to D'Angelo. I'd prefer to look Jacob in the eyes, but that's not going to happen. I believe it was your man Roarke who thought it in the first place."

"Yes, it was. It didn't earn him any new fans with the FBI, though." President Taylor stood up, circled his desk, and sat on the edge. Evans stood over him a few feet away.

"So we make a definitive joint statement. We put this to rest," Taylor said.

"Begging your pardon, Mr. President, the story has taken on a life of its own. It's going to be hard to mitigate it," Bernsie said.

"Tell you what, Bernsie: You find a way. Say it often enough and loud enough and make it stick." The president now stood and raised his voice. "A young woman was set up to embarrass this administration. It may have contributed to Henry Lamden's heart attack. And I'm not about to be dragged down by it. End of story."

"There's more, Mr. President," Jack Evans said. "Wurlin gave us something; call it a tip. Political good will to help balance the ledger."

"Oh?" Bernsie said, already feeling right at home back in the Oval Office.

"He gave D'Angelo a name he thought we'd be interested in and a story to go with it."

"Will I know the name?" Taylor asked.

"No, but you're going to be very interested in the story."

Chicago, Illinois

Luis Gonzales wasn't his favorite identity. He missed Miami and the life he lived as Ibrahim Haddad. The weather in Florida was more to his liking. It reminded him of the Mediterranean of his youth. And though he was a faithful Muslim, if only behind closed doors, he yearned for the ease at which women in Miami Beach were attracted to money...and the men who had it.

In addition to being rich, Haddad was also mysterious enough to make him desirable to some women. When finished, he rewarded his companions for their service. Diamonds. A necklace, earrings, a pin. They would all get something—except a second visit. This is the way it had been for decades. In Chicago, his guards did his bidding. They found women in their mid-30s, brunette, hair trimmed at the neckline, no taller than five-five or five-six. They always had the same look. Nobody with dyed hair. That would be obvious to him, and there would be consequences for making that mistake. They bought the jewelry, they took the women home after, and they made it abundantly clear that no one should *ever* return.

Haddad used women and dismissed them. In Miami, his urges were met more frequently. It was definitely more difficult in Chicago. This was true partly because of the different nightlife, and partly because Gonzales wasn't as visible as Haddad.

Tonight his needs were being met again, fast and emotionless in a hotel suite. Throughout the lovemaking, or more aptly, fucking, Gonzales insisted on keeping the radio on to a talk show. His consort tried to get him to tune to something more appropriate. But like everything else in his life, he controlled this moment, too. He never drifted too far, and when he did, it was to only one memory that he never shared with anybody.

Lebanon, Kansas
the same time

"Thomas Jefferson, people. These are Thomas Jefferson's words, not mine. Thomas Jefferson, one of the founding fathers. Write it down. E-mail it to your friends. It'll be online at www.strongnation-radio.com. But its real power comes in the telling," Elliott Strong emphasized. "And I quote, *'Experience hath shown, that even under the best forms [of government] those entrusted with power have, in time, and by slow operations, perverted it into tyranny.'*"

The talk show host cleared his throat for effect, and continued with a greater sense of urgency.

"*'Perverted it into tyranny,'* ladies and gentlemen. *'Tyranny.'*"

Strong brought his voice down at the end of the quote, but he wasn't finished. *'Unless the mass retains sufficient control over those entrusted with the powers of their government, these will be perverted to their own oppression.'*" He paused to let it sink in. "Thomas Jefferson. Makes me think he'd calling in if he could."

The number of Strong's listeners had spiked over the past week. Ninety-five new stations signed onto his daytime lineup, 107 to his overnight show. Strong spoke to the nation, and like Father Coughlin so many years before him, Elliott Strong was now speaking *for* the nation.

"Tyranny, ladies and gentlemen. Tyranny of those entrusted with the awesome powers of their government. Our government. You're finally getting it, aren't you? We're in the middle of 'Spygate' and the big cover-up. We're governed by an unelected government. And now Taylor sits like the king atop a Capitol Hill of lies. He does not represent our interests. He does not represent the people of the United States. And we cannot let him determine our future. It is time to raise your voice louder. It is time to end the perversion. It is time to end the tyranny. It is time to end the oppression. It is time to change the Constitution. And it is time to recall the president!"

Starista, Russia

As he listened to the Internet transmission, Dubroff pondered his immediate problems.

The American Embassy? *No, out of the question.* Brush an American businessman or a tourist? Leave a note? *Absolutely not.* He had to be more resourceful, even in today's Russia.

These were the concerns that kept him awake at night. *Who? How?* Perhaps he could get word out through a friend. *No. Everyone's dead.* Besides, he'd built his career on the foundation of never trusting anyone.

So *who* and *how* haunted him. His worry grew with every hour he lay awake.

Chicago, Illinois

Gonzales moved faster to the rhythm of the words on the radio. He thrust harder as the talk show host emphasized more. He felt the pressure inside, and the need to release just as the host finished.

"To recall the president!" was nearly drowned out by his own scream of pure, selfish pleasure.

The White House
Washington, D.C.

"Haddad," Evans said. "Ibrahim Haddad. Exporter. Lived on Fisher Island, off Miami Beach."

The president picked up the nuance. "Lived?"

"Lived," the intelligence chief continued. "Past tense."

"Lived as in no longer lives?" Bernsie asked.

"Lived as in no longer lives *there.* He disappeared the night of January nineteenth along with his very seaworthy boat and his staff. The implication is that he died in a boat accident. That's the connection that I think we're supposed to make."

"Before we get to the rest, and I assume there is more..."

"Yes, Mr. President."

"What is Jacob Schecter's connection with this Haddad?"

"None. According to the Mossad, Haddad is a businessman with strong ties to the Middle East and bank accounts a mile long. The Israelis started watching him in the mid seventies, when he was seen with Hafez al-Assad in Syria, and later his sons. He was also photographed in Iraq with Udai Hussein, and later in Libya."

The president sat straight up. "*Ashab al-Kahf,*" he whispered. *The People of the Cave.* It was all Haddad's operation?"

"There are strong indications," Evans declared.

"Then why the hell didn't our good friends in Israel let us know about this clown years ago?" the new chief of staff demanded.

Evans took the question. "Because they only knew where he traveled, not what he may have done. They still don't. But they read *The New York Times,* too. Someone must have compared the details of what occurred and what they knew. The meetings, the years, the characters matched up. One to one."

"Weren't we looking for a man named Abraham last year?"

"Absolutely. Our asset in Libya learned that Fadi Kharrazi had talked of an *Abraham,* or so we thought. We linked him to Fadi's plans here, not knowing what they were and who this Abraham was. But it wasn't Abraham at all. His name was Ibrahim."

"So Ibrahim Haddad ran the sleeper operation that elected Teddy Lodge."

"Most likely and conceivably more, Mr. President. The files the Special Forces team brought out of Libya suggested that former Soviet sleepers are quite comfortably embedded in the United States."

"Run by Haddad?" Bernsie asked.

"Unknown. But likely."

"But Lodge was a Libyan plant, not a Russian," Taylor added.

"Yes, from the beginning a Muslim plot, traded from country to country, ultimately designed to end our relationship with Israel. That's not the case with your average run-of-the mill Cold War Russian sleeper. Lodge and his friend Newman were the only real threats to come out of Libya." He added a word of caution. "Others may have been co-opted to Haddad's cause by money, not politics. They're the ones that don't show up in *Ashab al-Kahf.*"

"Back to Haddad," Taylor said, rising to pour himself a cup of coffee from a porcelin pitcher embossed with the White House seal. "He hightailed it out of Dodge?"

"Yup," Evans said, in keeping with the question.

"And you don't think he went down in his ship."

"Not a chance," Evans said, pointing to a cup for himself.

Taylor knew he liked it with a touch of cream, just to lighten it up.

The chief of staff rose and threw his hands in the air. "I don't believe it. You've got the fucking French Connection of politics here, and you're taking a calm coffee break!"

"Oh, quite the opposite, Bernsie. I'm just waking up to the real worry, which we haven't heard yet. Have we, Jack?" The president turned to his head of National Intelligence.

"You know me too well, Mr. President. There is more. After D'Angelo debriefed us on his meeting with the Mossad, I asked Bob's boys over at the FBI to check out Haddad's condo. Right out of *Architectural Digest*. Every room was designer perfect. Everything was just as he left it the night he disappeared, except for one thing."

The NDI pointed to the president's computer.

"There's a nice empty place on his desk where a big old computer sat. My guess is that it's at the bottom of the ocean, along with his very expensive yacht. That's not good news. We would have loved to get our hands on it, because that's where he must have done all of his correspondence."

"Phone records. Has Mulligan checked the phone records?" Bernsie appropriately asked.

"Completely. Bessolo, the team leader the FBI sent, went through years of calls from Europe and the Middle East. So far they're consistent with an importer/exporter. The numbers appear legit. But here's one you'll like: There's a call last year from Lodge's law office in Boston, too."

That got everyone's interest. Suddenly, a back channel that made an important connection.

"Bessolo picked up prints, too. Not ones that match his files. Which either means what we have are bogus, or the ones Bessolo got aren't Haddad's. We also have pictures and descriptions."

"Which all means what?" Bernsie asked.

"For all intents and purposes, we believe that while our man disappeared from sight, he has not vanished from the face of the earth. Ibrahim Haddad is gone, but he could be in the U.S. under another identity—still dedicated to his original purpose."

"Which is bringing us down."

"Not really. I think even he realizes that's not possible. But changing our allegiances in the Middle East? For my money, that *was, is,* and *always will be* his ultimate goal." Evans wanted to drive the point home. "In my estimation, he's out there, and he's not finished."

While this was not good news or even unexpected news, it was apparent that the combined intelligence forces were making progress.

"I don't mean to state the obvious, Jack, but what about the bank accounts you mentioned. Is anything traceable?" Taylor wondered.

"Yes and no. Some of his money is, in fact, large transactions in the last year. Anywhere from a half a million to millions. Each closely following the date of a completed act."

"Completed act?" This was Bernie Bernstein's question.

"Murders, Bernsie. Mrs. Lodge. Marcus. At least two others. Probably dozens more over the years. Cash went its merry way to one foreign account into another, and eventually to God-knows-where."

"The assassin's account," the president stated.

"Yes. But who and where? It's probably all in his rusting computer at the bottom of the ocean."

"Can't we send the Navy to find it?" Again, Bernsie's question.

"The Atlantic is as much as six miles deep in some places," Evans replied. "Off Puerto Rico, they call it *the trench*. Maybe it's there. Maybe he scuttled it in the Bahamas. We'll never find it. But we can look for people who came back into the U.S. after the Inauguration. People who might match Haddad's description."

"You think he'd return?"

"Yes, Mr. President. He's lived in America for decades. This is where he can most effectively continue. He's urbane, so we should be looking for him in major cities. He's rich, so he'll live high on the hog. He's back here. He's just slipped into another life. If we don't know who he is now, we sure as hell can find out who he was. The Mossad is going to help. It's at the top of my list."

The president finished his coffee and looked around the room. This is where he belonged. These are the people he belonged with. He was not going to act like a caretaker. He was going to be the President of the United States. Morgan Taylor buttoned his suit jacket, and stood before his chief of staff and the nation's intelligence director.

"Make no mistake, the election was stolen from us. Lodge was a fraud. He was elected because of the murders. Had he not been there, we would have beaten Henry."

"Remember, Lodge wasn't even Lodge," Bernsie explained. "He was the sleeper who assumed Lodge's identity."

"So noted, Bernsie. But where was the Constitution when we needed it? There was no remedy. Post-nine-eleven, it's all so different. We tread on very murky legal ground. What would have happened if Lodge had been killed after the election, but before the Inauguration? Lamden, too? Who would have been sworn in? Who would have succeeded me on January twentieth? The Speaker of the House? He's new to his job, and only there because of the turnover in Congress. Would there have been a new election? These are unknowns, gentlemen. Today, reality resembles fiction—movie plots and novels. In my mind, if we're to be fully prepared to face the tenuous future, we must consider that *everything* is possible. We've learned that the enemy is much more patient than we are. They will wait years. Decades, if necessary. We're an impatient people. As kids, we became bored with rock songs after a few weeks on the charts. Our children grew up with the pace of *Sesame Street*. Look at the cuts in commercials—two seconds or less. This is the appetite of the American viewer and the American voter, but not so in the rest of the world. Some will plot with great patience. Some will wait for opportunity. Some have a deep sense of history. They're concerned with more—much more—than whether they're the lead story on the news for a while. Yet we think that if our sound bites play often enough, then the world must be agreeing with us. Not so.

"We are going to look to the future, gentlemen. We are going to attack it. We are going to reshape the laws of the land to respond to a world of threats our ancestors could have never imagined.

"You've heard the debate about the Constitution; about an amendment intended to remove us. The truth is, these people are partially right. The Constitution must be readdressed, but not to kick our sorry asses out the door. No, we must be better prepared to provide governance and continuity, no matter what surprises our enemies have in mind."

The president hadn't intended on turning the briefing into a full-scale study. It all came spontaneously, driven by Evans's revelation about Haddad. Bernsie took mental notes. Everything Taylor said was on point. The president would need research to sell the idea. He'd need a special, independent White House counsel to vet the options. Someone Taylor could trust. Someone prepared to take the worst that

Supreme Court Chief Justice Leopold Browning would inevitably dispense. Someone with no bias. He smiled to himself. He had the perfect person in mind.

Lexington, Massachusetts
FBI Safe House

"Are you up for it, Katie?" Roarke asked.

"Oh, am I ever," she said.

"It's going to take a little finessing, but I think it'll have the desired effect."

"When?"

"In the morning. Witherspoon is running around in circles. He's worried. Tomorrow we surprise him. You and me."

"And the rest of tonight?" Katie asked.

"What do mean?"

Katie took his hand and led him to their bedroom in the safe house. Shop talk was over. "I want to see what you're up for." Once the door was closed, she unzipped him. "What's this?" she asked, kneeling down.

Roarke had become a very giving lover. This seemed too selfish. "No, no, no. Up, let me...."

Her lips closed around him tighter, but her tongue gave away her full intentions. She wanted all of him, and this was only the beginning.

Roarke sighed. He stood for awhile, but when she realized his legs were getting wobbly, she carefully walked him backward to the chair. Katie's hands cupped him as he arched up into her mouth. He moved with her now, matching her actions in an equal and opposite way, slowly, gently, until he couldn't hold it any longer. Then, sensing the moment, Katie was there for him.

He relaxed back into the chair. Katie stood, then slowly and sensually undressed. She took five minutes. The lights in the room were off, but her body was backlit by the moon. She looked so sensual, so appealing, so inviting, that he began to respond.

Katie stepped closer. Roarke reached for her hips. He wanted to pull Katie onto his lap.

"Not yet," she whispered. She leaned forward and kissed him gently, sharing the tastes. "That's *us*."

"I love *us*," Roarke sighed.

"Good," she whispered. "Now me."

Roarke stood up. He took her into his arms, continued the kiss, and gingerly walked her backward to the bed. He would gladly return the wonderful pleasure she'd given him...and more.

CHAPTER
40

Boston, Massachusetts
Friday, 29 June

"**D**amn!" Donald Witherspoon shouted. He nicked himself shaving. Blood oozed down his cheek. He dug through a drawer for a styptic pencil. He dabbed the medicine on his cut and cursed Katie Kessler again. He hated her when she was alive, and she was still able to torment him even though she was dead.

Witherspoon believed his benefactor would be proud. But the man who had paid him to watch Heywood Marcus also paid someone else to watch Witherspoon.

Roarke's target was sufficiently rattled now. He might expect to meet Roarke again, even FBI investigators. But the way they played it so far, no one came by to Freelander, Connors & Wrather. Until today. Roarke reasoned that the sight of a very-much-alive Katie Kessler would put him over the edge.

Katie and Roarke drove into Boston from Lexington. They parked his rented car in the lot beneath her downtown law offices, and started toward the elevator.

"Hey, let's get a coffee first. We're way early."

Roarke looked at his watch. Six thirty-five. "Okay." They didn't expect Witherspoon for more than an hour. Katie reported that he always made it in at 7:45. Not before. Not after. Like his wardrobe, which was always the same, Witherspoon was a creature of habit.

They took the elevator to the ground floor, walked half a block, and cut across the street.

Six forty A.M. There were just a few people in line at Starbucks. They fell in behind a pair of women, both talking on their cell phones. Roarke automatically scanned the room: three commuters sat on stools at the window reading. Two had *The Boston Globe*. One read *The Herald*. A couple seated at a table held hands. *A budding office romance?* he thought. Satisfied that everything was okay, he picked up the first section of *The Globe*. There was an account in the right column about some sort of protest march schedule for D.C. He made a mental note to find out more later. He unconsciously heard the women in front order their drinks. "Grande Chai latte with extra foam and a tall skim latte."

"Anything else?" a perky young woman clerk at the register asked.

"Sure, a pumpkin scone and a cinnamon twist."

The next thing Roarke caught was the barista repeat the order. "Got it. Grande Chai latte with extra foam and a tall non-fat latte."

Roarke looked up, not really knowing why. He put the paper back on the newsstand. The aroma of the coffee brought him back to his senses, and he sidled next to Katie. They were next. He kissed the back of her neck.

"Mmmm," she whispered. The woman at the counter smiled. She thought the same thing Roarke had before. *An office romance.*

Katie chuckled when she asked, "Do you know what you'd like?" Roarke was still kissing her.

Katie nodded. "Ah, yes." She realized she answered the question in her head, not the one asked. Kate moved her neck forward and ordered for the two of them. "One tall regular black, one tall skim latte." She turned around, and into Roarke's eyes she added, "Nothing else...now."

The clerk smiled again. "Names?" With a number of cups lined up, Starbucks employees usually relied on customers' names to get the orders into the right hands.

"The skim—Katie. The tall black is for Scott."

The man making the coffee repeated the order. He was just a few feet to her right. "Tall black and one tall non-fat latte."

Roarke reached into his pocket for a ten. He paid and they moved behind the people ahead of them to wait for their drinks.

Kate cuddled up to Roarke, cocked her head to the side, and smiled. "I love your eyes."

"You do?"

"Yes, because they're windows into who you are. I think I see further than anyone ever has."

"I take it you like what you see?"

She patted down Roarke's black T-shirt under his light summer sports coat. "Yes, I do." She leaned into his ear, kissed it, and whispered, "And don't worry. I'll do exactly as you told me. When he opens the door, he'll see you sitting at the desk. I'll be behind the door. He'll step forward, start talking, then on your cue I'll say, 'Hello, Donald.' That's all."

"That's all you'll need to say," Roarke answered. "It'll hit him all at once." She nodded. Katie was ready to meet up with Witherspoon again.

The people ahead of them took their drinks. Roarke and Katie stepped forward. The barista was very quick. Perfect for the morning rush.

Roarke whispered in her ear as they stood at the counter, "Then I'll tell him that he'll have just one opportunity to cooperate."

"And I just smile?"

"That's all you need to do."

"Katie," the barista called out. Roarke automatically tilted his head toward the voice. The man smiled as he moved the coffee cups up the line on the stand adjacent to his machine. "The black for Scott is up, too."

The barista wore a big broad smile, but quickly stepped behind the coffee machine to wipe his steamer. His blonde ponytail whipped around and landed on the collar of his tan shirt. He stood about the same height as Roarke. He was fit. Extremely fit. Roarke detected strong neck muscles and bulk on his arms. The man obviously exercised, but in a more rigorous regimen than the average health club member.

Roarke peered around. The barista caught Roarke's glance, and his expression changed marginally.

The woman at the register called out a new order. "Venti triple-shot caramel latte." The barista took the cup and kept his eyes down. He didn't repeat the order.

Katie grabbed Roarke's arm. "Come on. Gotta go, Mr. Roarke."

Roarke uttered a guttural "Yah," and took the two cups. She continued to talk to him, but the words just floated over him. His mind was elsewhere.

They were at the front door when a simple thing hit him. *Skim latte.* He'd heard it a lot recently. But most of the country referred to skim milk as non-fat. The guy doing the drinks called back *non-fat. From out of state?* he wondered.

That alone would not be a problem, but there was something about the man himself. *His face. His jaw line. The angle of his nose. The closeness of his eyes.*

Outside, more thoughts rushed forward. He felt a coldness that cancelled out the man's smile. A tight body under his shirt that trumped the relaxed dude manner. *Lose the smile. Ignore the ponytail.*

Now well outside Starbucks, Roarke stopped.

"Come on," Katie insisted.

The Secret Service agent ignored the request and sidestepped Katie. He wanted another glimpse of the man. She stopped to see what he was doing.

"Scott!"

Roarke stared into the shop, still ignoring her. Katie walked to his side and saw a dangerous look on his face. She followed his line of sight. Inside, the barista, working much slower now, was also looking at Roarke. He had the same expression. She glanced back at Roarke.

Roarke and the man's eyes locked in a suspended moment, absent of anyone else.

Roarke's memory ran through a catalogue of other faces. An insurance broker, an antique's dealer, a man on a train, a Capitol Police officer. He added an overlay of the man in his sight. When he finished, it settled on one image in Touch Parson's computer: *Depp.*

"What?" Katie asked.

Roarke hadn't realized he actually said the name aloud.

The man mouthed a word back. *Roarke!*

Roarke shoved his latte at Katie. "Here! Take this!" He bolted for the Starbucks door. His hand was already inside his jacket pocket, his fingertips on his holstered Sig Sauer.

As Roarke swung the door open, Depp launched the venti cup full of hot coffee into the air. It smashed to the ground. The drink splashed up, scalding the customer. She immediately jumped, only to slip on the slick floor. Another woman went to her side and knelt down. Two other patrons crowded closer to help. The commotion served to create immediate mayhem and block Roarke's quick passage to the counter. Depp tore into a storeroom and out of sight.

Roarke was now fully inside, his gun in his hand. The woman working the counter screamed at the sight.

"Where does that room go?" Roarke shouted.

She froze.

"Where?" he demanded. "Is there a back way out?"

"Yes," she managed.

"Out to the alley," the clerk said as he stepped over the downed woman's legs.

No more questions. Instead of navigating around the people, Roarke vaulted over the center counter. He made a left behind the coffee machine and a quick right to the back room where Depp had gone.

The assassin had a good ten seconds on Roarke and, if training proved right, the benefit of knowing where he was going.

Depp was as surprised as Roarke, and as off-guard. If it hadn't been for the name on the cups—Katie and Scott, and the mention of *Roarke*—he might not have even noticed. But, he had learned those names, first Roarke's, then Katie's. He also had another advantage. He'd seen Roarke at the Capitol and knew what he was capable of doing.

Fighting Roarke was not on his agenda. It was not something he'd been paid to do and it wasn't something he relished. Today was the day he was going to treat Donald Witherspoon to a Grande Soy Cap with extra foam, and an unhealthy double shot of ricin. The taste of the processed castor beans would have been masked by the aroma and flavor of the cappuccino.

Although ricin has potential medical uses in bone marrow transplants and cancer treatments, the barista had chosen it because of its other attributes. He had a vial in his pocket with 900 micrograms. In comparative terms, it could have fit on the head of a pin.

Somewhere along the way Witherspoon would have finished his coffee, tossed it, or left it on a desk to be thrown out by an assistant.

The assassin knew how effectively ricin worked. Ingestion leads to stomach cramps, quite normal for a harried attorney under pressure. Cramps give way to diarrhea, which are accompanied by uncontrollable waves of nausea and vomiting. As the poison works its way through the body, protein production in the cells is prevented. Without any known antidote, liver, kidneys, and spleen shut down.

It should have been a simple kill, worth 150 grand. But the plan fell apart, the mark was still alive, and the man known as Paul Erskine was running for his life.

By the time he cleared the outside door, his wig was off and curled up in his hand. He grabbed the top of his shirt and pulled hard and fast. Buttons flew in every direction. He didn't stop to recover them. But as he ran, he yanked the shirt over his head and rolled it up. Next, he tipped over a trash can, which would be rolling to the right when the Secret Service agent emerged from Starbucks. Finally, he doubled back, darting diagonally across the alley to an open service entrance leading to the mailroom of a 12-story office building. He reached into his back pocket for a perfectly crafted laminated building ID. He clipped it to his belt buckle, slowed down, found the clipboard he'd left hanging the day before, picked it up, and casually walked in.

He'd plotted an emergency escape route before taking the job. It was always his first priority. And while he had counted on a calm departure later that day through the front door, he was prepared.

A moment later, Roarke flew out of the Starbucks. He scanned the alley. *Two ways to go.* To the left, the alley extended some 200 feet; the right, only 25 feet before it intersected Federal Street. Depp had a 20-second lead, enough time to make the street. A trash can was still rolling in that direction. Roarke took off.

At Federal, he had another decision to make. He looked both ways. *Now which direction?*

Once inside, the assassin ran down three halls and into a stairwell. He bounded up two steps at a time, purposely skipping the first landings. He counted the floors as he climbed, not even breaking a sweat. When he arrived where he planned, he opened the hall door, stepped inside, and calmly walked to the men's room. The night before, he visited the bathroom and hid a number of items in a box under the sink. *Good. Still there.* He removed the articles and went into the farthest stall.

Roarke decided to go left. Only a few people were to the right. None of them running or walking away from him. But to the left, there were two clumps of pedestrians. He could be in either one.

Roarke ran to the first group, keeping his gun out, but behind him. *Not here,* he said to himself as he passed the last man. He caught up with the second. *Damn!*

"See anyone running?" he asked.

No one had. He doubled back to the first group and asked the same question.

"No."

Roarke stopped and calculated the possible escape routes. He quickly broke the street into quadrants and gave each a quick, but experienced, study. This took another 15 seconds. There was no sign of Depp. Then he realized, *Because he didn't come this way!*

Roarke returned to the alley, looking for any door or window that might have been broken into. He found something even better: a service entrance to a building across from Starbucks. Roarke cursed his stupidity. He'd fallen for Depp's deception. The trash can.

The door was not open, but it wasn't locked. He went in, cautiously. The safety was off the Sig. He backed up against the wall and turned the corner fast, with his gun in the lead.

Clear.

He repeated the action through the second corridor, and the third, where a shriek echoed off the walls. A middle-aged woman saw a gun round the corner. Roarke quickly raised it into the air.

"Secret Service. Did you see a man come this way?"

"No!" she said, frozen in place.

Roarke looked around her. An elevator bank and a stairwell were ahead.

Another decision.

He chose the stairs, calculating the best place to get lost was higher up. With his gun still out, Roarke climbed. He contemplated opening the door to the second floor, then the third, but he decided on the fourth. Once through the door, he checked the offices, one by one, turning each doorknob. They were all locked.

The bathroom. Roarke entered quietly. The mirror provided an instant reflection of the urinals. They were empty. Further down, three toilet stalls. The doors were open to two. The very last one appeared closed.

Roarke walked slowly toward the back of the bathroom. He peered down, looking for shadows or motion. Nothing, but Depp could be standing on the seat.

He needed Depp alive. He didn't know if he was armed, but he had to assume he was. Surprise was not an option.

"Secret Service! Come out now! Hands in the air." He stepped silently to the side, away from where he shouted the orders.

No response.

Roarke crept closer, cutting an obtuse angle to the stall, hugging the wall where the urinals were. "Now!" he repeated. Once again, he moved away from where he spoke in case Depp aimed there.

He calculated that Depp couldn't see him. He held his breath and listened for breathing or the shifting of weight on the toilet seat. He waited for 30 seconds and shook his head. Worse than hearing something was the absence of sound itself.

Roarke walked forward, barely sliding his neck around the partition. The door to stall three was only partially open, and at this angle, he could now see that no one was there.

He'd chosen the wrong floor.

At the same moment, a man one floor directly below Roarke adjusted his conservative blue-and-green-striped tie. He looked roughly 55. He pushed a pair of metal frame glasses into place, and ran his hand through his graying hair. He stood over six-feet. Then he let his body collapse into his suit. In that instant, he easily lost two inches. He exited the bathroom, walked to the far end of the hall, and stopped in front of a locked office. He reached in his right front pocket and removed a key which perfectly fit the lock. He entered and immediately immersed himself in meaningless paperwork, which he'd also left the day before. Everything was as he'd left it in the rented efficiency office suite.

Roarke covered the next five floors as fast as he could. They were empty. By the time he made it up to eight, people were beginning to file in. Now he needed a team to locate Depp.

Reluctantly, he gave up. He walked down the stairs to the first floor and entered the lobby. *No guard. No one to question.* Roarke departed through the front door, crossed the street, and looked up and down Franklin one last time. He turned back to the building and looked up.

Two women were talking in a window on four. He could see a man on the phone on five. And on three, a businessman in a white shirt and suspenders was pacing with the phone in his hand. He was gesturing with broad movements, as if he was arguing with someone on the other end and looking out into nothingness.

"Damn!" was all Roarke could manage.

The man pretending to be on the phone was thinking something entirely different.

41

SASR Command
Swanbourne, Australia
the same time

"**T**en minutes out," the voice announced calmly. "Target in range."

Ricky Morris looked at his ops screen. "Roger that. You are go. Repeat, you are go." Morris was the operation's commander. He was on a live link to the lead pilot of the twin Royal Australian Air Force F/A-18Ds, carrying out the mission objectives. The attack was the work of the SASR, the Special Air Service Regiment. In addition to the real-time displays radioed back to the Swanbourne, Australia HQ, Morris had satellite imagery, courtesy of the Americans.

"Target acquired," the pilot said with no hint of tension.

"We're fully committed now," Morris barely whispered to the man next to him. The prime minister's defence secretary, Chris Wordlow, nodded acceptance.

The room fell silent as two Lockheed Martin F-35 (JSF) Strike Fighters closed the distance in seconds.

"Warning, attack command received." This time the voice was from a computer onboard the lead F-35.

Come on, Wordlow mouthed. An SASR Tactical Assault Group (TAG) had located the terrorist base just days earlier. It hadn't been all that difficult. Once the bomb squad disabled the device discovered in the Sydney hotel, the SASR analyzed the parts. Everything had its own history, and everyone who fused a bomb left a signature of his handiwork. Sometimes it was a fingerprint, other times the wire or solder was a giveaway. It could be serial numbers or the origin of the

C-4. In this case, it was a combination of the markings on the explosives and the radio transmitter.

The device was amateurish and familiar, the work of a small insurgent group holed up in the Solomon Islands, northeast of Australia.

The Australian government had been watching the Solomons since the Bali bombings years earlier. Instability in the archipelago made it a natural habitat for terrorists. The Solomon Islands government invited "cooperative intervention." Prime Minister David Foss willingly agreed. Intelligence determined that, while most of the terrorist cells operated in Indonesia, the 992 islands of the Solomons—some of them very isolated—provided terrorists with the same degree of shelter. Even worse, they were too close to Australia.

That's where the group was hiding—one of the small islands off Rennell, to be exact. The TAG advance squad confirmed their identity and location, about 300 kilometers south of Guadalcanal. The Royal Air Force was going to do the rest.

"Attack commit," the monotone computer voice stated.

"We're going in with AGM-65 Maverick and AGM-88 HARM on the first pass. The knockout punch will come when we drop the GBU-12 Paveway laser-guided bombs," Ricky Morris said without taking his eyes off the three computer screens.

"Attack target."

This was Wordlow's first time witnessing an actual strike and it seemed all too much like a videogame. The Strike Fighters were represented by moving triangles. The target was boxed. The missiles, small circles, separated from the planes. As they converged on the box, he shifted his eyes to another screen. There he saw what the missiles saw: live video of the terrorist camp looming closer and closer.

"Seconds now." Morris pointed to the satellite feed. Barely two seconds later, the circle met the box, the missile-view cameras went black, and the satellite showed massive explosions. The base was obliterated.

"They'll go in for another run, but it's over," Morris stated.

Wordlow leaned back and let out the breath he'd been holding. As many as 100 men, maybe some women, were incinerated in a thousandth of a second. They had no warning, no chance to look to Allah for deliverance. It was the price they paid, he thought without remorse, for planning to blow up the Ville St. George Hotel and the President of the United States.

Jack Evans thought the same thing, watching the attack from his command center in the Pentagon.

CHAPTER 42

The New York Times editorial offices
New York, New York

"Hey, I got this odd e-mail. It's short and kinda weird."
Michael O'Connell handed it to his editor at *The New
York Times*. "What do you make of it?"

Andrea Weaver read it and quickly dismissed the content. "These
unsolicited e-mails are useless."

O'Connell would normally agree. Internet tips hardly ever amount
to much. The correspondence is usually comprised of verbose, argumentative complaints from disgruntled, anonymous readers. This, too,
was anonymous, but there was something that piqued O'Connell's
interest.

"No phone number. No contact. No information," Weaver complained. "Pass." She returned it to O'Connell.

"That was my first reaction," he explained. "But check it out again."
He gave it back to her.

She nodded affirmatively. "Bad English."

"Maybe intentionally bad."

She re-read the e-mail.

Andrea Weaver had been transferred to the news desk from Moscow
only two months earlier. She had limited contact with O'Connell, but
she'd been told to give the reporter, who was likely to earn a Pulitzer
for his inside reporting of the Lodge investigation, room to work.

"You think this is about Lodge?"

"Yes."

"There's nothing that directly indicates that, Michael."

"There's nothing that precludes it."

She read the correspondence a fourth time, then handed it back. "You probably don't even need my approval on a travel voucher," she said, acknowledging his star status at the paper.

"I know, but I do need to pick your brain. You've been there. I haven't. Where should I go?"

He could see Andrea Weaver's whole manner change. He'd worked her and she just realized it. "You are good."

"Why, thank you," he said through a laugh.

"Okay, sit down. Let me grab a map and we'll see what looks most promising."

Staritsa, Russia

Deep down, Aleksandr Dubroff hoped that nobody cared about him. He hoped that the State had forgotten him. But the very fact that he received pension payments reminded Dubroff that at least one department knew *where* he was, whether or not they knew *who* he was. Futhermore, he wasn't naïve. The FSB wouldn't welcome him speaking to the West. Not with what he knew.

Dubroff's career was built on secrets, deceptions, outright lies, and murder. He'd trained countless good young men to become merciless killers. He'd transformed medical students—who may have once dreamed of healing people—into torturers who inflicted unimaginable pain. He turned innocent girls into mistresses who would get their bedfellows to admit crimes against the State. And he taught everyone the lesson he believed the most: *Trust no one.*

While the Western press reported that Russia was transformed under democratization, Dubroff knew otherwise. *Nations with no concept of democracy cannot suddenly be democracized. It was the way of Russia. For hundreds of years.* He thought it was amazing that the Americans failed to realize that, even after Iraq. *People need to be told. People need the State to make their decisions.*

And now he was selling out the State—at least, the *old* regime. He feared the new leadership would not make the distinction.

Dubroff had already taken the first dangerous step. He sent an e-mail to the reporter O'Connell. But would the American be smart enough to act on the invitation? He hoped so.

The New York Times

> Your reports fine.
> Why do you write about things you not know?
> You need information good.
> Bearly a friend.

Michael O'Connell analyzed the printout at his desk. There were only four sentences to the e-mail, in obviously poor English. *A trick, or a clue to the sender's identity?* He considered each word important and possibly meaningful on multiple levels.

Your reports fine.

For more than a year, O'Connell's beat had been Teddy Lodge. He'd covered the origins of the sleeper spy plot that won Lodge the election and almost put him in the White House. President Taylor had given him complete access to the military mission that garnered the proof. Other news sources quoted him. *The author of the note had to be referring to the coverage.*

Based on information recovered in the American raid on Libya, O'Connell knew that the plot had been handed off from one Arab country to another, but it originated in Russia. The e-mail is from Russia.

Why do you write about things you not know?

This was more puzzling. *Is this criticism? An observation from someone who does know?* This is what he immediately concluded. Even working with the White House and his ex-CIA sources, O'Connell knew very little, and understood even less. *But the person who sent this to me does know.*

You need information good.

O'Connell got excited every time he read the line. The awkward English syntax aside, he felt this could be an invitation. *You need...* It sounded like an offer more than a criticism. And...*information good.* He believed that *good* meant *correct.* He believed the writer was indicating he or she had intelligence on the matter, and was interested in offering it up.

The letter was intentionally vague. The reporter reasoned it was written in such a way as to also pass as a complaint if intercepted. It might read that way to someone else, but in Michael O'Connell's hands, it told another story.

Bearly a friend.

O'Connell saw the connection immediately. The root of the word— bear. This wasn't about an animal. From his knowledge of the Cold War, "bear" meant only one thing. He was getting an invitation to come to Russia.

Starista, Russia

Dubroff moved cautiously. He smiled to neighbors when he left the house. *They see my suitcase.* It was a terribly weathered two-suiter. The leather was dry and flakey. "I'm going to visit my wife's ailing sister," he told the old woman who sold him eggs and milk.

"Where?" she asked. "You never mentioned..."

See? Everyone is suspicious. The Soviet way.

"In St. Petersburg. She has been failing for a long time," he added.

Dubroff waved to his butcher, and when the vegetable seller asked when he'd be back with more mushrooms, Dubroff said in a week-and-a-half.

In *truth*, something he had little experience with, he didn't know when or if he'd return to Staritsa. He wondered whether the FSB would detain him the moment he tried to board the bus at Tver, or later. Would he feel a cold hand yank him on the shoulder, steps away from his Moscow-bound, not St. Petersburg, train? That's how he often did it, theatrical and forceful. He simply slipped out of the shadows when his subjects were most focused on blending in; when they were convinced they had succeeded in tricking Mother Russia. That's when he loved making his arrests. In public, with no equivocation. No sympathy. Everyone would talk about what happened. Few would dare it.

Yet, now Aleksandr Dubroff looked for movement in the shadows. He glanced around to see if someone from the FSB would make an example of him.

Yes, the train. Two hundred fifty kilometers. That's when. It's such a good time to *instruct* rookies, he thought. No, Moskovia. So many more people to witness my capture. Maybe, he thought.

The bus door opened and Dubroff climbed the stairs. *Then again,* giving himself credit, *maybe not.*

CHAPTER

43

Russia

A leksandr Dubroff could feel it. He blamed his own stupidity. *Too much time on that damned computer.*

He didn't know where they were, but he was certain they were watching. Maybe it wasn't the man two rows behind him on the bus, or the attendant who stared far too long at his window as they rolled away. Maybe it was someone he hadn't noticed yet. The farmer in overalls in the aisle opposite him. He looked at the man's fingers. Rough and dirty? No. He strained to glance over his shoulder. Then what about the woman another row back. She seemed to be reading, but she hadn't turned a page yet.

Dubroff spent the next two hours sneaking looks and evaluating everyone. He knew he'd be doing the same thing on the train at Tver, assuming he made it that far.

There's an expression that goes to the very heart of the paranoid: *Sometimes they really are following you.*

A car pulled up onto the dirt driveway in front of the old Russian's dacha. Two men in poorly fitting suits stepped out. The driver walked around to the passenger side and motioned to the back of the house. The second man went where he was told.

The driver walked to the front door. His orders were to knock solidly and wait. If, after an appropriate amount of time, the door didn't open, he was authorized to break in. His supervisors told him that his subject was old. He'd also been warned: "He's a former colonel in the KGB. The man is resourceful." He wasn't informed about his status in the Politburo. No one cared anymore.

When the second knock went unanswered, he unholstered his revolver and put all his might against the wooden door. It gave way, probably needing only half the effort.

"This is the FSB! Show yourself!" There was a noise at the rear of the house. Another door opening. The Russian agent leveled his gun in the direction of the sound.

"In!" called Number Two from the back. *Damn. He was supposed to stay and wait! Doesn't anyone pay attention to training anymore?*

The agent worked his way around the first floor. There were old pictures of a beautiful young woman, books on horticulture, an upright piano. He touched a few keys. Instead of recognizable notes, the piano produced discordant tones and thuds. He continued his search. A collection of shot glasses. Dog-eared books of Russian poetry. A box of letters in a woman's hand. He looked at the postmarks. Nothing newer than the mid-1980s.

The agents converged at the steps leading upstairs. A worn carpet covered the scuffed brown hardwood floors, long in need of a good sanding and stain. The head agent nodded for Number Two to accompany him.

Worry hit the agent. *What did they say? Former colonel in the KGB.* They weren't just looking for an old man, they were here to take in a dangerous man.

The agent-in-charge had a printout of the Web sites Dubroff had logged onto, the length of time he spent on each, and the contents of the webpages. The psych ops shrink, assigned to evaluate Dubroff's motivation, concluded:

"The behavior of the subject is consistent with one who is absorbed in self-evaluation or end-of-life reflection. The tools of the technology allow him to search for references to his own career; to create meaning for his life's work, for his existence on the face of the earth. Finding little, yet seeing accounts of colleagues, many of whom he views as lesser, fosters a growing anger. First it is directed at them—people who have achieved fame, perhaps wealth, by violating their allegiance to country. Worse still is when they exploit their achievements at the expense of the subject. But soon this anger transfers to the State. Not only the former Soviet Union, but today's State. It is the recommendation of this department that the subject be questioned, that his computer be confiscated, that his actions cease. While he poses no immediate security risk, his archival know-ledge could be embarrassing."

The report was initialed and dispatched to a bureau supervisor who bucked it up. The name Dubroff, though not instantly recognizable to everyone in the FSB hierarchy, was familiar to a senior control, Yuri Ranchenkov. He was the man who ultimately decided to round up Dubroff.

Ranchenkov recalled a pain-in-the-ass teacher many years ago at the famed Andropov Institute. He made everyone who entered wish they'd never enrolled and turned anyone who graduated into a pro-fessional. His name was Dubroff, too. *But he still couldn't be alive?*

If he was the same man, he held important secrets. Between his KGB work and his years at the Politburo, he was a walking encyclo-pedia of every Cold War trick in the book. The shrink's summation was vastly understated. He called for an assistant to pull all the records on "an Aleksandr Dubroff, retired, Politburo, 1984 or 85. Mid-'80s at least. Ex-KGB field officer and teacher at Andropov." Then he added for good measure, "Confirm if he is deceased; if so, where he is buried. If he is alive, tell me where he lives!"

They found the information. Dubroff, Aleksandr, was alive. Ranchenkov sent investigators to his home without complaint from subordinates. He had an old-guard sensibility, left over from the Communist regime. He demanded obedience and loyalty. Ranchenkov supervised the secret branch of the DII—the Department of Internal Investigations—the newest version of the Secret Police. In a strange turn of events, he was tracking down his mentor.

After listening for any sound of life in the bedroom and hearing none, the lead FSB agent swung open the door with a simple nudge. Like every other room they checked, it had the musty smell of an old house. This did not make Sergei Ryabov any less cautious. The dossier on Dubroff was impressive. He had been a master spy. That meant he was proficient with a gun.

While both men were relieved the entire house was clear, Dubroff's absence presented another problem. *Where was he?*

"He picks mushrooms. He's probably out in the forest," said Number Two.

Ryabov had more experience, but only a little. Still, he bullied his partner as if he had years of experience. "And if he is not, then we have wasted hours."

His Number Two reluctantly nodded.

"Look in his drawers. I'll check his closets."

"What am I looking for?"

"What's there and what's missing!" exclaimed Ryabov.

The chief officer surveyed Dubroff's closet. He ran an elimination list. *Suitcase. Not here.* He looked under the bed, then in the guest room, in the hall closets, and finally in a quarter basement that housed the boiler and hot-water heater. There, he found four bulky, dusty suitcases, stacked one on top of another. The top one had a thick layer of dust on it, but curiously, a rectangle within that was dust free. There had been a fifth, smaller suitcase. He glided his finger across the clean portion of the top suitcase and looked at it. *Clean. Dubroff left recently!*

Sergei Ryabov shot upstairs and called into FSB headquarters the same moment Aleksandr Dubroff boarded the train.

CHAPTER 44

Boston, Massachusetts

Roarke's Secret Service credentials went a long way in defusing the momentary excitement. He explained to the police that he had been tracking a fugitive who, using a new identity, took a job at the coffee bar. Katie confirmed what she could, which helped. Unfortunately, for Roarke's sake, more damage had been done in the minutes while he was chasing Depp.

Another Starbucks employee took it upon herself to clean up. That included wiping the pots, trashing the cup that Depp used as a diversion, and restoring everything back to spic and span, customer-friendly normal. The possibility of lifting usable latent prints quickly went from 100 percent to basically zero.

Also, despite Roarke's protestations, the police were not inclined to declare Starbucks a crime scene. "You tell me what crime was committed here," the officer declared. He walked away from Roarke and got himself a free coffee.

Ten minutes later, Roarke and Katie were back on the street.

"What now?" Katie asked.

"So much for surprise." Roarke looked at the time. "Witherspoon would have been here by now. If he has a half a brain, he's taken off."

Katie shared the thought.

"Wait a second—Starbucks!" Roarke exclaimed.

"Yes," Katie said.

"Why was Depp here?"

Katie never asked herself that question. "I don't know."

"Come on, Katie. Here, across the street from your office."

"Oh, my God!" She started shaking. "Me?"

Six minutes earlier, Donald Witherspoon approached his regular Starbucks. He was drawn to the commotion and pushed his way through the large crowd that had quickly gathered.

"What's going on?" he asked no one in particular.

"The police are in there," a woman said.

"I heard somebody had a gun," added another.

Witherspoon saw another lawyer from the firm. He maneuvered close enough to call out. "Hey, Rog!"

The man, dressed in the same pinstripe uniform, turned to the voice. "Donald," he said with no particular enjoyment.

Witherspoon worked his way closer to his colleague and the front of the crowd. "I heard 'gun.'"

"Me, too. The police are in there now. Apparently there was some sort of chase. Don't really know. See." He pointed to the left side of building. "They're talking to somebody now."

They were about 15 feet from the front door. He couldn't see anything from his angle. Glare from the morning sun reflected off the glass. He sidestepped to the left and looked inside. A cop held a walkie-talkie to one ear. He had what looked like a license or ID card in his other hand.

"Did they catch anyone?" Witherspoon asked.

"Dunno. Just got here a few minutes ago."

He continued talking, proposing a theory, but Witherspoon stopped listening. He felt his chest tighten with anxiety, and his heart begin to race. Beads of perspiration immediately formed on his forehead. His palms got sweaty. *Kessler!*

He could easily see her. She'd stepped away from the door frame and faced the outside. Witherspoon turned 90 and leaned behind the other lawyer, avoiding her line of sight. A few seconds later, he slid around ever so slightly and looked up.

Now she was gesturing in the direction of their law offices. He slid behind his colleague again and let his mind race through what he had just seen and what it meant. *Kessler. Alive. And the man with the ID. Roarke?* He couldn't quite make him out. *And the chase? What kind of chase? Who was he after?* It almost didn't matter. The fact that Kessler was alive was enough.

Witherspoon faded back. The other attorney felt him leaving. "Hey, where you going?"

"Coffee down the street," he called out without looking back. He didn't offer to get his colleague any. He wasn't returning.

Russia
the same time

Neither was Aleksandr Dubroff. The old man felt like he was back in the game. He let a lot of himself die when he buried his wife. Now, the blood pumped through his veins with renewed vigor. His brain calculated options ten steps ahead. He weighed each move, but not as someone on the run, but from the perspective of the hunter. After all, even today, the FSB taught from the book he wrote.

Will they come looking for me? Absolutely.

Do they have orders to detain me? Now that I'm fleeing, yes.

Will they shoot if I don't stop? Without hesitation.

Will they know where to look?

The final question brought a broad smile to him. *No.* Search as they may, they weren't going to find Dubroff at the typical places. He wasn't going to the American Embassy or the airport. He didn't intend on sneaking across the border in the dead of night. Aleksandr Dubroff had other notions. He decided to switch trains, taking a roundabout route to Moscow, and cash in a few chits from someone who owed him.

Boston, Massachusetts

Katie didn't realize that she was standing on Milk Street with her mouth wide open. "Will he still try?"

If he wants to get paid, he'll try again, Roarke thought. "He's not foolish. He's seen me," Roarke said, trying to console her. He took Katie into his arms. She was shaking.

In less than a year, Katie Kessler had crossed over into a different world than she'd ever known or imagined. Roarke's world was full of death and deceit, power and politics. People weren't beaten in court, they ended up dead on city streets, or at the bottom of the Charles.

"Is this the way it's always going to be with us?" she asked softly.

Roarke squeezed harder. He could answer with a lie or tell the truth.

"For now, yes," he said. Roarke released her and took half a step back. He angled Katie's chin up toward his eyes, so she would clearly see him, and said, "Not forever."

"Why? Why me? I haven't done anything."

The question gave him pause. *Why Katie?* It actually didn't make sense. *Why would Depp be waiting for Katie to return to her old routine—including a morning coffee? If he wanted to kill her, he had ample time and opportunity, and much earlier. And Depp would have succeeded where the other contract killer had failed.*

"What a second." Roarke was thinking it through. "How many people come here before work?"

"What?" Katie asked.

"Starbucks. Who comes here?"

"I don't understand."

"Katie, I don't think you were the target. At least it's possible you're not. So who else stops for a coffee before work?"

"God, lots of people."

"Anybody relevant?"

"Well, yes. Donald Witherspoon."

Witherspoon wasn't a talented fugitive. He didn't know where to go. Returning to his Back Bay apartment was out of the question. He had cash, but not enough to get far. The most he could get out of an ATM was five hundred. He'd need help.

The summer heat began to rise off the pavement, making Witherspoon even more uncomfortable. He took off his suit jacket, speeded up his walk, and crossed Franklin, heading deeper into the maze of downtown office buildings. He turned his head slightly to the side every half-block to see if he was being followed.

"Ah!" Witherspoon slammed into an oncoming pedestrian with such force that he knocked the man down. Without realizing it, he stumbled as well, tumbling right on top of the man.

"Excuse me. Sorry, I wasn't watching," he stammered.

"No problem. Just help me up, old boy." The man held out his hand for Witherspoon to grab onto. Witherspoon's instinct was to continue, but the man's hand remained outstretched. "Come on," he said with a clipped British accent. "Help a friend up. No harm."

Witherspoon looked over his shoulder again, thinking twice. "Okay." He met the man halfway and they locked hands.

Witherspoon was instantly aware of a warm, comforting grip.

"That's it. 'Up, up and away,' as Superman would say," the man added in a soothing voice. He sized up Witherspoon. "You're all dusty on my account." Without stopping to ask, he patted Witherspoon's jacket and pants. "How clumsy of me. In such a rush."

Witherspoon felt the man's hands lightly brush across his crotch. It was soft, but intentional.

"I'm okay," Witherspoon said.

"Good. I do apologize. I insist that I pay for a cleaning."

"No, no, that's not necessary. Look, I have to go."

Witherspoon took a step forward, but the man grabbed his hand again. He felt the warmth once more. "Please, then. Let me buy you a breakfast. You look hungry. It's the least I can do."

Witherspoon hesitated as if to say, *Well, maybe.*

"My name is Mycroft. Terrence Humphrey Mycroft. My friends call me Terry." He still held onto Witherspoon's hand, and squeezed it ever so gently. "Really, let me make it up to you."

Witherspoon was on the run. The man offered him refuge. *Probably more.* He always had a hard time saying no. And he was definitely being asked. *I can disappear with him.*

"Okay. Where?"

"Well, I'm just in for business, but the restaurant at my hotel is just around the corner. What do you say?"

Witherspoon thought for a second more.

"I've just been out for a morning constitutional. My meetings aren't until much later, and I'd love the company. Truly."

"Where did you say you're from?"

"Oh, I didn't, but my accent must be a giveaway. London. I'm an attorney."

"As am I," Witherspoon offered.

"Fine, then let's bore ourselves to death," the Brit joked.

Witherspoon pursed his lips, giving the invitation one last thought.

"Thank you, Terrence. I'm Donald, and that sounds absolutely perfect."

Roarke and Katie went up to Witherspoon's office as planned. After twenty minutes it was apparent he wasn't going to show up.

"Damn!" Roarke exclaimed. "Too much time here. Ten-to-one...no, one-hundred-to-one he spotted us; probably when we were talking to the cop. He split."

"But you'll find him?" Katie was worried.

"I don't know. Maybe. He better hope so."

"Why?"

"Depp doesn't collect if he walks away. My guess is he's out there looking for Donald Witherspoon while I sit around with my thumb up my ass."

"Oh, Mister Roarke, such talk," she joked.

But Roarke wasn't in the mood. He headed toward the door. "Look, pull your things together. Call Davis at the FBI. Tell him you need a ride." He wrote down the number. "You can say your hello's here, then go back to *our place*." He didn't say where, for fear that the room had ears. "Don't leave with anyone Davis can't personally vouch for."

"Yes, sir." She saluted. "You mean I'm still under house arrest?"

"Damned straight. Until Witherspoon's put away."

Roarke left, but only for a moment. "I forgot something."

"What?"

"To kiss you." He took her with both arms and pulled Katie close so their lips met. The kiss took her breath away, and he lowered her slowly to the ground. Before leaving, he softly added, "Be careful."

He was well down the hall by the time she whispered, "You, too."

Witherspoon casually talked to his new friend. If Roarke enlisted the police, which he may have by now, they'd be keeping an eye out for a man on the run, not two businessmen engaged in a spirited conversation.

The farther they walked, the more at ease Witherspoon became. The man touched his back at an intersection; a friendly way to say *let's cross*. His hand lingered longer than necessary. It felt good. Witherspoon relaxed more. *This is going to be just fine.* He was certain that he was in good hands.

The two men rounded the corner onto Broad Street. Terry gently nudged Witherspoon onward with his arm around his shoulder. "Here we are."

Witherspoon had been in the Wyndham Downtown Boston for meetings with clients. It was convenient for the trade, just two blocks from the wharfs, three from Government Center, and only a few minutes' walk from work.

The Wyndham was actually a converted office building; Boston's first skyscraper. Redesigned as a hotel, it blended the original 1928 art deco décor of brass, rich woods, and brick with modern touches.

The lobby was spacious and, fortunately, fairly empty. Still, Witherspoon walked as close to Terry as he could, hoping to hide from anyone who might recognize him. Mycroft steered him toward the Caliterra Bar & Grille, then stopped, allowing his companion to look in.

"A bit crowded, I'd say."

"Yes." Witherspoon backed away. "Is there any place a little quieter?"

Mycroft checked his watch. "High time for breakfast. I'm afraid we're going to find this everywhere." He paused and read his companion's face. "Of course..." he stopped in mid-sentence. "We could take the lift upstairs and order room service."

Witherspoon nodded. "That would be fine."

"Oh, wait. I'm sure the maid hasn't had a chance to tidy up. Why don't you give me a few moments. Then you can join me."

"No, we can go right up," he said, having no desire to wait in public.

"Then up it is."

They walked to the elevator. Mycroft politely held back, allowing Witherspoon to press the button. Ten seconds later, the doors of an elevator to their left opened.

"Here we are. The gentleman first," Mycroft said. "Eighth floor."

Witherspoon did the honors. When the door opened again, Mycroft led Witherspoon to the right. Number 823. "Are you sure you wouldn't like to wait while I straighten up?"

Witherspoon laughed at the double entrende, not his first. "No, I'm ready now."

"Very good then." He fumbled with his electronic pass card. It dropped on the floor. "How clumsy of me." He was slow to bend down.

"Allow me," Witherspoon offered.

"Thank you."

Witherspoon inserted the card into the slot and turned the handle when the green indicator flashed.

"Thank you again, Donald. Just go right in."

Witherspoon led the way. The room, a mini-suite, was immaculate. "Well, look at this. The bed is made already. Bravo." It was as if no one had slept in it overnight.

Witherspoon smiled as he let his hand glide over the bedspread on the way to the windows. "Very nice," he said, looking out onto the harbor.

"Quite so, but I think we can close the shades, don't you?"

Witherspoon saw his smile reflected in the window in front of him. *This is the best place to be for now.* As he drew the drapes over the reflection, the room got darker. His back was still to the Englishman. Witherspoon sensed his presence. He turned around and faced him.

Witherspoon felt Mycroft's hands brush his crotch. "Well, breakfast did sound good, but...."

"My sentiments exactly." Mycroft said softly. He pushed closer. Witherspoon responded by pressing right into his companion's hand. He let out a quiet sigh.

"Why don't you lay down on the bed like a good boy."

Witherspoon obeyed.

"Just relax. Well, not completely. And I'll be right with you."

Mycroft went to his suitcase, which lay on the stand provided by the hotel. He opened it up, with the top blocking Witherspoon's view. "I've got a little surprise for you, Donald."

"Oh?" Witherspoon leaned forward on the bed a little.

"No, back down you go. I want you to be perfectly still." Mycroft busied himself. "What's that on your neck? A little cut?"

"Yes. Shaving this morning."

"What a shame. Such a pretty face, too."

Witherspoon was feeling very comfortable and safe. He all but forgot that he was running for his life less than 30 minutes ago.

"What do you have, Terry?"

"You'll see," the British visitor said seductively.

Witherspoon thought he heard the sound of something being screwed together.

"What is it?" he repeated.

"Something to die for, Donald."

Witherspoon flashed on a funny notion. Everything Mycroft said had been provocative and sexy. But not this time. An uneasy feeling came over him.

Mycroft's hand rose from behind the suitcase. Something long and cylindrical emerged.

"Something naughty?" Witherspoon asked.

"Naughty indeed," Mycroft replied in a soothing voice. A fraction of a second later, he pulled the trigger on his 9 mm Heckler & Koch P7 pistol. The MX12 Reflex Suppressor stifled the sound of the bullet, which created a hole directly between Donald Witherspoon's rather dead eyes. It produced less blood than Witherspoon had shaving.

Mycroft returned the gun to the suitcase and closed the top. He wore thin leather gloves, which he'd slipped on before attaching the silencer. He'd keep them on until he was far from the hotel. There would be no fingerprints, and no trace of a Terrence Humphrey Mycroft. He never stayed in the room. It was merely a backup.

He'd intended to take out Witherspoon with less fanfare, but the encounter with the Secret Service agent required a change in venue. And the assassin was always prepared.

CHAPTER

45

The White House
Monday, 2 July

"**C**an you possibly visit Boston without killing someone?" the president asked.

Roarke shrugged off a laugh. *Yes. Two men in two years. Both hired killers, both dead because they were after Katie.* But now Witherspoon was also dead. This one went into Depp's column, not his. "You can't blame me for Witherspoon," Roarke said.

Roarke explained how a hotel maid discovered Witherspoon's rather ventilated body late in the day when she went in to turn down a bed. Police were all over the room in a matter of minutes. The victim definitely was not the *woman* who had checked into the Wyndham. They quickly ID'd him as a Donald Witherspoon, resident Back Bay, Boston. But the woman? The police sent out an APB for a 35-year-old, lanky blonde from Sante Fe, New Mexico, who checked in with a Mastercard. They couldn't have known that they were looking for someone who didn't exist.

Roarke learned about Witherspoon's death shortly after his plane landed at Reagan National. Earlier in the day, he had alerted the Boston Police that someone may try to kill Witherspoon. Someone did. They told him what happened and where, but that they were looking for *a woman.* Roarke tried to set them straight, but the hotel clerk was insistent that the guest was a woman.

"So why was it necessary to kill Witherspoon?" Taylor asked.

"Because he colored outside the lines. And because Depp can't walk away from money."

"But why?"

Roarke explained his theory. "Witherspoon probably learned she was helping me again. With or without—and I'm inclined to believe *without* approval—I think he ordered a hit on her. It failed."

"Thankfully," Morgan Taylor added.

"Thankfully," Roarke sighed. "But the secret got out. Somehow. Not me. I kept it out of the news. I even stuck Katie in a safe house for a couple of days in Lexington. Still...."

"Haddad," the president said to himself.

"Who?"

"A name. Go on."

"So Witherspoon steps out of line, and whoever the hell he's working for finds out." He picked up a pen on the president's desk and worked it through his fingers. "Just like he finds out about everything," he continued. "And in comes our friendly assassin to clean up the mess. This time he posed as a coffee grinder in a Starbucks opposite the law offices."

When Roarke finished telling the story, Morgan Taylor let out an exhausted breath. "Oh, Jesus."

"We've got to find this guy," Roarke said. "He's positively incredible. He can turn into anybody—a man, a woman. And fast."

"A real chameleon."

"A viper. He sheds one skin and puts on another. All different. All distinctive. And all believable."

"Like an actor?" Taylor asked.

"Someone with phenomenal acting skills."

"And a killing machine," the president said.

"Effective, professional, efficient," Roarke said. "He knows how to complete a mission."

Neither Roarke nor the president had taken seats since their conversation began. They were barely two feet from one another. No microphones, like the ones used by Nixon, were there to record the next part of the conversation.

"I'm going after him, boss. I swear to God I'm going to hunt him down."

"That's still going to leave the man who is making your assassin very rich. He's the one we really need to find."

"Have Mulligan do that. I want the killer."

"Maybe you've forgotten how I like to do things," Taylor scowled. "Everybody's going to work together. No Lone Ranger shit. Do you have that?"

Roarke nodded.

"Good. There's enough crap flying around here now. I don't need you off doing your own thing. You report everything to me."

"And you tell me what *you* know?"

The president was taken back by such a direct comment. "What?"

"The *name*. I believe it was Haddad."

Morgan Taylor let a slow smile spread over his face. He snorted and took his seat, and motioned for Roarke to sit from across the desk.

"Okay, smart-ass, sit down. I've got a little time to kill before I head out to Andrews."

"Where'd we get his name from?"

"Not pertinent to this discussion."

Roarke knew not to press. If Taylor had wanted, he would have told him. "Does he have a full name?"

"Matter of fact he does. Haddad. Ibrahim Haddad. Miami, Florida. Of late, but not recently."

"What a surprise."

CHAPTER

46

Andrews Air Force Base
Suitland, Maryland

Colonel Peter Lewis had the credentials. And he had the stomach. The credentials required him to have more than 2,000 hours in the cockpit, an unimpeachable career record, and worldwide flying experience. The stomach prepared him for being called at the last minute to fly the President of the United States anywhere at a moment's notice.

It had been quiet for a while. *Too long,* thought the pilot of *Air Force One.* He liked being in the air better than on the ground. He felt in control there. He walked around the great plane with the 89th Airlift Wing's chief maintenance officer. "We're wheels up at sixteen fifty-five. We looking good, Rossy?"

"Always," answered Lt. Eric Ross. He cocked his head toward the twin 747 some 200 yards away. "Same for two-niner," indicating that SAM-29000, the twin 747 in Hangar 19, was ready as well. "We'll roll her out in thirty minutes."

"You swap out the nose tires on our bird?" Lewis hadn't liked the feel the last time he landed *Air Force One.*

"Yes, sir. You'll be riding with the Michelin Man. Smooth and comfy."

When Colonel Lewis heard it from Rossy, he believed it. The lieutenant was the best. He ran system checks twice a day and again right before any flight. What he couldn't personally get to, his men did. The next full review was scheduled for 2010, when the twin planes logged 20 years in service. But as far as Lt. Eric Ross was concerned, 2010 came each and every morning.

Still, Lewis kicked the tires. Old habits die hard for the colonel of *Air Force One.* "It'll be good to have Top Gun back aboard." Top Gun was the handle the Secret Service gave to Morgan Taylor, in honor of his years as a fighter pilot.

"Yes, sir." Ross was just as surprised by Taylor's return to the White House as everybody else. He knew the president had more than a basic understanding of *Air Force One.*

Lewis turned the page on the clipboard he held in his hand. "This is not a social visit. We're in and out of Honolulu in four hours."

The flight plan was set. Rossy had been briefed on the itinerary, the number of passengers, and any special requirements for the trip.

"Pretty light in the cabin."

"Right. No press. Just..." Lewis turned two pages to the manifest. "...the chief of staff, sec defense, the press secretary, and J3."

J3? thought Rossy. That stepped up the importance of the flight another notch. J3 was an extremely well-respected and important member of the president's team; a holdover from Taylor's last administration. J3 was the nickname of General Jonus Jackson Johnson. The general, the biggest, toughest officer he'd ever encountered, headed USASOC, America's largest command component of SOCOM, U.S. Special Operations Command. SOCOM answered to the president. It had a wide range of worldwide activities, from covert counterterrorism activities to highly visible military operations.

"Any idea who they're all meeting with?" the lieutenant asked. It was an out-of-line question.

"Not for me to reason why." The colonel stopped himself from reciting the rest of the phrase.

"Four hours."

"Real fast. We're back by twenty-two oh five tomorrow. Just a warm-up. Taylor's got a bigger one coming up soon. Sydney's on the schedule for August."

Lt. Ross glanced up at the underbelly of the jet, hardly giving the comment a second thought. "Yeah, I saw that, sir. I'll be ready."

Katie's apartment
Boston, Massachusetts
that night

"I can't ask you. And I won't," said Roarke over the phone.

"Won't what?" Katie asked. The bugs had been removed.

"I won't ask you to look at Marcus's old phone files or his computer," Roarke said.

"You're right, you can't ask that."

"I didn't. I can't."

"Good. Just so long as we're clear on that," Katie added.

"Completely. Because it would violate your company's lawyer-client privilege to see if Marcus ever spoke to an Ibrahim Haddad who lived in Fisher Island, Miami."

Katie rested the pewter Jefferson cup she was drinking from on her coffee table. Now with Witherspoon dead, she was back in her own home. For safety's sake, an FBI agent still guarded her building from a car on Grove Street. She cradled the phone on her neck and rummaged through her briefcase for a yellow pad and clicker pencil.

"Absolutely a clear violation, even though the lawyer in the relationship is dead," she said while writing the name down. *Abraham Haddid.*

"Well, it's a good thing you're not checking. Because I'd be wrong to ask, and you'd be wrong to check on any *Ibrahim,* with an *I,* Ibrahim Haddad. H-A-double D, A, D."

She crossed out what she had written, getting the correct spelling this time. "No matter how you spell it, it would be unethical."

"And I completely understand that, even considering he may have been involved in a seditious act, punishable under Federal law. You just can't do it."

"That's right. But it's surprising no one thought of this before," she offered.

"Yeah, you'd think," Roarke added.

"Of course, you know it would take a court order. The firm would have to vet the files, making sure only the pertinent ones were pulled. All of that could take a great deal of time."

Katie created a quick chart with arrows.

HADDAD → Marcus/Witherspoon

She looked at it and decided somebody else was needed. *The somebody on Scott's mind.* She added it at the end.

HADDAD → Marcus/Witherspoon ← ASSASSIN

Finding Haddad might help him find the assassin.

"I'm glad you understand the law," she stated.

"That's why I wouldn't ask you to consider this," he responded. "Anyway, where could Marcus lead us? He's dead."

"Exactly." She circled the word *ASSASSIN*.

"Then we understand each other?"

"Precisely. We're in complete agreement on this, Agent Roarke."

"One hundred percent, counselor?"

"One hundred percent."

"Now tell me what you're wearing."

CHAPTER

47

CIA Headquarters
Langley, Virginia

D' Angelo put down his coffee mug on the left side of his desk, away from the computer hard drive. He pressed the power button and waited for his start-up programs to load. When his sign-on page came up, he typed in his password. It also happened to be his childhood dog's name. Moments later, the overnight e-mail dumped into his file from the secure CIA server. The one that quickly caught his attention had no body, just a subject from a Web address he immediately recognized:

Want to take a trip? Ira.

"Yes!" Vinnie D'Angelo yelled. No one heard him, however. After the first day, he beat everyone else in to work. The CIA agent immediately dialed a classified phone number, which connected him to an office in Israel.

"Shalom," the voice answered after one ring.

"D'Angelo," was the simple reply.

"Well, hello," Wurlin said. "I expected I'd be your first call of the day. Do you ever sleep?"

"I sleep. Usually when I'm staring at our surveillance reports on the Mossad. You think you can give our boys something interesting to write about?"

Wurlin laughed. "You're only seeing what we want you to see."

D'Angelo suspected there was a good deal of truth in the remark. The Mossad was one of the world's most effective spy agencies—some days, the best. "Well then, tell me something I don't know."

Now Wurlin added a solemnity to his voice. "There is a man. He can be found in Damascus. He may have information you seek. He worked inside the Capitol under Hafez Al-Assad. I've been told he was privy to who came and went and, to some extent, who said what. He has indicated that he remembers certain things that you might find important."

"Why?" It was always important to understand the motivation of people who felt compelled to reveal national secrets to a foreign government. Money was the worst reason. It made everything suspect.

"He believes that fundamentalists are going to do great harm to Syria...that for Syria to survive as a modern Islamic state, it needs Western friends. You're about to become one."

He doesn't want money. "When can we meet?" D'Angelo asked. He clicked on his desktop calendar.

"You will meet this man in Damascus in three days. Have you been there before, Vincent?"

"No," D'Angelo quickly stated, never wishing to volunteer inform-ation. Even to Wurlin.

"Well, there is a great deal for you to see. You'll especially want to take in the Omayyad Mosque."

Lebanon, Kansas

Elliott Strong was clearly the most influential talk-radio host in the nation, conservative beyond definition; successful beyond the competition. Nobody on the left could touch him. But there was nothing new about that.

Liberal or progressive hosts pretty much faced an uphill struggle. Their primary challenge: attract like-minded listeners *to* talk radio, and *away* from news, classical, oldies, and rock stations.

Generally speaking, they weren't as good as their ultra-conservative counterparts at manipulating the facts and turning public opinion in their favor. Only a few influential voices emerged. No superstars like Limbaugh or Strong. Why? Because too often they used humor, a poor defense against hate. They appealed to logic, easily dismissed by the opposition. When a progressive host succeeded in building a constituency, he, or she, became a target, systematically ridiculed, criticized, demeaned, and, if possible, destroyed. Many didn't have the stomach for it. Most willingly stepped out of the line of fire.

Strong loved letting his rage fly. "Look, I know you liberals don't like me. You've taken great pains to label me the king of *hate* radio. You think by calling me that you'll rally support for yourself. You think that hate will get your leftist buddies in Congress all worked up. You go on and on, whining how Elliott Strong needs to be muzzled. Well, my friends, let me tell you. It's not going to work. Hate's not the issue—truth is, and I'm the king of *truth*. You come to me for the truth. I'm here to give it to you. It doesn't get any simpler than that, not if you care about your country. So listen to old Elliott, the real *heir of America*," he said mocking the progressive radio network.

"Now, let's talk about the truth. Here's what the liberals and the centrists are doing." Strong stepped up the pace. "They're attacking me, which I really don't give a damn about. But I do care that they're trying to discredit a true patriot—General Bridgeman. When liberals can't defend their own flimsy positions, and they can't admit that all they care about is tax and spend, tax and spend, tax and spend, they go after the messengers. Well, *Mister* Taylor—" Strong rarely called him president and always stretched out *Mister*, "—we do have a message for you: You and your imperial cabinet don't represent the American people. You do not represent the majority. Give America back to the people. It's not yours!"

Strong felt he had stirred the pot enough for awhile. "Let's go to the phones."

All the lines were lit up. He'd have another entertaining show, heard across the country and online around the world.

Andrews Air Force Base
Suitland, Maryland

Air Force One gently lifted off the ground with President Morgan Taylor in the forward compartment of Level 2. He'd said his hellos to Rossy, Colonel Lewis, and the rest of the crew before takeoff. Now he wanted to get caught up on his reading. Taylor brought aboard a file from the CIA. It was marked *Libya. Operation Quarterback, Post Game.*

In it were copies of materials extracted from the raid in Tripoli, and a summary of opinion collected by Jack Evans.

Original documents were in Russian and Arabic. Taylor perused the English translations. He was most interested in information pertaining to Russian sleeper spies trained at Andropov Institute under the Red Banner 101 program. The names Teddy Lodge and Geoff Newman were highlighted throughout the document. The president skipped them now. He wanted to re-read the sections that dealt with *other* sleeper spies still at large in the United States. The documents indicated the presence of men and women trained to advance in state legislatures, *Fortune* 500 corporations, the media, federal bureaus, Congress, and the courts.

There were five different references. *Nothing specific anywhere.* Evans had gone to former KGB agents now residing in the U.S. for information. Either no one had anything or they weren't talking. The U.S. Ambassador to Russia made specific inquiries to the FSB, but the intelligence chief of the new Russian spy agency claimed to have no knowledge of other sleeper spies.

And yet, here was the red flag in the recovered documents. *Elected officials, businessmen, who knows? Nearly a President of the United States.*

Taylor wondered whether he had any latitude under the Patriot Act to intensify a national search.

The Pentagon
Arlington, Virginia

"Okay, Penny. What do you have?"

"Nothing *you're* going to get anymore."

Ordinarily, Roarke enjoyed the playful, sexual tension from his former partner. Not today. He'd been through too much recently. He nearly lost Katie, and Depp got away.

"Right," he grunted over her shoulder.

She swiveled around in her chair, away from the computer screen. "You're no fun anymore."

"Sorry. Can we just get to what you've found?"

Captain Walker took Roarke's hands and looked deeply into his hazel eyes. "Scott, I know you better than almost anybody in the world. I know when you're hurt and when you're angry. I even know when you're ready to kill. But before I tell you what I've found, which you'll want to discuss with your friend Parsons, let me ask you one important question."

Her warmth broke through his concentration. He didn't say yes, but he gave her a trusting smile.

"You don't have to go after him, Scott. You have so much more in your life now. We can give all this to someone else. Let the FBI track him down, bring him in, or take him down. You finally have someone you love, someone who makes you happy. Why don't you just go to her." Penny choked on her own words and squeezed his hands, showing how much she cared. "I don't want anything to happen to you. But now there's someone more important than me."

Penny could still touch Roarke, almost as deeply as Katie. He nodded, stifled an affirming sigh, and smiled at her.

"You know, I'm a very lucky man. You've reminded me. I promise you, if I need help, I'll call for the cavalry. I want to get Depp, and if both of us walk away alive, all the better." He let go of her hands. "Does that help?"

"No, you asshole," she chided him. "But I'm sure it'll be the best I'll get from you! Now here, take a gander."

The captain swiveled her chair back around and punched up a master file she'd assembled. "I've sent each of the pictures and backup information I'm about to show you over to your buddy. He'll do more with it than I ever could. But if you want my two cents..."

"I do," he interrupted.

She smiled again. "I thought I'd never hear those two words from you," she said, speaking into the computer screen.

"Oh, you'll trick some innocent fool into saying them, someday," he added. "Besides, I think Parsons wants to meet you."

"Oh? Tell me more."

"Later. Show me what you have," he appealed.

"Okay, like you've said, we're looking for a man highly trained in the fine art of killing. He's also an accomplished actor, probably professionally or collegially trained. Proficient in makeup and dialects."

"Right, and..."

"I followed up on schools, then I thought, how do you go from acting to military service?"

Again, Roarke asked a simple question. "And?"

"Where are you likely to find practical training in both disciplines?"

"I'll bite."

"Come on. Think, sweetheart. Acting and military training?"

"Well, not the Army. Special Forces doesn't have a program of that sort. Neither do the Marines or the Navy. As far as I know, same for the Air Force. I'd have to check if the Pentagon or the NSA has anything."

"Think...."

"Help me out, captain."

"ROTC, Agent Roarke. ROTC. He's in college. The service is helping pay for school. I don't know, maybe he realizes he's not going to really make it as an actor. He advances, moves into one of the special forces divisions."

"How do you run this down?"

"I'm already on it. I cross-referenced ROTC against schools with theater arts departments. I was amazed at how many smaller arts colleges have military programs. About eighty-five schools out of more than seven hundred."

"Pretty daunting," he offered.

"Damned straight. I started limiting the years, sending out e-mails to each of the schools, and lighting candles every night."

"At first?"

"I didn't get very far. But I realized I was going at it ass-backwards. I needed to run a military search on theater majors who entered through ROTC." She clicked her mouse on an on-screen icon, and her computer took her to the first of ten pages of names.

"Jesus!" he exclaimed as she quickly scrolled through the pages.

"About twenty-five hundred names in the last fifteen years. From there, it's just a process of elimination. "I adjusted the search to match your estimates for height and weight." She went to her pull-down menu and clicked onto another file. The list got shorter.

"Next, I entered tighter age factors. No one younger than thirty, no one older than forty-two. You've run into the guy. Safe enough?"

"Safe enough."

She clicked again, another page came up with fewer names.

"Caucasian." Another mouse click.

Now there were only a few dozen names. "Still a lot. So I went one by one. I tossed out the upstanding citizens in the group who had a day job and a solid record. I eliminated anyone living at the poverty level, and I chucked the NASCAR driver in the group."

Roarke gave her a glance that asked *why?*

"Not available for hits on most weekends."

Walker clicked on the menu a final time. "Here's what I ended up with: eight strong possibilities. I sent pictures of seven of them over to your buddy Parsons for further analysis."

"What about the eighth?" Roarke asked.

"No need. He looked good until I found out the guy died in Iraq."

This was better news than Roarke expected. Seven solid leads. He was about to congratulate her when he thought of a question.

"Did you cross-check their acting experience in school? Any idea what their teachers might remember about them?"

"Very good question." Penny paused, then added sarcastically, "Of course I did!"

"Care to tell me?"

"Most of them did better in the theater of battle. A couple had some promise. But what do I know? I always fall asleep at plays."

Hickam Air Force Base
Honolulu, Hawaii

Hickam Air Force Base shares landing strips with the adjacent Honolulu International Airport. It suffered extensive damage and losses, both personnel and equipment, when Japanese planes rained bombs on December 7, 1941. In October 1980, Hickam AFB was designated a National Historic Landmark for its significance in the first day of World War II, and as a staging area for the ultimate defeat of Japan.

Air Force One was on its final approach, two miles out from Runway 4R, the 9,000-foot runway at Hickam that handled wide-bodied jets. Colonel Lewis was in communication with Honolulu Tower. All other traffic was held up as he gently landed SAM 28000. Nothing took off or landed until the president's escorts were also safely down.

Once on ground, *Air Force One* taxied to the Hickam side of the airport and came to a stop. A gangway was rolled up. The presidential retinue quickly appeared at the door. They took in the fresh salt air, then walked down the steps to meet the base commander. After the perfunctory salutes and greetings, the commander ushered them into two waiting limos for a short drive to Pacific Air Force Headquarters. While they made the ride, another 747 landed. Prime Minister David Foss and key members of his government were onboard.

Taylor chose the location—a mid-point, accessible on short notice, with none of the security risks that accompanied a more public visit. The plan was to talk about their next meeting. The one scheduled in Australia.

They all sat at one table. No one wore ties. There would be no photographs to record the session.

The president asked the leading question. "Are you positive it'll be safe?"

Prime Minister Foss, a veteran like Taylor, was not thrown by the directness.

"I cannot guarantee that, Mr. President. But I recommend that we make no public announcement about a change in venue. We simply make a last minute switch, passing up the pre-announced location for a secondary destination."

Taylor looked around the table. J3 agreed. The same for the secretary of state. "One you *can* guarantee?"

"One that we are able to completely sweep. Believe me, this incident has taught us a great deal."

"It's taught all of us, David." It was the first sign that the session was going to be productive. "No chances anymore."

Aboard *Air Force One*
the same time

"Just about fueled up," Rossy said over the field phones from under the plane.

"Roger," Lewis replied. He wanted to stay close to his bird until fueling. Only then would he try to catch a little rest. The president's primary pilot would be back at work in two hours, checking every compartment. Rossy would be on the line with him. The two of them were a team. They relied on each other to make *Air Force One* work. *No chances* was also Lewis's rule. *No chances.*

Lt. Ross believed in the same thing.

CHAPTER 48

FBI Labs
Quantico, Virginia
Tuesday, 3 July

"**H**ere's what I want you to do, Touch. Add a sandy brown ponytail to each of these guys. Give 'em all tans, and narrow their eyes. Make them colder. Can you do that?"

"I can do anything, Roarke. But if you're trying to turn these guys," he pointed to the computer screen, which had snapshot-size photos of the seven "—into *your* suspect, then you're going at it ass-backwards. The whole idea behind FERET is not to turn someone into the person you want. We try to find a *match* for the person *he could be*— like we were doing before. Then you throw this stuff away and get real evidence."

"I got that, but this time I saw him. As close as I am to you right now." Roarke stood beside Duane Parsons, who was at his console. "His guard was down, and he sure didn't expect to be recognized."

Roarke leaned into the screen. He rested his left hand on the photo analyst's chair, and pointed with the right to the eyes. "It's in the eyes. Fix that, and we might get closer to knowing who this guy is."

"I can make his damn dick three inches longer if you want, but like I said, it'll mean diddlysquat if you get to court."

Roarke stepped back. He was getting worked up, and he was pushing too hard. "Sorry."

Parsons swiveled his chair around. He felt Roarke ease up a bit. "Look," he offered, "you want him. He's bad news. He kills people pretty artfully. But because I don't have a real picture to go on, we won't get much more than false positives, matches that look promising but don't deliver. So here's what I'll do. I'll make the changes you want and give you the prints. Then go do your thing. If you do some good surveillance work and e-mail me good pictures—"

Roarke completed the sentence. "Then you'll be able to run a real match. I know. I know."

Parsons laughed. "Well, well, you are learning. It's only taken you a year."

"Right."

"I'm not telling you it's unreliable. But it comes down to photographs. Take the Pakistan program, for example. In oh-four they issued readable passports and national IDs that utilized finger and face biometric technology. They could ensure proper identity verification with a swipe of the card and see if it set off any alarms in counter-terrorism databases. *Viisage* got the contract. They've been able to use face-recognition technology to conduct one-on-one searches against forty million archived images. Forty million, Roarke. But *real pictures* as the base line." He turned his chair back toward the computer. "I'm still making cartoons for you."

Roarke fully understood. After saying thank you, he walked out the door, thinking that the only photo he'd probably get of Depp would be when he was dead on a slab in the morgue.

CHAPTER

49

Verona, Wisconsin
Wednesday, 4 July

Morgan Taylor kept Henry Lamden's appointment with the people of Verona, Wisconsin. It was the first of the semi-regular town meetings Lamden promised to hold. Taylor didn't expect he'd be half as good as Lamden at these events, but it was important to demonstrate that the coalition government worked.

Verona bubbled up from the Office of Strategic Affairs; a recommendation of Lynn Meyerson. She'd discovered that Verona, barely five miles from Madison, was the self-proclaimed "Hometown USA" of America.

"It's the perfect place to kick off your town meetings," she told President Lamden months earlier. "Imagine: 'Hometown USA.' It doesn't get any better than that." She explained that Verona earned the name in 1966, after an army detachment in Vietnam adopted Verona as their "foster village," representing the spirit of American life. "It all began when a GI named Ronald R. Schmidt thanked townspeople for sending the local newspaper, *The Verona Press,* to him overseas. The newspaper printed his letter of appreciation. They loved the fact that Schmidt said getting the paper was one of the few things he had to look forward to. Well, the town rallied around the entire troop and, lo and behold, the moniker 'Hometown USA' was invented."

Lamden had enjoyed the story and appreciated Meyerson's political savvy. Ironically, neither the president nor his aide was onboard *Air Force One* as it touched down in Madison. The day, the parade, and the town meeting belonged to Morgan Taylor.

"Good evening," the president said in greeting. Nearly 1,000 of Verona's 8,912 residents were packed into the Verona Area High School. Taylor thanked the mayor and other notables by name for making him feel so welcome. "First, let me tell you that President Lamden says he'd much rather be here than in his hospital bed." The line received some light applause. "The food is better." More reaction. "And, although he looks good in a gown, I know he'd rather be wearing something like this." Taylor unbuttoned his jacket to reveal a "Hometown USA" T-shirt. The gym erupted, and Morgan Taylor said a silent thank you to Lynn Meyerson.

"But in life, we don't always get to make the choices we'd like. So you've got this old warhorse, and I hope I'm a good substitution."

The crowd applauded until Taylor insisted they stop. "Enough! Most of you didn't vote for me!" The comment brought even more applause. He won them over. What a gratifying feeling.

"Okay, what do you say I hold court for a while, then I'll take your questions?" For the next twenty minutes Taylor gave a solid, off-the-cuff assessment of the first six months of the new adminstration. He talked about the positives and the negatives, the spirit of cooperation, and the attacks on White House policy. He took the citizens of Verona around the world, talking about Middle East tensions, the fragile peace between Pakistan and Afghanistan, and the upcoming summit. Taylor concluded with an appeal for support. "Something happened a few years back. Reason got supplanted by hatred; the calming voice has been replaced by stinging criticism. It's the same everywhere. New York to Los Angeles, El Paso to Verona. It's ruining our country. We are a nation divided by anger, increasingly intolerant and hopelessly driven by rhetoric. We used to have statesmen in government; people who answered the call for public service. Now, I honestly don't know why anyone would even consider running for public office.

"I can't fix this with a signature on a bill anymore than Congress can legislate it. I'm afraid it's up to you to change the political climate. Blow the ill winds away and welcome the goodness that made America great...welcome it back into your hearts and your homes, your community and your country. It's time. And what better place to start than right here in 'Hometown USA.'"

On one hand, it was a pure political play. On the other, it was the absolute truth. Verona agreed. There was no better place to start.

Morgan cut off the applause again. "I promised to take your questions. How about we start with a graduating senior?"

The president fielded questions about the environment, Medicare and Social Security, and even the Packers. Then a 64-year-old, gray-haired man ambled up to the microphone and nervously asked a question. He was hard to hear through the lingering laughter from Taylor's response about Green Bay.

"Again, if you could," the president said. "A little louder."

"Yes. My name is Nicholas Petchke. I drive the bus to the school."

Taylor tuned out his accent and keenly listened for the gist of the question.

"I came from a place where children were killed by suicide bombers, and yet the United States waited years to help. Schools like this were not even safe. Everyone was a target. Now I am here in America. I have a good life. But I am afraid; afraid because I see terrorism coming closer; afraid that America's own people will have to wait years for help, too." The entire gymnasium fell silent as Petchke concluded. "Mr. President, I ask: what's America doing to stop them?"

Morgan Taylor stood some forty to fifty feet from the immigrant, but it felt like the man was breathing into his face. "Well..." he began. But *well* wasn't good enough. Neither was a stock answer, nor a stump speech. Taylor turned around and reflected a moment. The American flag served as a backdrop. He pointed to it.

"Mr. Petchke, you came to this country for the freedom that flag represents, and now you believe that the dangers of the world have followed you here. Regrettably and undeniably, it is true. If I argued otherwise, every paper in the country, including your own *Verona Press*, would prove me wrong. What's America doing to stop them? That's your question?"

He heard a "Yes, sir" across the gym.

"Not enough."

A woman stood from her bleacher seat close to him. She identified herself as a Dane County clerk. "Mr. President, I lost a son in Iraq to a car bomb. My youngest, a graduate this year from this very high school, has just enlisted." She fought her tears, wanting to finish her thought. "Please tell me the same thing won't happen to him. Tell me what you're going to do to protect my son."

It wasn't simply the woman's question, or the man's; not merely a clerk's or a bus driver's. It was America's question. *Tell me what you're going to do to protect my son?*

Morgan Taylor didn't know.

CHAPTER

50

Russia

Anyone expecting Aleksandr Dubroff to take the most direct route to Moscow would have been wrong. Recognizing that he might never be able to return home, he was in no particular rush to get where he was going. Besides, purchasing a ticket for St. Petersburg to the northeast would draw less suspicion from the FSB. But Dubroff wasn't going to St. Petersburg. He got off at Bologoe, 164 km away, had a quiet dinner, purchased a round-trip ticket to Yaroslav, and waited for the eastbound train. Late in the evening he checked into the Kotorosl Hotel, about a ten-minute walk from the Yaroslavl Glavny train station. He produced an identity card—a fake, complete with a bar code, date of birth, and home address. It identified him as V. A. Zastrozhnaya, a grocer from Pskov. Dubroff picked up the card hours earlier from a retired forger who was quite surprised to see him. It had *fallen* out of the pocket of the real Zastrozhnaya, was copied, then returned. The forger prayed that the favor made them even, and this would be the last he'd ever see Dubroff.

The next day, "Zastrozhnaya" returned to the train station and headed south to Aleksandrov. The train ride was pleasant enough. His two-day stay at the Hotel Ukraina was even better. He visited the town, which was his namesake. It had a fascinating history. In the 16th century, Aleksandrov was the unofficial capital of the Russian State under Tsar Ivan IV, a man better known as Ivan the Terrible. For years, the city was recognized as the Russian Versailles, the home of great royal treasures. It was also noted for its prisons, and the horrors its inhabitants endured. Dubroff lost himself in the history and the remarkable Italian architecture. He visited Aleksandrovskaya

Sloboda, the Tsar's former residence and one-time Kremlin, which now served as a museum and nunnery. He avoided conversations with locals, keeping a keen eye out for anyone possibly following him. To the best of his knowledge, no one was.

On the third day, Dubroff continued the remaining 112 kilometers to Moscow, just under two hours. He still traveled as Zastrozhnaya; Aleksandr Dubroff had completely disappeared. Here he checked into the Sovietsky Hotel, a ten-minute drive from Red Square. He booked a third-floor room facing Lenningradsky Prospect. He regularly peered outside through the break in the two drapes to see if the Federal Security Service posted anyone across the street. Dubroff decided not to go out for another day. *That should allow for enough time,* the old agent thought.

FSB Headquarters
Moscow, Russia

"We lost him, sir." The younger FSB agent was fidgety, and with good reason. He was facing Yuri Ranchenkov in the downtown offices of the Federal'naya Sluzhba Bezopasnosti at Lubyansky Proyezd. He was up enough on recent history to know that some of the people who entered these chambers never left. Life—or death—was returning to the buildings that once housed the KGB.

"He's an eighty-eight-year-old pensioner! What do you mean you lost him?"

Sergei Ryabov explained what had happened. It didn't go well.

"He tells someone he's off to see a sick friend in Saint Petersburg. Does he book a train to St. Petersburg? Does he arrive there? No! Why? Because he had no intention of visiting a relative of his wife's. None of his relatives, or his wife's relatives, are still alive. It's all in his fucking biography!" Ranchenkov threw it at the bungling agent. "If you had read it, you would have known!"

Ryabov stood at attention.

"He stopped somewhere. Bologoe? Chudovo? Tosno? Did you check for anyone bearing his description? Did you look in any other cities along the way?"

"No, sir."

"He slipped through your fingers like sand. Will you remember that this man is a master at what he does? Even though he hasn't practiced his craft for years, he hasn't lost it. You better hope that you have a tenth of his ability if you are to make lieutenant...or live."

"Yes, sir," he said. Without asking, he knelt down to pick up the papers.

"You *will* find Aleksandr Dubroff before he is out of our reach. When you find him, you will report directly to me. You will not do anything on your own. That way, we shall discover what the traitor plans to do."

United States

Roarke followed President Taylor's orders. He called his friend from the service. Shannon Davis was very much like Roarke, but blonde and two inches taller. While Roarke went into the Secret Service at Taylor's behest, Davis joined the FBI. They remained close, and kept a running score of who broke the rules more. Right now, Scott Roarke was in the lead.

They figured if they fanned out from Washington, hitting the closest locations first, they could cover the country in two weeks.

The first stop was Maysville, Kentucky, a small town southeast of Cincinnati along the Ohio River. The subject was a high school football coach and history teacher. History was important to Maysville. The Underground Railroad, the pathway to freedom for many slaves, passed through Mason County, Kentucky.

After an hour's observation, from the school to home, Roarke and Davis concluded they could cross the first man off the list. He was a model citizen with a great deal of responsibility and no time to take off.

They had a similar experience at another river town to the south. Their second suspect resided in Knoxville, Tennessee. He was a lineman for the phone company and one glance eliminated him. He'd put on 30 pounds since his years in the service. Apparently his acting career hadn't worked out, either.

Next, Starkville, Mississippi. The two men split up, one checking out the subject at work, the other looking into his family. Bob McCallum looked like he might be their man. His flexible hours as a part-time cop made him suspect. Even more interesting was his work with the Starkville Community Theater. Roarke caught his picture on a poster for *Arturo Ui*. It made his skin crawl. He looked like Depp. He had the intensity and coldness Roarke had seen in person. His pulse quickened. The play was that night. He bought two tickets at the box office.

Meanwhile, Davis stopped by the police station, where he asked to talk to McCallum. He was told he wasn't in. "He's doin' that weird play this week," the desk sergeant reported.

"I was in the service with him. Just passing through," Davis said. "I bet he hasn't changed a bit."

The police officer grimaced. "Guess you haven't seen him in a-while."

"What do you mean?"

"Bob?"

"Yes."

"He lost an eye. Cancer. Just awful for awhile, but he's still at it. Say, what's your name?"

"Ah, Davis." Shannon had already backed up to the door. "Look, tell him hello. I'll try to see him later."

"I probably won't catch him until later in the week."

"That'll be great. Thanks."

Davis left and met Roarke at Cappes Steak House. Roarke was excited to see him. He had a copy of the poster with McCallum's picture.

"I think we've got him. And guess what? He's on stage tonight." He produced two tickets.

"I hope you didn't spend money on these," Davis said.

"Yeah, I did."

"Well, unless we're looking for a one-eyed sharpshooter, I think we should order dinner and hit the road," Davis explained.

"Damn!" Roarke uttered. He looked at the picture and let out a long sigh.

"Sorry, buddy. I'll have the bureau double-check, but I think we're three down, four to go."

Lebanon, Kansas

"Friends, here we are at a crossroads. General Bridgeman is going to go to Washington. Are you going with him? Arm-in-arm. Are you going to show the country that we don't need an election year to be heard? That our voice counts right now? That the administration does not have your confidence and never had your vote?"

Elliott Strong added more timber to his speech. "General Robert Woodley Bridgeman supports you. Do you support him? One by one, members of Congress have contacted the good general since he made his announcement on this show. One by one, they are taking the time to listen to what he has to say. One by one, they are coming to believe that change must occur, and that three-and-a-half years away is too long."

Elliott Strong had launched what amounted to a countrywide political movement. The national media had picked up on the wave of excitement emanating from the center of the country. Thanks to radio, General Robert Bridgeman was heading for the front page.

Washington, D.C.
NBC News, Studio A
Nebraska Ave. NW

"Today, on *Meet the Press*, retired Marine Corps General Robert Woodley Bridgeman," the host began. "General Bridgeman served in Operation: Enduring Freedom in Afghanistan, and Operation: Iraqi Freedom, where he was wounded in battle and decorated with the Purple Heart. He also has been honored with the Navy Cross and the Distinguished Service Medal. He has been recognized for his command of mountain and urban warfare, and now, as a civilian, he represents a growing coalition." The host stopped, and turned into a two-shot on another. He faced General Bridgeman across the table.

"A coalition of what, General? I know I'm not the only one scratching my head in recent weeks, wondering who and what you represent. You have emerged as something of a phenomenon on the public scene. What is your message?"

"Well, first and foremost, thank you for having me on today," the general said, slowly and with warmth. He smiled and stretched out

GARY GROSSMAN

both hands, as if to welcome the audience. The TV director, Ben Bowker, cut to a single shot, which accentuated the expression. "It's a fair and appropriate question. I am, of course, a civilian. My title, these days, is one of a retired serviceman. And I thank you for employing it. But in truth, I am just Bob Bridgeman. A regular guy who's seen an awful lot. Maybe too much for one man in a lifetime."

The host could have jumped in to focus the answer, but he decided to stay out and see where this was going.

"I love my country. I proudly served in the armed forces for twenty-six years. Since retiring, which in itself is hard for me to grasp, my wife has been trying to get me out of the house. She says I'm far too young to hang it up," he joked. "Well, she's right." Bridgeman suddenly turned serious. "I have seen our nation slip and slide into a quagmire of political uncertainty. After all, do we really have an elected official leading the United States?"

"Excuse me, sir, but we do. There was a legal election and the succession acts, enumerated by the United States Constitution, provided us with a stable and orderly process."

"Stable and orderly is quite correct. But now, with Mr. Taylor in the White House, we can't really say that he is the man most voters or electorates wanted. Can we?" It was not a question, and he pressed on. "At no other time in American history has a defeated candidate assumed the role of president. Yes, duly appointed vice presidents have succeeded presidents following their death, but not one who was nominated only minutes after the Inauguration."

"The Constitution," interrupted the host, "does not look at such technicalities."

General Bridgeman rose up in his chair. He found the camera, glanced away from the host opposite him, and said the most profound words of the interview: "It should." *Meet the Press* had been on the air continuously since November 6, 1947. It was the longest-running program in television history; no small achievement in the competitive, cutthroat world of TV news.

Every week, *Meet the Press* not only reported the news, it made it.

Senator Joseph McCarthy attacked his enemies and defended himself on the program. A young Massachusetts Congressman named John F. Kennedy found a national constituency through his appearances. After leaking the Pentagon Papers, Daniel Ellsberg first came out of hiding in front of the show's cameras, during a remote broadcast from

312

the NBC affiliate in Boston. Vice President Dick Cheney disclosed the Bush administration had videotape proof of Osama bin Laden's involvement in the terrorist attacks of 9/11. Every important politician in America used *Meet the Press* to his or her advantage at some time in their political careers. Today, it was General Bridgeman's turn, and the next question was inevitable.

"General Bridgeman, many people have appeared on *Meet the Press* to announce their aspirations for political office. The highest, of course, the presidency. We are years away from an election..."

"A *scheduled* election," the general politely inserted.

The host bore down. "As *presently* enumerated in the Constitution, the first Tuesday following the first Monday in November, General. Every four years. We are more than three years from a presidential election. Will you be on the ticket? And if so, for which party?"

Robert Woodley Bridgeman cocked his head slightly and thought for a moment. "As you have noted, the presidential election is pretty far down the pike. But I intend to take the pulse of the country and determine two important things. Are people happy now? That is to say, will they accept the administration for another forty-two months? That's roughly one hundred sixty-eight weeks. Twelve-hundred sixty days is a long time, and a lot can happen when people want it to."

The host began to cut in, but General Bridgeman continued unabated. "We must listen to the will of the country. It was, after all, the people who established the Republic. Let's just say we'll see what the people want."

The host broke for the first commercial, and worried what would happen if it were really left to the people.

A Hotel Room in rural Kansas

"I got your e-mail." Roarke now traveled with a Treo. "You have some news?"

"Yes. Keeping it simple, you were right," Katie explained. "They spoke. I think it's time for that subpoena. I'll talk to the senior partners and let them know *why* they should cooperate."

"Great, honey. I'll call Mulligan and keep you out of it."

"Thanks, but you know I'm knee-deep already and..." There was excitement in her voice, which Roarke detected.

"Yes?"

Roarke juggled the cell phone to his right ear. His left was actually still blocked from his underwater fight. It was more of an annoyance than a problem.

"I got an unusual call today."

"From who?" he asked.

"Well, if you want to know, it was from the president's chief of staff."

"Bernsie?"

"Mr. Bernstein?" she asked.

"Yeah, that's what the boss calls him. Why did he—"

"With a question," she said. "He wanted to know if I'd be available right away to head up a White House study on possible revisions to the succession laws."

"What?" Roarke exclaimed.

"Hey, I'm allowed."

"I didn't say you weren't. It's just that..."

"Just what, Mr. Roarke? That I'm in Boston? That I'm seeing you? That—"

"Wait a second, I'm happy for you. This is great news, and I'm not surprised. You deserve it."

"But you're upset that he didn't clear it with you first?" she added.

"I'm not upset. He's making a great choice. And if you'd let me finish, counselor, my *what* was leading to a complete sentence: What's the rush?"

"I suspect recent history, for one."

"Point taken," Roarke granted. "So you'll be moving to Washington?"

"Nope," Katie replied. "Maybe some trips down, but most of it can be done on the Internet, at law libraries, on the phone. I will have to interview the leadership in both the House and Senate who have already held hearings and drafted bills. And I'll have to venture back into Justice Browning's lair."

"Brave."

"It does mean I can kiss Freelander, Connors, & Wrather goodbye. Which is fine by me. *If* I take it..."

"Of course you will."

"If I take it," she continued, "there will probably be talk about us."

Roarke smiled. She was absolutely right. It could get in the way, but of all people, Katie could handle it. "Maybe."

"Definitely. But the thing that I'm most worried about..." she started to say.

"Yes?"

"...is how you feel about it. Whether you think I'm encroaching on your turf."

Roarke recognized that this was a serious question that deserved a serious and honest answer. "I think it'll be a real challenge. I think you should take it. I'm proud of you, sweetheart. And I understand you're not ready to completely change your life." He was referring to her reluctance to relocate.

"How'd you get so smart for a man?" she asked quietly. "Thank you."

"I love you."

"I love you more," Katie rejoined. After a beat, she picked up the pace, her nervousness gone. "Again, I don't know if I'll take it."

"You'll take the job."

"But if I do, I'll need clearance to talk with anybody and everybody. I'll need autonomy. I'll need to know the White House's expectations, and I'll need to be above the politics."

"Right," Roarke offered, again in that same tone as before. If one thing was true about Washington, it's that nothing is accomplished *without* politics.

CHAPTER

51

Moscow, Russia
Wednesday, 11 July

Michael O'Connell settled into his room at The National, Moscow's most centrally located four-star hotel. It's conveniently situated opposite the Kremlin on Tverskaya, the city's most chic street, and close to all of the principal locales.

"Public places. Public places only. You have to stay on the tourist routes," Andrea Weaver had explained before he left. "Otherwise you'll draw attention to yourself. In the mid-nineties it was wide open. Not so now. Restaurants, museums, or the shopping destinations only.

"There's GUM Department Store. It's right next to your hotel in Red Square. Americans are expected to go there and drop lots and lots of rubles on designer labels. It'll be very busy and the perfect place to strike up a casual conversation with a Russian. But you're not a woman and your friend knows that. So I'm not sure I'd make a shopping mall the first spot."

"But wouldn't that make it a reason to consider it? Because it isn't the natural place for me to be?" O'Connell asked.

"Possibly," she'd said, though not convinced. "I'd try the museums. The Pushkin. It has the best collection of European and Impressionist art in Russia, second only to the Saint Petersburg Hermitage. Or the Tretyakov Gallery. Absolutely beautiful masterpieces, more Russian."

"I wouldn't do a surreptitious meeting in a museum. Too damned quiet. Where else?"

"Well, outside in Red Square. It's where everyone starts sightseeing."

"Yes. Good idea. That's where I'll start. He'll find me there. Then where?"

"You'll have to play that by ear. "Lenin's Tomb?"

"I wouldn't be caught dead there."

"Restaurant Silla?"

"What kind of food?" O'Connell asked.

"Korean, Japanese, Chinese."

"No. Too exotic.

"Guantanamera?" she offered.

"Sounds Cuban."

"It is. Too un-American. Even for a *New York Times* reporter."

"Besides, I need someplace I can speak English."

"Okay then, the American Bar & Grill. There are two of them. You've got your basic burgers and sandwiches." She'd pulled out a map from her shelf, which O'Connell now had with him. "They're close to the Metros Mayakovskaya and Yaganskaya. A bit odd, though. They've got a Wild West motif: buffalo heads on the wall, saddles, even American road signs."

O'Connell went back to his original thought: the tourist destination GUM. That's what he told Andrea. That's where he decided to go.

Now, with the tourist pamphlets spread out on the bed, he read the history of *Gosudarstvenny Universalny Magazin,* which in English translates as State Department Store. The building was erected in the 19th century as an exhibition hall, and was eventually converted for shopping. At one point in its more than 100-year history, GUM, pronounced GOOM, was the largest department store in Europe. However, calling GUM a department store is actually a misnomer. It's comprised of hundreds of stores. Many closed in the Communist era, due to the fact that there were so few Soviet-made goods people wanted. Today, it's an impressive, three-level privatized shopping mall with brilliant glass ceilings, housing many of the world's most famous chains.

O'Connell didn't assume that the man who contacted him knew where he would be staying, *but he'd certainly count on me hitting the tourist spots.*

Still, O'Connell figured that this man, a former *something* in the Soviet era, had to be old. At least in his late 70s. Maybe even older. So O'Connell would be on the lookout, too, but it probably wouldn't make a difference. The Russian would find him.

Washington, D.C.

General Bridgeman followed his *Meet the Press* interview with a stop across town at CNN, where he was only politely received, and then to Fox News, where the anchors enthusiastically embraced him. He talked about the upcoming march on Washington, and gave them usable sound bites that would last the news day.

"I'm considering my options. If you would have asked me the same question six months ago, I wouldn't have given it a second thought. But now, America is in peril. We are faced with the prospect of nearly four more years of an unelected administration. Never has this happened. Just take the temperature of the country and you'll see how people feel. But the White House wants you to put the thermometers away. They're afraid to read the results. Well, I can tell you, here and now, people are beginning to say that four years is four years too long."

"You have to admit that the Constitution does not allow for a new election," the anchor stated.

The general continued so smoothly as to make everything seem entirely plausible. "Have you counted the mail, the e-mail, and the phone calls Congress has been getting on this? Every single one is from a voter. Voters in states across the nation. Red states. Blue states. That's where the Constitution is changed, state by state."

"Are you suggesting an Amendment that allows for a recall, General Bridgeman?"

"I would support such a proposal."

"And for an accelerated presidential election?"

"I would support such a proposal."

"And would your name be at the top of the ballot?"

"Well, not to beat around the bush, but as I've said before, let's just say we'll see what the people want."

The Fox News anchor broke for the commercial and extended his hand to the guest opposite him. "You know, General," he whispered, "I think it goes without saying that you can count on us for *fair and balanced* coverage."

"I was counting on it."

Damascus, Syria

D'Angelo's last visit to Damascus was with a Congressional delegation. He'd bleached his hair blonde, and passed himself off as a quiet and bored aide to the Senate Commerce Committee. He'd failed to distinguish himself on the trip, and his firing was easily explained to the rest of the group upon their return to the States. During that visit, however, he learned the location of a key al Qaeda training camp from an Iranian rug dealer whose brother drank too much. The compound was obliterated by missiles two days later. The businessman found 500,000 tax-free dollars in his hotel room the next day.

This time, D'Angelo entered the country as Rateb Samin, an Iranian expatriate stockbroker living in America. He told immigration officials in perfect Arabic that he was on a short holiday and he came to visit the major religious sites. He drew no attention to himself. However, for added impact, he observed Muslim law by praying at the appropriate hours.

Actually, D'Angelo considered the 5,000-year-old Damascus one of the most beautiful destinations he'd ever seen. As the oldest continuously inhabited city in the world, founded in the third millennium B.C., Damascus is noted for classic architecture. The buildings date back to the time when the city was the center of the Aramaic kingdom. It thrived through the Greek and Roman eras, and continued to flourish with the Byzantines.

Some scholars maintain that the name is owed to *Damaskas*, son of Hermes. Others attribute the origin to the myth of Askos or Damas who offered Dionysias a skin (skene), a *Damaskene*. Still other historians argue that the designation belongs to *Damakina*, the wife of the god of water.

No matter the correct derivation, Damascus has figured into the Old and New Testaments and the Qur'an. It served as the capital of the first Arab state during the time of the Omayyads in 661 A.D. The Omayyads were dedicated to building a workable infrastructure, organizing the city into districts, and providing potable water to the inhabitants, as well as erecting hospitals, palaces, and churches.

One of their great wonders is the Omayyad Mosque. It was constructed on the site of an earlier Aramaic temple, which, if history served D'Angelo correctly, provided a degree of irony. That temple was dedicated to the Aramean god of the ancient Syrians: the god *Hadad*.

CHAPTER 52

Shawnee Mission, Kansas
Saturday, 14 July

Roarke grew anxious. Three dead ends turned into four. Four obvious cases of mistaken identity. Then five. Now they were onto the next target, a possibility in Shawnee Mission, Missouri.

The suspect performed at one of the local community playhouses, The Barn Players. He didn't seem to have a day job, which certainly fit Depp's profile. He lived in a recently built three-bedroom house on East Green Gables, traveled a great deal, and had just returned home.

Roarke and Davis trailed him for about an hour. He made stops at the theater, a watch repair store, and now he drove his Mercedes, an expensive car for someone without work, into a parking lot at Town Center Plaza, not far from the Sprint World Headquarters on 119th.

"This looks like as good a place as any," Davis said.

"Might as well be here," Roarke agreed.

They held back as the man parked about 50 yards up from the stores.

"Let's see where he goes, then we'll move," the FBI agent added.

Once out of the car, the man walked toward a Sharper Image. "Boy toys!" Roarke exclaimed enthusiastically. It made sense that Depp would want anything and everything on the shelves. But it was his appearance that really made Roarke's heart race.

"This is the guy," Davis affirmed. Roarke silently hoped he was right. His height and weight were dead on. Too bad a baseball cap made it difficult to get a closer look at his face.

"Sure you don't want me to go in after him?" Roarke asked.

"Absolutely not. He could nail you in a second. He doesn't know me from Adam. I'll shop around a little, then hang back when he leaves. You stick by his car. He'll come around, and when his back is turned to unlock the car door, we'll nail him."

The plan was sound. They talked more about whether to call in backup, but ruled it out. It would take another 30 minutes to get more FBI officers to Shawnee Mission from Kansas City, Missouri.

"You just shop. No grandstanding. You have that?" Roarke demanded.

"Hey, it's one of my favorite stores. No problem." But Davis was nervous. He hadn't worked a takedown in years. He sucked in his gut, gave Roarke a salute, then briskly walked to the store. Roarke watched him enter, but that was all he saw—the afternoon glare off the floor-to-ceiling windows obliterated his view. He didn't like it. *Shit!* He wished he'd gone in.

Moscow, Russia
the same time

O'Connell was back at Red Square for the third day. He wasn't used to waiting. He didn't like it, and now everyone was beginning to look like an old KGB operative. He started each of the two previous mornings feeding the pigeons across from the Kremlin. He hadn't seen blue sky yet. Smoke from forest and peat fires outside of Moscow made the gray city even gloomier. After an hour's opportunity to get spotted, he walked to GUM. He spent time going in and out of the stores, visiting only the ones that might be on an American tourist's itinerary. When that failed, he picked up the Metro at nearby Ploschad Revolyutsii Station and spent the afternoon at the museums his editor recommended.

So far, no one approached O'Connell. Not even another American, which he would have welcomed. By the third day—today—he admitted to himself he was ready to call it quits. Even getting through the typical mess at Moscow's Sheremetyevo Airport would be a welcomed change. He'd be happier still after his Aeroflot jet touched down at JFK. O'Connell didn't like playing where the rules were different and so final. And he just kept worrying, *What if they think I'm a spy?*

Shawnee Mission, Kansas

Roarke drew his Sig from his shoulder holster and brought it down to his side. He didn't want to be caught with it in the open, yet at the same time, he couldn't be unprepared. "Nobody come, nobody come," he whispered.

Roarke ducked down and went between the rows of cars until he got a good 25 feet closer to the store. It took six cars before he lost the sun's reflection. He leaned against a Ford Focus. His gun was flat to his stomach with the safety off. He thought he could see his man browsing. Davis was behind him and off to the side.

Two minutes. Three. Roarke wished that he had gone to the bathroom before they started the surveillance. *Stupid,* he thought. Four minutes. *Come on already. Don't you read the catalogue? You should know what you want!* Five. That's when he saw his man making a purchase at the counter.

Roarke took that as the cue to get back into position. This is where it would happen. This is where he would take down Depp. *Right here. Right now.*

Moscow, Russia

It came from out of nowhere. A little shove from the side, and a hint of a thickly accented "Excuse me."

"What?" O'Connell turned to his left, but no one was there. Then he looked ahead. *Yes.* O'Connell caught a glimpse of a man, an older man, already steps ahead of him heading through Red Square in the direction of GUM. He wore a tweed sports jacket with worn elbow patches, black slacks, and dirty, beat-up shoes. He walked slowly, occasionally giving a fleeting, yet thorough, glance back.

The reporter's heartbeat quickened. *That's him!* He had been right. *Red Square and GUM.* O'Connell congratulated himself for his skills as a spy, then quashed the thought. That's not who he was.

No quick movements. Do what you've been doing, he said to himself. *Finish feeding the pigeons and go shopping.* When he picked his head up again, the man was gone. He remembered what he had been wearing. The man also had a newspaper rolled up in his left hand. *A gun?*

O'Connell was suddenly overwhelmed by fear. He found his man.

So had Sergei Ryabov of the Federal'naya Sluzhba Bezopasnosti. A tip from a bell captain at the Sovietsky, one of dozens of hotels he visited, paid off. It seemed money still talked louder in Russia than threats. Ryabov paid 200 U.S. dollars for the information, which led Ryabov to Aleksandr Dubroff in Red Square. He spotted Dubroff walking among the tourists feeding the pigeons. He observed him for five minutes when he thought he saw Dubroff make contact. *A brush pass? A comment? Possibly.* He held back. Dubroff continued through the landmark square. Ryabov looked for the man he bumped, but he lost him. Ryabov decided to stay with Dubroff. He knew he should call Deputy Ranchenkov, but he wanted to redeem his standing; he wanted to bring in the traitor himself.

Shawnee Mission

The man stepped off the curb. He wore jeans and an unzipped black leather jacket. He held a Sharper Image shopping bag in his left hand, keeping his right hand free. Roarke never took his eyes off that hand; the hand that would go for his gun.

He waited for the cars to go by, then crossed to the parking lot. Roarke was able to get a partial view through the window. *Watch his gun hand.* Davis was twenty steps away, at a slight angle, suggesting he was heading to a car parked a few spaces away. He slowed down and reached inside his jacket for his pistol, the 10-mm. Colt.

A few more seconds. Roarke ran the possibilities. *Keep down until he's at the door. Can't make a sound. No reflections in the tinted window. Same for the side mirror.* Roarke looked over his shoulder for a split second to see what his subject could use as cover. *Damn, a van's pulling out!*

The man in the baseball cap halted. A woman with two kids backed out. They could see Roarke. He slid his gun under his jacket. The driver seemed to take forever, actually seven attempts to make what was a three-point turn.

Roarke's target waited, but now the van blocked his view. He lost his line of sight on the gun hand. Roarke hoped that Davis had a clear view, if not a clear shot.

Moscow

By now, O'Connell knew the layout of GUM. The shops opened at 8:00 A.M. and, among the busiest were the ones which sold Krasny Oktyobr (Red October) Chocolates and the lacquered wood Matroishka dolls. Roarke went into the store he thought would work the best: Gallery Bosco di Ciliegi, with its rows and rows of clothes. The boutique was crowded with foreign posh shoppers excitedly browsing through the stylish clothing.

O'Connell entered, knowing the Russian would find him again. He went directly to the far end of the store, where a mirror provided him with a good way to see who came in. He surmised that the man would take his time, first making certain it was safe to enter. He would not rush forward. He would approach calmly.

O'Connell considered how times had changed. Russia was becoming increasingly closed and more secretive. The hammer and sickle were long gone; so were the daily fears of American missiles. But even his newspaper reported on an almost daily basis how the new regime embraced the return of autocracy. Citizens again served the State, not the other way around. Initially, the political shift was blamed on Russia's own war on terrorism. Yet, in too short a time, power consolidated in the hands of a virtual dictatorship that could fight anarchists, or any enemies within, with greater effectiveness. That's what Michael O'Connell thought about as he held up a leather jacket into the mirror. That's what went through his mind when he saw the old man saunter into Bosco di Ciliegi.

Shawnee Mission

Roarke heard some humming as the man got closer. *An oldie. What was it?* He tried to concentrate on getting Depp, but the name of the song was bugging him. A few more seconds. *What the hell is the song?*

The subject rounded the back of the car. Roarke knelt behind the rear and saw his own reflection in the green Toyota parked next to the Mercedes. He quickly adjusted, but the move meant he gave up his vantage point. Roarke heard a bag rustle and the sound of keys. *Bag's on the ground. Keys in his hand.* Then the unmistakable quick beep of the wireless lock unlocking. Roarke stood up and stepped out from behind the Mercedes.

"Stop!" he shouted.

"FBI!" Davis yelled from the front. "Freeze!"

Roarke didn't anticipate what happened next.

Moscow

The man stopped to examine a few items of clothing: a woman's silk scarf, an argyle cashmere sweater, a sports jacket. He appeared to leisurely work his way to the far end of the store. The reporter kept his eye on the mirror. Something new caught his eye. Another man rushed in through the entrance to Bosco di Ciliegi, looking as if he were late for something. He frantically scanned the room.

A frumpy jacket, loose pants. The man was totally out of place, even to O'Connell's thinking. He was definitely searching for someone. *Christ!* O'Connell automatically turned to the side, away from the new man.

Where's...? He caught sight of the old man who brushed him in Red Square. He was a few rows away, walking toward him, seemingly unaware of the danger. O'Connell caught his eye and nodded his head slightly. The *no* was instantly understood. O'Connell cocked his head in the direction of the other man, now fifteen feet away. The old man was able to see his reflection in a store mirror.

O'Connell watched as his contact quickly broke right, putting racks of clothes between him and the second man. Suddenly, a gun was out.

Russians automatically froze. It was impossible for anyone not to recognize the distinctive demand to "Halt!"—which the old man did not heed.

Shawnee Mission

The man froze in place. Roarke issued his next order. "Drop the keys and raise your hands!"

"What?" the man said.

"Arms out. Lie down, face on the ground."

The man's left hand went up slowly. His right hand remained at his side.

"I said, on the ground! Arms out. Legs spread. Now!"

Davis was now ten feet behind and off to the side, avoiding Roarke's potential direct line of fire.

The man was still looking down. He hadn't moved yet, and his hat obscured most of his face.

"FBI! Do as he says. This is your last warning."

The quarry looked to his left, to Davis, and back to the right, to Roarke. Roarke lowered his gun, aiming at the man's kneecap. "You'll be on the ground one way or another."

The man knelt, stretching his left arm forward, but his right was not.

"Arms out!" Roarke demanded!

"I can't!" the man finally said.

"I said arms straight out!"

"I can't!" There was desperation in the man's voice.

Acting? Roarke wondered.

"For God's sake, man, I'm disabled!" The man did his best to get into the spread-eagle position between his car and the Toyota, but his right arm wouldn't move where Roarke demanded.

With the man on the ground, Roarke stepped closer to cover him. Davis closed in from behind. He shoved the man's right arm forward and patted him down.

"He's clean." With his knee grinding into the man's shoulder blades, Davis pulled his hands together and threw on the handcuffs.

"Okay, now up!" Roarke ordered. "We've got a lot to discuss."

Moscow

A shot rang out as the old man made for the door. The old Russian stumbled into a group of Canadian tourists. There were screams. O'Connell froze, waiting for the policeman to find him. But a store manager tackled the gunman. The old man continued a few steps into the common area, finally crashing into a food cart of Krasny Oktyobr Chocolates.

Some people froze, others darted in every direction. O'Connell joined the runners trying to escape. Nobody really knew what to do or what had happened. O'Connell saw the old man on the ground. He stayed with the flow, pushing closer. O'Connell calculated that he only had a moment before the policeman would be on him. He leaned over. The Russian was bleeding, but he was still alive, laying on his side. His eyes were open, but cloudy. A pool of blood formed, soaking the crushed chocolates. O'Connell was a foot from his face.

"It's me. Michael O'Connell," he whispered.

Nothing. He inched closer. "O'Connell. You needed to see me."

The man's eyes widened. He managed a glimpse of recognition that seemed to say, *I know.*

O'Connell glanced over to the store. He saw that the policeman was engaged in a heated conversation with the man who had tackled him. He produced a badge.

With more urgency, O'Connell asked, "Please, what can you tell me?"

"Move out of the way," the policeman called out in Russian. Those who could understand him moved. Others didn't.

The old man grimaced with pain. He blinked once, uttered just one word, then closed his eyes. Even through his thick Russian accent it was distinctive enough to be understood. But it made no sense.

Shawnee Mission

As the man awkwardly rose to his feet, Roarke got a better, closer look. The features were slightly different. His eyes were bluer. He had a thin, but unmistakable scar above his lip. Most importantly, the man didn't show a hint of recognition of Roarke. Not a glimmer of the defiance he expected. It wasn't just good acting.

"Who are you?" the man asked.

"FBI," Davis said, which kept Roarke quiet. A crowd was beginning to draw around. Someone had called the Shawnee Mission police; a siren sounded from a few blocks away.

"Why?"

"Are you Charles Corbett?" Davis said, coming around front now.

"Yes," he managed.

"Former Army Special Forces."

"Yes."

"You're wanted for questioning for—"

"No," Roarke said under his breath.

Davis quickly glanced over, still keeping his gun on Corbett.

"He's not Depp," Roarke said.

"Are you certain?"

Roarke gave him an almost disappointed, "Yes." He holstered his pistol, then stooped down and picked up the man's shopping bag. "I'm sorry."

"Are you sure?" Davis asked again. His gun was still on the man.

"Absolutely."

The local police car rolled into the Town Center Plaza parking lot. Davis returned his Colt to his shoulder holster. "We're going to have some explaining to do."

"Yes, I know." The song Corbett had been humming finally came to him. A Broadway tune, not an oldie. He must have been practicing for a play. *The Impossible Dream.*

Moscow

O'Connell quickly drifted back in with a group of people making for an exit. Once clear, he decided not to return to his hotel. Instead, he went to St. Basil's Cathedral to do something he hadn't done in years—pray. He prayed that he would get out safely, and he prayed that he could figure out what the old man meant.

CHAPTER

53

Moscow

O'Connell IM'd the international desk for any news on a shooting at GUM. The editor pulled up an extract. "Something. Not much."

"What?"

The *New York Times* editor copied the text and sent it. According to a carefully worded *Izvestia* report, a Chetchnian terrorist was tracked by Russian security from Red Square to the GUM department store, where he was shot.

O'Connell IM'd another question. "Was he killed?"

The response. "No mention." Then a question from the editor, who'd suddenly became curious. "Why?"

O'Connell quickly typed in, "Just checking." He shut his laptop down and packed it in his attaché case. He hailed a cab for the airport, anxious to leave Russia. One word played in his mind the entire ride. It echoed through the long wait at the terminal, and it was with him as he finally fell asleep on the nonstop flight home.

Lebanon, Kansas

Elliott Strong chastised his listeners. "I'm telling you right now, you better book your hotel. Three weeks. If you wait much longer, you'll be sleeping on the Mall...which wouldn't be so bad," the talk show host offered with a half laugh. "George Washington's troops camped out there. So did Lincoln's Union forces. The Bonus Army in the nineteen thirties."

Every night he nudged his audience more. The printouts on his desk, sent to him by a friend on the Hill, confirmed the point. Hardly a hotel room was left within the Beltway. General Bridgeman's army was taking form. The networks estimated as many as two-and-half-million protestors were making travel plans for August 18. Strong was right. They were running out of beds.

He switched tones. "Now I just want to hear from people who are going." He gave the call-in phone numbers. "Open lines tonight. Hello, you're on the air."

"My wife and I are," the first caller said.

"Where are you coming in from?" The accent should have been enough to give it away, but the host loved letting people say where they lived. It reinforced the national reach of his show.

"Outside of Mobile."

Strong acknowledged the affiliate station the caller listened to. He didn't have to memorize them. They were always on-screen.

"What's the schedule, Elliott? I haven't heard much about that."

"It's online. We have the link to General Bridgeman's Web site. It starts with a prayer at ten A.M, the Pledge of Allegiance, 'The Star Spangled Banner.' A rock concert until noon, and then the general speaks."

"You're introducing him, right?" A perfect question.

Strong looked at his watch and smiled to himself. "Oh, thank you, but I think General Bridgeman deserves someone far more worthy than me."

Washington, D.C.
the same time

They met for dinner at Washington's Hotel Tabard Inn, a quaint Victorian watering hole and eatery made famous long before novelists like John Grisham wrote about it. The maitre' d placed them in a discreet room up a short flight of tin-lined stairs. Many secretive meetings had been held in this room with presidents and men who would be presidents, political enemies who broke bread together, and allies who broke their promises to one another. If only these walls could talk. So many conversations, so much strategizing, and so much lying over Grilled Hereford Ribeye, Marinated Ostrich Steak, and Rack of Lamb.

Duke Patrick wasn't sure what it would be tonight. Still, the invitation intrigued him.

Patrick, the speaker of the house, was the first to arrive. He passed the time with a vodka martini. Normally he could pack away a half dozen and not slur a line of speech. Tonight, he would make one last.

The general arrived with no fanfare. He was quietly led up the stairs by the owner, assured that they would not be bothered except for the food order, which he would personally handle.

"Well, well, Congressman Patrick, it's so good to see you," General Bridgeman said. He opened his arms to the speaker, who stood to greet him.

"General," Patrick said tentatively. He rejected the bear hug and opted for a handshake.

"No, please. First names. I never want to hear you say 'General' again." He let out a laugh. "Unless it's in public."

Duke Patrick didn't find the comment humorous. "If you don't mind, let's keep it at the general and congressman level for awhile," Patrick said, not giving into the cordiality.

"Well, that would be fine, but I'm sure we're going to find we have a lot in common before the evening is out." Bridgeman motioned to the owner, who had stayed at the door. "Scotch on the rocks, please." Once they were alone, Bridgeman took his seat. Patrick joined him, trying to figure out what political advantage he could garner from the unexpected meeting.

The White House
the same time

The chief of staff asked to have dinner with the president. He had a good deal to go over, and there never seemed to be enough time during the day. They were hardly into their first course, a simple arugula and pear salad, when Bernsie launched into his agenda.

"You're being skewered on the air."

Taylor kept chewing.

"They've accused you of just about everything from a cover-up to a coup."

The president still chomped away.

"Especially on radio. They want you out. They want a Constitutional amendment, and they can get it."

The president wouldn't give up his salad.

"Remember the recall in California? How quickly did they get Gray Davis out of office? Four months? Three? Less? Do you think you're immune?"

Morgan Taylor put down his fork.

"They can do it. You want to know how?"

The president nodded.

"We can thank prior administrations. They pretty much dismantled everything that guaranteed fairness in the media. It worked for Republican and Conservative administrations until now. These days they'll go after anyone because it makes for good ratings."

Taylor eased back in his chair. "Go on."

"A handful of corporations own 100 percent of the broadcast outlets and 90 percent of the cable companies. They own newspapers and radio stations. They own the billboards that the shows are promoted on, and when they decide to go after someone, there's no fighting back because they don't have to provide any airtime."

"So how do we throw these broadcasters off the air?"

"Throw them off? Don't even try to go there. They'll all hide behind the First Amendment. They exist and thrive because they have the right to be on the air. In good conscience, both sides of the aisle said, 'Okay, we'll get rid of all this regulation. Who needs a multitude of opinions? The people will decide what they want to hear and who they want to hear it from.'

"And what do we have? On a national scale, there's Elliott Strong. But locally, some of them are even worse. If you can believe it, there's a guy in North Dakota who goes after the church, the NAACP, and the Jews. In Georgia, there's a host who espouses a manifesto directly from the Klan. We have news directors who won't report the news unless it represents their owner's point of view, and stations that have no community affairs because a) they're not required to; b) they're programmed from miles away; and c) the operators probably don't give a damn what's going on. All together, radio and most of the TV talk is filled with hate beyond anything ever known. Congratulations, Mr. President, you're the most loathed person in the ether. And if you haven't noticed, radio isn't the only place where you're the main course for these media monsters. The worst of it is that the way the laws are *currently* written and enforced, there's no way to cut them off."

Taylor smiled. "You phrased that just a certain way, Bernsie. Complete the thought."

The president followed his argument perfectly.

"Well, you're right. I'm working on an idea. In its purest form it's very simple. Implementation could take some time."

"What do they say about me? I'm all ears." The president referred to his defining feature, which political cartoonists found endless ways to caricature.

"Okay, here it is. Require opposing points of view again. The worst of them will be gone, unable to stand up to any real political debate."

Morgan Taylor pushed his food aside and asked a White House waiter to hold the main course.

"Bernsie, I'm quite aware of these guys, but realistically, America's hooked on opinion. Arguing it, listening to it, and I dare say even complaining about it. We're too far down the line to turn back the clock. And hell, for a long time, I thought these guys were on my side."

"If they were, they're not any longer."

"You're right about that," the president admitted.

"And, we need to change that. *You* need to change that. Make a policy issue." Bernstein stopped, but only to phrase his next comment correctly. He delivered it in a whisper. "You owe it to President Lamden."

Morgan Taylor did not rush to answer, so his chief of staff went on. "Try this on for size. Call for the resignations of every FCC commissioner, no matter who they are—even your appointments. Then reconsider them on a one-by-one basis. After that, meet with the majority and minority leadership of the House and Senate. Bring in the chairs of the Communications Committees and Subcommittees, too. The Secretary of Labor can determine whether the giant media conglomerates fail to meet the test of *any* anti-trust laws, and the attorney general can examine the holdings of all these vertically integrated companies."

Bernstein hardly paused to take a breath. He was wound up tighter than an eight-day clock. "I'll get you lid-tight examples—and I mean lid-tight ones—on TV station abuses that under the Fairness Doctrine would never have happened. We'll revisit the deregulated license renewal procedures and prosecute clear violations. Finally, you order a Justice Department review of station news operations and call for the drafting of a new Doctrine. You can announce all of this at a press conference after your trip. Hell, if Janet Jackson's tit was worthy of front-page news, then let's strip the whole industry bare!"

The president politely listened to Bernstein. When his chief of staff finished, Taylor pointed out, "Just one problem, Bernsie."

"What's that?"

"It's not our party's fight."

"It has to be somebody's," Bernstein replied. "Because if we don't do something, it's going to get a whole helluva lot worse."

U.S. Interstate 735 North

A summer storm pelted the rental car on the way to the airport. The rhythmic whoosh of the windshield wipers lulled Shannon Davis into a deep sleep. Roarke was at the wheel. He aimed an air-conditioning vent at his face to help him stay awake. He also tried to find a radio station worth listening to; the choices were either country music or talk. One show in particular seemed to be everywhere up and down the AM dial. He gave up on AM and chose an FM jazz station. But Roarke didn't listen. He kept replaying an old conversation with Penny Walker that was still fresh in his mind.

"Eight strong possibilities," Penny Walker had said. "I sent seven of them over to your buddy Parsons for further analysis."

"What about the eighth?" Roarke remembered asking.

"No need. The guy died while on a mission in Iraq."

Roarke shut off the radio. "Damn it!" he said aloud.

Davis stirred. "What?" He'd only been asleep for ten minutes. It felt like ten hours. "Are we there?"

"No. But we may have another stop."

"There's no other stop."

Roarke checked his rearview mirror, signaled, slowed down, and pulled off onto the side of the road. "Here—you drive."

"Why? What?"

"I need to talk to Walker, and I need to concentrate."

"Okay?" Davis said, not hiding his confusion. They switched positions. "Still heading to the airport?"

"Yes...no...probably." Roarke hit speed dial on his Treo. "Hell, I don't know."

"It's a little late, Agent Roarke."

"Sorry, Penny, but I need you to go back to work. Please," Roarke pleaded over the phone. He was not cheerful. "Come on...."

"Look, sweetie," she said, "I get it, but if we're going to start from scratch, it'll take more than a quick trip tonight. Give a girl a break. Come home, we'll do this together tomorrow."

"We don't have to start over, Penny. I just need background on the last guy."

"What last guy? You checked out all seven."

"Yes, but it's number eight I want."

"Number eight? There is no number eight. Just seven. Remember?"

"Seven live ones. But you had an eighth that you threw out."

"Because he was dead! KIA!"

"I want to see the details in his file, Penny."

"He's dead and I'm tired."

"Penny...."

Cpt. Walker fell silent for a moment.

"Penny, I need it. I need you to get it for me. I'm tired, too. I'm pissed off. You're only twenty minutes away and I have to find this guy. Please!"

"Okay, okay. You still carrying your Treo?"

"Yes."

"Then sit tight."

"About how long?"

"Roarke, you just got me out of bed at home. You do remember where that bed is." There was a seductive edge to her comment. Then she got sharper. "And it's not in the Pentagon! I'll e-mail you with anything I can find. Hometown, parents, who he took to the prom. Whatever I can dig up. Now leave me alone!"

Walker hung up, and Roarke turned to Davis. "We're on."

"How soon?" he asked. "And where to?"

"Dunno. She'll let us know where." The bigger question was *who?* Would she find anyone who might be able to lead them to a dead soldier?

By the time they returned the car to the airport drop-off, it was too late to get a plane out. The last of the night's outgoing flights to the Washington or Baltimore area left at ten forty. Roarke and Davis opted for two rooms at the Marriott, located on the property a few minutes away. Roarke sent Shannon to bed, warning him to be ready to roll at 0500. Once in his room, Roarke ordered a club sandwich from room service and waited.

Sixty minutes passed. Roarke was tempted to call Walker at her office, but he resisted. *Don't bug her.* At 0030, an hour later for Cpt. Walker in Virginia, the e-mail arrived on his phone. Roarke pushed his half-eaten sandwich to the side and read the full file. There wasn't much. He finished it in three minutes. However, another e-mail followed with more...then another. Penny Walker was going much further than he expected.

At 0112, after e-mailing Penny a thank you, Roarke logged onto Orbitz. He booked two tickets to Columbus, Ohio. He called the front desk for a 4:30 wake-up call. The last thing he remembered was willing himself to sleep.

"Rise and shine," Roarke said over the phone. "We're out at oh seven fifteen on Delta to Columbus. We get into Cincinnati at twelve oh one."

"Got it," a tired Shannon Davis replied. Roarke heard a big yawn. "And then?"

"I'll fill you in on the way. You ready?"

"Yup. Your guy's still dead, right?"

"We'll find out."

54

Sunday, 15 July

R oarke spoke from memory just above the din of the jet engines. His notes were in his attaché case. Davis leaned into him and sipped a virgin bloody mary. Roarke was in mid-thought.

"High school in Cincinnati. College in Chicago. ROTC. Then a distinguished service record. Army Rangers. He was sent to Iraq. While on a patrol, his squad was lured into an apartment building. They thought they were freeing hostages. It was a trap. Once they were inside, terrorists remotely detonated a bomb. Everyone was lost."

"Jesus." Davis remembered reading about the deadly attack. "So he's dead."

"On paper," Roarke observed. "We're going to talk to his parents about his life."

West Chester Township, Ohio

They drove up a beautiful, tree-lined street in the Cincinnati suburb of West Chester Township, roughly 20 miles from downtown. West Chester was emerging as one of the fastest-growing and most desirable communities in the U.S. The homes ranged in value from under $200,000 to a half-million on up.

"Just ahead," Davis said, acting as navigator in their latest rental car, ironically, a blue Kia sedan.

They rolled up to a custom-built, three-story brick and wood colonial on Hidden Oaks Road. "Nice digs," Roarke observed. He wrapped up a half-eaten club sandwich and took the last swig of to-go coffee.

"You bet." The house definitely appeared to be on the the high-end of the homes in the area.

The lawn was immaculate, with seasonal flowers outlining a walkway through the quarter-acre front lawn. The entrance, faced with warm white shale, welcomed the two unannounced visitors. "This place takes real money to keep up," Davis concluded.

But another feeling came to Roarke. "I have a strange sense of déjà vu," Roarke volunteered as they got out of the car.

"Meaning?"

"That I feel his touch here."

"How so?" asked Davis, coming around the car.

"Hard to describe." Roarke continued to stare at the striking home. "It's not the house that's similar, not at all. It's the feeling. It reminds me when I visited a woman in Massachusetts last year. Her place was simple. She was the mother of Teddy Lodge's high school girlfriend. She died in a hit-and-run accident. The killer wasn't found." Roarke stopped and completed the thought directly to Davis. "Imagine that."

"The work of your infamous Mr. Depp?" Davis asked.

"Not impossible."

"Well, then, let's meet Bill and Gloria Cooper and see what happens to that feeling."

The humidity hit them halfway to the house. But both men couldn't take their jackets off. Visible guns, even holstered, were not a good way to say hello.

Roarke rang the door bell. "Coming," they heard from inside. A beautiful inlaid wooden door opened a few moments later.

"Hello," said a rather formal, almost stiff woman. She looked to be in her early seventies.

"Mrs. Cooper?" Roarke asked.

She sized up the visitors and didn't like what she saw. "Yes," she said coldly.

"My name is Scott Roarke." He turned to Davis to do the rest of the introductions, which deftly spared him from actually saying where he worked.

"And I'm Shannon Davis, from the Federal Bureau of Investigations." He produced his ID.

This reinforced her instant dislike. She barred the door.

"Mrs. Cooper, we'd like to talk to you."

"Why?"

Davis looked behind him and down the street, a move which suggested the conversation really should move inside. "It's about your son."

"Considering you're from the government, Mr. Davis, you know full well he died years ago in Iraq. There's nothing more to talk about." Her voice cracked. Tears were just behind her bitterness.

"Yes, we know that. We'd just like to learn more about him, what he was like as a boy, what his aspirations were."

"Why?"

They knew this question would come, and they had rehearsed the answer. Davis continued to take the lead.

"Leadership characteristics, Mrs. Cooper. He had such special talent, from football to theater. And he gave his life for his country."

"You took his life."

"We know what happened, Mrs. Cooper. We'd like to talk about it," Roarke tendered.

After a long thought, where Davis was certain she would close the door on them, she finally stepped aside. "Come in, I'll get my husband."

The New York Times
New York, New York

Michael O'Connell walked into his editor's office, dumped his backpack on the floor, and parked a rolling Travelpro suitcase against Andrea Weaver's wall.

The city desk editor looked up and smiled. "I don't suppose you have a story yet?"

He'd called two hours earlier from customs. He didn't get into anything at that time. "No."

"Any chance you'll be coming up with one soon?" Weaver asked quite seriously.

"Not unless you'd be interested in a one-word story."

"What do you mean?"

O'Connell launched into an explanation, including the Chechen cover story.

"That's all you got? That's all he said?"

"That's it. I still don't know who the hell he was."

"Are you sure you heard him right?"

"I think so. He had a thick accent, but it's not as if he gave me a lot to memorize."

"I don't get it. It must have been something else," Weaver proposed. "Have you checked with any translators? It probably isn't even English."

"I swear to God. That was all he said. It was in English. But I will check."

"It doesn't make any sense. Do you think it's some kind of threat?"

"Don't know. But I think he would have added *missiles* or *bombs* to it."

"And he's dead?"

"I didn't stick around to find out. But I think so."

"You sure he didn't whisper anything else?" Weaver asked.

"Look, we didn't have a chance to go out for a drink. He got fucking shot!" The reporter exhaled deeply. "Apparently, the FSB was onto the man. I'm lucky I got away."

"Tell you what," she recommended. "Go to the Internet. Type in the word, add any other fields you can think of, and see if something registers."

He'd already planned on doing that.

"I think you better consider all the possibilities," she added. "You have an expensive trip to account for."

O'Connell picked up his bags and left, not worrying about the cost of the trip, but the cost of *not* finding out what the man meant. He headed straight for his desk in the City Room. He ignored the e-mails and started with Google.

"Okay, Ivan," O'Connell said to himself, "what the hell were you trying to tell me?" He typed in the letters and waited to see what his first search produced.

West Chester Township, Ohio

Roarke and Davis were led into an airy living room with a vaulted ceiling. Gloria Cooper then excused herself to talk to her husband.

Roarke's eyes wandered from the cherry cabinets and leather furniture that defined the room, to the French doors leading to the back yard. He looked through the glass. A garden pathway led past a small stream. The property stretched on into the woods, which bordered the Cooper's home. It all appeared beautiful and, to Roarke, pristine.

Roarke turned back to the room. It was dark and cold, and although it was completely decorated, it also had an unused quality about it. The focal point was a shale fireplace. Above the mantle was a large photograph of a young man in a uniform, set off by an ornate frame. Richard Cooper.

Roarke stepped closer, utterly transfixed. He turned away only when he heard the footsteps of the Coopers coming into the room. Roarke and Davis had been alone for five minutes. Gloria Cooper obviously had used the time to convince her husband to come downstairs and listen to the visitors.

"Mr. Davis, Mr. Roarke, this is my husband, Bill."

"Hello," he said. Roarke gave him a quick study. Five-eleven, once taller, 210 to 220 pounds. High cheekbones. Thin lips. Short hair. Not unlike the man in the photograph.

"Mr. Cooper, thank you for inviting us into your house without any notice." Davis continued to do the talking for the team. "We appreciate it."

Davis restated the lie that brought them there. Mrs. Cooper invited them to sit down on the couch. The conversation started awkwardly. The Coopers were visibly guarded.

Roarke remained quiet through the first five minutes, encouraging them with smiles and nods. He continued to look around the room, often coming back to the picture above the fireplace.

"Richard got the acting bug in high school?" Roarke finally asked.

"Yes," said Bill Cooper. "He was a great football player, but in the off-season he discovered acting through Moeller's improvisation group."

"Moeller?"

"Moeller—it's a Catholic school that had a powerhouse football program for years. Probably will again. But while he was there, it lost ground to other schools and Richard tried acting. He loved it. Pretty soon, he told us he needed more than what Moeller offered."

"Yes, but remember what he said?" Mrs. Cooper asked her husband. "He wanted to do *important plays and grand roles.*"

"That's right," he agreed. "Grand roles, so he told us he wanted to transfer."

"I remember sitting in our house, not here, our old house, and talking to Richard about his choices," Mrs. Cooper explained. "We didn't really understand theater. We sure knew football. Everybody in Cincinnati does. After all, Bill was a running back in high school. That's where I met him. And Richard had all his talent—"

"And more," Bill added.

"But we didn't want to tell Richard what to do. Not that he would have listened," continued Gloria Cooper. "He was always so head-strong. So one day he announced that he wanted to apply to a high school across town. The School for Creative and Performing Arts."

Bill Cooper picked up the story. "He felt he would get more out of a theater program than sports. That's where he went. He did every play he could and never looked back at football again. He said he wanted to go into acting. He checked out colleges and chose North-western. He got a partial scholarship, but he still needed more help. We wouldn't have been able to do it without that."

Roarke held onto that thought for a moment. The Coopers were certainly living well. *Very well for a retired auto mechanic and dental hygienist,* he judged. He made a mental note to have their financial records pulled.

"Army ROTC?" Davis asked.

"Yes, they helped pay for school," Bill said, suddenly losing his enthusiasm. "I wish..." He stopped short of completing the thought. He reached for his wife's hand, but she pulled away.

Roarke immediately sensed the change of heart. He steered the conversation back in a lighter direction. "Tell us about the plays he did." He wanted to learn about specific roles.

It was a better place to go. Gloria Cooper found happier thoughts again. "Oh, everything. More improvisation, musicals, dramas." She went on to list his credits—Shakespeare, Ibson, Miller.

Roarke memorized them all. *Important plays and grand roles.* After the Coopers shared more recollections, Roarke was ready to return to Richard Cooper's early Army training, but in a less direct way than Davis had chosen. "Now, ROTC isn't quite the ticket to Broadway."

Mrs. Cooper looked at her husband. He waved her off. He wasn't prepared to tell the story.

"As we said before, we needed the money," she stated. "Richard told us that it would help him."

Bill Cooper interrupted. "They trained him to kill. And then they took him to Iraq. He never did another play."

Tears formed in Mrs. Cooper's eyes, but only for an instant. The coldness she exhibited at the door returned. She willed the tears away. Her resolve drove the next thought. "I'll tell you what *your* government did to our boy," she said directly. "It's in all his letters. You took his dreams away from him. You killed his spark, his joy. Oh, not at first. He couldn't wait to get back, to find his way to New York or Los Angeles. But, as so many of his friends died, I felt like he was driven by something awful. His letters got more depressing. He wanted to leave and he couldn't. So I think he acted his way through what he had to do. God only knows what that was. He never told us. And then one day, the boy we raised was gone."

The New York Times

"Damnit!" O'Connell cursed. The word produced too many random hits.

Weapon. Bomb. Army. Navy. Air Force. Submarine.
Spy.

He ate at his desk, trying other word combinations. O'Connell didn't know whether he'd even recognize a clue if he stumbled onto it.

West Chester Township, Ohio

The Coopers recounted the horrific story that Roarke had read about the night before. It was tenfold more difficult to hear in person.

"It was an afternoon in September two thousand four." She gave the exact date, something Roarke already had in his file. "Richard was part of an Army Special Forces squad that was sent to clear out Iraqi terrorists from an apartment building in Baghdad. I still don't know who they were. Sunnis or Shiites? They're all the same to me," Gloria said, dissolving into tears.

Bill cleared his throat and continued for her. "Richard and his buddies were lured into the building. It was pretty crazy just before the election. Everyone seemed to have a gun and Americans were being picked off right and left. It was insidious. They never should have been sent in. A CNN reporter said so. I have the tape. Apparently they heard that from a colonel who admitted it after the fact. After the fact! Why didn't he make that decision before he sent those boys in? They pleaded with their commander. The whole thing was up in the air for an hour. The news interviewed someone who said that they were being pushed in to show the Iraqi Interior Ministry that the U.S. was fully committed. Well, the order stood. Richard and the others did what they were told."

Gloria squeezed her husband's wrist. "Richard was one of six. All brave boys. All with dreams, too. All with parents like us, still wondering who in their right minds could have ordered them into that death trap. No more than a minute after they went in, the apartment building exploded. Five floors. The whole thing collapsed in seconds."

Bill fought back his own tears, determined to finish. "No one else was there. Only the six of them. It took weeks before they cleared out the rubble. They found parts of them, Mr. Roarke. Only parts of them. Arms, legs. Faces blown off." He stopped one more time to collect his thoughts. "It was a huge explosion. One of the most destructive. You want to know the worst of it?"

Roarke and Davis didn't need to acknowledge the question. The answer was already on Bill Cooper's lips.

"We don't even have Richard back. His body vaporized in the explosion."

There was a long silence, which no words could effectively fill.

"Oh, we did get a letter from the secretary of defense. It was signed by a machine."

The proud, lonely parents talked about their son for another 20 minutes. For part of the time, he wasn't dead. Richard Cooper was alive and vibrant.

Eventually, they ran out of things to say, or at least the desire to talk anymore. The Coopers retreated to the quiet sadness that had engulfed them for years. They buried him again, and it was time for Roarke and Davis to leave.

"What will you be able to do with what we've told you?" Gloria asked as they approached the door.

They looked at each other, not wanting to lie, yet not able to tell the truth. "We'll discuss the command issues you brought to our attention," Davis offered.

"And I promise you, we'll look at every aspect of the investigation into his death," Roarke added.

"Thank you," Gloria Cooper quietly responded.

"There is an additional thing that could help us," Roarke said.

"Yes?"

"Can you loan us any photographs of you with Richard."

The Coopers showed their confusion over the request.

"Family shots. Maybe over the years of all of you together."

"I don't understand."

Roarke tried his best to deflect the question, not wanting to explain the real need. "I think the nation owes you a debt of gratitude. You have a story that should be heard. Also, I can tell you right now that you and the other parents of your son's squad will receive a proper letter. That will happen if I have to go to the president myself."

Davis swallowed hard. Of all things, that would be the easiest for Roarke to accomplish. But they didn't know that. They really thought he was with the FBI.

Roarke continued. "It may be of little consequence now, but that's one wrong that will be righted."

"Thank you," Mrs. Cooper said, forgetting she'd actually asked a question. She went back for the photographs, taking pictures out of frames that lined the hallway. While she was away, Roarke let his eyes wander around the house. It was decorated with new furniture, original paintings, crystal fixtures, and marble. Everything was beautiful, as if chosen by a designer with little regard to budget.

"Here you are," she said. She let her hand lovingly graze across the top photograph. "This is the last picture we took together. At our old house."

Roarke saw proud parents and a handsome son. They stood at the front door of a modest Cincinnati home.

"Our neighbor took it." She was about to hand it to Roarke when she asked, "We'll get these back soon?"

"Yes, I promise. Thank you again for inviting us into your home," Roarke added. He gazed around one final time. "It is magnificent."

"We can thank Richard," Bill Cooper volunteered.

"Oh?"

"In a manner of speaking," he added. "Insurance policies he got abroad. We didn't know about them, but then Richard always was dramatic. We went from living paycheck to paycheck to having money in the bank. It was quite a surprise to us. But he always said he'd take care of us. I guess he has." He opened the door for his guests. There was nothing further to say.

CHAPTER 55

West Chester Township, Ohio

Shannon Davis tugged at Roarke's arm before they were at their rental car. "What was that all about?"

"What was what?" Roarke looked like the cat that swallowed a canary.

"How long have I known you?"

"Fifteen years."

"Since service."

"Yes," Roarke answered.

"So I can tell when you flash onto something. It just happened in there," Davis explained.

"When we get in the car," Roarke said. He tossed Davis the keys.

A block away, Roarke got the third degree again. "So?"

Roarke turned in his seat to face the FBI man. "You saw their house. Pretty spectacular for two blue-collar retirees."

"Cooper said it. Their son's insurance policy kicked in."

"For that?" Roarke pointed his thumb in the direction of the house. "That's more than insurance."

"Come on, not if he had a million-dollar policy. And what's to say it wasn't more?"

"And the premiums? Not on the pay of a Ranger. No, there's more money there than from an insurance company check. Besides, Cooper said it came from an insurance payment abroad. What's the chance of that?"

Davis steered to the side of the street and rolled to a stop.

"Their son sent the money?"

"Somehow, yes," Roarke answered. "Stay with me for a minute. He goes into a death trap, furious over the command decision. Everyone dies—well, maybe everyone. His body is never recovered. Assume he survives the bomb blast. The only one. He's obviously changed by the experience. He comes out vowing revenge. He blames his immediate supervisors. He blames the president. Hell, I wouldn't be surprised if we check the record and discover that people involved in the decision to take the building met a rather sudden and tragic end. Okay, he's officially dead. Figure he wants to come back to the States. But he needs money. He makes some inquiries, probably internationally. What does he do? He acts and he kills people. Coldhearted. Cold-blooded. He becomes an assassin—a highly paid assassin. Maybe the highest the world has ever known. The new Jackal. He has money in offshore accounts. He sends a little stipend to Mom and Dad."

"That would be hard to do. The Patriot Act's banking provisions flag anything over $10,000 from a foreign bank. That's why there are a lot of transfers for $9,999.00. But even then, it starts getting suspect."

"Okay, that's assuming it came in through normal channels. What if it didn't? What if they were given an offshore account to draw on? What if they got cash? What if a Lamborghini showed up in their driveway and they sold it? I don't know how, I'm sure you have ways to find out."

Davis seemed to be on board. "You think they know he's alive?"

"I don't know." Roarke thought for a second. "I don't think so, unless Gloria and Bill are as good at acting as their son. But I'd say no. Maybe he'll make an entrance someday, but right now he's dead. He's provided for them. That gives them comfort. Beyond that, I don't know what to think. I'm sure he's kissed off everyone else who used to be important to him, too. But it's worth checking. Old girlfriends, teachers, anyone we can come up with."

"The money still has me stymied. I can't quite figure how he could have done it without setting off alarms."

"Maybe he had some help."

Davis gave the idea some thought. "Like Haddad?"

"Exactly," Roarke said.

Chicago, Illinois

Luis Gonzales listened to his dreams. Since he was a child he felt the Prophet himself spoke to him through dreams. He saw signs and faces. There were words that showed him the way, and warnings that foretold where he would fail. For years his dreams provided encouragement and comfort. Then, shortly before Teddy Lodge was to ascend to the presidency, they became darker. His sleep turned fitful. His plan failed.

Now his sleep brought new dreams. *Millions of people in a wide shot. A thunderous, rumbling crowd but with only one voice. Individuals pop into view. They're hypnotized by the speaker. Phrases, not sentences. No one blinks. The wide shot again. There's movement to the crowd. First a gradual wave in one direction. Wider. Suddenly, it changes. A million people scattering in a million directions. The one voice is replaced by shrieks and screams. A wall rises around them; a wall of marble buildings and monuments. Wider still. Smoke begins to obscure the masses. Wider. Now the outline of the United States. Smoke engulfing the entire nation. Then he zooms through the smoke to another part of the world. A flashback. More screams, but this time his own. He is a young man sitting alone in a courtyard, rocking back and forth. Holding a little girl in his arms.*

Gonzales suddenly awoke. Everything remained clear: The Prophet speaking to him...connecting present to past...past to present. Today he was Luis Gonzales. In another time, Ibrahim Haddad. He was both the man wreaking havoc and the tortured soul.

He needed his inhaler.

Lebanon, Kansas
Monday, 16 July

"I really do worry about my liberal friends."

Actually, Elliott Strong had no liberal friends. For that matter, he had few friends at all. But he continued to pummel the enemy. "They're living in a fantasy world. The liberals complain, *'Nobody likes us. Nobody. Not the French. Not the British. Germany, no. Japan, no. We're all alone.'* Well, they're right about part of that. But do they do anything with the knowledge? No! Well, let me tell you, having alliances with countries that don't stand by us are a waste of time. Their armies are a joke. Their economies couldn't last a day without our help. It's time we all recognize that everything comes down to one little area of the world; one plot of land where the future—whether it's peace or the end of days—will be determined. Not Europe. Not Asia. Not Africa. The Middle East, people. Wake up to reality. If we're to survive, we need to make friends with the people we've made enemies of. It doesn't take a rocket scientist to figure that out. Forget these Machiavellian wars, people. Islam is spreading, even in the United States. The most recent census? Well, let me give it to you in broad terms. According to the U.S. Department of State, Islam is one of the fastest-growing religions in the country. Within a few years, America's Muslim population is expected to surpass the Jewish population. Did you get that? Let me say it again slower. Soon, there will be more Muslims in America than Jews. That will make Islam the country's second-largest faith after Christianity, my friends.

"They're here in the United States of America. And they're not leaving. They come as immigrants. About seventy-eight percent versus twenty-three percent who are born here. I can't give you exact numbers, but best estimates indicate there are approximately six to eight million American Muslims. And if you think this is anything new, read your history books! The earliest Muslims to arrive in this country came as slaves from West Africa in the mid-fifteen-fifties.

"So what will happen when they become the number-two religion? They'll demand more. They'll get their people elected. They'll get their agendas through Congress—all within their rights as Americans." He let that thought settle in before continuing. "Their right and their privilege. They're not going away. How's that for a reality check? And what are we doing to prepare for this inevitable shift in American culture? I could go to the phones and let you try to guess, but I'll make it easy for you, because I know what we're doing for that eventuality. Exactly the wrong thing! We keep supporting the *one* nation in the world that turns all these people, every one of them, into our enemies." He finally drew in a breath. "No wonder we're so damned hated."

Strong felt he had lectured enough. He lightened his voice, seeking to take the edge off his attack that never once mentioned Israel directly. "There's room for all of us. I'm not saying don't support an old ally. But we need to create new ones." This was Teddy Lodge's position for anyone smart enough to notice. "New ones," he repeated. "Nations that will become more important to the well-being of the world. I wish my liberal friends would understand that."

Elliott Strong's circle of friends couldn't make up a good card game. He always explained he didn't get out much because he slept when everyone else was awake. And the few daytime hours he had, he spent preparing shows or on the air.

Most of his outside contact came through e-mails. He used the Internet to find out what was happening in the world, not to help him shape his views.

Strong's only real relationship was with his third and current wife, Darice. She doubled as his producer, and like the other women he married, she was mainly around to cook and occasionally screw. Since there was no place to go, she never went out. On the rare occasion Strong ventured beyond Lebanon, Kansas, Darice stayed home.

He eventually expected there'd be a number-four in his life. *When?* Maybe after he moved his show to Washington. Strong went to his callers.

"Elliott, you haven't said whether you're going to Washington. What's the story?"

Strong shot Darice a cold glance. He wanted to avoid the question. She needed to do a better job screening.

"Well, I want *you* to go," he declared. He gave a cut sign, a slice across the throat. Darice dropped the caller. "On August eighteenth, you and the others will all be our reporters for the general's great march," he continued. "You'll give us the experience of being at the biggest rally ever held in Washington, D.C." He leaned back in his chair. *They'll have a great deal to describe,* he thought.

"Use your cell phones. Call. We'll be on the air with nonstop, commercial-free programming. If America wants to hear what's really going on, they'll tune to *Strong Nation*."

The New York Times

Another day at the computer. Michael O'Connell added more words to his hit list:

Secret. KGB. FSB. Kremlin. Russia. Enemy. Conspiracy.
Virus.

Nothing triggered a sensible response, or even supported a reliable hunch.

Boston, Massachusetts

Years ago, research of this nature would have required Katie Kessler to visit a solid law library, meticulously search through periodicals and papers, call up volumes of law books and scholarly texts, hand write her notes, then distill the information either in free hand or on a typewriter.

Now Katie pointed and clicked. She had access to Nexus/Lexus, and the findlaw.com and westlaw.com databases through her Internet connection at home. The ease of it made her decide this is where she'd do most of her work.

Considering she wasn't assigned to a current case at work, and given the complicity, though unwitting, of her law firm in a near coup of the Executive Branch, the senior partners wished Katie well. They hoped that her departure for the White House might even help restore their firm's corporate image.

Kessler's web-browsing sent her to recent speeches by members of Congress and testimony at open hearings. She downloaded a 2002 article from *The Hill*, a key Beltway publication, written by California Congressman Brad Sherman, an analysis by Texas Senator John Cornyn, opinion papers written by the Congressional Research Service of The Library of Congress, and newspaper articles from *Wall Street Journal, The Washington Post,* and *The New York Times.*

Some of her research brought Katie back to the work she'd done on the eve of the Inauguration. She re-read Article II, Section 1 of the Constitution, the Presidential Succession Act of 1792, The First Presidential Succession Act of 1886, the Presidential Succession Act of 1947, and the 25th Amendment. After her first pass, she went back and highlighted key words in the passages. Next, she copied them to a master file. She found particular merit in the 1886 Act. Unlike the present law, the succession line went from the president to the vice president, then on to the Secretary of State, followed by the Secretary of the Treasury, the Secretary of War, and the rest of the cabinet. She added an exclamation point in the margin. *Interesting,* she said to herself. While it was too early to come to any conclusion, she intuitively felt that *1886*, dismantled 61 years later, had merit.

Soon, Kessler would be calling on Chief Justice Leopold Browning. She knew by experience that if she wasn't prepared to argue her position on firm legal ground, the esteemed Supreme Court jurist would curtly dismiss her...or worse: he'd lecture her to death.

Kessler vowed to be ready. She looked away from her screen to a calendar on her desk. She traced the dates with her pencil. *Not this week. Not next. Maybe the week after.* She added a few days for good measure. *August 18.* She decided Saturday, August 18 would be the date. *Three weeks. That's enough time,* she thought. She picked up the phone and dialed the United States Supreme Court. *Three weeks. I'd better be ready!*

Maluku, Indonesia

Commander Umar Komari reviewed the inventory. He now had the weapons he needed—more than he ever imagined, including his prized SAMs, the deadly surface-to-air missiles. He looked to the heavens with tears in his eyes. *Muhammad surely approves.*

Komari's reverie was interrupted by the voice of his lieutenant.

"Yes, yes. What is it, Atef?" Komari gave permission for only one man to proceed beyond the guards he posted.

"You wanted a report on the training, sir," Musah Atef said.

"Enter."

Atef moved the canvas door to the side and walked into the largest tent he'd ever seen. It was decorated with the bed and furniture his men had stolen from a Christian fisherman's home in a nearby town. Neither the man nor his wife needed it any longer.

"So spacious. Truly fit for a commander."

"Or a president," Komari corrected him.

"Yes, but after we take the capitol, you shall have a palace."

"Quite so. And do we have the army that will take us there? Are they ready?"

"Soon. In a matter of weeks."

"Not sooner?" Komari asked with annoyance.

"Please, just a little more time. It would prove disastrous to move too early. The men need more training with the new weapons."

Komari turned away from Atef. He recently saw what happened to an army when it wasn't prepared. An encampment in the Solomons was attacked by Australians or Americans. He didn't know for sure. Though they had weapons to defend themselves, the men were not ready. A survivor reported that two hundred Muslim warriors died trying to figure out how to load their grenade launchers and fire a surface-to-air missile. Their leader, Komari's older brother Omar, was killed in the assault.

Komari spoke to Atef with his back to his aide. "One month, Atef. I want to strike on my brother's birthday."

"On my word, we will be ready by then."

"Then we will honor Omar's name with our victory over the infidels, and drive the Christians into the ocean."

The White House
Tuesday, 17 July

"Mr. President, just a reminder. Dr. Kaplan will be along in ten minutes."

"Thank you, Louise," Taylor said over the intercom. "I can always count on you to let me know when someone's going to poke and prod me."

The president didn't want to see the doctor, but Presley Friedman, chief of the Secret Service, reminded him that he had to get *tuned up*.

Morgan Taylor hated the invasive procedure. It made him feel like a dog on a leash. But this was one of those things even the President of the United States couldn't say no to.

It was over in seven minutes.

"You may pull up your pants, Mr. President," the doctor said.

Morgan Taylor rubbed his butt. Dr. James Kaplan quickly packed his bag and was ready to leave, but Presley Friedman held him up. He was on the phone. "Let's just see if everything's all right."

"Of course it's *not* all right. I've just been stabbed."

Kaplan laughed. "For the record, sir, you're such a baby."

"For the record, Doctor, try being president and see how much you like this."

Kaplan let out a louder laugh.

Friedman missed the exchange. He was talking to the Secret Service communications office. "Done," he said. "See you in February, Doc."

"Every six months, like a good teeth cleaning," Kaplan added at the door.

"Teeth, my ass," the president said to his director of the Secret Service. It was good for another laugh.

CHAPTER

56

The Pentagon
Arlington, Virginia
Wednesday, 18 July

R oarke bolted through the door with a quick, urgent hello.
Captain Walker recognized his voice and swiveled around,
away from her computer screen, to face him.

"Well, you've certainly been busy," she began.

"And?" Roarke said before he was all the way to her desk.

"Impatient, are we?"

"Anxious."

"Anxious? Are you sure?"

"Yes, I'm sure. Did you get my message?"

"Of course. But I'm stuck on anxious," Walker said mockingly. "You
know you're wrong."

"Wrong? About what?"

"The word. You're looking for *eager*. You get anxious over fear or
frustration, failure or disappointment. You're anxious if you're full
of worry, dread. Anxiety. See, it's even part of the same word. *Eager*
is all about enthusiasm, interest. Oh, and desire."

"Penny," he said with a scowl.

She smiled, but continued. "When you use eager, you'll often follow
it with *to*, then the infinitive. Anxious gets a preposition. *Anxious
about*. So you're not anxious about what I've found. You're eager *to*
hear it."

Roarke shook his head. "Sorry. Maybe I should start again." She
agreed. "Good morning, Captain. How are you today."

"Quite fine, in fact, Agent Roarke," she said, with an exaggerated delivery. "Thank you for asking. And you'll be happy to know that I've been working rather hard since you called from the road yesterday. It's been productive. I've come up with a good deal."

Roarke kissed her forehead. "That's nice," he said in an equally affected tone. But his eyes lit up and he couldn't contain himself any longer. "Now what the fuck is it?"

The Army intelligence officer laughed. "Eager are we? Here it is." She unlocked a drawer and removed a stack of files "Take a look."

Roarke obliged, joining Walker on her side of the desk. The top page was a summary of the attack in Baghdad. Pictures followed on subsequent pages. He leafed through them coming to the findings marked **U.S. Army EOD/Report/Baghdad, Ghazalia district**. It was signed and dated by the EOD (Explosive Ordnance Disposal) senior officer. Walker had highlighted the most important points in a bright yellow marker, which Roarke scanned.

> ...anonymous report six...Army Rangers respond...squad entered...command reports pairs cover building quadrants...sudden explosion...estimate 2,000 lbs...remote detonation...building reduced to rubble...brick, furniture, air conditioners, other debris one-hundred yards away...trees ignited...collateral damage...partial destruction of nearby buildings...car hurled by blast into passing truck...RECOVERED unexploded artillery shells, wires...1st Armored Division secured site...KIA six...

The remainder of the details included the itemization of body parts, skull fragments, and other coldly clinical information. Roarke let out a heavy and needed sigh. The description put him right in Baghdad, making him an eyewitness. It reminded him of too many things he'd seen himself. He returned to Walker's findings.

> ...dental reports...identities confirmed...exception, US Army Lt. Richard Cooper...search ended...

It went on, but Roarke had read enough. "Your take, Penny?" There was nothing but sadness in Roarke's voice.

She'd read everything a number of times anticipating his questions. "It was a complete investigation. By the book. Thorough forensics. I found no oversights."

"And they found no body."

"It's not unusual given the size of the blast."

"Is it impossible, though?"

"It's not impossible. He could have been at ground zero. Between the heat and the force of the blast, he could have been instantly incinerated."

"And if he wasn't at ground zero? If he was at the opposite end of the blast? Protected somehow. Covered. Behind something that shielded him?" Roarke asked.

"Possible."

"Do we know where he was at the time of the blast? His proximity to the bomb?"

"Well, now you're going where I went. We don't. But apparently no one was at the precise point of detonation based on the SOP that the men moved in pairs." She pointed to a schematic included in the report. There were X's for five of the six bodies. All died in pairs except for one GI near the back of the building.

Roarke's eyes widened with anticipation. He stared at the layout. "Is that a supporting column?"

"Looks like it could be," she responded.

"And given the fact that only one body was recovered in that part of the building, is it reasonable to believe that Lt. Cooper could have been the other man in the pair...that he could have been protected from the explosion by that column?"

Penny raised her eyebrow now validating his belief. "He got out. He ran out!"

"Or he was thrown out by the explosion. Either way, he's alive!" Roarke concluded.

FBI Labs
Quantico, Virginia

Next, Roarke visited Touch Parsons. He handed over various pictures of Bill, Gloria, and Richard Cooper. "Good boy, Roarke. You even got me different ages."

"Of course." The FBI man had drummed the idea into Roarke. Shots of parents over the years vastly helped map the facial structure of a child into middle age. The last photo of Richard was age 24, in uniform. He asked Parsons to add 13 years to his face, then morph the new extrapolation into various interpretations based on the eyewitness descriptions of Depp.

"Well, well, I think you're finally getting it, Roarke," Parsons said. He moved over two half-filled cups of cold coffee and a plate of Entemann's coffee cake crumbs to make room for Roarke's material.

"Funny, my teachers thought I was a slow learner, too."

Parsons said his usual *hmm* a lot as he looked at photographs. "I don't suppose you'll tell me who this guy really is?"

"Nope," Roarke offered.

"Why did I even ask?" After more *hmm's* he continued, "When do you need this by?" He followed up his question even before Roarke could get the answer out. "Why did I even ask? Immediately."

"Sooner."

Parsons got to work, narrating the entire process for Roarke. "I'll scan these, then I'll really start playing. There are remarkable similarities to the sketches. I can see why you think this might be your guy."

"*Is* my guy," Roarke corrected him with great certainty.

"Ah, you're getting cocky. But remember, nothing will hold up in court. But if I do say so myself, you're going to end up with some fucking incredible pictures that will look great on the front page!"

"That's what I'm counting on."

The White House
Thursday, 19 July

"This is the man you've been calling Depp?" Morgan Taylor asked. He studied the Army photograph Roarke brought to the White House.

"Yes. His name is Richard Cooper and officially he's dead."

"According to?"

"The United States of America, boss." Roarke ran the entire story for the president. He concluded by adding, "And we created this monster who's out for revenge. He's not just killing people for money. He's taking jobs that will cripple, maybe even destroy us. That makes him more dangerous."

"How so?" the president asked.

"Because he's extremely careful. He's not out to build a bank account. This is a means to an end. Somehow he hooked up with the right person who shares his anger and has ample funds to keep him going." Roarke now offered another belief that he had kept to himself. "And call me crazy, but I have a hunch it was back in Iraq."

Taylor tilted his head to the side and pressed his lips together. There was nothing in the reaction for Roarke to read. He kept his eyes on the president as he walked to his humidor on a table near the wall. Taylor kept a stash of cigars which he rarely smoked. Roarke watched him light up and take a long puff. Taylor held the humidor open for Roarke, but the Secret Service agent politely declined with a wave of his hand.

After a second long drag, the president examined his cigar. "You know why I like to smoke, Scott?"

"Yes, sir, I think I do. It gives you time to think. It makes you slow down."

"You do know me. But it also makes me feel like I'm doing something a little bit wrong in the White House. It is a federal building and the laws do not permit smoking."

"I'm sure your successor will pardon you."

Taylor chuckled. "My successor? Now will that be Henry Lamden if he recovers? Perhaps someone new to the White House after the next election? Or maybe even the speaker of the house, should something happen to me?"

Roarke suddenly looked stunned. The thought of Duke Patrick as president had never crossed his mind. But he was next in the line of succession.

"You see, there is so much to consider, Scott. Your Mr. Depp, aka the late Lt. Cooper and his *friend* may have me in their sights. So I might as well enjoy my cigar now."

Roarke nodded.

"Are you sure you wouldn't like one?" Taylor asked again.

He reconsidered and reached for the smoke.

"Good," Taylor said lighting him up. "Now sit down and let me tell you about a mission Vincent D'Angelo's on. I'm sure the two of you will want to chat when he's back.

CHAPTER

57

Omayyad Mosque
Damascus, Syria
Sunday, 22 July

Rateb Samin spotted the man. He looked nervous. His eyes
darted from side to side as he recited the *Zhuhr* (noon) prayer.
Samin, dressed in a classic gray embroidered dishadasha,
took a place near him in the spacious prayer hall. He knelt on a hand-
woven Asian rug, one of many that completely blanketed the floor.
He joined in the *Salah*, or ritual prayers. Islamic law decreed it must
be said in Arabic, which was not a problem for the Dutch businessman
on holiday. Samin covered his head, but keep the left side open to
peer out. As he chanted, he took in the remarkable mosaics and the
shrine erected in tribute to the Prophet. D'Angelo was fully engaged—
in the job, the people around him, and the magnificent architecture.

He casually glanced to his left. The man, barely ten feet away, fit
the description he'd gotten from the Mossad. *Approximately 70 years
old. Pock-marked, olive skin. Full beard, thick moustache. Round,
black-rimmed glasses framing his face.* He wore a brown salwar
kameez with quarter-inch thick black piping. A dark star-shaped
bruise or birthmark under his right thumbnail seemed to confirm
Jamil Laham's identity. To be certain, D'Angelo employed a pre-
arranged signal. He cleared his throat once, then twice, then once
again. It would be unmistakable to Laham, yet an insignificant act
to others within earshot at the Omayyad Mosque.

The man replied by raising his left hand to his nose and scratching.
He followed the initial reply by reaching his left hand behind his back
to satisfy another itch.

D'Angelo cleared his throat two more times. The man scratched his right ear.

That was all either of them needed to do except find the opportunity to talk. After 20 minutes they converged from two different directions into the immense courtyard. Both had put their sandals back on. D'Angelo was admiring the beauty of the arches with their inlaid mosaics when he heard "*Marhuba Al salaam a'alaykum.*" Peace be with you.

Without turning to the voice behind him he replied, "*Wa alaykum as-salaam.*" And with you peace.

"It is a fine day to take in the beauty of such a holy site," D'Angelo continued. "It's a wonder to behold."

"Yes, but we must remember that the beauty exists only to remind us of the goodness of the Prophet. It's a gift for all time," the older man said.

"Resplendent." D'Angelo's comment came from his heart. He said it in Arabic without even thinking. His command of the language was that good.

"This is your first visit here?"

"Yes. But I am a student of architecture. The marvels of the Omayyad Mosque have long been part of my dreams. Seeing it exceeds all expectations."

"Come then, I will describe what I know," Laham offered. "My name is Jamil Laham."

"And I am Rateb Samin," D'Angelo said.

They started through the courtyard. Laham walked with a limp. D'Angelo had to compensate with his own stride. They passed under the al Arous Minaret which sharply stood out against the blue sky.

"I detect a hint of British in your words."

"You have a very good ear, my friend. I am from Lebanon, but I now live in Amsterdam. The English accent you hear is from Oxford; my old school ties."

Of course, it was a fabrication. But Laham didn't need to know the truth. He just had to speak it himself.

"Perhaps you can point out the history *I* seek," the CIA agent asked. "They say knowledge is its own reward."

Laham noted the comment, but continued to lead him back inside. "There," he whispered as they approached another part of the vast building. "You have read that the Omayyad Mosque is the fourth holiest site of Islam?"

"Yes."

"First Mecca, then Medina, and the Dome of the Rock. The fourth is Omayyad. Well, this is one of the reasons." He pointed to a shrine. "There, within, is the head of al Hussein, grandson of the Prophet Mohammad. He was killed in a revolt that split our people in 680 A.D." The way he explained it seemed to devalue D'Angelo's cover. But he didn't question the visitor, he simply continued. "There were those who believed that only someone directly descended from Mohammad has the divine right to act as *caliph*, the leader of all Islam. Al Hussein did. And he was killed for his blood line. His followers became the Shi'ites. The Sunnis, the followers of the well-trodden path, the *sunnah*, remain the majority. They banned descendants of Mohammad from the caliphate for all time. It is the rift that still divides us. It is why we fight amongst ourselves. It is why the West fails to understand us. It is why they don't know whom to support. And yet, the religion that the Prophet founded will become the most powerful force in the world."

D'Angelo felt humbled by the explanation. This was not a weak man. He was here because he had lived through much and believed that helping the West might make them better understand the Arab world. He dropped all pretensions.

"You understand why I am here?"

"I do. And you understand the danger in my speaking to you?"

"Yes, I do."

"We shall continue to walk." Laham ordered.

The former government worker further described the history of the Mosque, even recalling the days of the god *Hadad*. Finally, in a garden by a striking blue arch gate, Laham got to the point of their meeting.

"I could die a thousand horrible deaths by talking with you."

"I believe you seek to save millions," D'Angelo guessed.

"You are right. And perhaps I take too much credit. Perhaps what I keep in my head has no importance to my government today. Perhaps I am just an old man with delusions."

D'Angelo now understood the man. He was well-read. He saw what was happening to his country and the world. It was no accident that Laham took him to see the head of al Hussein. There was a real message there. He didn't want to lose his.

Washington, D.C.
the same time

Roarke was mid-way through an evening workout when he felt his cell phone vibrate.

"Hello, love." Katie's caller ID gave her away.

She heard the pounding music in the background and quickly figured out she wouldn't get the personal time she craved. "You're exercising."

"Yeah, but it's okay." He stepped off the treadmill and grabbed a towel. "We can talk."

"Not about *everything*."

"No, you're right. Not about everything. Because I'm wearing gym shorts and just your voice can set me off."

Everything also included all of Roarke's work, so their phone conversations were typically limited to small talk and Katie's research.

"We can talk later," she proposed.

It was already close to midnight. It would be another hour before he was home. "How about a little now and a little later. We'll get the business stuff out of the way. So later...." He left the rest of the sentence unsaid. "How's your progress?"

"Mind boggling," she said. "I've come to the conclusion that change is long overdue. A number of key congressmen have already floated their idea of what it should look like. But nothing's happened. I guess even after nine-eleven, succession is too hot for most legislators to touch. I think I'm going to have a helluva time when I hit the Hill."

"Why?" Roarke really didn't know the answer.

"The honorable speaker of the house, for one. He leads the majority party. He's a Democrat. Taylor's a Republican. Democrats hold both houses. Do you think anything I come up with that moves him out of the way will get attention?"

"Not if you put it that way. But doesn't this come down to a state-by-state referendum? A Constitutional Amendment?"

"Yes and no. Acts passed by Congress govern the procedure. The Constitution covers *when*, not necessarily *how* and *who*. So one of the things that I'll propose is a new *what*."

"I'm glad that's cleared up," Roarke joked.

"Excuse me, but you're the one who sets all the rules on what we can and cannot get into on the phone." She had him. "Everything I read makes me feel like we're sitting on a ticking bomb."

"What do you mean," he asked.

"Well, the current law makes it relatively easy to foster what amounts to executive treason."

Treason was a word he didn't like. "Explain."

"We have the potential for a classic case of *The Law of Unintended Consequences*. A president of one party is replaced by the successor from another; unelected by popular vote."

"Isn't Taylor the beneficiary of that already?"

"Again, yes and no. Taylor was picked by President Lamden. The speaker is from the same party as President Lamden. Even though Taylor is something of a political wild card, the present line does not present any disruption. If Taylor dies, a Democrat takes office again, in what was a Democrat-elected administration. The unintended consequence I'm looking at is probably in the future. A new party fully takes over from the elected party. Different interests are represented. We could have a real political crisis."

Roarke listened, but he couldn't let go of the last point. It had come up in the president's office, too. Taylor had no vice president, and wouldn't until the long-range medical condition of President Lamden was settled. That would make Congressman Patrick president in the event of Taylor's death. Right away that was an *Unintended Consequence* that scared the hell out of him.

Damascus, Syria

"First, you must understand, I do not do this to help the Zionists. Although I cannot deny that they may ultimately benefit," Jamil Laham explained. "Though we and the Jews spring forth from the same seed, sons of Abraham, the gulf that spans between us is far greater than the differences that separate the Sunnis and the Shi'ites. Nonetheless, I am a realist. Creating peace in the world rests on individual efforts. The Prophet himself said, *'Do you know what is better than charity and fasting and prayer? It is keeping peace and good relations between people, as quarrels and bad feelings destroy mankind.'* There are those whose actions would destroy mankind: ideologues with weapons of mass destruction, terrorists with no regard for order, fundamentalist clerics, and yes, even American presidents. That is why I'm willing to talk to you. But it's puzzling to me why it has taken so long."

"I am sorry," D'Angelo didn't really understand the intent of the remark. He only heard of Laham a few days ago. "But you have my full attention now," D'Angelo offered in consolation.

"Very well. Many years ago I was chief of the Palace Guards. It may be hard to believe looking at me now, but I was a strong man without this cursed limp." He slapped his right leg with his hand.

D'Angelo automatically looked down.

"A teenager with a gun. He called himself a fighter in the army of Allah. Thanks to my men, he met Allah well before me. But I digress. I fought with General Hafez al Assad against the Israelis in what you call the Six Day War. I proudly stood by him when he became president. I am proud of my service with him. I was faithful in that service until the day he died." Laham lowered his eyes in deference to the man he obviously admired.

"You were not born then. You probably have very little knowledge of our president. But I can tell you that he was a great man with great ideas and important dreams. Foremost was his hope of bringing the Zionists to the bargaining table. He tried many ways, short term and long. The most extraordinary was to steer American politics toward a greater understanding of the Muslim world."

Right, D'Angelo said to himself. *What a nice way of saying you planted sleeper spies to take over the presidency.*

"He got very close to succeeding," D'Angelo volunteered. He figured the observation was less volatile than admitting what he really thought. "Congressman Lodge nearly became president."

"You do not mince words," Laham noted. "I was there when he conceived the plan. The Russians were more than interested in taking our money to facilitate the training of this man and, I understand, others like him. While I did not know who was recruited or the purpose of their assignments, I did have contact with the individual who oversaw it."

"Ibrahim Haddad," D'Angelo said.

"He went by that name, and others," Laham acknowledged.

"What can you tell me about this man?"

"Ah, I see I have your attention. Well then, Ibrahim first met with President Assad in nineteen seventy-two. Do you know he was already a rich businessman by the time he was in his mid-twenties?"

"What kind of business?"

"Import. Some rugs. Most notably art work. Expensive art that he sold to French, German, American, British, and Iranian dealers and collectors. His trade often took him to Russia without a blink of an eye. He traveled freely, and eventually took more interest in the president's plan than his own work."

"How would you describe him?"

"He was a tall man. Taller than me. Handsome, lean, arrogant, and bitter, but I will return to that later. He struck me as highly educated and he had a distinctive air about him. You'd be drawn to him, but never feel close. President Assad had many meetings with Ibrahim. And I have no doubt, the president made him a much richer man. How rich, I cannot say. When President Assad died, I initially believed that the plans died with him. I was removed from office when Bashir ascended to the presidency. A short while later, I suffered this wound." He gestured to his leg again. "I became a functionary in the finance department."

"And when you read the news earlier this year?"

"I learned that the dream of Hafez al Assad continued, but in the hands of others. Ultimately the Libyans. It was plain to see I had underestimated the character of the man my president chose to administer his plan."

"You say he went by many names?"

"Yes. In fact, I don't know his real identity. To me he was Hassan Kassir, but we shall continue to call him Haddad. It might be possible to find out, particularly when I tell you the rest of his story. Come, let's walk again. I tighten up if I don't move often."

There was nothing suspicious about the two men. Many tourists came to the Omayyad Mosque. For a few minutes Laham pointed out other sites including the mausoleum of Salah ad-Din. Salah was a noted hero and one of Islam's great commanders who re-took Jerusalem from the Crusaders in 1187. Unlike other conquerors, he spared his victims, allowing them time to leave with their lives. Laham also noted the three vibrant domes and the varying styles of the minarets which dramatically rose above the mosque.

After a time they stopped again. Laham faced D'Angelo. He sharpened his focus; peering directly at his companion. "You are American, though you disguise it well."

D'Angelo blinked acceptance that he'd been found out.

"Now I will enlighten you with a part of your history that your own texts have forgotten."

"**O**n June fifth, nineteen sixty-eight, the American senator Robert Kennedy won the California primary election," began the Syrian. "Arguably, it virtually handed him the presidency, but June fifth was also the anniversary of the outbreak of the Six-Day War. And that night, a Jerusalem-born Muslim named Sirhan Bishara Sirhan assassinated your beloved Bobby. Sirhan was immediately arrested, and eventually put on trial, sentenced, and sent to one of your maximum-security jails. The story does not end there," explained Jamil Laham.

D'Angelo was intrigued by Laham's story. The fact was, he didn't know Kennedy was killed on the anniversary of the war.

"Yitzhak Rabin, then Israel's Ambassador to the United States, was scheduled to meet with Senator Kennedy. Rather than meet about Israel's future, he was left to contemplate the impact of Senator Kennedy's death. He later wrote in his memoirs that Americans, so dazed by what everyone considered the 'senseless act of a madman,' couldn't begin to recognize the real political significance.

"And what, my friend, might that have been?" It was a rhetorical question. "No matter what your historians report, Sirhan was not a madman. He planned the act. At his trial he even proclaimed, 'I killed Robert Kennedy willfully, premeditatedly, and with twenty years of malice aforethought.'"

"Twenty years?" D'Angelo asked.

"From nineteen forty-eight through nineteen sixty-eight. The year nineteen forty-eight being when Israel declared nationhood."

The CIA agent listened intently.

"I have become something of an expert on the assassination. You'll soon see why. Just after Robert Kennedy graduated from Harvard

University, he reported from Israel for the *Boston Post*. Why is this significant? He was there when the Zionists established their state. He was there through the earliest days of their war for independence. And he was there when his brother, John Kennedy, visited with a congressional delegation in nineteen fifty-one. From that day on, the Kennedys resolved to help Israel 'bear any burden.'"

"That was many years ago."

"Indeed it was, yet still relevant. Robert Kennedy supported Israel from its birth. As president, he would have furthered the cause of the Jewish state. Many Muslims saw him as a threat. Sirhan Sirhan pulled the trigger for them all. To your people, he was an assassin—to us a hero who deserved to be free."

"I understand that. But...."

"Patience. I'm getting to what you must really grasp. In March of nineteen seventy-three, a group known as Black September stormed the Saudi Embassy in Khartoum. They took a United States Ambassador hostage, along with others. What was one of their principal demands?"

D'Angelo shrugged his shoulders, embarrassed he didn't have the answer.

"The release of Sirhan Sirhan," Laham asserted. "The release of the hero."

"My God!"

"President Richard Nixon refused to consider the demand. No negotiation. A foolish decision? You decide. All of the hostages, including the ambassador, were executed. Each of them was shot to death. I can recite their names and the names of their family members if you wish. I'm sure that's more than *any* American can do.

"You *will* recognize the name of another man in my story," Laham said resuming the saga. "A man who—according to Israeli intelligence and your infamous NSA—issued the order."

"Who?"

"I did start by saying that this is history your own texts have forgotten."

"Yes, you did."

"The order, according to many, came from the head of the Black September terrorist group." He stopped to see if that sparked a recollection. It did not.

"Yasser Arafat."

"Arafat!" exclaimed D'Angelo. "I never—"

"Your government and your media chooses not to remember," explained Laham quite correctly. "Of course, Arafat publicly disassociated himself from the murders, but there were reports that he discussed the assassinations during a private dinner with Romanian dictator Nicolae Ceausescu. A defector also at the dinner claimed that Arafat bragged about the Khartoum operation. That report was published in the *Wall Street Journal*. I can give you the date if you wish."

"Just go on."

"Eventually, a Palestinian analyst for the National Security Agency went public with charges that Arafat's role in planning the kidnappings and execution had been suppressed. Other reports to surface even include the exact single-side band radio frequency he used to communicate with his aide. Would you like that? 7150 kHz. Or the text of the message?"

D'Angelo interrupted. "Look, nothing you've said directly links Sirhan Sirhan to Black September or confirms that he took orders from Arafat."

"Perhaps. But in turn, I must ask why would Black September make Sirhan's release a condition of the hostages' freedom?"

"Publicity?"

"Perhaps. The United States did not have a counter-terrorism force at that point. Maybe they thought it would work. But what if it was not for publicity? What if they really believed their actions could return a hero to the Palestinians?"

D'Angelo vowed to read the reports when he returned home.

"Now for the connection that I believe you're most interested in," Laham stated. "While the United States did not make a punitive strike against Black September, Israel did. They sent a squadron of F-4 Phantoms, armed with Shrike and Maverick missiles into Palestinian camps in Jordan and Syria. Little is known about this attack except that more than one hundred men, women, and children were killed. In addition to the missiles that destroyed the camps, another air-to-ground rocket went astray into a nearby town. Forty-five more people died, including an old couple visiting their son, his wife, and their newborn granddaughter. The baby's father escaped the blast. He was buying food for dinner at the souk. He came back to the devastation and found his family. They were all dead. His wife and parents were burned to death in the fire. His daughter was blasted through the house and impaled on the front gate. He lifted the girl off the iron rail and gently laid her down in front on a carpet remnant. He went back to what was left of the house and carried his wife out, then his parents. When help came the man was sitting on the ground, gently rocking his daughter to her eternal rest. His tears were gone by then. Those who tell the story have said he was quite composed. He thanked everyone for their concern, but he explained he would take care of things in due time. They thought he was talking about burying his family. But there was more to his statement. In that one hour of his life, he vowed revenge against the Zionists, against the State of Israel, and against the American presidents who supported them. He changed that day into the man you seek. Into Ibrahim Haddad."

"This is all personal," D'Angelo concluded.

"I'm afraid you're right."

"Which explains his utmost patience. He's put more than thirty years into his hatred. How can anyone live like that?"

"For the Muslim world, that hatred is fueled every day the Zionist flag flies."

"That won't change." D'Angelo instantly wished he hadn't said that, but it was too late. Laham broke eye contact and shook his head. He raised his head to the heavens and uttered a quiet prayer. *Oh God, You are Peace. From You comes Peace. To You returns Peace. Revive us with a salutation of Peace. And lead us to your abode of Peace.*

D'Angelo recognized Mohammad's Prayer for Peace and Laham's sincere hope that the world would find it. "I'm sorry."

Laham, still with his eyes to the sky, nodded. "I wouldn't be talking to you if I didn't recognize the Jewish state as permanent. But peace should be just as permanent, and yet it is hardly evident." He lowered his head and stared deeply into D'Angelo's eyes. He saw sincerity. "I hope our conversation will help."

"I do as well. Finding Ibrahim Haddad is key."

"Yes it is; which is why I'm surprised it's taken so long to talk."

D'Angelo recalled Laham saying that earlier in their conversation. "It's only been a matter of a few days," he said.

"A few days?" Laham appear utterly confused. "I first approached the Israelis three years ago with this information."

CHAPTER 59

CIA Headquarters
Tuesday, 24 July

D'Angelo was furious. He did nothing to hide his anger from the NDI. "It's bullshit! They sat on this for three years?"

"Schecter *never* said a word, not on my watch," Evans stated.

"Come on, Jack. You can't tell me—"

"I can tell you anything I want." The National Director of Intelligence stopped his agent in midsentence. "Anytime I want. Am I clear?"

"Yes."

"That stated, it *is* the truth. They never informed us."

D'Angelo settled down. "But it is absolute bullshit," he said again. "This guy told the Mossad about Haddad. They had to tell us."

"They had to? Why?" Evans asked.

"Because."

"Come on, Vinnie, how long have you been doing this? It's all about secrets. Learning them, evaluating them, holding onto them, and maybe trading them. Rarely does anyone just hand them out. Not us. Not them."

"But they had his name. We could have nailed Haddad years ago. God knows how many people have died because of him," D'Angelo said. "We're their fucking friends!"

"Friends? We spy on each other, we use the promise of money to try to influence their politics. We walk away from their peace talks at the worst times. Then we make demands and they laugh at us. Friends? I'm really not so sure."

"But they knew." By now it was becoming a desperate argument.

"Maybe at the time they didn't value the information. It could have been filed away or lost. Maybe they realized it after the fact. Maybe with my call...or yours. It could be as simple or as complicated as that. Remember how ineffective we were in tying intel together prior to nine-eleven, despite reliable information? People didn't know how to read it or they ignored it. That's why I'm here, now, in this office. Why would we expect any better from the Israelis?"

"Because they have been better at it. Because their survival has always depended on it. What if Schecter wanted to see how far the plot would go?"

"Well, if that's the case, Vincent, we've got a chit in our column. And someday I won't be shy about asking them to make good on it."

The White House
Washington, D.C.

"I need to get everyone on the same page," Morgan Taylor said. "You all know each other. I think it's fair to say you all trust each other. Now let's find out how you can help one other."

FBI Director Robert Mulligan, NDI Evans, the Army's General Jonas Jackson Johnson, and Bernie Bernstein were joined by Scott Roarke, Vinnie D'Angelo, and Shannon Davis.

"Bob, you go first," the president suggested.

"Okay. Bessolo and his team have gone through Haddad's condo in Florida. As hard as it is to believe, there's nothing there. No note-pads, no computer files, and no smoking gun. We lifted a few finger-prints; they're no help. We're delving into his bank transactions. Local, off-shore; anything we can track. Interpol is running searches for us, too. If he is our man, I can't prove it."

"Not yet," Morgan Taylor noted. "Keep on it." Next, the president went to his National Intelligence chief.

"If you don't mind, I'll defer to D'Angelo." The NIA sat next to his man and tapped his arm twice.

"Ditto to everything Director Mulligan said. We're also working with the FBI on his banking. But from my sources," D'Angelo remained intentionally vague, "Haddad feels like the linchpin to the plan and his ultimate agenda is revenge."

"Revenge?" the FBI chief asked.

"Yes, he holds a personal grudge against the United States, against the presidency in particular."

"Why? How do you know?"

Again D'Angelo phrased his answer carefully. Evans warned him the FBI had a leak. "Let's just leave *how* out of it. *Why?* Because his family was killed by an Israeli strike in Syria in nineteen seventy-three."

Bernstein spoke up next. "Wait a second, the Israelis, not us? So why blame the U.S.? I don't get it.

"He holds the U.S. responsible for Israeli's existence."

"So we have a nutcase on our hands," the chief of staff declared.

The president disagreed. "Not a nutcase. A man who is hell-bent on revenge. He has all his wits about him and the patience of Job."

"Except for the fact that he's Muslim," D'Angelo continued.

"Do you know where he is?" This was Mulligan's question.

"No, but I've learned how we might be able to find him." This drew everyone's attention. "He's a reputable art dealer. That's apparently where some of his money comes from. I suggest we work together to track major transactions over the last five to ten years. Because so much art is now traded on the Internet, we should look there, as well as galleries. Oh, and one other thing. He uses a variety of aliases and he speaks a number of languages. Consequently, our search should broaden to include French, German, Spanish, and Russian art dealers. I think it's fair to assume that he has as many passports as he does identities. We should see what comes up in the database with minor changes to his appearance."

D'Angelo stopped. Evans had gently pressed against his arm. He said enough for the room, despite the fact that it was the Oval Office.

Without a thank you, the president turned to Roarke.

"Scott, you and Shannon have the floor."

Roarke jumped in. "Shannon and I, with the help of DIA and the FBI labs, have been working on the identity of the assassin. We feel we've ascertained who he is, or more accurately, who he *was*."

"What?" was everyone's reaction.

Bernstein looked most shocked, so the Secret Service agent played to him. "He was an officer in the United States Army. Officially, he was killed in action in Baghdad. However, his body was never recovered. Like Haddad, he has a motive for revenge. He was sent into a building in what was arguably a suicide mission. His squad

had challenged the order, but their objections were dismissed. Everyone died, including—for the record—our subject. We visited his parents,
who have benefitted greatly from an insurance policy, for which there
is no record. With their permission, we borrowed family photographs
and ran them through the FBI photo recognition labs. We have a very
reliable match with witness descriptions of the suspect. I should add
that I've seen this man twice, once in Washington and again, recently
in Boston. He *is* the man in the picture." Roarke reached into his
attaché case. "This picture." He held up an enlargement of the photograph the Coopers gave him. "Meet Richard Cooper."

The New York Times editorial offices
the same time

O'Connell typed every conceivable word pairing into the search
box. Nothing hit him right.

He re-read the initial e-mail from the Russian.

Your reports fine.
Why do you write about things you not know?
You need information good.
Bearly a friend.

*I'm thinking too big. Not weapons or armies. If it's about Lodge
and the presidency, then forget bombs. I have to think smaller.*
O'Connell went back to his computer and tried new fields.

Congress, Representative, Senator

The White House

"Total speculation now, but for argument sake, Cooper is captured
by insurgents. Somehow he talks his way out of being killed and
works his way up the system," Roarke postulated.

"Or an alternative," Davis added. "He's taken in by an anti-American
individual or family. They get him on his feet and introduce him to
people who ultimately lead to Haddad. This could have taken months

or years. I'm sure we won't know what actually happened until we have either Haddad or Cooper in our hands. But with the president's permission, General Johnson could reopen the investigation of the building blast..."

Everyone waited for the president's blessing which came in a concise order. "J3, make it so."

"Yes, sir," the general answered.

"Let's make some progress on this before I board *Air Force One* for Australia."

"Yes, Mr. President."

"Three days, J3." The general acknowledged the deadline. "Do you have any more, Scott?

"Yes I do."

The New York Times

O'Connell felt he was on a better track. However, none of the hits seemed dead on. Not yet. As he read through the material he continued to write down other words that came to mind.

Judge, Politician, Businessman, Election

He'd get to those later.

The Oval Office

"In addition to the training he picked up in the military, which is considerable, Cooper is an accomplished actor," Roarke explained. "And I mean accomplished. He's adept at creating truly distinct personas by becoming different people. It's not just makeup and hair, this guy is incredible."

Roarke talked through the inevitable silence that followed. "He could probably get credentials to your next press conference and nobody would know it."

"Jesus Christ," Bernsie gasped. "How the hell do you find him?"

"I don't," Roarke said. "We let him find me."

The New York Times

O'Connell leaned back in his chair. He rubbed his eyes and shook his head. He needed a break. The reporter pushed away from his desk, stood, and stretched. *I've gotta get out of here.* He headed out, first grabbing a copy of the day's paper, which he hadn't read. *Some fresh air and a little coffee.*

The Oval Office

"How?" the FBI chief asked.

"Through Cooper's parents," Shannon Davis said joining the conversation.

"But they think he's dead."

"And he'll stay that way, at least for now," Roarke explained. "But here's what we've come up with." Roarke outlined the plan.

New York City

O'Connell sat in the corner of the diner with steam rising from his cup of strong black coffee. A piece of coffee cake lay on his plate. Half of the topping was on O'Connell's red plaid L.L. Bean shirt.

The reporter read nearly every page of the paper, but not from top to bottom. He had his own ritual. First he turned to the domestic political stories, sorting by by-line the other reporters he considered closest to their sources. After working his way through those stories he went for global news. Then he was onto business stories with a political slant, the editorials, and the op-ed page. He always finished with a review of the radio and TV appearances by polls.

He followed the Redskins during football season and little other sports. The food pages meant nothing to him. The stocks depressed him. O'Connell didn't care about Hollywood. The only DVDs he owned were *All the President's Men*, *The Candidate*, *The Best Man*, and *All the Kings Men*.

O'Connell could digest *The New York Times* in twenty to thirty minutes. He also tried to go through *The Washington Post* and *The Washington Times*. Recently, he'd been so focused on his inquiry that he skipped his own paper. The same would have happened today if he didn't feel fried.

The story that most caught his attention was President Taylor's upcoming trip to Australia. *Times* correspondents reported on the agenda, which was to solidify the changes in the nuclear proliferation agreement among Southeast Asian countries. The threat of increased terrorist activities in the region made the conference a priority. Unconfirmed rumors of a bomb threat earlier in the summer added to the tension. Sydney police denied the reports, which they attributed to a water main break below the Ville St. George Hotel. However, an unnamed military source indicated that the SASR, the Australian Special Forces Regiment, had carried out a seek-and-destroy mission against a terrorist stronghold in the Solomon Islands. That report remained unconfirmed.

All of this interested O'Connell and he followed the story as it jumped from page one to inside the first section. As he turned the pages his left hand accidentally hit his coffee cup. It went over, spilling the remaining half on the plate holding his cake and the newspaper. "Damn!" he shouted at himself.

Patrons hardly lifted their eyes from their papers, laptops, or books, and no one rushed over to help him. He used the Arts Section to pat down the spill. When his table was sufficiently dry he returned to the paper, forgetting where the article jumped.

O'Connell gave it a rest. He walked over to the counter and asked for a refill. Minutes later he was back at his table finding his place in the *Times*. Page ten. He slid the paper to the left side of the table and placed his cup and what was left of his pastry directly on a full-page coffee-stained ad on page eleven. He finished reading the story and wondered whether there was anything to the bomb threat. He decided to write himself a reminder. O'Connell automatically reached for a pen in his pocket. It wasn't there. He had left it at his desk. The reporter looked around. He caught the waitress's attention.

"One minute," she signaled.

He sipped his coffee. The second cup was just as bad as the first.

"What's up?" the waitress asked.

"A pen I can borrow?"

"Sure, here."

He took her ballpoint and tried to write in some white space on the adjacent page. But the pen wouldn't ink over the wet paper. O'Connell ate the last of his cake, which partially covered a dry portion of the same page. Her pen worked where the food had been.

Check with Sydney bureau

While he scribbled some additional notes, his eye caught the ad copy on the page. It was a simple advertisement. *Catchy*, he thought. He took another sip of coffee and turned the page.

The Oval Office

"He won't do it!" Bernsie declared.

"I think he will. And as soon as he writes about it, others will pick up on it," Roarke predicted.

"No way, he'll see that he's being used," the chief of staff maintained.

J3 just laughed. It was as if no time had elapsed. Bernstein the naysayer, arguing with everybody. It was one of the things that made the Taylor White House work. The president had the same feeling, which was why he cut the argument off.

"You're both right. But O'Connell *will* do it. We tell him just enough to make it interesting. He'll want to break it. Then the story will take on a life of its own. The nets will call it another Iraqi blunder. But in order to get it, he has to embargo the privileged information until we have Mr. Cooper in custody."

Taylor read the room. Everyone seemed to be in agreement except for his chief of staff. "Bernsie, what's wrong?"

"It's a bad idea. And it's dangerous. You're using the press again. It'll backfire. It's..."

"How much different is it from what my predecessors have done?" Taylor argued. "You gave me the lecture yourself. So the big difference is they fed radio and TV shows to get and stay elected. Remember the conservative commentator who was paid in oh-four? Whole agendas were pushed without disclosing that fact. We'll just be feeding a reporter a *true* story to catch a fucking killer."

Even Bernsie had to take note of the difference.

"Well then, gentlemen," Morgan Taylor said, "Mr. O'Connell doesn't have an end to his Pulitzer prize-winning tome yet. Why don't we help him find it?"

The New York Times

O'Connell suddenly shivered. He clenched his fists and held his breath. It was as if a bolt of lightning electrified him with awareness. He stared out at the rest of the patrons. Everyone was calm, self-absorbed, and unaware of his epiphany.

The words! He tore through the *Times* trying to find the page again. He went so fast he missed it the first time. *There!* He patted down the page. *Son of a bitch!* Everything connected: What the old Russian said and what he meant...the political implication and the tremendous impact on the country.

It was there in his own newspaper—in bold **Times New Roman** over the otherwise blank page; the last two words of a simple print advertisement. The first word, uttered by the Russian; the second word which completed the thought. Connected, they gave him his answer. *Strong Nation.*

CHAPTER

60

Walter Reed Army Medical Center
Bethesda, Maryland
Thursday 2 August

"**G**ood morning, Mr. President. Early day?"

"They're *all* early, and they're rarely good," Morgan Taylor joked. "How's the president doing?" he asked the head cardiologist on Henry Lamden's team.

"A little stronger. You'll be starting the day for him. Mrs. Lamden doesn't usually come by until oh-nine-hundred these days."

The doctor led Morgan Taylor to President Lamden's heavily guarded room. The president was sleeping, but he had more color in his face than the last visit. Taylor gently rested his hand on Lamden's arm. "Henry," he whispered.

Lamden stirred, opened his eyes, and slowly focused on his visitor. "You're a sight for sore eyes. Have you ruined everything yet?"

"No, but I haven't been at it long enough. Give me time." Taylor wished he hadn't said that. "How you doing?"

"Been a lot better. But that's when I was twenty. It's been downhill from there."

"Oh, cut the crap, you'll be back in the hot seat. I'm just keeping the damned thing warm for you."

Lamden breathed deeply. "Not so sure, Morgan. The doctors may want to go back in." He'd already had quadruple bypass surgery two weeks after the heart attack. "They're not saying very much. Too afraid of what the stock market will do or that you'll load the place back up with your Republican friends."

Morgan Taylor laughed, but he actually wanted to have a serious conversation. He stepped away from the bed and quietly asked the doctor, "Can you give us a few minutes?"

"Certainly, Mr. President. I'll be outside if you need me."

Once they were alone, Taylor pulled a chair over to Lamden's bed. "Henry, I'm heading to Australia in a couple of hours and I want to talk over some strategy."

"Oh?"

"I have a two-stage plan for the conference that will play a whole helluva lot better if it's from both of us."

"A plan? Does Foss know anything? It's his ball game."

"No, but I have a feeling he won't be the problem. It's some of the others." Taylor explained what he had in mind. It actually made Henry Lamden sit up.

Andrews Air Force Base
later that day

"Mr. President."

Lt. Eric Ross was at the base of the gangplank to greet him.

"Afternoon, Rossy. Everything shipshape?"

"Yes, sir. Next stop Honolulu. Then onto Sydney."

"You're with us the whole way?" the president asked.

"I wouldn't miss this trip for the world."

PART III

CHAPTER

61

Washington, D.C.

After a short discussion, it was decided that a Pentagon spokesperson would make the call to *The New York Times* reporter.

"Mr. O'Connell, this is Nanette Lambert with the Army Office of Public Affairs. I'd like to give you first crack at a story."

O'Connell hated when some government functionary called in with a useless pitch. He blamed himself for even answering. "Sorry to waste your time, but I'm on a deadline." O'Connell was already sorting through his initial Internet searches on Strong and he definitely didn't want to be distracted by a pitch on a puff piece. Besides, he was miffed Taylor never called him back. "I'm not the one you want anyway. You need to speak to someone in features."

"Mr. O'Connell, you are the right person. The story concerns an investigation. That's something of your specialty," the career officer explained.

Investigation definitely caught his attention. O'Connell clicked to a clean screen on his computer to make notes. "On the record, Ms...?"

"Lambert, Nanette Lambert. Lt. Lambert. And no. Call it deep background. The rest is up to you. Agreed?"

O'Connell thought for a requisite moment. "Agreed."

"Okay, in brief, we're reopening an inquiry into a bombing in Baghdad that occurred a number of years ago. A special forces team went into an apartment building. The entire team was killed. Do you recall the story?"

"Not off-hand."

Lambert read the next words off a script. She needed to get it right. "All the officers and enlisted men were accounted for—except one. We're unlocking the files." She stopped there to allow O'Connell to catch up on his keyboard.

"Where did you say you're calling from?"

"The Pentagon. Army Office of Public Affairs. I am an unnamed source. Are we clear on that?"

"Yes. And when was this? I'll need dates."

"I'll give you all the basics."

"Why are you reopening this particular investigation?"

Lambert read again from her script. "There were some unanswered questions. We're doing this on behalf of the family of one of the soldiers."

"And his name is?"

"Lt. Richard Cooper. That's Cooper. C-o-o-p-e-r."

O'Connell rested his hands on the computer keys. A bell went off; a bell he didn't like. He suddenly felt he was being used.

"Why me?"

"We thought this was *your* kind of story, Mr. O'Connell."

"And who exactly is the *we*?"

"Off the record?"

"If that's the only way to get it."

"Off the record, Mr. O'Connell, a friend across the river."

Aboard *Air Force One*

"Morning, Colonel."

"Well, good morning, Mr. President," Colonel Peter Lewis said.

"Mind if I join you?" Morgan Taylor stepped into the cockpit.

"Our pleasure." Lewis got an agreeable nod from his co-pilot, Air Force captain Barnard Agins.

"Take a seat, Mr. President," Agins said. "I've been meaning to stretch my legs." The co-pilot removed his headphones and slid his seat back. The president stepped to the side, allowing Agins to pass. In thanks, he patted him on the back.

Morgan Taylor slid into the seat and scanned the display. He didn't need any explanations. Taylor kept current with flight ops, if only through computer simulators. He read the fuel gauge and altimeter and precisely saw where they were via the GPS—over the South Pacific

Even though Morgan Taylor hadn't asked, Lewis knew what the president really wanted.

"Sir, it's been a while. Would you like to fly her?" *Air Force One* was on autopilot.

"Yes, sir," said the former Navy commander.

Taylor fastened his safety belt, grabbed hold of the yoke, and gave Lewis a thumbs-up to disengage the autopilot, transferring control of the 747 to the president.

"She's all yours."

Taylor didn't answer, he just smiled.

Only one person noticed a change in the way the plane handled— Lt. Eric Ross. Rossy's senses were attuned to the plane more than anyone's. He was in an aft compartment when the president took control. He felt a slight surge of power and an almost imperceptible dip in altitude. After a second, he relaxed. Confident that all was well, he returned to his favorite reading—tech updates from Boeing.

The New York Times

The library shelves were filled with biographies and autobiographies of Limbaugh, Savage, Franken, O'Reilly, Hannity, and other talk-show hosts. But no one had written anything comprehensive about Elliott Strong. O'Connell quickly learned that a number of publishing houses had approached the Kansas-based talker, however Strong rejected every offer and threatened to sue anyone who proceeded with an unauthorized biography in print, on A&E, or in magazines. Until recently, the established media hardly cared.

So Michael O'Connell went back to the tried-and-true method for his initial research. He made phone calls.

The *New York Times* reporter soon discovered that none of the individual radio stations that had employed Strong during his ascension were still run by the same owners. No matter the size, the stations now belonged to media conglomerates which acquired them in the media buying frenzy that followed deregulation.

Many of the radio stations weren't even operated in the local communities they served. They were programmed from miles away.

A call to a main station number might trigger an answering machine or an automatic transfer to an office in another town.

That point was no more clearly demonstrated than in January 2002, when a train transporting 10,000 gallons of anhydrous ammonia derailed in Minot, North Dakota. O'Connell learned that the contents spilled, sending a toxic cloud into the sky. Authorities who responded to the danger attempted to warn residents to stay indoors. However, when they called the six local commercial radio stations, no one was there to make an announcement. The stations were automated and programmed remotely. *So much for local radio*, thought O'Connell.

Some congressmen used the Minot case to explore the impact of the 1996 Telecommunications Act. The facts were clear. The law prompted consolidation. Roughly 9,000 out of 10,000 existing radio stations across the U.S. were bought and sold at least once within a five-year period, including the stations where Strong worked.

Minot was allowed to happen. And Elliott Strong remained an enigma.

The reporter had no previous concept of the impact of deregulation. He vowed to find a way to work it into his story. That still left him with an immediate problem. *Where do I go now?*

Lebanon, Kansas

There wasn't going to be a hotel room left in Washington between August 15th–19th. The Bridgeman March accounted for every bed, except those already booked by vacationers.

Anyone dawdling found themselves either out of luck or forced to stay north of Baltimore or deep in Virginia.

"I warned you," Elliott Strong said to his listeners. "But hey, we've secured permits from Parks and Recreations, so bring your sleeping bags. The Mall's all yours."

Estimates for the march now exceeded two million. Almost half would have to sleep on the grass. The entertainment was booked and the networks were already adjusting their lineup. *Dateline* and *Primetime Live* put in requests to follow Bridgeman through the day. CNN and FOX committed their anchors to non-stop coverage. Ironically, there would be more live programming for the one-day march, which was really a rally, than the networks devoted to the last two party conventions. Strong gloated. *All this for a political movement that didn't exist much more than a month earlier.*

Elliott Strong smiled into the mirror that sat on his desk. "Sixteen more days," he said. "I can't wait."

The New York Times

Strong's early history was a matter of public record, posted on www.elliottstrong.com. It was a story he often told on the air. O'Connell read how Strong talked his way into his first radio job by mowing the lawn and how, by being in the right place at the right time, he earned an on-air shift. After that, there was truly no biographical information, only a list of radio stations which carried *Strong Nation*. When the Fresno station, now owned by one of the nation's largest holders of radio properties, couldn't help him, the reporter phoned the local Fresno newspaper.

That call, and the two that followed, eventually put him in touch with a senior residence, where the station's general manager now lived.

O'Connell waited on the telephone for nearly ten minutes until the person front the desk pulled the retiree away from lunch.

"Hello!" Overstreet yelled into the phone. The old, but booming, radio voice startled O'Connell.

"Hello, Mr. Overstreet?"

"What?"

"Mr. Overstreet?" he asked louder, realizing the old man was hard of hearing.

"Yes, who's there?"

O'Connell explained. He finished the thought with, "...and I'm calling regarding Elliott Strong."

"Who?"

"An announcer you hired years ago. "Strong. Elliott Strong." By now O'Connell wrote off the interview.

"Strong, you say?"

"Yes."

"The kid?"

The reporter was surprised. "Yes, yes. The kid. Do you remember him?"

"Of course I do. He was boffing my secretary behind my back," he laughed. "Didn't know for the longest time. Did he tell you I canned them both?"

O'Connell ignored the question.

"Then he left her waiting at the bus station while he high-tailed it out of town."

"I didn't know that. Do you remember her name?"

"I remember the dimple on her left cheek. And I'm not talking about the one she could see in the mirror. Of course I remember her god-damned name! Sally. Got to give it to the kid. He surprised the hell out of me."

"Is she still around?"

"Nope. She married some car salesman in town. Funny about things. Heard she died in a car accident years back."

O'Connell was disappointed. "What else can you tell me about the kid?"

"Luckiest guy in radio." Then Overstreet opened up.

Chicago

Luis Gonzales's fortune was built on the sales of artwork—both legitimate and illegal. While money bought everything and everyone he needed, information was also a highly valuable commodity. Certain facts came from people who thought they were contributing to Middle East think tanks, but they were actually reporting to Gonzales via shell organizations.

He also had moles inside the government. A new message just arrived for him from an officer in the FBI.

Gonzales decoded the message, contained in an eBay sales posting. As each word formed, his body tensed more. Even though his informant didn't understand the significance of the communiqué, the impact was profound.

Florida rez subject of fed conspiracy.
Agency investing. Subject: Haddad, Ibrahim.

Not that Gonzales was really surprised. *It was only a matter of time.* He thought again about the night he abandoned his last life and identity. He was amazed that it had taken this long. Gonzales blamed the Libyan, Fadi Kharrari. *The idiot archived everything. The U.S.*

Special Forces obviously found files with the name Haddad during their raid.

Anticipating discovery, Haddad left Fisher Island, Florida, on the eve of the Inauguration. His computer, like his yacht, went to the bottom of the Atlantic. He counted on the amply compensated cleaning crews to scrub his condo of any fingerprints. All vestige of Haddad's presence should have been erased in the days after his disappearance.

So they found where Ibrahim Haddad lived. So what. Haddad no longer existed.

Sydney, Australia
Friday, 3 August

Morgan Taylor's bullet-proof limousine, shuttled aboard one of two C-5s, now powered through the highways from Glenbrook Air Force Base to Sydney. Actually, three limos left the belly of the Galaxy transports. Two of them were decoys; one was the true presidential limousine. For nearly 60 kilometers, they jockeyed position in a high-speed shell game. Sometimes decoy number one moved in front. Then an identical car took the lead before it dropped back in favor of one of the others. They made the move so many times that it would have been difficult for an observer to tell which limo carried the president.

As the cars approached The Ville St. George, one limo peeled off and entered the underground garage. The president's?

The two remaining cars continued at full speed with police and military escort. A kilometer away, the second limousine broke for the Park Hyatt on Hickson Road. The third did the same a minute up the line, pulling into the Mariott Sydney Hotel, a block away from the harbor.

This ruse was the design of Presley Friedman, the president's Secret Service chief. The St. George was out of the question. He didn't want to put the president up in the other hotels either; not this trip. But Morgan Taylor needed to stay somewhere, so it was decided he would eventually end up at Kirribilli House.

Since 1957, Kirribilli House has welcomed royalty, heads of state, and Congressional and Parliamentary members, in addition to serving as the residence for the Prime Minister and his family.

Taylor changed modes of transportation in an underground loading dock at the Park Hyatt. He completed his ride in a laundry van.

When it came to safety, the usually boisterous Taylor remained quiet. He didn't argue with Friedman. Taylor wasn't the boss of this part of the trip.

The New York Times
the same time

"Hello, this is Michael O'Connell. I'm with the *New York Times* and..."

"I'm sorry. I'm not interested in a subscription."

O'Connell often got this reaction when he didn't explain what he did fast enough. "I'm a reporter working on a story about Elliott Strong. Is this Bill Bueler?"

"Yes," the caller responded with trepidation.

"Well, can I speak with you for a few minutes?"

O'Connell found his first lead through the Grants, New Mexico, Chamber of Commerce. Bueler was an old deejay, presumably around the time that Strong worked at the same station. Now he was a manager at a local McDonald's.

"Strong, you say?"

"Right. You worked together about eighteen years ago."

"Can't help you," Bueler interrupted.

"Just a few questions." O'Connell said lightly. "I understand you had the morning shift. Strong followed you."

"I don't remember." It was a cold response.

"Oh? Didn't you spend some time together?"

"I said I don't remember."

O'Connell sensed real hostility. "Mr. Bueler, it's really a simple matter. Strong's gone onto become one of the nation's most popular syndicated hosts. I'm sure that you..."

"It was a long time ago. A lot of people came and went."

"Strong used Grants as a jumping-off point for a station in Arizona."

"Once and for all, I can't help you."

"Can't or won't, Mr. Bueler?"

"Goodbye, Mr. O'Connell." The former deejay hung up.

Sydney, Australia
Government House
Saturday, 4 August

"Ladies and gentlemen, welcome to the first session of what we trust will be an historic conference," Prime Minister Foss said resolutely. "We have a great deal of work ahead. Preliminary sessions with members of our staffs have paved the way. Now it is our job to forge a new South Pacific Alliance—a model for the four corners of the world that will proclaim we stand united against terrorists and those nation states, individuals, organizations, or even corporations that support or shelter them. Ironically, it is an ancient Arab proverb that best describes our union—'The enemy of my enemy is my friend.' I see new friends joining us at this table. May we all have the resolve to make the world safer."

Foss looked around the State Room of the Government House. The Colonial Building, the most sophisticated example of Gothic Revival in all New South Wales, had been closed to the public since Australia's SASR approved it as the secure site for the summit. In attendence were leaders from seventeen nations including Japan, South Korea, Indonesia, Malaysia, Vietnam, Thailand, Cambodia, the United States, India, Pakistan, and Afghanistan. Foss removed his suit jacket and rolled up his sleeves.

"What do you say we get to work?"

The New York Times

The *New York Times* reporter tracked down Marcy Ripenberg in Prescott, Arizona. It was a brief call. Ripenberg didn't want to talk about Strong. But as she hung up, O'Connell was certain he heard the word, "fucker."

His next series of phone calls focused on a similar set of characters in Phoenix, Arizona—an old program director who was out of the business and another former secretary Strong slept with, Sheila Stuart. She was the first person who was really willing to talk.

"Yeah, he was a real mover and a shaker. And I'm not just talking about his announcing," she said through a fit of coughs. She sounded like she'd smoked for far too long. "I knew he wasn't going to spend much time here. Just passing through." She laughed. "Phoenix and me."

O'Connell ignored the comment. "Where did you think he was going?"

"To the top. Any way he could."

"What kind of person was he?"

"He read like crazy. Sometimes I couldn't get him to put his book down, no matter what I did."

"And what did he like to read?"

"That's a very good question. Is this going in the newspaper?"

"Possibly."

"Oh. You'll leave out the part about..."

"Yes."

She coughed more. "Tons of history. I guess it was for his radio show. He was always quoting this president or that president. I couldn't keep them straight, but Elliott knew them all. And nothing could break his concentration. Not even when I was under the desk when he was.... You won't use that either, will you?"

"No."

"On account of my husband," Stuart added.

"I understand," O'Connell replied. "But it sounds like you really wish the two of you could have made a go of it."

"Yeah, I guess that's right. But I wasn't part of his plans. Never really was."

"He was that talented?"

"Talented? I don't know about that. He was good. But he was better than good. He was lucky."

O'Connell bolded **luck** on his computer notes. It was the second time he heard it in context with Strong.

"Don't get me wrong," she added. "He was damned good on the air. He could think fast and, for someone his age, he really had a knack for politics. But it was the accident that helped him the most."

"What accident?" This came out of nowhere.

"The crash. The car crash that killed Buck Roberts, the drive time, you know, the afternoon host. Elliott was doing weekends. Roberts was heading home one night and he ran off the road into a ravine. Killed. Just like that. Elliott got called to cover the next day. It was just before an L.A. outfit bought the station. They were putting together a regional block of stations. A month after Elliott took over for Buck, he was on seven stations. That's what I call lucky."

"Damned lucky, Mrs. Stuart."

Washington, D.C.
the same day

"Now what?" Roarke asked Shannon Davis.

"We wait."

"I hate waiting. I'm not good at it. Besides, what do we wait for? For Cooper to say, 'Here I am!' That's not going to happen."

Davis put his feet up on the table in a conference room in the White House basement—their war room. They knew who the enemy was, but aside from the story leaked to the *Times,* they didn't have a clue what to do next.

"Start with the assumption that he saw the report. He could go into deep hiding, which would be the smartest and easiest thing. Does he do that, or does he come after us?"

"Not *us.* Me," Roarke corrected. "He knows me by sight now and I'm sure he's realized I'm after him." Roarke craned his neck, moving his head from shoulder to shoulder. He felt tense and frustrated. He finally sat down next to his friend. "That means he's more likely to go on the offensive."

Neither man added to the conversation for two solid minutes. Roarke finally broke the silence. "Another assumption: Cooper's got more than enough money to live his life out. He also has the ability to pass himself off as just about anybody."

"So that and his shoe size are supposed to deliver him to us?"

"No, it won't. As far as we've seen, this guy doesn't do a thing without surveillance and preparation. There's a better-than-fair chance that he's the most skilled assassin that's emerged in a long time. And if he's not the most skilled, he's at least the most careful."

"Which leaves us at square one."

They sat quietly for another few minutes, sharing only deep, frustrating sighs.

Davis tried another approach. "We do know his assignments came from a man named Haddad. What if we announce we've caught him; that he's talking to us. That might snarf him out."

Roarke didn't like the idea.

"Okay then, we pull in Cooper's parents. Hold them on conspiracy charges. Hell, they might even be involved and..."

Another *no* from Roarke. "Unless we catch the right man, with the proper proof, the press will fry us. Remember, it's been a year since he killed Jennifer Lodge and six months since he shot Teddy Lodge. The story's already off everyone's scope. We bring in the wrong man and the FBI takes the fall. Probably the president, too."

"So I guess that's it," Davis said getting to his feet. He reached for his dark blue suit jacket which was draped over the back of his chair. Roarke had nothing to add that would keep the conversation going.

"Write if you get work," Davis said. Roarke saluted with two fingers.

That was it. They were in the middle of a chess match, not knowing whether the other guy even wanted to play. To make matters worse, the opponent was winning.

The New York Times
the same time

The impact of being on one Houston radio station was far greater than the seven New Mexico, Arizona, and Nevada stations. That's where Elliott Strong went next. O'Connell spoke to Linda Dale Lockhart, the retired media critic of the *Houston Chronicle*. She was quite familiar with O'Connell's writing, which made it easier for him.

"Yup, he was in this market about eighteen months; maybe closer to two years," the critic remembered. "He stirred up all sorts of shit. I think he really found his voice here—a pretty angry one at that. As I recall, he never had guests; not that he had to. When they threw out the Fairness Doctrine, stations had no reason to broadcast balanced shows. So a lot stopped trying. But as I understand it, there was a loophole, anyway. Call-in shows weren't really governed by the Fairness Doctrine."

"No?" This was different from what O'Connell had generally heard and what most critics understood.

"Well, presumably by inviting a cross section of the community to express their opinions, the scope of the opinion broadened—at least on paper. Of course, things were tame back then anyway. Who knew where it was all going? It was all pretty local. Now? Seems whoever's the loudest gets the most attention. And for a while in this market, Strong was the loudest of them all."

"How so?"

"Well, remember, he was preaching to the converted. That's what talk-show hosts generally do. But he must have slipped something in Houston's Kool Aid, because his ratings took off here."

O'Connell asked the next question with some notion of what he might hear.

"Would you describe him as *lucky*?"

"Funny you mention it. Now that I think of it, yes."

"How so?"

"Well, let's see, he was on the number-two talker in town. The number-one was a powerhouse station with a bonafide Houston legend. Race was his name, Bill Race. Well, he had a heart attack. Forty-four."

"He died?"

"Yup. Deader than a doornail. And Strong moved right in on his audience."

O'Connell kept the critic engaged for a few more minutes, but he had learned enough.

FBI Headquarters
Washington, D.C.
the same time

"What about other prints from Haddad's condo?" Mulligan asked Bessolo.

"Some illegals on the cleaning staff. And one that matched a California driver's license.

"You have a name with that?"

"Ali Razak."

"Razak." He spelled it. "No police record. We're checking with the IRS on anything they may have. I have a picture of him from California. I'll forward it up to you. A big guy."

"Big, like *bodyguard* big?"

"Try Godzilla."

CHAPTER

62

The GAO report was more of an indictment than a study. The investigative arm of Congress, the Government Accounting Office, charged that the Pentagon couldn't reconcile where all its Category I weapons were. Translating the GAO paper into people-speak, the military simply did not know how many Stinger missiles—believed to have been shipped to the Middle East during the Gulf War and through the subsequent war in Iraq—were missing. Inventory records of man-portable air defense systems (MANPADS) differed from GAO's physical count, not by dozens or even hundreds, but by thousands of missiles.

Since 1970, several hundred thousand MANPADS were manufactured and issued to American military. Thousands were sold internationally through the Foreign Military Sales Program. Problems in record keeping, storage, theft, and black market trade revealed that the armed services could not account for the actual number of missiles that had been in their stores. The reason? Lax reporting on serial numbers of MANPADS produced, fired, destroyed, sold, or transferred.

To put it another way, there are better records on who owns America's laptop computers than who's holding Stinger missiles capable of downing an aircraft.

And what of personal arms? In Vietnam alone, some 90,000 semi-automatic pistols were abandoned by American combatants during the troop evacuation. Add to that 791,000 M-16A1 rifles, 857,600 other non-classed rifles, and thousands of other weapons, including 550 tanks, the total of arms left behind reached an estimated 1,882,238.

The number of deaths these weapons have inflicted by guerilla fighters and terrorists around the world is impossible to calculate because there are no end-use controls that prevent them from getting into the hands of undesirables. The potential destruction from the MANPADS on the market is even worse and less excusable.

More recently, a combat theater commander in the Persian Gulf relaxed administrative requirements permitted by operational regulations, which ultimately led to missiles being transported on unguarded trucks and driven by third-country nationals. In addition, ammunition sites were left wide open.

In Europe at one depot, facility managers' records recorded that 22,558 Category I missiles were in storage. The CAO counted 20,373, a frightening difference of 2,185 missiles.

The GAO's conclusion, enumerated in GAO/NSIAD-94-100:

> "It is impossible to accurately determine how many missiles are missing at the item manager or storage level because the services did not establish effective procedures to determine what should be in their inventories."

In hard numbers, it is estimated that one percent of the worldwide total of 750,000 MANPADS—or 7,500 missiles—were beyond the control of the U.S. military or formal governments.

Luis Gonzales had two.

Paris, France
Sunday, 5 August

The wires picked up the *New York Times* story. Cable news ignored it. There were no visuals. But the foreign press took note. Two days after Michael O'Connell's brief article ran, the *International Herald* gave it a paragraph on page six.

> The United States Army has reopened an investigation into the deaths of seven members of a Special Forces team killed in Baghdad, September 2004. The combatants died during a devastating apartment building explosion. Reports at the time indicated that it was a trap. The exact reason for renewing the inquiry is unknown, but a Pentagon source told the *New York Times* that some irregularities have recently surfaced...

Canadian Robby Pearlman sipped his latte on the balcony of his suite at the Hotel Meurice. He looked over the Tuileries and the city beyond. It was the Vancouver real estate developer's third trip to Paris. By far, it was his best.

The tall, athletic businessman turned back to the bedroom where a 26-year-old blonde lay naked on the bed they shared. They'd met the previous afternoon at the Louvre, on a *DaVinci Code* museum tour. She was on holiday from London where she worked as a teacher. She was hoping for a suave Frenchman, but the handsome, soft-spoken, well-read Canadian caught her eye.

She slept as he read the newspaper and contemplated what to do.

Lebanon, Kansas
the same time

"Bring your cell phones with you and call in. And you can text message friends, because I guarantee you, it's going to be too loud to hear any rings." The phones were an important component to the real success of the Bridgeman March on Washington.

"We're days away from the biggest political show of force ever to be witnessed in America. You'll be part of it. You'll make history. You'll show the rest of the country and the entire world that we demand change. We demand it now."

Bridgeman's picture was on the cover of *Time*. Inside, there was a sidebar on Elliott Strong. They printed only what they knew; O'Connell had more.

The New York Times
the same time

O'Connell discovered that in Atlanta, Strong benefited from another timely merger which put him on stations across the state.

Another announcer was supposed to get the syndication gig, but coincidently, he was the killed in a brutal, unsolved car jacking.

Paris, France
an hour later

Robby Pearlman ran his fingers down the back of his newest con-quest and pressed into her. She felt his hardness against her ass and responded with a tired moan. She really wanted to rest and couldn't understand how he was ready again.

"In a little while, I'm so tired."

He pushed closer to her. She reached back and held him in her hand. "Please. Just a few minutes." Up until now he had been attentive to her needs and pleasure. But now he showed an insatiable appetite. He rolled her on her back and climbed over her. "In a while."

Pearlman wouldn't stop. It was as if he stalked her and now it was time to take her down. She tried to resist, but couldn't. He was too strong; too determined. The man she'd spent the last 24 hours with suddenly changed. He became a sexual predator.

"Please! You're hurting me."

Pearlman didn't stop. He didn't hear her. And least of all, he didn't care. He was some place far away.

Boston, Massachusetts

"What's the matter?" Katie asked. They were already into their nightly phone call and it was clear to her that Roarke wasn't himself.

"Nothing. I'm okay."

"Come on, honey, are the bad guys getting you down."

He was constantly amazed at how well she read him.

"I can't."

"You can tell me how you feel," she offered.

"How do you know me so well?" Roarke asked in return.

"I know you because I love you."

This was still all so new to him. "And why do you love me?"

"I love you because I know you so well."

With that, Roarke opened up. Tonight, they wouldn't have a romantic or sexy conversation. This was a pouring out, equal to what Katie had done when she was in Roarke's arms. He spoke like they were in bed; lovingly, openly, and honestly. Through it all, he blessed the day they met. Katie vowed to catch an early flight out in the morning. It was time she took her research to Washington; time she tried out Roarke's bed.

two hours later

Katie Kessler's first round of research covered everything from prestigious legal journals to Gore Vidal's novels. She reviewed Congressional testimony from 2004 and studied fundamental arguments offered by the Founding Fathers. Some of them seemed relevant enough to be heard in the halls of the House and Senate chambers today. When it came to constructing a new framework for presidential succession, there was certainly no shortage of opinion. Kessler read hundreds of briefs; thousands of pages of testimony. But coming up with solid arguments that would stand up to the Constitution was another thing entirely.

As Katie packed her suitcases and stacked her boxes of research by the front door of her Grove Street apartment, she wondered whether she would be able to accomplish what Congress hadn't achieved in more than fifty years.

Recently, many of the country's greatest legal scholars went to the Capitol to offer their proposals for amending the succession laws. Nothing came of the testimony. Leading representatives filed a variety of bills. Again, nothing happened. Now Ms. Kessler was going to Washington. She asked herself how she could make a difference. It seemed like an impossible task until she had an epiphany. *I don't have to get a bill passed.* She needed to deliver the groundwork. Others would supply the muscle for the heavy lifting. By working *for* the White House, she could approach succession from the inside, much like Harry Truman had in 1947. Another realization came to her. *That's how it gets done! Not when Congress wants it, but when the president does.*

Ideas were taking shape now. They were a combination of disparate thoughts from both sides of the aisle, with a little political dynamite thrown in for good measure.

It all came down to one experience that occurred before her time. In 1968, when a majority of Americans voted for Richard Nixon, they also voted for his choice as vice president, Spiro Agnew. The majority of the country didn't want Democrat George McGovern. They got Republicans Nixon and Agnew. Agnew eventually resigned. Nixon chose Ford to replace him. When Nixon resigned, Ford chose Nelson Rockefeller as his vice president. The term that started out with the election of Nixon-Agnew ended with the unelected Ford-Rockefeller.

This was consistent with the will of the people. But what if something catastrophic happened to the new president and vice president? The speaker of the house would have become president. Speaker of the House Carl Albert was a Democrat.

The will of the people? Kessler asked herself again. *Presidential succession, no matter what form it takes, should reflect the will of the people.*

To shape her arguments she needed counsel from the *other* man she'd grown to respect over the past year—Supreme Court Chief Justice Leopold Browning.

Maluku, Indonesia
the same time

Komari called himself commander. It wasn't an official rank in anyone's army except his own. He established his own rules of discipline and loyalty. He presided over the most undemocratic of court martials, and punishment always came swiftly. In Komari's world, there was no imprisonment.

Umar Komari's force grew by the day. Although the Indonesian government had heard rumblings of his activities, they didn't consider the insurgent, who confined his operation to the remote islands, a real threat. Anti-Christian sentiment continued to grow, but the occasional report of violence attributed to Komari was far less important to the TNI than maintaining order in Jakarta. That was a mistake.

Komari hadn't begun wholesale slaughter of the hated Christians, but his nightly raids were striking fear in the small fishing villages of the Malukus. He killed, stole, and recruited Muslim conscripts, and rewarded them with some of the spoils. His drug production increased, as he knew it would, and his weapons cache expanded. So the would-be commander actually had a command. Soon he would be addressed by a new title. He repeated it in his mind.

President.

Sydney, Australia
Monday, 6 August

Morgan Taylor listened to the Indonesian leader's remarks, showing only a blank stare. Since Taylor took office, he'd expressed his disappointment numerous times about Indonesia's inability to drive terrorists out. Now he was worried that the country was becoming a training ground from which terrorism was being exported. However, nine minutes into the speech, the Indonesian president claimed his government had addressed the problem.

"Terrorists will find no sanctuary in my country. As we gather under the umbrella of freedom, our military carries on a vigilant search for the last remnants of *Jemaah Islamiyyah*. We have dealt deadly blows to the rebels. According to the reports I read, we are more safe today than in previous years. I am encouraged by our progress, as you should be." He continued to spout platitudes for another two minutes, then concluded with a request for substantially more aid.

"The chair thanks you for your comments," said Prime Miniser Foss, "and now recognizes the representative from the United States of America, President Morgan Taylor."

"Thank you, Prime Minister Foss." Taylor turned over his prepared remarks. For a protracted moment, he was back at the town hall meeting at Verona Area High School. *What can we do?* That was the overriding question he heard that night. He read the same concern on many of the the faces in the room now—at least those who weren't posturing for the sake of the summit.

Morgan Taylor didn't have the answer for the Verona bus driver who asked, *What's America doing to stop them?* The same was true when the Dane County, Wisconsin, law clerk explained that her oldest son had been killed by a suicide bomber in Baghdad, and now she was afraid for her youngest who just enlisted. *Tell me what you're going to do to protect my son.*

He moved onto other issues during the town hall meeting in the gym, but personally, he never moved off the question. He was going to answer it today.

"With all due respect to the remarks of President Ramelan Djali, the Indonesian leader must recognize that we are his partner in the defense of his country. Is that true, sir?"

He got an affirmative nod.

"And as such, we share intelligence."

Another *yes*.

"Then I think we are in a perfect position to assess that things are *not* better!"

Taylor stepped on the gasps. "Sir, there's nothing to indicate that you're striking deadly blows. The opposite is true. The United States provides you with weekly, sometimes daily intelligence. You have done little with it. And, sadly, we have done little to encourage you." Now he broadened his argument. "The same can be said of almost every nation at this table, save Australia which recently struck back in the Solomons. Who else can honestly say they have gone after the terrorists in a manner that would benefit peace?" He looked at every leader at the table. Some averted their eyes.

Taylor reached behind him. On cue, Secretary of State Poole handed him a folder. "Let me share a number of reports compiled by the intelligence services of the United States government. Some of these will be familiar to President Djali. They paint a very different picture than the one presented here today. Since he didn't share them with you, I will."

The Indonesian was offended. He tried to speak, but Taylor over-powered him. "Mr. President, I'm sure everyone will want to hear from you again. But if you please..." He opened the file and slid a dozen photos across the table in different directions.

"These satellite photos show terrorist encampments in twenty-three locations. They were taken as long ago as last November and as recently as last week. Each has one or more areas circled in red. Inside those circles are training camps and weapons stores. Mr. Djali's island country is the perfect setting for playing hide and seek. The same can be said for areas of the Solomons and Malaysia, Pakistan, India, of course, Afghanistan, Thailand, and even Japan. I have satellite photographs of your countries as well." Poole disseminated them. "They're not good."

Taylor noted the shock in the room as the men and women sorted through the photographs of their countries up-to-date photos that revealed operational terrorist camps.

"Mr. Chairman, I'm not here to undermine the good intentions of a respected ally," he said returning to the topic of Indonesia. "However, American lives have been lost in bombings in Mr. Djaili's country.

Recent activity makes it undeniably apparent that Indonesia is on the verge of a religious holy war, a jihad against Christian nationals and westerners. It is supported by al Qaeda funds and the sale of drugs, and it is hardly acknowledged because of corruption within lower levels of Mr. Djali's government.

"I suggest that if we're to claim any victory, it's time to—as we say—come clean." Everyone seemed to get the meaning. "Put away your speeches. There are no reporters here. So no more grandstanding. Stop your posturing. We're here to fight these bastards at the root level—with arms, troops, intelligence, and yes, Mr. Djali, what you also need, hard cash."

"Your insinuations are the height of insult," Djali finally managed. He turned to Prime Minister Foss, "I will not stand for this."

Foss didn't have a chance to respond; Taylor jumped right back into the debate.

"Mr. President, they are not insinuations and I haven't intended to insult you; only correct you. But your comment reminds me of President Truman's meeting in nineteen forty-five with Russian's foreign minister, Vyacheslav Molotov." He removed his reading glasses and stared at his Indonesian counterpart. "Molotov came to the White House to discuss the future of Poland. Truman believed the Russians were reneging on what Roosevelt and Stalin had agreed upon four months earlier. Russia was imposing communism on Poland. Truman had been warned by Henry Stimson, his secretary of war, to be careful dealing with the Soviets. Truman dismissed Stimson's advice and told Molotov that the Russians were not true to their word. 'We are!' demanded Molotov. Truman then explained to him, in words of one syllable, exactly why they were not. Molotov argued, as you have, Mr. President, 'I have never been talked to like that in my life.' Do you know how Truman responded?"

Djali raised an eyebrow.

"'Carry out your agreements and you won't be talked to like that.'"

Morgan put his glasses back on and re-addressed Djaili. "So, Mr. President, why not start over and explain what's really going on in your country."

Djali had been quite unprepared for Taylor's direct assault, which effectively stripped away all diplomatic formality. With the niceties off the table, Taylor went one very American step further. He added, "This time without the bullshit."

The Indonesian reached for his glass of water and took a sip. His hands shook. All eyes were on President Djali as he cleared his throat. "Chairman Foss, members of the committee, I need your help."

Paris, France

Robby Pearlman got the girl out of his life by changing hotels. Even if they bumped into one another later, she wouldn't recognize him. Pearlman was going to morph into another character.

A new offer had come in. It was high-paying and risky. The contract was just shy of the amount he received for the business he did in Hudson, New York, a little over a year ago. At first, he wasn't sure if he wanted to take it. Something about it. He'd have to take more chances than normal, work with shoulder-fired missiles, and there would be multiple deaths.

He considered the dangers while he dyed his hair. *Where's the optimum strike zone? Close-in or far away? Certainly not in full view. A roof? Not a car.* He weighed the job against the report he read in the *International Herald Tribune.* Although not specific, the story about the army investigation reminded him that he could never be too careful or too conservative.

Roarke's behind this. He thought about finding and killing the Secret Service agent. He knew where he lived and who he slept with. But, he asked himself, *Why take the chance?* If he did take the agent out, there'd be others like him. They'd keep coming.

Another thought about the article nagged at him. It felt more and more like a plant. *If it is...* He made some adjustments to his latest identity and pulled away from the mirror. He sharpened his focus, looking straight into the eyes of his latest creation. He was moody, quick-thinking, and guarded. The talkative Canadian real estate developer was gone. A critical California psychologist stood in his place. The new guise gave him renewed perspective. An idea slowly formed. *It would take some doing,* he said to himself. *But this job definitely provided an interesting opportunity.*

He pulled his hair extensions back into a ponytail, peered at his reflection again, and decided where he had to go. *Belgrade.* He had unique contacts in Belgrade. There, he could get meetings with certain people willing to do anything for money. There, he could make his payday and solve his personal problem at the same time.

Richard Cooper smiled into the mirror, but someone else entirely new looked back.

Washington, D.C.

It was their second meeting. This one was at Duke Patrick's Georgetown brownstone.

"General," Patrick said answering the door.

"Mr. Speaker, so good to see you again. Thank you for having me."

"Well, I figured if we're going to go down this road together, we sure as hell have to open our homes to one another."

"Yes, quite so. I've already told Lily that I want to get you down for a good old Texas barbeque after the speech. She's cleaning the grill right now," Bridgeman laughed.

"I'd be delighted. But first things first. Shall we?" Patrick motioned to his study where their conversation would continue. The speaker invited the general to sit down. "What's your pleasure?"

"I'm a scotch man. On the rocks."

Patrick poured a glass of an average supermarket scotch.

He handed Bridgeman the glass. "To the future."

"To the future together," he replied.

Over the next two hours the men discussed how the next administration would take shape and how soon that might actually occur.

Lebanon, Kansas
Tuesday, 7 August

"Hi Elliott, you've been talking about it for a while now, but what's the chance we can get Taylor out? These amendment things take a long time. You gotta go state by state. It could take forever, or at least until the next election."

"Good question," Elliott Strong said to the caller. It took him right where he wanted to go tonight. But that wasn't a coincidence. The caller was another plant. "...and after re-reading my American history, I've come up with some fascinating points. Are you ready for a lesson that will make your head spin?" he asked rhetorically. "Pay attention now." He could imagine listeners turning up the volume or telling their spouses to be quiet. "Revelations like this don't come down the pike every day."

He rustled some papers unnecessarily. "Here it is. Thomas Jefferson, one of the Founding Fathers, was way ahead of his time. You have to admire the old boy, he really had a sense of what's going on right now. What is it? Well, Jefferson was worried about the power of the dead over the living. He feared that an unchanged Constitution was the last thing we needed." He left room for a *wow*. "Now I'm getting to the good part. He proposed that each generation have a real say in what they needed and that the Constitution should expire after nineteen or twenty years. Twenty years, people! Boy are we overdue. Jefferson wanted us to draft a new one, not just once, but every twenty years!"

Strong's voice boomed over the airwaves. He slapped his hand on the table and argued, "By my count, we're ten Constitutions behind!" The talk-show host failed to point out that the notion was dismissed by Jefferson's contemporary, James Madison, who contended that the mechanism for change was implicit in the way the Constitution was drafted.

"Ten Constitutions behind, my friends. Would we have such an unbelievable situation today if the Constitution had been updated? Would a defeated president be serving as commander in chief? Would he be holding the nation's highest office?"

Strong raised his hand in the air, conducting himself. As he lowered it, he brought his voice down. "I don't think so." Listeners heard him take a deep sigh; one of his trademarks. "Now I'm a realist. My critics might take exception with that, but it's true. You come to me for the truth. Well, here it is. We're not going to change the Constitution overnight. I was wrong to suggest it. It was naïve, and yes, you heard me right, I was wrong."

The host fell silent for five seconds. He watched the second hand on the wall clock tick by. "Okay. So what now? We're days away from the biggest march on the Capital in the history of the Republic and suddenly I tell you it's unlikely we can get an amendment through. You've booked your planes, you made arrangements to give your kids to the grandparents, the hotel has your credit card number, and crazy Elliott Strong says it ain't gonna happen? Well, hold on. I started by telling you that I've been reading up on my American history, folks. You know I started that when I was just a kid doing the farm reports on the radio outside of Fresno. But I missed something. And this one is going to make you very happy."

Another five seconds ticked off, which further added to the audience's anticipation.

"You're going to demand a recall of the administration! Taylor goes—like he was supposed to. He lost, for God's sake. And this will be the way you—citizens of a *Strong Nation*—can hand him his walking papers."

Glenbrook Air Force Force Base
New South Wales, Australia
Wednesday, 8 August

He took his break and plugged in his laptop computer. Nothing unusual. Everyday, the *Air Force One* mechanic checked his e-mail and surfed the Net. Anyone looking over his shoulder would be amazed at his interests: Classic baseball cards, lunchboxes, comic books. His hobby was buying and selling. He did most of his work over eBay.

He scanned the list of new postings for 1955 Bowman baseball cards. Although they weren't the most valuable cards in the market, collectors considered them unique because of their design. Pictures were framed horizontally in a wood-grain color TV monitor, rather than a typical vertical pose in a plain border.

Finding cards in great condition was the challenge. The 320-card 1955 set was the last issued by the Bowman Gum Company of Philadelphia. The cards are susceptible to easy corner chipping. The slightest flaking on the edges generally leads to exposure of the white cardboard underneath the photograph, which immediately downgrades a card's worth. Also, the cards were routinely printed off center; another reason why the set, though singularly distinctive, isn't among the most popular.

The mechanic was only interested in one card: #37 with famed Brooklyn Dodgers' shortstop, Pee Wee Reese. The card depicted the star third baseman on his right knee. He held a baseball bat upside-down. The name REESE appeared as black capital letters over a white bar. The back had his personal stats and his batting records. The face value, in mint condition was an affordable $150. The card often showed up in Internet auctions. He could have bought it any number of times over the years, but he hadn't.

He typically logged on once or twice a week to check the postings. He actually found this American hobby fun, and a way to turn a buck. But he never completed his Bowman set collection, which would have been worth a little over $5,000. *Maybe this trip*, he thought.

He scrolled down the postings, expecting this to take no more than a few moments. Three '55 Reese cards were listed. One was a more expensive Topps card, two were Bowmans. He read what the collectors had written. The first Bowman advertised a card in fair condition, with an opening bid established at $19.50. The other offered a Reese in better shape and with the following description.

Harold "Pee Wee Reese" Brklyn Ddgr lft hander, Excellent to Nr Mint—slight grease stain on back smudges birthdate 7/22/18

He almost missed it the first time. On the second pass the Air Force officer's eyes widened. *Lft hander.* He looked over his shoulder. No one was nearby. He turned back to the computer screen. *Birthdate 7/22/18.* He'd waited years for this specific card listing. Now it had come.

He rested his fingers on the keys for three minutes without typing.

Reese threw and batted right handed and his correct birthday was a day later, July 23rd.

The asking price was a sensible $111.50. He typed his bid, which was a tad higher.

5,000,000 Euro. Bidder 34423.

He'd thought for years about the exact amount to quote. Today's price was higher due to the location and heightened security. But the seller obviously knew where he was. *Glenbrook.* He wanted the job done on the way back home.

He took a deep breath before hitting send. *Yes.* He was ready. He pressed enter. The information immediately charged through the Internet via a WiFi connection. To anyone else clicking on the auction it would look like a joke. But it was far from it. If the seller accepted the offer, half of the stated amount would be wired into an account under his *real* name. The remainder would be paid upon the successful completion of the mission.

Considering it might take a few hours before he had his answer, the officer powered down his computer and went back to work.

A few other crew members of *Air Force One* saw him smiling as he climbed back aboard the plane. *Odd,* they must have thought. *He rarely smiles.*

The New York Times
the same day

O'Connell's four calls to Strong's syndicator earned him little more than an exercise in futility. His first request was forwarded to the company publicist. No response. The second, for some reason, was routed to an accountant, who couldn't understand why he got the call. The next two calls went to the president of the company, Charlie Huddle. O'Connell stated his request to the secretary, but was promptly returned to the publicist. He called back, complaining that he wanted to speak directly to Huddle. After being put on hold for nearly five minutes, during which time he had to listen to one of Strong's broadcasts, the secretary finally punched back only to tell him, "Mr. Huddle is not available, but he recommends you visit *StrongNation-Radio.com* for all information pertaining to the talk-show host."

That's where he began. *Goddamned runaround!* O'Connell spent most of his life discovering new ways to get around functionaries, road blocks, and corporate assholes. *Okay, let's try the back door,* he thought.

He used his cell phone this time, dialed the main number again, and started walking down the hall at a fast clip. The switchboard answered.

"Hello. Sales department, please."

"Just a moment."

By the time an assistant answered, O'Connell sounded out of breath—which he was.

"Hi there. Hope you can help me." He kept walking. He seemed harried. "I've got a copy change on a web address for a commercial."

"So?"

"So, it's on Strong's show. Today! Gotta get it right to him. What's his direct?"

"Just a second, I'll..."

"I don't have any time. Got to get this right to him. You have the control room?"

"Well, yes, but..."

"The fucking URL is wrong. The client is going apeshit. If it hits the air that way, we're gonna have a suit on our hands!"

"Okay, okay. Here it is." She read off the number from a contact sheet.

"Got it," O'Connell said. "Thanks."

"What did you say your name is?"

He pressed end on his Blackberry and kissed the device. "Thank you, sweetheart."

Kirribilli House
Sydney, Australia
that night

The two men sat and nursed their drinks and puffed on their Monticristos, quite legal in Australia.

"There's no balls to it yet," Morgan Taylor told the Australian prime minister. "Until this agreement grows some serious balls, it's not going to mean a damned thing."

"Morgan, these people can't move as fast as you want. They're afraid."

"David, there's an ancient Sephardic expression. You're either on the train or under it. I want to be on it."

"I know. So do I, but what do you want to do? Go in and punish Malaysia if they don't weed out the *Kumpulah Mujahedeen*? Or the same with the *JI* in Indonesia? We can't sanction our allies like that, Morgan."

"No? Then we might as well hand over the keys to the front door to the enemy. Whoever they are. I'm sick and tired of signing agreements that don't mean a fucking thing. They get our money. We offer protection. Do they really do anything in return to fight terrorists in their own backyard? No. And, they hate us no matter what."

"They fear you, Morgan, and they fear the people who can bring them down."

Prime Minister Foss gently flicked the ashes from his half-smoked cigar into a crystal ashtray. "But, of course you're right. It's the reality of the 21st century. We're allied with sprawling third-world countries that are spread out over thousands and thousands of square kilometers of ocean. The leaders can barely hold on to their own power base let alone keep their enemies in check. In many places, the growth of Islam is out-pacing Christianity. Muslim majorities are finally gaining political power. In any given year, Japan may have more terrorist groups than baseball teams, South Korea has its maniac neighbor to the north, and you tell me how much help Pakistan is?"

"They sign everything and do nothing, David."

"So what do you propose? Another American land grab? I don't think you're about to follow Bush."

President Taylor took his last puff of the night and crushed out his cigar. He leaned across the small table that separated the two men and said, barely above a whisper, "Supply and demand, David. We cut off the supply line that's arming the terrorists."

The prime minister frowned. He wasn't certain what Morgan Taylor was suggesting.

"We're in a war on terrorism. Who the hell are we fighting? The bin Ladens? Some rogue governments? I don't know from day to day and I'm the President of the United States with all the military power imaginable. I can order a strike anywhere in the world. But what are my targets?"

"That is the nature of things today."

"Come on, David. These guys are armed to the teeth. So we cut off their supply."

"Where?" Foss asked.

"Everywhere. From the source," Taylor said.

"You're not planning on bombing gun manufacturers."

"Bombing them? No. Examining their books, yes. If that's not possible, then we look at *other* options." He didn't explain the point further. "So, yes, we do go after the mass producers of arms, but also the arms dealers who traffic in them, the governments that help them, the corporations that shelter them."

Foss was clearly surprised by the proposal. "Morgan, they'll kill you in your own country. You're a hunter yourself. I'm even versed on your 2nd Amendment debate—the right to bear arms. They'll impeach you."

"Hell, they're already looking for ways, David. But this isn't about me. That's why this needs to be *our* initiative, agreed upon by *our* allies."

Taylor pressed closer. "We destroy cocaine fields in Venezuela. We target planes and ships transporting contraband. Hell, you saw the pictures of Indonesia. I can call the NSA right now and get you another fifty hard targets where weapons are stored in the South Pacific; places where there are enough weapons to wipe out Sydney tomorrow. And I'm not counting the dirty bombs. I have no idea where they're hidden. Think about it. We'll really make war on terrorism if we go after the weapons. We out the countries that don't do it themselves. We give them fair warning. If they don't solve the problem, we'll do it for them."

"WMDs all over again? You don't want another Iraq."

"Doesn't have to be. And I won't be drawn into that kind of quagmire. We don't invent a search. We seek, we evaluate, we confirm, we share our discovery with the host government, and then we destroy. Every action is a front-page victory."

"A Taylor Doctrine?" Foss concluded.

"Absolutely not! It can't be. It has to come out of our talks. It's the balls."

"How do you explain it to the doves in your own party? And what about collateral damage? Civilians will be killed."

"Yes," Taylor lowered his eyes. "That will happen. But after every strike, we show what the enemy had in store for us. This is war, David. How many innocent civilians would have died if that C-4 had gone off at the St. George?"

"Hundreds. Probably a thousand or more."

"And the reaction from Hezbollah or *JI*?"

"Celebration," the prime minister admitted.

"So to answer your question about how I'll do back home? First of all, I'm not calling for individuals to disarm. I'm not shutting down Remington, Colt, or Heckler & Koch. And we're certainly not planning on bombing Walther in Germany, or Beretta over in Italy. Hell, Beretta is the army standard in the U.S. We'd be shooting ourselves in the foot."

"Or my Glock factories?" Foss noted.

"Or Glock. Our principal targets are the hiding places. We crash the arms deals, we cut off the money supply worth billions, and most importantly, we take out the stores. We do it with the authority of the agreement forged here and subsequent alliances in Europe, Africa—even the Middle East."

"We'll be labled *one-worlders*. It'll play into every conspiracy theorist's wet dreams," the prime minister added.

"They're already calling me every name in the book. But if we're ever going to succeed at this so-called war, we have to fight it—for better or worse. I don't know if we can make it better, but I can promise you, if we don't put some bite into this session, things *will* definitely get worse. Not temporarily worse. Worse forever."

The night was coming to an end. Foss extinguished his cigar. He noticed that they'd both finished their drinks. "Another before we call it a night, Morgan?"

"No thanks," Taylor replied.

Foss rose and started for the door. "May they never claim that two old drunken warhorses concocted this plan. How about we sleep on this a bit? Let's get together a half hour before the first session and see how it looks in the morning."

Foss offered his hand to his friend. Morgan Taylor took it and repeated the overarching truth. "David, remember, this can't be termed 'the Taylor Doctrine.' It has to be bigger than that."

Glenbrook Royal Air Force Base
Friday, 10 August

The outrageous bid for an inexpensive 1957 Bowman baseball card looked like a teenager's prank. The anonymous person who posted the card responded accordingly.

> Bidder 34423
> You express serious offers now.
> Others will not be considered.

EBay was filled with ludicrous offers. This was not one of them. 2,500,000 euros were already transferred from one account to another. This e-mail confirmed the terms of the transaction.

Before clicking off, the Air Force mechanic re-read the message. The answer was contained in simple code on the second line.

> You express serious offers now.

Years of training, preparation, and waiting came down to one message: *Y-e-s o-n.*

Chicago, Illinois

Luis Gonzales made the transfer without a concern for the amount. Some of it was his money, most of it came from long-held accounts funded by special interests in Saudi Arabia and Syria. He'd earned good interest on it. Now it belonged to a highly skilled mechanic.

Amazing. Gonzales thought about the fortuitous turn of events. *Lamden's illness returns the presidency to Taylor. There's no vice president.* Things were better than he planned. It was the perfect political storm, and it would build to Category 5 in a matter of days. He would achieve so much at once—revenge and chaos. All of this was for his wife and daughter, killed by the Israelis because of the Americans. Both nations would be punished, and as a result, a true Palestinian state would rise and the Zionists would fall.

Gonzales admitted this would still take a few years. The American public needed more conditioning. A new president would help propagate the paradigm shift. Then, the map would be redrawn. Money destined for Israel would go to Palestine.

The fee for this part of the operation was insignificant. Two-and-a-half-million euros today; an equal amount when the job was completed. Gonzales considered it a small price to pay a sleeper spy on the job aboard *Air Force One.*

Langley, Virginia
CIA Headquarters
the same day

"Any progress?" D'Angelo asked Jassim at the start of the day. His team leader did have some new information.

"Actually, yes." Jassim read from a report culled from FBI and NSA searches. "Ali Razak, came to the U.S. in ninety-nine from Syria. No army record, probably because of his height, but according to Interpol, Razak showed up in interesting places at interesting times."

"Meaning?"

"London. Same date as that big department store bombing. Remember?"

"Yes." Evans had assigned him as a CIA liaison to the MI-5 investigation.

"Portugal, when the air base was hit."

"Is he tied to Hezbollah?"

"No record of it. No associations with known terrorist organizations either. Just sightings of a really big man at both places."

"He's hard to hide. Ultimately that should work in our favor. It would have been hard to keep Shaq a secret in Miami. Razak has to show up again."

Jassim added his hope, then noted, "He'd make the perfect body-guard. Don't you think?"

"Haddad!" Vinnie D'Angelo concluded. "You're right."

"Guess, what? We've got a positive ID on him from people in his building in Florida. Right off his driver's license photo."

"California?"

"Yeah, we tracked that down. Probably his point of entry. A job there years ago? I don't know. Not yet. We'll find out. There's no police record. Tax report from a year ago is clean. Nothing filed yet for this year."

"Because?"

"I don't know. Out of country? Dead?"

"You wish," D'Angelo joked. "Try a new identity."

"Which brings me to my next point. I don't think Razak is his real name."

"Why?"

"Because of its meaning in Arabic."

"Which is?" D'Angelo asked.

"Protector. This guy wears his job like a label. We find him, we find Haddad."

This made D'Angelo even more convinced. "Get his picture and fingerprints out to every police database. And while you're at it, let's have conversations with every big men's shop in the country."

"Beg your pardon?" Jassim asked.

"Razak sure isn't running around naked. The man has to dress. It's the obvious place to check. Rochester Big and Tall. Lots of others. Fax that picture to every single one by the end of the day." D'Angelo was pleased with Jassim's work. "And you're right. We find him, we find Haddad."

Sydney, Australia
Saturday, 11 August

While Morgan Taylor outlined his proposal, Foss studied the presidents, prime ministers, and premiers. The Pakistani president was the first to express his outrage.

"Are you suggesting American B-1s will be dropping bombs in my country on the suspicion that I am harboring terrorists? If you are, Mr. President, then this summit is over!"

A similar complaint was made by the Indonesian president. "I have never heard of such a thing. The other day you complained that I'm not doing enough. Now you say that my borders are meaningless to you."

India joined its neighbor Pakistan's objections. Malaysia agreed. Even New Zealand, Vietnam, and Cambodia. Foss allowed everyone to express their positions. He did it with a certain degree of delight, knowing that Morgan Taylor would not give in. He never did.

When the fury died out, Prime Minister Foss addressed the group. "The President of the United States has offered a radical notion. If action is taken solely on the authority of an American president, be it Morgan Taylor, President Henry Lamden, or their successors, then I join you in unconditionally voting this down."

He was answered by a chorus of, "Here, here!"

"However," he said with authority, "taken as the will of a majority of signatory nations eager to seek out and destroy the very forces that threaten us, then I wholeheartedly embrace Mr. Taylor's proposal." He stunned the room back into silence. "We are living on borrowed time. There's not a woman or man among us who isn't at a loss for the ways and means to combat terrorists. They have crossed our borders, either legally or illegally. They are hell-bent on bringing us down one way or another. They are patient. They have vast resources to build stockpiles of arms and to recruit followers. Unarmed, they can be swatted dead. Armed, as they are, we are the ones who face oblivion. President Taylor proposes that we change the rules of engagement. Is that what you really object to? I, for one, want to hear more." Without asking for a consensus, he nodded to Taylor.

"Mr. Prime Minister, fellow members of this esteemed league of nations, I am not the world's policeman and I don't want to be. However, we have a global enemy. Undeniably, this enemy is hiding in your countries. I know they are in mine. They build their armies and traffic their weapons. But too often, we wait until *after* they've struck to track them."

Taylor cocked his head, a signal to Jack Evans. The U.S. national director of intelligence was ready with a handful of poster boards, which he put on the table in front of the president. Taylor slid one to his right, another to his left, and two across the table. Another dozen remained in front of him. "I've shared other satellite photographs with you. These were taken in the last twenty-four hours. You may not be able to identify the locations, but they are *all* from the countries represented here. Once again, weapons caches and encampments are circled. In most cases, these locations are out of reach of your own troops. So they remain in operation.

"These photos, and ones like them, are regularly sent to your military commands. You tell me what action has ever been taken? With the exception of an airstrike by Australia barely a month ago—none. The SASR destroyed the stronghold in the Solomons where the attack against our summit was planned. Were there any objections to that reprisal?"

Taylor reminded everyone how the remote-controlled bomb was discovered quite by accident at the Ville St. George. "We're all alive today because of chance. Nothing more. How much longer can we play the odds? And yet you have no interest in annihilating the very forces which seek to kill you? You have no interest in at least destroying their weapons stores?"

Thailand's leader had been studying one of three photographs that showed areas within his country. He lifted his head. "If the Chair will allow a question?"

Foss saw that Taylor was willing to relinquish the floor.

"You have a way of making a convincing argument, Mr. President. I have never seen these photos, or any like them. I assure you, I will speak with my commanders about this *oversight*. It will be corrected immediately."

No one dared asked what that meant.

He continued, "Suffice it to say, I am troubled, but I need to understand more. Tell us how this strike force could work. Why wouldn't it be a United Nations force?"

"Because we want it done in our lifetime," Taylor said without a hint of humor. "I would like to believe that our own alliance will serve as a model to the U.N. But with Russia's increasing proclivity toward censure and the profits they earn through arms sales, forget it."

"We'd have to explain a great deal to our people. I'm not sure how to do it," admitted the Thai leader.

"Tell them the truth," Taylor replied. "You commit yourself to the fight. The United States will provide you with the necessary, irrefutable intelligence to act. But then you must act. If you do not, within twenty-four hours—under the jurisdiction of the agreement I hope to forge—an international force will do the work for you. You will then have the ability to announce that you accepted the invitation of the international strike team. It is a face-saving consideration. Make no mistake, this is a zero-sum proposition. We are past the point of options." Morgan Taylor raised his left index finger and Jack Evans produced another satellite photograph. He stood and personally walked it over to Prime Minister Foss.

"This Liberian ship is carrying grenade launchers and an estimated twenty-five hundred automatic weapons, along with Japanese cars. She sailed from Kyoto two days ago. She's due in Melbourne later this week. What do you want to do, Mr. Prime Minister?"

CHAPTER

64

Washington, D.C.
the same day

Roarke ran harder to relieve the stress. Until the various investigative agencies came up with anything on Cooper, he was desk-bound. He started going stir-crazy by the second day. Now nearly two weeks had elapsed since he returned from the field. His mentor Morgan Taylor was out of town and Katie was busy. So he ran.

Sometimes ideas came to him while he exercised. But recently—nothing. He felt brain dead. Roarke had gone as far as he could with Touch Parson's FRT pictures. They were already in wide distribution, courtesy of the FBI. The finances of Cooper's parents were still being examined, and Morgan Taylor's idea of planting the story about Cooper's squad still hadn't paid off; at least to his knowledge.

Nothing, he thought. Roarke hated *nothing*.

Belgrade, Serbia

"I see no problems with what you'd like to do," said the arms dealer, known only as Old Serbe. "I'll give you some choices in a moment." The grizzled man in a flannel shirt excused himself. This was not the first time he had worked with the American shrink. The Californian willingly paid him in whatever currency he requested. Today they agreed on euros. The exchange rate was more favorable than dollars. After a few minutes, the trader returned with a handful of photographs. "Take a look. You choose the best one."

After a half hour looking at the prospects, the American picked three possibilities.

"Indeed, my choices, too," Old Serbe laughed. "Come back in two hours and you shall examine the prospects."

"Thank you," said the Los Angeles psychologist. "I'll do a bit of shopping in the meantime. But I do need to conclude this today. Time is a factor."

"Undoubtedly. Your satisfaction is my first priority."

Precisely two hours later they met. It took one more hour to decide on the finalist and conclude the transaction. The Californian and the man he hired through Old Serbe went to dinner to discuss the specifics that would change both of their lives.

Washington, D.C.

The Capitol Police were getting their assignments in a morning briefing. Nobody was happy. Extraordinary numbers of protestors were expected to descend on the nation's capital. Estimates compiled from hotel and airline reservations, combined with assumptions about day trippers, conservatively edged toward 2.5 million. The vendors and tourist-based businesses might revel in the numbers, but not the police. The names Elliott Strong and Robert Bridgeman were not bandied about warmly. This march was going to cost the District upwards of $12 to 15 million—and that's if everything went well.

Across town, Duke Patrick worked on his speech. He sat at his dining room table writing in long hand. He studied what he had composed, still not pleased. It had to be inspiring. He needed to rally the crowd in D.C., yet simultaneously connect with the TV audience. Most of all he had to provide the country with a dynamic and authoritative presence; a leader who spoke with the voice of reason amidst growing discontent. He also needed to introduce General Robert Bridgeman.

Patrick tried out the phrases. Nothing felt right yet. He crumpled the latest page of handwritten notes and tossed it toward a small wastebasket. *Toward*, not in. He missed. His tenth miss in a row.

Patrick always struggled like this. He had to work at getting to his folksy style. Once there, he'd quickly memorize his speech and deliver it as if it were a rousing Sunday sermon. He avoided anything fancy.

He was a good old boy. That's what got him his first seat in the House and what won over fellow Democrats after the last election. His ascension to speaker, number-three in the line of succession, was the affirmation he initially sought. Now he had a new goal.

Patrick tolerated Henry Lamden, but he hated Morgan Taylor. He vowed to do anything to bring him down.

Lamden's heart attack opened the door to some interesting possibilities. The invitation to introduce General Bridgeman was a pure gift.

Taylor ridiculed me. He did it in the White House. Never again, Patrick thought as he tried out another sentence. *Never again.*

Tyler, Texas

Across the country, General Bridgeman was busy with his own speech. His rise to national prominence was on the lips of every political pundit on the airwaves. For someone who was neither a declared Republican nor Democrat, Bridgeman presumed to speak for all the people.

Who's tired of the way things are? Who's ready for the way things ought to be? That was the approach he decided to take. He had little concern that the actual presidential primary was years off. Robert Bridgeman was on his own timetable. And who better to lead the charge than a Washington outsider. Four years earlier, Taylor proved that voters still took a shining to military brass. But in his mind, a Marine general outranked a Navy commander any day...particularly August 18.

Washington, D.C.

Katie put down her boxes and suitcases outside Scott's apartment.

Roarke heard the doorbell as he was toweling off from his shower. He didn't rush to the door. He never opened it without first identifying who was there; and second, determining if he wanted to let in that *who.*

He tuned his bedroom TV to Aux. An image appeared, captured by the pencil-thin fiber optic camera he placed within the door frame.

"Holy shit!" he exclaimed. Roarke ran to the door, unlocked the dead bolt, and threw it open.

"Katie! Oh my God!"

She responded with equal surprise to the sight of him. "My goodness! I hope you don't greet everyone like this." She looked down.

He did the same. "Oh Christ!" He had lost his towel on the way. "Quick! Come on in."

"No," she said pushing past him with her suitcases. "You come in."

Katie kicked the door closed with her foot and took him right on the hallway floor.

Maluku, Indonesia
Sunday, 12 August

"Atef, a question while we eat."

"Yes, Commander," the subordinate said.

"You have served me well in the mountains. How shall I reward you in the city?" the insurgent commander asked.

They discussed many things over their tasteless meals, but this was the first time Komari ever asked him what he might want.

"To continue to serve you, sir."

Komari laughed so hard, he spilled his tea onto his thick, filthy beard. "Spoken like a politician, not a soldier." He wiped the mess with his shirt sleeve. "Atef, we will take Jakarta and rule all Indonesia. You will be at my side. But you must have expectations. So I ask again, what reward do you seek from me? Money? The power that comes from being a senior secretary?"

"Actually, a bath," Musah Atef said through a mouthful of overcooked beef with rice.

Komari enjoyed this next laugh even more. Then without warning, he changed the tone with a pointed question. "To bathe your body or to wash away your sins?" To punctuate the directive, he quickly reached down and removed a hunting knife from a sheath in his boot and plunged the blade into the wooden table.

Atef swallowed hard. "What do you mean, sir?"

"Many people will die. Christian women and children among them. Thousands. You will share responsibility for the cleansing of our nation. At some point a thought may enter your mind. 'Have I done the right thing?' My back may be turned and you, Musah Atef, would have the occasion to do the work of our enemies."

"Commander, I am, and forever will be, your instrument. I should die in your service tonight, here and now, if you believe I would ever betray you."

Commander Umar Komari stared deeply into the dark brown eyes of the young man who sat before him. He saw fear in the young lieutenant he had plucked from a fishing village two years earlier. There was fear where he had expected loyalty.

No, thought Komari, *this one will not be at my side when we liberate the people.*

CHAPTER 65

The New York Times
the same day

Now Michael O'Connell had to decide what to do. He read his notes again. His research fell into two categories: *So what* and *Holy shit!*

The *so what* side was filled with unsubstantiated reports, unrelated facts, and personal assumptions; not enough on which to base a *New York Times* article. Moreover, if somehow the story did go to print at this point, he'd leave the paper open to libel.

On the other hand, there was the *Holy shit!* factor, filled with the same unsubstantiated reports, unrelated facts, and personal assumptions that, libel or no libel, led to a shocking conclusion.

O'Connell drummed his fingers on the desk. This was too big for him to decide on his own. He took all of his work and marched into his editor's office.

"I'm on a deadline, go away," Weaver demanded.

"You say that to everybody," O'Connell replied and made his unwelcomed way in. "Besides, I need your help."

"Am I hearing Michael O'Connell correctly? He needs help?"

"Come on, Weaver. Really."

"Well, I'm just a little surprised. Nothing from you in days. Not a word on paper. Not an e-mail." The *Times* editor had expected *something* from O'Connell. "You know, they've been asking about you upstairs. I've been covering for you. If you can't make this story work, we'll get you onto another."

"That's the problem. I can make it work. But we have to be dead certain we're ready to go all the way with it." O'Connell purposely chose his words.

"Go all the way with it?" Weaver gave up her editing and motioned for O'Connell to sit.

The *Times* reporter outlined what he'd discovered on his initial round of calls.

Taking into account O'Connell's recent escapade in Russia, Weaver immediately went to the *Holy shit!* side.

"My sentiments exactly." He leaned forward in his chair. "So what do we do?"

"We don't run it. But you stay on it. How much time do you think you need?"

"The question we should be asking is whether we've run out of time."

O'Connell's desk
later

O'Connell based his worry on the notion that Strong had a great deal, if not everything, to do with Robert Bridgeman's sudden ascent. Another concern came to him. The march on Washington might be more than advertised.

His sense of duty now competed with his duty to country. O'Connell seriously thought about notifying President Taylor, but he was out of town. *Maybe Roarke?* He dismissed the notion, at least for now. He had to have more.

The reporter typed a quick e-mail and added the web address to the top. He hit send and waited to see whether Elliott Strong would reply.

Ninety minutes later he had his answer, apparently written by Strong's producer/wife.

> Elliott Strong does not consent to interviews.
> He conducts them with his listeners.
> Thank you for your inquiry.

At least I got a reply, he said to himself. Undaunted, he dialed the number he coaxed out of the sales department secretary at Strong's syndicator.

After four rings a man answered with a sharp, "Yeah?" It wasn't Strong.

"Hello. Is Elliott there?" O'Connell asked as if he were the man's best friend.

"He's just getting off the air. Wanna hold?"

"Sure."

The engineer didn't ask anything else. Most people didn't have this phone number and the guy seemed like he knew Strong. Besides, he was busy running the audio board. He put the phone down on the desktop and forgot about it.

O'Connell listened to the last few minutes of the afternoon show. That was followed by the sound of doors opening and closing. He was sure he heard Strong in the background talking to a woman. Then, "Who is it?" Something unintelligible was followed by Strong saying, "Yeah, yeah, okay."

"Hello."

"Elliott?" came the greeting from O'Connell.

The host strained to place the voice. He couldn't. "Who is this? Do I know you?" he asked suspiciously.

"No, but you've read my stories on the air. I'm Michael O'Connell. From the *New* Yuck *Times.*"

Strong cupped the phone over his hand, but O'Connell could still make out the reaction. "Christ! Why did you give this to me!"

"Sorry, it sounded like a friend," the engineer apologized.

"Look," Strong said back on the line and without any of the friendliness he used on the radio, "I have a firm policy of no interviews!"

"Just one question, Strong. Is it pure luck or coincidence that *every* break in your career came at someone else's expense?"

Strong answered by slamming the phone onto the cradle. O'Connell was left with a dial tone, but he got more than he hoped. He got a glimpse of the real man.

Washington, D.C.
that night

Roarke and Katie sat across from each other at a café near his apartment. They shared a sausage and spinach panini and Caesar

EXECUTIVE TREASON

salad. She was trying to figure out the best ways to navigate the District. The small Metro map she'd picked up wasn't helping much.

"Use a driver, or at least a cab," he said with some concern.

"But I believe in public transportation."

"I don't think Bernstein wants you trekking around underground. And I sure as hell don't."

"It's safe."

"Katie, you're working for the White House, for God's sake. There are perks. It's not going to break the president's budget."

"Well, maybe. I'll probably have too much to carry around anyway."

"Thank you. Now with that settled, are you coming to an overall opinion yet?" Since she arrived, they hadn't talked about work. His or hers.

"Overall? I still don't know why *me*. I'm not an expert on the Constitution. I'm not a Constitutional attorney. I've been reading briefs from real scholars and members of Congress who have given this incredible time and thought, mostly since nine-eleven."

"But nobody's done anything."

She agreed. "Maybe because there are too many points of view. Too many possibilities to consider."

"Enter Katie Kessler," he proudly offered. "You can sort it out. Make total non-partisan recommendations to a Republican administration serving at the pleasure of a Democrat."

"Makes my head spin," she said while feeding him a bit of the panini.

"So, back to my question," he said chewing the sandwich. "Overall opinion?"

"The law is based on an incredibly faulty premise. Stop me if I've already told you all of this, but in nineteen forty-five, after President Truman succeeded Franklin Roosevelt, he decided to change the first line of succession from cabinet to Congress. In fact, he didn't name a vice president until he ran for re-election in nineteen forty-eight."

"Really?"

"Really. And without a vice president serving under him, George Marshall, his secretary of state, would become his immediate successor if he died. Now a couple of relative points. Some claim that Truman didn't necessarily believe he, or any president, should be appointing his own successor. In a democracy, the position of president is elective, and therefore it should fall to someone who had stood the test of the

433

electorate. He pointed to the speaker of the house, the leading officer of Congress."

"But he's not nationally elected."

"You're right." The speaker is elected every two years by constituents in his district. But he's elevated to national prominence by gaining the support and vote of the majority of the members of the House.

"But here's the rub. The seventeen ninety-two Statute named the president *pro tempore* of the senate as the first officer in the line of succession, not the speaker of the house."

"So why the change for Truman?"

"On the surface, Truman wanted the power to stay with the party of the presidency. The House was more likely to be controlled by the president's party than the Senate. But there was more to it than that. Truman's relations with the president pro tem wasn't, what shall I say, *cordial*. He was a wily, vindictive powerful seventy-eight-year-old named Kenneth McKellar from Tennessee. He was known as a real patronage guy. Truman knew him from the Senate. Not his favorite. On the other hand, Speaker of the House Sam Rayburn was a good friend; good enough that Truman was said to have visited Rayburn's office for a glass of bourbon after he learned he was going to be sworn in as president."

"Politics," Roarke sadly concluded.

"And faulty reasoning," Katie added. "We've had long periods since nineteen forty seven when the president's party is not the majority party in either the House or the Senate, or both."

"So much for Truman's logic."

"Right again. And wouldn't you think that it's *more* likely for a cabinet member appointed by a president to continue his policies than a legislative officer with a different political agenda?"

"Makes sense to me." He was thinking about Duke Patrick right now. "But Truman got his way. What was it like before that?"

"Good question. Let's go back to eighteen eighty-six. President Grover Cleveland's vice president died in office. Congress was out of session and according to the seventeen ninety-two act, there were no statutory successors to take over if Cleveland croaked or he couldn't discharge his duties. So Congress reconvened and pulled together The First Presidential Succession Act, which set the line of succession after the veep with the secretary of state, followed by the rest of the cabinet department heads, in order of their department's establishment. The eighteen eighty-six Act required the successor to convene Congress, if it wasn't already in session, to determine whether or not to call for a special presidential election."

"It's getting complicated again."

"Oh, it's very complicated and full of holes. Big ones. Like the whole question of who's an '*officer*?'"

"Meaning?"

"Well, Duke Patrick, for example. Would the house speaker be considered an *officer* in Constitutional terms?"

"Of course he is," Roarke said, totally engaged. "He was elected..."

"Not so fast. The Constitution, Article II, section 1, clause 6 says..."

Roarke smiled. "You really have this down."

"Stop it. I have it memorized, I'm trying to act like I have it down...clause 6 specifies that Congress may, by law, specify what *Officer*—capital *O*—shall act as president if both the president and vice president are unavailable. That's the foundation of all the laws that followed. But does the Constitution view elected *officials* as *Officers*? No one knows for sure how the Supreme Court would ultimately rule. Cabinet members, yes. They're *officers* appointed by the president, ratified by the Senate."

"And what do you think?"

"Well, my buddy James Madison and I think officers are those appointed rather than elected."

"You are good," Roarke added.

"And there's more if you're still with me."

"Forever."

Katie liked that a lot. It deserved a kiss, which she gave him by sitting up and stretching across the table.

"Ummm," he said enjoying his reward.

"Now I know you're dying to ask me where we stand now."

"Where do we stand now," Roarke chimed in.

"On very shakey ground. Here's why. Under the current law, the 25th Amendment to the Constitution focuses primarily on how the president is succeeded in office, under the terms of the nineteen forty-seven Act. But did you realize that someone could be bumped out of office?"

"No. How?"

"Imagine there's a catastrophe. The president, vice president, speaker, and senate *pro tem* are killed. The secretary of state is next in line to become the chief executive."

"I'm with you."

"Okay, but then the Senate acts very quickly. It elects a new president *pro tempore*. The senator conveniently bumps the secretary of state out. But then the House names a new speaker. He, or she," Katie smiled at the thought, "would bump the Senate president."

"It'd be chaotic."

"Worse. We'd have numerous politicians and officers—see the distinction now—laying claim to the presidency. It would have to get settled by the Supreme Court. Not a good time after a tragedy."

"This is amazing," Roarke observed.

"I wish I could take credit for it, but the arguments have been around for a long time."

"Okay. So, in short, it's a mess. One terrorist strike could throw us into a huge constitutional crisis. How, my dear, are you proposing we get out of it?"

"That, my love, is something I'm still sorting through."

Glenbrook Royal Air Force Base
New South Wales, Australia
the same day

The down payment was in his account. The remainder would be his very soon. Just a few more details and his work would be done.

Colonel Lewis gave the *Air Force One* crew and the support team word that they were still a few days away from wheels up. There were rumors that they might have a quick stopover in Kandahar airport in Afghanistan. *Is that good or bad?* The engineer borrowed the navigation charts from the cockpit. *Good.*

He mentally calculated the distances and considered the likely flight plan. *Better, in fact. Much better.*

CHAPTER

66

Sydney Australia
Wednesday, 15 August

"Done!" Prime Minister Foss proclaimed.

The pronouncement was followed by silence. The representatives, all of them leaders of their own nations, looked around at one another. Something momentous had happened here, but it was hard to grasp the full significance. Morgan Taylor began to clap. He was joined by the prime minister of Japan. The Indian president joined in. One by one, the heads of state of the rest of the countries applauded. Foss acknowledged the achievement himself by standing and nodding his appreciation.

The formal agreement would be drawn up shortly. The basic language of the pact endorsed Morgan Taylor's plan to seek and destroy terrorist weapons stores anywhere in the South Pacific. The policy, once ratified by the U.S. Senate, would serve as a blueprint for similar sweeping treaties he hoped to broker in other parts of the world. In its final form, it was titled "The Southeast Asia and Pacific Anti-Terrorist Act," or SAPATA.

Photographers were called in to record the moment for posterity. Taylor and Foss shook hands for the cameras. They'd successfully hammered out the means to be pro-active. They could take action outside their own borders. They could with a formal invitation. They could do it without a signatory nation's full approval. It represented a sweeping change in the way the war on terrorism would be fought.

SAPATA would also help stabilize smaller governments; those with insurgent forces they could not uproot themselves.

Taylor requested that the countries sign in alphabetical order, based on an English standard. That placed the United States at the bottom. The president wanted to erase any notion that SAPATA was actually a "Taylor Doctrine." Foss may have felt blindsided by Taylor's strong-arming tactics at the session, but even the prime minister agreed mutual "defense" agreements were outdated. Today's global threats required a posture that embraced the notion of mutual "offense." SAPATA was it.

"Congratulations, Mr. President," Foss said as Morgan Taylor came up to add his name to the document.

"The same to you, Mr. Prime Minister."

The two old warriors stood at attention as the still cameras and TV crews shot their pictures. Then Foss explained to the world the momentous step they'd taken together at Government House.

Chicago, Illinois
two hours later

What the hell is this all about? Gonzales wondered after decoding the message encrypted in an eBay bid for classic rock and roll '45s. It worried him. Midway through the communiqué was the heart of the problem:

> He asked if it was pure luck or concidence that every break came at somebody else's expense?

The question was so pointed, so specific.

> How does he know?

There was more.

> Can you get into the *New York Times*?

Gonzales could. *A complication?* he wondered. *Yes, but not insurmountable.*

CIA Headquarters
Langley, Virginia

"Philadelphia, Detroit, Miami, Buffalo, Indianapolis, and Chicago," reported Jassim. "Dixon's personally talked to many of the leading big and tall men's stores."

"And?" D'Angelo asked.

"Based on purchases in the last six months, we had likelies in each of those cities. Factor in the exact measurements, and we narrow the possibilities to Detroit, Indie, and Chicago."

"Any name matches?"

"Let me get Dixon. He can fill you in more."

Dixon, the CIA liaison to the FBI, was on a call. When he finished, he joined Jassim and D'Angelo.

"What's the latest on Razak," Jassim prompted.

"Still nothing one-to-one, but we are assuming he could be using a different name."

"Correct," D'Angelo replied.

"Well, based on that last call, I'm down to two cash customers who fit the description of a six-four-to-five-plus Middle Eastern weightlifter. One who gave a name and address and another who didn't. We're checking on the one who did. He's in Indianpolis. Right measurements. Right age. Right look."

"And the other?"

"Chicago. A guy who shopped earlier in the year at Rochester Big & Tall. He came in wearing summer clothes...in January. He needed a lot to keep him warm."

The New York Times
the same time

"Can you help me out, Robin?" O'Connell asked one of his friends on the business desk.

"Whatcha want?" the Wall Street writer asked, looking up from her computer.

"I'm working on an article on Elliott Strong."

"Strong the yahoo?"

"That's the one. I have his radio stuff down, but I need info on his net value. Can you run down his financials?"

"I don't know, Mike."

"Just get me started."

"I'm on a deadline," she said.

"You know where to look. Please." This should have been a simple yes or no. Instead it was a negotiation.

"What do you need?"

"Everything. Loans, leans, holdings, tax history, tax problems, partnerships. The whole nine yards."

"That's an awful lot."

Yup, she's negotiating, O'Connell thought.

"I hope this isn't a rush, Mike."

"It's a big rush. Weaver is on my ass to get an article out before the march on D.C. Strong's talking it up on his show."

"I don't know, I've got this enterprise piece of my own."

"Come on, get me started." *Time to pay up.* "Look, if there's a solid business angle, we can team up on a sidebar."

This was just what the business reporter wanted to hear. She smiled thinking she'd gotten the best of O'Connell. She had a lot to learn.

"Okay, but just one hour. I'll e-mail everything over to you."

Lebanon, Kansas
that night

"Let's talk a little about the political parties in the U.S. of A." Elliott Strong represented neither and attacked both. Some people tried to describe him as a libertarian, but they'd be wrong. Strong defined himself as a cultural conservative, an anti–Belt way, and "the living, breathing voice of the Founding Fathers."

"They aren't representing you. They're not doing the work of Jefferson, Adams, Madison, and Washington. They've allowed the government to grow to suit their own needs, not yours. They come at it from different sides and say the same things. The Republicans argue against big government, but they've added new Cabinet departments and ballooned deficits to the trillions. And the *Dimo*crats?" The jab was deliberate. "They're the greatest social spenders of all time. The *Dimo*crats have run up bills we'll never afford to pay from here to

Hyannis Port. Well, maybe not *from here*," he joked. "Don't count on either party to be the loyal opposition. They're both the loyal resistance; the resistance to the future. They're not the ones to lead. For God's sake, they don't even see where the country is already going; where you want it to be; the nation your children deserve to inherit. There is a man who does see it right; who does see the light. Bob Bridgeman." He decided Bob sounded better than Robert.

Strong was getting to his point. "He's already a leader. He's a leader you can count on. He's a leader you can trust. He's a leader who can end the January Siege."

The host had been looking for another way to describe the Inauguration of Lamden and Taylor. Now it just rolled off his tongue. "The January Siege." He smiled in his mirror, quite proud.

"The January Siege! January 20, the day we lost control of the country. Well, Bob Bridgeman is going to Washington and you're his army. You're his instrument of justice. Show America that we are united and that you want Congress to change the laws or get out of the way.

"General Bridgeman stands *with* you. And unlike the parties which created the travesty of the January Siege, Bob Bridgeman also stands *for* you." Strong was leading up to his final point. "Bob Bridgeman won't suppress your freedom of speech. He supports your right to assemble, and he will not take away your ability to own and bear arms. He'll tell you as much in Washington. So come ready." The word *ready* was an intentional choice. The implication, though unstated, was for protestors to come *armed* and ready.

"Your calls coming right up." He threw to a McDonald's commercial. *Strong Nation* was sailing down the main stream.

Glenbrook Royal Air Force Base
New South Wales, Australia
Thursday, 16 August

The president's motorcade pulled up alongside *Air Force One*. Colonel Peter Lewis saluted from the cockpit window when Morgan Taylor stepped onto the tarmac. His favorite mechanic leaned into the cabin.

"You called?"

"Yes, Rossy. Check out number three. Agins caught a power flux."

"Oh? Like what?"

"Nothing below normal," co-pilot Bernard Agins added. "But she could use your eyes."

"Anything else?"

"Not from me. Milkis?" Colonel Lewis asked.

The navigator, Greg Milkis, said he was fine.

"Okay, I'm on it. I'll let you know. Don't leave without me."

"Not a chance," Lewis replied.

Forty minutes later, with everyone satisfied and the president in his forward compartment, *SAM 28000* rolled down the runway. In four hours they'd be in Afghanistan for a quick conference with the military leadership and time to greet the troops. After that, they'd be on the way home, a few days ahead of the much-ballyhooed march.

Washington, D.C.
the same day

The hotels were all booked, but he hadn't planned on checking in anywhere, under any name. The man had another way to find a room. He stood outside Reagan National Airport. To any passerby, it appeared as if he were waiting for someone. Occasionally, he rubbernecked around some departing travelers, trying to spot a friend. But there were no friends here. The buff man with a baseball cap and a blonde, ponytail was actually searching luggage tags. He already spotted three names and addresses he liked. He was still looking for others; people who lived closer in; within walking distance to the Mall.

The reason he wanted a family was quite simple. It was more likely that they'd be traveling for a longer period of time. He would slip into their apartment with some viable excuse should a neighbor raise a question. But these days, neighbors rarely spoke to one another.

By seven o'clock, he felt confident he had enough locations. *At least one should work.* He preferred multi-unit buildings.

"Couldn't find your friend?" one American Airlines baggage handler asked when he saw the man start to leave.

"No," he said. "Must have missed 'em."

They had talked off and on through the last hour. It helped him get close enough to the bags to read and memorize the tags.

"I'll call them later. Thanks." He tipped the skycap ten dollars, not once worrying about fingerprints. It was all too benign.

Kandahar, Afghanistan
8 hours later

Rossy was about to check the re-fueling of the president's plane when a member of his crew radioed for some assistance from the twin 747. Twenty-nine's got a cargo door problem."

"What kind?" he said over his com link.

"The latching. I think we gotta check the mechanism."

Colonel Peter Lewis wouldn't take off unless every door closed and sealed properly on both planes. Any loss of pressurization caused by a malfunctioning latch could be deadly. Rossy quickly found another member of his team to take over his job.

By the time Ross solved the problem, which turned out to be minor, fueling was complete.

Lewis was nearly through his final pre-flight check when he got the heads-up that the commander in chief was on the way. He called in for the latest weather advisory. Aside from a band of seasonal thunderstorms over the Banda Sea, they'd have clear skies.

Morgan Taylor boarded and went straight to the flight deck. "Colonel."

"Mr. President, all set for the long haul?" Lewis asked. They carried enough fuel to make Los Angeles or San Francisco. But the flight plan called for them to touch down in Hawaii. If necessary, both were capable of docking with a KC-10 tanker midair.

"Am I! After I give the Mrs. a call, I'm getting some shut-eye." Taylor automatically scanned the flight controls and gauges knowing what to look for. "If I wake up in time, maybe I'll join you later. Tell you what, Colonel, we can swap. You figure out how to balance the damned budget and I'll do what I really enjoy."

"Half of that deal sounds good," Lewis laughed. He had his headphones in his hand, so he didn't hear the radio clearance from ground control. His co-pilot, Bernard Agins, tapped the right cup of his phones. "Excuse me sir, we're cleared to go."

"Then that's my cue," the president said. "See you gentlemen later." He said goodbye to Agins, Milkis, and Lewis; all good men.

Two minutes later, the entourage rolled to the end of the runway. The escorts lifted off first. Most of the transports had departed straight for Washington from Glenbrook. Three minutes later, *Air Force One* was aloft. Lewis reported all was well on take-off, though the plane handled more lightly than expected.

Morgan Taylor was asleep by the time they climbed to cruising altitude. He lost himself in his favorite dream—he was at the controls.

Over the Pacific

The roving mechanic followed his routine. He did it throughout the flight. It started with a check of the visible systems on the plane. Then he went to the guts. He opened panels containing internal wiring and sub systems. Everything was in order.

He made his way toward the flight deck, up the stairs from the first level rear stairs, where he nodded politely to the members of the president's staff and basically ignored the reporters. Some people were already asleep, a few were typing updates they'd e-mail out via *Air Force One*'s satellite com center, others were playing poker. He spoke to the crew, making sure they were okay. He was surprised he didn't find Brady at his post.

Rossy considered Mark Brady solid back-up. Brady was relatively new to the president's bird; if three years was new. He worked with Ross on both planes. About the only thing he couldn't do was pilot. But he was always there, diagnosing onboard problems almost as fast as his supervisor.

Rossy cued his com set. "Brady, Rossy, over."

No response.

The lieutenant took a few steps to the side in case the plane's frame blocked his signal. "Brady, this is Rossy, over." He waited a beat, then keyed the mike again. "Brady, give me your location, over."

Each request was met with silence. Rossy spotted another of his engineering crew members in the galley. "Seen Brady?"

"No, sir. Not since pre-flight."

Odd. Rossy found another engineer, a corporal who, in a few years, might show the right stuff for the job.

"Blumie, have you seen Brady?"

Blumenstein shot a surprised expression. "He didn't tell you?"

"Tell me what?"

"Stomach cramps. He said he spent the morning in the john and after refueling he ran back to the head."

"Not the plane's?"

"Ah, no. On ground, sir," Blumie stated.

"Are you sure?"

"Absolutely."

Rossy turned away to the side and tried his radio again. "Lieutenant Brady. Report! This is Rossy, over." He waited no more than ten seconds, enough time for Brady to call in, then barked an order for Blumenstein. "Assemble everyone on our team in two minutes! Right here. Check all the johns. Call me if you find Brady!"

"Brady said he was just sick, I don't think..."

"Do it!"

Two minutes. Enough time for Rossy to make it to the cockpit and back.

The secure door was closed and guarded. Rossy needed to pass through the Secret Service detail.

"What's up, Rossy?" asked the agent.

"I need the colonel to radio the CO at Kandahar."

"You know we don't like to bother the flight crew."

"One of my men may be missing."

Normal 89th Airlift Wing security procedures require the crew and passengers to be fully boarded prior to the arrival of the president and his party. The agent was miffed that he was hearing this problem now.

"One second." The secret service officer notified Colonel Lewis that Lt. Ross wanted in. He then called the supervising agent on duty. Rossy didn't dissuade him.

"Colonel," Rossy said before making it all the way into the cockpit, "Get Kandahar on the horn. I need to know if my man Brady's there. Try the infirmary."

"Why wouldn't he be onboard?"

"That's what I want to find out. I'll be on the radio," he said while backing out. "Let me know as soon as you hear." Lewis nodded affirmatively.

Rossy's men were now assembled, with one exception—Mark Brady. "Does anyone know if Brady opted off?"

"No, sir," came the replies.

"He's always here," offered a corporal.

"Well not this time." Peter Lewis cut through on his radio. "Rossy, negative. Repeat. Negative. No report of Brady at the infirmary."

"Ask them to check with their security. Did he leave the base?" By now two of the Secret Service agents flanked Rossy.

"Do we have a situation we need to know about, Lieutenant?"

Washington, D.C.
the same time

"We've gotta match, Roarke," Shannon Davis phoned excitedly.

The Secret Service agent had to think for a moment. "A match?"

"Yes, put your pants on lover-boy and get over here right away." Davis had heard that Katie Kessler was in town.

"Depp?" he asked chosing to use his own nomenclature.

"Just step on it. We'll talk about it when you're here."

Roarke raced across town in a cab. He was in Davis's office in under twenty minutes.

"Let's have it."

"Miami. Here take a look. Surveillance cameras at Customs ferreted him out." It was a nod to the FRT technology. Davis clicked on the photo which Customs e-mailed. Roarke leaned in. Despite the poor resolution and low lighting, it looked enough like Richard Cooper to take it seriously.

"Jesus, what the hell are they trying to do? Save a few bucks on electricity," Roarke complained.

"Yeah, you'd think."

"Tell me we have him in custody?"

"Sorry buddy."

"Shit! Where'd he come in from?"

"Miami, via Madrid."

Roarke stamped his foot. "Damn it!"

"They did get another picture of him."

Davis called up a less fuzzy head-and-shoulder shot. "There."

Roarke studied every detail of the picture, looking beyond the casual clothing, the blonde ponytail, and what could have been a fake scar across his chin. His eyes were narrow. His jaw line was square. The ears were set as he remembered. On personal observation, it appeared to be Cooper, but he wanted Parsons to run a closer scan.

"Who's he now?"

Davis read off a sheet he'd already printed out. "A Kelvin Ruffin. New Zealand passport. Other than that, I don't know. Nothing that triggered any alarms. The system is a little sluggish and they cleared him along."

"Have you talked to the Customs agent?"

"Way ahead of you. He remembered him. Said he was polite. A visiting journalist."

Journalist? "Why journalist?" He racked his brain.

Davis smiled blankly. Roarke came up with the answer without him. "Jesus, to cover the march! He's going on another kill!"

"Run his name against all foreign press. New Zealand. Everywhere. You'll need to connect with Interpol. Send them the picture, too. And e-mail this over to Touch Parsons." Roarke was already dialing the FBI computer analyst. "I want his unequivocal assurance that this *is* Richard Cooper."

CIA Headquarters
Langely, Virginia

"It's him!"

"Are you sure?" D'Angelo asked.

"Yes," Dixon insisted. "Two people in the store ID'd him from the picture."

"Almost six months later? How could they possibly remember him?"

"His attitude. He wasn't exactly Mr. Personality. He tried to bargain. Pretty stupid. They said he was belligerent when they told him *no*. The clerk was ready to call the police. Then he calmed down, bought what he wanted off the rack, and left two suits for tailoring."

"But no name and address?"

"Just his last name. Alley."

"Spell it," D'Angelo said.

"A-l-l-e-y. Like in back alley."

D'Angelo thought for a second. "Last name, not first?"

"Right. But it's close."

D'Angelo realized the same thing. *Alley for Ali. Ali Razak.* "Very close," he admitted. "What do you bet he's our man?"

"Redskin tickets." Dixon asked.

"You're on. And if he is in Chicago, then Haddad is too," the CIA agent concluded. "Let's start talking with hotels and realtors. Try running Razak with it. Maybe we'll get lucky."

"Consider it done."

"And keep it close to the vest. This one's ours."

Aboard *Air Force One*

They were taking Brady's disappearance very seriously. Lewis radioed the air base in Afghanistan and the Air Force F-15 Eagle commander on his left wing, while the Secret Service alerted Presley Freedman's office at the White House.

Lewis asked Milkis to plot a course to the nearest airport.

Milkis scanned his charts. "Jakarta." He calculated the time. "Fifty minutes."

"That's where we're going. Get us straight into..." Milkis was interrupted by a newly installed alarm in the cockpit; a series of fast, high-pitched bursts. It was triggered when an engine was failing or was within known limits of failing.

"Talk to me," Lewis ordered. He automatically held the yoke steady.

"Number one's showing failure," Agins called out as calmly as possible. He scanned the panel. "Fuel looks good." There are numerous reasons for sudden engine failure. Fuel flow and quantity usually are not a cause.

The ear-shattering alarm continued, suddenly compounded by another piercing tone. "Shit! Number three's shutting down," Lewis called out.

The plane began to rumble and dip. More alarms sounded.

"Rossy!" Lewis shouted out over the com.

"I'm on it!" he radioed back.

Lt. Ross rushed from the mid section, now concluding why Brady wasn't aboard.

The plane's unusual movement woke the president. The Secret Service agent guarding his door called out.

"Sir!" the agent shouted, not really knowing what to do. The president, still dressed, bolted out of bed, grabbed a leather flight jacket from a hook, and opened the door.

"We've lost an engine," his experience told him.

"I don't know."

"Maybe more," the president said. "We've got to get to the cockpit." A third alarm was sounding now. "Three!" He started for the stairs. The agent took the lead. At that moment, a massive blast knocked him back in his compartment and onto the floor. A door flew passed him. Then smoke. Shattered glass floated in air for a second, then reversed direction, sucked out by sudden decompression. *Air Force One* yawed to the left. Oxygen masks dropped. The sound was deafening.

All of this was in the first three seconds.

Taylor had been here before. The plane was going down. He put the oxygen to his mouth, took in a deep breath, and counted to ten to get his heart rate down. The president surveyed the rubble. The Secret Service agent who had come to get him was dead. The door which had blown across the compartment broke his neck.

Air Force One nosed down. Morgan Taylor dropped his mask and struggled up the stairway against the building G-force. He strained to reach the cockpit...

....or what was left of it.

CHAPTER

67

Taylor grabbed the side of the demolished cabin door and swung it aside. It came off its hinges and he peered inside. Lewis, Agins, and Milkis—all strapped to their seats—were dead. Milkis's chair was blown completely off its bolts and nearly upside down. A gaping hole through the structure opened up to the second level below. Everything that wasn't attached was gone; out the window. To balance himself, Taylor stretched his arms out and used the walls of the cabin for support.

There was nothing he could do for the men. *The plane?* Virtually all of the displays were out. Other operating systems still seemed functional. Taylor struggled to keep his eyes open. The force of the wind blasting through the windshield was almost unbearable. *Oxygen!* He needed more oxygen. He reached for the mask, filled his lungs, then unbuckled Lewis and tried to slide him out of his seat; an impossible task considering the air blast and the G loads. But out of nowhere, another pair of hands reached in to help him.

Rossy.

"Explosion on *Air Force One*. Repeat, explosion on *Angel*," radioed Strike Eagle pilot Chester Pike. *Angel* was the Secret Service's unclassified designation for the president's plane.

"Say again," responded the commander of the AWACS, ten miles to starboard and 6,000 feet higher.

"An explosion in or near the cabin. Colonel Lewis was in the process of reporting multiple engine malfunctions. *Air Force One* is rapidly losing altitude quickly. I'm staying with her."

"Roger."

"One hundred yards off the left wing. Can't see any activity in the cockpit. Assuming flight crew is disabled or dead. Request air-sea rescue emergency assistance below."

"Roger. Scrambling ASR emergency assistance." With the touch of a computer screen a flash message went out to the 7th Fleet. Word simultaneously was sent via satellite to the USASOCOM, the Pentagon, and Jack Evans.

Meanwhile, all planes except for the Pike's Strike Eagle and two other escorts peeled off. They received orders to secure the area against enemy aircraft.

It took the strength of both men to pull Lewis out of his chair. Once done, Taylor jumped in, buckled, and grabbed the yoke. He pulled it back with all his strength. "Get Agins out!"

Rossy unbuckled the dead co-pilot and dragged him over the hole. He returned to the president's side and shouted over the wind. "A bomb."

"I don't care what the fuck it was now. Help me pull the nose up!"

Lt. Ross helped. The president tried his foot rudder pedals to stabilize the yawing. The airplane responded. "We'll need full flaps, Rossy. The second we get her leveled out, get those flaps down!"

They were burning off 1,000 feet of altitude every 10 seconds. At this rate, they'd crash in a matter of minutes. "Harder!" They were fighting overwhelming and asymmetrical forces, the power of a 747 in an uncontrollable dive, and the increasing air speed. Everything was working against them. "Come on, Goddammit! Come on!" Thankfully, they still had thrust from number four. They'd need it if they got the nose up.

Rossy put all of his effort into the struggle. The great plane slowly angled up.

"More!" Taylor called out. The plane bucked, not wanting to be tamed. "More!"

The nose continued to rise. Every degree up gave them extra seconds of life. If they could level, they might be able to stabilize *Air Force One* enough to make it to an airport—somewhere, or ditch.

"More!"

SAM 28000 never came completely level, but its angle of descent shallowed. "Now, Rossy! Full flaps."

The engineer obeyed. The flaps on each wing extended out and down, increasing the drag and the lift, which slowed their speed. An immediate effect—they could hear better. The wind still rushed in, but with the flaps down, they seemed to have a fighting chance. Thirty seconds later Morgan Taylor let out his first real breath.

"Okay, emergency procedures."

"Yes, sir."

"Radio?"

Rossy tested the system. "Dead."

"GPS?"

"Inoperable. All three."

"Lights?"

Rossy threw the toggles. "Landing lights only functional on the right side."

"Keep them off."

"Any idea what our fuel situation is?"

"Looks like we bingo'ed on one and three. But I can't tell you if any of the tanks were ever filled."

"What?" the president demanded.

"Possible sabotage at fueling."

"Who? Why?"

"One of my crew. I don't know why."

Rossy was amazed the cockpit was still intact. He looked around. "The bomb could have been planted for good measure. Looks like it didn't do all the damage it could have. It was under the navigator's seat. His metal briefcase helped contain the blast."

"You call this contained?" the president said.

In the midst of the crisis, Lt. Ross had to smile. "Poor choice of words, sir."

"Roger that," Taylor said. "Now, let's talk through the rest. We may not be able to later." The moon, nearly full, illuminated the sky. Taylor saw blackness below, but it wasn't the ocean. Lewis said they'd be above a storm center. They were going down through it and the turbulence could give them more trouble before impact. "How's the cabin?"

"A mess. We've got casualties. Only a few people were buckled in when we decompressed. I don't know for sure," Rossy explained.

"Let's see if they can hear us back there." He tried the public address system. "This is Taylor," he said showing as much confidence in his voice as possible. "We've leveled out. If you can hear me, send someone forward. Just one person. Everyone who's not doing anything essential buckle up in secure seats." He didn't explain what happened in the cockpit, but if the message went out it would be clear. The flight crew was dead and the former Navy commander was flying *Air Force One*.

"All right. Deactivate landing gear warning system."

"Roger," Rossy responded. He pulled the circuit breaker even though the landing gear warning lights were inoperative.

"Deactivate TAWS and GPWS."

Rossy turned off the terrain awareness and warning system and the ground-proximity systems to prevent unnecessary warnings.

"No change in fuel status?"

"No idea sir."

"Then set radio altimeter to fifty feet."

"Done. We just don't know what's true, sir, and it's going to be dark down there beneath the clouds."

"Do we know how low our ceiling is?"

Rossy had seen the weather forecasts before take-off. *What did they say?* He tried to remember.

"Ah. I think it called for fifteen hundred to two thousand."

The president quickly calculated. "At our current rate, we'll have five minutes to see where the hell we are. Then..." He stopped short of finishing the thought. Another more urgent one came to mind. "Any idea how much fuel we are carrying?"

"No."

"Check," the president ordered. "She's holding now, but if we lose number two or four, we'll have to burn off more altitude. I'm gonna take her under ten thousand. We won't need oxygen." Without power, it was conceivable that the plane could glide. If he handled it right, they'd head down at around 240 knots; about 3,000 feet per minute. But he wanted more than three minutes to get his bearings.

"Roger," Rossy said, unbuckling.

Air Force One picked up speed as Morgan Taylor nosed down, right into the storm center.

The New York Times
the same time

"We can't run this," Andrea Weaver argued. She was on the phone with Michael O'Connell after reading his first draft. He was at his desk looking at the copy on his computer screen. "You've danced around everything. Come on, O'Connell, we talked about this."

"I had to," he countered.

"And without any facts, you don't have a story."

"The facts support Strong's rise to national prominence through a series of accidents and misfortunes. It's all there Andrea. Read it again."

"I've read it once. That's enough."

"But it's all there!"

"Nothing's there."

"It is," he pleaded. "Strong's entire career is based on doors miraculously opening for him. There's a pattern, which I've substantiated."

"And your conclusion?"

O'Connell had the answer; or at least he assumed he did. However, he couldn't put it in print. "We both know," he said.

"Correction. *We* don't know. *You* believe," the editor argued. "And beyond that very significant issue, what is the point of view of your story? You're this close to calling it a conspiracy. So far, all unfounded. How different is that from what Strong does?"

"Jesus Christ! You don't think I know that?" He wheeled his chair away from his desk. "Why don't we just call it a feature story on America's most persuasive radio talk-show host and give it to Arts?"

"Why?"

"Why? To flush him the fuck out."

She was right on top of him. "That's not our job, Mr. O'Connell!"

O'Connell realized he'd overstepped his bounds. He needed to calm down. "Okay, then what do you suggest?" He was being sincere, not contrite.

"You're an investigative reporter. Don't give me any crap about feature stories. Investigate and file something I can print!"

Weaver was quite finished. They hung up. O'Connell faced his computer again and saw his reflection in the monitor. It was as blank as the screen.

Over the Banda Sea
the same time

Air Force One's communication center was coming to life. When the plane leveled, crew members carefully made their way to their consoles, sent out emergency messages, and radioed the AWACS and the F-15 escort.

"What is your status?" asked the commander aboard the AWACS.

"Casualties. Maybe thirty. We're still getting a count. Computers back online."

"Roger. The F-15 pilot reports extensive damage in the cockpit."

"Affirmative."

"Who the hell is flying the bird?"

"The president."

"Say again," the com officer in the AWACS asked. "Did not fully copy that."

"Roger. The President of the United States."

Now Morgan Taylor mentally ran through the ditching procedures. He'd never done it before, but it was survivable—in simulators.

Hit the water as slowly as possible. Keep the nose up; avoid stalling. Keep the wings parallel with the water as the point of impact approaches. Absolutely avoid one wing tip striking the water first. That would invariably result in uncontrollable, violent slewing.

He remembered more. *Into the wind. But which way was the wind blowing down there? Bleed off more speed; less damage on impact. Maintain sufficient air speed to take any last minute action. Don't stall. Depressurize.* He smiled to himself. *No problem there.* Most importantly, he recalled, *ditch alongside a swell. But how will I know which way the swells are aligned?* Experienced pilots understood that ditching into a swell would be tantamount to crashing into a brick wall. *Anything else?* he asked himself. He lost his concentration when he heard Secretary of State Poole.

"I had to come up and see for myself!" Poole held a towel across a large gash that went from his forehead to his right eye. He stepped into the cockpit carefully, avoiding the sharp surfaces everywhere.

"Norman!" The president recognized his voice without turning around.

"Mr. President. I'm the appointed representative," he said above the howling wind. "We heard you loud and clear."

"Good," Taylor yelled over the wind. "Is everyone on oxygen?"

"Yes. We knew to do that." He held on as the plane rumbled.

"We should be below ten thousand feet soon. Everyone will be able to breath normally, but I'll be damned if I know exactly when."

"Good." After he inhaled another breath he asked, "What do you need me to do?"

"Get back and appoint some officers to stand by the emergency exits. When we're down, get those doors open."

"Then?"

"Then we'll find out how good a boat *Air Force One* makes."

"Yes, sir. Anything else?" Poole asked.

"Just brace. Heads down. Glasses off. Knees up. It'll be rough, no matter how lucky we are. And evacuate immediately."

"I'll get the Secret Service guys up to help you."

"They'll be no help to me or anyone else unless they're strapped in tightly. Now go."

"Godspeed, Mr. President."

Morgan Taylor managed to raise one hand off the yoke and wave. He wasn't about to give *Air Force One* up to God quite yet.

The Pentagon
the same time

General Jonas Johnson Jackson was aware of the crisis one minute into it. He was at his desk at the Pentagon when his pager went off, his phone rang, and an instant message hit his computer screen; all simultaneously—all bad news.

USAPACOM was on the phone from the South Pacific. The IM came from Langley and his pager showed a discreet White House number which belonged to Presley Freedman, head of the Secret Service. He took them in order of personal priority. Phone and IM at the same time; the pager last.

The word was the same. **Emergency aboard Air Force One.** General Jackson stayed on the telephone. USAPACOM handled all of the traffic out of the South Pacific. The 7th Fleet, under the command of Admiral Clemson Zimmer, was in the area.

"Talk to me, Clem."

"Still getting assessments. Hold."

J3 was snapping fingers at assistants in the outer office and shouting down the hall for maps.

"Confirmed. Catastrophic event on *Air Force One*." He was relaying information as he was hearing it. "Two engines out. Stabilizing. What?"

"What?" J3 asked in kind.

"General, ah, the flight crew is dead."

"Then who's flying the bird?"

"Hold."

J3 distinctly heard Zimmer request a repeat of the latest information.

"Roger, I copy." He came back to the call. "J3, the president."

"The president—what?" He didn't understand.

"The president is flying his plane!"

"Good God!"

Admiral Clemson continued to give J3 updates as fast as he could relay them. Aides brought maps to General Jackson who quickly pinpointed *Air Force One*'s location based on the last coordinates.

"The Banda Sea. Got it. Can he make Halim?" Jackson thought that the Indonesia Air Force Base, located outside of Jakarta, might be the closest facility.

"Don't know. Top Gun's burned off a lot of altitude. Looks like he's preparing to ditch."

"What do you have there, Clem?"

"Most of the fleet is gathered closer to the Solomons, some thirty-six hours out. But I've got some assets closer. The *Blue Ridge* for one. And the *Kitty Hawk*'s search and rescue planes could be in the area in two hours."

"Roger. Stand by." The president's head of USASOC, America's largest command component of SOCOM, U.S. Special Operations Command, punched in one of one hundred numbers on his speed dial.

"J3. We have a situation."

"Monitoring it," reported a desk at Special Operations Command at MacDill Air Force Base in Florida.

"Patch in the F-15 escort and the AWACS. Sixty seconds."

"Affirmative, General."

As J3 waited, three words that Clemson stated came to mind: *Search and Rescue.*

Washington, D.C.
the same time

Roarke's cell phone issued the tone that accompanied a text message. He was working with Shannon Davis at the FBI.

"Freedman. Ten-ninety."

Ten-ninety was a simple police code. It meant *alarm.* Accompanied by the name Freedman, it stood for only one thing: *National emergency. Come in!* He didn't need to ask why.

The White House
the same time

Presley Freedman dispatched extra Secret Service to the Capitol. He did so without thinking of the consequences. Duke Patrick could soon be president. He also placed a call to Henry Lamden's principal physician at Walter Reed.

Aboard *Air Force One*

Rossy's worry multiplied the moment he read the computer display at his master engineering station. It had been his idea to install a virtual cockpit where he could check on key flight deck data during the course of a journey. But what he saw was absolutely wrong. The fuel tanks showed full. They'd been flying for under two hours, two engines were starved, yet the readouts were still reporting fuel capacity at 100 percent. He typed in a command. The screen blinked once, then confirmed full status on all engines. He typed an override command. The screen blinked again. Full. "Shit!" he exclaimed.

He ran to the steps leading up to the cockpit. Rossy slumped into the co-pilot's seat, attached the face mask, took in the needed oxygen, then pointed down.

"Get down to the deck fast, sir."

Without further instruction, Morgan Taylor nosed down. He traded altitude for speed. The extended flaps made a rough ride even rougher as they were buffeted by the winds.

"The fuel tanks were sabotaged," Ross explained. "The computers were re-programmed to read full. No one caught it. I can't tell you how many tons are left or whether we'll be sucking air in another second."

"You're sure?" the president shouted over the onrushing wind.

Rossy looked out at one and three; both dead. "Yes, sir. I'm sure."

The president switched on the PA. "Attention! This is Taylor. Secure yourself immediately. Prepare for ditching. I repeat, prepare for ditching. Fuel supply is critical. We're getting out of these clouds now. Brace! Brace!"

The radio operator communicated the president's news to the orbiting AWACS. The report was flashed halfway across the world to the Pentagon, the White House Situation Room, Langley, and MacDill. At the same time, crew members cleared the aisles as best they could, then strapped in for impact.

Air Force One broke out of the clouds just above 2,300 feet. The moonlight, blocked by the storm, cut visibility down to almost zero.

"See anything, Rossy?" Taylor asked.

Rossy squinted. "Not sure, sir." The onrushing wind didn't help. He checked the sides. "Maybe land mass off to the right. Three o'clock. Hard to tell."

"What's the direction of the swells?"

The lieutenant looked straight down. "Can't see 'em yet."

"Going to take the edge off our descent. We can't afford to hit the water at this speed." Taylor estimated it to be around 230 knots as he leveled out.

"Smell that?" Rossy asked.

Fresh salty air rushed in. "Yes," Taylor noted. He was glad he had pulled out.

"There!" Rossy shouted. "I see white caps. Flowing...toward us!"

"Distance?" Taylor shouted.

"Maybe five hundred feet."

Good, Taylor thought. Enough room to bring the 747 parallel to the waves. He dipped his left wing and lost another 200 feet. That's when his two remaining engines died.

CHAPTER 68

Aboard *Air Force One*

"**F**laps up to twenty degrees," Taylor called out. Without the thrust to keep the nose up, *Angel* lost altitude faster. Retracting the flaps could help compensate.

"Roger," Rossy said, using only his feel to tell him what was right. "What do you see below?"

"Catching some wave crests. But we're too low or it's too dark to see the swells."

The president held the yoke steady. "Try the landing lights."

They didn't respond. "Negative." He tried again. "Looks like we'll be doing this in the dark, sir."

The president's immediate problem—and one that no simulator could have prepared him for—was estimating when his undercarriage would hit the water. The profile of a 747 was far higher than anything he flew for the Navy. The cockpit was perched even higher. If he misjudged and hit the water too low, *Air Force One* would stop dead in place and flip. If he extended his glide path too long, he would collide with a wave, which was probably inevitable anyway.

"Brace, Rossy," Morgan Taylor said more softly.

The president summoned a mental picture of the fuselage. *Nose up.* The 747 was well-served by its straight fuselage. The angle of attack on the water could make the difference. A swept-up rear fuselage could, at impact, bring the plane to an almost vertical attitude before smashing down and most likely nosing under water. *Rear first, Taylor,* he said to himself again.

Rossy gripped the sides of his seat. He readied himself for the impact and what was to follow. Death would come with a violent backwards shock, followed by a forward catapult through the window, and the brick wall of water ahead. Altogether, they faced a second, maybe two, of pain; if that.

Aboard the F-15 Eagle

Major Pike hung to the side and three hundred feet over *Air Force One* when a thought occurred to him. Pike instantly dropped down, parallel and close to Taylor's wing; possibly too close. But he had something *Air Force One* didn't have. Lights.

Aboard *Air Force One*

The ocean suddenly brightened. Taylor whispered a quiet thank you to the F-15 pilot. His act might prove to be the difference. Now he could judge the distance of the waves and his height above them. Less than Rossy thought. He was coming in at too steep an angle. He brought the nose up, getting the feel of the ocean rising and falling beneath him for the last 200 feet. Another adjustment. *Twenty seconds.* A wave passed under. He pulled the yoke toward him again, lifting slightly. *Fifteen seconds.* Another wave. The next one would be his.

A lifetime of memories were knocking at the door, but Morgan Taylor barred them all. He held the plane steady; nose up. There was a sudden boom as the rear of *Air Force One* slammed into the ocean. But the 747 didn't flip. They lifted up, skipping like a rock across a pond. Then a second impact. This one harder. A powerful whiplash effect jerked him forward. He sensed Rossy's body snap with his, however he couldn't look over. He had to control the plane.

The entire fuselage of the 544,000-pound plane raced across the water at more than 140 miles an hour. Taylor needed to keep the wings parallel above the oncoming wave, which was about to crash over them.

Rossy was amazed they were alive. The salt-water spray rushing through the broken glass actually invigorated him. He glanced over to Taylor. He was struggling to hold the great plane steady against a wall of water. *The yoke!* Rossy unbuckled his safety belt and reached in to help.

The president was grateful for the extra muscle and equally surprised he was around to need it.

The plane road out the waves every fifteen seconds. So far three. With each one, *Air Force One*'s speed decreased. Taylor and Rossy fought to control the angle until finally, forward speed was so slow, they had no more maneuvering ability. *Air Force One* came to a stop.

Some airplanes will float for only a few minutes, if at all. Others, according to reports, have drifted for days. Taylor wasn't going to wait to find out how *Air Force One* would do. He unsnapped his harness.

"Evacuate now! Out! Fast!" he announced.

Rossy slumped back into his seat. "You did it, sir."

"*We* did it. But we're not safe yet. Now get your ass out of here!"

"You too, Mr. President."

"I haven't come this far to sit around and sink. Right after you."

As he stood, Rossy had to steady himself. The plane rose and fell with every new wave. "Thank you."

"Save it. Now get moving!"

Further back, the doors and emergency exits were open. Rafts, which automatically deployed, were already in the water. White House staff, *Air Force One* crew, reporters, and members of the president's delegation made their escape.

Then there was the matter of the sensitive files and equipment onboard *Air Force One*, including the "football" with the go-codes for a nuclear strike. Should the plane remain afloat, its secrets could be mined. However, contingency plans were already in play.

Just as Rossy was at the flight deck door, two Secret Service agents shoved past him and grabbed Morgan Taylor by the arms.

"Mr. President, you have to go."

The president only had a fleeting moment to survey the horrific scene. What had been *Air Force One* was reduced to a virtual war zone. There were fatalities—those who were not buckled when the plane decompressed; the injured—some close to death; and the dazed. He prayed that there would be time for everyone to escape. But he would not be allowed to supervise the process. Now, Morgan Taylor was going to the head of the line.

The Banda Sea
The Malukas

"Again!" Musaf Atef yelled out to Commander Komari. "The jet!" He pointed skyward. Although it was hard to determine, it appeared to be an American military plane. It over-flew them at no more than 300 meters. On its third pass, just to their right, two missiles ignited, leaving a flame of fire streaming behind them. The jet pulled up. Seconds later, maybe a kilometer away, one missile, then the next, found their target. The flashes, against the night sky, blinded the Indonesian terrorists who were onboard the stolen trawler. They were returning with another cache of weapons, bought from the Chinese. As their eyes adjusted to the explosion, Atef saw a raft approaching. The flames backlit what must have been survivors from the crash of the first plane—a bigger plane, they realized.

"Look!" Atef called.

"Yes, I see." Komari signaled for his men to have their guns ready. He strained his eyes. "Two, no, three rafts!"

"What shall we do?" Atef asked.

"If they are friends, they will join us. If they are our enemies, they must die."

The boat quickly cut the distance. Komari commanded his men to stand at the ready. He called to two of his more elite soldiers to unlatch the cases carrying black market Stinger missiles. They'd become quite proficient over the last weeks, and he was confident they could take out the jet, should it return.

New York City
a bar
the same time

Michael O'Connell was unaccustomed to having a crisis of conscience. Things were usually very clear to him. The tequila only reinforced his basic philosophy: *Dig for facts, write your story, print it, and let the chips fall where they may.* But not this time. He had some facts, he had written a story, but his editor wouldn't run it. Now it was unlikely that he'd get much more, and yet he was absolutely convinced that everything he learned about Elliott Strong was true.

The old Russian knew I'd find out. He knew I'd come and he expected I'd know what to do with it.

O'Connell's dilemma was simple. He struggled over whether to leak the story to the government. To make such a move would compromise his integrity as a journalist. He might never be able to go back. Sources would dry up. His credibility would be ruined. *But?* The third shot of tequila wasn't helping him make up his mind.

Goddammit, I tried! He was arguing with the old communist; a conversation he'd been having for days. *You had no right to contact me. Why me?* The only thing the Russian said back in these mental exercises was the one word he shared with him in Moscow. *Strong.*

"Fuck it!" O'Connell uttered aloud. The reporter slapped down a 20 and left.

Washington, D.C.
minutes later

"What is it?" O'Connell's name and number came up in the caller ID display. "I'm a little busy right now." Roarke was sprinting through the White House.

"I gotta see you," the reporter quickly admitted.

"It's going to have to wait." Roarke didn't want to say too much. "It can't."

Roarke stopped dead on the spot. "What is it?"

"We need to talk about it in person, Roarke. Tonight. Where?"

"Not on the phone. In person."

"Can you come up?" O'Connell asked.

"No." The news about the president's crash hadn't broken yet. Roarke wasn't about to tell the *Times* reporter why he couldn't leave. "What's so important that you..."

"I know the identity of another sleeper."

Roarke instantly switched gears from the president's crisis to O'Connell's bombshell. "Get down here!" The agent checked his watch. He calculated the flights out of LaGuardia and proposed a meeting time. "Eight-thirty. I'll clear you through the North Gate."

New York City

O'Connell made it to his condo at the Bromley at 83rd and Broadway. He threw a few overnight items together and hit the street to catch a cab at the corner. A taxi heading uptown caught his hand signal, but another sitting on 83rd honked and moved up. The reporter grabbed the door and climbed in.

"LaGuardia."

"Very good," replied the driver. He had an Indian accent.

O'Connell automatically looked at his name and picture. *Ishmail* something. The plastic was cracked.

"What airline?"

"American," O'Connell answered. He saw the reflection of the man in the rearview mirror. He smiled at his passenger.

"Very good. Very, very good."

The cab drove uptown. "What is your profession?" Ishmail said.

"A reporter." O'Connell was not in a talking mood.

"Ah, very good. A reporter. You report the news. Breaking news very good."

"Right," O'Connell said not loud enough to be heard.

"Very good profession."

At 110th, the taxi made a right turn, crossing above Central Park to the East Side. O'Connell hated when cab drivers talked endlessly for the sake of talking. He decided to close his eyes, hoping the cabbie would get the message.

"Very good," the driver whispered.

The Banda Sea
the same time

The trawler came up to the first raft. Commander Komari signaled one of his men. He hit it with the boat's searchlight.

"Hey! Kill the light!" yelled a man in a uniform.

The man at the lamp ignored the request for two reasons. He didn't understand English and he was ordered to shine it.

Another raft drifted up. The beam swung over. A third raft came toward the trawler. Some of the men had guns. Many wore American military uniforms. Komari shouted an order in Bahasa Indonesian.

The beam swung back over to the second boat. "Allah be praised!" he exclaimed.

Musaf Atef wondered why Komari should call to the Almighty at such a time. "Commander, what is it?"

"Look, even a fool's eyes can see who God has delivered to us."

"I don't understand."

"They are Americans."

"Yes."

"And the leader of the great Satan is among them." He yelled to the soldier on the lamp. "There!" The light settled directly on Morgan Taylor.

Next, Komari gave Atef very specific instructions. If he followed them, Atef might redeem himself.

Atef had his men toss nets over to the president's raft. Komari shouted out in halted English, "Come aboard! Yes, yes, come aboard!"

In the distance, the last of the flames turned to smoke as *Air Force One* slipped beneath the surface. With the backlight gone, the only illumination on the ocean was from the trawler. It held on the first raft until each of the seventeen men and two women were safely onboard.

Atef gave the soldier aiming a light a slicing motion across his throat. The beam went dark. At the same moment, the engines kicked in and the boat moved away 20 yards, then idled.

"Wait!" shouted one of the American officers. "The others!" He stepped forward. "You can't leave..."

"Oh?"

A dozen guns were on the people pulled out of the boat. Three Secret Service officers automatically surrounded the president. Taylor dropped back.

"Who the hell are you?"

"Commander Umar Komari, leader of October 12. Right now your superior."

"Bull shit!" the officer stepped forward. Shots rang out from three guns. He and the two other agents directly behind him were cut down.

Atef screamed another order. The light turned on again. It lit up the closest raft. The gunmen filled it with bullets. When they had done their work there, they turned on the remaining raft. In the course of a minute, both were gone, along with the thirty-one men and women aboard.

The fourteen remaining prisoners stood in silence, hardly believing what they had just witnessed. At that moment, the F-15 swooped overhead, rocking the trawler. Two terrorists fell overboard. Another Secret Service agent pushed the president behind him, thinking for an instant that they could use the jet's distraction to strike, but the guns were right on them again.

"Atef!"

"Yes, commander."

"How well have you trained your men?"

He completely understood the question. The lieutenant screamed out to two subordinates who didn't have military rank yet. They readied their shoulder-fired Stinger. It took another moment to calibrate the targeting. The shooter turned in the direction from which the American plane was likely to come. He brought the missile tube up and prepared to fire. But he was wrong. The F-15 cut across at a perpendicular angle this time. It took a moment to adjust, then he whipped around and fired. The Stinger flamed across the sky in a race to catch up with the Eagle.

Aboard the F-15 Eagle

The F-15's defensive systems came alive. An unmistakable alarm alerted Pike. His heads-up display revealed the full picture. Twenty-two seconds to impact. "Under attack!" he radioed out. There was no time to say anything more.

He quickly ran through a set of maneuvers designed to shake and distract the Stinger. He was so low to the deck that he had to confine his defensive flying to lateral moves. There was no down, and up would burn off too much speed. He sharply dodged left, then right, releasing countermeasures at the same time, including a new towed decoy system, dubbed "soap on a rope." The decoy proved effective over the Balkans, Iraq, and Afghanistan. What about the South Pacific at low altitude? Another left turn. A right. A sharper right.

Dweedle dweedle. The sound of the missile alarm. More chaf. *Dweedle dweedle.* The missile was still on him.

An explosion, about 5 kilometers away on the horizon, illuminated the sky for the second time that night. Komari's men cheered.

"You have fallen into the wrong sea," the commander told his captives in English. "I will decide what to do with you soon. But first, the American president step forward."

Everyone stood still. The Secret Service agents blocked Morgan Taylor.

"I will only ask one more time. Then the first row will die." He gave the order for the guns to take aim. "Now."

The president pushed his protectors aside and walked forward. "I'm Morgan Taylor."

"And so you are," Komari observed. "You are a much smaller man than I imagined. Older."

Taylor did not engage the terrorist.

"Older and weaker, too."

"I believe that you will not find any of us weak."

Komari laughed. "Like your supersonic jet? We plucked it from the sky like a kite."

Don't be so sure, Taylor thought. Heat from the flares had drawn the Stinger's sensors. Experience told him the missile had detonated, not the fully armed Eagle. The F-15 was gone, but there were still eyes and ears overhead.

"Are we prisoners of war, commander?" Taylor asked.

"War? I suppose so," Komari boasted. "Your own well-publicized 'War on Terror.'"

"Then we shall be afforded proper treatment under the Geneva Accords."

The terrorist laughed, as Taylor was certain he would. "No, Morgan Taylor. You shall suffer the same fate as the Christian infidels who, for too long, have controlled my country."

The lunatic plans to attack Jakarta!

"Take them under. Kill anyone who resists." The instructions were in Bahasa, but the captives understood the threat.

There was another raft.

The fourth inflatable raft, the last to get clear of *Air Force One*, was out of view when the trawler came upon the others. Secretary of State Norman Poole ordered it to stay back when he heard the yelling and gunshots. Twenty-nine men and women were safely on board. Another eleven clung to the side. They escaped by diving off their rafts when the terrorists fired their rounds.

Poole, the defacto captain, instructed everyone to remain low and quiet. Help would come. The ELT, or emergency locator transmission, should be doing its job. Based on what the survivors of the attack told him, the terrorists knew who they had in hand.

Pike kept his plane on the deck and flew 10 miles due west before climbing to 10,000 feet.

"Roger that," Major Pike radioed to J3. "Assumption is that Top Gun *is* aboard." His pictures would confirm that fact when he landed at Andersen Air Force Base on Guam. Command redirected him there after the Stinger launch.

He hoped that his presumed death could buy the president and USAPACOM needed time.

New York City

Not such a good reporter, thought the cabbie. *He didn't comment that the man pictured in the license had a moustache. The driver didn't.* He gazed into his rearview mirror. *He should have sensed that we never got on the East Side Drive. But he's sleeping.* The cab kept heading north into the Bronx, missing the last exit for the Triboro Bridge. *And he failed to notice that the bulletproof glass between the front and back seats was gone. Very foolish. No, he just sleeps.*

The taxi continued to drive north, taking turns slowly. The cabbie came to a gradual, almost imperceptible stop in an alley. *Why wake him?* He reached to his right and quietly put his hand under a copy of the *New York Times* and raised a 9 mm Glock. The silencer was already attached. *Just let him sleep.*

He actually wondered what it would be like not to wake; not to know that you had fallen asleep, never to breathe again. No fear. No knowledge. No goodbyes.

Just let him sleep. "Very good."

CHAPTER 69

Cannon House Office Building
the same time

Duke Patrick nearly had his speech down, but an argument in the outer office broke his concentration. *Now what?* He waited for the talking to die down. It didn't. There was a knock at his door. "I said no interruptions!"

His chief of staff was the first in. A number of other men—all looking serious, all with Secret Service pins on their lapels—followed. "I couldn't stop them," he said.

"Mr. Speaker," began the lead agent. He muscled his way right around Patrick's staffer. "You need to come with us. There's an urgent meeting at the White House."

"What? Why? I'm in the middle of something important."

"I'm sorry for the interruption, but please. Now, sir."

"I demand to know why?"

"I'm not at liberty to discuss it."

"Then I won't be joining you." He turned his back to the agents and silently returned to his speech.

"Sir..."

Patrick ignored him.

"Mr. Speaker, I have my orders."

Patrick blew his temper. He reeled around and shouted, "Is this one of Taylor's tricks? Get me out of the way so I can't deliver my speech?"

"No, Mr. Speaker."

"Then why on God's earth should I go with you?"

"Because the White House needs you there."

Patrick remained obstinate.

The Secret Service agent stepped away and spoke into a small microphone in his sleeve. He pressed one finger to his ear, seating the earpiece tighter. Congressman Patrick watched, broadly smiling as if he had won something. The agent finished and walked directly up to the speaker and whispered into his ear.

"Mr. Speaker, I've been instructed at the highest levels to bring you to the White House. It is your Constitutional duty."

"Highest levels? What the hell is that supposed to mean? I don't believe the president has returned yet."

Duke Patrick was living up to his reputation, thought the Secret Service agent. *Insolent, intractable, and officious.* The agent radioed back, "Negative on John Wayne. Repeat. John Wayne will not comply." John Wayne was the agency's handle for the current speaker of the House. It was an homage to Hollywood's Duke.

Ten seconds later the speaker's private phone line rang.

"I think that's for you, Congressman."

It rang three more times. Patrick finally picked it up, showing his extreme displeasure.

"Congressman Patrick."

The Secret Service agents and Patrick's chief of staff watched; unaware of what was being said, but totally interested. The congressman's expression dropped.

"Okay," was all he said.

He hung up, and ignoring the Secret Service detail, told his chief, "I'll be at the White House. Stay by the phone."

On board the AWACS

"Still tracking the craft." The navigator gave the heading, which was plotted by Pentagon analysts back home. "Course is for an island. Two point two miles." He changed screens. "Landfall likely at any number of potential coves. Other islands ahead through narrow passageways." It wasn't his job to assess the potential destinations, but it didn't look good. The terrain was rocky and mountainous. Dense vegetation would make a rescue mission extremely difficult. He typed in more information on his computer. It got worse. The immediate islands were known for their caves—hundreds, if not thousands of them. He revised his opinion. If they took the president there, it might be impossible to find him. *Like a needle in a haystack.*

Outside the Dirksen Senate Office Building
the same time

Katie expected to hear sirens. After all, it was Washington, D.C. There was a fair chance that at any given moment, one dignitary or another needed to be hustled somewhere fast. But in the five minutes since she left the Rayburn Building, it seemed like there were nothing but screaming sirens.

She was on the corner of Constitution and C trying to hail a cab when she realized that all the noise was heading in the same direction—away from the Capitol. A taxi eventually stopped for her. She gave Roarke's address and asked the obvious. "What's going on?"

"Dunno," the driver answered.

"Is it usually this crazed?"

"Oh, sometimes. You never know." Two black Lincolns with blaring sirens passed them on Constitution. "Could be anything."

The explanation sounded good enough until another two cars raced by. She took her cell phone out of her pocketbook and dialed Roarke.

It rang three times. "Yeah, honey. Can't talk."

Not good, she thought. "Just tell me, is everything all right?"

"Why? What do you know?"

"Nothing, except that every car with a siren has it turned on."

"Where are you?"

"Heading home." *That has a nice ring to it.* "Will you be...?"

"Later," he interrupted.

"Call me when you can. Please." She let her concern show.

"I will. Love you."

She added, "I love you more," but Roarke was already gone.

Lebanon, Kansas

"They're going to feel the love, Elliott," said a caller.

"They better feel what we hate," the talk-show host said. "That's what the march is all about."

Elliott Strong brokered in hate, day and night. He had delivered his single-minded message for years: You're either for a *Strong Nation* or against it. Now his philosophy had a face attached—General Robert "Bob" Woodley Bridgeman.

Over the years, he never embraced Democrats. Now he finally turned on Republicans, as he always planned. Strong was leading millions of disenfranchised Americans toward a new political movement; a new party which would soon have a new name.

"This isn't a protest march, for God's sake. You go to Washington and show Bob Bridgeman that you're there for him. You're there to demand change. If the power brokers don't do it themselves, well then, I suppose we'll have to do it ourselves."

This was the first time he raised the specter of seizing political power. He slammed his hand on the table to get his listeners' attention. "You have that? No more calls to congressmen we don't trust. No more e-mails to a president, hell, two presidents, that don't mean anything to us! No more pleading with senators. We'll take this country from the ground level up. It's time for a recall! We'll get people in government who can do what needs to be done. And believe me, there's only one man who can lead us out of the mess we're in. General Bob Bridgeman."

Strong shuffled some papers. He looked at his computer screen. He had enough calls to last a month. *They're getting it*, he thought.

The White House

"Where are you?" Roarke asked urgently.

"Ah, almost at your apartment."

"Still driving?"

"Yes," Katie replied. "Scott, what's going on?"

"Change of plans. Get over here."

"Here? Where's here?"

"The White House. North Entrance. I'll meet you," he explained.

"But..."

"Just do it."

Washington, D.C.

T he capital was packed with protestors and the vendors were thrilled. They were stocked up with *Bridgeman Rules, March2Washington,* and *Bridgeman for President* t-shirts, sweatshirts, and buttons. Everything was designed in bold red, white, and blue with a single, approved photograph of General Bridgeman against a fully unfurled American flag. It was the work of a New York designer; organized and distributed; definitely not a fly-by-night operation.

The Associated Press had already estimated that more than $2 million would be spent by marchers on souvenirs. Hotel rooms and meals could account for $20 million over the next few days. Overtime for police and support services, another $1.5 million according to the wire service quotes. It was all for a man the public knew nothing about little more than a month earlier...and all because of one radio talk-show host.

Fox News scored another sit down with Bridgeman, while CNN had to settle for a quick run-and-gun interview with the general. No matter the bias, everyone talked about the meteoric rise of the Texas general. As the host of *The McLaughlin Group* termed it, opinion weighed heavily over traditional reporting in this new age of journa*less*dom. Fact-based coverage was becoming a dying art.

"So, Roger Deutsch, political contributor to *Vanity Fair,* I ask you, can General Bridgeman muster a vote of confidence?" The McLaughlin host always employed tight, staccato phrasing in his questions.

"A vote of confidence? Yes. But if the endgame is to unseat the president, he'll flame out long before the election. This is too early; three years before the next election, two years before the primaries. I can't even tell you what party he's aligned with, or more to the point, what party is aligned with Bridgeman."

"Any party he wants!" interrupted the *Philadelphia Inquirer's* Victor Monihan. "When was the last time we saw a political rally this size for a declared candidate? Never. Both the Republicans and the Democrats would love to have him lead their party. Now if you're asking me if it's a good thing?"

"Is it a good thing?" the host prompted.

"Who knows? I can't even articulate who he represents, other than an amorphous radio constituency."

"I can tell you what he wants, though," argued Peter Weisel, the Washington bureau chief of the *Chicago Tribune.* "He's for a recall and totally anti-Lamden, anti-Taylor, anti-Constitution, anti-process, anti-procedure, and anti-protocol. And just check his military record— he's anti-establishment."

Weisel was not the first to recognize it, but he was the first to state it.

"Page One, the *Chicago Tribune,*" the host read. "It's right here. You say General Bridgeman was not the leader he claims to be, but an arrogant maverick who ignored military command in Bosnia."

"Worse," explained Weisel. "Under his command, he very nearly restarted the war. The Pentagon sent him to Afghanistan to cool off. He was ordered to lay low, but he couldn't. He called the new leadership a joke and he held the prime minister under house arrest on suspicion of drug trafficking. Unproven, I might add. That wasn't the last of Bridgeman's brilliant military career moves. He came back to a desk job and promptly pissed off then–President Morgan Taylor for deploying troops to Lebanon. It's all true, and yet you don't hear any of this on the radio."

"For good reason," offered the *Dallas Morning News's* Christy Castle. "It's triple X material. *Ex*cessively misstated. *Ex*tremely inaccurate. *Ex*ceptionally partisan. The man is a true military hero. Distinguished Service, Silver Star, Navy Cross; the whole nine yards. You've ignored how he prevented war from breaking out again in Bosnia, how he uncovered the largest drug smuggling operation in Afghanistan, let alone how, in the Middle East, General Bridgeman saved his own men in the heat of battle. This is a good man, a dedicated American. How he got to national prominence? Well, I suppose that's because we need him."

71

The White House

"**K**essler." Katie identified herself to one of the two White House guards who stopped her cab. She noticed far more security than normal; more Secret Service and Marines; more guns. "I'm here to see Scott Roarke."

While one guard stayed with her, another looked at a list. Her name was not on it. "You have an appointment?"

"Mr. Roarke just called. I got here quickly and..."

"May I see your license, please."

Katie complied, also producing a temporary White House ID she'd forgotten to mention.

The marine stepped aside and radioed inside. He had to speak loudly over the sirens from other cars rolling into the driveway.

While the Marine was making his call, Katie paid the driver, but was careful not to get out of the cab until the Marine okayed her.

"You're cleared Ms. Kessler," the guard said a minute later. "Agent Pino will escort you through security."

"Thank you."

The woman agent appeared almost out of nowhere and led Katie to the metal detectors. She handed Katie's purse and attaché case to another guard at an X-ray machine.

"Is this your first visit to the White House? Ms. Kessler," Agent Pino asked.

"No, my third." Her first meeting was immediately after the Inauguration. The second was only a few days ago with Bernie Bernstein and White House counsel, Brad Rutberg. Now she sensed that this visit was going to be different for entirely new reasons, still unknown.

There was a profound change in everyone's manner. People were quickly racing through the halls. The urgency from outside carried right inside, or, as she realized, *vice versa*.

"This way, please." Pino ushered her to an elevator and accompanied Katie down. When the doors opened, Katie entered a whole new world. Marines were posted everywhere. Officers with uniforms from almost every branch of the military scurried from room to room.

"Just ahead." They continued to even more guarded quarters, the White House Situation Room. The Secret Service agent spoke to a huge Marine posted at the door. He radioed inside showing no hint of emotion. A minute later, Scott emerged. It wasn't the Scott Roarke she'd left earlier that morning. His face was ashen; he looked pained.

"What's wrong?"

Roarke pulled her inside and closed the door. What he had to say was not even for the guards. Not yet.

"The president's plane went down."

Katie suddenly knew why she was there. It wasn't because Scott needed his girlfriend at his side. All her work was coming to bear.

Roarke explained what he could. With news of the crash of *Air Force One* came the inevitable question:

"Who's in charge?"

Without another word, Roarke accompanied Katie to Brad Rutberg and Supreme Court Chief Justice Leopold Browning.

"Ms. Kessler," Justice Browning said, "circumstances have moved up our meeting."

"Yes, sir," she replied. She firmly shook the hand of the man she deeply respected. She hadn't seen the chief justice since their spirited conversations in January. "We have much to discuss."

"Indeed." The chief justice was 68, which made him younger than most of his colleagues, yet he was more knowledgeable than anyone else on the bench. It was difficult to argue Constitutional wisdom with the former Illinois prosecutor. Katie had tried. And though she was persuasive in their last meeting, she learned that when it came to law, no one in the country had a more brilliant mind than Browning. *What can I possibly tell him that he doesn't already know?*

Haruku, Indonesia

The prisoners were marched blindfolded from the shore, up a rocky incline, through a dense tropical jungle, to a flat area. By the sound of things, they settled in a tent. The fact was confirmed when the rebels removed their hoods. "At least we're not in a cave," Taylor whispered to Rossy.

"Silence!" Komari's order was followed by the butt of a rifle across the back of the president's head.

Taylor fell to the ground. Komari barked something else in Indonesian, which the president quickly realized were instructions to tie the prisoners together in pairs, back-to-back. Taylor was lashed to Ross. Considering what they had gone through together, the president couldn't have asked for a better partner.

"Sorry I put us down in these waters, Rossy," the president whispered when Komari and his men were working on the others.

"You saved a lot of lives, sir."

"Did I?" They were surrounded by a dozen men with guns.

The soldier closest to them couldn't stop gaping at Taylor. He'd seen the look before. Pride over a valued prize. Word had spread that the prisoners included the American president. But Taylor assumed that very fact created a serious problem. *They have to figure out what to do with me.*

"Surely the infidels will pay handsomely for their leader," Atef boasted. "We will trade the keys to the capitol for his life. Right?"

Komari wasn't so sure. *Bargaining would surely give us away. The Americans can trace radio signals. Far better to kill them now and forget that we ever found the infidels.* But another thought called out to the commander.

"The Prophet may be testing us, Atef."

"Testing? Why?"

"To see if we have the strength to demonstrate our commitment."

The commander's junior didn't understand. "How? We have done what no army has ever done in history. We have captured the American president."

"We have done little more than put ourselves in the enemy's sight. Unless, this is the Prophet's way of determining whether we deserve to continue." Komari actually believed what he was saying. "Perhaps we can take the heads of our prisoners?"

Atef was aghast. "Sir!"

"Atef, the Great Satan is certain to try to hunt us down. We shot a boat load of unbelievers. We destroyed their jet fighter. But they don't know who or where we are. If we try to bargain for the president's life, we will reveal ourselves. They are smart. They have their technology. But if we kill them and wait for their searches to end, we will be free to strike again. After all, as it was with the revelation of God to the Prophet Muhammad, our *jihad* demands we *command the right and forbid the wrong.* Our right is to kill the Americans. We forbid them from interrupting our holy cause. We must, as in the *hadith*—the word of the Prophet—avert injustice by action."

It seemed to make sense to Atef. "So it is a test. Allah be praised."

The Pentagon

"Issue the Warning Order," J3 declared. The commander of USASOCOM didn't want to lose another moment.

"Yes, sir," replied Admiral Zach Standish of NAVSPECWARCOM. The Navy Special Warfare Command oversaw the SEALs and their two other components, the Special Boat Squadron (SBS) and the SEAL Swimmer Deliver Vehicles (SDVs).

"Where are the nearest SDVs?" the general asked.

Standish replied, "The 7th Fleet has two on the *Essex*."

"No subs?"

"Too far away. But here's the problem, we don't have a full team onboard right now."

"Why not?"

"They went into the Solomons after the attack," Standish explained. "So, we'll have to bring in another platoon to hook up with the *Essex*."

J3 asked the obvious. "Where's the nearest? Coronado?"

"No, luckily Pearl." Pearl Harbor.

J3 calculated the number of men the two submersibles could transport. *Eight.* It would have to be enough. Actually, SEALs were known to work best in tight eight-man groups.

"Deploy them."

"Yes, sir."

"And confirm when the Warning Order has been received and what time the Team will be airborne."

"And their mission, sir?"

"We're a go for a D.A." A *Direct Action;* military-speak for a combat operation.

The Warning Order set a number of critical things in order. It put the U.S. Navy SEALs on notice, it established the operational chain of command, it readied combat and tech support, and it got SEALs where they needed to go. Heaven and Earth opened with the issuance of a Warning Order. Generally the act provided SEALs with up to twelve hours to prepare. They'd have a lot less today.

The White House Situtation Room

"What are we looking at?" Katie was confused by the banks of monitors. The chief justice was by her side.

"Satellite views fibered in from the Pentagon's National Military Command Center, the NMCC," explained Roarke. "They're fed from various agencies including the National Geospatial Agency in Herndon, Virginia, west of D.C. There's also intel from surveillance planes over the target area and we're seeing tactical maps of the Indonesian islands. But I can't help you there."

"There are so many," she observed.

"Thousands. But," he pointed to a large hi-def monitor, "fewer in the immediate vicinity. That's what they're focusing on."

"Then he's alive? The president is alive?"

"We don't know. All we're doing is tracking a boat we presume he's on. We're waiting for infrared, closer satellite pictures, and more telemetry."

Eve Goldman walked in with Bernie Bernstein. He was just finishing briefing her when Chief Justice Leopold joined them.

"Madame Attorney General," the austere Supreme Court judge said.

"Chief justice," she replied. Both sounded grim. "We have some work to do." It was an understatement.

Katie stepped forward and said hello to Eve Goldman. "Attorney General, good to see you again. I mean..." She tried to apologize for her flub. *Good* was out of place.

"We're all frazzled, Ms. Kessler. And under the circumstances, it is good to see you."

Katie immediately felt better.

The AG continued. "I understand you've been doing some comprehensive research. Anything that bears discussion now?"

Brad Rutberg and Bernie Bernstein moved closer to the conversation.

"I'm afraid I have a great deal of long-range thinking. Succession is inherently flawed as legislated. But as far as today?" Katie looked to Chief Justice Browning for support. "There is only the law."

He agreed without opinion.

"But," she said surprising everyone, "I actually do have one thought."

"Ms. Kessler, not another of your polemics," the nation's senior justice contended.

"If you'll allow me, sir. I've read a great deal about bumping."

"We're not facing that situation," he pointed out.

"No, but for argument sake, if the speaker of the house is not able to assume office at the moment that a successor must be named, then the senate *pro tem* serves as acting president. Right?"

"That's right," Rutberg chimed in.

"It could be because the speaker was killed in a catastrophic event," Katie continued.

"Arguably so," the chief justice remarked.

"But the House majority could quickly elect a new speaker and according to law, he or she would bump the acting president."

Browning failed to see where her argument was going. "You're outlining a completely different scenario, Ms. Kessler."

"I am, your honor."

"Then what is your point?"

The attorney general also wanted to know. "Please, counselor. Congressman Patrick is on his way. With the president down and presumed incapacitated, perhaps even dead, we must proceed accordingly." *Even if it means making that moron Patrick president,* she said to herself.

"Really?" Katie said. "I think there may be another possibility." She showed a devilish, almost political smile. "A bit of bumping, but quite within reason."

"What? What kind of possibility?" Chief Justice Browning deman-ded.

"A decision designed to buy us some time."

"No more riddles, Ms. Kessler! State what you mean."

"It will require an additional call before the speaker is informed. When he is, I don't think he'll like it."

"I don't care what the hell he likes!" blurted Bernie Bernstein, quite in character.

The lawyers politely ignored the comment even though they agreed. Chief Justice Browning raised his eyebrow. Kessler had a way of get-ting to him.

"Ms. Kessler," Browning commanded, "Let's hear it. The Constitution is calling."

The Cabinet Room
White House
minutes later

"Mr. Speaker, please take a seat," the marine guard said. "Someone will be up to see you shortly."

"Up?" *Up meaning up from the Situation Room or the War Room?* "Look, Colonel." Patrick got right in the officer's face. "I don't like surprises. I was ordered here; told that there was a matter of national urgency." He was actually told *emergency,* but he remembered wrong. "The Secret Service didn't say a goddamned thing about what's going on. Bernstein didn't either when he called. Now you. I don't like guessing games."

The marine locked eyes with the Speaker. "Congressman, friends don't consider me much of a game player either."

"Then we understand each other."

"Not at all, Mr. Speaker. Now if you'll excuse me."

The White House War Room
fifteen minutes later

While the discussion about succession stayed in the Situation Room, military planning moved into the White House War Room. The FBI's Robert Mulligan was invited in, along with Presley Freedman and

Scott Roarke. So were the secretaries of defense and homeland security.

"What do we know about this place?" Mulligan asked Secretary of Defense T.J. Harriman.

"Lots. And it all speaks to the president's initiative in Australia. The Malukus consist of one thousand twenty-seven islands. Only seven of them are considered big. About six hundred twenty-two are uninhabited. And that's only a fraction of Indonesia," explained the SecDef, a former CEO of Ford. "You want to start a revolution? That's the place. You can strike and hide with ease. That's what a Muslim vigilante group called Laskar Jihad—or Holy War Forces—have been doing for years. And for years they were just playing with matches. Now they're into their own scorched earth program. The worst part is they've got plentiful fuel—the country's Christians. Since ninety-nine, they've been burning their way through the islands, picking up recruits and trading drugs for weapons. The NDI tells me that a considerable amount of their firepower comes from the Chinese."

"And no one's done anything about them?"

"Mr. Director, it's a fucking huge country. In fact, Indonesia is the biggest Muslim nation in the world. Let's just say that up till now, except for some training initiatives we coordinated for the Indonesian Army, it ain't been our problem."

"I guess that's changed," Roarke remarked.

"Yes, it has."

The National Director of Intelligence finished scanning a file and joined the conversation. "To the secretary's point, this is a copy of a letter written to United Nations Secretary General Kofi Annan in two thousand. It was signed by members of the Moluccan Christian Communication Forum." He gave it to Harriman. "The Forum asked for help. They reported that jihad forces vowed to fight to their last drop of blood. They claimed that rebels were preparing for a more deadly attack. The Forum pleaded for the international community to step in. They argued that the stability of the region is threatened and the Malukus are becoming a terrifying breeding ground for international terrorism."

"And what did the U.N. say?" Roarke asked, following up on his previous question.

"Basically, paraphrasing the secretary's words, ain't been their problem."

"Jesus Christ! Why doesn't everyone just open their borders and tell the terrorists to come right in. No taxes and kill as many people as you want," Bernstein complained.

"My sentiments exactly," the secretary of homeland security added.

"Well, that's exactly the point President Taylor was arguing in Australia," said Jack Evans. "So let's talk about how we free him and get on with it."

At that moment, General Johnson called the briefing to order.

"All right everybody, listen up. As Secretary Harriman began explaining, the target is in the Banda Sea." He called up a computer map on one 42" plasma TV screen. "It's a nearly enclosed sea, occupying about one hundred eighty thousand square miles. The Banda is bounded by the southern Malukus and Ceram, Buru, and Sula to the north." He kept the map on one screen and called up a closer view on another plasma.

"Intel suggests the terrorists have landed on Haruku Island in the southeastern portion of the Banda. Haruku is one of a pair of islands, separated by a narrow passageway." J3 walked in front of the screen and pointed to a cove, between two marked points: Naira and Timitu. "These were Christian cities. But a Laskar Jihad-led revolt put them in Muslim hands. Now most of Haruku, and its neighbor Saparua, is Muslim-held territory. The Christians who survived were relocated to the north. That means we will be going into an extremely hostile zone."

"How big a force will we send?" FBI Director Robert Mulligan asked.

"Not how big, Mr. Director," J3 responded. "How small."

The Pentagon

"Status?" demanded General Johnson.

"Just confirmed from CTF-71—in a manner of speaking, they're halfway there and getting closer." Rear Admiral Erwin "Skip" Gatson explained that the team had been on leave in Honolulu. "They were due to ship back to Coronado in two days." Gatson referred to the West Coast home of the SEALs at the Navy Amphibious Base in Coronado, California. "But we got them in the air twenty-two minutes ago."

"Good, Skip," J3 said over the secure telecom line. Gatson was Commander, Battle Force, 7th Fleet aboard the USS *Blue Ridge,* and a life-long personal friend of Johnson's. J3's next addition to the conference call was Air Force General Reed Heath.

"Talk to me, Reed. What are the AWACS seeing?"

"The signal is five by five. Transit has stopped."

Stopped? J3 wondered if that was good or bad, whether the enemy knew who they had, and if that would even make a difference.

"Assume they know what kind of package they have, Reed. What do you think they're doing?"

"Easy. Same thing we are. Trying to figure out what the hell to do."

J3 had come to the exact same conclusion.

General Jonus Jackson Johnson shot a glance at the two clocks on the wall—the time in D.C. and the clock he set to Maluku time sixteen hours ahead. Halfway around the world it was 0417 hrs. "They barely have an hour of darkness left. Okay, they rushed to cover. They took Top Gun with them. So he's alive. Given that, they're going to wait until darkness again. They'll hunker down, maybe weigh the benefits of negotiating, and delay any action until night. Any alternate views?"

"No," the two others said in unison.

"Then that gives us fifteen hours to launch an offensive. Your boys up to it?" J3 asked Gatson.

"Yes, sir. We're just going to need some good eyes overhead. Ours and Reed's."

"Anything you need, Skip," the Air Force officer added.

"Good. We'll get Predators up from Anderson." The low-altitude, quiet unmanned aerial drones or UAVs, launched from Guam, would provide the SEALs with real-time guidance.

"We'll give you all the pictures you need, Skip," General Heath added.

"Thank you. Pull all your thoughts together and get back to me in thirty. Make sure your SEALs are rested, Skip. We'll need them sharp."

"Yes, sir."

SEALs, an acronym for SEa, Air, and Land, are the Navy's foremost special operations force. If the U.S. needs an enemy ship destroyed in a buttressed harbor, the job goes to the SEALs. When a beach needs to be "softened up" before a large-scale attack, SEALs get the call. They take out bridges, roads, railway lines, and communications centers. They parachute into global hot spots, though they're more likely to swim into an area of operation. And they can swim for a very, very long time. Water is a SEAL's best friend.

President John F. Kennedy commissioned the SEALs, the Navy's former Underwater Demotion Team, on January 1, 1962, as an elite maritime special operations unit capable of striking anywhere in the world.

Skip Gatson tagged SEAL team THREE, one of eight operational platoons. The platoons are comprised of sixteen SEALs, which are divided into two squads of eight or four of four. Each SEAL platoon is generally commanded by a Navy lieutenant (0-3 grade). Today, the honors went to Lt. James Nolt. On Gatson's call, Nolt selected the seven men he wanted *with* him. He was going in, too.

Over the Pacific

"Gentlemen, we have ourselves a genuine situation."

Nolt shouted over the light whine of the C-17 Globemaster III engines. The SEAL team commander was ordered to brief his men in two parts. The first, while in the air; the second, after they parachuted to their South Pacific LZ near the USS *Essex*.

Much of Nolt's Louisiana drawl fell off as he yelled. Not that it mattered. He only used it for effect and the SEALs knew it.

"If you didn't believe me before we took off, believe it now. This is not a drill. We're flying due west, then south. In six hours we'll jump, you do the math and figure out where we're going. A buddy in the 7th Fleet will lend you a shower. We'll have a full briefing, a little trip in a pair of SDVs, and then a nice swim. Our mission is pretty straightforward. Enemy forces have taken a VIP and his entourage. Our job is to locate and neutralize the enemy, and get our people out for their first class trip home. Questions?"

"Who's the bigshot?" asked Mario Pintar, one of the snipers in the team. He was laying out his gear in the C-17's voluminous interior cabin. The space was large enough to play a regulation basketball game.

"Next question," Nolt replied.

Pintar stopped his work. "Come again?"

Ordinarily, Special Ops forces heading into action would never be denied the identity and nature of the target. But Nolt had been instructed to wait for more ISR—intelligence, surveillance, and reconnaissance information. They wanted to know whether the president was alive.

"Next question," Nolt repeated.

"Okay, don't tell me," Pintar said under his breath.

"What's the size of the enemy force?" Julio Lopez asked.

"Undetermined at this time."

"Unified army or guerillas, sir?" This question came from the youngest SEAL on the team, Brian Showalter. He still used "sir," something SEALs generally ignored.

"Guerilla rebels. We suspect they've been supplied by the Chinese and other non-allied countries. But that's an assumption only."

"Any injured in the VIP's party?" SEAL Harold Chaskes asked. He was a combatant who also served as medic.

"Unknown. Possibly."

There were no further questions except for the ones that Nolt wouldn't answer now. "So, what do you say we sit around the campfire? For old times' sake."

The SEALs grumbled. They knew what was coming.

"Lopez, let's hear it."

"Never underestimate the enemy," he yelled over the whine of the engines. "No matter how untrained or disorganized."

"Expect the worse and prepare for it," added Chaskes.

"Never fight fair," Pintar piped in.

"Talk the assholes back home out of proposing commando ops during daylight hours," added SEAL Derek Shaughnessy.

Then, one after another they chimed in with the other rules that would keep them alive.

"Conserve your rounds...HQ might not know what the fuck is going on...Bad weather is your buddy...Review procedures...Review maps...Wire cutters come in handy...Be ready to kill."

"And?" Nolt called out as a cue to a well-rehearsed line.

"Get the job done!" they all shouted.

They were pumped up. Soon they would sleep. He left them with one other thought for now.

"Once again, I remind you, this is not an exercise," Nolt stated. "We are in an operation fully sanctioned by the government of the

United States of America, under the command and coordination of General Jonus Jackson Johnson and the Joint Chiefs. We even have ourselves a code name. OPERATION EAGLE CLUTCH."

"Ouch!" yelled Pintar.

"Snatch and grab," Lt. Nolt summarized. "Our claws are going to be sharp."

The Cabinet Room

"Speaker Patrick, I'm sorry I kept you waiting."

Eve Goldman, the attorney general, had been appointed to talk to the congressman.

Patrick stood, but that was his only nod to decorum. "Attorney General," he blustered, "I've been wasting my good time for over an hour. I demand to know what is going on!"

"And so you will. Have a seat, Congressman Patrick."

"I'll stand," he said defiantly. He never liked Goldman. In fact, he opposed all of Taylor's appointments when he was part of the minority. If she, or any of his other cabinet members ever came up for another assignment, Patrick, now leader of the democratic majority would make life impossible for them.

"Fair enough, congressman. Here it is. *Air Force One* went down in the Pacific earlier today."

"What?" Even this was too much for Patrick to comprehend. His knees buckled and he sank into the chair he wasn't going to take.

She chose her words carefully. She was speaking to one of the country's greatest leaks, let alone the man next in line to succeed Morgan Taylor. "Roughly three hours ago, the president's plane encountered a series of mechanical problems." She kept the actual details off the table. "We're still determining the exact cause."

"And Taylor?"

"*President* Taylor," she said correcting him.

"President Taylor," he noted without a hint of respect.

"That's a question, Mr. Speaker?"

"Yes, it's a goddamned question. What about President Taylor?"

"We haven't heard from him since the crash."

"And that was hours ago?"

"Yes, his plane went down in the South Pacific. The Navy has been overflying the area."

"Then?" he asked anticipating his immediate future.

"We have a decision to come to, Congressman."

"There's no decision to come to, Madame Attorney General. It's already been made for you. The 25th Amendment. Remember? I'm next in line."

"Well, yes, and no, Mr. Speaker."

"What do you mean, Goldman?" He was completely full of himself. "This is the law!" The door to the Cabinet Room suddenly flew open. "You can't stop me."

Two Secret Services agents entered. Duke Patrick ignored them.

"You need to swear me in. The country has to have a president!"

Patrick was so self-absorbed that he didn't see who followed the Secret Service agents into the Cabinet Room.

"The country has a president," pronounced a frail, but authoritative Henry Lamden.

"I believe you're in my seat, Mr. Speaker."

Patrick had to look down. Lamden was in a wheelchair, rolling under his own steam. "Mr. President, I had no idea," he said more angry than embarrassed.

"Apparently not. But then, you had no reason to think otherwise." Lamden pulled up next to his chair at the cabinet table.

Still shocked, Patrick remained in the seat at the middle of the table.

"My chair? Mr. Speaker?" In a completely awkward moment, Patrick stood and made way for the president to transfer from his wheelchair.

Henry Lamden had lost a good deal of weight, but none of his acrimony for Duke Patrick. They were from the same political party. That was the end of what they had in common.

"Gentlemen, Attorney General Goldman," Lamden said, "can you give us a few minutes alone?"

The Secret Service agents filed out with a great story to tell their colleagues. Eve Goldman would have given her eyeteeth to stay and listen, but she took President Lamden's cue.

"You may sit down," the president said.

"I think I'd like to stand."

"I would feel more comfortable if we saw each other eye-to-eye, Congressman."

Another awkward moment. Patrick looked around the room, hoping one of the statues or paintings might feed him the right line. None came and he sat down opposite Lamden. When the door was closed, the president continued.

"So, my friend, three quick surprises for you in one day. *Air Force One* goes down. For a fleeting instant you see yourself in the White House, then an old pol crashes your party. I can't begin to imagine what you're feeling."

"I'm relieved to see you, Mr. President."

"Oh, cut the bullshit. Of course you're not. You're pissed as hell. You got this close! Right here. But not today, Patrick. Not this day, or God willing, any day soon. It'll have to be over *my* dead body. And as you can see, I'm not quite there yet."

"You have me all wrong, Mr. President. The country needs you."

"That is debatable. The real truth is the country *doesn't* need you."

Patrick bolted to his feet in defiance. "Mr. President, obviously you're not well. You should be back in the hospital. You can't run the country. You don't have the strength. You're irrational. Listen to yourself. You're attacking the speaker of the House of Representatives. Me." He started for the door. "I'm going to talk to the attorney general and the White House lawyers."

"Mr. Speaker, I'm here because of them, and a smart young woman attorney who encouraged them to get me out of bed. She's the one who spoke to the doctors. They cleared me. I guarantee you, if you go down that road, you will not win. More importantly, you will not survive another week in this town."

For one of the first times in his life, Duke Patrick decided to shut up.

"While we're talking man-to-man, in another day, you'll introduce the biggest single danger to the American public since Joe McCarthy. Maybe I underestimated you. You're a better politician than I thought. But I have to ask you—what the hell do you think you're doing tying in with that crackpot? The best Bridgeman will give you is VP. And let me tell you, if you think that sychophant behind him has an ounce of interest in you, you're crazy. Strong will eat your heart out right on national radio. You're not in his great plan for the country. He's designing a hate-filled America, with laws that serve the extreme. There's no room in his nation for the Constitution, and there's no room in it for you, Mr. Speaker. So again I ask—what the hell do you think you're doing?"

"You may dismiss the voice of the people. You can call Strong and all of the others like him sychophants or egomaniacal hate-mongers— whatever you want. But the power is shifting. There is a tyranny of words mounting, and it's going to take you down, along with every other old-time politician. People don't listen to you anymore. You're a sound bite. Seven seconds, eight. If you're lucky, ten. They're the whole show. A caller on the radio gets more airtime. The only rule is you have to agree with the host. So what am I doing? I'm joining the new media, Mr. President. I'm agreeing with the host. And I'm going to be heard. Not you. Me. Enjoy your presidency while you can, because this isn't over. You just kicked the can down the road a little bit. We'll see who will or won't survive in this town."

The speaker of the house left the Cabinet Room, and with it, any tie with the administration.

The White House Press Room

"I have a brief announcement to make," Bill Bagley said. "I'll take questions for a short period after."

Ninety-minutes earlier, the White House press corps received an advisory that a major announcement would be forthcoming. They'd been waiting and speculating. Advance word had not leaked, so the press secretary's statement caught everyone off guard.

"The Pentagon received a report early this morning that *Air Force One* crashed into the South Pacific Ocean. The president's plane was enroute to Andrews Air Force Base from Afghanistan. At present, I am unable to give you the exact location of the crash due to security in the area." His voice cracked. Bagley fought back his grief, then continued with a hollow and labored delivery. "I can tell you that President Morgan Taylor was onboard along with members of the White House cabinet and staff, and colleagues of yours. Contact was lost with the president's plane west of Indonesia. The 7th Fleet has been assigned the task of rescue and recovery. I have no further details on cause of the disaster. I'll share what I can throughout the day."

Hands shot up in the air. A dozen voices yelled out questions. However, Bagley had more to say.

"According to the 25th Amendment, ratified in 1967, succession would pass to the speaker of the House, in this case Congressman Duke Patrick." He paused, sensing the anticipation in the room. "However..."

The *however* brought instant gasps.

"...when appraised of the situation, President Henry Lamden, recovering at Walter Reed Army Medical Center in Bethesda, advised Attorney General Eve Goldman that he would resume his duties as president, pending discharge by his doctors. President Henry Lamden has since returned to the White House. At this hour he is conferring with his cabinet and he'll speak to the nation tonight at nine o'clock, eastern time. He has informed the speaker, who was 'relieved to see' the president."

"Questions?" Bagley asked. They all came at once:

"How long were we without a president?"

"Is President Lamden healthy enough?"

"Do we know if there are survivors?"

"What happens if...."

Lebanon, Kansas

Midway through his next call, Strong's wife frantically waved a paper at him. She was in the control room, trying to get his attention. Strong, annoyed by the distraction, ignored her. She then spoke into the intercom. "Look at your computer." While the caller from New Hampshire rambled on about how he was going to be in the first row for Bridgeman's speech, Strong read the message screen.

"Oh my God!" he blurted.

"What?" asked the caller.

Strong's reaction was genuine; maybe his first honest one in years. "Bring it in," he said over the air.

His wife ran in with the bulletin from the Associated Press. As he scanned it, she typed a quick Internet link on his computer. The full story appeared.

Elliott Strong rarely read anything cold on the air. He usually marked pages with one-word cues for adlibs and practiced what he wanted to say. Not this time. He got the gist of the news brief, dropped the caller, who was talking again, and began.

"Darice has just handed me a story from the Associated Press. Honey, keep on this," he said off mike. "We aren't the first to report this, but here it is. From AP, maybe a minute ago, '*Washington, D.C.— White House Press Secretary Bagley announced that* Air Force One *has crashed in the South Pacific, near a chain of islands that comprise Indonesia. President Morgan Taylor, and a contingent of administration staff and reporters, were returning from Kandahar, Afghanistan, when* Air Force One *suffered a catastrophic incident. No further details are known at this time. When notified, President Henry Lamden returned to the White House to assume the office of president.*"

Strong's voice wavered as he read the news. *An accident? Intentional?* This was different than anything he'd been told. *What's it going to mean to the plans?* He'd send an e-mail out during the break to see if there were any new instructions. For now, he decided to stay the course.

"Tragic news. But the march will go on."

Chicago, Illinois

Luis Gonzales switched off his radio and stared out the window at the city below. Taylor was gone. The Prophet's hand was evident. But a final act was yet to come. Chaos and death. Lamden would be blamed. He would follow the news enroute to his next destination. It was time to leave Chicago now. He had things to attend to in Paraguay. Business. The kind that filled his pocketbook and the kind that filled his heart. Money and revenge. Both made him happy.

The White House War Room
0534 hrs ET

"Oh, Christ!" Roarke caught the time. *Where the hell?* he asked himself. Hours had gone by and he'd completely forgotten about his meeting with O'Connell.

"Give me a sec," he told Evans backing away. The National Director of Intelligence was going over the latest recon photos. "I have to check on something."

He went to the closest phone and called the White House switchboard.

He asked for the marine guard at the North Entrance. "Roarke," he said getting connected. "Do you have a visitor there for me. O'Connell? Michael O'Connell?"

"No, sir," the marine replied. "I have his name, but he hasn't shown up yet."

Roarke was clearly perplexed. "Okay, thanks. Call me if he does."

Next Roarke scrolled down to O'Connell's number in his Treo's call log. He pressed the center oval button to connect him. After five rings, the reporter's voice mail message engaged.

"O'Connell, Roarke. You said you were coming down? Where the hell are you?"

With that, he hung up, not entirely disappointed that he didn't see the *Times* reporter. *Not today. Not now. Too much going on.*

Roarke rejoined the conversation with Evans.

"Is everything okay?" the intelligence czar asked.

"Yeah. Any change?"

"Quiet." The latest satellite intel showed rugged mountain terrain with ample cover. "But we've got heat signatures for some three hundred. Until the SEALs are in place, we're not going to know much more."

"What's J3 say about the chances?" He hated asking a question like that. There's never a good answer. Roarke knew. He'd been in Special Forces.

Evans shook his head. "Surprise will be on our side. That's all I can tell you."

Roarke examined the computer printouts of the terrain. "It's rough going."

"Most of it up. And not along the paths." Jack Evans pointed out the route of ascent the SEALs would take, compared to the way the terrorists went.

"What about noise?" Roarke asked.

"Oh, there will be a lot of it," Evans added. "But not from the SEALs." He explained what J3 had in mind. Roarke actually smiled. He wished he could be there.

Arafura Sea

"**S**omebody up there likes us," Rear Admiral Clemson Zimmer explained to J3, who was enroute to the Special Ops C2, the Command Center at MacDill AFB in Florida. Zimmer was 12,000 miles away aboard the USS *Blue Ridge*. "We've got a pair of SDV MK VIII's on the USS *Essex*. Pure luck."

General Johnson breathed a sigh of relief. *Actual good news*; or what could be termed as good news.

"I suppose we can thank the terrorists who planted the bomb in Sydney. When Australia invoked ANZUS, we spread the 7th Fleet out. The *Essex* was assigned to the Malukus, right where we need to be," Zimmer added. "SEAL Team THREE will drop in the Banda Sea, about fifteen kilometers off shore. They'll get a swift, all-expenses paid trip to Huruku, with an on-time arrival."

"And their cover?" J3 asked.

"We're ready. Targets have been set. What's your ETA for MacDill?"

General Jackson didn't have to consult his watch. His internal clock had been ticking off the time since he left. "Thirty-eight minutes."

"Roger. The details will be there waiting for you. But here's the general idea."

Haruku Island

Every time the prisoners started falling asleep, the terrorists roamed the tent and kicked the captives. "Where is your American strength now?" asked one of the guards in broken English. He stood over the president who was gagging on blood from his last beating. He couldn't spit it out; his mouth was covered with tape. "The Great Satan doesn't look so great tonight," he boasted.

The rebel circled to the president's back. Ross was tied to him. They were both covered in mud from being dragged up a hillside. They itched and smelled of urine. They sat on hard, unforgiving, dusty ground. Ants crawled around and while the hostages did their best to kick them away, the ants, like the insurgents, were winning.

Without warning the guard rammed his rifle butt into Rossy's ear. The lieutenant fell over, pulling the president with him. The other prisoners looked on. Some had broken ribs, a few suffered broken noses.

The beatings came every fifteen minutes, each time from a different terrorist. It was as if the leader was putting his men to the test. Did they have the stomach for the job? One after another, they did.

Taylor shifted his weight to the side, helping Ross back up. The lieutenant whispered his thanks, knowing that if the guard heard him, he'd earn another, more crippling blow.

"We're gonna start losing guys pretty fast, Mr. President," he said.

Rossy was right. The president felt like he had a rat's-eye view of the *Titanic*.

3,500 feet over the Banda Sea
2320 hrs local time

"Coming around again," reported the pilot to the ramp of the C-17. The SEALs would jump momentarily. Their equipment and specialized gear had been dropped on pallets with flotation devices on a first pass, released by a series of automated floor locks, controlled by the C-17's loadmaster.

"Go, go, go, go!" The command from Nolt came right after a green "on" light signaled the SEALs were over the DZ. The first four SEALs, comprising Bravo Team, jumped out of the rear of the C-17 that had ferried them from Hickam. Then came Alpha. Their drop zone put them ahead of the USS *Essex*, a Waspclass landing ship. Two Navy HH-60H Seahawks, equipped for Combat Search and Rescue (CSAR), were ready to lift off as soon as the SEALs cleared the airspace and dumped in the sea.

Now it was Nolt's turn. He saluted to the Air Force major who supervised their drop. "Thanks for the lift. You know where to send the bill." On his way down, he thought about the shower he'd be enjoying in twenty minutes, and the one he hoped to take about six hours later.

Aboard the USS *Blue Ridge*
The Banda Sea
Sunday, 19 August local time
0116 hrs
(Saturday, 18 August ET)

"Misdirection," Adm. Zimmer explained from the command ship. Nolt's SEALs listened over their radio. J3 was connected from MacDill. President Lamden was on in the White House War Room. "They're going to think *we think* we're pounding them." The Admiral described his plan.

"The target is here," he used a tele-strator, visible via computer links. Everyone saw a small rugged island, 12 kilometers from the target. "The purpose is two-fold. We're going to light up the sky in the distance and draw their eye while the SEALs come in from their blind side. And we're going to use the noise to mask the incursion. The window of opportunity is twelve minutes. We'll start with a heavy bombing run that will shake them all out of bed. They'll see missiles launched to the South, they'll feel the shock. And they'll drop their defenses. Psych Ops says that they'll be drawn to the light-show feeling pretty good about themselves. That's when the SEALs strike. Then phase two of EAGLE CLUTCH."

"I suppose you've blown up your fair share of things, Lieutenant Nolt," Zimmer gathered.

Nolt laughed. "Yes, sir, I have."

"And you've trained for hundreds of hours, and for virtually any contingency."

"Yes, sir. The same is true for all my men."

"But this is one hell of an assignment."

"Yes, sir."

"Do your men know the nature of the mission?"

"They understand that we are to infiltrate a terrorist camp and secure the release of a group of kidnapped VIPs, sir." As instructed, Nolt had not explained the actual identity of the number-one VIP.

"And your men are ready?" Zimmer asked.

"Yes, sir."

Nolt's team listened intently, so far unfazed by what seemed like a typical pre-mission pep talk.

"I'm sorry you were not informed earlier. However, there is an extraordinary aspect to this operation," Zimmer continued.

A few of the men chuckled. They'd heard this kind of thing before.

"The operation has only come together in the last few hours. We believe there are only a few hours left to act. VIPs were taken. I stress, *very* important persons. You were called together minutes after the Navy reported that the hostages were taken. The details are known by a handful of people, for good reason. You're about to join the short list."

The SEALs began to feel a greater sense of urgency.

"Approvals have gone up the chain of command faster than any action in American history. Any. You have trained for this, without ever knowing who you were training to free. And now the time has come."

The SEALs looked at Nolt. He kept a poker face.

"Gentlemen, you are about to rescue the President of the United States."

Nolt watched as surprise registered on everyone; man by man. They shot hard stares at one another.

"He was captured following the ditching of *Air Force One*. We believe that was an act of sabotage. It is unknown if the capture of the commander in chief is related. But now it's your job to get the president and the other hostages out. Eight SEALs against hundreds of guerillas. You must succeed. You will succeed."

Heightened fervor spread through the briefing room aboard the *Essex*. Pintar immediately checked his handgun; Lopez felt for his knife. The others found their own way to toughen up.

"That is your mission. Are you ready?" Zimmer asked.

"We're SEALs," offered Showalter, without regard to rank. "God help anybody who gets in our way."

Lamden heard exactly what he needed. "EAGLE CLUTCH is *go*."

The *Essex* came dead in the water and a series of ballast tanks in the stern flooded down. A rear gate lowered and the two Mark VIII Swimmer Delivery Vehicles, essentially sub-surface "wet" submarines, floated out of the well deck. The SEALs were all on board.

"Ready, Nolt," called out to the members of the Alpha Detachment.

"Ready," reported Shaughnessy, Pintar, and Lopez. Nolt would take the lead submersible with them. He received a similar acknowledgment from Bravo Detachment—Harold Chaskes, Todd Roberts, Mark Polonsky, and Brian Showalter. Four men in each SDV, along with the pilot and navigator.

The Mark VIII's computerized mixed-gas on-board breathing systems were already fired up, and the canopies were closed. The crew reviewed their checklists, engaged the Doppler navigation systems (DNS), the obstacle-avoidance sonar subsystem (OAS), and tested the ballast and trim systems and the horizontal and vertical planes. These were controlled through a manual stick to the rudder, elevator, and bow planes.

All of the electronics of the SDVs were housed in airtight, dry canisters, designed to withstand seawater pressure to a depth of 500 feet. Today, they'd shuttle to Haruku at a maximum depth of 30 feet; less for the last 100 yards.

With the signal from the pilot of Alpha, all was set. The first Mark VIII's five-bladed propeller began turning. The 254-inch-long craft moved forward. The pilot flooded all of the compartments and began a slight descent. The Bravo SDV followed.

The sea was still rising to swells of 15 feet, but below the surface, all was calm. The eight SEALs got into a relaxed breathing pattern. This was the last time for private thoughts and personal prayers. In another few minutes they'd be on the clock.

Washington, D.C.
the same time

He relaxed in the hotel's luxurious bathtub, clearing his mind and thinking through the details. Success always depended on the right state of mind.

Except for the crowd, there wasn't anything especially difficult about the job. People might see him move about, but they'd take little notice. Their attention would be elsewhere—to the podium or the TV projection screens placed at intervals down the Mall.

Once he accomplished his assignment, he'd simply become one in a million of confused, perhaps riotous marchers, hiding in plain sight.

He rarely liked to be told exactly where, how, and when to perform an assignment, but the instructions had been specific.

In another two hours, he would leave Washington a far richer man than when he arrived. He slid his torso under the bath water and held his breath. He kept his eyes open. It was a comforting sensation. He saw everything through a slowly shifting, thick, out-of-focus lens. So peaceful. It cleansed him; not that he needed it. He felt no guilt.

The Banda Sea
Off Saparua Island

Lt. Commander James Nolt knew very little about the enemy. More time, more recon would have been extremely helpful. For now, he had only his intuition and text-book analysis.

Guerilla fighters. They had weaknesses, he thought. The SEALs would have to take advantage of them. *They have a loose organization and possibly a poorly trained command.* Next, he put himself in their position. *Arrogant. Self-deluded. Fanatical. Strong belief in their political and religious cause. Willing to become martyrs. Capable of taking the hostages with them.*

To successfully complete the mission, Nolt and his men needed to remain stealth, maintain the offensive, and operate in a limited-visibility environment. *Raid, kill, gain ground.* The team leader ran the play book in his head. He was 100 percent certain that each of his SEALs was doing exactly the same.

The two jet-black SDVs slowed and finally came to a stop. The navigator delivered them to the precise coordinates, about 900 yards off the rocky shore.

Nolt's squad unhooked from the Mark VIII's breathing apparatus and engaged their own tanks. They opened the canopies and silently floated above the submersibles. When they were at a depth of 15 feet they swam toward land.

The SDVs would stay in place until 0700 hours. or later, if ordered by C2. They were the backup means of exfiltration, should EAGLE CLUTCH go wrong. But like the trip out, the Mark VIIIs could only transport the SEALs. A lot had to go right before they'd be safely on their way home.

The SEALs swam in pairs. One diver-buddy held a board, which included a compass, as well as depth and watch gauges. The basic equipment kept the teams on course. Meanwhile, the other partner held onto his arm just below the triceps. He served as the lookout and counted kicks calculated to get them to the shore. The pairs communicated in non-verbal codes, consisting of squeezes and alternating pauses. The swim represented the fundamental of SEALs training: Teamwork is everything. Seemingly impossible tasks are made possible by working together.

Everything they needed for the ops was attached to their wetsuits: grenade and ammo pouches, secondary magazines, medical kits, helmet radios, night vision equipment, and their weapons. They chose Heckler & Koch MK23's, Sig Sauer 9 mm automatics, Beretta M92-Fs with slide locks and Qualatech silencers, and K-Bar survival knives

Pintar and Shaughnessy also carried their Knights SR25 sniper rifles, critical for the first phase of the mission.

Lebanon, Kansas

"How many times can the presidency be stolen?" Strong asked his listeners. "This amounts to a coup." He read from the wire service report about Lamden's return. His real information came from an e-mail on the Hill. "So they trot Henry Lamden out so they don't have to swear in the speaker of the House."

Strong had to be careful; he hadn't laid the groundwork on why Patrick, a Democrat, would be better than another Democrat. He decided to give it a more politically motivated spin.

"They know that Congressman Patrick was coming out in support of General Bridgeman; that he was all set to introduce him today. So, rather than make him president, they punish him. They bring out an invalid instead of naming Duke Patrick the rightful president." He slammed his hand down hard.

"How do I know this? Because I've been told by my sources in Washington." *Patrick.* "Conspiracy at the highest level. Congress must open an investigation immediately. This is the last straw!"

Strong thought he turned the negative into a true positive. *More for Bridgeman to talk about today. More to anger the crowd. More reason to incite....*

Haruku Island

They quietly emerged from the sea, timing their run to shore—two SEALs at a time—with the crashing of the waves. They regrouped 50 yards inland at the base of a cliff—their first obstacle.

The clouds obscured the moon, which cut down on the enemy's ability to see them. It also made their passage more difficult. They had a 100-foot slippery vertical surface to climb and no time to waste.

The SEALs continued to use hand signals. Nolt indicated where they should ascend. The first men up had the hardest job—finding the best place to grip. Each footing was marked with luminous powder, visible through the night-vision goggles.

Alpha took six minutes to scale the rock face. Bravo needed an extra 90 seconds, which put them behind schedule.

Speeding up could be dangerous, but they were on a timetable which was out of their control. Nolt pushed his men through the underbrush due north for a quarter of a mile, then northwest until they came to a thick bamboo forest. They made up two minutes. The next 200 yards would take additional time. They had to navigate around gullies and swamp.

"Shit!" Showalter cursed. He slid knee-deep into a bog. The more he tried to pull himself out, the harder it became to move.

Polonsky avoided the same mistake, stopping short of the mud. Roberts came to Showalter's aid. Chaskes circumvented the area, but doubled-back.

Polonsky motioned for Showalter to stand still. He looked overhead. Bamboo branches shot through the jungle canopy. "Push that one down," he signaled Roberts. If Showalter could grab hold of the branch, then at least he'd stop sinking.

Roberts shimmied up the tree, high enough to reach a point where he could force down the trunk and get it within reach of Showalter.

All of this was accomplished silently, but it was taking too much time.

"Got it," Showalter whispered. He reached as high up the curved wood as possible and slid the top of the trunk between his legs. The flexibility of the branch worked in his favor. But there wasn't much he could do yet.

Roberts then bent over another trunk, a few feet from the first. The trapped SEAL grabbed the second shaft and forced it under him as he had done before. The two trees effectively created a ladder. With a combination of pulling and climbing, Showalter cautiously inched out of the mud that had trapped him.

Polonsky checked the time. *Two minutes behind schedule.*

Nolt looked at his watch. The massive batteries of the USS *Cowpens*, an Aegis cruiser off the coast, were loaded and ready to fire. According to the GPS direction finder on Nolt's wrist PDA, they still had another 50 yards to go. He waved Alpha forward into their attack position.

Shaughnessy identified nine targets on the perimeter. He rolled on his stomach and showed Pintar, who was behind him, nine fingers. The word went back to Lopez, and ultimately to Nolt.

The nine were only the first kills they'd have to make. Beyond them, the rest of the militia. Shaughnessy panned his night-vision sight across a grove, which abutted a cliff. He could see three encampments. Each housed at least 100 troops. The men milled around. The light from their cigarettes created hot spots on the infrared goggles. Another, smaller group gathered around a camouflaged tent. It was large enough to hold a dozen or more prisoners.

Shaughnessy looked at his palm device. He was receiving LINK 16-type data, down-linked and culled from intelligence sources including AWACS telementry, a RC-135 Rivet Joint ELINT/SIGINT/COMINT aircraft, and an E-8B/C J-STARS ground surveillance plane. With it, he had a solid lock on the primary objective: the tent and a pulsing beacon from within.

Lt. Nolt gave his watch one more glance. *Forty-five seconds.* He inched forward through the underbrush toward Shaughnessy, careful not to show a profile to the enemy. The two men would come in from the southwest. Pintar and Lopez to their left. Bravo Team—Chaskes,

Showalter, Roberts, and Polonsky—would circle around from the north. *Twenty seconds.*

Ten seconds. Nolt steeled himself for his first kill. *Five seconds.* His target stood 20 feet ahead. His automatic weapon was down at his side.

Suddenly and without warning, the sky brightened to the south. Flashes of light, all coming from one point well off shore, illuminated the night sky. Trails of fire streamed across the horizon.

The guerillas watched, mesmerized. Then they realized they were under attack. With nowhere to run, they fell to the ground and covered their heads waiting for the explosions.

The explosions came, but not at their encampment. They were a few kilometers away, at a neighorboring island.

Gradually, the troops rose to their feet and cheered at the stupidity of the Americans.

Now.

The targets closest to Alpha Team had their weapons down. They were pointing to the destruction of the island in the distance.

Nolt stepped out of the shadows. Shaughnessy was by his side. The SEALs moved in perfect synchronicity. They approached from the rear, stretching a thin cord into a wide noose. In one quick, stealth move, they slipped their devices over the unsuspecting victims' heads. The rebels' hands reflexively went up, but there was nothing they could do. Each SEAL kicked his target's knees. The victims were thrown off balance. Neither man could steady nor protect himself.

Nolt and Shaughnessy drew their nooses back under their victims' chins until their work was done. Their first kills went down without a whisper rising above the explosions. Nolt and Shaughnessy slowly lowered the bodies to the ground.

Three men, barely 15 feet in front of them, paid no attention. Nolt again took the lead and flared to the target on the left. Shaughnessy would take the man on the right. They counted on Lopez to drop the target in the middle.

This time, they'd use their UDT knives. Again, as in a mirror image of one another, the two SEALs advanced from behind. Their blades came up as they grabbed their targets heads with their left hands and quickly slit their throats. Simultaneously, the guard between them crumpled to the ground, felled by a bullet from 30 yards away. But death would not be so immediate for Nolt and Shaughnessy's two, unless they ended it with a back-entry slash to the kidneys and another front plunge into the heart. It took all of another second.

Now Pintar did more of the cleanup. He fired four perfectly aimed shots through his noise-suppressed SR45.

Plus 30 seconds. On schedule, Nolt reported to himself. *Two more men at the edge of the guerilla's compound.* He signaled Shaughnessy. Suddenly, the man on the right stepped forward, then turned to address his compatriot. He spotted Nolt.

"Kunjungi!"—Look! the sentry exclaimed. His automatic instantly came up. The other Indonesian guerilla whipped around.

"Apa?" he asked. *What?* His confusion bought Nolt his life. The first guard started to explain rather than fire a round.

From his blind side came Lopez. He slammed the butt of his Sig Sauer up and under the skull of the combatant. He dropped him with the other end of his weapon, plunging his K-Bar into the man's heart. This drew the second man's attention, which prevented him from detecting Shaughnessy. He worked his knife in around the front of the Indonesian's chest and dropped him with one blow.

There was no time for thanks or congratulations. The camouflaged tent was ahead.

Haruku Island

Based on the number of seconds between the flashes and the sound, Taylor calculated that the bombs were exploding eight-to-ten miles away. He didn't know for sure what they were, but he had a strong feeling about the possibility.

Five minutes into the bombardment, the terrorist commander returned to the tent. He strode right to the president and laughed aloud.

"Do you hear your bombs?"

Taylor ignored Komari.

"All your American technology and you can't find the right target? Your soldiers are blind. They attack the wrong island. But listen."

Another volley passed overhead, exploding miles away. "That is the sound of their disdain for you. No helicopter gunships to rescue you. Why? Because that is how you infidels fight. Missiles from the sky. Bombardment from a ship. There is no substitution for a man on the ground. For loyalty. For a true jihad."

Komari laughed heartily again and kicked two of the nearest captives; one was a woman reporter for the *Miami Herald*.

Morgan Taylor never took his eyes off the commander. *Keep him talking. Engage him.* He wanted Komari to remove the tape over his mouth. He tried to speak through the gag.

"What? Are you ready to plead for your life?"

Taylor continued to make noise. Komari came back to him.

"At first, you presented a problem to me. But I realized the Prophet himself delivered you. You, the President of the United States; the enemy of my brother. My enemy. You were a gift from Heaven. The Prophet Muhammad rewarded me with the honor of punishing you."

Taylor tried to speak again. Komari felt no reason why he shouldn't be heard. With one quick, painful tug, he tore the duct tape from the president's mouth.

"There. You deserve to plead for your life; not that it will matter. Your fate is sealed."

Taylor spit out a mouthful of blood and took in a deep, refreshing breath. *Salt air.* They were so close to the ocean. Close to an infiltration point. *Stay alive,* he said to himself.

"Your English is quite good," Taylor managed. His mouth and lips were so dry it was hard to talk. "May I learn the name of my judge, jury, and executioner."

"You may. I am Umar Komari, Commander of the October 12th Allegiance."

"October 12th?" The president searched his memory for the meaning. There was always a meaning.

"Come now, you have to be a student of history. October 12, 2002? Kuta on Bali? The news called it the deadliest act of terrorism in Indonesian history. It was an act of war on Christian colonialism."

The president remembered. *Keep him talking.* "Hundreds died. Mostly tourists. The Jemaah Islamiah."

"Yes, my brother was JI. He moved to the Solomon Islands, where you and your godless allies launched an indefensible attack only weeks ago. You killed him."

Taylor remembered. The recollection was in his face.

"Ah, you can't deny it. So your judge is right."

Keep him talking. "The Australians found a bomb in a hotel. He could have killed many people."

"I know this plan. What great patience my brother had. One of many such bombs."

Keep him talking. More bombs. A diversion?

"Ready to be detonated at the proper time. But it was discovered. Yes, and somehow your spies found him."

"He would have killed hundreds of innocent people."

"There are no innocent people in this war," Komari shouted. "You, yourself have proven that with your decision to bomb encampments. To kill my brother." He stood up and kicked the president squarely in his stomach. "To kill my brother!" The sheer physical act of hurting the president made Komari happy.

"Was one of my brother's bombs intended for you?"

The president grimaced at the pain. He feared another rib was broken. As Komari's foot landed a second blow, he nodded *yes.*

The commander knelt down again. An almost spiritual glow came over Komari's face. "I understand the meaning of it all now." He leaned into the president and whispered in his ear. "The Prophet has truly delivered you to me, so I may complete my brother's work. Praise be Allah."

CHAPTER 73

Washington, D.C.

K atie fumbled for her cell phone, which was under a stack of papers. Her work was spread out on Roarke's IKEA desk in his apartment. She already vowed that his furniture had to go. She just hadn't told him yet. "Coming!" she yelled, willing the phone to keep ringing. She missed it. "Caller ID Unknown." *Okay, no one to call back.* Katie was about return to her work when her phone rang again.

"Hello," she quickly answered.

"Ms. Kessler?" It was a man's voice. He sounded official. There was urgency in his voice.

She didn't recognize it. "Yes."

"Where are you right now?"

"What? What's the matter?" She straightened up. "Who is this?"

"Agent Roarke instructed me to call you. You must meet him precisely at three thirty PM."

"Where is he? Who is this?"

"I work with Agent Roarke. He's in a briefing and he can't be disturbed. He's asked that you not call his cell phone, but it's extremely important you meet him as he requested. He said you'd understand."

"But why?" This was a little too cloak-and-dagger for her. She remembered the Charles River. "What going wrong?"

"All he said was you must meet him. He told me three-thirty, Ms. Kessler."

"Okay, okay. Where?"

It still didn't make sense when he told her, but the past few days had been full of surprises. *Why should today be any different*, she thought.

"All right, I'll be there. But can I call?"

"No. Absolutely not. He'll explain when he sees you."

"Do I need to bring anything?"

"No. But be there on time."

"I will." She asked another question about reaching someone else who could help, then realized the caller had dropped off. Katie was having a hard time getting used to Scott Roarke's world. She also realized that so much seemed to be played out between the lines of the law. Most of that was never reported.

the same time

Roarke dialed the New York number again.

"Hello."

This wasn't the voice he expected to hear. "Who is this?" Roarke demanded. He looked at his Treo. He'd dialed the right number, but a stranger answered.

"First, who are you?" came the reply from a very serious sounding man.

Roarke strained to hear the ambient noise in the background. There was a good deal of conversation and the distinctive wail of sirens.

"I'm calling for my friend who was supposed to meet me last night."

"And who exactly is your friend?"

Roarke suddenly sensed that it was the kind of question a police officer asks, especially when the answer isn't known.

"He's a reporter for *The New York Times*."

"Oh?"

A cop, he thought. "Michael O'Connell. What's happened to him?"

"You say you're a friend? What kind of friend?"

Roarke wasn't sure he wanted to say quite yet. "Look, you've answered O'Connell's phone. This is *his* number. You're not him, so how about explaining who you are first."

There was a slight pause, then the man spoke. "Coates—NYPD."

Roarke knew the name. He strained to remember. *Coates. Coates!* "Detective Harry Coates." *Shit. That was a mistake.*

The cop was caught off guard. "You know me?"

Roarke recalled that Coates was one of the investigating officers for the New York Police Department when it looked into one of Cooper's killings during the campaign. He hit a brick wall with the CIA, but Roarke read the brief and knew a good deal about the 53-year-old policeman. *Shit, shit, shit!* Roarke said to himself and hung up.

Roarke's number couldn't be traced. In fact, it didn't really exist, but he cursed at his stupidity. *Something's wrong.* He needed information quickly. *Davis can find out.*

Haruku Island
the same time

Komari was satisfied with the way that his men took pleasure torturing the Americans. Even Musaf Atef. The commander's doubts about his lieutenant disappeared when he delivered a nose-breaking punch to one of the bound and gagged officers.

"See how the Prophet gauges our commitment? If we have the will to inflict pain on Taylor and his thugs, then we are prepared for our destiny; to liberate our land from the Christians."

"Commander, the Americans will pay a great deal for their leader. Are you certain you want to kill him?" he said over the sound of the shelling.

"Atef, this is not a transaction. There is no monetary gain to be realized. This is fate. Ours and theirs. Listen to their bombs. Are they raining money?"

"No."

"What kind of negotiations would we have?"

Komari didn't expect a response. He didn't get one. "What a shame our prisoners don't understand the role God has given them. We have become a true army through their deliverance; truer still when we take the president's head."

The thought made Atef shiver. A quick death was one thing, but a traditional beheading—especially of the American leader—was another. He bravely called the decision to question. "Commander, should anyone ever find out how he died, they shall search us down to the ends of the earth. But if we execute him as a common criminal—the world will understand that. Our Muslim brothers would welcome us."

Once again Komari saw weakness that worried him. Perhaps he should be put to the ultimate test. "The Qur'an says, '*When you clash with unbelieving infidels in battle, strike and overpower them. Thus you are commanded. He lets you fight in order to test you.*' You are a reader of the Holy Qur'an, a true believer of the Prophet, Atef?"

"Yes, commander." His pulse quickened in anticipation of what Komari was about to demand. "Then it shall be you who proves it, to me, and to all who are witness to *your* faith."

Komari went to a hope chest he'd stolen from a fisherman's wife. He opened it and extracted a long, beautiful ceremonial sword.

"Atef, you are a leader, are you not?"

He would feel one end of the sword or the other.

The Washington Mall
the same time

"There are far too few," Duke Patrick proclaimed to the marchers—all 2.4 million of them. Another 46 million people watched on TV and listened on the radio. The speaker stood alone on a stage in front of the Capitol. The platform was decorated only with American flags—fifty of them. They waved in the background, providing an animated backdrop for the cameras.

Patrick hid his anger for Lamden and his hatred of Taylor. For now, he would be a statesman. One day soon he would have his revenge.

"Too few. Too few great generals—defenders of our freedom—have become commander in chief. Yes, George Washington, Ulysses S. Grant, and Dwight Eisenhower. But do you remember the others: William Harrison, Rutherford B. Hayes, James A. Garfield, Chester A. Arthur, Benjamin Harrison..."

The crowd sensed where he was going with his run of names. Applause began to build.

"...Andrew Jackson, Franklin Pierce, Andrew Johnson, and Taylor. Oh, but not Morgan Taylor—he was only a commander." His line got a laugh. "I'm talking about Zachary Taylor. Twelve great men. Twelve extraordinary generals. Throughout our history, America has depended on men who are willing to lay down their lives for us. America has stood behind twelve exceptional military leaders in the past. We can make it thirteen! Are you ready?"

The crowd roared back with a booming "Yes!" that crescendoed across the Mall.

"Are you ready to send a signal to every city and town, every county, and every state that it is time for a new American revolution, the way the Founding Fathers intended...where the Constitution *can* be re-written?"

"Yes!" echoed the marchers.

"I'm ready, too!" That was Patrick's personal adlib.

"Yes!"

"We are at the dawn of a new day. We have in our midst a different kind of man; a true leader; a real hero who can usher in a new era of greatness we, as Americans, deserve. Are you ready for that day?"

"Yes!"

"Did you see the dawning light?"

"Yes!"

"Are you prepared to welcome the future?"

"Yes!"

"Then I give you the man to take us there. Ladies and gentlemen assembled here...and to all Americans across the country, that future begins now with United States Marine Corps General Robert Woodley Bridgeman!"

Thunderous shouts filled the air as the general walked onto the stage. He wore a sharply tailored blue suit. His white shirt was set off by a bold red tie. Bridgeman fit in perfectly with the flags.

Duke Patrick shook his hand and hugged the general. The stage belonged to the man Elliott Strong catapulted to national attention, but in wake of the day's news, he shared it with Duke Patrick. Bridgeman saluted and extended his arms in appreciation. The crowd cheered for another three minutes.

Lebanon, Kansas

Elliott Strong watched a TV monitor on a bookshelf across the room and described the scene to his listeners as if he were there. He made special note of the injustice Patrick suffered and the way Bridgeman would correct it. And he smiled.

Chicago, Illinois
the same time

"The car is in front."

"What?" Gonzales slid off a pair of earphones and turned down his walkman. He was listening to Strong.

"We're ready."

"Thank you," Gonzales told his man, Roger Alley, the former Ali Razak—the Miami man wanted by the FBI. "The rest of the suitcases are on my bed. Get them."

"Certainly, Mr. Gonzales." The name was finally coming automatically to him. He wondered if it would change again now that they were on the move. "And your computer drive?"

"Take it. Did you double check with the cleaning crew?"

The bodyguard had. He also confirmed that movers would be arriving in another hour. By midnight, the luxurious condo would be empty and wiped clean. A bank would handle the sale.

"Then let's go."

Gonzales breezed through the lobby without a word to the building guard at the front desk. He was happy to be heading to a warmer climate and out of the United States, where soon there would be hell to pay.

The Washington Mall

"Thank you, Congressman Patrick," Bridgeman began. The nation saw the two men together. "You are a true American, who like everyone here today, deserves far better. We'll see that day together."

The crowd cheered again for the duke and the general. The opening line gave further credence to the rumor circulating the country: A Bridgeman-Patrick ticket would be on the ballot. Patrick waved for the cameras and left, as ordered. Now it was time for Bridgeman to get to his prepared remarks. He did so with great gusto.

"America—our defenses are down," Bridgeman said quietly. The powerful opening salvo surprised the crowd. It instantly silenced them. "Our defenses are down. They are down to nothing. These are not the technological defenses that protect our skies. No, they're the defenses that protect our God-given personal freedoms. Those defenses have eroded to nothingness, not by enemies from foreign lands, but from those at home who seek to destroy our way of life."

In another time, Bridgeman could have been inspiring the colonial army to cross the Delaware, or the American forces to take the beaches at Normandy. He was that kind of leader; inspiring and charismatic. Soon he might lead America's voters to the polling booth for another victory. For without announcing his intentions, John Bridgeman was already the people's candidate. He was preaching to the converted in a populist movement where people believed that America was being destroyed from within.

"But there is hope," General Bridgeman continued, "Because of you. The torn fabric of ideas, the fading words on the parchment are replaced by the strength of your presence. The heart of our nation boldly beats again because of you. So, right here, right now, in this very place, we stand together and pledge ourselves to a new American revolution. And no one will be able to rise above our defenses!"

The multitude, which had remained utterly silent, suddenly broke into a deafening cheer that eclipsed anything in Washington's history.

As Richard Cooper listened to the radio coverage, the intensity of the moment, the mood of the crowd, the very feel of the event took him back a year earlier, when he was peering out of a hotel room in Hudson, New York. He shouldered a Galil sniper rifle then. He remembered the ease at which he set up his shot. That day, his target was merely 50 yards away. It wasn't a matter of sharp shooting as much as timing. His view was partially obstructed. It was only when Congressman Teddy Lodge moved that he had the clear shot of his target.

He remembered listening to the cadence of Lodge's speech. At the appropriate moment in his delivery, the congressman bowed his head forward. That's when Cooper pulled the trigger and Jennifer Lodge breathed her last. Pandomonium replaced calm that day in the small upstate New York community. No one suspected—at least for months— that the candidate wasn't the target. The deception worked that day, as another one would today.

Cooper smiled and listened to the rambling of another would-be president.

CHAPTER 74

The White House

"Hello."
        "Yes, who is this?"
        "Mr. Roarke? Mr. Scott Roarke?"

Roarke didn't recognize the voice. Louise Swingle put it through because the caller insisted he had to speak to Agent Roarke about Katie Kessler.

"Yes! Who the hell are you?"

"Go to the Washington Monument now," the deep, deadly serious voice intoned. "Your girlfriend is approaching the west side. She is in great danger. If you expect to save her, you must get there immediately. She will be dead by fifteen-thirty."

"What? Who..." His caller disconnected. Roarke caught a clock straight ahead. 1517 hours. *Thirteen minutes!*

The Washington Mall

"Our defenses are down at our borders, too," Bridgeman exclaimed. "Foreigners easily walk across, taking American jobs and exhausting American resources. Our defenses are down on our morals. The media programs indecency as it deprograms and desensitizes our minds. Our defenses are down on our values. We have divorced ourselves from the traditional family unit. And, our defenses are down on our faith, for we have taken God out of our laws, our schools, and our lives. But, here, in this place; now, where we stand, we will lead a new American revolution." The crowd could feel where he was going. The cheering started anew. "And no one will be able to rise above our defenses!"

Jesus! Katie exclaimed to herself after pushing through at least a hundred Bridgeman supporters. That was simply to cross Constitution Avenue. She couldn't imagine getting through the crowd ahead and making her way to The Washington Monument. *But Roarke said...*

After enough "Excuse me"s, she gave up on pleasantries. The only good thing about trekking toward her destination was that she could at least see it. *Why in the world did he pick this spot? And today?* It suddenly didn't seem right.

She twisted and turned her way through the crowd. Katie heard General Bridgeman echoing across the Mall, amplified through speakers under the television projection screens. All in all, she hated it. It was hot and muggy. She wished she had worn lighter clothes and her heels were absolutely ridiculous. She felt like turning around. *But according to the guy on the phone, Roarke said...* When another person bumped her from behind, she cursed. This was too much. *Fuck it! I'm calling Scott.*

Katie stood in the shadow of the Washington Monument and dialed. She thought she heard Scott's "Hello," but no matter how high she turned up the volume or how hard she pressed the phone to her ear, she couldn't hear.

"Scott! I can't hear you. I'm on my way. Are you coming?"

He wore a loose-fitting *March2Washington* sweatshirt and faded jeans, and size 12 cowboy boots. His stature gave him more mobility than most others. And yet, he remained invisible. No one paid attention to the man with the ponytail stuck out the back of a Washington Nationals baseball cap. No one saw that he kept his right hand under his shirt. He was very close to where he wanted to be; close enough to do what he'd been contracted to do; precisely the way he'd been told. Everyone else wanted to press nearer to Bridgeman or a TV monitor. He wanted to stay where he was...until it was time.

Katie still had a few hundred yards to reach the Washington Monument. While she made her way, she tried to catch some of what Bridgeman was saying...why the crowd was cheering.

"America is watching us. America is listening to us. We are the new voice of politics. The new face of reason. Together, we are a mighty instrument of change."

So many people came out for this?

"Congress! Can you see us? Do you hear us? If you don't now, you will! Look across the street. To the Supreme Court. Those great justices. Do you see us? Do you hear us? If you don't now, you will! Now look to the White House, to Henry Lamden who sits again in his chair. Do you see us? Do you hear us? If you don't now, you will! For we are here to stay!"

Katie tuned out. She finally saw some breathing room that led to the west side of the monument. That's where she was supposed to meet Scott. It looked fairly open. *Probably because the view sucks.* She looked at the time. *Come on Scott, spare me from being a political casualty out here!*

Roarke flew through the halls, hitting his speed dial to Katie when his phone rang. He stopped.

"Katie!" He could barely make her out over the rumble of sound. "Katie!"

"Scott! I can't hear you," she said. "I'm on my way. Are you coming?"

"Katie!" It was useless. Too much noise.

As soon as Roarke was out the door he spotted a Capitol Policeman's motorcycle.

"Keys! Where are the keys?"

The officer stood by the cycle. "No way." He was waiting for orders to lead a motorcade across town.

"Keys! I need your bike."

"I can't."

"Yes, you can." Roarke flashed his badge. "And you can get me backup! Send them to the Washington Monument, west side.

"Now. Give me the fucking keys!"

The Capitol police officer hesitated.

"Now!"

He took them out but still held them. Roarke shot his hand up from under the policeman's arm; a karate move from his training years ago. The keys flew up. Roarke snatched them midair and saddled the motorcycle. "Get that backup to the Washington Monument!" He turned the key, gunned the engine, and lurched forward.

The shortest distance was across the White House lawn, but he couldn't jump the gates. So Roarke peeled out of the driveway, making a right onto Pennsylvania Avenue and another quick right at 15th St. N.W.

Marchers at the corner of 15th and Constitution blocked his way. He stopped, bolted forward, slowed, stopped, then jumped the curb. The White House was directly north of the monument, but he had to come up from the west where there were fewer people and a better line of sight.

What's she wearing today? What the hell is Katie wearing? He tried to recall.

Roarke stood up on the bike to see over the crowd as he raced down Constitution. Just before 17th street, he made a sharp left onto the Mall, avoiding a marcher, but catching the corner of a table full of commemorative t-shirts. The goods went flying and the vendor screamed a stream of obscenities which Roarke ignored. He was bearing down fast on the base of the 550-foot-high, Egyptian-style obelisk; the largest masonry structure in the world.

Haruku Island
the same time

With a slight hand signal, Nolt ordered his men down. Now they were ahead of schedule and the schedule ruled. He cupped his hand over the display of his PDA. Once again, the GPS-relayed pulse confirmed the objective. Nolt would take his next cue in 30 seconds.

The Washington Mall

She was 25 feet away. He decided to walk right up behind her, pop the woman twice with his Heckler & Koch Compact USP 45, let her collapse into his arms, and lay her on the ground. He could accomplish this quickly and invisibly, then be on his way.

The woman looked about nervously and turned to him. She froze as if she recognized him. *But how?* Her eyes darted about as if asking for help.

That man? She'd seen the look before. Roarke taught her to pay attention to everything. Now the lesson was paying off. *He looks like...*

He sped up. Twenty feet. She was staring at him. He had his gun under his loose shirt. Fifteen feet. People were walking past, getting closer to the nearest screen. Another few feet and he'd bring his gun up. The speech was the only sound filling the air except for a yell and the roar of a motor behind him and to the side.

"Cooper!"

He distinctly heard the name, but he didn't turn around. He was ten feet away. The woman hadn't moved. He should shoot now. He slid his 45 out.

"Cooper!"

He kept going. His gun came up.

"Cooper, stop!"

He wasn't going to get closer, as planned. But it didn't matter. Too much noise, too much activity, too much attention elsewhere.

"Katie, down!"

That registered.

The woman instantly dropped and he adjusted his aim.

The detonation of an unsilenced gun rose above the speech and the cheering. *What?* That was the first of three confused thoughts. The second was that the woman was not looking at him, but beyond— to someone else. And the third, was that he was feeling cold and disoriented. *What?* he asked himself again. He heard the name *Cooper* from someone behind him, but he couldn't turn to it. He looked at his gun. That simple, direct act was answered by another bullet to his side, from a different direction.

He dropped to his knees with the most perplexed expression. Then he fell backwards, his pupils reflecting the monument honoring the first president of the United States.

CHAPTER
75

Haruku Island

The shock was overwhelming. A sonic boom. Then another. A pair of Super Hornets overflew, barely above tree-top level. Komari's men instinctively threw themselves on the ground and covered their ears and opened their mouths. It was completely reflexive and exactly what Nolt counted on. But the distraction was not yet complete. A second, then a third wave of Navy F/A-18s buzzed the camp, keeping the terrorists pinned. As each crossed above, they flared out and released AGM 65 Maverick missiles, further terrifying the untrained troops. The missiles shot through the air to the offshore target, but the very proximity of the jets—only meters above them—kept the rebels down. The noise, the photo-flash bombs, chaff, and flares blinded and deafened the terrorists. The spectacle numbed them.

"Go, go, go!" radioed Nolt. Shaughnessy and Nolt were the first through the tent flap. They moved wide to the left and right. Showalter and Pintar were footsteps behind, and split 10 feet apart. Roberts and Polonsky backed them up and were prepared to enter if any of the first team went down. Chaskes and Lopez fired at any of the huddled terrorists who dared raise their heads.

Komari had killed the lights on the first assault; a quick and smart decision. But the SEALs, with their night-vision goggles, could see perfectly.

Nolt's PDA told him exactly where the president was. Two-o'clock, 22 feet ahead.

Lopez, looking through his own night-vision goggles, dispatched two guards standing inside the tent.

Now, Nolt's way was clear. The president was ahead, and apparently bound back-to-back with another captive. Even through his infrared sight, he could tell that the president was injured...and in danger. A man stood over President Taylor with a machete raised high. Someone to the side was yelling an order. The blade started sweeping down. Nolt fired his laser-aiming handgun. The guerilla took three hits between the eyes. The blade fell to the side, barely missing the president, but catching the man behind him in the leg.

Another guerilla stood close to the first man. *The one who gave the order!* He wore a beret and held a gun with one hand and a riding crop or whip in another. His eyes burned with hatred, but his reaction time wasn't as great as his fury. His pistol came up.

Nolt didn't have the angle to take him out. Another rebel was coming toward him, blocking his shot. He fired. The man dropped to his knees. The SEAL angled sideways. The man with the beret was laughing. He had his shot.

"Lieutenant, down!" It was Shaughnessy's voice from the opposite end of the tent. Nolt dove as a shot rang out. It hit the rebel and continued through his shoulder to where Nolt had stood. The terrorist spun around thinking the shot came from Nolt. Not finding him, he re-acquired his target—the president. He took aim. But Shaughenessy's final shot went through his left eye socket. All that had been Commander Umar Komari ceased to be.

Roberts and Polonsky finished off the rest of the terrorists in the tent. Chaskes and Pintar found two targets of their own outside. They were dead in the time that it took Komari to hit the floor.

Washington, D.C.

Roarke slid the motorcycle to a stop and maneuvered over the borrowed vehicle. He kept his pistol on the deadman. He knocked the would-be assassin's gun to the side and checked for a pulse. *It's over.* He thanked God for the tip that saved Katie's life. *But who fired the second shot?*

Katie rushed into Roarke's arms, but he suddenly angled her behind him. He heard someone running toward them from his left and he sensed that a gun was on him. Roarke swiveled, still offering his body as a shield. He took quick aim at the man approaching.

"Jesus!" he yelled.

"Put that thing down! You could hurt someone," Shannon Davis said.

Roarke was completely surprised to see his friend, but he knew who fired the shot that ended it.

"How did you..."

"Katie called me," the FBI agent explained. "Smart thinking, too." He kept his gun trained on the dead man. "Said you might be in trouble."

Roarke sighed. "*Me*? But she was the one..."

Katie looked up. His unfinished thought brought her to tears.

"Everything's all right. It's over. It's all over," Roarke said looking around her to make sure. Davis was doing the same. "Cooper's dead."

Haruku Island

Nolt radioed the *Essex*. "Clear, clear, clear. Objective achieved. Top Gun secure. I repeat, Top Gun is secure." He then sent out a verifying instant message on his PDA. "TG-okay. Send birds." That was the signal for the five Seahawks, which had been hovering out of the target area, to converge on the camp. They arrived with lights aimed at the now-frightened guerillas, huddled in three groups.

A handful of rebels foolishly tried to take on the first helicopter. They, and their compatriots nearest them, were cut down in a hail of fire from the Seahawk's M240 7.62 mm machine guns in flexible door mounts.

While the SEALs swept the ground for any remaining dangers, Nolt went to aid the president. He lifted his night-vision goggles, holstered his gun, and put out a welcomed hand.

The ear-pounding sound of the Seahawks made it necessary for Nolt to shout. "Mr. President, my name's Nolt, lieutenant, U.S. Navy. It's a real pleasure to meet you."

"SEALs?"

"Yes, sir. Proud of it."

"Clemson's?"

"Affirmative. Directly under Admiral Zimmer."

"Well, thank you, son. But the man you really want to meet is right behind me. He needs some attention."

"I'm doing okay," Rossy volunteered, though his leg was badly cut by the machete.

Nolt radioed for Chaskes to come back and treat the wound.

Morgan Taylor gestured to the ties. "And as close as we are, I'm sure he'd be happier than a clam at high tide if you cut these damned things off."

Nolt laughed. "No problem." He sliced through the plastic ties with his knife.

"Now get the others free, will you?" the president asked.

The SEAL obliged.

Five minutes later, Nolt and the SEALs of Team THREE accompanied the hostages out to a designated LZ. Two new platoons of special forces rappelled from the forward Seahawks and took control of the area, while the other three Seahawks kept their weapons trained on the captives.

"I can only imagine how you found me, Lieutenant," the president said.

"Your personal Lo-Jack, sir." He was referring to the low-powered transmitter doctors implanted in Taylor's backside. The signal told the GPS satellites and command where Taylor was, right down to one meter. "The AWACS tracked you all the way. Let's just say your butt preceeded you, sir," Nolt joked.

For a second, Taylor vowed never to complain about anything again.

CHAPTER 76

Chicago, Illinois
Kennedy Expressway

G onzales listened to the news on the car radio. He was furious.
Patrick's speech revved up the crowd. Bridgeman mesmerized
everyone. *But what happened?*
The answer was *nothing.*

What happened to the two MANPAD missiles? They should have
been fired into the crowd. Hundreds, if not thousands, were supposed
to have died. The deaths were intended to cause a riot. In defiance,
the mob should have stormed the Capitol Police or fired on them.
And what happened to the cell phone text messages? Gonzales planned
for team leaders to unknowingly steer the crowd into the line of fire.

Something went wrong; terribly wrong. The day was an unmitigated
disaster.

Cooper failed to fulfill his contract. Instead of the media reporting
from the worst riot in American history, they simply described how
calm the marchers remained. Instead of furthering Gonzales's personal
cause, the crowd lined up for the portable potties and left.

Gonzales expected commentators to draw direct comparisons with
the attack on the Bonus Army in 1932. He counted on the press to
draw a parallel between Henry Lamden and Herbert Hoover. He
expected the administration to take a hard and instant fall. He anticipated Robert Bridgeman's immediate rise to mythical stature.

Instead, Bridgeman walked off the stage to cheers and people went
home peacefully.

*The handheld missiles? The spark that was to start a political war?
Nothing?*

Gonzales ordered Alley to switch radio stations, hoping he'd find better news. "Change it! Get me something else." But all the reports were the same.

A calm and orderly protest.

Fox radio reported that some marchers voiced dissatisfaction with the Lamden-Taylor White House, but there was hardly any real negative commentary. Even Elliott Strong noted that, "the day fell short of expectations." He left it at that.

Gonzales kept demanding his driver find better coverage. "Again!" A mistake. Alley was so distracted that he failed to notice that an Illionis State Trooper who clocked him at 30 miles per hour over the speed limit on the Kennedy Expressway.

"Mr. Gonzales...behind us."

Gonzales craned his neck. "What?"

"A police car. He's got his lights on." Gonzales saw him. "Why?"

The driver's foot was on the break. He slowed down considerably. "I don't know."

"Of course, you do, you idiot. You're speeding." The speedometer was still over 80.

"What should I do, sir?"

"Pull over, of course. Show him your license. Take the ticket and don't say anything other than you're sorry."

Alley slowed and eased onto the shoulder. He came to a gradual stop. Gonzales slid back into his carseat. He wanted to disappear, or at least look like a fare on the way to the airport.

"No problems," Gonzales reminded Alley.

"It'll be okay."

The officer pulled up behind the BMW, but he didn't get out of his vehicle.

"What's he waiting for?" Gonzales asked.

"He's checking our plates. It's normal. We just sit tight."

Gonzales tried to relax.

"Here he comes," Alley said.

The State Trooper motioned for the driver to roll down the window. Alley complied.

"Is something wrong, officer? We're on our way to the airport."

"May I see your license and registration, please." The please wasn't necessary.

"Our flight is..."

"Your license," the trooper demanded.

Once he had Alley's license, he stepped back, behind the car.

"What's he doing?" Gonzales whispered.

"Just checking. Everything will be fine."

The officer returned to the car and peered inside. "Mr. Alley, you were traveling at more than 30 miles per hour over the limit."

"I'm sorry. I'm trying to make a plane. May we..."

Without responding, the officer stepped back again, keeping the license and registration. He returned to his squad car and sat inside.

"What's he doing?"

"They do this sort of thing. It's all normal."

No it's not, Gonzales thought. *No it's not.*

"Step out of the car and put your hands on the roof!"

The State Trooper's order, amplified through a PA, came so suddenly and with such intent, that Gonzales's chest tightened in the time it took for the policeman to complete his sentence. Gonzales reached inside his jacket pocket for his inhaler. After fumbling for a few seconds he found his medication. He took a fast puff and struggled to say, "Don't!"

Alley looked in the rearview mirror. The policeman was crouched behind his open car door. He had a microphone in one hand and a shotgun aimed at the back of the car.

"Out, now!" the trooper demanded.

Gonzales responded to the second demand by looking around. The action brought him right into view of the video camera mounted on the dashboard.

"What should I do?" the driver asked.

Gonzales's chest ached. *To get this far. How did they know? I can't...* He figured that by now, other officers were on the way; maybe even with a helicopter. "Back up! Smash him fast! Then go!"

"He's got a gun!"

"Do it!"

Alley started the car and jammed it into reverse. His foot slammed on the gas pedal. The 25 feet that separated the two vehicles immediately disappeared. Before the officer could get off a proper shot, the impact knocked him down. His shotgun discharged in the air and the door broke his arm.

"Go, go! Now!" Gonzales cried out. He filled his lungs with another puff from his inhaler. The acceleration pressed him into the back of his seat and then tossed him to the right as Alley swerved onto the road. He swore in Arabic at the cop, at the traffic, and under his breath, at everyone in America.

"That field! There!" Gonzales pointed about a quarter-mile down the road. "Pull over, I'm going to jump out. Then you keep going."

"To where?"

"Anywhere. Jamaica." Gonzales made that up. "I'll find you. And destroy the computer! You must destroy the computer." It was in the trunk.

Gonzales whipped around to see if they were being followed. *Not yet.* He tapped Alley. "Now! Get over!" The driver steered to the side, applied the breaks and came to a quick stop.

"Jamaica?"

"Yes, Jamaica!" Gonzales shouted as he put his hand on the door. "In ten days." With that he was gone. He ran down an embankment and hid, waiting for Alley to peel out again. When he was certain that his man was a good distance down the Kennedy, and the sirens were well past him, he walked toward an opening in a fence and the world that lay beyond.

CHAPTER
77

Andrews Air Force Base
Suitland, Maryland
the next day

The VC-25, the twin of the downed *Air Force One*, landed at Andrews Air Force Base without fanfare. The SAM 29000 rolled up to the gangway, and was met by a contingent of Secret Service officers, a marine detail, General Jackson, and one other friend.

Only one man had seen Taylor as he looked now—Scott Roarke. That was years ago in Iraq.

Taylor held his side and walked slowly. He escaped with three broken ribs, a severely scarred cheek, black eyes, and a gash across his forehead. He'd soon recover from the injuries, but the experience had changed him. He was hardened and eager to help Henry Lamden get on with the business of destroying terrorist camps and weapons supplies.

General Jackson was the first to greet him. "Mr. Vice President, you're a sight for sore eyes."

"General, I'm just happy to be alive." He shook J3's hand, then hugged him, carefully. "Thank you for getting those boys in there."

"Sorry we called it so close. I think it was the time difference."

Taylor tried to laugh, but it hurt too much. He saw Roarke standing off to the side.

"Get on over here. I'm sure as hell not coming to you!"

Roarke did as ordered. "I see you're no worse for the wear. But don't you think this rescue-behind-enemy-lines-thing is becoming a little old?" Roarke offered lightly.

"No thanks to you."

"Hey, I had my hands full."

"So I heard. Nice work."

"Thank you."

"Now let's get going. There's a hot bath with my name on it wherever the hell I'm sleeping tonight."

Everyone laughed. Taylor was due to move back into Number One Observatory Circle, the vice president's residence.

Taylor was escorted to one of the 23 new AgustaWestland EH101 helicopters operated under the Marine One squadron. Like its fixed-wing counterparts in the Air Force, an EH101 in the fleet assumes a special call sign whenever the president is aboard—*Marine One*. Today it flew as *Marine Two*, reflecting the vice president's position in the political food chain.

As soon as they were airborne, J3 handed Morgan Taylor a sealed file. "It didn't take much. The president talked to Prime Minister Foss. It's done."

Taylor broke the seal and scanned the first page of the secret report. There was Lamden's name, signed in ink, along with fax signatures by Foss and the leaders of six other Asian nations. The report identified hard targets that the United States was authorized to attack under the terms of "The Southeast Asia and Pacific Anti-Terrorist Act." The first was the Liberian tanker heading toward Sydney. SAPATA, quickly passed by overwhelming Senate approval, was going active.

Lebanon, Kansas
the same time

Millions of listeners were waiting to hear what Elliott Strong had to say today. Bridgeman had been chased out of the headlines by his nemeses, Lamden and Taylor. How would their bombastic talk-show host respond?

"Good afternoon. Unless you've been living under a rock, or with your head in the sand, you've probably noticed something very important about the political climate in America...about the leadership issues...about the construction of the government." He waited for his audience to fill in the blanks, then Strong responded in a booming voice. "Nothing's changed!"

True to form, Strong ignored what he couldn't overcome. Instead of even acknowledging the breaking news he redefined the debate. "I'm happy for Mrs. Taylor. I'm glad to see our military demonstrate its might. But members of our *Strong Nation*, we're right back with the mess we had before. Worse. We saw yet another example of the arrogance of this administration. They prevented a true man of the people, a man willing to break from the system from taking power— if only for a short time. They stopped Speaker of the House Duke Patrick. And why? They were afraid of him; afraid because he was willing to recognize that General Bridgeman deserves to be the leader of the Free World."

Elliott Strong smiled into his mirror. He was proud of how he twisted the argument in his favor. Now, with the issue settled for his listeners, it was time to move on.

"So, let's look at the real news."

He didn't know the half of it.

The White House
four hours later

A showered and refreshed Morgan Taylor walked into the Oval Office. He wore khakis, a light blue shirt, and a blue double-breasted jacket without a tie. This was informal for him.

Louise cleared him through, which was, in itself, somewhat awkward. Morgan Taylor thought about what he was going to say. The vice presidency wasn't for him. A good president needed a good vice president; not somebody who didn't want to be there. Lamden deserved his own man, from his own party.

"Morgan," Henry Lamden said with real affection.

Taylor quickly observed that the heart attack had aged the president. He was thinner, weaker, and smaller. His suit was too big for him. Lamden slowly came to his feet and stepped away from the desk used by Franklin Roosevelt, John F. Kennedy, George W. Bush, and Henry Lamden. It had been given to the U.S. by Queen Victoria. Roosevelt added a front panel to cover the mid section so that visitors wouldn't see his wheelchair. The desk seemed to dwarf Lamden now.

"Well, Henry, you're looking good."

"Don't bullshit a bullshitter, Morgan," Lamden countered. He braced himself against the desk top, right in front of the hinged panel, which could swing open. Years ago, little John-John Kennedy played with the door while JFK worked.

Taylor came the rest of the way into the Oval Office and shook Lamden's hand. He got half the energy in return.

"Looks like you took quite a beating," the president offered.

"Sons of bitches," was Taylor's reply. "Call it serendipity, but I suppose by being there we prevented one helluva bloodbath. They planned on taking Jakarta. I can't even imagine how many hundreds of thousands of Christian Indonesians would have been killed."

"Just serendipity?" asked Lamden. He was a religious man; more so than Taylor.

Taylor hadn't really thought about the circumstances that brought him to Haruku Island. "Makes you wonder."

Lamden closed his eyes believing there was more to it. When he opened them again, he returned to the leather chair behind the Victorian desk—the power seat.

"I'm exercising my right as president. I'm going to talk and you're going to keep your damned trap shut, which I know isn't your nature."

"Henry, I need to talk to you, too."

"No, you don't."

Taylor laughed. This was his old friend. He brought up one of his favorite chairs—the Colonial Adams. It's what he used for personal conversations. He felt that's where they were going.

"Good, now listen. I'm not going to give you a long speech and I'm not taking questions after like a goddamned press conference."

"Okay, okay," Taylor said obligingly.

"I'm happy to have my picture in the history books. Maybe someday they'll even put me on a fifty-cent stamp. But I have to tell you, Morgan, I'm not up for this job anymore."

Taylor leaned forward; clearly caught off guard. *This isn't what...*

"Look at me," Lamden said rolling on. "They say I'll get stronger with time, but the doctors admit it'll never happen with the pressure of this place. Personally, I like hanging around here. But I've spent enough years away from my wife; first on ships with nothing but smelly men, and then on the Hill with men whose politics stank. Quite honestly, I missed a lot of years getting laid. Given the choice, if my wife's willing and there's enough Viagra in the world, I'd rather be in bed with my wife than being fucked by voters who didn't want me in the first place.

"Morgan, you're the president the country needs, whether or not they know it. You've proven it to them once and again. Get yourself a vice president you can really trust and do what you need to do.

"If you really feel you have to, parade me out on holidays and special events. Send me to meet the Pope; I think I'd like him. Or get me over to England for a royal wedding. My wife loves Wedgwood. But don't argue with me now. Not one word. My mind is made up. This is your job, Morgan. You've got the balls for it. And for God's sake, between you, me, and the lamppost, you even have the heart. But you won't hear me admit that in public. You'll get too many votes from Democrats next time. Which leads me to an important question: Can you even run again? After all, you didn't get elected last November. But hell, that's your problem, not mine."

Taylor fought the tears back. He did have the heart.

"So, do what the country needs you to do. Become president for the third time."

78

The New York Times
Two days later

"**T**his is Weaver," the *Times* editor answered.
"Ms. Weaver, my name is Roarke. Scott Roarke. I'm with the Secret Service."

"Yes, Mr. Roarke." She was nervous; distracted. "I know who you are."

"Can we talk about Michael O'Connell?" Shannon Davis passed along the details, or at least what was known by NYPD, to Roarke.

She had trouble replying. "You heard?" she managed to say.

"Yes, what happened?"

"He was robbed and killed." Weaver's voice cracked. "His body was found in the Bronx. Why, for God's sake?"

Roarke decided to volunteer information; something he rarely offered. "He was on the way to see me, Ms. Weaver. He had something to tell me. Do you have any idea what that was?"

She hesitated. The time it took her to respond told Roarke she did. "Please. What was it."

"I can't," she said. Andrea Weaver was falling on a useless sword.

"Look, who robs someone in the middle of Manhattan and drives them to the Bronx? He was on his way to see me at the White House. He had something to tell me in person. You know what it was."

Still silence.

"It's what got him killed," he continued. "If you want to help, tell me."

He could almost hear her thinking.

"It was important enough to cost him his life."

"The police were here," she said weakly.

"Did you tell them anything?"

"No."

"Why not?"

"For the same reason I haven't told you. We're the press and...."

"He's dead, Weaver. Michael O'Connell is dead. Because of a story he was working on? Something he discovered? He had to see me. Me! And he pretty much hated me. But still, O'Connell had to come down in person. He didn't want to do it over the phone. He was grabbing a cab for the airport." He raised his voice, something Roarke rarely did with a woman. "For that reason alone, I have to assume that it was too important to discuss on the telephone. So, what was it?"

"But the robbery?"

"Come on."

"And the Bronx?"

"He was dumped there." An uneasy thought started forming in his mind. *The taxi driver.* It evaporated as soon as she spoke.

"What's your e-mail address?"

"My e-mail?" he responded.

"I'll send you the story Michael was working on. I've only got part of it. We got hit by a weird computer virus the other day. His computer got fried, most of my files were lost."

The e-mail dumped into Roarke's mailbox a minute later. He opened it and read what remained of Michael O'Connell's last story. It was a saga that began years ago on a California back road and led to U.S. Route 281 in Lebanon, Kansas. Time after time, according to the report, Strong's career advanced, as if orchestrated by an outside force.

The next two pages were a jumble of words. The computer gibberish cleared up midway through O'Connell's description of his trip to Russia. The reporter intimated that a famous American radio talk-show host may have been there as well. The article became incomprehensible again. Roarke scanned ahead until he came to a section which covered Andropov Institute's Red Banner curriculum, where Russians and Middle East agents were trained to become Americans. Michael O'Connell made the leap of faith that the sleepers could have found their way to positions in the U.S. media; including radio. The loosely connected dots formed a picture of Elliott Strong.

Roarke sat back in awe. Of course, the *Times* couldn't print the story. In its current draft, it was largely composed of hearsay and supposition. But in Roarke's mind, it was true. All of it.

The Secret Service agent considered what happened. *O'Connell put out feelers. Word got back to Strong, or O'Connell talked to him directly. Given O'Connell's reputation, Strong, or whoever he worked for, considered O'Connell too much of a threat. So he was killed.*

Roarke printed the story and ran up to the Oval Office. "Louise, is he in?"

"He's with the NDI."

"Good. Buzz him."

Roarke started for the door.

"Scott, you can't..."

But he could, and Louise knew it.

"Boss!"

Louise barely got word to the president when Roarke was through the door. Few people in the world could get into the Oval Office on a sprint.

"Scott, we are in the middle of something." Jack Evans and the president were working on strategies that would take out more terrorist camps around the world. Roarke got to share a great deal of Morgan Taylor's presidency, but not this. The intelligence director turned over the map, which earmarked targets. "I'd appreciate it if you would wait a few minutes." It wasn't really a request.

"I can't, sir."

When Roarke added *sir,* even the president knew the seriousness.

"I'll be quick."

"Okay, let's have it."

"Mr. Director, this is for you, too." Evans blinked acceptance. "You know I got that call from Michael O'Connell."

"Yes." The president was also all too aware that O'Connell had been killed.

"He had to talk to me. It was urgent. I know why."

Taylor looked at Evans. They both sensed the conversation was going to take a turn for the worse.

Roarke handed both men a copy of the reporter's virus-scrambled article. "O'Connell's editor sent this to me. It was his last story...I think the one he died for."

The president and his chief intelligence officer eyed the article.

"Str+@dvjfng Ties fr Stro8fg Opinions"
By Mic&t#) NBl O'C890$$ll, Sn. P37d0fal Wr9&tr

Roarke explained why it was hard to read.

"But what's this say?" Evans asked.

"'Strong Ties for Strong Opinions,' By Michael O'Connell, Senior Political Writer."

"And?"

"I believe O'Connell had first-hand information that Elliott Strong is a foreign agent."

Roarke left. Evans remained. It was clear that President Taylor and the National Director of Intelligence were now going to talk about the new crisis and not the agenda Jack Evans had set.

"We'll have to vet this with Mulligan and our sources from the old KGB," the NDI stated. "I'll also call Jacob Schecter and see if he can shed any more light on this."

"And when we determine it's true—that the whole damned thing is true?" the president asked. "What then? Strong is the extremists' messiah." He reflected on his appraisal. "No, that's understating it. He's the voice of a whole new movement, which makes Bridgeman the front man and Patrick, God only knows!"

"Maybe you'll want *me* to deal with this, Mr. President."

There was a coldness to Evans' delivery and the message behind it. It was a calculated declaration which required no further response from the president.

Chez Black Restaurant
Positano, Italy
three days later

Vinnie D'Angelo and Ira Wurlin were seated at their old table behind the sliding partition. They were there at the behest of their superiors. No one except Guiseppie, the waiter of nineteen years, or Mr. Black, the legendary proprietor of *Chez Black*, would be allowed in. And that wouldn't be for a while.

D'Angelo wasted no time getting to the point of the meeting. Once again, the topic was Israeli agents working in the United States. The American CIA agent did all the talking. Wurlin spared the denials. D'Angelo's information was unassailable. When D'Angelo finished laying out the foundation he simply said, "Ira, you're going to solve a problem for us."

CHAPTER
79

Lebanon, Kansas
Monday, 3 September

"Last caller. Hello, you're on *Strong Nation*."

"Elliott, now that Taylor is back in the White House, what do you think our chances are of really getting him out?"

Strong smiled into the mirror in front of him. He loved calls like this, especially at the end of the night. It gave him a chance to pontificate, and that always went over well with his listeners.

"Our chances? This isn't a game of chance. We're not spinning a wheel here, hoping our number comes up. Anyway, the basic rule of gambling is the house always wins. In this case, it's been the White House. But here's what I think. From now on, no more house rules. We're a few votes closer to having our debate on a recall. And I'll tell you plain and simple, we are going to win that battle. That's how we'll get Taylor out. That's how we'll steer our country into the future."

The host's closing music, *Don't Back Down*, was creeping up under him as the second hand ticked toward the hour. He timed his goodbye's perfectly.

"That's it. Good night, good morning, good luck, good day. Remember, together a *Strong Nation* is ours."

Elliott Strong signed off.

Strong never went straight to bed after his late-night show. He was too wound up. He had a routine that worked, though. First, he checked his e-mail. There'd be the usual spam that got through filters, an occasional note from his syndicator, and some correspondence from corporate executives who were aligned with his politics. Tonight, there was also a note from Duke Patrick's office—a vitriolic rant about Taylor that went nowhere, and a leak from another source on the Hill about a senator who might be willing to throw his support to Bridgeman for the right payback. *Interesting,* he thought. *The defections begin.*

However, while Strong projected bravado on the air, he inwardly recognized that something wasn't right. He had been warned to expect breaking news from the march. Nothing occurred. Bridgeman remained an item in the news, but if an incident was supposed to put him over the top, it failed to transpire. Aside from a sketchy report about a shooting near the Washington Monument, everything was calm. The status quo returned to the country and Taylor was president again.

Strong leaned back in his chair and reflected on the recent events. *What went wrong? First, Taylor's airplane crash should have put Patrick in the White House. It didn't. Lamden re-emerged. That turned him into a hero and Bridgeman's coverage was eclipsed by what happened a few blocks away. Then the biggest surprise of all. Taylor returned from the dead!*

What the hell went wrong? he wondered. He couldn't answer the question himself. And in the days since the march, Strong hadn't heard from the one man who might know. *Maybe tonight.*

He logged onto eBay to check the bidding of some paintings he'd never buy. He was looking for a specific price on a special painting, Richard Merkin's *Charlot*. It wasn't there. If it had been, the amount would have provided him with a phone number to call for one-time use. Months often went by between contacts; sometimes years. *But there should be...*

The last part of Strong's nightly routine before sleeping was walking his dog, Grant. At four-thirty A.M. the Labrador retriever was at the door, waiting in anticipation.

At that hour, or any hour for that matter, Lebanon was quiet. No one was around to tell Strong to use a leash. Grant bounded out. He ran in circles, checked his favorite scents, then 20 yards down the street he found a tree to claim as his own.

By the time Strong caught up with his dog, he noticed that Grant was staring into the darkness, sniffing the air. The playful three-year-old was easily distracted by squirrels, cats, and mice. He barked. "Come on, leave them alone." The dog barked again, but didn't move. "Shhh," Strong said automatically. There were no houses nearby, no neighbors to distract, but there was still something about a dog barking in the middle of the night that prompted the response.

Grant ignored him. Untethered, he took off into the darkness to chase down whatever was tempting him.

Strong continued his walk, feeling refreshed in the cool morning air. There was already a hint of fall from the north. Strong smiled inwardly. *It'll be okay in the morning. Another beautiful September day; one day closer to the next election.*

He noticed that Grant had stopped barking. Strong whistled. His dog didn't respond. He whistled again. No sounds, not even crickets. He clapped his hands and called out, "Grant! Come!"

The ELCAN SpectrIR SP50B Thermal Weapon Sight was designed for Homeland Security, police, the military, and *other* professionals. It utilizes heat-imagery technology; true "see-in-the-dark" infrared vision which can reveal what the human eye can't. It works in rain and fog, dust and smoke, and, of course, in the dead of night.

The SpectrIR can distinctively detect a moving target up to 650 feet away. It works by separating living, breathing objects from their surroundings by reading their heat signatures.

Security forces at nuclear plants, oil refineries, and port authorities have added the night-vision scope to their arsenals. Interestingly, the scope can be hooked up with a wireless RF video-port to provide real-time remote viewing. Mounted on an AR15 assault rifle with an extendable shoulder stock, and in the right hands, it served as the perfect nighttime sniper weapon.

It was unfortunate about the dog. The shooter liked dogs. He had one just like him back home.

The man had been in the area for two days, scouting and determining how to complete his mission. No one had seen him. No one would. *Odd*, he thought, *coming to this Lebanon.* He had done the same thing in the country with the same name.

He wanted the perfect shot. The dog delayed his first attempt along the road. Now his target faced him full-on. He lined up the crosshairs between his target's eyes. One bullet. One fraction of a second between life and death. One more more voice silenced, caught on TV; beamed out on 2.46 Hz through a scrambled command RF link.

Elliott Strong looked off into the darkness. He had an awareness of a flash, like a firefly. It was something so uniquely American. He'd never seen it back home as a child in Syria, nor in Russia where he had been trained. *So American...*

The Israeli sniper slipped further into the darkness and disappeared. There were dangers working in the United States, but this time Ira Wurlin assured him everything would be fine.

CHAPTER 80

The Oval Office
Tuesday, 4 September

This was Katie's meeting. In attendance were President Morgan Taylor, Bernsie Bernstein, White House counsel Brad Rutberg, Attorney General Eve Goldman, Secretary of the Treasury David Jaburi, and Lynn Myerson's old boss—Office of Strategic Affairs chief Michael Safron. Everyone was seated in a circle. Katie shared the couch with Goldman.

She chose a conservative gray suit, her mother's pearls, and low black heels. That was a conscious decision. The last thing she wanted to do was trip in front of the president.

Taylor welcomed everyone. "Thank you for coming. I think the events of the last year, let alone the past few weeks, underscore the need for this dialogue. Our goal is to formulate and advance a new approach to the line of succession; one that ensures that the objectives of an elected administration can withstand a crisis and the nation can count on a stable transition. We've weathered two rocky tests of the current law. I think we can all agree that in the post-nine-eleven era, the process needs reinventing."

Katie had a simple yellow pad on her lap. The president set up the agenda perfectly, as promised.

"Ms. Kessler has, under my instructions, thoroughly researched the law and listened to learned opinion from the Hill. I dare say, she's also probably gotten an earful of contrary, partisan viewpoints. We're ready to hear your thoughts. Ms. Kessler."

"Thank you, Mr. President." Katie remained seated. It seemed appropriate. Besides, Roarke advised her not to stand over Taylor. "I appreciate the confidence you've expressed in me. I hope I live up to your expectations."

"Oh, you will. I'm a good judge of character."

Katie smiled inwardly.

"As you noted, since September 11, 2001, we have lived in an age faced with the possible decapitation of the United States government. Mass terrorism, or as we've recently seen, even smaller acts of executive treason, bring into question the flaws in the Succession Act of 1947.

"Of course, it will not be the Office of the President that makes any change. It is clearly Congress's constitutional right, granted by Article II, Section 1, Clause 6, modified by the 25th Amendment. But I believe the proposal I have for you today takes partisanship out of the equation, and speaks to the greater need—continuity of leadership and continuity of policy.

"This is a new approach; a variation on earlier iterations, but clearly something different. It correctly addresses the longstanding constitutional debate over the definition of '*Officer,*' and it eliminates a scenario whereby an acting president could be bumped. It sidesteps the potential for the speaker of the house or president *pro tem* of the Senate from having to resign his position to serve as president, and it provides solutions for succession—should a president-elect be killed following an election and before the Inauguration."

In years past, such a notion would have been unthinkable, let alone unspeakable. Today it has to be considered.

"I weighed many of the ideas already on the table. There have been some very thoughtful bills offered up; notable proposals from Representative Brad Sherman, Senators John Cornyn and Trent Lott, as well as propositions from a wide range of groups, including The Continuity of Government Commission."

Eve Goldman, the only one in the room making notes, raised her pencil tip. "Excuse me, but do you have a sense of whether any of these proposals would stand a constitutional test?"

"The fundamental question, Attorney General. In my estimation, the more carefully crafted bills would. But are they the right proposals and would they even get out of a conference committee? After all, many sidestep Congressional leadership, so why would the House or Senate leadership basically vote themselves out of a job."

"Oh?" Secretary Jaburi responded. "How so?"

"Well, that's the political side of this whole debate and well beyond my experience." *What experience?* she thought. Katie reached into her attaché case and removed spiral-bound copies of a position paper. "Sticking to the basics, I believe what I'm about to propose *is* legally sound. My proposal addresses two main points: First of all, it preserves the Office of President from a catastrophic attack against Washington; second, it assures that a president can emerge to lead the nation."

Katie had just cleared the land for the political bomb she was about to drop.

"I propose that the speaker of the house and the president *pro tempore* of the Senate be removed from the line of succession."

Bernsie gasped.

"It's not without precedent," she continued. "This was the law from 1886 to 1947."

"Then we sell it in that way," Bernsie said, relieved that they could rely on some history.

"Well, there's more." *Here goes.* "I also recommend that the order not fall to the Cabinet secretaries."

"Then who on God's earth becomes president after the vice president?" he stammered.

"The president or president-elect—directly following a national election—will nominate a well-respected, above-reproach candidate outside the fundamental operation of the government and even outside of Washington, D.C., as next in line after the vice president. This could be a former president or vice president, a governor, a former key cabinet member or someone equally experienced and worthy. The nominee would be subject to Senate confirmation and once confirmed, receive regular intelligence reports and Secret Service protection."

"But, your recommendation would put someone in line who hasn't been elected. At least the speaker and the president *pro tem* are elected officials," the Office of Strategic Affairs chief complained.

"Not nationally, Mr. Safron. They become national figures only through their elevated positions in Congress," Eve Goldman noted. "In that sense, they're nominated peers and confirmed through majority vote, just like the secretaries of state, defense, right through the cabinet."

"Thank you, Attorney General," Katie said appreciatively. "I should add that the creation of a president-designate post would be subject to the same Congressional scrutiny, perhaps more."

Bernsie decided to listen. No further interruptions.

"Preferably, he or she would represent the party of the elected president," Katie contended. "This is crucial. Every four years, the direction of the federal government is determined by the public's decision in the voting booth. I'm sorry, Mr. President, but if the nation votes Democratic, they should have a president from that party."

"Apology accepted," Taylor said lightly. "And vice versa."

"Yes, sir. By having a qualified, informed, and pre-confirmed president-designate in the wings, we are assured that America can survive even the most cruel and deadly attack imaginable."

Katie needed a sip of water.

"Ms. Kessler," the president said.

"Yes?"

"You have some backup you want us to read?" He pointed to Katie's lap. She'd forgotten to hand out the paperwork.

"Oh, yes." She passed copies to everyone.

"What do you say you give us a few minutes to review this?"

Katie obliged. She poured herself a glass of water, then waited while everyone absorbed her written arguments. After nearly five minutes, Morgan Taylor broke the silence. "Questions? Comments?"

Eve Goldman went first. "You seem to have covered the issue quite thoroughly. But I see you also have other designees. Can you talk about them?"

"Certainly. Just as my proposed changes to the Succession Act establishes a president-designate, I think we should consider one for a vice president. The VP-designate would also be subject to Senate confirmation and live outside the metropolitan D.C. area."

"So you would completely eliminate the secretary of state, the attorney general, the homeland security secretary, and other cabinet members from the line?"

"I would. Currently, they have to resign their offices in order to be sworn in. Consider what the law is now. Assume that the president dies. Those next in line—the vice president, the speaker, and the Senate *pro tem* are also killed. The secretary of state becomes acting president. But the House of Representatives could immediately vote in a new speaker of the house. Maybe that person is from a different political party than the president; maybe not. But the new speaker, according to the 1947 Act, can bump the acting president out. The former secretary of state is now out of a job. In a nutshell, that's the issue of 'bumping.' My approach avoids that possibility."

Brad Rutberg nodded his overall acceptance of the plan, but still asked, "How do you convince Congress?"

"I don't. I help frame the arguments. I think the president carries it to the nation directly. We've seen the fragility of the office and the strength of the institution; the best of what works and the inherent flaws in what doesn't." She carefully avoided mentioning Duke Patrick by name. "The president tells the American people that the need to protect the Office far outways any individual's job in Congress or the cabinet. The future is too precarious to rely on an antiquated practice, at least in my estimation."

Katie was finished. She'd made her case. *Successfully?*

"Ms. Kessler..." Taylor slowly started.

"Yes, Mr. President?"

"Have you run this by Chief Justice Browning?" He raised his eyebrow. This would be the real test.

Katie smiled confidently. "As a matter of fact, I have." The room fell completely silent. "He wishes I'd come to work for him instead of you."

Epilogue

Special Operations Command
MacDill Air Force Base, Florida
one week later

G eneral Jonas Jackson Johnson and Jack Evans monitored the attacks from the Integrated Battle Command Center at MacDill Air Force Base. The strikes were executed from the deck of the USS *Kitty Hawk* and Australian Royal Air Force bases at Tindal and Amberley. The Liberian tanker was the first target. Wisely, the captain stopped shy of Sydney. He acquiesced to the SASR team, rather than face scuttling. The Australian special forces quickly found what they sought.

All told, sixteen other targets were being pounded by F/A 18s and F-111s flown by the two nations under SAPATA authority. Satellite imagery, in large part provided by the KH-12s, showed massive explosions at seven locations in Indonesia, two in the Solomons, five more in the Malaysian islands, and two in Pakistan.

The satellites, dubbed Improved Crystal, are assets of the National Reconnaissance Office (NRO), located near Washington Dulles Airport and the National Security Agency. They capture new images every five seconds. The shots are relayed through Milstar satellites to the National Photo Interpretation Center, then—within five minutes—onto National Command Authority at MacDill.

J3 and Jack Evans monitored the images on hi-def television screens deep within the concrete-reinforced, blast-secure facility. Live audio transmission from the fighters accompanied the pictures.

Down-looking *before* photos were on a separate bank of monitors. They showed amazing detail even through clouds; direct evidence of heat sources created by thermal plumes. These and other analytical markers gave J3 the data on which he based the SAPATA attack order.

Unlike in the movies, the images were black and white and somewhat grainy. In time, computer enhancement would clean them up. But the pictures were sharp enough to tell the story. The terrorist camps, storage centers, and training areas were disappearing from the face of the earth in a hail of allied firepower.

"From now on we go to the terrorists, no matter where they are—Afghanistan or the Arizona desert. We remove them with extreme prejudice," the general observed.

J3 wasn't so far off. Although he didn't know it yet, Evans had satellite reconnaissance photos pinpointing another target—an al Qaeda training camp in Mexico, and another in Peru. He was certain Taylor would pull the trigger on those targets as well.

"Why didn't we do this years ago?" J3 asked. He watched as the latest images downloaded. Each one had a human toll that would be calculated in the thousands once the clean-up teams were on ground.

"Because patriotism played better than militarism," Evans admitted. "But we're in a new World War, General. And you're right. This is the way it has to be fought. Thankfully, we have the man willing to do it."

The Oval Office

"Mr. President, Mr. Hernandez is on the phone.

Taylor had Louise schedule the call with the Mexican leader. It would be brief.

"Mr. President, so good of you to make yourself available."

"The pleasure is mine," Hernandez said, not really knowing what to expect.

"Don't be too hasty. I know we have been having some disagreements about the stepped-up security at the border."

"Yes, yes we have, Mr. President. Is this the reason for your call? It would be most appreciated."

"No, Mr. President. It isn't. To tell you the truth, things are about to get more intense." Morgan Taylor explained how, in four days, the Air Force was going to cross the border to do something Hernandez hadn't.

The Mexican leader realized an appeal wouldn't get him anywhere. He was hearing a new, uncompromising policy and the debate was over. Morgan Taylor definitely wasn't an *acting president* any longer.

"Roarke, what kind of trick are you trying to pull?"

The call from Touch Parsons came out of nowhere.

"What the hell do you mean?" Roarke answered. He heard the FBI photo analyst type on his keyboard and he could almost see the phone tucked between his ear and shoulder.

"Come on, Roarke. We both know."

"Know what?"

Parsons sensed that maybe Roarke didn't have any idea. "You're serious?"

"Serious about what?"

"Just get over here."

Roarke made it to the FBI Labs in Quantico in an hour. He tore into Duane Parsons's inner sanctum. His first question was out before any hellos. "Okay, what's going on that was so important you couldn't explain."

"Your buddy, here," Touch said.

"What buddy?"

"This one." He wheeled around to his computer and placed a stylus on a paint box palate. It matched up to a cursor on a computer scroll down file. Parsons tapped the first line; his most recent work. A photograph popped up that Roarke had seen enough.

"What of it?" he asked coldly.

"I'm just doing what you asked"

"Refresh my memory. And get that picture off the screen."

Parsons didn't clear the computer screen, but he turned around and faced Roarke. "Make sure. You said, make sure."

Roarke finally recalled the conversation. "And?"

"I said I would *after*. Well, this is after."

Roarke frowned, still uncertain of the point Touch Parsons was making.

"Here, look," the FBI's computer photo expert said. Parsons addressed the screen again. The photograph was there. He quickly moved the stylus to the corner of the pad and the picture receded into the left side, paired with a second shot. "Okay, side by side, now."

Roarke leaned in. He stared at the FBI photograph of the lifeless Richard Cooper, taken at the Mall where he and Davis killed him. He shifted his glance to the right. Parsons had paired it with the photograph captured by the Immigration camera. He'd seen them both hundreds of times.

"They're the same man."

"Yes," Parsons noted.

"FERET confirmed that," Roarke stated for clarity. "*You* even told me."

"Yes, I did."

"The man on the left is the same as the man on the right," Roarke stated again.

"Yes."

"Then what's the mystery?"

"You didn't ask me the most important question."

"Parsons, you are, by far, the most impossible, most insolent, most annoying human being I've ever worked with. What the hell are you talking about?"

"How many times do I have to explain things to you, Roarke? Bring me the right photographs and I can take the guess work out of anything."

"I did. I personally brought you the right photographs!"

"Yes, you did. Yes, you did."

Parsons called up another photograph—Richard Cooper in his military outfit. "The question, my friend...," he adjusted the screen again. The photograph of Cooper seated on the right side; the shot from the Mall remained on the left, "...is, whether these two photographs are of the same man?"

"Of course they are!" Roarke shot back.

Parsons typed in a command. Each photograph zoomed in on a sequence of tight frames matching feature-by-feature: eyes, mouth, nose, ears, eyebrows, chin. Then, on a separate screen the computer mapped three-dimensional models. Parsons let the program cycle twice. He stopped it on an extreme close-up of Cooper's eyes.

"Are you sure?"

Roarke leaned in again. His own eyes widened, as did his mouth. He wasn't proficient in *how* Facial Recognition Technology worked, but Parsons convinced him FRT *did* work. The truth was in the mapping. The God awful truth was right in front of him.

Bali

He was dead again. Rich and dead, with no regrets. He set up another assassin to take the fall, to bury Richard Cooper a second time. Even his benefactor would think he was gone. That was fine. The fact that he didn't fulfill his contract and ignite the riot, as agreed, was of no concern. Now, he had no ties and no identity. He hadn't felt any loyalty for years. There was only the sun and the sand—and time to think more about how to punish the government responsible for sending him into that building in Iraq.

GARY GROSSMAN's first novel, *Executive Actions,* propelled him into the world of political thrillers. *Executive Treason* continues to tap Grossman's experience as a journalist, documentary producer, and reporter. He has written for *the New York Times,* the *Boston Globe,* and the *Boston Herald American.* He is also the author of *Superman: Serial to Cereal* and *Saturday Morning TV.* He covered presidential campaigns for WBZ-TV in Boston, and produced television series for NBC News, CNN, ABC, CBS, and FOX. He taught at Emerson College, Boston University, and USC, and is now co-owner of Weller/Grossman Productions, a Los Angeles-based Emmy Award-winning television production company.

To discover more about *Executive Treason,*
you can log onto the Web site
www.executivetreason.com